borrowed & blue

Praise for *Something Borrowed*

"Page-turning, heartbreakingly honest."

—*Entertainment Weekly* (Grade: A)

"What kind of self-described 'nice girl' would sleep with her best friend's fiancé? One who's seriously flawed, like this delightful debut novel's heroine, but also surprisingly winning and real."　　—*Glamour*

"Hilarious and thoughtfully written. You may never think of friendships—their duties, the oblique dances of power, and their give-and-take—quite the same way again."　　—*The Seattle Times*

"Sharply observed and beautifully etched."

—*The Star-Ledger* (Newark)

"Dead-on dialogue, real-life complexity, genuine warmth."

—*Seattle Post-Intelligencer*

"A thrill to read."　　　　　　　　　　—*The Washington Post*

Praise for *Something Blue*

"Warm and engaging; readers will find themselves cheering for Darcy as she proves people can change, in this captivating tale."

—*Booklist* (starred review)

"Giffin's plotting and prose are so engaging that she quickly becomes a fun, friendly presence in your reading life."　　—*Chicago Sun-Times*

"Highly entertaining."　　　　　　　　　—*The Boston Globe*

borrowed & blue

emily giffin

ST. MARTIN'S GRIFFIN ✺ NEW YORK

BORROWED & BLUE. SOMETHING BORROWED. Copyright © 2004 by Emily Giffin. SOMETHING BLUE. Copyright © 2005 by Emily Giffin. All rights reserved. Printed in the United States of America. For information, address St. Martin's Press, 175 Fifth Avenue, New York, N.Y. 10010.

www.stmartins.com

Grateful acknowledgment is made for permission to print excerpts from the following:

"Thunder Road" by Bruce Springsteen. Copyright © 1975 Bruce Springsteen. All rights reserved. Reprinted by permission.

"Lookin' Out My Back Door" by John Fogerty. Copyright © 1970 Jondora Music (BMI) Copyright renewed. Courtesy of Fantasy, Inc. All rights reserved. Used by permission.

ISBN 978-1-250-07083-8 (trade paperback)

St. Martin's Griffin books may be purchased for educational, business, or promotional use. For information on bulk purchases, please contact the Macmillan Corporate and Premium Sales Department at 1-800-221-7945, extension 5442, or write to specialmarkets@macmillan.com.

First Edition: June 2015

10 9 8 7 6 5 4 3 2 1

something borrowed

For my mother, with love

acknowledgments

I would like to thank my parents, sister, family, and friends for their love and support.

I am grateful to my agent, Stephany Evans, and my editor, Jennifer Enderlin, for believing in me.

I owe a huge debt to my earliest readers, Sarah Giffin, Mary Ann Elgin, and Nancy LeCroy Mohler, for their tireless input on every draft of the manuscript.

And most of all, I thank Buddy Blaha, for everything.

one

I was in the fifth grade the first time I thought about turning thirty. My best friend Darcy and I came across a perpetual calendar in the back of the phone book, where you could look up any date in the future, and by using this little grid determine what the day of the week would be. So we located our birthdays in the following year, mine in May and hers in September. I got Wednesday, a school night. She got a Friday. A small victory, but typical. Darcy was always the lucky one. Her skin tanned more quickly, her hair feathered more easily, and she didn't need braces. Her moonwalk was superior, as were her cartwheels and her front handsprings (I couldn't do a handspring at all). She had a better sticker collection. More Michael Jackson pins. Forenza sweaters in turquoise, red, *and* peach (my mother allowed me none—said they were too trendy and expensive). And a pair of fifty-dollar Guess jeans with zippers at the ankles (ditto). Darcy had double-pierced ears and a sibling—even if it was just a brother, it was better than being an only child as I was.

But at least I was a few months older and she would never quite catch up. That's when I decided to check out my thirtieth birthday—in a year so far away that it sounded like science fiction. It fell on a Sunday, which meant that my dashing husband and I would secure a responsible baby-sitter for our two (possibly three) children on that Saturday evening, dine at a fancy French restaurant with cloth napkins, and stay out past midnight, so technically we would be celebrating on my actual birthday. I would have just won a big case—somehow proven that an innocent man didn't do it. And my husband would toast me: "To Rachel, my beautiful wife, the mother of my children, and the finest lawyer in Indy." I shared my fantasy with Darcy as we discovered that her thirtieth birthday fell on a Monday. Bummer for her. I watched her purse her lips as she processed this information.

"You know, Rachel, who cares what day of the week we turn thirty?" she said, shrugging a smooth, olive shoulder. "We'll be old by then. Birthdays don't matter when you get that old."

I thought of my parents, who were in their thirties, and their lackluster approach to their own birthdays. My dad had just given my mom a toaster for her birthday because ours broke the week before. The new one toasted four slices at a time instead of just two. It wasn't much of a gift. But my mom had seemed pleased enough with her new appliance; nowhere did I detect the disappointment that I felt when my Christmas stash didn't quite meet expectations. So Darcy was probably right. Fun stuff like birthdays wouldn't matter as much by the time we reached thirty.

The next time I really thought about being thirty was our senior year in high school, when Darcy and I started watching the show *Thirtysomething* together. It wasn't one of our favorites—we preferred cheerful sitcoms like *Who's the Boss?* and *Growing Pains*—but we watched it anyway. My big problem with *Thirtysomething* was the whiny characters and their depressing issues that they seemed to bring upon themselves. I remember thinking that they should grow up, suck it up. Stop pondering the meaning of life and start making grocery lists. That was back when I thought my teenage years were dragging and my twenties would surely last forever.

Then I reached my twenties. And the early twenties did seem to last forever. When I heard acquaintances a few years older lament the end of their youth, I felt smug, not yet in the danger zone myself. I had plenty of time. Until about age twenty-seven, when the days of being carded were long gone and I began to marvel at the sudden acceleration of years (reminding myself of my mother's annual monologue as she pulled out our Christmas decorations) and the accompanying lines and stray gray hairs. At twenty-nine the real dread set in, and I realized that in a lot of ways I might as well be thirty. But not quite. Because I could still say that I was in my twenties. I still had something in common with college seniors.

I realize thirty is just a number, that you're only as old as you feel and all of that. I also realize that in the grand scheme of things, thirty is still young. But it's not *that* young. It is past the most ripe, prime child-bearing years, for example. It is too old to, say, start training for an Olympic medal. Even in the best die-of-old-age scenario, you are still about one-third of the way to the finish line. So I can't help feeling uneasy as I perch on an overstuffed maroon couch in a dark lounge on the Upper West Side at my surprise birthday party, organized by Darcy, who is still my best friend.

Tomorrow is the Sunday that I first contemplated as a fifth-grader playing with our phone book. After tonight my twenties will be over, a chapter closed forever. The feeling I have reminds me of New Year's Eve, when the countdown is coming and I'm not quite sure whether to grab my camera or just live in the moment. Usually I grab the camera and later regret it when the picture doesn't turn out. Then I feel enormously let down and think to myself that the night would have been more fun if it didn't mean quite so much, if I weren't forced to analyze where I've been and where I'm going.

Like New Year's Eve, tonight is an ending and a beginning. I don't like endings and beginnings. I would always prefer to churn about in the middle. The worst thing about this particular end (of my youth) and beginning (of middle age) is that for the first time in my life, I realize that I don't know where I'm going. My wants are simple: a job that I like and a guy whom I love. And on the eve of my thirtieth, I must face that I am 0 for 2.

First, I am an attorney at a large New York firm. By definition this means that I am miserable. Being a lawyer just isn't what it's cracked up to be—it's nothing like *L.A. Law,* the show that caused applications to law schools to skyrocket in the early nineties. I work excruciating hours for a mean-spirited, anal-retentive partner, doing mostly tedious tasks, and that sort of hatred for what you do for a living begins to chip away at you. So I have memorized the mantra of the law-firm associate: *I hate my job and will quit soon.* Just as soon as I pay off my loans. Just as soon as I make next year's bonus. Just as soon as I think of something else to do that will pay the rent. Or find someone who will pay it for me.

Which brings me to my second point: I am alone in a city of millions. I have plenty of friends, as proven by the solid turnout tonight. Friends to Rollerblade with. Friends to summer with in the Hamptons. Friends to meet on a Thursday night after work for a drink or two or three. And I have Darcy, my best friend from home, who is all of the above. But everybody knows that friends are not enough, although I often claim they are just to save face around my married and engaged girlfriends. I did not plan on being alone in my thirties, even my early thirties. I wanted a husband by now; I wanted to be a bride in my twenties. But I have learned that you can't just create your own timetable and will it to come true. So here I am on the brink of a new decade, realizing that being alone makes my thirties daunting, and being thirty makes me feel more alone.

The situation seems all the more dismal because my oldest and best friend has a glamorous PR job and is freshly engaged. Darcy is still the lucky one. I watch her now, telling a story to a group of us, including her fiancé. Dex and Darcy are an exquisite couple, lean and tall with matching dark hair and green eyes. They are among New York's beautiful people. The well-groomed couple registering for fine china and crystal on the sixth floor at Bloomingdale's. You hate their smugness but can't resist staring at them when you're on the same floor searching for a not-too-expensive gift for the umpteenth wedding you've been invited to without a date. You strain to glimpse her ring, and are instantly sorry you did. She catches you staring and gives you a disdainful once-over. You wish you hadn't worn your tennis shoes to Bloomingdale's. She is probably thinking that the footwear may be part of your problem. You buy your Waterford vase and get the hell out of there.

"So the lesson here is: if you ask for a Brazilian bikini wax, make sure you specify. Tell them to leave a landing strip or else you can wind up hairless, like a ten-year-old!" Darcy finishes her bawdy tale, and everybody laughs. Except Dex, who shakes his head, as if to say, what a piece of work my fiancée is.

"Okay. I'll be right back," Darcy suddenly says. "Tequila shots for one and all!"

As she moves away from the group toward the bar, I think back to all of the birthdays we have celebrated together, all of the benchmarks we reached together, benchmarks that I always reached first. I got my driver's license before she did, could drink legally before she could. Being older, if only by a few months, used to be a good thing. But now our fortunes have reversed. Darcy has an extra summer in her twenties—a perk of being born in the fall. Not that it matters as much for her: when you're engaged or married, turning thirty just isn't the same thing.

Darcy is now leaning over the bar, flirting with the twenty-something, aspiring actor/bartender whom she has already told me she would "totally do" if she were single. As if Darcy would ever be single. She said once in high school, "I don't break up, I trade up." She kept her word on that, and she always did the dumping. Throughout our teenage years, college, and every day of our twenties, she has been attached to someone. Often she has more than one guy hanging around, hoping.

It occurs to me that I could hook up with the bartender. I am totally unencumbered—haven't even been on a date in nearly two months. But it doesn't seem like something one should do at age thirty. One-night stands are for girls in their twenties. Not that I would know. I have followed an orderly, Goody Two-shoes path with no deviations. I got straight As in high school, went to college, graduated magna cum laude, took the LSAT, went straight to law school and to a big law firm after that. No backpacking in Europe, no crazy stories, no unhealthy, lustful relationships. No secrets. No intrigue. And now it seems too late for any of that. Because that stuff would just further delay my goal of finding a husband, settling down, having children and a happy home with grass and a garage and a toaster that toasts four slices at once.

So I feel unsettled about my future and somewhat regretful about my past. I tell myself that there will be time to ponder tomorrow. Right now I will have fun. It is the sort of thing that a disciplined person can simply decide. And I am exceedingly disciplined—the kind of child who did her homework on Friday afternoons right after school, the kind of woman (as of tomorrow, I am no longer any part girl) who flosses every night and makes her bed every morning.

Darcy returns with the shots but Dex refuses his, so Darcy insists that I do two. Before I know it, the night starts to take on that blurry quality, when you cross over from being buzzed to drunk, losing track of time and the precise order of things. Apparently Darcy has reached that point even sooner because she is now dancing on the bar. Spinning and gyrating in a little red halter dress and three-inch heels.

"Stealing the show at your party," Hillary, my closest friend from work, says to me under her breath. "She's shameless."

I laugh. "Yeah. Par for the course."

Darcy lets out a yelp, claps her hands over her head, and beckons me with a come-hither expression that would appeal to any man who has ever fancied girl-on-girl action. "Rachel! Rachel! C'mere!"

Of course she knows that I will not join her. I have never danced on a bar. I wouldn't know what to do up there besides fall. I shake my head and smile, a polite refusal. We all wait for her next move, which is to swivel her hips in perfect time to the music, bend over slowly, and then whip her body upright again, her long hair spilling every which way. The limber maneuver reminds me of her perfect imitation of Tawny Kitaen in the Whitesnake video "Here I Go Again," how she used to roll around doing splits on the hood of her father's BMW, to the delight of the pubescent neighborhood boys. I glance at Dex, who in these moments can never quite decide whether to be amused or annoyed. To say that the man has patience is an understatement. Dex and I have this in common.

"Happy birthday, Rachel!" Darcy yells. "Let's all raise a glass to Rachel!"

Which everyone does. Without taking their eyes off her.

A minute later, Dex whisks her down from the bar, slings her over his shoulder, and deposits her on the floor next to me in one fluid motion. Clearly he has done this before. "All right," he announces. "I'm taking our little party-planner home."

Darcy plucks her drink off the bar and stamps her foot. "You're not the boss of me, Dex! Is he, Rachel?" As she asserts her independence, she stumbles and sloshes her martini all over Dex's shoe.

Dex grimaces. "You're wasted, Darce. This isn't fun for anyone but you."

"Okay. Okay. I'll go . . . I'm feeling kind of sick anyway," she says, looking queasy.

"Are you going to be okay?"

"I'll be fine. Don't you worry," she says, now playing the role of brave little sick girl.

I thank her for my party, tell her that it was a total surprise—which is a lie, because I knew Darcy would capitalize on my thirtieth to buy a new outfit, throw a big bash, and invite as many of her friends as my own. Still, it was nice of her to have the party, and I am glad that she did. She is the kind of friend who always makes things feel special. She hugs me hard and says she'd do anything for me, and what would she do without me, her maid of honor, the sister she never had. She is gushing, as she always does when she drinks too much.

Dex cuts her off. "Happy birthday, Rachel. We'll talk to you tomorrow." He gives me a kiss on the cheek.

"Thanks, Dex," I say. "Good night."

I watch him usher her outside, holding her elbow after she nearly trips on the curb. *Oh, to have such a caretaker.* To be able to drink with reckless abandon and know that there will be someone to get you home safely.

Sometime later Dex reappears in the bar. "Darcy lost her purse. She thinks she left it here. It's small, silver," he says. "Have you seen it?"

"She lost her new Chanel bag?" I shake my head and laugh because it is just like Darcy to lose things. Usually I keep track of them for her, but I went off duty on my birthday. Still, I help Dex search for the purse, finally spotting it under a bar stool.

As he turns to leave, Dex's friend Marcus, one of his groomsmen, convinces him to stay. "C'mon, man. Hang out for a minute."

So Dex calls Darcy at home and she slurs her consent, tells him to have fun without her. Although she is probably thinking that such a thing is not possible.

Gradually my friends peel away, saying their final happy birthdays. Dex and I outlast everyone, even Marcus. We sit at the bar making conversation with the actor/bartender who has an "Amy" tattoo and zero interest in an aging lawyer. It is after two when we decide that it's time to go. The night feels more like midsummer than spring, and the warm air infuses me with sudden hope: *This will be the summer I meet my guy.*

Dex hails me a cab, but as it pulls over he says, "How about one more bar? One more drink?"

"Fine," I say. "Why not?"

We both get in and he tells the cabbie to just drive, that he has to think about where next. We end up in Alphabet City at a bar on Seventh and Avenue B, aptly named 7B.

It is not an upbeat scene—7B is dingy and smoke-filled. I like it anyway—it's not sleek and it's not a dive striving to be cool because it's not sleek.

Dex points to a booth. "Have a seat. I'll be right with you." Then he turns around. "What can I get you?"

I tell him whatever he's having, and sit and wait for him in the booth. I watch him say something to a girl at the bar wearing army-green cargo pants and a tank top that says "Fallen Angel." She smiles and shakes her head. "Omaha" is playing in the background. It is one of those songs that seems melancholy and cheerful at the same time.

A moment later Dex slides in across from me, pushing a beer my way. "Newcastle," he says. Then he smiles, crinkly lines appearing around his eyes. "You like?"

I nod and smile.

From the corner of my eye, I see Fallen Angel turn on her bar stool and survey Dex, absorbing his chiseled features, wavy hair, full lips. Darcy complained once that Dex garners more stares and double takes than she does. Yet, unlike his female counterpart, Dex seems not to notice the attention. Fallen Angel now casts her eyes my way, likely wondering what Dex is doing with someone so average. I hope that she thinks we're a couple. Tonight nobody has to know that I am only a member of the wedding party.

Dex and I talk about our jobs and our Hamptons share that begins in another week and a lot of things. But Darcy does not come up and neither does their September wedding.

After we finish our beers we move over to the jukebox, fill it with dollar bills, searching for good songs. I push the code for "Thunder Road" twice because it is my favorite song. I tell him this.

"Yeah. Springsteen's at the top of my list, too. Ever seen him in concert?"

"Yeah," I say. "Twice. *Born in the U.S.A.* and *Tunnel of Love.*"

I almost tell him that I went with Darcy in high school, dragged her along even though she much preferred groups like Poison and Bon Jovi. But I don't bring this up. Because then he will remember to go home to her and I don't want to be alone in my dwindling moments of twenty-somethingness. Obviously I'd rather be with a boyfriend, but Dex is better than nothing.

It is last call at 7B. We get a couple more beers and return to our booth. Sometime later we are in a cab again, going north on First Avenue. "Two stops," Dex tells our cabbie, because we live on opposite sides of Central Park. Dex is holding Darcy's Chanel purse, which looks small and out of place in his large hands. I glance at the silver dial of his Rolex, a gift from Darcy. It is just shy of four o'clock.

We sit silently for a stretch of ten or fifteen blocks, both of us looking out of our respective side windows, until the cab hits a pothole and I find myself lurched into the middle of the backseat, my leg grazing his. Then suddenly, out of nowhere, Dex is kissing me. Or maybe I kiss him. Somehow we are kissing. My mind goes blank as I listen to the soft sound of our lips meeting again and again. At some point, Dex taps on the Plexiglas partition and tells the driver, between kisses, that it will just be one stop after all.

We arrive on the corner of Seventy-third and Third, near my apartment. Dex hands the driver a twenty and does not wait for change. We spill out of the taxi, kissing more on the sidewalk and then in front of José, my doorman. We kiss the whole way up in the elevator. I am pressed against the elevator wall, my hands on the back of his head. I am surprised by how soft his hair is.

I fumble with my key, turning it the wrong way in the lock as Dex keeps his arms around my waist, his lips on my neck and the side of my face. Finally the door is open, and we are kissing in the middle of my studio, standing upright, leaning on nothing but each other. We stumble over to my made bed, complete with tight hospital corners.

"Are you drunk?" His voice is a whisper in the dark.

"No," I say. Because you always say no when you're drunk. And even though I am, I have a lucid instant where I consider clearly what was missing in my twenties and what I wish to find in my thirties. It strikes me that, in a sense, I can have both on this momentous birthday night. Dex can be my secret, my last chance for a dark twenty-something chapter, and he can also be a prelude of sorts—a promise of someone like him to come. Darcy is in my mind, but she is being pushed to the back, overwhelmed by a force stronger than our friendship and my own conscience. Dex moves over me. My eyes are closed, then open, then closed again.

And then, somehow, I am having sex with my best friend's fiancé.

two

I wake up to my ringing phone, and for a second I am disoriented in my own apartment. Then I hear Darcy's high-pitched voice on my machine, urging me to pick up, pick up, *please pick up*. My crime snaps into focus. I sit up too quickly, and my apartment spins. Dexter's back is to me, sculpted and sparsely freckled. I jab hard at it with one finger.

He rolls over and looks at me. "Oh, Christ! What time is it?"

My clock radio tells us it is seven-fifteen. I have been thirty for two hours. Correction—one hour; I was born in the central time zone.

Dex gets out of bed quickly, gathering his clothes, which are strewn along either side of my bed. The answering machine beeps twice, cutting Darcy off. She calls back, rambling about how Dex never came home. Again, my machine silences her in midsentence. She calls back a third time, wailing, "Wake up and call me! I *need* you!"

I start to get out of bed, then realize that I am naked. I sit back down and cover myself with a pillow.

"Omigod. What do we do?" My voice is hoarse and shaking. "Should I answer? Tell her you crashed here?"

"Hell, no! Don't pick up—lemme think for a sec." He sits down, wearing only boxers, and rubs his jaw, now covered by a shadow of whiskers.

Sick, sobering dread washes over me. I start to cry. Which never helps anything.

"Look, Rachel, don't cry," Dex says. "Everything's going to be okay."

He puts on his jeans and then his shirt, efficiently zipping and tucking and buttoning as though it is an ordinary morning. Then he checks the messages on his cell phone. "Shhhit. Twelve missed calls," he says matter-of-factly. Only his eyes show distress.

When he is dressed, he sits back on the edge of the bed and rests his forehead in his hands. I can hear him breathing hard through his nose. Air in and out. In and out. Then he looks over at me, composed. "Okay. Here's what's going to happen. Rachel, look at me."

I obey his instructions, still clutching my pillow.

"This will be fine. Just listen," he says, as though talking to a client in a conference room.

"I'm listening," I say.

"I'm going to tell her I stayed out until five or so and then got breakfast with Marcus. We got it covered."

"What do I tell her?" I ask. Lying has never been my strong suit.

"Just tell her you left the party and went home . . . Say you can't remember for sure whether I was still there when you left, but you think I was still there with Marcus. And be sure to say you 'think'— don't be too definite. And that's all you know, okay?" He points at my phone. "Call her back now . . . I'll call Marcus as soon as I leave here. Got it?"

I nod, my eyes filling with tears again as he stands.

"And calm down," he says, not meanly, but firmly. Then he is at the door, one hand on the knob, the other running through his dark hair that is just long enough to be really sexy.

"What if she already talked to Marcus?" I ask, as Dex is halfway out the door. Then, more to myself, "We are so screwed."

He turns around, looks at me through the doorway. For a second, I think he is angry, that he is going to yell at me to pull myself together. That this isn't life-or-death. But his tone is gentle. "Rach, we are not screwed. I got it covered. Just say what I told you to say . . . And Rachel?"

"Yeah?"

"I'm really sorry."

"Yeah," I say. "Me too."

Are we talking to each other—or to Darcy?

As soon as Dex leaves, I reach for the phone, still feeling dizzy. It takes a few minutes, but I finally work up the nerve to call Darcy.

She is hysterical. "The bastard didn't come home last night! He better be laid up in a hospital bed! . . . Do you think he cheated on me?"

I start to say no, that he was probably just out with Marcus, but think better of it. Wouldn't that look too obvious? Would I say that if I knew nothing? I can't think. My head and heart are pounding, and the room is still spinning intermittently. "I'm sure he wasn't cheating on you."

She blows her nose. "*Why* are you sure?"

"Because he wouldn't do that to you, Darce." I can't believe my words, how easily they come.

"Well, then, where the fuck is he? The bars close by four or five. It's seven-freaking-thirty!"

"I don't know . . . But I'm sure there's a logical explanation."

Which, in fact, there is.

She asks me what time I left and whether he was still there and who he was with—the exact questions that Dex prepped me on. I answer carefully, as instructed. I suggest that she call Marcus.

"I already called him," she says. "And that dumbass didn't answer his goddamn cell."

Yes. We have a chance.

I hear the click of call-waiting and Darcy is gone, then back, telling me that it is Dex and she'll call me when she can.

I stand and walk unsteadily to my bathroom. I look in the mirror. My skin is blotchy and red. My eyes are ringed with mascara and charcoal liner, and they burn from sleeping in my contact lenses. I remove them quickly just before dry-heaving over my toilet. I haven't thrown up from drinking since college, and that only happened once. Because I learn from my mistakes. Most college kids say, "I will never do this again," and then do it the following weekend. But I stuck to it. That is how I am. I will learn from this one too. *Just let me get away with it.*

I shower, wash the smoke from my hair and skin with my phone resting on the sink, waiting to hear from Darcy that everything is okay. But hours pass and she does not call. Around noon, the birthday well-wishers start dialing in. My parents do their annual serenade and the "guess where I was thirty years ago today?" routine. I manage to put on a good front and play along, but it isn't easy.

By three o'clock, I have not heard from Darcy, and I am still queasy. I chug a big glass of water, take two Advil, and contemplate ordering fried eggs and bacon, which Darcy swears by when she's hungover. But I know that nothing will kill the pain of waiting, wondering what is going on, if Dex is busted, if we both are.

Did anybody see us together at 7B? In the cab? On the street? Anyone besides José, whose job it is to know nothing? What was happening on the Upper West Side in their apartment? Had he gone mad and confessed? Was she packing her bags? Were they making love all day in an attempt to repair his conscience? Were they still fighting, going around and around in circles of accusation and denial?

Fear must supersede all other emotions—stifling shame or regret—because crazily enough, I do not seem to feel guilty about betraying my best friend. Not even when I find our used condom on the floor. The only real guilt I can muster is guilt over not feeling guilty. But I will repent later, just as soon as I know that I am safe. *Oh, please, God. I have never done anything like this before. Please let me have this one pass. I will sacrifice all future happiness. Any chance of meeting a husband.*

I think of all those deals I tried to strike with Him when I was in school, growing up. *Please don't let me get any lower than a B on this math test. Please, I will do anything—work in a soup kitchen every Saturday instead of just once a month.* Those were the days. To think that a C once symbolized all things gone wrong in my tidy world. How could I have ever, even fleetingly, wished for a dark side? How could I have made such a huge, potentially life-altering, utterly unforgivable mistake?

Finally I can't take it any longer. I call Darcy's cell phone, but it goes straight to voice mail. I call their home number, hoping she will pick up. Instead Dex answers. I cringe.

"Hi, Dex. This is Rachel," I say, trying to sound normal.

You know, the maid of honor in your upcoming wedding—the woman you had sex with last night?

"Hi, Rachel," he says casually. "So did you have fun last night?"

For a second, I think that he is talking about us and am horrified by his nonchalance. But then I hear Darcy clamoring for the phone in the background and realize that he is only talking about the party.

"Oh yeah, it was a great time—a great party." I bite my lip.

Darcy has already snatched the phone from him. Her tone is chipper, fully repaired. "Hey. I'm sorry I forgot to call you back. You know, it was high drama over here for a while."

"But you're okay now? Everything's all right with you—and Dex?" I have trouble saying his name. As if it will somehow give me away.

"Um, yeah, hold on one sec."

I hear her close a door; she always moves into their bedroom when she talks on the phone. I picture their four-poster bed, which I helped Darcy select from Charles P. Rogers. Soon to be their marital bed.

"Oh yeah, I'm fine now. He was just with Marcus. They stayed out late and then ended up going to the diner for breakfast. But of course, you know, I'm still working the pissed-off angle. I told him he's totally pathetic, that he's a thirty-four-year-old engaged man and he stays out all night. Pathetic, don't you think?"

"Yeah, I guess so. But harmless enough." I swallow hard and think, yes, that *would* be harmless enough. "Well, I'm glad you guys made up."

"Yeah. I'm over it, I guess. But still . . . he should have called. That shit does not fly with me, you know?"

"I hear you," I say, and then bravely add, "I told you he wasn't cheating on you."

"I know . . . but I still pictured him with some stripper bimbo from Scores or something. My overactive imagination."

Is that what last night was? I know I'm not a bimbo, but was it some conscious choice of his to get laid before the wedding? Surely not. Surely he wouldn't choose Darcy's maid of honor.

"So anyway, what did you think of the party? I'm such a bad friend— I get wasted and leave early. And, oh shit! Today's your actual birthday. Happy birthday! God, I'm the worst, Rach!"

Yeah, you're the bad friend.

"Oh, it was great. The party was so much fun. Thank you for planning it—it was a total surprise . . . really awesome . . ."

I hear their bedroom door open and Dex say something about being late.

"Yeah, I actually gotta run, Rachel. We're going to the movies. You wanna come?"

"Um, no, thanks."

"Okay. But we're still on for dinner tonight, right? Rain at eight?"

I totally forgot that I had plans to meet Dex, Darcy, and Hillary for a small birthday dinner. There is no way I can face Dex or Darcy tonight— and certainly not together. I tell her that I'm not sure I'm up to it, that I am really hungover. Even though I stopped drinking at two, I add, before I remember that liars offer too much extraneous detail.

Darcy doesn't notice. "Maybe you'll feel better later . . . I'll call you after the movie."

I hang up the phone, thinking that it was way too easy. But instead of feeling relieved, I am left with a vague dissatisfaction, wistfulness, wishing that I were going to the movies. Not with Dex, of course. Just someone. How quickly I turn my back on the deal with God. I want a husband again. Or at least a boyfriend.

I sit on the couch with my hands folded in my lap, contemplating what I did to Darcy, waiting for the guilt to come. It doesn't. Was it because I had alcohol as an excuse? I was drunk, not in my right mind. I think of my first-year Criminal Law class. *Intoxication, like insanity, infancy, duress, and entrapment, is a legal excuse, a defense where the defendant is not blameworthy for having engaged in conduct that would otherwise be a crime.* Shit. That was only *involuntary* intoxication. Well, Darcy made me do those shots. But peer pressure does not constitute involuntary intoxication. Still, it is a mitigating circumstance that the jury might consider.

Sure, blame the victim. What is wrong with me?

Maybe I am just a bad person. Maybe the only reason I have been good up to this point has less to do with my true moral fiber and more to do with the fear of getting caught. I play by the rules because I am risk-averse. I didn't go along with the junior-high shoplifting gags at the White Hen Pantry partly because I knew it was wrong, but mostly because I was sure that I would be the one to get caught. I never cheated on an exam for the same reason. Even now I don't take office supplies from work because I figure that somehow the firm's surveillance cameras will catch me in the act. So if that is what motivates me to be good, do I really deserve credit? Am I really a good person? Or just a cowardly pessimist?

Okay. So maybe I am a bad person. There is no other plausible explanation for my lack of guilt. Do I have it in for Darcy? Was I driven by jealousy last night? Do I resent her perfect life—how easily things come to her? Or maybe, subconsciously, in my drunken state, I was getting even for past wrongs. Darcy hasn't always been a perfect friend. Far from it. I start to make my case to the jury, remembering Ethan back in elementary school. I am on to something . . . *Ladies and gentlemen of the jury, consider the story of Ethan Ainsley* . . .

Darcy Rhone and I were best friends growing up, bonded by geography, a force greater than all else when you are in elementary school. We moved to the same cul-de-sac in Naperville, Indiana, in the summer of 1976, just in time to attend the town's bicentennial parade together. We marched side by side, beating matching red, white, and blue drums that Darcy's father bought for us at Kmart. I remember Darcy leaning in to me and saying, "Let's pretend we're sisters." The suggestion gave me goose bumps—*a sister!* And in no time at all, that is what she became to me. We slept over at each other's houses every Friday and Saturday during the school year and most nights of the week during the summer. We absorbed the nuances of each other's family life, the sort of details you only learn when you live next door to a friend. I knew, for example, that Darcy's mother folded towels in neat thirds as she watched *The Young and the Restless,* that Darcy's father subscribed to *Playboy,* that junk food was allowed for breakfast, and the words "shit" and "damn" were no big deal. I'm sure she observed much about my home too, although it is hard to say what makes your own life unique. We shared everything—clothes, toys, yards, even our love of Andy Gibb and unicorns.

In the fifth grade we discovered boys. Which brings me to Ethan, my first real crush. Darcy, along with every other girl in our class, loved Doug Jackson. I understood Doug's appeal. I appreciated his blond hair that reminded us of Bo Duke. And the way his Wranglers fit his butt, his black comb tucked neatly inside the back left pocket. And his dominance in tetherball—how he casually and effortlessly socked the ball out of everyone's reach at a sharp upward angle.

But I loved Ethan. I loved his unruly hair and the way his cheeks turned pink during recess and made him look like he belonged in a Renoir painting. I loved the way he rotated his number-two pencil between his full lips, making symmetrical little bite marks near the eraser whenever he was concentrating really hard. I loved how hyper and happy he was when he played four square with the girls (he was the only boy who would ever join us—the other boys stuck to tetherball and football). And I loved that he was always kind to the most unpopular boy in our class, Johnnie Redmond, who had a terrible stutter and an unfortunate bowl cut.

Darcy was puzzled, if not irritated, by my dissent, as was our good friend Annalise Giles, who moved to our cul-de-sac two years after we did (this delay and the fact that she already had a sister meant she could never quite catch up and reach full best-friend status). Darcy and Annalise liked Ethan, but not like *that*, and they would insist that Doug was so much cuter and cooler—the two attributes that will get you in trouble when you choose a boy or a man, a sense that I had even at age ten.

We all assumed that Darcy would land the grand Doug prize. Not only because Darcy was bolder than the other girls, strutting right up to Doug in the cafeteria or on the playground, but also because she was the prettiest girl in our class. With high cheekbones, huge, well-spaced eyes, and a dainty nose, she has a face that is revered at any age, although fifth-graders can't pinpoint exactly what makes it nice. I don't think I even understood what cheekbones and bone structure were at age ten, but I knew that Darcy was pretty and I envied her looks. So did Annalise, who openly told Darcy so every chance she got, which seemed wholly unnecessary to me. Darcy already knew she was pretty, and in my opinion she didn't need daily reinforcement.

So that year, on Halloween, Annalise, Darcy, and I assembled in Annalise's room to prepare our makeshift gypsy costumes—Darcy had insisted that it would be an excellent excuse to wear lots of makeup. As she examined a pair of rhinestone earrings freshly purchased from Claire's, she looked in the mirror and said, "You know, Rachel, I think you're right."

"Right about what?" I said, feeling a surge of satisfaction, wondering what past debate she was referring to.

She fastened one earring in place and looked at me. I will never forget that tiny smirk on her face—just the faintest hint of a smug smile. "You're right about Ethan. I think I'm going to like him too."

"What do you mean, 'going to like him'?"

"I'm tired of Doug Jackson. I like Ethan now. I like his dimples."

"He only has one," I snapped.

"Well, then I like his dim-*ple*."

I looked at Annalise for support, for words to the effect that you couldn't just *decide* to like someone new. But of course she said nothing, just kept applying her ruby lipstick, puckering before a handheld mirror.

"I can't believe you, Darcy!"

"What's your problem?" she demanded. "Annalise wasn't mad when I liked Doug. We've shared him with the whole grade for months. Right, Annalise?"

"Longer than that. I started liking him in the summer. Remember? At the pool?" Annalise chimed in, always missing the big picture.

I glared at her, and she lowered her eyes remorsefully.

That was different. That was Doug. He belonged in the public domain. But Ethan was exclusively mine.

I said nothing else that night, but trick-or-treating was ruined. The next day in school, Darcy passed Ethan a note, asking him if he liked me, her, or neither—with little boxes next to each selection and instructions to check one. He must have checked Darcy's name because they were a couple by recess. Which is to say that they announced that they were "going out" but never spent any real time together, unless you count a few phone calls at night, often scripted ahead of time with Annalise giggling at her side. I refused to participate in or discuss her fledgling romance.

In my mind, it didn't matter that Darcy and Ethan never kissed, or that it was only the fifth grade, or that they "broke up" two weeks later when Darcy lost interest and decided that she liked Doug Jackson again. Or that, as my mother told me for comfort, imitation is the sincerest form of flattery. It only mattered that Darcy stole Ethan from me. Perhaps she did it because she really did change her mind about him; that's what I told myself so I would stop hating her. But more likely Darcy took Ethan just to show me that she could.

So, ladies and gentlemen of the jury, in a sense, Darcy Rhone had this coming to her. What goes around comes around. Perhaps this is her comeuppance.

I picture the faces of the jury. They are not swayed. The male jurors look bewildered—as if they miss the point altogether. Doesn't the prettiest girl always get the boy? That is precisely the way the world *should* work. An older woman in a sensible dress purses her lips. She is disgusted by the mere comparison—a fiancé to a fifth-grade crush! Good heavens! A perfectly groomed, almost beautiful woman, wearing a canary-yellow Chanel suit, has already identified and allied herself with Darcy. There is nothing I can say to change her mind or mitigate my offense.

The only juror who seems moved by the Ethan tale is a slightly overweight girl with a severe bob the color of day-old coffee. She slouches in the corner of the jury box, occasionally shoving her glasses up on her beak of a nose. I have tapped into this girl's empathy, her sense of justice. She is secretly satisfied by what I did. Maybe because she, too, has a friend like Darcy, a friend who always gets everything she wants.

I think back to high school, when Darcy continued to get any boy she wanted. I can see her kissing Blaine Conner by our locker and recall the envy that would well up inside me when I, boyfriendless, was forced to witness their shameless PDA. Blaine transferred to our school from Columbus, Ohio, in the fall of our junior year, and became an instant hit everywhere but in the classroom. Although he wasn't bright, he was the star receiver on our football team, the starting point guard for our basketball team, and, of course, our starting pitcher in the spring. And with his Ken-doll good looks, the girls loved him. Doug Jackson, part two. But alas, he had a girlfriend named Cassandra back in Columbus to whom he claimed to be "110 percent committed" (a jock expression that has always bugged me for its obvious mathematical impossibility). Or so he was before Darcy got in the mix, after we watched Blaine pitch a no-hitter against Central and she decided that she had to have him. The next day she asked him to go see *Les Misérables*. You'd think a three-sport jock like Blaine wouldn't be into musicals, but he enthusiastically agreed to escort her. After the show, in Darcy's living room, Blaine planted a large hickey on her neck. And the following morning, one Cassandra of Columbus, Ohio, was dumped on her ear.

I remember talking to Annalise about Darcy's charmed life. We often discussed Darcy, which made me wonder how much they gossiped about me. Annalise contended that it wasn't only Darcy's good looks or perfect body; it was also her confidence, her charm. I don't know about the charm, but looking back I agree with Annalise about the confidence. It was as if Darcy had the perspective of a thirty-year-old while in high school. The understanding that none of it really mattered, that you only go around once, that you might as well go for it. She was never intimidated, never insecure. She embodied what everyone says when they look back on high school: "If I only knew back then."

But one thing I have to say about Darcy and dating is this: she never blew us off for a guy. She always put her friends first—which is an amazing thing for a high school girl to do. Sometimes she blew her boyfriend off altogether, but more often she just included us. Four of us in a row at the theater. The flavor of the month, then Darcy, then Annalise and me. And Darcy always directed her whispered comments our way. She was brash and independent, unlike most high school girls who allow their feelings for a boy to swallow them up. At the time, I thought she just didn't love them enough. But maybe Darcy just wanted to keep control, and by being the one who loved the least, that is what she had. Whether she did care less or just pretended to, she kept every one of them on the hook even after she cut them loose. Take Blaine, for example. He is living in Iowa with a wife, three kids, and a couple of chocolate Labs, and he still e-mails Darcy on her birthday every year. Now that is some kind of power.

To this day Darcy talks wistfully of how great high school was. I cringe whenever she says it. Sure, I have some fond memories of those days, and enjoyed moderate popularity—a nice fringe benefit of being Darcy's best friend. I loved going to football games with Annalise, painting our faces orange and blue, wrapping up in blankets in the bleachers, and waving to Darcy as she cheered down on the field. I loved our Saturday-night trips to Colonial Ice Cream, where we always ordered the same thing—one turtle sundae, one Snickers pie, one double-chocolate brownie—and then split them among us. And I loved my first boyfriend, Brandon Beamer, who asked me out during our senior year. Brandon was a rule-follower too, a Catholic version of me. He didn't drink or do drugs, and he felt guilty even discussing sex. Darcy, who lost her virginity our sophomore year to an exchange student from Spain named Carlos, was always instructing me to corrupt Brandon. "Grab his penis like this, and I guarantee, it's a done deal." But I was perfectly happy with our long make-out sessions in Brandon's family station wagon, and I never had to worry about safe sex or drunk driving. So if my memories weren't glamorous, at least I had a few good times.

But I also had plenty of bad times: the awful hair days, the pimples, the class pictures from hell, never having the right clothes, being dateless for dances, baby fat that I could never shed, getting cut from teams, losing the election for class treasurer. And the overwhelming feeling of sadness and angst that would come and go willy-nilly (or, more accurately, once a month), seemingly out of my control. Typical teenager stuff, really. Clichés, because it happens to everyone. Everyone but Darcy, that is, who floated through those tumultuous four years unscathed by rejection, untouched by the adolescent ugly stick. Of course she loved high school—high school loved her.

Many girls with this view of their teenage years seem to really take it on the chin later in life. They show up at their ten-year reunion twenty pounds heavier, divorced, and reminiscing about their long-gone glory days. But the tide of glory days hasn't ebbed for Darcy. No crashing and no burning. In fact, life just keeps getting sweeter for her. As my mother once said, uncharacteristically, Darcy has the world by the balls. It was—and still is—the perfect description. Darcy always gets what she wants. And that includes Dex, the dream fiancé.

I leave Darcy a message on her cell, which will be turned off during the movie. I say that I am too tired to make it to dinner. Just getting out of going makes me less queasy. In fact, I am suddenly very hungry. I find my menus and call to order a hamburger with cheddar and fries. Guess I won't be losing five pounds before Memorial Day. As I wait for my delivery, I picture Darcy and me playing with the phone book all those years ago, wondering about the future and what age thirty would bring.

And here I am, without the dashing husband, the responsible baby-sitter, the two kids. Instead my benchmark birthday is forever tainted by scandal . . . Oh, well. No point beating myself up over it. I hit redial on my phone and add a large chocolate milk shake to my order. I see my girl in the corner of the jury box wink at me. She thinks the milk shake is an excellent idea. After all, doesn't everyone deserve a few weak moments on her birthday?

three

When I wake up the next morning, the cavalier girl sucking down a milk shake is gone, caved to guilt and thirty years of rule-following. I can no longer rationalize what I did. I committed an unspeakable act against a friend, violated a central tenet of sisterhood. There is no justification.

So on to Plan B: I will pretend that nothing happened. My transgression was so great that I have no choice but simply to will the whole thing to go away. And by proceeding with business as usual, embracing my Monday-morning routine, this is what I seek to accomplish.

I shower, dry my hair, put on my most comfortable black suit and low heels, take the subway to Grand Central, get my coffee at Starbucks, pick up *The New York Times* at my newsstand, and ride two escalators and one elevator up to my office in the MetLife Building. Each part of my routine represents one step further from Dex and the Incident.

I arrive at my office at eight-twenty, way early by law-firm standards. The halls are quiet. Not even the secretaries are in yet. I am turning to the

Metro section of the paper, sipping my coffee, when I notice the blinking red message light on my phone—usually a warning that more work awaits me. Some jackass partner must have called me on the one weekend in recent memory when I failed to check my messages. My money is on Les, the dominant man in my life and the biggest jackass partner amid six floors of them. I enter my password, wait . . .

"You have one new message from an outside caller. Received today at seven-forty-two A.M. . . . ." the recording tells me. I hate that automated woman. She consistently bears bad news and does so in a chipper voice. They should adjust that recording at law firms, make the voice more somber: "Uh-oh"—with ominous *Jaws* music in the background—"you have four new messages . . ."

What is it this time? I think, as I hit play.

"Hi, Rachel . . . It's me . . . Dex . . . I wanted to call you yesterday to talk about Saturday night but—I just couldn't. I think we should talk about it, don't you? Call me when you can. I should be around all day."

My heart sinks. Why can't he adopt some good old-fashioned avoidance techniques and ignore it, never speak of it again? That was my game plan. No wonder I hate my job; I am a litigator who hates confrontation. I pick up a pen and tap it against the edge of my desk. I hear my mother telling me not to fidget. I put the pen down and stare at the blinking light. The woman demands that a decision be made with respect to this message—I must replay it, save it, or delete it.

What does he want to talk about? What is there to say? I replay, expecting the answers to come to me in the sound of his voice, his cadence. But he gives nothing away. I replay again and again until his voice starts to sound distorted, just as a word changes in your mouth when you repeat it enough times. *Egg, egg, egg, egg.* That used to be my favorite. I'd say it over and over until it seemed that I had the altogether wrong word for the yellow substance I was about to eat for breakfast.

I listen to Dex one final time before I delete him. His voice definitely sounds different. This makes sense because in some ways, he is different. We both are. Because even if I try to block out what happened, even if Dex drops the Incident after a brief, awkward telephone call, we will forever be on one another's List—that list every person has, whether recorded in a secret spiral notebook or memorized in the back of the mind. Whether short or long. Whether ranked in order of performance or importance or chronology. Whether complete with first, middle, and last names or mere physical descriptions, like Darcy's List: "*Delta Sig with killer delts . . .*"

Dex is on my List for good. Without wanting to, I suddenly think of us in bed together. For those brief moments, he was just Dex—separate from Darcy. Something he hadn't been in a very long time. Something he hadn't been since the day I introduced the two.

I met Dex during our first year of law school at NYU. Unlike most law students, who come straight from college when they can think of nothing better to do with their stellar undergrad transcripts, Dex Thaler was older, with real-life experience. He had worked as an analyst at Goldman Sachs, which blew away my nine-to-five summer internships and office jobs filing and answering phones. He was confident, relaxed, and so gorgeous that it was hard not to stare at him. I was positive that he would become the Doug Jackson and Blaine Conner of law school. Sure enough, we were barely into our first week of class when the buzz over Dexter began, women speculating about his status, noting either that his left ring finger was unadorned or, alternatively, worrying that he was too well dressed and handsome to be straight.

But I dismissed Dex straightaway, convincing myself that his outward perfection was boring. Which was a fortunate stance, because I also knew that he was out of my league. (I hate that expression and the presumption that people choose mates based so heavily upon looks, but it is hard to deny the principle when you look around—partners generally share the same level of attractiveness, and when they do not, it is noteworthy.) Besides, I wasn't borrowing thirty thousand dollars a year so that I could find a boyfriend.

As a matter of fact, I probably would have gone three years without talking to him, but we randomly ended up next to each other in Torts, a seating-chart class taught by the sardonic Professor Zigman. Although many professors at NYU used the Socratic method, only Zigman used it as a tool to humiliate and torture students. Dex and I bonded in our hatred of our mean-spirited professor. I feared Zigman to an irrational extreme, whereas Dexter's reaction had more to do with disgust. "What an asshole," he would growl after class, often after Zigman had reduced a fellow classmate to tears. "I just want to wipe that smirk off his pompous face."

Gradually, our grumbling turned into longer talks over coffee in the student lounge or during walks around Washington Square Park. We began to study together in the hour before class, preparing for the inevitable—the day Zigman would call on us. I dreaded my turn, knowing that it would be a bloody massacre, but secretly couldn't wait for Dexter to be called on. Zigman preyed on the weak and flustered, and Dex was neither. I was sure that he wouldn't go down without a fight.

I remember it well. Zigman stood behind his podium, examining his seating chart, a schematic with our faces cut from the first-year look book, practically salivating as he picked his prey. He peered over his small, round glasses (the kind that should be called spectacles) in our general direction, and said, "Mr. Thaler."

He pronounced Dex's name wrong, making it rhyme with "taller."

"It's 'Thaa-ler,'" Dex said, unflinching.

I inhaled sharply; nobody corrected Zigman. Dex was really going to get it now.

"Well, pardon me, Mr. Thaaa-ler," Zigman said, with an insincere little bow. "Palsgraf versus Long Island Railroad Company."

Dex sat calmly with his book closed while the rest of the class nervously flipped to the case we had been assigned to read the night before.

The case involved a railroad accident. While rushing to board a train, a railroad employee knocked a package of dynamite out of a passenger's hand, causing injury to another passenger, Mrs. Palsgraf. Justice Cardozo, writing for the majority, held that Mrs. Palsgraf was not a "foreseeable plaintiff" and, as such, could not recover from the railroad company. Perhaps the railroad employees should have foreseen harm to the package holder, the Court explained, but not harm to Mrs. Palsgraf.

"Should the plaintiff have been allowed recovery?" Zigman asked Dex.

Dex said nothing. For a brief second I panicked that he had frozen, like others before him. *Say no,* I thought, sending him fierce brain waves. *Go with the majority holding.* But when I looked at his expression, and the way his arms were folded across his chest, I could tell that he was only taking his time, in marked contrast to the way most first-year students blurted out quick, nervous, untenable answers as if reaction time could compensate for understanding.

"In my opinion?" Dex asked.

"I am addressing you, Mr. Thaler. So, yes, I am asking for your opinion."

"I would have to say yes, the plaintiff should have been allowed recovery. I agree with Justice Andrew's dissent."

"Ohhhh, really?" Zigman's voice was high and nasal.

"Yes. Really."

I was surprised by his answer, as he had told me just before class that he didn't realize crack cocaine had been around in 1928, but Justice Andrews surely must have been smoking it when he wrote his dissent. I was even more surprised by Dexter's brazen "really" tagged onto the end of his answer, as though to taunt Zigman.

Zigman's scrawny chest swelled visibly. "So you think that the guard should have foreseen that the innocuous package measuring fifteen inches in length, covered with a newspaper, contained explosives and would cause injury to the plaintiff?"

"It was certainly a possibility."

"Should he have foreseen that the package could cause injury to *anybody in the world?*" Zigman asked, with mounting sarcasm.

"I didn't say 'anybody in the world.' I said 'the plaintiff.' Mrs. Palsgraf, in my opinion, was in the danger zone."

Zigman approached our row with ramrod posture and tossed his *Wall Street Journal* onto Dex's closed textbook.

"Care to return my newspaper?"

"I'd prefer not to," Dex said.

The shock in the room was palpable. The rest of us would have simply played along and returned the paper, mere props in Zigman's questioning.

"You'd prefer not to?" Zigman cocked his head.

"That's correct. There could be dynamite wrapped inside it."

Half of the class gasped, the other half snickered. Clearly, Zigman had some tactic up his sleeve, some way of turning the facts around on Dex. But Dex wasn't falling for it. Zigman was visibly frustrated.

"Well, let's suppose you *did* choose to return it to me and it *did* contain a stick of dynamite and it *did* cause injury to your person. Then what, Mr. Thaler?"

"Then I would sue you, and likely I would win."

"And would that recovery be consistent with Judge Cardozo's rationale in the majority holding?"

"No. It would not."

"Oh, really? And why not?"

"Because I'd sue you for an intentional tort, and Cardozo was talking about negligence, was he not?" Dex raised his voice to match Zigman's.

I think I stopped breathing as Zigman pressed his palms together and brought them neatly against his chest as though he were praying. "I ask the questions in this classroom. If that's all right with you, Mr. Thaler?"

Dex shrugged as if to say, have it your way, makes no difference to me.

"Well, let's suppose that I accidentally dropped my paper onto your desk, and you returned it and were injured. Would Mr. Cardozo allow you full recovery?"

"Sure."

"And why is that?"

Dex sighed to show that the exercise was boring him and then said swiftly and clearly, "Because it was entirely foreseeable that the dynamite could cause injury to me. Your dropping the paper containing dynamite into my personal space violated my legally protected interest. Your negligent act caused a hazard apparent to the eye of ordinary vigilance."

I studied the highlighted portions of my book. Dex was quoting sections of Cardozo's opinion verbatim, without so much as glancing at his book or notes. The whole class was spellbound—nobody did this well, and certainly not with Zigman looming over him.

"And if Ms. Myers sued," Zigman said, pointing to a trembling Julie

Myers on the other side of the classroom, his victim from the day before. "Should she be allowed recovery?"

"Under Cardozo's holding or Justice Andrews's dissent?"

"The latter. As it is the opinion you share."

"Yes. Everyone owes to the world at large the duty of refraining from acts which unreasonably threaten the safety of others," Dex said, another straight quote from the dissent.

It went on like that for the rest of the hour, Dex distinguishing nuances in changed fact patterns, never wavering, always answering decisively.

And at the end of the hour, Zigman actually said, "Very good, Mr. Thaler."

It was a first.

I left class feeling jubilant. Dex had prevailed for all of us. The story spread throughout the first-year class, earning him more points with the girls, who had long since determined that he was totally available.

I told Darcy the story as well. She had moved to New York at about the same time I did, only under vastly different circumstances. I was there to become a lawyer; she came without a job, or a plan, or much money. I let her sleep on a futon in my dorm room until she found some roommates—three American Airlines flight attendants looking to squeeze a fourth body into their heavily partitioned studio. She borrowed money from her parents to make the rent while she looked for a job, finally settling on a bartending position at the Monkey Bar. For the first time in our friendship, I was happy with my life in comparison to hers. I was just as poor, but at least I had a plan. Darcy's prospects didn't seem great with only a 2.9 GPA from Indiana University.

"You're so lucky," Darcy would whine as I tried to study.

No, luck is what you *have,* I'd think. Luck is buying a lottery ticket along with your Yoo-hoo and striking it rich. Nothing about my life is lucky—it's all about hard work, it is all an uphill struggle. But of course, I never said that. Just told her that things would soon turn around for her.

And sure enough, they did. About two weeks later a man waltzed into the Monkey Bar, ordered a whiskey sour, and began to chat Darcy up. By the time he finished his drink, he had promised her a job at one of Manhattan's top PR firms. He told her to come in for an interview, but that he would (wink, wink) make sure that she got the job. Darcy took his business card, had me revise her résumé, went in for the interview, and got an offer on the spot. Her starting salary was seventy thousand dollars. Plus an expense account. Practically what I would make *if* I did well enough in school to get a job with a New York firm.

So while I sweated it out and racked up debt, Darcy began her glamorous PR career. She planned parties, promoted the season's latest fashion trends, got plenty of free everything, and dated a string of beautiful men. Within seven months, she left the flight attendants in the dust and moved in with her coworker Claire, a snobbish, well-connected girl from Greenwich.

Darcy tried to include me in her fast-track life, although I seldom had time to go to her events or her parties or her blind-date setups with guys she swore were "total hotties" but that I knew were simply her castoffs.

Which brings me back to Dex. I raved about him to Darcy and Claire, told them how unbelievable he was—smart, handsome, funny. In retrospect I'm not sure why I did it. In part because it was true. But perhaps I was a little jealous of their glamorous life and wanted to juice mine up a bit. Dex was the best thing in my arsenal.

"So why don't *you* like him?" Darcy would ask.

"He's not my type," I'd say. "We're just friends."

Which was the truth. Sure, there were moments when I felt a flicker of interest or a quickening of my pulse as I sat near Dex. But I remained vigilant not to fall for him, always reminding myself that guys like Dex only date girls like Darcy.

It wasn't until the following semester that the two met. A group of us from school, including Dex, planned an impromptu Thursday evening out. Darcy had been asking to meet Dex for weeks, so I phoned her and told her to be at the Red Lion at eight. She showed up, but Dex did not. I could tell Darcy viewed the whole outing as wasted effort, complaining that the Red Lion wasn't her scene, that she was over these grungy undergrad bars (which she had been into just a few short months ago), that the band sucked, and could we please leave and go somewhere nicer where people valued good grooming.

At that moment Dex sauntered into the bar wearing a black leather coat and a beautiful, oatmeal-colored cashmere sweater. He walked straight over to me and gave me a kiss on the cheek, which I still wasn't used to—Midwesterners don't kiss and greet like that. I introduced him to Darcy, and she turned on the charm, giggling and playing with her hair and nodding emphatically whenever he said anything. Dex was pleasant to her but didn't seem overly interested and, at one point, as she was dropping Goldman names—*Do you know this guy or that guy?*—Dex actually appeared to be suppressing a yawn. He left before the rest of us, waving good-bye to the group and telling Darcy that it was nice to meet her.

On the walk back to my room, I asked her what she thought of him.

"He's cute," Darcy said, giving the minimum endorsement. Her lackluster response irritated me. She couldn't praise him because he hadn't been dazzled enough by her. Darcy expected to be the one pursued. And that's what I had come to expect too.

The next day, as Dex and I had coffee, I waited for him to mention Darcy. I was sure he would, but he didn't. A small—okay, a *big*—part of me enjoyed telling Darcy that her name hadn't come up. For once, somebody wasn't falling all over themselves to be with her.

I should've known better.

About a week later, out of the blue, Dex asked me what the story was with my friend.

"Which friend?" I asked, playing dumb.

"You know, the dark-haired woman from the Red Lion?"

"Oh. Darcy," I said. And then cut right to the chase. "You want her phone number?"

"If she's single."

I delivered the news to her that evening. She smiled coyly. "He *is* pretty cute. I'll go out with him."

It took Dex another two weeks to call her. If he waited on purpose, the strategy worked wonders. She was in a frenzy by the time he took her to Union Square Cafe. The date obviously went well, because they went to brunch the next morning in the Village. Soon after that, Darcy and Dex were both off the market.

In the beginning, their romance was turbulent. I always knew Darcy loved to fight with her boyfriends—it wasn't fun unless high drama was involved—but I viewed Dex as this rational, cool creature, above the fray. Maybe he had been that way with other girls, but Darcy sucked him into her world of chaos and high emotion. She'd find a phone number in one of his law-school notebooks (she was a self-proclaimed snoop), do the research, trace it back to an ex-girlfriend, and refuse to speak to him. One day he came into Torts looking sheepish, with a cut on his forehead, right above his left eye. Darcy had hurled a wire hanger at him in a jealous rage.

And it worked the other way, too. We'd all go out and Darcy would cozy up to the bar with another guy. I'd watch Dex steal casual glances their way until he could stand it no longer. He'd go to collect her, looking angry but composed, and I'd overhear her justifying her flirtations with some tenuous connection to the guy: "I mean, we were just talking about our brothers and how they were in the same freaking fraternity. Jesus, Dex! You don't have to overreact!"

But eventually their relationship stabilized, the fights grew less intense and more infrequent, and she moved into his apartment. Then, this past winter, Dex proposed. They picked a weekend in September, and she picked me as her maid of honor.

I knew him first, I think to myself now. It is no more ironclad than the Ethan defense, but I cling to it for a moment. I picture my sympathetic juror, leaning forward as she absorbs this revelation. She even raises the point during deliberations. "If it weren't for Rachel, Dex and Darcy would never have met. So, in a sense, Rachel deserved one time with him." The other jurors stare at her incredulously, and Chanel Suit tells her not to be ridiculous. That it has nothing to do with anything. "In fact, it might even cut the other way," Chanel Suit counters. "Rachel had her chance to be with Dex—but that window has long passed. And now she is the maid of honor. *The maid of honor! It is the ultimate betrayal!*"

I work late that night, delaying my call back to Dex. I even consider waiting until tomorrow morning, mid-week, not calling at all. But the longer I wait, the more awkward it will be when I inevitably see him. So I force myself to sit down and dial his number. I hope for voice mail. It is ten-thirty. With any luck, he will be gone, home with Darcy.

"Dex Thaler," he answers, his tone all business. He is back at Goldman Sachs, having wisely chosen the banker route over the lawyer route. The work is more interesting, and the money much better.

"Rachel!" He sounds genuinely happy to hear from me, although somewhat nervous, his voice a bit too loud. "Thanks for calling. I was starting to think I wasn't going to hear from you."

"I've been meaning to call. It's just that . . . I've been really busy . . . Crazy day," I stammer. My mouth is bone-dry.

"Yeah, it's been nuts here too. Typical Monday," he says, sounding a bit more relaxed.

"Yeah . . ."

An awkward pause follows—well, it feels awkward to me. *Does he expect me to bring up the Incident?*

"So. How do you feel?" His voice becomes lower.

"How do I feel?" My face is burning, I'm sweating, and I can't rule out the possibility of regurgitating my sushi dinner.

"I mean, what do you think about Saturday?" His voice is lower still, almost a whisper. Maybe he is just being discreet, making sure nobody in the office hears him, but the volume translates as intimate.

"I don't know what you're asking me . . ."

"Do you feel guilty?"

"Of course I feel guilty. Don't you?" I look out my window at the lights of Manhattan, in the direction of his downtown office.

"Well, yeah," he says sincerely. "Obviously. It shouldn't have happened. No question about that. It was wrong . . . and I don't want you to think that, you know, that it's typical practice for me. I've never cheated on Darcy before. Never . . . You believe that, don't you?"

I tell him that of course I believe him. I want to believe him.

Another silence.

"So, yeah, that was a first for me," he says.

More silence. I picture him with his feet up on his desk, his collar loosened, tie thrown over his shoulder. He looks good in a suit. Well, he looks good in anything. And nothing.

"Uh-huh," I say. I am gripping the phone so tightly that my fingers hurt. I switch hands and wipe my sweaty palm on my skirt.

"I feel so bad that you've been friends with Darcy forever, and this thing that happened between us . . . it puts you in a really atrocious position." He clears his throat and continues. "But at the same time, I don't know . . ."

"What don't you know?" I ask, against my better judgment to end the conversation, hang up the phone, choose the flight instinct that has always served me well.

"I don't know. I just . . . well, in some ways . . . well, objectively speaking, I know what I did was so wrong. But I just don't feel guilty. Isn't that awful? . . . Do you think less of me?"

I have no idea how to answer this one. "Yes" seems mean and judgmental; "no" might open the floodgates. I find safe, middle ground. "I have no room to judge anyone, do I? I was there . . . I did it too."

"I know, Rachel. But it was my fault."

I think about the elevator, the feel of his hair between my fingers.

"We were both at fault . . . We were both drunk. It must have been the shots—they just sneaked up on me and I hadn't really eaten much that day," I ramble, hoping that we are nearly finished.

Dex interrupts. "I wasn't that drunk," he states plainly, almost defiantly.

You weren't that drunk?

As though he has read my mind, he continues. "I mean, yes, I had a few drinks—my inhibitions certainly were lowered—but I knew what I was doing, and on some level, I think I wanted it to happen. Well, I suppose that's a rather obvious statement . . . But what I mean is that I think I *consciously* wanted it to happen. Not that it was premeditated. But it had crossed my mind at various points before . . ."

At various points? When? In law school? Before or after you met Darcy?

I suddenly recall one pre-Darcy occasion when Dex and I were studying for our Torts exam in the library. It was late and we were both punchy, almost delirious from lack of sleep and too much caffeine. Dex started imitating Zigman, quoting certain pet phrases of his, as I laughed so hard that I started to cry. When I finally got ahold of myself, he leaned across the narrow table and wiped a tear off my face with his thumb. Just like a scene in a movie, only usually those are sad tears. Our eyes locked.

I looked away first, returning my eyes to my book, the words jumping all over the page. I couldn't for the life of me focus on negligence or proximate cause. Only the feel of his thumb on my face. Later, Dex offered to walk me back to my dorm. I politely declined, telling him that I'd be fine on my own. As I was falling asleep that night, I decided that I had imagined his intent, that Dex would never care for me as more than a friend. He was only being nice.

Still, I sometimes wondered what would have happened if I hadn't been so guarded. If I had said yes to his offer that night. I am wondering now in a big way.

Dex keeps talking. "Of course, I'm well aware it can never happen again," he says with conviction. "Right?" The last word is earnest, almost vulnerable.

"Right. Never *ever* again," I say, immediately regretting my juvenile choice of words. "It was a mistake."

"But I don't regret it. I should, but I just don't," he says.

This is so weird, I think, but say nothing. Just sit dumbly, waiting for him to speak again.

"So anyway, Rachel, I'm sorry for putting you in this position. But I thought you should know how I feel," he finishes, then laughs nervously.

I say okay, well now I know, and I guess we should move on and put this behind us, and all of those other things that I thought Dex was calling to tell me. We say good-bye, then I hang up and stare out my window in a daze. The call that was supposed to bring closure only ushered in more uneasiness. And a tiny little stirring inside me, a stirring that I resolve to squelch.

I stand up, turn off my office light, and walk down to the subway, trying to put Dex out of my head. But as I wait on the subway platform, my mind returns to our kiss in the elevator. The feel of his hair. And the way he looked sleeping in my bed, half-covered by my sheets. Those are the images that I remember the most. They are like the photographs of ex-boyfriends that you desperately want to throw away, but you can't bring yourself to get rid of them. So instead you store them in an old shoe box, in the back of your closet, figuring that it doesn't hurt to save them. Just in case you want to open that box and remember some of the good times.

four

We are days away from the official start of summer and all Darcy can talk about is the Hamptons. She calls and e-mails me constantly, forwarding information about Memorial Day parties, restaurant reservations, and sample sales where we are guaranteed to find the cutest summer clothes. Of course, I am absolutely dreading all of it. Like the four previous summers, I am in a house with Darcy and Dex. This year we are also sharing with Marcus, Claire, and Hillary.

"You think we should've gotten a full share?" Darcy asks for at least the twentieth time. I have never known such a second-, third-, fourth-guesser. She has buyer's remorse when she leaves Baskin-Robbins.

"No, a half share is enough. You never end up using the full share," I say, the phone tucked under my ear as I continue to revise my memo summarizing the difference between Florida and New York excess insurance law.

"Are you typing?" Darcy demands, always expecting my full attention.

"No," I lie, typing more quietly.

"You better not be . . ."

"I'm not."

"Well, I guess you're right, a half share is better . . . And we have a lot of wedding stuff to do in the city anyway."

The wedding is the only topic I wish to avoid more than the Hamptons. "Uh-huh."

"So are you going to drive out with us or take the train?"

"Train. I don't know if I can get out of here at a decent hour," I say, thinking that I do not want to be stuck in a car with her and Dex. I have not seen Dex since he left my apartment. Have not seen Darcy since the betrayal.

"Really? 'Cause I was thinking that we should definitely, *definitely* drive . . . Wouldn't you rather have a car the first weekend out? You know, especially because it's going to be a long weekend. We don't want to be stuck with cabs and stuff . . . C'mon, ride with us!"

"We'll see," I say, as a mother tells a child so that the child will drop the topic.

"Not 'we'll see.' You're comin' with us."

I sigh and tell her that I really should get back to work.

"Okay. Sheesh. I'll let you go work at your oh-so-important job . . . So we still on for tonight?"

"What's tonight?"

"Hello? *Ms. Forgetful.* Don't even tell me you have to work late—you promised. Bikinis? Ring a bell?"

"Oh, right," I say. I had completely forgotten my promise to go bathing-suit shopping with her. One of the least pleasant tasks in the world. Right up there with scrubbing toilets and getting a root canal. "Yeah. Sure. I can still do it."

"Great. I'll meet you at the yogurt counter in the basement of Bloomie's. You know, next to the fat-women's clothes. At seven sharp."

I arrive at the Fifty-ninth Street station fifteen minutes after our desig-nated meeting time and run into the basement of Bloomingdale's, nervous that Darcy will be pouting. I do not feel up to cajoling her out of one of her moods. But she looks content, sitting at the counter with a cup of strawberry frozen yogurt. She smiles and waves. I take a deep breath, reminding myself that there is no scarlet letter on my chest.

"Hi, Darce."

"Hey, there! Omigod. I'm going to be so bloated trying on suits!" She points at her stomach with her plastic spoon. "But whatever. I'm used to being a fatty."

I roll my eyes. "You're not fat."

We go through it every year during bathing-suit weather. Hell, we go through it virtually every day. Darcy's weight is a constant source of energy and discussion. She tells me what she is weighing in at—always hovering around the mid-to-high-one-twenties—always too fat by her rigorous standards. Her goal is one-twenty—which I maintain is way too thin for five nine. She e-mails me as she eats a bag of chips: "Make me stop! Help! Call me ASAP!" If I call her back, she'll ask, "Is fifteen fat grams a lot?" Or "How many fat grams equal a pound?" The thing that irritates me, though, is that she is three inches taller than I am but five pounds lighter. When I point this out, she says, "Yes, but your boobs are bigger." "Not five pounds bigger," I say. "Still," she'll say, "you look perfect the way you are." *Back to me.*

I'm far from fat, but her using me as a sounding board on this topic is like me complaining to a blind woman that I have to wear contacts.

"I am so fat. I totally am! And I chowed at lunch. But whatever. As long as I'm not a fat cow in my wedding dress . . ." she says, finishing her last spoonful of yogurt and tossing the cup into the trash. "Just tell me I have plenty of time to lose weight before the wedding."

"You have plenty of time," I say.

And I have plenty of time before the wedding to stop thinking about the fact that I had sex with your husband-to-be.

"I better rein it in, you know, or else I'm gonna have to shop here." Darcy points at the plus-size section without checking to see if any larger women are within earshot.

I tell her not to be ridiculous.

"So anyway," she says, as we ride the escalator up to the second floor,

"Claire was saying that we're getting too old for bikinis. That one-pieces are classier. What do you think of *that*?" Her expression and tone make it clear what she thinks of Claire's view on swimwear.

"I don't think there are precise age limits on bikinis," I say. Claire is full of exhausting rules; she once told me that black ink should only be used for sympathy notes.

"Ex-*act*-ly! That's what I told her . . . Besides, she's probably just saying that because she looks kind of bad in a bikini, don't you think?"

I nod. Claire works out religiously and hasn't touched fried food in years, but she is destined to be lumpy. She is redeemed, however, by impeccable grooming and expensive clothing. She'll show up at the beach in a three-hundred-dollar one-piece with a matching sarong, a fancy hat, and designer glasses and it will go a long way toward disguising an extra roll around her waist.

We make our way around the floor, searching the racks for acceptable suits. At one point, I notice that we have both selected a basic black Anne Klein bikini. If we both end up wanting it, Darcy will either insist that she found it first or she'll say that we can get the same one. Then she will proceed to look better in it all summer. No, thanks.

I am reminded of the time that she, Annalise, and I went shopping for backpacks the week before we started the fourth grade. We all spotted the same bag right away. It was purple with silver stars on the outside pocket—way cooler than the other bags. Annalise suggested that we get the same one and Darcy said no, that it was way too babyish to match. Matching was for third-graders.

So we rock-paper-scissored for it. I went with the rock (which I have found to be a winner more than its share of the time). I pounded my jubilant fist over their extended scissor fingers and swept my purple book bag into our shared cart. Annalise balked, whining that we knew purple was her favorite color. "I thought you liked red better, Rachel!"

Annalise was no match for me. I simply told her yes, I did prefer red, but as she could plainly see, there were no red bags. So Annalise settled for a yellow one with a smiley face on the pocket. Darcy agonized over the remaining choices and finally told us that she was going to sleep on the decision and come back with her mom the next day. I forgot about Darcy's bag choice until the first day of school. When I got to the bus stop, there stood Darcy with a purple bag just like mine.

I pointed at it, incredulous. "You got my bag."

"I know," Darcy said. "I decided I wanted it. Who cares if we match?"

Hadn't she been the one to say that matching was babyish?

"I care," I said, feeling the rage grow inside me.

Darcy rolled her eyes and smacked her gum. "Oh, Rachel, like it matters. It's just a bag after all."

Annalise was upset too, for her own reasons. "How come you two get to be twins and I'm left out? My bag is gay."

Darcy and I ignored her.

"But you said we shouldn't match," I accused Darcy, as the bus pulled around the corner and screeched to a stop in front of us.

"Did I?" she said, fingering her stiff, feathered hair, freshly sprayed with several layers of Breck. "Well, who cares?"

Darcy used "who cares" (later replaced by "whatever") as the ultimate passive-aggressive response. I didn't recognize her tactic as such at the time; I only knew that she always managed to get her way and make me feel stupid if I fought back.

We boarded the bus, Darcy first. She sat down and I sat behind her, still furious. I watched Annalise hesitate and then sit with me, recognizing that I had right on my side. The whole purple backpack issue could have escalated into a full-fledged fight, but I refused to let Darcy's betrayal ruin the first day of school. It wasn't worth going to battle with her. The end result was seldom satisfying.

I covertly replace the Anne Klein suit on the rack as we make our way to the long line for the dressing rooms. When one becomes available, Darcy decides that we should share a room to save time. She strips down to her black thong and matching lace bra, contemplating which suit she should try on first. I steal a look at her in the mirror. Her body is even better than it was last summer. Her long limbs are perfectly toned from her wedding workout regimen, her skin already bronzed by routine applications of tanning cream and an occasional trip to the tanning beds.

I think of Dex. Surely he compared our bodies after (or even during, since he "wasn't that drunk") our night together. Mine isn't nearly as good. I am shorter, softer, whiter. And even though my boobs are bigger, hers are better. They are perkier, with the ideal nipple-to-areola-to-breast ratio.

"Stop looking at my fat!" Darcy squeals, catching my glance in the mirror.

Now I am forced to compliment her. "You're not fat, Darce. You look great. I can tell you've been working out."

"You can? What body part has improved?" Darcy likes her praise to be specific.

"Just everywhere. Your legs look thin—good." That is all she is getting from me.

She studies her legs, frowning at the reflection.

I undress, noting my own cotton underwear and nonmatching, slightly dingier cotton bra. I quickly try on my first suit, a navy-and-white tankini, revealing two inches of midriff. It is a compromise between Claire's one-piece edict and Darcy's preference for bikinis.

"Omigod! That looks so awesome on you! You gotta get it!" Darcy says. "Are you getting it?"

"I guess so," I say. It doesn't look awesome, but it's not bad. I have studied enough magazine articles about suits and body flaws over the years to know which suits will look decent on me. This one passes.

Darcy puts on a tiny black bikini with a triangular top and bare coverage in the bottom. She looks straight-up hot. "You like?"

"It's good," I say, thinking that Dex will love it.

"Should I get it?"

I tell her to try the others on before making a decision. She obeys, taking the next one off the hanger. Of course, every suit looks amazing on her. She falls into none of those categories of body flaws in the magazines. After much discussion, I settle on the tankini and Darcy decides on three tiny bikinis—one red, one black, and one nude-colored number that is going to make her look naked from any kind of distance.

As we go to pay for our suits, Darcy grabs my arm. "Oh! Shit! I almost forgot to tell you!"

"What?" I ask, unnerved by her sudden outburst, even though I know she isn't going to say, "I forgot to tell you that I know you slept with Dex!"

"Marcus likes you!" We might as well be in the tenth grade, from her tone and use of the word "likes."

I am intentionally obtuse. "I like him too," I say. "He's a nice guy." *And a hell of an alibi.*

"No, silly. I mean, he *likes* you. You must've done a good job at the party because he called Dex and got your number. I think he's going to ask you out for this weekend. Of course, I wanted it to be a double date, but Marcus said no, he doesn't want witnesses." She drops her bikinis onto the counter and fumbles in her purse for her wallet.

"He got my number from Dex?" I ask, thinking that this is quite a development.

"Yeah. Dex was cute when he told me about it. He was . . ." She looks up, searching for the right word. "Sort of protective of you."

"What do you mean by 'protective'?" I ask, way more interested in Dex's role in this exchange than in Marcus's intentions.

"Well, he gave Marcus the number, but when he got off the phone he asked me all these questions, like were you seeing anyone and did I think you would like Marcus. And you know, was he smart enough for you. Stuff like that. It was really cute."

I digest this information as the store clerk rings up Darcy's bikinis.

"So what did you tell him?"

"I just said that you were *totally* single, and that of course you'd be into Marcus. He's such a sweetie. Don't you think?"

I shrug. Marcus moved to New York from San Francisco only a few months ago. I know very little about him, except that he and Dex became friends at Georgetown, where Marcus's claim to fame was graduating dead last. Apparently Marcus never went to class and got high all the time. The most infamous story is that he overslept on the day of his statistics final exam, showed up twenty minutes late only to discover that he had thrown his remote control into his backpack instead of his calculator.

I haven't yet determined whether he is a free spirit or simply a buffoon.

"So are you psyched? If you get a date in with him before our share starts, you will have dibs on him over Claire and Hillary."

I laugh and shake my head.

"Seriously." Darcy signs her receipt and flashes a smile at the clerk. "Claire would love to sink her nails in him."

"Who said I'm going on a date?"

"Oh, puh-lease. Don't even start with that shit. You're going. (A) he is such a cutie. And (b) Rachel, no offense, but you can't exactly afford to be all picky, Ms. Haven't Been Laid in—what? Over a year?"

The store clerk looks up at me sympathetically. I glare at Darcy as I slide my tankini across the counter. *Yeah, right—a year.*

We leave Bloomingdale's and look for a cab on Third Avenue.

"So, you'll go out with Marcus?"

"I guess so."

"Promise?" she asks, getting her cell phone out of her purse.

"You want me to take a blood oath? Yes, I'll go," I say. "Who are you calling?"

"Dex. He bet me twenty bucks that you wouldn't go."

Darcy's right—I have nothing else going on. But the real reason I say yes to Marcus when he calls and asks me out is that Dex said I wouldn't go. And just in case he thought he had cast some sort of spell over me and I was going to turn Marcus down because I'm preoccupied with the Incident, I will go out with Marcus.

But as soon as I say yes, I start obsessing about what Marcus *really* knows. Did Dex tell him anything? I decide that I must call Dexter and find out. I hang up three times before I can dial the full number. My stomach is churning when he answers on the first ring. "Dex Thaler."

"So what does Marcus know about what happened last Saturday?" I blurt out, my heart racing.

"Well, hello to you too," he says.

I soften slightly. "Hi, Dex."

"Last Saturday? What was last Saturday? Refresh my memory."

"I'm being serious! What did you tell him?" I am horrified to find myself talking in the girly, whiny way that Darcy has perfected.

"What do you think I told him?" he asks.

"Dexter, tell me!"

"Oh, relax," he says, his tone still one of amusement. "I didn't tell him anything . . . What do you think this is? A high school locker room? Why would I tell anyone our business?"

Our business. *Our. We. Us.*

"I was just wondering what he knew. I mean, you told Darcy you were with him that night . . ."

"Yeah. I said, 'Marcus, I was with you last night and we had breakfast together this morning—all right?' And that was that. I know that's not how it works with you girls—women."

"What is that supposed to mean?"

"I mean you and Darcy share every exhaustive detail with one another. Like what you ate that day and what brand of shampoo you plan on purchasing."

"And like when you sleep with one another's fiancés? That sort of detail?"

Dex laughs. "Yeah, that would be another example."

"Or like your bet that I'd say no to Marcus?"

He laughs again, knowing that he is busted. "She told you that, did she?"

"Yeah. She told me that."

"And did it offend you?"

I realize that I am starting to relax, almost enjoying the conversation. "No . . . but it made me say yes to Marcus."

"Oh!" he laughs. "I see how it works. So you're saying that had she not shared that piece of information with you, you would have turned my boy down?"

"Wouldn't you like to know?" I ask coyly, hardly recognizing myself.

"I would actually. Please enlighten me."

"I'm not sure . . . Why did you think I'd say no?"

"Wouldn't you like to know," he retorts.

I smile. This is full-fledged flirtatious banter.

"Okay. I thought you'd say no because Marcus doesn't seem to be your type," he finally says.

"And who is?" I ask, and then feel instantly remorseful. Flirting like this is not the path to redemption. It is no way to right my wrong. This is what my brain tells me, but my heart is galloping as I await his answer.

"I don't know. I've been trying to figure that out for about seven years."

I wonder what he means by this statement. I twist the cord around my fingers and can think of nothing to say in response. We should hang up now. This is going in a bad direction.

"Rach?" His voice is low and intimate.

I feel breathless, hearing him say my name like this. The one syllable is familiar, warm. "Yeah?"

"You still there?" he whispers.

I manage to say, "Yes, I'm still here."

"What are you thinking?"

"Nothing," I lie.

I have to lie. Because what I am thinking is, *Maybe you are my type a little bit more than I once thought.*

five

Maybe I don't have a type at all.
When I consider my past relationships there is no composite picture. Not
that the sample would be considered statistically significant—other than
Brandon in high school, I have had only three boyfriends.

My real dating history began my first semester of college at Duke. I
lived in a coed dorm, and every night we all gathered in the lounge to
study (or pretend to), hang out, and watch shows like *Beverly Hills,
90210* and *Melrose Place*. It was in that lounge that I developed a serious crush on Hunter Bretz from Mississippi. Hunter was scrawny and
nerdy, but I was crazy about him. I loved his intelligence, his slow,
smooth drawl, and the way his brown eyes fixed on you when you
talked, as though he really cared about what you had to say. My roommate Pam, a Jersey girl with big hair, declared my feelings a "total fucking mystery" but still encouraged me to ask Hunter out. I didn't, but I
did work hard at developing a friendship, cracking through his shy

exterior to talk to him about poetry and literature. I really believed that I was making progress with Hunter when Joey Merola came in for the kill.

Joey was the opposite of Hunter—a boisterous sports guy with a loud laugh. He played every intramural sport in the book and was always strolling into the lounge all sweaty with a story about how his team came from behind in the last second to win the game. He was the kind of guy who was proud of how much he could eat and the fact that he could get by in literature classes without ever reading a book.

One Thursday night, Joey, Hunter, and I were the last three in the lounge, talking about religion, the death penalty, and the meaning of life, the stuff I had imagined discussing in college, away from Darcy and her more shallow pursuits. Joey was an atheist and for the death penalty. Like me, Hunter was Methodist and against the death penalty. All three of us were unclear on the meaning of life. We talked and talked, and I was determined to outlast Joey and end up with Hunter. But sometime after two, Hunter threw in the towel. "Awright y'all, I have an early class."

"C'mon, man. Skip it. I never make my eight o'clock," Joey said proudly.

Hunter laughed. "I figure I'm payin' for it, I should go."

This was another thing I liked about Hunter. He was paying for his own education, unlike most of the rich kids at Duke. So he said good night, and I wistfully watched him amble out of the lounge. Joey didn't miss a beat, just kept yapping, rehashing the fact that we were both from Indiana—just two towns apart—and that both of our fathers had attended Indiana (his dad had been a walk-on for the basketball team). We played the name game and got two hits. Joey knew Blaine, Darcy's ex-boyfriend, from reading the local sports page. And we both knew of Tracy Purlington, a promiscuous girl from the town between ours.

Finally, when I said I really must get to bed, Joey followed me upstairs and kissed me in the stairwell. I thought of Hunter, but I still kissed Joey back, excited to be getting some real collegiate experience. Annalise had already met her now-husband Greg (and lost her virginity to him), and Darcy had hooked up with four guys by my latest count.

The next morning I regretted kissing Joey. Even more so when I spotted Hunter hunkered down in the library stacks, his head bent over a textbook. But not enough to keep me from kissing Joey again that weekend, this time in the laundry room as we waited for our clothes to dry. And so it continued until everybody in our dorm, including Hunter, knew that Joey and I were an item. Pam was psyched for me—said that Joey blew Hunter away and had the cutest butt in the dorm. I wrote to Darcy and Annalise, telling them about my new boyfriend and how I was over Hunter (only partly true) and how happy I was (happy enough). They both had one question: was I going to go *all the way* with Joey?

I was ambivalent on the subject of sex. Part of me wanted to wait until I was deeply in love, maybe even married. But I was also intensely curious to find out what all the fuss was about, and desperately wanted to be sophisticated and worldly. So after Joey and I had been together a respectable six weeks, I marched over to the school health clinic and returned to my dorm with a prescription for Lo/Ovral, the birth-control pill that Darcy guaranteed would not cause weight gain. A month later, with the added protection of a condom, Joey and I did the great deed. It was his first time too. The earth didn't move during those two and a half minutes, as Darcy claimed it did during her first time with Carlos. But it also didn't hurt as much as Annalise had warned me it would. I was relieved to have it out of the way and happy to join my hometown friends in all their womanly glory. Joey and I embraced in my bottom bunk and said that we loved each other. Ours was a better first time than most.

But that spring, there were two red flags indicating that Joey wasn't the man of my dreams. First, he joined a fraternity and took the whole thing way too seriously. One night when I teased him about the frat's secret handshake, he told me that if I disrespected his brotherhood, I was disrespecting him. *Please*. Second, Joey became obsessed with Duke basketball, sleeping out in tents for tickets to big games and painting his face blue, jumping up and down courtside with the other "Cameron Crazies."

The whole scene was a bit much, but I guess I would have been fine with his enthusiasm if he had been from New Hampshire or another state with no huge basketball ties. But he was from Indiana. Big Ten country. His father played for the Hoosiers, for God's sake. And there he was, this sudden die-hard "I've liked Duke since the dawn of time and I'm all tight with Bobby Hurley because he once drank at my frat house" kind of a fan. But I looked beyond these imperfections, and we forged ahead to sophomore and then junior year.

Then one night, after Wake Forest beat Duke in hoops, Joey showed up at my place in a foul mood. We began to argue about nothing and everything. First it was petty matters: he said that I snored and hogged the bed (how can you *not* hog a twin bed?); I complained that he consistently mixed up our toothbrushes (who makes that mistake?). The arguing escalated to more significant issues. And there was no turning back when he called me a boring intellectual and I called him a shameless bandwagoner who actually believed that his painted blue face contributed to Duke's championships. He told me to lighten up and get some school pride, before storming off.

He returned the next day with a solemn face and his scripted "we need to have a talk" introduction followed by the "we'll always be close" conclusion. I was more stunned than sad, but I agreed that maybe we should be having a more diverse college experience, which really meant dating other people. We said we would always be friends, even though I knew we didn't have enough in common for that to happen.

I didn't shed a tear until I saw him at a party holding hands with Betsy Wingate, who had also lived in our freshmen dorm. I didn't want to be holding his hand, so I knew my reaction was only a mix of nostalgia and hurt pride. And regret that maybe I should have pursued Hunter, who had long since been snatched up by another discerning undergraduate.

I phoned Darcy in a rare case of role reversal, seeking comfort from the relationship pro. She told me not to look back, that I had some good, rah-rah college memories with Joey, something I wouldn't have had with Hunter, who would have dragged me down socially. "Besides," she said earnestly, "Joey taught you the basics of predictable, missionary-style sex. And that's worth something, right?" It was her idea of a pep talk. I guess it helped a little.

I kept hoping that Hunter and his girlfriend would break up, but it never happened. I didn't date again at Duke, nor did I through most of law school. The long drought finally ended with Nate Menke.

I met Nate our first year of law school at a party, but for the next three years we barely talked, only said hello in passing. Then we both found ourselves in the same small class—The Empowered Self: Law and Society in the Age of Individualism. Nate spoke in class often, but not just to hear himself speak, as half the people in law school did. He actually had interesting things to say. After I made a decent point one day, he asked if I wanted to grab a coffee to discuss it further. He ordered his black, and I remember copying him because it seemed more sophisticated than dumping milk and sugar into my cup. After coffee, we took a long walk through the Village, stopping in CD stores and used-book shops. We went to dinner after that, and by the end of the evening it was clear that we were going to become a couple.

I was thrilled to have a boyfriend again and became quickly enthralled with most things about Nate. I liked his face, for one. He had the coolest eyes that turned up slightly in a way that would have made him look Asian but for his light coloring. I also liked his personality. He was soft-spoken but strong-willed and politically active in a defiant, angry sort of way. It was hard to keep track of all his causes, but I tried, even convinced myself that I felt the same way. Compared to Joey, who could only muster passion for a basketball team, Nate seemed so real. He was intense in bed too. Although he had had few partners before me, he seemed very experienced, always urging me to try something new. "How's this?" "How's that?" he would ask, and then would memorize his position and get it just right the next time.

Nate and I graduated from law school and spent the summer in the city, studying for the bar exam. Every day we went to the library together, breaking only for meals and sleep. Hour after hour, day after day, week after week, we crammed thousands of rules and facts and laws and theories into our crowded brains. We were both driven less by the desire to succeed than by an all-pervasive fear of failure, which Nate chalked up to our being only children. The relentless ordeal brought us closer. We were both miserable, but happy in our misery together.

But that fall, only one of us stayed miserable. Nate began working as an assistant district attorney in Queens, and I started my law firm job in Midtown. He loved his job, and I hated mine. As Nate interviewed witnesses and prepared for trial, I was relegated to document productions—the lowliest task in the legal profession. Every night I'd sit in conference rooms studying piles of papers in endless cardboard boxes. I'd look at the dates on those documents and think, *I was just getting my driver's license when this letter was typed, and here it is, still caught in an endless cycle of litigation.* It all seemed so pointless.

So my life was bleak—except for my relationship with Nate. I began to rely on him more and more as my sole source of happiness. I often told him that I loved him, and felt more relief than joy when he said it back. I started to think about marriage, even talked about our theoretical children and where we all might live.

Then one night Nate and I went to a bar in the Village to hear a folk singer from Brooklyn named Carly Weinstein. After her performance, Nate and I and a few other people chatted with her as she put her guitar away with the gentleness of a new mother.

"Your lyrics are beautiful . . . what inspires you?" Nate asked her, big-eyed.

I was instantly worried; I remembered that look from our first coffee date. I became even more distressed when he bought a copy of her CD. She wasn't *that* good. I think Nate and Carly went on a date a week later, because there was one night when he was unaccounted for and didn't answer his cell phone until after midnight. I was too afraid to ask where he had been. Besides, I already knew. He had changed. He looked at me differently, a shadow over his face, his mind somewhere else.

Sure enough, we had the big talk soon after that. He was very forthright. "I have feelings for someone else," he said. "I always promised that I would tell you."

I remembered those conversations well, remembered liking the strong, confident way I sounded as I told him that if he ever met someone else, he should just tell me outright, that I could handle it. Of course, I didn't think at the time that it would ever leave the hypothetical realm. I wanted to suck back all my cavalier instructions, tell him instead that I would greatly prefer a gentle lie about needing some space or some time apart.

"Is it Carly?" I asked, a catch in my throat.

He looked shocked. "How did you know?"

"I could just tell," I said, unable to fight back sobs.

"I'm so sorry," he said, hugging me. "It kills me to hurt you like this. But I had to be honest. I owe you that."

So he got a new girl, *and* he got to be noble. I tried to be angry, but how can you be mad at someone for not wanting to be with you? Instead I just sulked around, gained a few pounds, and swore off men.

Nate kept calling for a few months after our breakup. I knew he was just being nice, but the calls gave me false hope. I could never resist asking about his girlfriend. "Carly is fine," he would say sheepishly. Then once, he answered, "We're moving in together . . . and I think we're going to get engaged . . ." His voice trailed off.

"Congratulations. That's great. I'm really happy for you," I said.

"Thank you, Rachel. It means a lot to hear you say that."

"Yeah . . . Best of luck and all, but I don't think I want you to call me anymore, okay?"

"I understand," he said, probably relieved to be off the hook.

I haven't heard from Nate since that conversation. I'm not sure if or when they married, but I still look for Carly Weinstein sometimes when I'm shopping for CDs. So far she hasn't made it big.

Looking back, I question whether I really loved Nate, or just the security of our relationship. I wonder if my feelings for him didn't have a lot to do with hating my job. From the bar exam through that first hellish year as an associate, Nate was my escape. And sometimes that can feel an awful lot like love.

A reasonable time passed after Nate. I lost my breakup weight, got my hair highlighted, and agreed to a string of blind dates. At worst they were awful. At best, simply uncomfortable and forgettable. Then I met Alec Kaplan at Spy Bar, down in Soho. I was with Darcy and some of her friends from work and he and his oh-so-hip friends approached us. Alec, of course, wooed Darcy at first, but she pushed him my way—literally, with her hand on the small of his back—with firm directions to "talk to my friend." To her, it was the ultimate in generosity. Even though she had Dex, she was never one to turn down male attention. "He's really cute," Darcy kept whispering. "Go for it."

She was right, Alec was cute. But he was also all about image. He was the kind of guy who retires his college cool-boy uniform of filthy, intentionally broken-in baseball caps, fraternity party T-shirts, and woven leather belts, swapping it for his twenty-something urban cool-boy uniform of gripping, cotton-spandex T-shirts, tight black pants with a slight sheen, and loads of hair gel. He told too many "a guy walks into a bar" jokes (none funny) and "I'm a badass trader" war stories (none impressive). When he bought me a drink on that first night, he threw down a one-hundred-dollar bill and told the bartender in a loud voice that he was sorry but he didn't have anything smaller. In a nutshell, he epitomized what Darcy and I call TTH—for Trying Too Hard.

But Alec was smart enough, fun enough, and nice enough. So when he asked for my number, I gave it to him. And when he called and asked me out to dinner, I went. And when he propositioned me, four dates later, ribbed condom in hand, I shrugged inside but said yes. He had a great body, but the sex was just average. My mind often wandered to work, and once when I heard *SportsCenter* in the background, I even pretended he was Pete Sampras. Many times I came close to breaking up with him, but Darcy kept telling me to give him another chance, that he was rich and cute. Way richer and cuter than Nate, she'd point out. As if that was what it was all about.

Then one night, Claire spotted Alec kissing a petite, somewhat trashy-looking blonde at Merchants. When the girl went to the bathroom, Claire confronted Alec, warning him that if he didn't confess his infidelity, she would tell me herself. So the next day Alec called and sputtered an apology, saying he was getting back together with his ex, who I assume was the girl at Merchants. I almost told him that I had wanted to break up too—it was the truth. But I cared so little that I didn't bother setting the record straight. I simply said okay, best of luck. And that was that.

Every now and then I run into Alec at the New York Sports Club near work. We are very cordial to each other—once I even used the StairMaster beside his, not caring that my face was broken out or that I was wearing my sloppiest gray sweats (Darcy says they should never be worn in public). On that occasion, we made small talk. I inquired about his girlfriend, letting him ramble on about their upcoming trip to Jamaica. It took no effort at all to be nice, another clear indication that I had nothing real invested in our relationship. In some ways, in fact, I shouldn't even put Alec in the serious-boyfriend category. But because I slept with him (and see myself as the sort of woman who would only sleep with someone in a legitimate relationship), I put him in that unfortunately exclusive club.

I review my three boyfriends, the three men I slept with in my twenties, searching for a common thread. Nothing. No consistent features, coloring, stature, personality. But one theme does emerge: they all picked me. And then dumped me. I played the passive role. Waiting for Hunter and then settling for Joey. Waiting to feel more for Nate. Then waiting to feel less. Waiting for Alec to go away and leave me in peace.

And now Dex. My number four. And I am still waiting.

For all of this to blow over.

For his September wedding.

For someone who gives me that tingly feeling as I watch him sleeping in my bed early on a Sunday morning. Someone who isn't engaged to my best friend.

six

On Saturday night, I cab down to Gotham Bar and Grill with an open mind and a positive attitude—half the battle before any date—thinking that maybe Marcus will be the someone I am looking for.

I walk into the restaurant and spot him right away, sitting at the bar, wearing baggy jeans and a slightly wrinkled, green plaid shirt with the sleeves rolled up haphazardly—the opposite of TTH.

"Sorry I'm late," I say, as Marcus stands to greet me. "Had some trouble getting a cab."

"No worries," he says, offering me a stool next to his.

I sit down. He smiles, exposing two rows of very white, straight teeth. Possibly his best feature. Either that or the cleft in his square chin.

"So what can I get you?" he asks me.

"What are you having?"

"Gin and tonic."

"I'll have the same."

He glances toward the bartender with a twenty extended and then looks back at me. "You look great, Rachel."

I thank him. It's been a long time since I've received a proper compliment from a guy. It occurs to me that Dex and I didn't get around to compliments.

Marcus finally gets the bartender's attention and orders me a Bombay Sapphire and tonic. Then he says, "So, last time I saw you we were all pretty wasted . . . That was a fun night."

"Yeah. I was pretty out of it," I say, hoping that Dex told me the truth about keeping Marcus in the dark. "But at least I made it home before sunup. Darcy told me you and Dex were out pretty late that night."

"Yeah. We hung out for a while," Marcus says, without looking at me. This is a good sign. He is covering for his friend but has trouble lying. He takes his change from the bartender, leaves two bills and some coins on the bar, and hands me my drink. "Here you go."

"Thanks." I smile, stir, and sip from the skinny straw.

An emaciated Asian girl wearing leather pants and too much lip liner taps Marcus on the arm and tells him that our table is ready. We carry our drinks, following her to the restaurant area beyond the bar. As we sit, she hands us two oversized menus and a separate wine list.

"Your server will be with you shortly," she says, before flipping her long, black hair and waltzing off.

Marcus glances at the wine list and asks if I want to order a bottle.

"Sure," I say.

"Red or white?"

"Either."

"Do you think you're going to have fish?" He looks at the menu.

"Maybe. But I don't mind red with fish."

"I'm not very good at picking wines," he says, cracking his knuckles below the table. "You wanna have a look?"

"That's okay. You can pick. Whatever is fine."

"All right then. I'll wing it," he says, flashing me his "I never skipped a night wearing my retainer" smile.

We study our menus, discussing what looks good. Marcus slides his chair closer to the table, and I feel his knee against mine.

"I almost didn't ask you out, since we're in the same summer house and all," Marcus says, his eyes still scanning the menu. "Dex told me that's one of the cardinal rules here. Don't get involved with someone in your house. At least not until August."

He laughs as I store away this fact for later analysis: *Dex discouraged our date.*

"But then I thought, you know, what the hell—I dig her, I'm going to call her. I mean, I've been thinking about asking you out since Dex first introduced us. Right when I moved here. But I was seeing this girl from San Francisco for a minute in there and thought I should wrap things up before I called you. You know, just to make it all neat and kosher. So I finally ended that deal . . . And here we are." He wipes his forehead with the back of his hand as if relieved to make this confession.

"I think you made the right decision."

"To wait?"

"No. To call." I give him my most alluring smile, fleetingly reminding myself of Darcy. *She doesn't have the market cornered on female attractiveness,* I think. *I don't always have to be the serious, dowdy one.*

Our waitress interrupts the moment. "Hello. How are you this evening?"

"Fine," Marcus says cheerfully, and then lowers his voice. "For a first date."

I laugh, but our waitress musters only a stiff, tight-lipped smile. "Can I tell you about the specials?"

"Go for it," Marcus says.

She stares into the space just above our heads, rattling off the list of specials, calling everything "nice"—"a nice sea bass," "a nice risotto," and so on. I nod and only half listen while I think about Dex telling Marcus not to ask me out, wondering what that means.

"So would you like to start with something to drink?"

"Yeah . . . Think we're going with a bottle of red. What do you recommend?" He squints at the menu.

"The Marjorie pinot noir is *superb*." She points down at the wine list.

"Fine. That one then. Perfect."

She flashes another prim smile my way. "And are you ready to order?"

"Yes, I think we are," I say, and then order the garden salad and tuna.

"And how would you like that done?"

"Medium," I say.

Marcus orders the pea soup and the lamb.

"Excellent choices," our waitress says, with an affected tilt of the head. She gathers our menus and turns on her heels.

"Man," Marcus says.

"What?"

"That chick has zero personality."

I laugh.

He smiles. "Where were we? . . . Oh yeah, the Hamptons."

"Right."

"So Dex says it's never a good idea to go out with someone in your own house. And I'm like, 'Dude, I'm not playin' by your dumb East Coast rules.' If we end up hating each other, we hate each other."

"I don't think we're going to hate each other," I say.

Our waitress returns with the wine, uncorks the bottle, and pours some into his glass. Marcus takes a healthy sip and reports that it's great, skipping the usual pretentious ceremony. You can tell a lot about a guy by watching him take that first sip of wine. It's not a good sign when he does the whole swirling thing, burying his nose into the glass, taking a slow, thoughtful sip, pausing with a furrowed brow followed by a slight nod so as not to appear too enthusiastic, as if to say, this passes, but I have had plenty better. If he is truly a wine connoisseur, that's one thing. But it is usually just a bunch of show, painful to observe.

As our waitress pours my wine, I ask Marcus if he knows about the bet.

He shakes his head. "What bet?"

I wait until we are alone again—it's bad enough that our waitress knows this is a first date. "Dex and Darcy had a bet about whether I'd say yes when you asked me out."

"Get outta here." He drops his jaw for effect. "Who thought you'd go and who thought you'd diss me?"

"Oh. I forget." I pretend to be confused. "That's not the point. The point is—"

"That they are so up and in our business!" He shakes his head. "Bastards."

"I know."

He lifts his glass. "To eluding Dex and Darcy. No sharing details of tonight with those nosy bastards."

I laugh. "No matter how great—or how bad—our date is!"

Our glasses touch and we sip in unison.

"This date is *not* going to be bad. Trust me on that."

I smile. "I trust you."

I do trust him, I think. There is something disarming about his sense of humor, and easy, Midwestern style. And he's not engaged to Darcy. A nice bonus.

Then, as if on cue, Marcus asks me how long I've known Darcy.

"Twenty-some years. First time I saw her she was all dressed up in this fancy little sundress, and I was wearing these dumb Winnie-the-Pooh shorts from Sears. I thought, now *there's* a girl with style."

Marcus laughs. "I bet you looked cute in your Pooh shorts."

"Not quite . . ."

"And then you were the one who introduced Darcy and Dex, right? He said you were good friends in law school?"

Right. My good friend Dex. The last person I slept with.

"Uh-huh. I met him first semester of law school. I knew right away that he and Darcy would make a good match," I say. A bit of an exaggeration, but I want to set the record straight that I never considered Dex for myself. Which I didn't. And still don't.

"They even look alike . . . No mystery as to how their kids will turn out."

"Yes. They will be beautiful." I feel an inexplicable knot in my chest, picturing Dex and Darcy cradling their newborn. For some reason, I had never thought beyond the wedding in September.

"What?" Marcus asks, obviously catching my expression. Which doesn't mean that he is perceptive, necessarily; my face is just less than inscrutable. It is a curse.

"Nothing," I say. Then I smile and sit up a bit straighter. It is time for a transition. "Enough about Dex and Darcy."

"Yeah," he says. "I hear you."

We start the typical first-date conversation, discussing our jobs, our families and general backgrounds. We cover his Internet start-up that went under and his move to New York. Our food arrives. We eat and talk and order another bottle of wine. There is more laughter than silence. I am even comfortable enough to take a bite of his lamb when he offers it to me.

After dinner, Marcus pays the bill. It is always an awkward moment for me, although offering to pay (whether sincerely or with the fake reach for the wallet) is so much more awkward. I thank him, and we make our way to the door, where we decide to get another drink.

"You pick a place," Marcus says.

I choose a new bar that just opened near my apartment. We get in a cab, talking the whole way to the Upper East Side. Then we sit at the bar, talking more.

I ask him to tell me about his hometown in Montana. He pauses for a beat and then says he has a good story for me.

"Only about ten percent of my senior class went to college," he starts. "Most students don't even bother with SATs at my high school. But I took the thing, did fine on it, applied to Georgetown, and got in. Of course, I didn't mention it to anyone at school—just went about my business, hanging with my boys and whatnot. Then the faculty catches wind of the Georgetown thing and one day my math teacher, Mr. Gilhooly, takes it upon himself to announce my good news to the class."

He shakes his head as if the memory is painful. "So everyone was like, 'So what? Big fucking deal.'" Marcus imitates his bored classmates by folding his arms across his chest and then patting his mouth with an open hand. "And I guess their reaction pissed Mr. Gilhooly off. He wanted them to truly grasp the depth of their inadequacies and future doom. So he proceeded to draw this big graph on the board showing my earning potential with a college degree versus their earning potential bussing tables at Shoney's. And how the gap would get worse and worse with time."

"No way!"

"Yeah. So they're all sitting there like, 'Fuck Marcus,' right? Like I think I'm hot shit 'cause I'm going to make six figures someday. I wanted to kill that dude." Marcus throws up his hands. "Thanks for nothing, Mr. Gilhooly. Way to win me some friends."

I laugh.

"So what the fuck am I supposed to do now? I gotta fight the image of dork gunner boy, right? So I go out of my way to show everybody I don't give a shit about academics. Started smokin' weed every day, and never stopped the practice in college. Hence, well, you know, my finishing next to last at Georgetown. I'm sure you've heard about the remote?" he asks, peeling the label off his Heineken.

I smile and tap his hand. "Yeah. I know the story. Except the version I heard was that you were dead last."

"Aww, man!" Marcus shakes his head. "Dex never gets that shit right. My one-point-six-seven beat someone out! Next to last, dude! Next to last!"

After two drinks, I glance at my watch and say it's getting late.

"Okay. I'll walk you home?"

"Sure."

We stroll over to Third Avenue and stop in front of my apartment.

"Well, good night, Marcus. Thank you so much for dinner. I had a really nice time," I say, meaning it.

"Yeah. So did I. It was good." He licks his lips quickly. I know what is coming. "And I'm glad we're in the same house this summer."

"I am too."

Then he asks if he can kiss me. It is a question I don't usually like. *Just do it,* I always think. But for some reason it doesn't bother me coming from Marcus.

I nod and he leans over and gives me a medium-long kiss.

We separate. My heart isn't palpitating, but I am content.

"You think Darcy and Dex bet on that?" he asks.

I laugh because I had been wondering the same thing.

"How did it go?" Darcy yells into the phone the next morning.

I am just out of the shower, dripping wet. "Where are you?"

"In the car with Dex. We're on our way back to the city," she says. "We went antiquing. Remember?"

"Yes," I say. "I remember."

"How did it go?" she asks again, smacking her gum. She can't even wait until she gets home to get the scoop on my date.

I don't answer.

"Well?"

"We have a bad connection. Your cell is breaking up," I say. "I can't hear you."

"Nice try. Give me the goods."

"What goods?"

"Rachel! Don't play dumb with me. Tell me about your date! We're dying to know."

I hear Dex echo her in the background. "Just *dying!*"

"It was a lovely evening," I say, trying to wrap a towel around my head without dropping the phone.

She squeals. "Yes! I knew it. So details! Details!"

I tell her that we went to Gotham Bar and Grill, I ordered the tuna, he had lamb.

"Rachel! Get to the good stuff! Did you hook up?"

"I can't tell you that."

"Why not?"

"I have my reasons."

"That means you did," she says. "Otherwise you'd just say no."

"Think what you want."

"C'mon, Rachel!"

I tell her no way, I am not going to be her car-ride entertainment. She reports my words to Dex and I hear him say, "Bruce is our car-ride entertainment. Tell her that."

Tunnel of Love is playing in the background.

"Tell Dexter that's Bruce's worst album."

"They're all bad albums. Springsteen sucks," Darcy says.

"Did she just say this album is bad?" I hear Dex ask Darcy.

Darcy says yeah and a few seconds later "Thunder Road" is blaring. Darcy shouts at him to turn it down. I smile.

"So?" Darcy asks. "Are you going to tell us or not?"

"Not."

"If I promise not to tell Dex?"

"Still not."

Darcy makes an exasperated sound. Then she tells me that she will find out one way or another and hangs up.

The next I hear from Dex is on Thursday night, the day before we are scheduled to leave for the Hamptons.

"Do you want a ride? We have room for one more," he says. "Claire's coming with us. And your boyfriend's in."

"Well, in that case, I'd love a ride," I say, trying to sound breezy and casual. I need to show him that I've moved on. I *have* moved on.

At five o'clock the next day, we are assembled in Dexter's car, hoping to get ahead of the traffic. But the roads are already clogged. It takes us an hour to get through the Midtown Tunnel and nearly four hours to make the 110-mile drive to East Hampton. I sit in the backseat between Claire and Marcus. Darcy is in a giddy, hyper mood. She spends most of the car ride facing the three of us in the backseat, raising various topics, asking questions, and generally carrying the conversation. She makes things feel celebratory; her good moods are as infectious as her bad ones are contaminating. Marcus is the second most talkative in our group. For a thirty-mile stretch, he and Darcy are a running comedy routine, making fun of each other. She calls him lazy, he calls her high maintenance. Claire and I chime in occasionally. Dex says virtually nothing. He is so quiet that at one point Darcy yells at him to stop being such a bore.

"I'm driving," he says. "I need to concentrate."

Then he looks at me in the rearview mirror. I wonder what he's thinking. His eyes give nothing away.

It is getting dark when we stop for snacks and beers at a gas station on Route 27. Claire sidles up to me in front of the chips, loops her arm through mine, and says, "I can tell he really likes you." For a second I am startled, thinking that she means Dex. Then I realize she is talking about Marcus.

"Marcus and I are just friends," I say, selecting a can of Pringles Light.

"Oh, c'mon now. Darcy told me about your date," she says.

Claire is always in the know about everything—the latest trend, the hot new bar opening, the next big party. She has her manicured fingers on the pulse of the city. And knowing the details of Manhattan's singles is part of her bag too.

"It was just one date," I say, happy that Darcy has not determined what happened with Marcus, despite a barrage of questioning. She even probed him with an e-mail; he forwarded me the message with his subject line reading "Nosy bastards."

"Well, the summer is long," Claire says wisely. "You're smart not to commit until you see what else is out there."

We arrive at our summer house, a small cottage with limited charm. Claire found it when she came out alone in mid-February, disgusted with all of us for not sacrificing a free weekend to house-hunt. She organized everything, including setting up the other half of the share. As we tour the house, she apologizes again for the lack of a pool, and laments that the common areas aren't really large enough for good parties. We reassure her that the big backyard with a grill makes up for that. Plus, we are close enough to the beach to walk, which, in my opinion, is the most important thing about a summerhouse.

We unpack the car and find our bedrooms. Darcy and Dex have the room with the king-sized bed. Marcus has his own room, which could come in handy. And Claire has her own room—a reward for her efforts. I am rooming with Hillary, who blew off work today and took the train in last night. Hillary is always blowing off work. I don't know anyone more laid-back about work, particularly at a big firm. She comes to work late every day—closer and closer to eleven with each passing year—and she refuses to play the games that other associates play, like leaving a jacket on the back of their chair or a cup full of coffee on their desk before leaving at night so that partners will think they've only left for a short break. She billed fewer than two thousand hours last year and therefore received no bonus. "Do the math and you'll realize that making a bonus comes out to less per hour than flipping burgers at McDonald's," she said this year on the day checks were handed out.

I call her on my cell now. "Where are you?"

"Cyril's," she shouts over the crowd. "Want me to stay here or meet you guys somewhere?"

I pass along the question to Darcy and Claire.

"Tell her we're going straight to the Talkhouse," Darcy says. "It's already late."

Then, as I expected, Claire and Darcy insist on changing their clothes. And Marcus, who is still wearing his work clothes, goes to change too. So Dex and I sit in the den, opposite each other, waiting. He holds the remote control but does not turn the TV on. It is the first time we have been alone since the Incident. I am conscious of sweat accumulating under my arms. Why am I nervous? What happened is behind us. It is over. I must relax, act normal.

"Aren't you going to doll up for your boyfriend?" Dex asks quietly, without looking at me.

"Very funny." Even the mere exchange of words now feels illicit.

"Well, *aren't* you?"

"I'm fine in this," I say, glancing down at my favorite jeans and black knit top. What he doesn't know is that I already put much thought into this outfit when I changed after work.

"So you and Marcus make a swell couple." He glances furtively at the staircase.

"Thanks. So do you and Darcy."

We exchange a lingering look, too loaded with potential meaning to begin to interpret. And then, before he can respond, Darcy bounds down the stairs in a curve-hugging chartreuse sheath. She hands Dex a pair of scissors and crouches at his feet, lifting her hair. "Can you cut the tag, please?"

He snips. She stands and spins.

"Well? How do I look?"

"Nice," he says, and then glances at me sheepishly as if the one-word compliment to his fiancée might somehow upset me.

"You look awesome," I say, to show him that it doesn't. Not in the least.

We pay the cover and make our way through the massive crowd at Stephen's Talkhouse, our favorite bar in Amagansett, saying hello to all of the people we know from various circles back in the city. We find Hillary at the bar with a Budweiser, wearing cutoff jeans, a white scoop-neck T-shirt, and the kind of plain blue flip-flops that Darcy and Claire would only wear to their pedicurist. There is not a pretentious bone in Hillary's body, and as always, I am so happy to see her.

"Hey, guys!" she yells. "What took you so long?"

"Traffic was a bitch," Dex says. "And then certain people had to get ready."

"Well, of *course* we had to get ready!" Darcy says, looking down to admire her outfit.

Hillary insists that we need a kick start to our evening and orders a round of shots. She hands them out as we stand in a tight circle, ready to drink together.

"To the best summer ever!" Darcy says, tossing her long, coconut-scented hair behind her shoulders. She says it at the start of every summer. She always has wildly high expectations that I never share. But maybe this summer she will be right.

We all throw back our shots, which taste like straight vodka. Then Dex buys another round, and when he hands me my beer, his fingers graze mine. I wonder if he does it on purpose.

"Thank you," I say.

"Anytime," he murmurs, holding my gaze as he did in the car.

I count to three silently and then look away.

As the night wears on, I find myself watching Dex and Darcy interact. I am surprised by the territorial pangs I feel as I observe them together. It is not exactly jealousy, but something related to it. I notice little things that didn't use to register. Like once, she slipped her four fingers into the back of his jeans right at the top. And another time, when he was standing behind her, he gathered all of her hair in one hand and sort of held it up in a makeshift ponytail before dropping it back at her shoulders.

Right now, he leans in to say something to her. She nods and smiles. I imagine that his words were "I want you tonight" or something along those lines. I wonder if they have had sex since he and I were together. Surely, yes. And that bothers me in some weird way. Maybe that happens whenever you watch someone on your List with someone else. I tell myself that I have no right to be jealous. That I had no business adding him to my List in the first place.

I try to focus on Marcus. I stand near him, talk to him, laugh at his jokes. When he asks me to dance, I say yes without hesitation. I follow him onto the crowded dance floor. We work up a good sweat, dancing and laughing. I realize that although there is no great chemistry, I am having fun. And who knows? Maybe this will lead to something.

"They're dying to know what happened on our date," Marcus says into my ear.

"Why do you say that?" I ask.

"Darcy inquired again."

"She did?"

"Yup."

"When?"

"Tonight. Right after we got here."

I hesitate and then ask, "Did Dex say anything?"

"No, but he was standing right next to her looking pretty darn interested."

"Some nerve," I say playfully.

"I know, the nosy bastards . . . And don't look now, but they're staring at us." His face touches mine, his whiskers scratching my cheek.

I drape my arms over his shoulders and move my body flush against his. "Well then," I say. "Let's give them something to look at."

seven

So what's the deal with you and Marcus?" Hillary asks me the next morning as she picks through the pile of clothes that have already accumulated beside her bed. I resist the urge to fold them for her.

"No deal, really." I get out of bed and promptly start to make it.

"Potential?" She pulls on a pair of sweats and ties the drawstring, cinching them at hip level.

"Maybe."

Last year Hillary broke up with Corey, her boyfriend of four years, a nice, smart, all-around great guy. But Hillary was convinced that as good as the relationship was, it wasn't good enough. "He's not *the One*," she kept saying. I remember Darcy informing her that she might revise that opinion in her mid-thirties, a statement Hillary and I both rehashed at length later. A classic, tactless Darcyism. Yet, as time passes, I can't help wondering if Hillary made a mistake. Here she is, one year later, embroiled in the fruitless blind-dating scene while, rumor has it, her ex has moved into a Tribeca loft with a twenty-three-year-old med student who is a dead ringer for Cameron Diaz. Hillary claims that it doesn't bother her. I find that very hard to believe, even for someone with her moxie. In any case, she doesn't seem to be in a hurry to find a Corey replacement.

"Summer potential or long-term potential?" she asks me, running her hands through her short, sandy hair.

"I don't know. Maybe long-term potential."

"Well, you looked like a total couple last night," she says. "Out there dancing."

"We did?" I ask, thinking that if we looked like a couple, Dex must know that I'm not dwelling on him.

She nods, finds her "Corporate Challenge" T-shirt, and sniffs the armpits before tossing it over to me. "Is this clean? Smell it."

"I'm not gonna smell your shirt," I say, throwing it back. "You're gross."

She laughs and puts on her obviously clean enough shirt. "Yeah . . . You two were out there whispering and laughing. I thought for sure you were going to hook up last night, and that I would get the room to myself."

I laugh. "Sorry to disappoint."

"You disappointed him more."

"Nah. He just said good night when we got home. Not even a kiss."

Hillary knows about the first kiss. "Why not?"

"I don't know. I think we're both proceeding with caution. We'll have a lot of contact between now and September . . . You know, he's in the wedding party too. If things blow up, it could be bad."

She looks as if she is considering my point. For one second I am tempted to tell Hillary everything about Dex. I trust her. But I don't share, reasoning that I can always tell her, but I can't untell her and erase the knowledge from her mind. When we are all together, I would feel even more awkward, constantly thinking that she's thinking about it. And anyway . . . it is over. There is really nothing to talk about.

We go downstairs. Our housemates have already assembled around the kitchen table.

"It's kick-ass outside," Darcy says, standing, stretching, and showing off her flat stomach under a cropped T-shirt. She sits back down at the table, returning to her game of solitaire.

Claire looks up from her Palm Pilot. "Perfect beach weather."

"Perfect golf weather," Hillary says, looking at Dex and Marcus. "Any interest?"

"Um, maybe," Dex says, glancing up from the sports page. "Want me to call and see if we can get a tee time?"

Darcy slams her cards onto the table and looks around defiantly.

Hillary doesn't seem to notice Darcy's objection to a round of golf because she says, "Or we could just pop over to the driving range."

"No! No! No! No golf!" Darcy pounds the table again, this time with her fist. "Not on our first day! We have to stay together! All of us. Right, Rachel?"

"Guess that means no golf today," Dex says, before I am forced to become involved in the great golf debate. "Darcy's orders."

Hillary gets up from the table with a disgusted look on her face.

"I just want us all to be together at the beach," Darcy says, putting a benevolent spin on her selfishness.

"And you make the prospect seem so pleasant." Dex stands, walks over to the sink, and starts making coffee.

"What's your problem, grouchy bottom?" Darcy says to his back as if he is the one who just told her how to spend the day. "You are being such an old stinkweed. Sheesh."

"What's a stinkweed?" Marcus asks, scratching his ear. It is his first contribution to the morning conversation. He still looks half asleep. "I'm not familiar."

"Just have a look at one right now," Darcy says, pointing at Dex. "He's been in a bad mood since we got here."

"No, I haven't," Dex says. I want him to turn around so I can read his expression.

"Have too. Hasn't he?" Darcy demands an answer from the rest of us, looking at me specifically. Being friends with Darcy has taught me the art of smoothing over. But sleeping with her fiancé has dulled my instinct. I am not in the mood to chime in. And nobody else wants to become embroiled in what should be their private argument. We all shrug or look away.

In truth, though, Dex *has* been somewhat subdued. I wonder if I have anything to do with his mood. Maybe it bothered him, watching me with Marcus. Not full-blown jealousy, just the territorial pangs that I experienced. Or perhaps he's only thinking about Darcy, seeing her for the controlling person she is. I've always been aware of Darcy's demands—you can't miss them—but lately, I have been less tolerant of her. I am tired of her always getting her way. Maybe Dex feels the same.

"What are we doing for breakfast?" Marcus asks through a loud yawn.

Claire glances at her diamond-studded Cartier. "You mean brunch."

"Whatever. For food," Marcus says.

We discuss our options and decide to skip the crowded East Hampton scene. Hillary says that she bought the essentials the day before.

"By essentials, do you mean Pop-Tarts?" Marcus asks.

"Here." Hillary sets bowls, spoons, and a box of Rice Krispies on the table. "Enjoy."

Marcus opens the box and pours some into his bowl. He looks across the table at me. "Want some?"

I nod, and he prepares my bowl. He doesn't ask anyone else if they want cereal, just pushes the box down the table.

"Banana?" he asks me.

"Yes, please."

He peels the banana and slices it into his bowl and mine, alternating every few slices. He takes the bruised section for himself. We are sharing a banana. This means something. Dex's eyes dart my way as Marcus flicks the last neat cylinder into my bowl, leaving the nasty end piece in its peel where it belongs.

Several hours later, we are finally ready to go to the beach. Claire and Darcy emerge from their rooms with their stylish canvas bags filled to the brim with plush new beach towels, magazines, lotions, thermoses, cell phones, and makeup. Hillary carries only a small bath towel from the house and a Frisbee. I am somewhere in between with a beach towel, my Discman, and a bottle of water. The six of us walk in a row, our flip-flops smacking the pavement with that satisfying sound of summer. Claire and Hillary walk on either end, flanking the house couple and the possible couple-to-be. We cross the beach parking lot and climb over the dune, hesitating for a second to take in our first collective glimpse of the ocean. I am glad that I no longer live in landlocked Indiana, where people call Lake Michigan "the beach." The view is thrilling. It almost makes me forget that I slept with Dex.

Dex leads the way down the crowded beach, finding us a spot halfway between the dunes and the ocean where the sand is still soft but even enough to spread our towels. Marcus puts his towel next to mine; Darcy is on my other side, Dex next to her. Hillary and Claire set up in front of us. The sun is bright but not too hot. Claire warns us all about the UV rays, that these are the days when you really have to be careful. "You can get severe sun damage and not even realize it until it's too late," she says.

Marcus offers to put suntan lotion on my back.

"No, thanks," I say. But as I struggle to reach the middle of my back, he takes the bottle from me and applies the lotion, meticulously maneuvering around the edges of my suit.

"Do mine, Dex," Darcy says cheerfully, shedding her white shorts and squatting in front of Dex in her black bikini. "Here. Use the coconut oil, please."

Claire bemoans the lack of SPF in the oil, says we are too old to keep tanning and that Darcy will be sorry when the wrinkles set in. Darcy rolls her eyes and says she doesn't care about wrinkles, she lives in the moment. I know I will get an earful later, that Darcy will tell me that Claire is just jealous because her fair skin goes straight from white to bright pink. "You'll regret it when you're forty," Claire says, her face shaded by a huge straw hat.

"No I won't. I'll just get laser resurfacing." Darcy adjusts her bikini top and then coats more oil on her calves, using quick, efficient strokes.

I have watched her grease up for more than fifteen years now. Every summer her goal was to have a savage tan. Often we would lie out in her backyard with a big tub of Crisco, a bottle of Sun-In, and a garden hose for periodic relief. It was absolute torture. But I suffered through it believing that dark pigmentation was a virtue of sorts. My skin is pale like Claire's, so every day Darcy would surge further ahead.

Claire remarks that cosmetic surgery won't cure skin cancer.

"Oh, for Pete's sake!" Darcy says. "Stay under your damn hat then!"

Claire opens her mouth and then closes it quickly, looking injured. "Sorry. I was just trying to help."

Darcy shoots her a conciliatory smile. "I know, hon. Didn't mean to snap at you."

Dex looks at me and makes a face, as if to say that he wishes both of them would shut up. It is the first direct communication we have had all day. I allow myself to smile back at him. His face breaks into a glorious grin. He is so handsome that it hurts. Like looking at the sun. He stands for a moment to adjust his towel, which has folded over in the wind. I look at his back and then down at his calves, feeling a surge of remembrance. *He was in my bed.* Not that I want a repeat performance. But *oh,* he has a nice body—lean but broad. I am not a body person, but I still appreciate a perfect one. He sits back down just as I look away.

Marcus asks if anybody wants to play Frisbee. I say no, that I am too tired, but what I am thinking is that the last thing I want to do is run around with my soft, white stomach poking out of my tankini. But Hillary is a taker and off they go, the portrait of two well-adjusted beachgoers leaving the rest of us to our trifling.

"Hand me my shirt," Darcy says to Dex.

"Please?"

"The 'please' is a given," Darcy says.

"Say it," he says, popping a cinnamon Altoid into his mouth.

Darcy hits him hard in the stomach.

"Ouch," he says in a monotone, to indicate that it didn't hurt in the slightest.

She winds up to hit him again, but he grabs her wrist.

"Try to behave. You're such a child," he says fondly. His edginess of this morning is gone.

"I am not," she says, sidling over to his towel. She presses her fingers into his chest, poised for a kiss.

I put on my sunglasses and look away. To say that what I am feeling is not jealousy is a stretch.

That night we all go to a party in Bridgehampton. The house is huge with a beautiful L-shaped pool surrounded by gorgeous landscaping and at least twenty tiki torches. I scan the guests in the backyard, noticing all of the purple, hot pink, and orange dresses and skirts. It seems that every woman read the same "bright colors are in, black is out" article that I read. I followed the advice and bought a lime green sundress that is too vivid and memorable to wear again before August, which means it will cost me about one hundred and fifty dollars per wear. But I am pleased with my choice until I see the same dress, about two sizes smaller, on a slender blonde. She is much taller than I am, so the dress is shorter on her, exposing an endless stretch of bronzed thigh. I make a conscious effort to stay on the opposite side of the pool from her.

I go to the bathroom, and on my way back to find Hillary, I get stuck talking to Hollis and Dewey Malone. Hollis used to work at my firm but quit the day after she got engaged to Dewey. Dewey is unattractive and humorless, but he has a huge trust fund. Hence Hollis's interest. It was amusing to hear Hollis explain to us that Dewey has such a "big heart," blah blah blah, trying in vain to disguise her true intentions. I am envious of Hollis's escape from firm hell, but I would rather be stuck billing than married to Dewey.

"My life is so much better now," she chirps tonight. "That firm was poison! It was so stifling! I thought I might miss the intellectual stimulation . . . but I don't. Now I have time to read the classics and think. It's great. So liberating."

"Uh-huh . . . That's nice," I say, taking mental notes to share with Hillary later.

Hollis goes on to tell me about their penthouse on the park and how she's been working so hard on decorating it and has had to fire three designers for not adhering to her vision. Dewey contributes nothing to the conversation, just crunches his ice and looks bored. Once I catch him staring at Darcy's butt, packed neatly into a pair of tight magenta Capri pants.

Marcus is suddenly beside me. I introduce him to Dewey and Hollis. Dewey shakes his hand and then continues to mouth-breathe and look distracted. Hollis promptly asks Marcus where he lives and what he does for a living. Apparently his Murray Hill address and his marketing job don't quite measure up because they find an excuse to move on to more worthy guests.

Marcus raises his eyebrows. "Dewey, huh?"

"Yeah."

"*Dooo heee* have a stick up his ass or what?"

I laugh.

He looks proud of his joke, pleased to make me laugh.

"So, are you having fun?"

"I guess so. You?"

He shrugs. "The people here kind of take themselves seriously, don't they?"

"That's the Hamptons."

I survey the party. It is a far cry from neighborhood barbecues back in Indiana. Part of me feels satisfied that I have expanded my horizons. But a larger part of me feels uncomfortable every time I come to a party like this one. I am a poser, attempting to mingle with people who consider Indiana to be mere flyover country—necessary terrain to cross on their trips to Aspen or Los Angeles. I watch Darcy making her rounds with Dex at her side. There is no trace of Indy left in her; to watch her you would guess that she grew up on Park Avenue. Her kids will grow up in Manhattan, for sure. When I have kids, if I ever have kids, I intend to move to the suburbs. I look at Marcus, trying to imagine him dragging our son's Big Wheel out of the street. He looks down at our little boy, whose face is streaked with dried Popsicle, and instructs him to stay on the sidewalk. The boy has Marcus's short eyebrows pointing up toward each other like an upside-down **V**.

"C'mon," Marcus says. "Let's get another drink."

"All right," I say, keeping my eye on the blonde in my dress.

As we walk toward the poolside bar, I think of Indiana again, picturing Annalise and Greg with their neighbors, all spilled out on the freshly cut Midwestern lawn. If somebody wore her same pair of khaki shorts from the Gap, nobody would care.

After the party, we find another party, and then do our usual finale at the Talkhouse, where I dance with Marcus again. Around three o'clock, we all pile into the car and go home. Hillary and Claire head straight for bed while the two couples remain in the den. Darcy and Dex hold hands on one love seat; Marcus and I sit next to each other, but not touching, on the adjacent couch.

"All right, kids. It's past my bedtime," Darcy says, standing suddenly. She glances at Dexter. "You coming?"

My eyes meet Dexter's. We look away simultaneously. "Yeah," he says. "I'll be right there."

The three of us talk for a few more minutes until we hear Darcy calling Dex from the top of the stairs. "Come on, Dex! They want to be alone!"

Marcus smirks while I study a freckle on my arm.

Dex clears his throat, coughs. His face is all business. "Okay then. Guess I'll head up. Good night."

"All right, man. See you tomorrow," Marcus says.

I just mumble good night, too uncomfortable to look up as Dex leaves the room.

"Finally," Marcus says. "Alone at last."

I feel an unexpected pang for Dex that is somehow reminiscent of Hunter leaving Joey and me alone in the lounge at Duke, but I push it away and smile at Marcus.

He moves closer and kisses me without asking first this time. It is a nice enough kiss, maybe even nicer than our first one. For some reason,

I think of the Brady Bunch episode when Bobby saw skyrockets after kissing Millicent (who, unbeknownst to Bobby, had the mumps). When I first saw that episode I was about Bobby's age, so that kiss seemed like serious stuff. Someday I will see skyrockets like that, I remember thinking. To date, I have not seen skyrockets. But Marcus comes just as close as anyone before him.

Our kissing escalates to the next level and then I say, "Well, I think we should go to bed."

"Together?" he asks. I can tell he is joking.

"Very funny," I answer. "Good night, Marcus."

I kiss him one more time before going to my room, passing Dex and Darcy's closed door on the way.

The next morning I check my voice mail. Les has left me three messages. He might as well be a Jehovah's Witness, for as much attention as he pays to the holidays. He says that he wants "to go over a few things tomorrow, early afternoon." I know he is vague on purpose, not leaving a specific time or instructions to meet him at the office or call in. This way he can be sure that my Memorial Day is slashed in half. Hillary tells me to ignore him, pretend that I didn't get the message. Marcus says to jam him with a message back, telling him to "jack off—it's a national holiday." But of course I dutifully check the train and jitney schedule and decide I will leave this afternoon to avoid the traffic. Deep down, I know work is only an excuse to go—I have had enough of this whole bizarre dynamic. I like Marcus, but it is exhausting being around a guy who, as Hillary would say, "is potential." And it is even more exhausting avoiding Dex. I avoid him when he is alone, avoid him when he is with Darcy. Avoid dwelling on him and the Incident.

"I really need to get back," I sigh, as if it is the last thing I want to do.

"You can't leave!" Darcy says.

"I have to."

As she sulks I want to point out that ninety percent of the time we are in the Hamptons, she is completely distracted, in social-butterfly mode. But I just say again that I have to.

"You're such a buzz kill."

"She can't help having to work, Darcy," Dex says. Maybe he says it because she often calls him a buzz kill too. Then again, maybe he just wants me to leave for the same reasons I want to go.

After lunch I pack up my things and go into the den, where everyone is lazing around, watching television.

"Can someone give me a lift to the jitney?" I ask, expecting Darcy, Hillary, or Marcus to volunteer.

But Dex reacts first. "I'll take you," he says. "I want to go to the store anyway."

I say good-bye to everyone, and Marcus squeezes my shoulder and says he'll give me a call next week.

Then Dex and I are off. Alone for four miles.

"Did you have a nice weekend?" he asks me as we are backing out of the driveway. Gone is any trace of the banter that surfaced right after the Incident. And he, like Darcy, has stopped inquiring about Marcus, perhaps because it is fairly evident that we have become some kind of item.

"Yeah, it was nice," I say. "Did you?"

"Sure," he says. "Very nice."

After a brief silence, we talk about work and mutual friends from law school, stuff we talked about before the Incident. Things seem normal again, or as normal as they can be after a mistake like ours.

We arrive at the jitney stop early. Dex pulls into the parking lot, turns in his seat, and studies me with his green eyes in a way that makes me look away. He asks what I am doing on Tuesday night.

I think I know what he's asking, but am not sure, so I babble. "Work. The usual. I have a deposition on Friday and haven't even started preparing for it. The only thing I have on my outline is 'Can you spell your last name for the court reporter?' and 'Are you on any medications that might impede your ability to answer questions at this deposition?'" I laugh nervously.

His face stays serious. He clearly has no interest in my deposition. "Look, I want to see you, Rachel. I'm coming over at eight. On Tuesday."

And the way he says it—as a statement rather than a question—makes my stomach hurt. It isn't really the stomach pain I have before a blind date. It isn't the nervousness before a final exam. It isn't the "I'm going to get busted for doing something" feeling. And it isn't the dizzy sensation that accompanies a crush on a guy when he just acknowledged your presence with a smile or casual hello. It is something else. It is a familiar ache, but I can't quite place it.

My smile fades to match his serious face. I would like to say that his request surprised me, caught me off guard, but I think part of me expected this, even hoped for it, when Dex offered to drive me. I don't ask why he wants to see me or what he wants to talk about. I don't say that I have to work or that it's not a good idea. I just nod. "Okay."

I tell myself that the only reason I agree to see him is that we have to finish sorting out what happened between us. And therefore, I am not committing a further wrong against Darcy; I'm simply trying to fix the damage already done. And I tell myself that if I do, in fact, actually want to see Dex for other reasons, it's only because I miss my friend. I think back to my birthday, our time in 7B before we hooked up, remembering how much I enjoyed his solo company, how much I enjoyed Dex removed from Darcy's demands. I miss his friendship. I only want to talk to him. That is all.

The bus arrives and people start to file onto it. I slide out of the car without another word between us.

As I settle down in a window seat behind a perky blonde talking way too loudly on her cell phone, I suddenly know what it is in my stomach. It is the same way I felt after sex with Nate in those final days before he dumped me for the tree-hugging guitar player. It is a mixture of genuine emotion for another person and fear. Fear of losing something. I know at this moment that by allowing Dex to come over, I am risking something. Risking friendship, risking my heart.

The girl keeps talking, overusing the words "incredible" and "amazing" to describe her "woefully abbreviated" weekend. She reports that she has a "vicious migraine" from "bingeing big time" at the "fab party." I want to tell her that if she takes her volume down a notch, her headache might subside. I close my eyes, hoping that her phone battery is low. But I know that even if she stops her high-pitched chatter, there is no way I am going to be able to sleep with this feeling growing inside me. It is good and bad at the same time, like drinking too much Starbucks coffee. It is both exciting and scary, like waiting for a wave to crash over your head.

Something is coming, and I am doing nothing to stop it.

It is Tuesday night, twenty minutes before eight. I am home. I have not heard from Dex all day so I assume we are still on. I floss and brush my teeth. I light a candle in the kitchen in case there is a lingering aroma of the Thai food I ordered the evening before for my solo Memorial Day dinner. I change out of my suit, put on black lacy underwear—even though I know, know, *know* that nothing is going to happen—jeans, and a T-shirt. I apply a touch of blush and some lip gloss. I look casual and comfortable, the opposite of how I feel.

At exactly eight, Eddie, who is subbing for José, rings my buzzer. "You have company," he bellows.

"Thanks, Eddie. Send him up."

Seconds later Dex appears in my doorway in a dark suit with faint gray pinstripes, a blue shirt, and a red tie.

"Your doorman was smirking at me," he says, as he steps into my apartment and tentatively looks around as if this were his first visit.

"Impossible," I say. "That's in your head."

"It's not in my head. I know a smirk when I see one."

"That's not José. Wrong doorman. Eddie's on tonight. You have a guilty conscience."

"I told you already. I don't feel that guilty about what we did." He looks steadily into my eyes.

I feel myself being sucked into his gaze, losing my resolve to be a good person, a good friend. I look away nervously, ask if he wants something to drink. He says a glass of water would be fine. No ice. I am out of bottled water so I run the tap until the water comes out cool. I fill a glass for each of us and join him on my couch.

He takes several big gulps and then puts his glass down on a coaster on my coffee table. I sip from my glass. I can feel him staring at me, but I don't look back. I keep my eyes straight ahead, where my bed is situated—the scene of the Incident. I need to get a proper one-bedroom or at least a screen to separate my sleeping alcove from the rest of the apartment.

"Rachel," he says. "Look at me."

I glance at him and then down at my coffee table.

He puts his hand on my chin and turns my face toward his.

I feel myself blush but don't move away. "What?" I release a nervous laugh. He doesn't change expression.

"Rachel."

"What?"

"We have a problem."

"We do?"

"A major problem."

He leans forward, his left arm draped along the back of the sofa. He kisses me softly and then more urgently. I taste cinnamon. I think of the tin of cinnamon Altoids that he had with him all weekend. I kiss him back.

And if I thought Marcus was a good kisser, or Nate before him, or anyone else for that matter, I thought wrong. In comparison, everyone else was merely competent. This kiss from Dex makes the room spin. And this time, it's not from booze. This kiss is like the kiss I have read about a million times, seen in the movies. The one I wasn't sure existed in real life. I have never felt this way before. Fireworks and all. Just like Bobby Brady and Millicent.

We kiss for a long, long time. Not breaking away once. Not even shifting positions on my couch even though we are at an unnatural distance for such an intense kiss. I can't speak for him, but I know why I don't move. I don't want it to end, don't want the next awkward stage to come, where we might ask the questions about what we are doing. I don't want to talk about Darcy, to even hear her name. She has nothing to do with this moment. Nothing. This kiss stands on its own. It is removed from time or circumstance or their September wedding. That is what I try to tell myself. When Dex finally breaks away, it is only to move closer to me and put his arms around me and whisper into my ear, "I can't stop thinking about you."

I can't stop either.

But I *can* control what I'm doing. There is emotion, and then there is what you do about it. I pull away, but not too far away, and shake my head.

"What?" he asks gently, his arm partially around me.

"We shouldn't be doing this," I say. It is a watered-down protest, but at least it is something.

Darcy can be annoying, controlling, and exasperating, but she is my friend. I am a good friend. A good person. This isn't who I am. I must stop. I won't know myself if I don't stop.

Yet I don't move away. Instead, I wait to be convinced otherwise, hoping he will talk me into it. And sure enough: "Yes. We should," he says. Dex's words are sure. No second-guessing, doubts, worry. He holds my face in his hands and stares intently into my eyes. "We have to."

There is nothing slick in his words, only sincerity. He is my friend, the friend I knew and cared for before Darcy ever met him. Why didn't I recognize my feelings sooner? Why had I put Darcy's interests ahead of my own? Dex leans in and kisses me again, softly but with a sense of absolute certainty.

But it's wrong, I silently protest, knowing that I am too late, that I have already surrendered. We have crossed a new line together. Because even though we have already slept together, that didn't really count. We were drunk, reckless. Nothing really happened until this kiss today. Nothing that couldn't have been stuffed into a closet, confused with a dream, maybe even forgotten altogether.

That is all changed now. For better or worse.

eight

I have always done my best thinking in the shower. The night is for worrying, dwelling, analyzing. But in the morning, under the hot water, I see things clearly. So as I lather my hair, inhaling my grapefruit-scented shampoo, I pare everything down to the essential truth: what Dex and I are doing is wrong.

We kissed for a long time last night, and then he held me for even longer, few words passing between us. My heart thumped against his as I told myself that by not escalating the physical part we had scored a victory of sorts. But this morning, I know it was still wrong. Just plain wrong. I must stop. I will stop. Starting now.

When I was little, I used to count to three in my head when I wanted to give myself a fresh start. I'd catch myself biting my nails, jerk my fingers out of my mouth, and count. *One. Two. Three. Go.* Then I had a clean slate. From that point forward I was no longer a nail-biter. I used this tactic with many bad habits. So on a count of three, I will shake the Dex habit. I will be a good friend again. I will erase everything, fix it all.

I count to three slowly and then use the visualization technique that Brandon told me he used during baseball season. He said he would picture his bat striking the ball, hear it crack, see the dust fly as he slid safely into home base. He focused only on his good plays and not the times he screwed up.

So I do this. I focus on my friendship with Darcy, rather than my feelings for Dex. I make a video in my head, filling it with scenes of Darcy and me. I see us hunkered down in her bed during an elementary-school sleepover. We are discussing our plans for the future, how many kids we will have, what we will name them. I see Darcy, ten years old, propped up on her elbows, pinkies in her mouth, explaining that if you have three kids, the middle one should be a different sex from the others so everyone has something special. As if you can control such things.

I picture us in the halls at Naperville High, passing notes between classes. Her notes, folded in intricate shapes, like origami, were so much more entertaining than Annalise's notes, which simply reported how bored she was in class. Darcy's were chock-full of interesting observations about classmates and snide remarks about teachers. And little games for me to play. She'd put quotes down the left-hand side of the page and people's names on the right for me to match. I'd crack up as I drew a line from, say, "Nice brights, buddy" to Annalise's father, who made that comment every time drivers forgot to turn off their high beams. She was funny. Sometimes cutting, even downright mean. But that only made her funnier.

I rinse my hair and remember something else, a memory that has not surfaced before. It is like finding a photograph of yourself that you never knew was taken. Darcy and I were freshmen, standing beside our locker after school. Becky Zurich, one of the most popular girls in the senior class (but not the nice kind of popular, more the mean, feared variety) walked by us with her boyfriend, Paul Kinser. With her virtually nonexistent chin and way-too-thin lips, she really wasn't pretty at all, although at the time she somehow convinced a lot of people, including me, that she was. So when Paul and Becky passed us, I looked at them, because they were popular seniors, and I was impressed, or at the very least, curious. I'm sure I wanted to hear what they were talking about so that I could glean some insight into being eighteen (so old!) and cool. I think it was only a casual glance in their direction, but maybe it was a stare.

In any case, Becky gave me an exaggerated stare back, making her eyes pop out like a cartoon. She followed this with a hyenalike, lip-curling sneer and said, "What're you lookin' at?"

Then Paul chimed in with "Catching flies?" (I'm sure dating Becky made Paul meaner, or maybe he just figured out that being mean earned him action later.)

Sure enough, my mouth was wide open. I snapped it shut, mortified. Becky laughed, proud to have shamed a freshman. She then reapplied her pink frosted lipstick, inserted a fresh piece of Big Red into her mean little mouth, and made one final face at me for good measure.

Darcy had been shuffling through books in our locker but clearly caught the gist of the exchange. She spun and eyed the pair with revulsion, a look she had practiced and mastered. She then imitated Becky's shrill laughter, craning her neck unnaturally backward and rolling in her lips to make them invisible. She was hideous—and looked exactly like Becky in midchortle.

I stifled a smile while Becky looked momentarily stunned. She then gathered herself, took a step toward Darcy, and spat out the word "bitch."

Darcy was unflinching as she stared right back at the senior duo and said, "It's better than being an *ugly* bitch. Wouldn't you agree, Paul?"

It was Becky's turn to stare, mouth agape, at her newly discovered adversary. And before she could formulate a comeback, Darcy threw in another insult for good measure. "And by the way, Becky, that lipstick you're wearing? It's *so* last year."

Everything about that moment is suddenly in sharp focus. I can see our locker decorated with pictures of Patrick Swayze in *Dirty Dancing*. I can smell that distinct, starchy, meat-based odor of the nearby cafeteria. And I can hear Darcy's voice, forceful and confident. Of course, Paul had no response to Darcy's question, as it was clear to all four of us that Darcy was right—she was the prettier of the two. And in high school that sometimes gives you the last word, even if you are a freshman. Becky and

Paul scurried off and Darcy just kept talking to me about whatever it was we had been talking about, as if Becky and Paul were totally insignificant. Which they were. It just took a lot to realize that at fourteen.

I turn off the water, wrap a towel around my body and another over my head. I will call Dexter as soon as I get to work. I will tell him that it has to stop. This time I really mean it. He is marrying Darcy, and I am the maid of honor. We both love her. Yes, she has flaws. She can be spoiled, self-centered, and bossy, but she can also be loyal and kind and wildly fun. And she is the closest thing to a sister that I will ever have.

During my commute, I practice what I will say to Dex, even talking out loud at one point on the subway. When I finally arrive at work, I have my speech so memorized that it no longer sounds scripted. I've inserted the proper pauses into my Declaration of Mind-set and Future Intent. I am ready.

Just as I am about to make the phone call, I notice that I have an e-mail from Dex. I open it, expecting him to have reached the same conclusion. The subject line reads "You."

You are an amazing person, and I don't know where the feelings that you give me came from. What I do know is that I am completely and utterly into you and I want time to freeze so I can be with you all the time and not have to think of anything else at all. I like literally everything about you, including the way your face shows everything you're thinking and especially the way it looks when we are together and your hair is back and your eyes are closed and your lips are open just a little bit. Okay. That's all I wanted to say. Delete this.

I am breathless, dizzy. Nobody has ever written words like this to me. I read it again, absorbing every word. *I like literally everything about you too,* I think.

And just like that, my resolve is gone again. How can I end something that I have never experienced before? Something I have been waiting for my whole life? Nobody before Dex could make me feel this way, and what if I never find it again? What if this is *it?*

My phone rings. I answer it thinking it could be Dex, hoping it's not Darcy. I can't talk to her right now. I can't think about her right now. I am buzzing from my electronic love letter.

"Cheers, baby."

It is Ethan, calling from England, where he has lived for the past two years. I am so happy to hear his voice. He has a smiling voice, always sounding like he's on the verge of laughter. Most things about Ethan are just as they were in the fifth grade. He is still compassionate, still has cherub cheeks that turn pink in the cold. But the voice is newer. It came in high school—with puberty—long after friendship had replaced my schoolgirl crush.

"Hi, Ethan!"

"What's the statute of limitations on wishing someone a happy birthday?" he asks. Ever since I went to law school, he loves throwing out legal terms, often with a twist. "Strawberry tort" is his favorite.

I laugh. "Don't worry about it. It was only my thirtieth."

"Do you hate me? You should have called and reminded me. I feel like an absolute ass, after eighteen years of never forgetting. Shit. My mind is going and I'm still in my twenties—not to rub it in."

"You forgot my twenty-seventh too," I interrupt him.

"I did?"

"Yeah."

"I don't think I did."

"Yeah—you were with Bran—"

"Stop. Don't say that name. You're right. I forgot your twenty-seventh. That makes this infraction somehow less egregious, right? I didn't break a streak . . . So how is it?" He whistles. "Can't believe you're thirty. You should still be fourteen. Do you feel older? Wiser? More worldly? What did you do on the big night?" He fires off his questions in his frenetic, attention-deficit-disorder way.

"It's the same. I'm the same," I lie. "Nothing's changed."

"Really?" he says. It is like him to ask the follow-up. It's as if he knows that I am holding back.

I pause, my mind racing. *Do I tell? Not tell? What will he think of me?*

What will he say? Ethan and I have remained close since high school, although our contact is sporadic. But whenever we do talk, we pick up where we left off. He would make a good confidant in this emerging saga. Ethan knows all the major players. And more important, he knows what it's like to screw up.

Things started out right for him. He did well on the SATs, graduated as our salutatorian, and was voted most likely to succeed, picked over Amy Choi, our valedictorian, who was too quiet and mousy to win votes for anything. He went to Stanford, and after graduation took a job at an investment bank even though he majored in art history and had no interest in finance. He instantly despised everything about the banking culture. He said pulling all-nighters was unnatural, and realized that he preferred sleep to money. So he traded his suits in for fleece and spent the next several years drifting up and down the West Coast snapping pictures of lakes and trees, gathering friends along the way. He took writing classes, art classes, photography classes, funded by the odd bartending job and summers in Alaska's fisheries.

That's where he met Brandi—"Brandi with an *i*" as I called her before I realized that he genuinely liked her, and that she wasn't just a fling. A few months into their romance, Brandi got pregnant (insisting she was part of that woefully unlucky .05 percent on birth-control pills, although I had my doubts). She said that abortion was out of the question, so Ethan did what he thought to be the right thing and married her at City Hall in downtown Seattle. They sent out homemade marriage announcements featuring a black-and-white photo of the two hiking. Darcy made fun of Brandi's way-too-short-and-tight jean shorts. "Who the hell hikes in Daisy Dukes?" she said. But Ethan seemed happy enough.

And that summer, Brandi gave birth to a baby boy . . . an adorable, bouncing *Eskimo* baby boy with eyes that turned coal black almost immediately. Brandi, with blue eyes that matched Ethan's, begged for forgiveness. Ethan promptly had the marriage annulled, and Brandi moved back to Alaska, probably to track down her native lover.

I think Brandi soured Ethan on the whole fresh-air, live-off-the-land kind of life. Or maybe he just wanted something new. Because he moved to London, where he writes for a magazine and is working on a book about London architecture, an interest he didn't acquire until he landed on British soil. But that's how Ethan is. He figures things out along the way, always ready to back up and start over, never bowing to pressure or expectations. I wish I could be more like him.

"So what did you do for your birthday?" Ethan asks.

I shut my office door and blurt it out. "Darcy had a surprise party for me, I got wasted, and hooked up with Dex."

I suppose this is what happens when you're not accustomed to having secrets. You don't learn the art of holding back. In fact, I am surprised I have lasted this long. I hear static in the line as the news travels across the Atlantic. I panic, wishing I could suck the admission back in.

"Get the fuck outta here. You're kidding me, right?"

My silence tells him that I'm serious.

"Ohhh, *shhhit*." His voice is still smiling.

"What? What are you thinking?" I need to know if he's judging. I need to know what he thinks of me, if he is siding with Chanel Suit.

"Wait. Whaddaya mean, hooked up? You didn't sleep with him, did you?"

"Um. Yeah. Actually I did."

I am relieved to hear him laugh, even though I tell him that it's not funny, that this is serious business.

"Oh, *trust* me. This is funny."

I picture the dimple in his left cheek. "And what exactly is so amusing?"

"Miss Goody Two-shoes screws her friend's fiancé. This is raw comedy at its best."

"Ethan!"

He stops laughing long enough to ask if I could be knocked up.

"No. We had that covered."

"So to speak?"

"Yeah," I say. Any pun I ever make is an accident.

"So no harm done, right? It was a mistake. Shit happens. People make mistakes, especially when they're wasted. Look at me and Brandi with an *i*."

"I guess so. But still . . ."

Ethan whistles and then says the obvious—that Darcy would flip if she ever found out.

My other line rings. "You need to get that?" Ethan asks.

"No. I'll let it roll to voice mail."

"You sure? It could be your new boyfriend."

"Ask yourself if you're being helpful," I say, although I'm relieved that he is not preachy and serious. That's not Ethan's style, but you never know when someone is going to take the moral high ground. And there is definitely moral high ground all around here, particularly considering that Darcy is a friend of his too. Not as close as he and I are, but they still talk occasionally.

"Sorry. Sorry." He snickers. "Okay. Just one more substantive question."

"What?"

"Was it good?"

"Ethan! I don't know. We were drunk!"

"So it was all sloppy?"

"C'mon, Ethan!" I say, as if I'm not thinking about the particulars. Meanwhile, a snapshot of the Incident flashes through my brain—my fingers pressed into Dexter's back. It is a perfect, airbrushed image. There is nothing sloppy about it.

"So you've spoken to him since?"

I tell him about the Hamptons weekend and the date with Marcus.

"Nice touch. Going for his friend. That way, if you marry Marcus, you guys can be swingers."

I ignore him and continue with the rest—the ride to the jitney, last night, a summary of the e-mail.

"Wow. Shit. So . . . do you have feelings for him too?"

"I don't know," I say, even though I know that the answer is yes.

"But the wedding's still on?"

"Yeah," I say. "As far as I know."

"As far as you know?"

"Yes. It is."

Silence. He is not laughing anymore, so my guilt returns in full force. "What are you thinking now?"

"I was just wondering where you want this to go," he says. "What do you want from it? Is it a fling, or do you want him to call off the wedding?"

I flinch at the word "fling." That's not what it is at all, but at the same time, I don't think I want Dex to call off the wedding. I can't imagine doing that to Darcy. I tell Ethan that I don't know, I'm not sure.

"Hmm . . . Well, has he mentioned the engagement at all?"

"No. Not really."

"Hmm."

"What? What does 'hmm' mean?"

"It means I think he should call the shit off."

"Because of me?" My stomach drops at the thought of being responsible for Darcy's canceled wedding. "Maybe he just has cold feet?"

I hear my voice rising hopefully at the suggestion of mere cold feet. Why does part of me want it to be that simple? And how can I be so thrilled to be near Dex, so deeply moved by his e-mail, and still want, on some level, for him to marry Darcy?

"Rach—"

"Ethan, I know what you're going to say."

I *don't* know exactly what he is going to say, but I have a hunch from his tone that it has something to do with where things are going to end up if I don't cease and desist. That it's going to blow up somehow. That someone—likely me—is going to get hurt. But I don't want to hear him say any of it.

"Okay. Just be careful. Don't get busted. Shit."

I hear him laughing again.

"What?"

"Just thinking of Darcy . . . It's sort of satisfying."

"Satisfying how?"

"Oh, come on. Don't even tell me that part of you doesn't like zinging her a little bit. There's some poetic justice here. Darcy's been riding roughshod over you for years."

"What are you talking about?" I ask, genuinely surprised to hear him describe our friendship like that. I know I've been feeling more irritated by her recently and I know that she has not always been the most selfless of friends, but I've never thought of her as riding roughshod over me. "No she hasn't."

"Yeah, she has."

"No. She *hasn't*," I say more firmly. I'm not sure who I am defending—me or Darcy. *Yes, there was the matter of you, Ethan. But you don't know about that.*

"Oh, please. Remember Notre Dame? The SATs?"

I think back to the day we all received our SAT scores, sealed in white envelopes from Guidance. We were all tight-lipped, but dying to know what everyone else got. Finally Darcy just said at lunch, "Okay, who cares. Let's just tell our scores. Rachel?"

"Why do I have to go first?" I asked. I was satisfied with my score, but still didn't want to go first.

"Don't be a baby," Darcy said. "Just tell us."

"Fine. Thirteen hundred," I said.

"What was your verbal?" she asked.

I told her 680.

"Nice," she said. "Congratulations."

Ethan went next. Fourteen ten. No surprise there. I forget what Annalise got—something in the low eleven hundreds.

"Well?" I looked at Darcy.

"Oh. Right. I got a thirteen hundred five."

I knew instantly that she didn't have a 1305. The SAT is not scored in increments of five. Ethan knew too, because he kicked me under the table and hid a smile with his ham sandwich.

I didn't care that she lied per se. She was a known embellisher. But the fact that she lied about her score to beat me by five—that part really figured. We didn't call her on it. There was no point.

But then she said, "Well, maybe we'll both get into Notre Dame."

It was her Ethan power move in the fifth grade all over again.

Like a lot of kids in the Midwest, my dream growing up was to attend

Notre Dame. We're not Irish or even Catholic, but ever since my parents took me to a Notre Dame football game when I was eight, I wanted to go there. To me it was what a college should be—stately stone buildings, manicured lawns, plenty of tradition. I wanted to be a part of it. Darcy never showed the slightest interest in Notre Dame and it irritated me that she was infringing on my terrain. But I wasn't too worried about her taking my spot. My grades were higher, my SATs were probably higher, and besides, more than one student from our high school got into Notre Dame every year.

That spring, the acceptance and rejection letters trickled in slowly. I checked the mailbox every day, in agony. Mike O'Sullivan, who had three generations of alumni in his family and was the president of our class, got into Notre Dame first. I assumed that I would be next, but Darcy got her letter before I did. I was with her when she got the mail, although she wouldn't open the envelope in front of me. I went home, hoping guiltily that she had received bad news.

She called an hour later, ecstatic. "I can't believe it! I got in! Can you believe it?"

In short, no. I couldn't. I mustered up a congratulations, but I was crushed. Her news meant one of two things: she had taken my spot, or we would both go to Notre Dame and she would upstage me for four more years. As much as I knew I would miss Darcy when I went away, I felt strongly that I needed to establish myself apart from her. Once she got in, there would be no perfect resolution.

Still, I wanted that acceptance more than I had ever wanted anything. And I had my pride on the line. I waited, prayed, even thought about calling the admissions office to beg. One sickening week later, my letter arrived. It looked just like Darcy's. I ran inside, my heart pounding in my ears as I sliced open the envelope, unfolded the paper that held my fate. *Close . . . you are very highly qualified . . . but no cigar.*

I was devastated and could barely speak to my friends in school the next day, especially Darcy. At lunch, as I fought back tears, she informed me that she was going to Indiana anyway. That she wanted nothing to do with a school that would turn me down. Her charity upset me all the more. For once, Annalise spoke up. "You took Rachel's spot, and you didn't even want to go there?"

"Well, it *was* my first choice. I changed my mind. And how was I supposed to know it would happen like this?" she said. "I assumed she would get in; I only beat her by a few points on the SAT."

Ethan had had enough. "You didn't get a damn thirteen hundred five, Darcy. The SAT is scored in increments of ten."

"Who said I got a thirteen hundred five?"

"You did," Ethan and I said in unison.

"No I didn't. I said a thirteen ten."

"Omigod!" I said, looking at Annalise for support, but her gumption had run out. She claimed that she had forgotten what Darcy said.

We argued for the rest of the lunch hour about what Darcy had said and why she had applied to Notre Dame if she didn't want to go there. We both ended up crying, and Darcy left school early, telling the school nurse she had cramps. The whole thing blew over when I got into Duke and talked myself into being happy with that result. Duke had a similar look and feel—stone buildings, pristine campus, prestige. It was just as good as Notre Dame and maybe it was better to broaden my horizons and leave Indiana.

But to this day I wonder why Notre Dame picked Darcy over me. Maybe a junior male member of the admissions staff fancied her photo. Maybe it was just Darcy's typical good luck.

In any case, I'm glad that Ethan refreshed my memory about Notre Dame. It replaces the Becky Zurich showdown in the forefront of my mind. Yes, Darcy could be a good friend—she usually was—but she also screwed me at a few pivotal moments in life: first love, college dream. Those were no small matters.

"All right," I say to Ethan. "But I think you're overstating the point a little. I wouldn't use the term 'roughshod.'"

"Okay, but you know what I mean. There's an undercurrent of competition."

"I guess so. Maybe," I say, thinking that it isn't much of a competition when one person consistently loses.

"So, anyway, please keep me posted. This is good stuff."

I tell him I will.

"Oh, one more thing," he says. "When are you going to visit me?"

"Soon."

"That's what you always say."

"I know. But you know how it goes. Work is always crazy . . . I'll come soon, though. This year for sure."

"Good enough," Ethan says. "I really do miss you."

"I miss you too."

"Besides," he says. "You might need a vacation by the time you're through with all of this."

After we hang up, I note with satisfaction that Ethan never told me to stop. He only said to be careful. And I will do that. I will be careful the next time I see Dexter.

nine

I avoid Darcy for three days, a very difficult thing to do. We never go so long without talking. When she finally reaches me, I blame my absence on work, say I have been unbelievably swamped—which is true—although I have found plenty of time to daydream about Dex, call Dex, e-mail Dex. She asks if I am free for Sunday brunch. I tell her yes, figuring that I might as well just get the face-to-face meeting over with. We arrange to meet at EJ's Luncheonette near my apartment.

On Sunday morning, I arrive at EJ's first and note with relief that the place is full of children. Their happy clamor provides a distraction and makes me slightly less nervous. But I am still filled with anxiety at the thought of spending time with Darcy. I have been able to cope with my guilt by avoiding all thoughts of her, almost pretending that Dex is single and we are back in law school, before I ever got the big idea to introduce Darcy to him. But that tactic will not be possible this afternoon. And I'm afraid that spending time with her will force me to end things with Dex, something I desperately don't want to do.

A moment later, Darcy barges in carrying her big black Kate Spade bag, the one she uses for heavy errand-running, specifically the wedding variety. Sure enough, I see her familiar orange folder poking out of the top of the bag, stuffed with tear-outs from bridal magazines. My stomach drops. I had just about prepared myself for Darcy but not for the wedding.

She gives me the two-cheek Euro kiss hello as I smile, try to act natural. She launches into a tale about Claire's blind date from the night before with a surgeon named Skip. She says it did not go well, that Skip wasn't tall enough for Claire and failed to ask if she wanted dessert, thus setting off her cheapskate radar. I am thinking that perhaps the only radar that had gone off was Skip's "tiresome snob" radar. Maybe he just wanted to go home and get away from her. I don't offer this suggestion, however, as Darcy doesn't like it when I criticize Claire unless she does so first.

"She is just *way* too picky," Darcy says as we are led to our booth. "It's like she looks for things not to like, you know?"

"It's okay to be picky," I say. "But she has a pretty screwed-up set of criteria."

"How do you figure?"

"She can be a little shallow."

Darcy gives me a blank stare.

"I'm just saying she cares too much about money, appearances, and how connected the guy is. She's just narrowing her pool a bit—and her chances of finding someone."

"I don't think she's *that* picky," Darcy says. "She'd have gone out with Marcus and he's not well connected. He's from some dumpy town in Wyoming. And his hair is sort of thinning."

"Montana," I say, marveling at how superficial Darcy sounds. I guess she's been like this since her arrival to Manhattan, maybe even our whole lives, but sometimes when you know someone well, you don't see them as they really are. So I honestly think I've managed to ignore this fundamental part of her personality, perhaps not wanting to see my closest friend in this light. But ever since my conversation with Ethan, her pushy, shallow tendencies seem magnified, impossible to overlook.

"Montana, Wyoming. Whatever," she says, waving her hand in the air as if she herself doesn't hail from the Midwest. It bothers me the way Darcy downplays our roots, even occasionally bagging on Indiana, calling it backward and ugly.

"And I like his hair," I say.

She smirks. "I see you're defending him. Interesting."

I ignore her.

"Have you heard from him lately?"

"A few times. E-mails mostly."

"Any calls?"

"A few."

"Have you seen him?"

"Not yet."

"Damn, Rachel. Don't lose momentum." She removes her gum and wraps it in a napkin. "I mean, don't blow this one. You're not going to do better."

I study my menu and feel anger and indignation swell inside of me. What a rude thing to say! Not that I think there is anything wrong with Marcus, but why can't I do better? What is that supposed to mean, anyway? For our entire friendship, it has been silently understood that Darcy is the pretty one, the lucky one, the charmed one. But an implicit understanding is one thing. To say it just like that—*you can't do better*—is quite another. Her nerve is truly breathtaking. I formulate possible retorts, but then swallow them. She doesn't know how bitchy her remark is; it only springs from her innate thoughtlessness. And besides, I really have no right to be mad at her, considering.

I look up from my menu and glance at Darcy, worried that she will be able to see everything on my face. But she is oblivious. My mom always says that I wear my emotions on my sleeve, but unless Darcy wants to borrow the outfit, she doesn't see a thing.

Our waiter comes by and takes our orders without a notepad, something that always impresses me. Darcy asks for dry toast and a cappuccino, and I order a Greek omelet, substituting cheddar cheese for feta, and fries. Let her be the thin one.

Darcy whips out her orange folder and starts to tick through various lists. "Okay. We have so much more to do than I thought. My mom called last night and was all 'Have you done this? Have you done that?' and I started freaking out."

I tell her that we have plenty of time. I am wishing we had more.

"It's, like, three months away, Rach. It's going to be here before we know it."

My stomach drops as I wonder how many more times I will see Dexter in the three months. At what point will we stop? It should be sooner rather than later. It should be now.

I watch Darcy as she continues to go through her folder, making little notes in the margins until the waiter brings our food. I check the inside of my omelet—cheddar cheese. He got it right. I begin to eat as Darcy yaps about her tiara.

I nod, only half listening, still feeling stung by her rude words.

"Are you listening to me?" she finally asks.

"Yes."

"Well then, what did I just say?"

"You said you had no idea where to find a tiara."

She takes a bite of toast, still looking doubtful. "Okay. So you did hear me."

"Told ya," I say, shaking salt onto my fries.

"Do you know where to get one?"

"Well, we saw some at Vera Wang, in that glass case on the first floor, didn't we? And I'm pretty sure Bergdorf has them."

I think back to the early days of Darcy's engagement, when my heart had been at least somewhat in it. Although I was envious that her life was coming together so neatly, I was genuinely happy for her and was a diligent maid of honor. I recall our long search for her gown. We must have seen every dress in New York. We made the trek to Kleinfeld in Brooklyn. We did the department stores and the little boutiques in the Village. We hit the big designers on Madison Avenue—Vera Wang, Carolina Herrera, Yumi Katsura, Amsale.

But Darcy never got that feeling that you're supposed to get, that feeling where you are overcome with emotion and start weeping all over the dressing room. I finally targeted the problem. It was the same problem that Darcy has trying on bathing suits. She looked stunning in everything. The body-hugging sheaths showed off her slender hips and height. The big princess ball gowns emphasized her minuscule waist. The more dresses she tried on, the more confused we became. So finally, at the end of one long, weary Saturday, when we arrived at our last appointment, at Wearkstatt in Soho, I decided that this would be our final stop. The fresh-faced girl, who was not yet jaded by life and love, asked Darcy what she envisioned for her special day. Darcy shrugged helplessly and looked at me to answer.

"She's having a city wedding," I started.

"I just *love* Manhattan weddings."

"Right. And it's in early September. So we're counting on warm weather . . . And I think Darcy prefers simple gowns without too many frills."

"But not too boring," Darcy chimed in.

"Right. Nothing too plain-Jane," I said. *God forbid.*

The girl pressed a finger to her temple, scurried off, and returned with four virtually indistinguishable A-lines. And that's when I made a decision that I was going to pick one of the dresses to be *the one.* When Darcy tried on the second dress, a silk satin A-line in soft white with a dropped waist and beading on the bodice, I gasped. "Oh, Darcy. It's gorgeous on you," I said. (It was, of course.) "This is it!"

"Do you think?" Her voice quivered. "Are you sure?"

"I'm positive," I said. "You need to buy *this* one."

Moments later, we were placing an order for the dress, talking about fittings. Darcy and I had been friends forever, but I think it was the first time that I realized the influence I have over her. I picked her wedding dress, the most important garment that she will ever wear.

"So you won't mind running some errands with me today?" she asks me now. "The only thing I really want to accomplish is shoes. I need my shoes for the next fitting. I figure we'll look at Stuart Weitzman and then zip up to Barney's. You can come with me, can't you?"

I plow a forkful of my omelet through ketchup. "Sure . . . But I do have to go in to work today," I lie.

"You always have to work! I don't know who has it worse—you or Dex," she says. "He's been working on this big project lately. He's never home."

I keep my eyes down, searching my plate for the best remaining fry. "Really?" I say, thinking of the recent nights Dex and I have stayed at work late, talking on the phone. "That sucks."

"Tell me about it. He's never available to help with this wedding. It's really starting to piss me off."

After lunch and a lot more wedding conversation, we walk over to Madison, turning left toward Stuart Weitzman. As we enter the store, Darcy admires a dozen sandals, telling me that the cut of the shoes is perfect for her narrow, small-heeled feet. We finally make our way to the satin wedding shoes in the back. She scrutinizes each one, choosing four pairs to try on. I watch as she prances around the store, runway style, before settling on the pair with the highest heels. I almost ask her if she is sure they are comfortable, but stop myself. The sooner she makes a decision, the sooner I will be dismissed for the day.

But Darcy isn't finished with me. "While we're over here, can we go to Elizabeth Arden to look at lipsticks?" she asks as she pays for her shoes.

I reluctantly agree. We walk over to Fifth, while I tolerate her yammering about waterproof mascara and how I have to remind her to buy some for the wedding day because there was no way that she was going to make it through the ceremony without crying.

"Sure," I say. "I'll remind you."

I tell myself to view these tasks with an objective eye, as detached as a wedding coordinator who barely knows the bride, rather than the bride's oldest but most disloyal friend. After all, if I am especially helpful to Darcy, it might diminish my guilt. I imagine Darcy discovering my misdeeds and me saying, "Yes, all of that is true. You got me. But may I remind you that I NEVER ONCE ABANDONED MY MAID OF HONOR DUTIES!"

"May I help you, ladies?" the woman behind the counter at Elizabeth Arden asks us.

"Yes. We are looking for a pink lipstick. A vivid yet soft and innocent bridal pink," Darcy says.

"And you are the bride?"

"I am. Yes." Darcy flashes one of her fake PR smiles.

The woman beams back and makes her decisive recommendations, swiftly pulling out five tubes and setting them on the counter in front of us. "Here you are. Perfect."

Darcy tells her that I will need a complementary shade, that I am the maid of honor.

"How nice. Sisters?" The woman smiles. Her big square teeth remind me of Chiclets.

"No," I say.

"But she's like my sister," Darcy says, simply and sincerely.

I feel low. I picture myself on *Ricki Lake*, the title of the show "My Best Friend Tried to Steal My Groom." The audience boos and hisses as I babble my apologies and excuses. I explain that I didn't mean to cause any harm, I just couldn't help myself. I used to wonder how they found people who had committed such acts of despicable disloyalty (never mind how they got these people to fess up on national television). Now I was joining the low-life ranks. Giving Brandi with an *i* a run for her money.

This has to stop. Right now. Right at this second. I haven't yet slept with Dex consciously, soberly. So we kissed again? It was only a kiss. The turning point will be the selection of the bridal lipstick. Right now. *One, two, three, go!*

Then I think of Dexter's soft hair and cinnamon lips and his words—*I like literally everything about you.* I still can't believe that Dex has those feelings for me. And the fact that I feel the same way about him is too much to ignore. Maybe it is meant to be. Words like "fate" and "soul mates" swirl around in my head, words that made me scoff in my twenties. I note the irony—aren't you supposed to get more cynical with age?

"You like this one?" Darcy turns to me with her full lips in a pout.

"It's nice," I say.

"Is it too bright?"

"I don't think so. No. It's pretty."

"I think it may be too bright. Remember, I'm going to be in white. It'll make a difference. Remember Kim Frisby's wedding makeup, how she looked like a total tart? I want to look hot, but sweet too. You know, like a virgin. But still hot."

I am suddenly and unexpectedly on the verge of tears—I just can't stand the wedding talk another second. "Darce, I really have to get to work. I'm truly sorry."

Her lower lip protrudes. "C'mon, just a little longer. I can't do this without you!" And then she says to our salesgirl, "No offense to you."

The girl smiles as if she totally understands, no offense taken. She recognizes the truth of what Darcy is saying and is probably wondering what kind of a maid of honor leaves the bride during such a pivotal moment.

I take a deep breath and tell her that I can stay a few more minutes. She samples more tubes, wiping her lips with a makeup-removing lotion between hues of pink.

"How about this one?"

"Nice." I smile earnestly.

"Well, nice doesn't cut it!" she snaps. "It has to be perfect. I have to look perfect!"

As I study her pouty, berry-stained, bee-stung lips, any trace of remorse is gone. All I feel is solid, full-blown resentment.

Why does everything have to be perfect for you? Why does it all have to be handed to you in a perfect package all wrapped up with a Martha Stewart bow? What did you do to deserve Dex? I met him first. I introduced him to you. I should have gone for him. Why didn't I, again? Oh, right, because I thought I wasn't good enough for him. Well, I was mistaken. I obviously misjudged the situation. It can happen . . . especially when one has a friend like you, a friend who assumes that she has a right to the best of everything, a friend who is so relentless in her quest to outshine you that you even begin to underestimate yourself, set your sights low. This is your fault, Darcy, for taking what should have been mine in the first place.

I am keyed up and absolutely desperate to get away from her. I look at my watch and sigh, almost believing that I really do have to go to work and that Darcy is being inconsiderate, as usual, taking advantage of my time. *I think my job is a little more important than your lipstick for an event that is still months away!*

"I'm sorry. Darce—it's not my fault that I have to work."

"Fine."

"It's not my fault," I say again.

Not my fault.

My feelings for Dex are not my fault.

And his feelings for me—and I know they are real—are not his fault.

Before I can escape, Darcy calls Claire on her cell. Has she tried Bobbi Brown? I can hear Claire inquire, and then state with the authority of *Bride's* magazine that they have a beautiful bridal line and their lipstick has plenty of moisture but not too much shine.

"Will you come meet me now?" Darcy pleads into the phone. Her sense of entitlement knows no bounds.

She hangs up the phone and tells me that I am free to go, that Claire will be straight over. She waves at me; I am being dismissed.

"Good-bye," I say. "I'll speak to you later?"

"Sure. Whatever. Bye."

As I turn to leave, she issues a final warning. "If you're not careful, I'm going to have to demote you to lowly bridesmaid and give Claire your honored position."

So much for just like sisters.

I call Dexter's cell phone the second I am out of sight. It is a low move, making the call while Darcy does wedding errands, but I am running off the steam of indignation. That's what she gets for being so demanding, domineering, and self-centered.

"Where are you?" I ask Dex after we exchange hellos.

"Home."

"Oh."

"Where are you? I thought you were shopping."

"I was. But I said I had to work."

I notice that we are both dancing around any direct mention of Darcy.

"Well, *do* you have to work?" he asks tentatively.

"Not really."

"Good. Me either. Can I see you?"

"I'll be home in twenty minutes."

Dex beats me to my apartment and is waiting in my lobby making small talk with José about the Mets. I am so happy to see him, relieved to be away from Darcy. I smile and say hello, wondering if José recognizes Dex from past visits with Darcy. I hope he doesn't. It's not just my parents from whom I want approval. I even want it from my doorman.

Dex and I ride the elevator and walk down the hall to my apartment. I am jittery with anticipation, eager for his touch. We sit on my couch. He takes my hands and we start kissing with an urgency that feels like an affair. It is a serious word—a scary word. It conjures images of Sunday school and the Ten Commandments. But it is not adultery. Nobody is married. Yet. I push it all out of my mind as I kiss Dex. There will be no more guilt, not for this next parcel of time.

Suddenly, perching on the couch seems ridiculous. My bed would be so much more comfortable. Nothing more has to happen just because we're on a bed. That is a teenager's perception. I am a grown woman with life experience (albeit limited), and I can control myself on my own bed. I stand up and lead him over to the other side of my studio. He follows me, still holding my hand. We sit on the foot of the bed. Dex slips his feet out of his loafers. He is not wearing socks. He moves his big toes up and down and then rubs his feet together. He has high, graceful arches and slender ankles.

"Come here," he says, pulling me against him and both of us up toward my pillows. He is strong, his skin warm. We are now on our sides, our bodies against each other. He kisses me more, and we topple over in his direction. He stops kissing me suddenly, clears his throat, and says, "It's so strange. Being with you like this. And yet it also feels so natural. Maybe because we've been friends for so long."

I tell him I know exactly what he means. I think back to law school. We weren't best friends in those days, but we were close enough to learn a lot about each other, stuff that comes out even when your focus is on contributory negligence and ways to rescind a contract. I mentally catalog all that I learned about Dex in the pre-Darcy days. That he grew up in Westchester. That he is Catholic. That he played basketball in high school and considered walking on at Georgetown. That he has an older sister named Tessa who went to Cornell and now teaches high school English in Buffalo. That his parents divorced when he was very young. That his father remarried. That his mother beat breast cancer.

And then there was all that I learned via Darcy, details of his personal life that I've found myself conjuring and pondering in recent days. Like that Dex is grouchy in the morning. That he does at least fifty push-ups before bed every night and that he never leaves dirty dishes on the counter. That he broke down when his grandfather died, the only time she has ever seen him cry. That he had two serious girlfriends before Darcy and that the one named Suzanne Cohen, who worked as a research analyst at Goldman Sachs, dumped him and broke his heart.

When I add it all up, I know a lot. But I want more. "Tell me everything about yourself," I say, sounding eighteen.

Dex touches my face and then draws an imaginary line along my nose and around my mouth, resting his finger on my chin. "You first. You're the mysterious one."

I laugh. "Hardly," I say, thinking that he is confusing being shy with being mysterious.

"You are. You were a closed book in law school. All quiet, not wanting to date anyone—despite plenty of guys trying . . . I could never get much out of you."

I laugh again. "What's that supposed to mean? I told you plenty in law school."

"Like what?"

I rattle off some autobiographical details.

"I'm not talking about stuff like that," he says. "I'm talking about the important things. How you *feel* about things."

"I hated Zigman," I offer weakly.

"I know. Your fear was all-consuming. And then you did a great job when he finally called on you."

"I did not," I say, remembering how I stumbled my way through a long, painful line of questioning.

"Yes you did. You just didn't think you did. You don't see yourself the way you are."

I avert my eyes, focus on a spot of ink on my comforter.

He continues. "You see yourself as very average, ordinary. And there is nothing ordinary about you, Rachel."

I can't look back at him. My face burns.

"And I know that you blush when you're embarrassed." He smiles.

"No I don't!" I cover my face with one hand and roll my eyes.

"Yes you do. You're adorable. And yet you have no idea, which is the most adorable part."

Nobody, not even my mother, has ever called me adorable.

"And you are beautiful. Absolutely, stunningly beautiful in the freshest, most natural way. You look like one of those Ivory girls. Remember those commercials? . . . You're probably too young. You're like a J.Crew model. All natural."

I tell him to please stop. Even though I love what he has just told me.

"It's true."

I want to believe him.

He kisses my neck, his left hand resting on my hip.

"Dex."

"Hmmm?"

"Who ever said I didn't want to date in law school?"

"Well, you didn't, did you? You were there to learn, not date. That was clear."

"I went out with Nate."

"Not until the very end."

"He didn't ask me out until the very end."

"Brave guy."

I roll my eyes.

"I almost asked you out, you know that?"

I laugh at this.

"It's true," he says, sounding a little bit hurt.

I give him a dubious look.

"Do you remember that time when we were studying for our Torts final?"

I picture his thumb on my face, wiping away my tear. So it *had* meant something.

"You know exactly what I'm talking about, don't you?"

My face feels hot as I nod. "I think so. Yeah."

"And when I asked to walk you home, you said no. Shot me down."

"I didn't shoot you down!"

"You were all business."

"I wasn't. I just didn't think at the time . . ." My voice trails off.

"Yeah, and then you introduced me to Darcy. I knew then that you had zero interest."

"I just didn't think . . . I didn't know you saw me that way."

"I loved spending time with you," Dex says. "Still do." He stares at me, unblinking.

I tell him that he blinks less than anyone I have ever met. He smiles, says he has never lost a staring contest. I challenge him, making my eyes as wide as his. I notice that he has a dark speck in his left iris, like an eye freckle.

Seconds later, I blink. He flashes a quick, jubilant smile and then kisses me more. He changes the intensity and pressure and amount of tongue, the kissing ideals that are all too often abandoned once in a long-term relationship. Kissing Dex would never become stale. He would never stop kissing me like this.

"Tell me about Suzanne," I say when we finally separate. "And your high school girlfriend."

"Alice?" He laughs, sweeps a piece of my hair behind my ear. "What about her? Ancient history."

Everyone knows that you don't discuss exes when you're in a fledgling relationship. Even though you are dying to know those details from the very beginning, that is something you bring up much later in the game. You don't have to be a Rules Girl like Claire to have that concept down. Dating someone new is a fresh start for both of you. No good can come from rehashing past—and by definition failed—relationships. But compared to the fact that he is engaged, ex-girlfriends are an innocuous topic. There is no need to strategize here in my safe studio. The rules don't apply. It might be the only advantage to our situation.

"Were you in love with them?" For some reason I need to know.

He rolls onto his back and stares at the ceiling, concentrating. I like that he thinks about my questions, just as he did during law-school exams. I remember him staring into space for the first forty-five minutes of an exam. Not writing a word on his blue book until he thought through his entire answer.

He clears his throat. "Not with Alice. But yes with Suzanne."

No wonder Suzanne has always bothered Darcy so much. She wants to be the only one he has ever loved. I remember how she used to beat down Blaine in high school: "You didn't love Cassandra, did you? Did you?" Until he finally just said no. Only you, Darcy.

"Why not with Alice?" I ask. I'd rather hear about the one he didn't love first.

"I don't know. She was a sweet girl. As sweet as they come. I don't know why I didn't love her. It's something you can't really control."

Dex is right. It has nothing to do with the other person's inherent worth, the sum of their fine attributes. It is something you can't will yourself to feel. Or not feel. Although I have done a pretty good job of it over the years. Just look at Joey. I dated him for two years and never felt even a fraction of what I'm feeling now.

"Of course, it was just high school," he continues. "How serious can you really be at that age?"

I nod, thinking of sweet little Brandon. Then I ask Dex about Suzanne. "So you loved her?"

"Yeah. But that wasn't going to work in the long run. She's Jewish and was very up-front about her expectations of me. She wanted me to convert, raise our kids Jewish, the whole nine yards. And maybe I would have been okay with that . . . I'm not very religious . . . but I wasn't okay with the fact that she made it a bright-line rule. I saw a life of her browbeating me into shit. Just like her mother does to her father. Besides, we were too young to commit. . . . It still killed me when she walked, though."

"Is she married now?"

"Funny you ask that. I actually just heard from a mutual friend that she got engaged. About a month after—" He stops, looks uncomfortable.

"After you did?"

"Yeah," he whispers. He pulls me against him and kisses me hard, erasing any thoughts of Darcy. We undress and slide under the covers.

"You're cold," he says.

"I'm always cold when I'm nervous."

"Why are you nervous? Don't be nervous."

"Dex," I say into his neck.

"Yeah, Rach?"

"Nothing."

His body covers mine. I am not cold anymore.

We kiss for a long time, touching everywhere.

I don't know the time, but it is just getting dark.

I almost stop him, for all of the obvious reasons. But also because I'm thinking we should wait until we can spend a night together. Then again, that might never happen. And likely I will never shower with him, watch him shave in the morning. Or read the Sunday *Times* over coffee, whiling away the hours. We'll never hold hands in Central Park or cuddle on a blanket in Sheep's Meadow. But I can have him now. Nothing is stopping us from this moment.

I can see just a fraction of Dexter as we move together—his sideburn with a trace of gray, his strong shoulder, his seashell of an ear. My fingertips graze his collarbone, then hold on more tightly.

ten

I can't stop thinking about Dex. I know that we won't end up together, that he will marry Darcy in September. But I am content to live in the moment, and allow myself the daily pleasure of obsessing. Nothing lasts forever, I tell myself. Especially the good stuff. Although typically you aren't faced with a hard deadline. I think of a few other examples of concrete, predetermined endings. Take college, for example. I knew that I would go away for four years, accumulate friends and memories and knowledge, and that it would all come to an abrupt end on a set date. I knew that on this day, I would collect my diploma and pile my belongings into a U-Haul bound for Indiana, and the Duke experience would be done. A chapter closed forever. But that awareness didn't stop me from enjoying myself, sucking all of the joy out of the deal.

So that is what I am doing with Dex. I am not going to dwell on the end at the expense of the here and now.

Tonight I am home when Dex phones from work to say a quick hello and tell me that he misses me. It is the sort of call a boyfriend makes to his girlfriend. Nothing covert or complicated about it. I pretend that we are together for real. The phone rings again a second after we hang up.

"Hey," I say, in the same hushed tone, thinking that it is only a follow-up call from Dex.

"What's that voice?" Darcy asks, yanking me back to reality.

"What voice?" I ask. "I'm just tired. What's going on?"

She launches into the details of her latest work crisis, which typically amounts to no more than a paper jam at the copier. This one is no exception. A typo on a flyer for a club opening. I resist the urge to tell her that the target audience won't notice a misspelling, and instead ask her who is going to the Hamptons this weekend. I feel my senses heighten, anticipating Dexter's name. He already told me that he was going, convincing me that I had to go too. It will be awkward, but worth it, he said. He has to see me.

"Not sure. Claire might be having friends in town. Dex is in."

"Oh, really? He doesn't have to work?" I ask, sounding a bit too surprised. I feel a stab of worry, but Darcy doesn't notice my false tone.

"No, he just finished with some big deal," she says.

"Which deal?"

"I don't know. Some deal."

Dexter's job bores Darcy. I have observed the way she can shut him down, interrupting him in the middle of a story, transitioning back to her own petty concerns. *Am I fat? Does this look good on me? Will you come there with me? Do that for me. Reassure me. Me. Me. Me.*

As if on cue, she tells me that she is considering sending in a tape to *Big Brother*, that it would be fun to be on the show. Fun for an exhibitionist. I can think of few things more horrifying than being on national television, out there for the world to judge, assess, tear apart.

"Do you think I'd get picked?" she asks.

"You'd have a good chance."

She is pretty enough to get picked, and she has a vivid personality—exactly what they look for on reality television. I study my own face in the mirror, think of Dex telling me that I look like a J.Crew model. Maybe I am attractive. But I am nowhere near as pretty as Darcy, with her precise features, incredible cheekbones, bow-shaped lips.

Now she is laughing loudly into the phone, telling me another story about her day. She hurts my ears. The word "strident" comes to mind, and as I study my reflection again, I decide that although I'm far from beautiful, perhaps I have a softness that she lacks.

It is Thursday, the day before we leave for the Hamptons. Dex is over. We had planned on waiting until next week to see each other alone, but we both finished work early. And well, here we are, together again. We have already made love once. Now I am resting my head on his chest. As he breathes, his chest lifts my face slightly. Neither of us speaks for a long time, then he asks suddenly, "What are we *doing*?"

There it is. The Question.

I have thought of it a hundred times, worded the inquiry exactly like that, with the same intonation, the same emphasis on the word "doing." But every time I answer it differently:

We are following our hearts.

We are taking a chance.

We are crazy.

We are self-destructive.

We are lustful.

We are confused.

We are rebelling.

He is afraid of marriage.

I am afraid of being alone.

We are falling in love.

We are already in love.

And the most common: we have no idea.

This is the one I offer up. "I don't know."

"Neither do I," he says softly. "Should we talk about it?"

"Do you want to?"

"Not really," he says.

I am relieved that he doesn't. Because I don't. I am too afraid of what we might decide. Either choice is scary. "Let's not, then. Not now."

"Then when?" he asks.

For some reason, I say, "After July Fourth."

It sounds arbitrary, but it has always been a benchmark of sorts, the summer midpoint. Even though more than half the summer is left after the Fourth of July, the part that follows is the faster half, the part that always flies by. June, although a day shorter, feels so much longer than August.

"Okay," he says.

"No examining anything until July Fourth." I state the rule clearly, as I would at the outset of a law-school exam. My voice is firm, even though I'm not sure what we've just decided. That we are finished as of July Fourth? Or maybe . . . no, he couldn't think that I meant that is when he would tell Darcy he can't go through with marrying her. No, that is not what we just decided. We simply decided to decide nothing. That is all.

Still, picking the date scares me. I picture a giant countdown of days, hours, minutes, seconds. Like the clocks set up in 1999 for the countdown to the new millennium. I remember watching the seconds roll off such a clock in the post office near Grand Central Station sometime in December. That clock made me nervous, frantic. I wanted to attack my to-do list, clear my desk of backed-up calls, finish it all immediately. At the same time, watching those numbers tick by paralyzed me. I had too much to do, so why do anything at all?

I try to calculate the number of hours left before July Fourth. How many nights we will have together. How many times we will make love.

My stomach growls. Or maybe it's his. I can't tell because I am flat against him. "Are you hungry? We can order food," I say, and kiss his chest. "Or I can make us something."

I imagine myself whipping up a tasty snack. I can't cook, but I would learn. I would make an excellent, nurturing wife.

He tells me that he doesn't want to waste time eating. He can get something on his way home. Or just go to bed hungry. He says he wants to feel me against him until it's time to leave.

The next day I ask Dex if there were any problems when he returned home. It is a vague question, but he knows what I am asking. He says that Darcy was not home when he got in, so he had time to shower, reluctantly wash me off him. He says that Darcy had left him a message: "It's eleven and you're not answering your cell or your phone at work. You're probably having an affair. I'm going out with Claire."

It is her usual tongue-in-cheek accusation when Dex works late. She asks him if he's having an affair, never believing that he would do such a thing. She changes the person every time, selecting a random female name from his office. The less attractive the woman, the more amused she is. "I know you're in love with Nina," she'll say, knowing that Nina is a chubby word processor from Staten Island with fake nails adorned with glitter art.

I think of Dex returning home last night. A whole scene unfurls in my mind—Dex stealing into his apartment, hurrying to shower and get in bed, waiting for the key to turn in the lock, pretending to be asleep when Darcy enters their room. She hovers over him, studying him in the dark.

"How was your date with Nina?" she asks in a wry, loud voice.

He wipes his eyes with his fists as people do on television when they're awakened from a sound sleep. "Hi," he says wearily and then pretends to fall back asleep.

She cuddles up to him in bed, tossing out an "I love you."

His jaw clenches, but he says it back. What choice does he have? He falls asleep thinking about me. Thinking that her chin is too sharp against his chest.

I am watching them on the beach, down by the water.

Darcy and Dex standing together in the not-too-hot June sun. This weekend is the first that I have seen them together since Dex and I soberly, willfully, made love. I am wearing dark sunglasses so I can study them from my towel without being obvious, while Claire babbles to me about—what else?—the wedding. What if the night is chilly? Should we buy matching wraps, a light, gauzy cardigan? I nod and murmur that it is a good idea.

Dex has just finished a quick swim, even though the water is freezing. Now they are talking, huddled close together. Perhaps he is giving her the report on the water temperature. She hesitantly steps closer to the ocean's reach, just enough to let the water coat her feet. They are both smiling. Dex kicks water onto her shins and she shrieks, turns, and scampers a few feet from him. I can see the muscles strain in her long, tanned legs. She is wearing the nude-colored bikini. Her hair is down, blowing around her face. He laughs, and she raises her index finger as if to scold him and then walks toward him again. They are engaged in a full-fledged frolic. It pains me to watch them, but I can't stop. I can't look away.

I feel as if they are putting on a show. Well, Darcy is always putting on a show. But Dex is a willing participant. Surely he knows we are all watching. That I am watching. It is always that way when you are in a group and someone decides to go for a swim or walk to the water. The ocean is like a giant stage. It is natural that the others watch, if only for a moment. Dex must be aware of this, yet he is still in full-throttle playful-couple mode. He should be brooding on his towel, napping, or reading a novel—something dark, to give me the impression that he is confused, upset, torn. But instead he is splashing Darcy and grinning.

Marcus cups his mouth with his hands, yells down at them. "How cold is it?"

"Freaking freezing!" Darcy announces, her hand stroking Dex's back, while he reports a manly "Nah, it feels good. Come on down!"

Rage commingles with hurt. For the first time, I completely regret having sex with Dex. I feel foolish, suddenly sure that it meant next to nothing to him. Tears sting my eyes as I force myself to turn away from them, slip on my headphones. I order myself not to cry.

Before I can hit play, Marcus asks me what I'm listening to. I have only seen him once since our date and that was just for a quick weekday lunch at a deli near my office, but we have talked several times, and one conversation lasted over an hour. The only apparent reason why date number two has not happened, at least as far as he knows, is mere circumstance. He's busy, I'm busy. Work has been crazy. That whole routine. So the door is still wide open, which I am very glad about. I need to focus more on him. Feelings for him might emerge once I put Dex behind me. I smile and say, "Tracy Chapman. It's a good CD. Wanna listen?"

I hand him my headphones as Dex and Darcy walk toward us. Marcus listens for a few seconds. "That's nice." He gives my headphones back to me and fishes a Coke out of our cooler. "Want a sip?" he asks just as Darcy and Dex are standing over us.

I tell him sure, take the can, and wipe the lid with the edge of my towel after I swallow.

He says with a knowing, goofy look, "I don't mind your germs. If you catch my drift."

I laugh and shake my head, as if to say, Marcus, you crazy nut, you.

Marcus winks. I laugh again.

Perfect timing. Dex catches the whole exchange. I do not look at him. I will not. "Is anybody else getting in?" he asks.

Claire gives him the standard response. "Not yet. I'm not hot enough."

Marcus says he hates to swim, particularly in freezing water. "Please make me see how that is fun."

Darcy giggles. "It's *not* fun. It's torture!"

I say nothing, hit the play button on my Discman.

"What about you, Rachel?" Dex asks, still hovering over me.

I ignore him, pretending that the volume is too high to hear him.

He and Darcy return to their towels on the other side of Claire. Darcy brushes sand from her feet and ankles, while Dex sits cross-legged, looking at the ocean. I can see his shoulder and back out of the corner of my eye. I try not to think about his smooth skin and how he feels against me. I won't be feeling it again. I tell myself it's not the end of the world. It is for the best.

Before dinner that night, as I am dressing, Darcy comes to my room to ask me if I brought an eyelash curler. I tell her no, that I don't own an eyelash curler. Maybe Hillary does, but she is showering. She sits on my bed and sighs, her features rearranging in a dreamy expression.

"I just had the best sex," she says.

I struggle to keep my composure. "Oh, really?" I know I am opening the door for more sharing, but I don't know what else to say. My face is on fire. I hope Darcy won't notice.

"Yeah, it was phenomenal. Did you hear us?" It is like Darcy to share such details. She has always been explicit in her sexual reports. She will tell you what words were exchanged at the moment of orgasm. I have always listened, usually laughed, occasionally even enjoyed her stories. But those days are long over.

"No. I must have been in the shower," I say.

"Yeah, we were in the shower too." She finger-combs her wet hair, then shakes her head from side to side. "Wow. Haven't had sex like that in months."

I think of their wet bodies pressed together and can't decide who I hate more.

It is late, after two A.M. I have avoided Dex all night, at the house and then at dinner. Now we are at the Talkhouse. I have just ordered two beers, one for me and one for Hillary, when Dex finds me at the bar.

"Hi, Rach," he says.

I am buzzed and brazen. The alcohol has dried up my hurt, leaving only resentment and anger. They are easier emotions to manage, more straightforward. "Yes?"

"What's going on?" he asks casually.

"Nothing," I snap, turning to leave.

"Wait a sec. Where are you going?"

"To take Hillary her beer."

"I want to talk to you."

"What about?" I make my voice icy.

"What's wrong?"

"Nothing's wrong," I say, wishing I could think of something pointed and vengeful. I have not had much practice being mean, but my tone of voice must do the trick because Dex looks hurt. Not as hurt as I was today on the beach or during Darcy's sex report. Not hurt enough. I raise my eyebrows, looking at him with a slight look of disgust, as if to say, Yes? Is there something I can do for you?

"Are you—are you mad at me?" he asks.

I laugh—no, it is more of a snort.

"*Are* you?" he asks again.

"No, Dex, I'm not mad at you," I say. "I really am not concerned with you at all. Or what you do with Darcy."

Now he knows that I know. "Rachel . . ." he starts, flustered. Then he tries to tell me it was her doing, that she initiated it.

"She said it was the best sex of her life," I say as I walk away, leaving him standing alone at the bar. "Good job. Congrats."

Even in the fog of my buzz, I know that I have no right to confront Dex like this. All he did was have sex with his fiancée. He has promised me nothing—we were not supposed to even discuss anything until the Fourth of July. No material misrepresentation has been made. In fact, no misrepresentation has been made at all, material or otherwise. I am in this situation of my own accord, have not been duped. But I still hate him.

I scan the crowd, trying to find Hillary. Dex follows me and grabs my arm right below my elbow. I drop one of the beers. The bottle breaks.

"Nice. Look what you did," I say, looking down at the mess.

"I'll get you another one."

"Don't bother."

"Rachel, please . . . I couldn't help that. It was Darcy, I swear."

Hillary suddenly appears beside us. "What's up?"

I am not sure if she heard any of our conversation.

"Nothing," Dex answers quickly. "Rachel's just mad at me for dropping her beer."

"You can have mine," Hillary says.

"No, take this one," I say, handing her the other beer.

She reluctantly takes it and asks where Darcy is.

"We were just looking for her," I say.

I glance at Dex. He is trying to cover up in front of Hillary, but he is not doing the best job of it. His eyes are wide with worry, his mouth stretched into an uneasy smile. I bet he didn't have that look on his face in the shower.

It is over, I say in my head, with the dramatic flourish of a woman wronged. Then I turn around to find Marcus. Sweet Marcus, who offered me his Coke on the beach and is not engaged to anyone.

eleven

Ahh. The bunny-in-the-pot routine," Ethan says when I give him the update on Monday morning.

"It was *not* a bunny-in-the-pot routine!" I protest, remembering that I saw *Fatal Attraction* with Darcy and Ethan. Darcy had major issues with the whole premise. She kept saying how unrealistic it was—no man would cheat on his wife with a much-less-attractive woman. I guess I am disproving her theory.

"Oh no?" Ethan deadpans. "Well, perhaps a variation on that theme. More subtle though. You just exerted slight pressure . . . and let him know that it is unacceptable to continue relations with his fiancée."

"Well, anyway . . . it's over," I say, realizing that those two words lump me right in with a hoard of naïve women who say it's over while praying it's not, looking for any shred of hope, insisting that they only want closure when what they really want is that one last conversation disguised as seeking closure while they work to keep the door open for more. And the pathetic truth is I *do* want more. I wish I could undo the confrontation at the Talkhouse. I should not have said a word to Dex. I feel an ache of worry that he is going to stop seeing me altogether. He will probably decide that it's not worth it, the situation is just way too complicated.

"It's over, huh?" Ethan asks dubiously.

"Yes."

"Bravo," Ethan says in his finest English accent. "Way to take a stand."

"So, anyway," I say, as if it is easy for me to transition away from Dex.

"Yeah. So anyway. Are you coming to London the week of the Fourth?" he asks.

I had mentioned it as a possibility in a recent e-mail, before Dex and I had established our date. Now I don't want to leave. Just in case things aren't completely over. "Um, I doubt it. I already committed to the Hamptons," I say.

"Won't Dex be there?"

"Yes, but I still want to get my money's worth out of the share."

"Right. Uh-huh."

"Don't say it like that."

"Okay," he says, changing his tone. "But are you ever going to visit me? You blew me off after your bar exam too. Because of that Nate guy."

"I *will* visit. I promise. Maybe in September."

"Okay . . . But the Fourth would have been fun."

"It's not even a holiday there," I say.

"Yeah. It's funny the way the Brits don't celebrate our independence from them . . . But it's a holiday in my heart, Rachel."

I laugh and tell him that I'll look into flights for the fall.

"All right. I'll e-mail you my free weekends—all my deets."

He knows I hate the word "deets." Just as I hate people who make a "rez" for dinner. Or ask you to get back to them "ASAP." And Ethan's favorite, designed especially to annoy me—"YOYO," i.e., "you're on your own."

I smile. "Sounds fab."

"Super then."

My phone rings as soon as I hang up with Ethan. Les's name shows up on my screen. I consider not picking up but have learned that avoidance techniques don't work well at a law firm. It only makes partners more irritable when you finally do talk.

"How did you serve the IXP papers?" he barks into the phone as soon as I say hello. Les always skips the pleasantries.

"What do you mean?"

"Your mode of service. By mail? By hand?"

I nailed it to his cottage door, jackass, I think, remembering the antiquated mode of service tested by the New York bar.

"By mail," I say, glancing down at my well-worn copy of the New York Rules of Civil Procedure.

"Great. Fucking great," he says in his normal snide tone.

"What?"

"What? *What?*" he shouts into the phone. I pull the receiver away from my ear but now I hear his voice in stereo, filling the hall. "You fucked up! That's what! The papers needed to go by hand! Didn't you bother to read the Court's order?"

I scan the letter from the judge. Damn, he is right.

"You're right," I say solemnly. He hates excuses and I have none anyway. "I screwed up."

"What are you, a goddamn first-year associate?"

I stare at my desk. He knows full well that I'm a fifth-year.

"I mean, Christ, Rachel, this is malpractice," he growls. "You're gonna get this firm sued and yourself fired if you don't get your head out of your ass."

"I'm sorry," I say, just as I remember that he hates you that much more when you're sorry.

"Don't be sorry! Fix the shit!" He hangs up on me. I don't believe Les has ever finished a conversation with a proper good-bye, even when he's in a decent mood.

No, I'm not a first-year, asshole. Thus your tirade has no effect. Go ahead, fire me. Who cares? I think back to when I first started working at the firm. A partner would raise his eyebrows, and it would send me back to my office with tears welling, panic mounting over my job security or at the very least my yearly evaluation. Over the years my skin has thickened somewhat, and at this moment, I don't care at all. I have bigger issues than this firm and my career as a lawyer. No, scratch the word "career." Careers are for people who wish to advance. I only want to survive, draw a paycheck. This is merely a job. I can take or leave this place. I start to imagine quitting and following my yet-to-be-determined passion. I could tell myself that although I lacked a meaningful, intense relationship, I had my work.

I call opposing counsel, a reasonable midfortyish associate with a minor speech impediment who must have been passed over for partner at his firm. I tell him that our papers were served incorrectly, that I would re-serve them by hand but they would arrive a day late. He interrupts me with a pleasant chuckle and says with a lisp that it is not a problem, that of course he wouldn't challenge service. I bet he hates his job as much as I do. If he liked it, he'd be all over this lapse like white on rice. Les would have a field day if the other side served a day late.

I send Les an e-mail message, one brief sentence: "Opposing counsel says they're fine with receiving papers by hand today." That will show him. I can be as curt and surly as the next guy.

Around one-thirty, after I have printed a new set of papers and turned them over to our courier for delivery, Hillary comes to my office and asks if I have lunch plans.

"No plans. You want to go?"

"Yeah. Can we go somewhere nice? Get a good meal? Steak or Italian?"

I smile and nod, retrieving my purse from under my desk. Hillary could eat a big lunch every day, but I get too sleepy in the afternoon. Once, after ordering a hot open-face turkey sandwich with mashed potatoes and green beans, I actually took the subway home for an afternoon nap. I returned to six voice-mail messages, including a ranting one from Les. That had been my last nap, unless you count the times I turn my chair to the window and balance a paper in my lap. The technique is foolproof—if someone barges in, it just looks as if you're reading. I sling my purse over my shoulder as

Kenny, our internal messenger from the mailroom, peeks around my half-open door.

"Hey, Kenny, come on in."

"Ra-chelle." He says my name in a French accent. "These are for you." He smirks as he produces a glass vase filled with red roses. A lot of roses. More than a dozen. More like two dozen, although I don't count. Yet.

"Holy shit!" Hillary's eyes are wide. I can tell that it takes tremendous effort for her not to grab the card.

"Where should I put 'em?" Kenny asks.

I clear a spot on my desk and point. "Here's fine."

Kenny shakes his wrists, exaggerating the weight of the vase, whistles, and says, "Woo-hoo, Rachel. Someone's diggin' you."

I wave my hand at him, but there is no way to deny that these are from anyone other than a guy with romantic interest. If they weren't red roses, I could pawn them off on some familial occasion, tell them it was some special day for me or that my parents are aware of my service error and are trying to comfort me. But these are not only roses, they are red roses. And bountiful. Most certainly not from a relative.

Kenny leaves after making one final remark about the roses costing someone some serious jack. I try to head out the door after him, but there is no chance that we are going anywhere until Hillary gets full information.

"Who are they from?"

I shrug. "I have no clue."

"Aren't you going to read the card?"

I am afraid to read it. They have to be from Dex—and what if he signed his name? It is too risky.

"I know who they're from," I say.

"Who?"

"Marcus." He is the only other possibility.

"Marcus? You guys barely hung out at all this weekend. What's the deal? Are you holding back on me? You better not be holding back on me!"

I shush her, tell her that I don't want everybody at the firm knowing my business.

"Okay, well then, tell me. What does the card say?" She is in interrogation mode. For as much as she hates the firm, she is one tough litigator.

I know I can't get out of reading the card. Besides, I, too, am dying to know what it says. I pluck the white envelope out of the plastic fork in the vase, open it very slowly as my mind races to make up a story about Marcus. I slide the card out and read the two sentences silently: I AM SO SORRY. PLEASE SEE ME TONIGHT. It is written in Dexter's all-capitals handwriting, which means he had to go to the flower store in person. Even better. He did not sign his name, probably imagining a scenario like this one. My heart is racing, but I try to avoid a full-on grin in front of Hillary. The roses thrill me. The note thrills me even more. I know I will not refuse his invitation. I will be seeing him tonight, even though I am more afraid than ever of getting hurt. I lick my lips and try to appear composed. "Yeah, from Marcus," I say.

Hillary stares at me. "Let me see," she says, grabbing for the card.

I pull it out of her reach and slip it into my purse. "It just says he's thinking of me."

She pushes her hair behind her ears and asks suspiciously, "Have you been on more than that one date? What's the full story?"

I sigh and head into the hallway, fully prepared to sell out poor Marcus. "Okay, we had a date last week that I didn't tell you about," I start, as we walk toward the elevator. "And, um, he told me his feelings were growing . . ."

"He said that?"

"Something like that. Yeah."

She digests this. "And what did you say?"

"I told him I wasn't sure how I felt and, um, I thought we should keep things low-key over the weekend."

Frieda from accounting darts into the elevator after us. I hope that Hillary will save further interrogation for after our elevator ride, but no, she continues as the doors close. "Did you guys hook up?"

I nod so that Frieda, standing with her back to us, won't know my business. I would have said no, but red roses would make less sense had there been no hook-up.

"But you didn't sleep together, did you?" At least she whispers this.

"No," I say, and then give her a look to be quiet.

The elevator doors open, and Frieda scurries on her way.

"So? Tell me more," Hillary says.

"It was pretty minor stuff. C'mon, Hill. You're relentless!"

"Well, if you'd told me the entire story up front, I wouldn't need to be relentless." Her face looks trusting again. I am out of the woods.

We talk about other things on our short walk to Second Avenue. But then, over steak at Palm Too, she says, "Remember when you dropped that beer on Saturday night, while you and Dex were talking?"

"When?" I ask, feeling panicked.

"You know, when you were talking, and I came up—right at the end of the evening?"

"Oh yeah. I guess. What about it?" I make my face as blank as possible.

"What was going on? Why was Dex so upset?"

"He was upset? I don't remember." I look at the ceiling, wrinkle my forehead. "I don't think he was upset. Why do you ask?"

When trapped, answering a question with a question is always a sound tactic.

"No reason. It just seemed odd, is all."

"Odd?"

"I don't know. It's crazy . . ."

"What?"

"It's crazy, but . . . you guys looked like a couple."

I laugh nervously. "That *is* crazy!"

"I know. But as I was watching you two talk, I thought to myself that you would be way better with Dex. You know, better than he is with Darcy."

"Oh, come on," I say. More nervous laughter. "They look great together."

"Sure. Yes. They have all of that surface stuff. But something about them doesn't fit." She brings her water glass to her lips and inspects me over it.

Keep your day job, Hillary.

I tell her she is nuts, even though I love what she has just told me. I want to ask her why she thinks this. Because we both went to law school? Because we have some shared trait—more depth or dignity than Darcy? But I say nothing more, because it's always wise to say as little as possible when you're guilty.

Les barges into my office after lunch to ask me about another matter for the same client. I have figured out over the years that this is his awkward way of apologizing. He only comes by my office after an explosion, like the one this morning.

I swivel in my chair and give him the update. "I've checked all of the cases in New York. And federal cases too."

"Okay. But keep in mind that our fact pattern is unique," Les says. "I'm not sure the Court will care much about precedent."

"I know that. But as far as I can tell, the general holding we rely upon in Section One of our brief is still good law. So that's a good first step."

So there.

"Well, make sure you check case law in other jurisdictions too," he says. "We need to anticipate all of their arguments."

"Yup," I say.

As he turns to leave, he says over his shoulder, "Nice roses."

I am stunned. Les and I do not make small talk, and he has never commented on anything other than my work, not even a "How was your weekend?" on a Monday morning, or a "Cold enough out there for you?" when we ride the elevator together on a snowy day.

Maybe two dozen red roses make me seem more interesting. I *am* more interesting, I think. This affair has given me a new dimension.

I am shutting down my computer, about to leave work, with plans to see Dexter. We have not yet spoken, only traded a series of conciliatory messages, including one from me thanking him for the beautiful flowers.

Hillary appears in my doorway, on her way out. "You're leaving now too?"

"Yeah," I say, wishing I had slipped out ahead of her. She often asks me if I want to get a drink after work, even on Mondays, which virtually everybody else considers the only stay-in night of the week. She isn't so much a party girl, like Darcy, she just isn't one to sit home and do nothing.

Sure enough, she asks if I want to grab a margarita at Tequilaville, our favorite place near work despite—or maybe because of—the stale chips and touristy crowd. It is always a welcome escape from the predictable New York scene.

I say no, I can't.

Of course she wants a reason. Every reason I think of she can and will refute: I'm tired (c'mon, one drink?), I have to go the gym (blow it off!), I'm cutting back on alcohol (a blank, incredulous stare). So I tell her that I have a date. Her face lights up. "So ole Marky Mark's flowers worked their magic, huh?"

"You got me," I say, glancing at my watch for good measure.

"Where are you going? Or are you staying in?"

I tell her we're going out.

"Where?"

"Nobu," I say, because I ate there recently.

"Nobu on a Monday night, huh? He *does* dig you."

I regret my choice; I should have gone for the no-name neighborhood Italian restaurant.

"If the date ends before two, call me and give me the scoop," she says.

"Sure thing," I say.

I go home forgetting all about Marcus and Hillary.

"Thank you so much for seeing me," Dex says, as I open the door. He is wearing a dark suit and white shirt. His tie is removed, likely stuffed into his briefcase, which he puts on the floor right inside my door. His eyes are tired. "I didn't think you would."

I never considered not seeing him. I tell him this, realizing that it might erode my power. I don't care. It is the truth.

Both of us begin to apologize, moving toward each other awkwardly, self-consciously. He takes one of my hands in his, squeezes it. His touch is both soothing and electrifying. "I'm so sorry for everything," he says slowly.

I wonder if he knows to be sorry about the beach too, if that is included in "everything." I have replayed that scene over and over, mostly in sepia, like Don Henley's "Boys of Summer" video. I blink, squeezing the images out of my mind. I want to make up. I want to move on.

"I'm sorry too," I say. I take his other hand, but there is still much space between us. Enough to fit another person or two.

"You have no reason to be sorry."

"Yes I do. I had no right to be angry at you. I was so out of line . . . We weren't going to discuss anything until after July Fourth. That was the deal . . ."

"It's not fair to you," he says. "It's a fucked-up deal."

"I am fine with the way things are," I say. It's not exactly true, but I am afraid of losing him if I ask for more. Of course, I am terrified of truly being with him too.

"I need to tell you about that afternoon with Darcy," he says.

I know he is talking about the shower episode, and I can't bear to hear it. The sepia beach frolic is one thing, the up-close and color porn scene is another. I don't want a single detail from his perspective. "Please don't," I say. "You really don't have to explain."

"It's just that . . . I want you to know that she initiated it . . . Truly . . . I've been avoiding it for so long, and I just couldn't get out of it." His face twitches, a mask of guilty discomfort.

"You do not have to explain," I say again, more firmly. "She's your fiancée."

He nods, looking relieved.

"You know when the two of you were on the beach?" I ask quietly, surprising myself by bringing it up.

"Yeah," he says knowingly, and then looks down. "When I came back up to the towels, I knew. I knew you were upset."

"How did you know?"

"You heard me say your name and ignored me. You were so cool. Chilly. I hated that."

"I'm sorry. It's just that you looked so happy with her. And I felt so— so . . ." I struggle to find the right word. "Well, obsolete, used."

"You are not obsolete, Rachel. You are all I think about. I couldn't sleep last night. Couldn't work today. You are anything but obsolete." His voice has lowered to a whisper, and we have assumed the position of slow-dancers, my arms around his neck. "And you must know that I'm not using you," he says into my ear. I feel the goose bumps rising.

"I know," I say into his shoulder. "But it's just so weird. Watching you with her. I don't think I should go to the Hamptons with you both again."

"I'm so sorry," he says again. "I know. I just wanted to spend time with you."

We kiss once. It is a soft, closed-mouth kiss, our lips barely touching. There is no connotation of lust or sex or passion. It is the other side of a love affair, the part I like the best.

We move over to my bed. He sits on the edge, and I am cross-legged beside him.

"I just want you to know," he says, staring intently into my eyes, "that I would never do this if I didn't deeply care for you."

"I know," I say.

"And I'm . . . you know . . . taking this whole thing very seriously."

"Let's not talk about it until the Fourth," I say quickly. "That was the deal."

"Are you sure? Because we can talk about it now if you want."

"I'm sure. Positive."

And I am positive. I am afraid of any leads he might give me about our future. I can't bear the thought of losing him, but have yet to consider what it would be like to lose Darcy. To have done something so huge and all-encompassing and wrong and final to my best friend.

He tells me that it scares him how much I mean to him, do I know how much I mean to him?

I nod. I know.

He kisses me again, more intensely this time. Then I experience my first truly unbelievable make-up sex.

The next morning Hillary visits me on the way to her office. She asks me how my date went. I tell her it was great. She plops down in one of my guest chairs, placing her bottle of Poland Spring water and her sesame bagel on my desk. She leans back and slams my door with her elbow. Her face is all business.

It turns out that Marcus did indeed opt for the no-name Italian restaurant in his neighborhood. The same no-name Italian restaurant that for whatever reason also struck Hillary's fancy last night. A city of millions, and Marcus and Hillary were seated two tables apart, over identical plates of ravioli on a random Monday night. Welcome to Manhattan, a smaller island than you'd ever think.

"The only thing you didn't lie to me about," Hillary says, shaking her finger at me, "is that Marcus was, in fact, on a date. Just not with your lying ass—although the girl resembled you in the mouth and chin region."

"Are you mad?"

"Not mad, no."

"What then?"

"Well, for one, I'm shocked. I didn't think you were capable of such deceit." She looks impressed by this revelation. "But I'm also hurt that you feel you can't confide in me. I like to think of myself as your best friend—not some figurehead, a throwback from your high school days—your present-day best friend. Which brings me to my next point . . ." she says knowingly. She waits for me to fill the silence.

I look at my stapler, then my keyboard, and then my stapler again.

Although I have pictured getting busted many times, it is always Darcy doing the busting. Because after all, if you're going to let your mind wander, go for the worst scenario, not some intermediate level of doom. It's like worrying about your boyfriend getting into a drunk driving accident—you don't think about him hitting a mailbox and splitting his lip. You picture lilies beside an open casket.

So I've had images of Darcy catching us. Not caught-in-bed-naked-in-the-act kind of busted—that is too far-fetched, particularly in a doorman building—but something more subtle. Darcy stops by unexpectedly, and José sends her up without buzzing me first (mental note to self: tell him never to do that). I answer the door assuming it is only the Chinese delivery guy bringing cartons of wonton soup and egg rolls to Dex and me, as we are understandably famished from our escapades (mental note to self, number two: always look through the peephole first). And there she stands, her big eyes taking it all in. Speechless in her horror. She flees the scene. Dex dashes into the hall in his gingham boxers, bellowing her name, like Marlon Brando in *A Streetcar Named Desire*.

Next scene: Darcy amid cardboard boxes packing her CDs with the ever-supportive Claire offering her Kleenexes at every turn. At least Dex would get all the Springsteen albums, even *Greetings From Asbury Park,* which someone had given Darcy as a gift. Most of the books would stay, too, as Darcy brought few books into the union. Just a few glossy coffee table numbers.

I read once—ironically, in one of Darcy's magazines—that you should engage in this visualization exercise when you're having an affair, that you should imagine getting caught and the grim aftermath. These images should snap you back to reality, get you thinking straight, make you realize what it is you'd be losing. Of course, the article presupposed a lust-driven affair, and the article was not directed at the unattached person in the triangle, but rather the participant in the committed relationship. Then again, the article also assumed that the third party was not the maid of honor in the upcoming wedding of the other two persons. Clearly our circumstances do not fit your typical adulterous mold.

In any event, I don't know exactly how I'd feel if Darcy busted us and my friendship with her ended. I can't really get there mentally. The fact is, Darcy is one hundred percent clueless, and she and Dex are still very much engaged. And likely, it will stay that way; they will get married and she will never discover the truth about our affair.

Hillary is a different story.

"Well?" she asks.

"Well, what?"

"Who were you *really* seeing last night? Who really sent you those?" She points at my roses.

"Someone else."

"No *shit*."

I swallow.

"Okay, look, I wasn't born yesterday. You get in a fight with Dex at the Talkhouse, you both clam up when I arrive on the scene. Then you leave the Hamptons early the next day, all down in the dumps, with false claims of imminent deadlines—I know your work schedule, Rach, and you had nothing due yesterday. And then these flowers arrive." She points at my roses, still in full bloom. "You name Marcus, whom you basically ignored over the weekend. Which is odd, even if you did decide to play it low-key. Then you tell me you have a date with Marcus, and I see him out sans you—with another woman!" She finishes her catalog of evidence with a jubilant smile.

"Was she cute?" I ask.

"The woman?"

"Yeah. Marcus's date."

"Actually, yes, she was quite attractive. As if you care."

She is right—I don't.

"Now quit stalling and address my point," she says.

"What point is that?"

"Rachel!"

"It certainly does look bad," I say, still reluctant to confess.

"Rachel. Who do you think I'm going to tell? I'm your friend. Not Darcy's. Hell, I don't even like her that much . . ."

I pick up my tape dispenser, pull out two inches of tape, and hold it between my index finger and thumb. For some reason, this is a harder confession than the one to Ethan. Maybe because it is face-to-face. Maybe because her past has not been as dicey as Ethan's.

"Okay." Hillary tries again. "Let me say the words for you, and you can just nod your head." Her voice is like that of a mother to a child.

I nervously play with the tape, wrapping it around my thumb. She is about to spell it all out, and I have two choices—admit or deny. An admission might be a huge relief. A denial will have to be accompanied by a suitably indignant expression and a barrage of "How could you think that? Are you crazy?" et cetera. I am in no mood for that charade.

"Dex is cheating on Darcy," she says. "With you."

Drum roll.

I raise my chin and return her gaze. Then I nod the smallest of nods, my head barely moving.

"I knew it!"

I consider telling her that I don't want to talk about it, but in truth, I *do* want to talk about it. I want her to tell me that I'm not a terrible person. I want her to expound upon her earlier statement that I would be better suited to him than Darcy. And most of all, I just want to talk about Dex.

"When did this all start?"

"The night of my party."

She stares at the ceiling for a second and nods as if everything makes sense now. "Okay, start from the beginning. Leave nothing out." She settles into her chair and tears off a piece of her bagel.

"The first time I slept with him was an accident."

"The *first* time? You've *slept* with him? Multiple times?"

I give her a look.

"Sorry, go on. I just can't believe this!"

"Okay. So yes, the night of my party, we were the last two out . . . we went for drinks, one thing led to another, and we slept together back at my apartment. It was an accident. I mean, we were both drunk. I was, anyway."

"Oh, I remember. You were a little bit out of it that night."

"Yeah. I was. But, interestingly, Dex says he wasn't that drunk." This detail not only shifts the responsibility his way, but simultaneously makes the genesis of the affair more meaningful.

"So he, what, took advantage of you?"

"No! I didn't mean to imply that . . . I knew what I was doing."

"Okay." She motions for me to go on.

I tell her about waking up the following morning, Darcy's frantic messages, our panic, and Dexter using Marcus as his alibi. "So that's it," I say.

"What do you mean, 'that's it'? Clearly not." She gives my roses a purposeful glance.

"I mean, that was it for a while. We both felt regretful and—"

"How regretful?"

"Regretful, Hillary! Obviously!" To myself, I recall that first day, and my complete lack of penitence. "So that was it. In my mind, it was over."

"But not in his, right?"

I choose my words carefully and tell her about his Monday call to me and the things he said. And then everything that happened in the Hamptons. And about our first sober kiss. The turning-point kiss. Sleeping with him for the real first time.

She takes another big bite of her bagel. "So is this—what? A purely physical thing? Or do you really like him?"

"I really like him," I say.

She digests this. "So is he going to break off the engagement?"

"We haven't talked about it."

"How can you not talk about it? Wait—was that what you were fighting about in the Talkhouse?"

I tell her that we weren't exactly fighting, but that I was upset about him having sex with Darcy. Hence the roses.

"Okay. So if he's sorry for sleeping with his fiancée, that sounds like he's headed in the direction of breaking up with her, right?"

"I don't know. We really haven't discussed it yet."

She looks confused. "When are you going to?"

"We said we'd talk about it around July Fourth."

"Why then?"

"Arbitrary. I don't know."

She takes a swig of water. "Well, you *do* think he's going to dump her, right?"

"I don't know. I don't even know if I want that."

She gives me a nonplussed look.

"You are forgetting an important piece of this whole thing, Hillary. Darcy is my longtime, lifelong friend. And I am her maid of honor."

She rolls her eyes. "Details."

"You just don't like her."

"She's not my favorite person in the world, but Darcy is not the point."

"She's a major point, in my opinion. She's my friend. And besides, even if she weren't, even if she were a random woman, don't you think I would have to confront the bad karma aspects of this?"

I wonder why I am arguing against myself.

She straightens in her chair and speaks slowly. "The world is not that black-and-white, Rachel. There are no moral absolutes. If you were sleeping with Dex for the sheer thrill of it all, then maybe I'd worry about your karma. But you have feelings for him. It doesn't make you a bad person."

I try to memorize her speech. *No moral absolutes.* That is good stuff.

"If the tables were turned," she continues, "Darcy would do the same thing in a heartbeat."

"You think?" I ask, considering this.

"Don't you?"

"Maybe you're right," I say. Darcy does, after all, have quite a history of taking. I give, she takes. That's the way it has always been.

Until now.

Hillary smiles and nods. "I say go for it."

More or less what Ethan said. That's two votes for me, zero for Darcy.

"I'm going to keep seeing him as much as I can. We'll see what happens," I say, realizing that just "seeing what happens" is my version of "going for it."

twelve

Darcy and I are flying home to Indianapolis for Annalise's baby shower, and I am stuck in the dreaded middle seat. Darcy was assigned the middle, but of course she wangled her way into my window seat, saying that if she can't look out the window she gets airsick. I wanted to tell her that this principle of car travel does not apply in a plane, but I didn't bother, just surrendered to her demand. In the past I would have done so mindlessly, but now I feel resentful. I think of Ethan and Hillary and their recent statements about Darcy. She is selfish, plain and simple. And this is the truth, regardless of my feelings for Dex.

A forty-something man with a crew cut has the aisle seat to my left. He has glued the entire length and width of his right forearm to our shared armrest, elbow to fingertip. He drinks and turns the pages of his magazine with his left hand so as not to lose ground.

The pilot announces that the skies are clear and we will be landing ahead of schedule. Darcy announces that she is bored. She is the only person I know, over the age of twelve, who says with great regularity that she is bored.

I glance up from my book. "Did you already read your Martha Stewart wedding issue?"

"Cover to cover. There's nothing new in there. And by the way, you're the one who should be reading it. There's an article on favors—you promised you would help me think of an original idea for favors," she says, as she adjusts her seat the whole way back and then up again.

"How about matchbooks?"

"You said original!" Darcy crosses her arms. "Everybody does matchbooks! That's just a given. I need a proper favor, in addition to matches."

"What does Martha suggest?" I ask, marking my place in my novel with my thumb.

"I dunno, hard stuff to make. Labor-intensive stuff." She looks at me plaintively. "You have to help! You know I'm no good at crafts."

"Neither am I."

"You're better than I am!"

I turn back to my book, pretending to be engrossed.

She sighs and chews her Juicy Fruit more vigorously. And when that doesn't work, she hits the spine of my book. "Raa-chel!"

"Okay! Okay!"

She smiles, unabashed, like a child who doesn't care that she's made her mother miserable, only that she got what she wanted. "So you think we should do something with *d?*"

"*D?*" I ask, playing dumb.

"You know, a *d* . . . for Dex and Darcy. Or is that cheesy?"

"Cheesy," I say, which would have been my answer even before the D and R days.

"Okay—then what?" She checks the number of fat grams in her snack mix before casting it into the seat-back pocket in front of her.

"Well, you have your sugared almonds in netting tied with pastel ribbons . . . or mints in a tin with your wedding date," I say as I exert slight pressure with my left elbow, trying to wedge it in a tiny crevice on my armrest. In my peripheral vision, I see Crew Cut flex his bicep in resistance. "Then you have permanent keepsakes like Christmas tree ornaments . . ."

"Can't. We have too many Jewish guests—and honestly, I think some people who celebrate Kwanza," she interrupts, proud of her diverse guest list.

"Okay. But you get the point. That genre. Permanent keepsakes: ornaments, homemade CDs with your favorite songs."

She becomes perky. "I like the CD idea! But wouldn't that be expensive?"

I give her a look that says, yeah, but you're worth it. She eats it up. "But what's another few hundred dollars in the scheme of things, right?" she asks.

I'm sure her parents would love this statement. "Right," I patronize.

"So we could have, like, *The Darcy and Dex Soundtrack* and put our all-time favorite songs on it," she says.

I wince.

"Are you sure it's not cheesy? Tell me the truth."

"No, I like it. I like it." I want to change the subject but worry that this will spark a discussion of my maid-of-honor shortcomings. So instead I strike a thoughtful pose and tell her that although the CDs would be time intensive and expensive, they would make a lovely, special favor. Then I ask her if Dex would like the idea.

She looks at me as if to say, who cares what Dex wants? Grooms don't matter. "Okay. Now help me think of some songs."

I hear Shania Twain singing "Whose Bed Have Your Boots Been Under?" Or maybe Diana Ross belting out "Stop! In the Name of Love!" No, all wrong, I think. Both songs cast Darcy in the role of noble victim.

"I can't think of one song. My mind's a blank. Help me think," Darcy says, her pen poised over her napkin. "Maybe something by Prince? Van Halen?"

"I can't think of any either," I say, hoping that Bruce Springsteen doesn't make the cut.

"You sure it's not cheesy?" she asks.

"It's *not* cheesy," I say, and then whisper, "This guy next to me is really pissing me off. He won't give me any of the armrest." I turn to quickly survey Crew Cut's smug profile.

"Excuse me! Sir!" Darcy leans over my lap and pokes his arm. Once, twice, three times. "Sir? Sir!"

He casts a disdainful eye her way.

"Sir, could you please share the armrest with my friend here?" She flashes him her most seductive smile.

He shifts his arm one centimeter. I mumble thanks.

"See?" Darcy asks me proudly.

This is the part where I'm supposed to marvel at her way with men.

"You just have to know how to ask for what you want," she whispers. My mentor in dealing with the opposite sex.

I think of Dex and July Fourth.

"I might have to try that," I say.

My parents call my cell right after we land, to confirm that Darcy's father picked us up and to ask if I ate on the plane. I tell them yes, Mr. Rhone showed up, and no, they stopped serving dinner on the New York to Indy flight about ten years ago.

As we pull into our cul-de-sac, I spot my father waiting for me on the front porch of our two-story, white-aluminum-sided, green-shuttered house. He is wearing a short-sleeved, peach-and-gray plaid shirt and matching gray Dockers. By any measure, it is an "outfit," and it has my mother written all over it. I thank Mr. Rhone for the ride and tell Darcy that I'll call her later. I am relieved that she does not ask if we can all get together for dinner. I've had enough wedding talk and know that Mrs. Rhone is incapable of discussing anything else.

As I cross Darcy's yard into my own, my dad throws up his arm and gives an exaggerated, overhand wave as if signaling a far-off ship. "Hello, counselor!" he belts out, all grins. The novelty of having an attorney daughter has yet to wear off.

"Hi, Dad!" I kiss him and then my mother, who is hovering at his side, already examining me for possible signs of anorexia, which is ridiculous.

I am nowhere near too thin, but my mom does not accept New York's definition of thin.

As I field their questions about my flight, I notice that the hall wallpaper has changed. I advised my mother against wallpaper, told her paint was the way to go for a fresher look. But she stuck with wallpaper, switching from tiny floral print to slightly tinier floral print. My parents' taste has not evolved since around the time that Ronald Reagan was shot. Our home still has lots of country touches—cross-stitched expressions of good cheer like "Back-door friends are best," a scattering of wooden cows and pigs and pineapples, stencil borders throughout.

"Nice wallpaper," I say, trying to sound sincere.

My mom doesn't buy it. "I know—you don't like wallpaper, but your father and I do," she says, motioning me into the kitchen. "And we're the ones who live here."

"I never said I liked wallpaper," my dad says, winking at me.

She shoots him a practiced look of annoyance. "You most certainly did, John." Then she tells me in a whisper, designed for him to hear, that, in fact, my father picked the new paper.

He gives me a "Who, me?" expression.

They never tire of their routine. She plays the fearless leader, corralling her unruly husband, the good-natured fool. Although I spent much of my adolescence irritated by the monotony of it, particularly when I had friends over, I have come to appreciate it in recent years. There is something comforting about the sameness of their interaction. I am proud that they have stayed together, when so many of my friends' parents have divorced, remarried, morphed two families into one, with varying degrees of success.

My mom points to a plate of cheddar cheese, Ritz crackers, and red grapes. "Eat," she says.

"Are these seedless?" I ask. Grapes with seeds just aren't worth the effort.

"Yes, they are," my mom says. "Now. Shall I throw something together or would you rather order pizza?"

She knows that I'd prefer pizza. First, I love Sal's pizza, which I can only get when I'm home. Second, "throwing something together" is an exact description of my mom's cooking—her idea of seasoning is salt and pepper, her idea of a recipe is tomato soup and crackers. Nothing strikes fear in my heart like the sight of my mother strapping on an apron.

"Pizza," my dad answers for us. "We want pizza!"

My mom pulls a Sal's coupon off the refrigerator and dials the number, ordering a large pizza with mushrooms and sausage. She covers the mouthpiece. "Right, Rachel?"

I give her the thumbs-up. She beams, proud to have memorized my favorite combination.

Before she can hang up, she is inquiring about my love life. As though all my phone updates informing them that I have nothing going on were just a ruse, and I've been saving the truth for this moment. My father covers his ears with feigned embarrassment. I give them a tight-lipped smile, thinking to myself that this inquisition is the only part of coming home that I don't like. I feel that I am a disappointment. I am letting them down. I am their only child, their only shot at grandchildren. The math is pretty basic: if I don't have children in the next five years or so, it is unlikely they will see their grandchildren graduate from college. Nothing like a little added pressure to an already stressful pursuit.

"Not one boy out there?" my mom asks, as my dad searches for the ideal slice of cheese. Her eyes are wide, hopeful. The probe might seem insensitive, except she truly believes I have my choice of dozens, that the only thing keeping me from her grandchildren is my own neurosis. She doesn't understand that the simple, straightforward, reciprocated love she has for my father is not so easy to come by.

"No," I say, lowering my eyes. "I'm telling you, it's harder to find a good guy in New York than anywhere." It is the cliché of single life in Manhattan, but only because it's true.

"I can see that," my dad says, nodding earnestly. "Too many people caught up in that rat race. Maybe you should come home. At least move to Chicago. Much cleaner city. It's because Chicago has alleys, you know." Every time my dad visits New York, he harps on the lack of alleys; why would they make a city without alleys?

My mom shakes her head. "Everybody is married with babies in the suburbs. She can't do that."

"She can if she wants to," my dad says with a mouthful of cracker.

"Well, she doesn't want to," my mom says. "Do you, Rachel?"

"No," I say apologetically. "I like New York for now."

My dad frowns as if to say, well, then there is no solution.

Silence fills the kitchen. My parents exchange a doleful glance.

"Well. There is *sort of* someone . . ." I blurt out, just to cheer them up a bit.

They brighten, stand up straighter.

"Really? I knew it!" My mom claps giddily.

"Yeah, he's a very nice guy. Very smart."

"And I'm sure he's handsome too," she says.

"What does he do?" my dad interrupts. "The boy's looks are beside the point."

"He's in marketing. Finance," I say. I'm not sure if I am telling them about Marcus or Dex. "But . . ."

"But what?" my mom asks.

"But he just got out of a relationship, so the timing may be . . . imperfect."

"Nothing is ever perfect," my mom says. "It is what you make of it."

I nod earnestly, thinking that she should cross-stitch that nugget of wisdom and hang it over my twin bed upstairs.

"On a scale of one to ten, how much do you dread this baby shower?" Darcy asks me the next day as we drive to Annalise's shower in my mom's '86 Camry, the car I learned to drive in. "Ten is total, total doomsday kind of dread. One is I can't wait, this thing will be really fun."

"Six," I say.

Darcy makes an acknowledging sound and then flips open her compact to check her lipstick. "Actually," she says, "I thought it'd be higher."

"Why? How much do you dread it?"

She closes her compact, examines her two-point-three-carat ring, and says, "Mmmm . . . I don't know . . . Four and a half."

Ohhh, I get it, I think. I have more reason to dread it. I am the one going into a room full of married and pregnant women—many of whom are fellow high school classmates—without so much as a boyfriend. Only one of us is thirty and totally alone, a tragic combination in any suburb. That is what Darcy is thinking. But I make her say it, ask her why she supposes that I dread the shower by a full point and a half more.

Shamelessly and without hesitation to consider a tactful wording, she answers me. "Be-*cause.* You're single."

I keep my eyes on the road, but can feel her stare.

"Are you mad? Did I say something wrong?"

I shake my head, turn on the radio. Lionel Richie is wailing away on one of my mother's preselected radio stations.

Darcy turns the volume down. "I didn't mean that that was a bad thing. I mean, you know that I *totally* value being single. I never wanted to marry before thirty-three. I mean, I'm talking about *them.* They are so narrow, you know what I mean?"

She has just made it worse by telling me that she didn't even want this whole crazy engagement. She would have preferred another three-plus years of bachelorettehood. And lo and behold, it all just fell in her lap. What's a girl to do?

"They're so narrow that they don't even know they're narrow," she continues.

Of course she is right about this. This group of girls, of which Annalise has been a member since the day she left college, lives like women in the fifties. They picked out china patterns before their twenty-second birthdays, married their first boyfriend, bought three-bedroom homes within miles, if not blocks, of their parents, and went about the business of starting a family.

"Right," I mumble.

"So that's all I meant," she says innocently. "And deep down inside, they are so jealous of you. You're a big-time lawyer at a big-city firm."

I tell her that is crazy—not one of those girls longs for a career like mine. Most don't work at all, in fact.

"Well, it's not only the career. You are free and single. I mean, they watch *Sex and the City*. They know what your life's all about. It's glamorous, full of fun, hot guys, cosmopolitans, excitement! But they won't let you see their insecure side. Because it would make their own lives that much more pathetic, you know?" She smiles, pleased with her pep talk. "Yeah. Your life is totally *Sex and the City.*"

"Yes. I am a lot like Carrie Bradshaw," I say flatly.

Minus the fabulous shoes, incredible figure, and empathetic best friend.

"Exactly!" she says. "Now you're talking."

"Look. I don't really care what they're thinking," I say, knowing it is only half true. I only care to the extent that I agree. And part of me believes that being thirty and alone *is* sad. Even with a good job. Even in Manhattan.

"Good," she says, slapping her thighs with encouragement. "Good. That's the spirit."

We arrive at Jessica Pell's—a fringe friend of ours from high school—exactly on time. Darcy consults her watch and insists on driving around for a few minutes, to be fashionably late.

I tell her it's not necessary to be fashionably late to a baby shower, but I oblige, and at her request, I take her through the McDonald's drivethrough. She leans over me and yells into the speaker that she "would love a small diet Pepsi." Now, I know that she knows that McDonald's has Coke, not Pepsi. She has told me before that she likes to test them, see if they'll ask. That the Pepsi people always ask if you order the Coke, but the Coke people don't always ask.

But it is an opportunity to make a stir, create an exchange. Pimply Suburbanite meets Big-City Supermodel.

"Is diet Coke awright?" the boy mumbles into his microphone.

"Guess it'll have to do," she says with a good-natured chuckle.

She finishes her diet Coke as we pull up to Jessica's house. "Well. Here goes nothing," she says, fluffing her hair, as if this shower were all about her instead of Annalise and her unborn child.

The other guests have already assembled in Jessica's well-coordinated blue-and-yellow living room when we arrive. Annalise screams, waddles over to us, and gathers us in a group hug. Despite the uncommon ground, we are still her best friends. And it is clear that we are the honored invitees, a role that makes me somewhat uncomfortable and Darcy bask.

"It's so good to see you guys! Thank you so much for coming in!" Annalise says. "You both look amazing. Amazing. You get more stylish every time you come home!"

"You look great too," I say. "Pregnancy agrees with you. You have that glow."

Like my parents' house, Annalise resists change. She still has the same hairstyle—shoulder-length with curled-under bangs—that was great in the eighties, horrible in the mid-nineties, and through sheer luck, slightly less awful now. It passes as a nice motherly cut. And her face, always round as a persimmon, no longer looks chubby, but simply part of the cute, pregnant package. She is the sort of pregnant woman that people gladly relinquish their seats to on the subway.

Darcy rubs Annalise's stomach with her jeweled left hand. The diamond catches the light and flashes in my face. "Oh my," Darcy coos. "There is a little naked person in there!"

Annalise laughs and says, "Well yes, that is one way of looking at it!" She introduces us to some of the guests, fellow teachers and guidance counselors from the school where she teaches, and other neighborhood friends. "And of course, you know everybody else!"

We exchange hugs with Jess and our other high school classmates. There is Brit Miller (who shamelessly worshiped and copied Darcy in high school). Tricia Salerno. Jennifer McGowan. Kim Frisby. With the possible exception of Kim, who was a bubbly cheerleader and, miraculously, also in the advanced science and math classes, none of the girls were particularly smart, interesting, or popular in high school. But as wives and mothers, their mediocrity matters no longer.

Kim slides down on the sofa and offers me a spot next to her. I ask her how Jeff (who also graduated in our class and played baseball with Brandon and Blaine) and her boys are doing. She says they are all doing great, that Jeff just got promoted, which was exciting, that they are buying a new house, that the boys are just perfect.

"What does Jeff do again?" I ask.

She says sales.

"And you have twins, right?"

Yes, boys. Stanley and Brick.

Now, I know Brick is her mother's maiden name, but I wonder again how she could have done that to a child. And Stanley? Who calls a baby Stanley, or even Stan? Stanley and Stan are man names. Nobody should have that name under the age of thirty-five. And even if the names were tolerable in their own right, they do not go together, my pet peeve in name selection. Not that you should choose rhyming names for twins, or even names beginning with the same letter, like Brick and Brock or Brick and Brack. Go with Stanley and Frederick—both old-man names. Or Brick and Tyler—both pretentious surnames. But Stanley and Brick? Please.

"Did you bring photos of the boys?" I ask the obligatory question.

"As a matter of fact I did," Kim says, whipping out a small album with "Brag Book" written on the cover in big, purple bubble letters. I smile, flipping through the pages, pausing for the requisite time before I go to the next. Brick in the tub. Stanley with a Wiffle ball. Brick with Grandma and Grandpa Brick.

"They're precious," I say, closing the album and handing it back to her.

"We think so," Kim says, nodding, smiling. "I think we'll keep them."

As she returns the album to her purse, I overhear Darcy telling her engagement story to Jennifer and Tricia.

Brit is egging her on. "Tell her about the roses," she prompts.

I had forgotten about the roses—perhaps blocked them out since the arrival of my own.

"Yes, a dozen red roses," Darcy is saying. "He had them waiting in the apartment for me after he proposed."

Not two dozen.

"Where did he ask you?" Tricia wants to know.

"Well, we went out for a really nice lunch, and afterward he suggested that we take a walk in Central Park . . ."

"Did you suspect it?" two girls ask at once.

"Not *at all* . . ."

This is a lie. I remember her telling me two days before Dex asked that she knew it was coming. But to admit this would detract from the drama of her tale, as well as diminish her image as the one pursued.

"Then what did he say?" Brit asks.

"You already know the story!" Darcy laughs. She and Brit still keep in touch occasionally due to Brit's diligence; her fascination for her teen idol has never eroded.

"Tell it again!" Brit says. "My engagement story is so lame—I picked out the ring myself at the mall! I have to live vicariously through you."

Darcy puts on her pretend-modest face. "He said, 'Darcy, I can't think of anything that would make me happier than having you as my wife.' "

Except being with your best friend.

"Then he said, 'Please share your life with me.' "

And share your best friend with me.

A chorus of oohs and ahhs follow. I tell myself that she is embellishing the tale, that he really just uttered the standard "Will you marry me?"

"Take off your ring," Brit clamors. "I want to try it on."

Kim says that it is bad luck to remove your ring during the engagement. *Take it off!*

Darcy shrugs to demonstrate that her free spirit is still very much intact. Or perhaps to point out that when you are Darcy Rhone, you don't need luck. She slips off her ring and passes it around the circle of eager women. It ends up in my hands.

"Try it on, Rach," Brit says.

It is a married girl's fun trick. Make the single girl try on the diamond ring so she can, if only for a moment, get one step closer to the unknown euphoria of betrothal. I shake my head politely as though I'm declining a second helping of casserole. "That's okay," I say.

"Rachel, any prospects?" Tricia asks tentatively, as you would inquire about someone's CAT scan results.

I am ready to report a firm no, when Darcy answers for me. "Tons," she says. "But no one special guy. Rachel is very picky."

She is trying to help. But somehow it has the reverse effect, and I feel even more like an emerging old maid. Besides, I can't help but think that she is only being charitable because I so clearly look like the odd woman out, the loser in the group. If I were engaged to, say, Brad Pitt, there'd be no way that Darcy would brag on my behalf. She'd be sulking in the corner, her competitive juices flowing in full force, telling Brit in the bathroom that yes, Brad is Brad, but Dex is so much cuter—just a little less pretty. Of course, with that, I would actually agree.

"I wouldn't say I'm that picky," I say matter-of-factly.

Just hopelessly alone and having an affair with Darcy's husband-to-be. *But you all do realize that I graduated from a top-ten law school and make six figures? And that I don't need a man, dammit! But when I do find one and have a baby, I will sure as hell pick a better name than Brick!*

"Yeah, you are picky," Darcy says to me, but for her audience. She takes a sip of punch. "Take Marcus, for example."

"Who is Marcus?" Kim asks.

"Marcus is this guy that Dex went to Georgetown with. Nice, smart, funny," Darcy says, waving her hand in the air, "but Rachel won't give him the time of day."

If she keeps it up, they are going to start wondering if I'm a lesbian. Which would make me a true freak show in their eyes. Their idea of diversity is someone who attended an out-of-state school and didn't rush a sorority.

"What, no sparks?" Kim asks me sympathetically. "You need sparks. Jeff and I had sparks in the eleventh grade and they never stopped."

"Right," I say. "You need sparks."

"Absolutely," Brit murmurs.

Their collective advice: don't settle. Keep looking. Find Mr. Right.

That is what they all did. And by God, I think they believe it. Because nobody who marries at the ripe age of twenty-three can be settling. Naturally. That is a phenomenon that only happens to women in their thirties.

"So, have you made a final decision on your baby names?" I ask Annalise, desperate to change the subject. I know she is considering Hannah and Grace if she has a girl, Michael or David for a boy. Wholesome, classic, solid names. Not trying too hard.

"Yes," Annalise says. "But we're not telling." She winks at me. I know that she'll tell me the final decision later, just as she has with the runner-up selections. I am safe. The friend who will never, can never, swipe your baby names.

My specialty is fiancé-stealing.

After we play a few silly shower games, Annalise opens her presents. There is a lot of yellow clothing because Annalise does not know whether she's having a boy or a girl. So no pink gifts except for a pink bunny bank from Tiffany, courtesy of Darcy, who says she knows for sure that Annalise is going to have a girl, that she has a very good sense about these things. I can tell that Annalise hopes she is right.

"Besides," Darcy says, "even if I'm wrong—and I'm not—did you know that at the turn of the century, pink was for boys and blue was for girls?"

We all say that we did not. I wonder if she is making it up.

Annalise comes to my gift. She opens my card, murmuring to herself. Her eyes fill with tears as she reads my words—that she is going to be the most wonderful mother and that I can't wait to watch it all. She waves me over to her, as she did with the other girls, and gives me a big hug. "Thank you, honey," she whispers. "That was so nice."

Then she opens my present, an off-white cashmere blanket with a teddy bear border. I spent a fortune on it, but I am glad that I splurged as I watch Annalise's expression. She gasps as she unfolds it, presses it to her cheek, and tells me it is perfect, that she will use it to bring the baby home from the hospital.

"I want to fly back when she's born!" Darcy says. "I better not be on my honeymoon!"

Whether she does it on purpose or it is simply the way she is wired, something she can't help, Darcy inserts herself into every moment. Usually I don't mind, but after spending ages finding the perfect gift for my second-oldest friend, I wish she would pipe down and stop overshadowing Annalise and me for a nanosecond.

Always the diplomat, Annalise smiles quickly at Darcy before returning her focus to me and the blanket. She passes it around as everyone agrees that it is the ideal receiving blanket, so adorable, so soft. That's what they're saying, anyway. But something tells me that they are all thinking, *Not a bad choice from a litigator with questionable maternal instincts.*

thirteen

When I return home from the shower, my mother follows me into the family room and bombards me with questions. I give her the highlights, but she is insatiable. She wants to know every detail about every guest, gift, conversation. I have a flashback to high school, when I'd come home, exhausted from a day of academic and social pressure, and she would inquire about Ethan's debate-team performance or Darcy's cheerleading tryout or what we talked about in English class. If I wasn't forthcoming enough, she would fill in the gaps, rambling about her part-time job at the orthodontist's office or what rude thing Bryant Gumble said on the *Today* show or how she ran into my third-grade teacher in the grocery store. My mother is an open-book chatterbox and she expects everyone to be just like her, particularly her only child.

She finishes her inquisition on the shower and moves on to—what else?—the wedding.

"So has Darcy decided on a veil?" She straightens a pile of *Newsweek*s on our coffee table, waiting for an in-depth answer.

"Yes."

She moves closer on our couch. "Long?"

"Fingertip."

She claps excitedly. "Oh. That will be beautiful on her."

My mother is, and has always been, a big Darcy fan. It didn't make sense back in high school given the fact that Darcy never put a premium on studying and promoted a certain unwholesome boy craziness. Yet my mother just plain old loved Darcy, perhaps because Darcy supplied her with the details of our life that she so craved. Even past the perfunctory parental pleasantries, Darcy would talk to my mother as a peer. She would come over to my house after school, lean against our kitchen counter, eating the Oreos my mother had set out for us while she talked and talked. Darcy would tell my mom about the boys she liked and the pros and cons of each. She'd say things like, "His lips are too thin; I bet he can't kiss," and my mom would become delighted and elicit more, and Darcy would give it, and I would end up leaving the room to start my geometry homework. Now what's wrong with that picture?

I remember once in the seventh grade, I refused to participate in the annual talent show, though Darcy incessantly heckled me to be one of her two backup dancers in her outlandish rendition of "Material Girl." Despite her own shyness, Annalise folded quickly, but I refused to succumb, didn't care that Darcy's choreography called for a three-girl act, didn't care that she said I was ruining her chances of a blue ribbon. Often I would let Darcy talk me into things, but not that one. I told her not to waste her breath, I had no intention of ever setting foot on a stage. After Darcy finally gave up and invited Brit to take my place, my mother lectured me on becoming more involved in fun activities.

"Aren't straight As enough for you?" I asked her.

"I just want you to have fun, honey," she said.

I lashed out, saying, "You just want me to be her!"

She told me not to be ridiculous, but part of me believed it. I feel the same way now. "Mom, no offense to you or the second daughter you never had, but—"

"Oh, don't start with that nonsense!" She pats her ash-blond hair which she has been coloring with the same Clairol hue for the past twenty years.

"All right," I say. "But truly, I have had it up to here with Darcy's wedding." I hold my hand four inches above my head and then raise it even higher.

"That's no attitude for a maid of honor." She purses her lips and scrapes one index finger across the other.

I shrug.

My mom laughs, the good-natured parent, refusing to take her only daughter too seriously. "Well, I should have known Darcy would be a handful as a bride. I'm sure she wants everything to be perfect . . ."

"Yeah, she deserves it," I say sarcastically.

"Well, she *does* deserve it," my mom says. "And so do you . . . your time will come."

"Uh-huh."

"Is that why you're sick of this?" she asks, with the accomplished air of a woman who has watched far too many talk shows on confronting your feelings and nurturing your relationships.

"Not exactly," I say.

"Then why, exactly? Is she being a pain in the you-know-what? What am I asking—*of course* she is! That's Darcy!" Another fond chuckle.

"Yeah."

"Yes, what, sweetie? What's on your mind?"

"Yes, she's being a pain in the ass," I say, reaching for the remote control to unmute the television.

"What is she doing?" my mom persists calmly.

"She's being Darcy," I say. "Everything is about her."

My mom gives me a sympathetic look. "I know, honey."

Then I blurt out that she doesn't deserve Dexter, that he is too good for her. My mother looks at me circumspectly. *Oh shit,* I think. Does she know? Ethan and Hillary are one thing—my mother's quite another. I was unwilling to tell her which boys I thought were cute in high school, so this one is certainly off the table. I can't stand the thought of letting her down. I am thirty, but still very much a parent-pleaser. And my mother, a woman who finds the keys to life in cross-stitched blurbs, would never understand this breach of friendship.

"She's driving him crazy too. I'm sure of it," I say, trying to cover.

"Did Dexter tell you this?"

"No, I haven't discussed this with Dex." Technically this statement is true. "You can just tell."

"Well, be patient with her. You'll never regret being a good friend."

I consider this gemstone from my mother. One would be hard-pressed to disagree with it. In fact, it is the way I have lived my entire life. Avoiding regret at any cost. Being good no matter what. Good student. Good daughter. Good friend. And yet I am struck by the sudden realization that regret cuts two ways. I might also regret sacrificing myself, my own desires, for Darcy's sake, in the name of friendship, in the name of being a good person. Why should I be the martyr here? I imagine myself alone at thirty-five, alone at forty. Or even worse, settling down with a dull, watered-down version of Dex. Dex with a weaker chin and twenty fewer IQ points. I would be forced to live with "What if" forever.

"Yeah, Mom. I know. Do unto others. Blah blah blah. I'll be a good friend to precious Darcy."

My mom looks down at her lap, smoothes her skirt. I hurt her feelings. I tell myself that I must be nice for one more evening. It is the least I can do. I don't have a sibling to pick up the slack and be the good child when I am off my game. I smile and change the subject. "Where's Dad?"

"He went to the hardware store. Again."

"For what this time?" I ask, indulging her in the "Dad can't get enough of hardware stores and car dealerships" joke.

"Who knows? Who ever knows?" She shakes her head, happy again.

I am half asleep, thinking about Dex, when my cell phone rings. I have it next to my bed, the battery fully charged and the ringer on high, hoping Dex will call. His number lights up my phone screen. I press it to my ear.

"Hi, Dex."

"Hi, there," he says, his voice low. "Did I wake you up?"

"Um, sort of. But that's okay."

He doesn't apologize, which I like.

"God, I miss you," he says. "When are you coming home?"

He knows when I'm coming home, knows that his fiancée has the identical itinerary. But I don't mind him asking. This question is for me. He wants me—not Darcy—back in his time zone.

"Tomorrow afternoon. We land at four."

"I'm coming over to see you," he says.

"Good," I say.

Silence.

I ask him where he is now.

"On the couch."

I picture him in my apartment, on my couch, although I know he is on their Pottery Barn pullout, the one that Darcy plans to replace with "a more high-end piece" as soon as they are married.

"Oh," I say. I don't want to hang up, but in my sleepy state, can think of nothing to say.

"How was the shower?"

"You didn't get a report?"

"Yeah. Darcy called."

I am glad he told me that she called him, wonder if he added this detail on purpose.

"But I was asking *you* how the shower was," he says.

"It was great to see Annalise . . . But it was miserable."

"Why's that?"

"Showers are just that way."

Then I tell him that I wish he were next to me. It is the kind of thing I don't usually say, unless he says something like it first. But the dark and the distance make me bold.

"You do?" he asks in the tone I use when I want more. *Guys aren't so different from us,* I think, which no matter how many times I think it will always seem like a remarkable revelation.

"Yeah. I wish you were right here with me."

"In your bed at home, right there with your parents in the next room?"

I laugh. "They're open-minded."

"Wish I were there, then."

"Although I have a twin bed," I say. "Not a lot of room."

"A twin bed with you is not a bad thing." His voice is low and sexy.

I know we are both thinking the same thing. I can hear him breathing. I say nothing, just touch myself and think of him. I want him to do the same. He does. My phone is hot against my face and, as usual when I'm on my cell, I wonder about the radiation I could be getting. But tonight, I don't care about a little radiation.

The next day Darcy and I share a cab home from LaGuardia. I am dropped off first. I phone Dex the second I hit the pavement, finding him at the office, working, waiting for my call. I am ready for you whenever, I say, happy that I already shaved my legs back in Indiana. He says he'll be right up as soon as she calls his office. You know, he says, sounding embarrassed by his newly acquired tactics. I understand. For a second, I feel bad that my life consists of these sleazy, adulterous strategies. But only for a second. Then I tell myself that Dex and I aren't in that camp. That in Hillary's words, life's not black-and-white. That sometimes the end justifies the means.

That evening, after Dex and I have been together for several hours, I realize that our visits are starting to run together in one delicious blur of talking, touching, dozing, and simply existing together in a warm, easy silence. Like the perfect beach vacation, where the routine is so blissfully uneventful that when you return home and friends ask how your trip was, you can't really recall what exactly you did to fill up so many hours. That is what being with Dex is like.

I have stopped counting our lovemaking but know that we are well past twenty. I wonder how many times he's been with Darcy. These are the things I think about now. So to say that she has nothing to do with us is not true. To say that it's not a contest is ludicrous. She is the measuring stick; I hold myself up against her. When we are in bed, I wonder, does she do it like this? Is she better? Do they follow a script by now or does she keep things fresh? (My vote, sadly, is fresh. And even more sadly, when your body is a ten, does it really matter if the sex is stale missionary?) I think of her afterward, too, when I often feel self-conscious about my body. I suck in my stomach, arrange my breasts when his back is turned, and never saunter around my apartment naked. I wonder how many times we'd have to be together before I would give up the pretty lingerie routine in favor of my gray sweats or flannel Gap pajama bottoms that I wear when I am alone. We probably don't have time for that stage to develop. At least not before the wedding. Time is running out. I tell myself not to panic, to savor the present.

But I can sense a recent shift. I allow myself to think of the future now. I've stopped feeling sick when I imagine Dex canceling the wedding. I've stopped feeling that my loyalty to Darcy should always come before all else, namely what I want. I'm still not sure where things will go, where I want them to go, but my fear of breaking the rules has dulled somewhat, as has my instinct to put Darcy above myself.

Tonight Dex talks about work. He often tells me about his deals, and although I am interested in the mechanics of it all, what I really like is the color that Dex provides about the major players at his firm, the people who fill his daily life. For example, I know that he likes working for Roger Bollinger, the head of his group. Dex is Roger's golden boy and Roger is Dexter's role model. When he tells a story about Roger, he imitates Roger's Boston accent in a way that convinces me that if I ever meet Roger it will seem as though Roger is imitating Dex imitating Roger. Roger is barely five feet four (my question—guys usually don't supply details on the appearance of other guys and are far more likely to report on wit or intelligence) but it doesn't hurt him with women, according to Dex. Incidentally, Dex reported this tidbit matter-of-factly, not admiringly, which reassures me that Dex does not have womanizing tendencies. Womanizers feel either (a) impressed by or (b) competitive with fellow womanizers.

He finishes telling me a story about Roger and then asks, "Did I tell you that Roger was engaged twice?"

"No," I say, thinking that he knows he hasn't. It's not the kind of thing you forget sharing, particularly given our circumstances. I feel suddenly chilly, and pull the sheet up over both of us.

"Yeah. He broke it off both times. He keeps saying things to me like, 'It's not ovah till it's ovah' and 'The fat lady hasn't sung yet.'"

I wonder if Roger knows anything about me, or if he's just doing the typical bachelor banter. "When?" I ask Dex.

"When does the fat lady sing?" Dex curls his body around mine.

"Well, yeah. Sort of." We are getting into sensitive territory, and I am thankful he can't see my eyes. "When did he break off the engagements?"

"Not sure about the first time. But the second time was right before the ceremony."

"You're kidding me."

"Nope. The bride was getting dressed when he went to her room. Knocked on her door and gave her the news right in front of her mother, her grandmother, and her ninety-five-year-old great-grandmother."

"Was she surprised?" I ask, realizing that it's a dumb question. Nobody expects the groom to barge in and call off the wedding.

"Apparently. But she shouldn't have been *that* surprised . . . She must've known he had done it once before."

"Was there somebody else?" I ask tentatively.

"Don't think so. No."

"Then why did he do it?"

"He said he couldn't see it lasting forever."

"Oh."

"What are you thinking?"

He must know what I'm thinking.

"Nothing."

"Tell me."

"Nothing."

"Tell me."

The dialogue of the new relationship. After a couple is established, the question becomes a relic.

"I'm thinking that I don't believe in that wedding-day, Julia Roberts *Runaway Bride*—or groom—routine."

"You don't *believe* in it?"

I am treading carefully. "I just think it's unnecessary . . . needlessly mean," I say. "If someone is going to call it off, they should do it before the wedding day."

My message isn't exactly subtle.

"Well, I agree, but don't you think it's better to pull the cord than make a mistake? Don't you owe it to the other person and yourself and the whole institution of marriage to say something, even if you come to the realization late in the game?"

"I'm *in no way* advocating the making of that sort of mistake. I'm just saying you should figure it out before the wedding day. That's what engagements are for. And in my book, by the wedding day it's a done deal. Suck it up and make the best of it. That's a cold move, telling her when the gown is on."

I picture Darcy in this humiliating scenario, and my empathy for her is unequivocal.

"You think? Even if it just ends up in a divorce?" he asks.

"Even if. You ask that girl if she'd rather be divorced or dissed in her dress in front of all those people."

He makes a noncommittal "hmmm" sound so I can't tell whether he agrees. I wonder what it all will mean for us. If he's even thinking about us at all. He has to be. I feel my muscles tense, my foot twitch nervously. I tell myself that it's not July Fourth yet. I don't want to think about it anymore at all.

I reach over Dex and turn up my stereo. Creedence Clearwater Revival is singing "Lookin' Out My Back Door." Talk about an upbeat song. It is exactly what I need to block out images of Dex and Darcy's wedding.

Instead, I picture a road trip with Dexter. We are in a white convertible with the top down, sunglasses on, trucking along a stretch of highway with no other cars in sight.

> *Bother me tomorrow, today I'll buy no sorrow.*
> *Doo, doo, doo, lookin' out my back door.*

fourteen

Every year over the July Fourth holiday, there is a mass exodus from Manhattan. People head for the Hamptons, the Cape, Martha's Vineyard, even New Jersey. Nobody stays. Not even Les. The summer of the bar exam, when Nate and I stayed in the city to study, I was amazed at what a different, downright peaceful place it was without all of the people. Of course, I plan on staying home this year too—I can't stomach the thought of seeing Dex and Darcy together. I call Dex and tell him this. He says what I have been hoping he would say.

"I'll stay too."

"Really?" My heart races just imagining spending the night with Dex.

"Yeah. Let's do it."

So we devise our plan: we will both "discover" at the last moment that we have to work. We will bitch and moan up a storm but insist to Darcy that she should go on and have fun without us. By then she will have a fresh pedicure, new outfits purchased, parties lined up, and reservations made at her favorite restaurants. So there's no way she'll stay home, and Dex and I will be together, uninterrupted for days. We will fall asleep together, wake up together, and eat our meals together. And although Dex hasn't confirmed it, I assume that at some point, we will have our big talk.

I share the plan with Hillary, who has high expectations. She is convinced that the long weekend will be the turning point in my relationship with Dex. As she leaves work at noon on the third, she stops by my office and tells me to have a great weekend. "Good luck." She crosses her fingers in the air.

"What do you mean? You think we're going to get caught?"

"No. That's not what I meant. I mean good luck with your talk. You are going to talk to Dex about what's going on, aren't you?"

"Yeah. I suppose so."

"You suppose so?"

"I'm sure we will. That is the plan."

"Okay. Make sure that you do." She gives me a stern look. "It's crunch time."

I grimace.

"Rachel, do not wimp out on this. If you want to be with him, now's the time to pipe up."

"I know. I got it," I say. And for a second I picture myself being Hillary-like. Strong, bold, and confident.

"I'll call you if your girl seems at all suspicious."

I nod, feeling a stab of guilt over such plotting against Darcy.

Hillary knows what I'm thinking. "You gotta do what you gotta do," she says. "Don't turn soft now."

At seven sharp, just as planned, Dexter arrives at my door with a fresh haircut that further accentuates his cheekbones. He holds a bottle of red wine, a small black duffel bag, and a bunch of white Casablanca lilies, the kind you find at every Korean deli for three bucks a stem. Even though they are inexpensive and somewhat wilted, I like them as much as my expensive roses.

"These are for you," he says. "Sorry. They're kind of dying already."

"I love them," I say. "Thank you."

He follows me into the kitchen as I look for a vase to put them in. I point to my favorite blue one in my top cupboard, just out of my reach. "Can you get that for me?"

He retrieves the vase and sets it on my counter as I begin trimming the stems and arranging them. I am a domestic goddess as far as he can tell.

"We did it," Dex whispers into my ear.

Goose bumps rise on my arms. I manage to get the flowers in the vase and add a little water before turning around to kiss him. His neck is warm, and the back of his hair is still damp from his haircut. He smells of cologne, which he doesn't usually wear. Of course, I am also wearing perfume, which I don't usually wear. But this is a special occasion. When you are used to snippets of time, our stretch of days might as well be forever. The way I feel reminds me of bursting off the bus on the last day of school before summer vacation. No worries except what to do first—ride bikes, go to the pool, or play Truth or Dare with Darcy and Annalise in my cool, unfinished basement. Today I know what I want to do first and I am pretty sure we will be doing it soon. I kiss Dex's neck as I inhale his sweet skin and the scent of lilies.

"This weekend is going to be out of control," he says, sliding my tank top over my head, letting it fall at our feet. He unhooks my bra, cups my breasts and then my face. His fingers press the back of my neck.

"I'm so glad you're here," I say. "I'm so happy."

"Me too," he says, as he works on my button-fly.

I lead Dex over to my bed and remove his clothes, admiring his body from every angle, kissing him in new places. On the back of his knees. On his elbows. We have time.

We make love slowly, each of us stopping the other at various points until we can't stand it any longer, and then reversing in the other reckless, breathless direction. He feels more mine than he ever has, and I know why: he is not going home to her tonight. He will not have to wash off, or check for signs of our togetherness. I sink my nails into his back and pull him harder against me.

After we make love, we order food from the diner and eat burgers by candlelight. Then we climb back into bed, where we talk and listen to music, fighting through waves of fatigue so that we can savor our time together, not waste it sleeping.

Our only interruption comes around midnight, when Dex says he should probably phone Darcy. I tell him it's a good idea, wondering whether I should give him privacy or stay in bed beside him. I decide to go to the bathroom, let him do his thing. I run water so I can't hear any piece of their conversation. A minute later, Dex calls my name.

I open the door a crack. "Are you off?"

"Yeah. C'mere. You didn't have to leave."

I get back in bed beside him, find his hand.

"Sorry about that," he says.

"No problem. I understand."

"Just taking precautions . . . I figure she won't call now. I told her I was on my way home to bed."

"What is she doing?"

"They're all at the Talkhouse. Drunk and happy."

But we are sober and happier, all tangled up in my sheets, our heads resting on one pillow. When Dex sits up to blow out the candle burning on my windowsill, I notice that trimmings from his haircut have transferred from his neck to my white pillowcase. There's something about those tiny black hairs that makes me so happy I want to cry.

I close my eyes so that I won't.

At some point, we fall asleep.

And then morning comes.

I wake up, remembering the first morning we woke up together, the panic that gripped my heart on that Sunday I turned thirty. The feeling I have now could not be more different. Calm joy.

"Hi, Rachel."

"Hi, Dex."

We are both grinning.

"Happy Fourth of July," he says, his hand resting on my inner thigh.

"Happy Fourth."

"It's not your typical Fourth. No fireworks planned, no picnics, no beach. You okay with that?" he asks.

"Yeah. I'm okay with that," I say.

We make love and then shower together. I am self-conscious at first, but after a few minutes, I relax and let him wash my back. We stay under the hot water (he likes his showers as hot as I do) long past the point of wrinkled fingers. Then we are out in the world, walking down Third Avenue to Starbucks. It is a humid, gray day, and rain feels likely. But we don't need good weather. Happiness wells inside me.

We are alone in line to order, Marvin Gaye singing over the sound system. I order a tall skim latte. Dex says, "Give me the same thing in a large with, um . . . just regular milk."

I like that he abandons the Starbucks terminology, skipping the word "grande" and ordering his coffee as a guy's guy should.

The perky girl behind the register bellows our order to her colleague, who promptly marks our cups with a black marker. Starbucks employees are consistently, freakishly chipper, even during the worst of morning rush hour when they have to deal with hordes of cranky people waiting impatiently for their caffeine fix.

"Oh wait," the girl says, beaming. "Are these together or separate?"

Dex answers quickly, "We're—they're together."

I smile at his slip. *We are together.*

"Will there be anything else?"

"Um. Yeah. I'll have a blueberry muffin," Dex says and then looks at me. "Rachel?"

"Yeah. I'll have one too," I say, resisting the urge to order a low-fat muffin. I don't want to be anything like Darcy.

"So two blueberry muffins." Dex pays and drops his change into the tip mug in front of the register. The girl smiles at me, as if to say, your guy is not only hot but generous too.

Dex and I both add a packet of brown sugar to our coffee, stir, and find a seat at the counter facing the street. The sidewalks are deserted.

"I like New York this way," I say, tasting my foam. We watch a lone yellow cab drift up Third Avenue. "Listen . . . no honking."

"Yeah. It really is dead," he says. "I bet we could get reservations anywhere tonight. Would you like to go out?"

I look at him. "We can't do that."

Getting coffee is one thing. Dinner is another.

"We can do whatever we please. Haven't you figured that out yet?" He winks and sips his coffee.

"What if somebody sees us?"

"Nobody's here." He motions out the window. "And so what if they do? We're allowed to eat, aren't we? Hell, I could even tell Darcy we're going to grab a bite together. She knows that we're both stuck here working, right?"

"I guess so."

"C'mon. I want to take you out. I've never taken you out on a proper date. I feel bad about that. What do you say?"

I raise my eyebrows and smirk.

"What's that look for?" Dex asks. His full lips meet the rim of his cup.

"It's just that 'proper' is not the word that comes to mind when I think about us."

"Oh, that," Dex says, waving his hand in the air, as though I have just stated an insignificant detail about our relationship. "Well, that can't be helped . . . I mean—yes, the circumstances are . . . less than ideal."

"That's an understatement. Let's call a spade a spade, Dex. We're having an affair."

It is the most I have ever said about what we are doing. I know Hillary wouldn't give me any awards for forthrightness, but my heart still skips. It is a bold comment for me.

"I guess so," he says hesitantly. "But when I'm with you, I'm not thinking about the impropriety of our . . . relationship. Being with you doesn't feel wrong."

"I know what you mean," I say, thinking that there would be a few people out there who might beg to differ.

I wait for him to say more about it. About us. Our future. Or at the very least our coup this weekend. He doesn't. Instead he suggests we take our coffee home and read the paper in bed.

"Sounds perfect," I say, wondering what section he reads first. I want to know every single thing about him.

It rains on and off all day, so we stay in, moving from bed to sofa to bed, talking for hours, never checking the time. We talk about everything—high school, college, law school, our families, friends, books, movies. But not Darcy or the situation. Not even when she calls his cell phone to say hello. I study my cuticles as he tells her he just stepped out of his office to get a bite to eat, and that yes, he's getting a lot done, been working on a pitch all day. He mumbles "Me too" at the end of their brief conversation, so I know what he has just told her. I tell myself that many couples punctuate their calls with "I love yous" in the automatic way other people say "good-bye." It doesn't mean anything.

As Dex snaps his cell phone shut, looking chagrined, my cell phone rings. It's Darcy. Dex laughs. "She just told me she had to run. Sure she did! To call you!"

I don't pick up, but I listen to her message afterward. She bitches about the weather but says that they are having fun anyway. She says she misses me. That it's not the same without Dex and me. I will not feel guilty. I will not.

That evening Dex and I separate for a few hours so that he can go home and change for dinner, as he has only packed jeans and shorts and basic toiletries. I miss him while he's gone, but I like the way the separation makes our dinner seem more like a date. Besides, I am grateful for the chance to primp alone. I can do the things that a guy you just started seeing should not see you do—pluck a stray eyebrow hair, strategically spray perfume (behind the knees, between the breasts) and apply makeup to make it look like you are wearing very little.

Dex picks me up at seven-forty-five and we cab it down to one of my favorite restaurants in Manhattan, Balthazar, where it is usually impossible to get a reservation unless you call weeks in advance or are willing to take a six o'clock or eleven-thirty seating. But we get in promptly at eight o'clock and are given an ideal, cozy booth. I ask Dex if he knows that Jerry Seinfeld proposed to his wife, Jessica Sklar, at Balthazar. Perhaps this is the exact spot where Jerry popped the question with the Tiffany ring.

"I didn't know that," Dex says, glancing up from the wine list.

"Did you know that she dumped her husband of four months for Jerry?"

He laughs. "Yeah, I think I heard that one."

"Soo . . . Balthazar must be the restaurant of choice for the scandalous."

He shakes his head and gives me an exasperated smile. "Please stop calling us that."

"Face facts, Dexter. This is scandalous . . . We're just like Jerry and Jessica."

"Look. We can't help the way we feel," Dex says earnestly.

Yeah. And perhaps that is what Jessica whispered to Jerry on her cell phone, while her unsuspecting husband sat guffawing at Must-See TV in the next room.

As I scan my menu, I realize that my opinion of Jerry and Jessica might be changing. I used to subscribe to the notion that he was a heartless home wrecker and she a shameless gold digger who coldly upgraded her Nederlander husband for a wealthier, wittier model the second the opportunity presented itself, which, I read, was at the Reebok Sports Club, the Upper West Side gym that Darcy also belongs to. Now, I'm not so sure. Maybe that *was* how it all went down. Then again, maybe Jessica married Eric Nederlander, whom she thought she loved by any relative measure in her life up to that point, and then she met Jerry, days after returning from her Italian honeymoon, and quickly realized that she had never really loved before, that her feelings for Jerry far surpassed whatever she felt for Eric.

What was a girl to do? Stay in a marriage with the wrong man, all in the name of appearances? Jessica knew the shit that she would get, not only from friends and family and her own husband, whom she had promised to have and to hold forever (not just a mere 120 days), but from the whole world—or at least those of us so bored with our own lives that we devour *People* magazine the second it hits the newsstands. Yet she went for it anyway, realizing that you only live once. She stuck her neck out in traffic, and like the frog in my all-time favorite video game, made it across the street, safely into the little box on top of the screen, or, as it were, into a six-million-dollar pad overlooking Central Park. Owning up to her mistake actually took real grit and courage. And maybe Jerry, too, deserved credit for ignoring the wrath of the world, following his heart at any price. Maybe true love just prevailed.

Regardless of what really happened with Jessica, Eric, and Jerry, my notions of rule-following in love are shifting.

"So, do you know what you'd like to have?" Dex asks me.

I smile and tell him that I am waiting to hear the specials.

After dinner Dex asks me if I want to go get another drink.

"Do you?" I ask, wanting to please him, give him the right answer.

"I asked you first."

"I would rather just go home."

"Good. Me too."

The night has cleared somewhat, and as we are dropped off on my corner, we see a few fireworks exploding in the distance over the East River. Blues and pinks and golds illuminate what feels like our own private city. We hold hands and stare up at the sky, watching silently for several minutes before we go inside and say good night to José, who by now thinks that Dex is my boyfriend.

We go upstairs, undress, and make love. It is not my imagination—it is better every time. Afterward, neither of us speaks or moves. We fall asleep, our legs and arms entwined.

In the morning, I wake up just as the light is returning to the sky. I listen to Dex breathe and study the sharp curve of his cheek. His eyes snap open suddenly. Our faces are close.

"Hi, baby." His voice is scratchy with sleep.

"Hi," I say softly. "Good morning."

"What are you doing awake? It's early."

"I'm watching you."

"Why?"

"Because I love your face," I say.

He looks genuinely surprised by my comment. How could he be? He must know that he is handsome.

"I love the way you look too," he says. His arms move around me, pulling me against his chest. "And I love the way you feel."

I feel myself blush.

"And the way you taste," he says, kissing my neck and my face. We avoid mouths, as you do after sleep. "And I guess all of that makes sense."

"Why's that?"

"Well, because . . ."

He is breathing hard now and looks nervous, almost scared. I reach for a condom from my nightstand drawer, but he pulls my hand back, and moves inside me, and says "because" again.

"Because why?"

I think I might know why. I hope I know why.

"Because, Rachel . . ." He looks into my eyes. "Because I love you."

He says those words exactly as I am thinking them, fighting a growing impulse to say it first. And now I don't have to.

I try to memorize everything about this moment. The look in his eyes, the feel of his skin. Even the way the light is slanting through my blinds. It is a moment beyond perfection, beyond anything I have ever felt before. It is almost too much to bear. I don't care that Dex is engaged to Darcy, or that we are creeping around like a couple of outlaws. I don't care that my teeth need a good brushing and that my hair is messy and limp around my face. I only feel Dex and his words and I know, without a doubt, that this is the happiest moment of my life. Snapshots flash through my mind. We are dining by candlelight, sipping fine champagne. We are curled up next to a raging fire in an old Vermont farmhouse with creaky floorboards and snowflakes the size of silver dollars falling outside. We are sharing a picnic lunch in Bordeaux in the middle of a meadow filled with yellow flowers, where he will give me a vintage diamond ring.

This might just happen. He loves me. I love him. What else is there?
Surely he won't marry Darcy. They cannot do happily ever after. I find
my voice and manage to say those three one-syllable words back to him.
Words I haven't uttered in a very, very long time. Words that meant nothing before now.

Neither of us acknowledges what we said that day, but I can feel it in the
air, all around us. It is more palpable than the thick humidity. I can feel
it in the way he looks at me and the way he says my name. We are a couple, and our words have made us brazen. At one point, as we are walking
through Central Park, he takes my hand. It is only for a few seconds, five
or six steps, but I feel a rush of adrenaline. What if we get caught? What
then? A small part of me wants that result, wants to run into an acquaintance of Darcy's, a coworker stuck in the city for work, going for a brief
stroll in the park. She will play informant on Monday morning, telling
Darcy that she saw Dex with a girl, holding hands. She will describe me
in detail but I am generic enough that Darcy won't suspect me. And if
she does, I'll just deny it, say that I was at work all day. Say that I don't
even own a pink shirt—which is new, one that she has never seen. I will be
wildly indignant, and she will apologize and then turn back to the issue of
Dex cheating on her. She will decide to dump him and I will be supportive,
tell her she is doing the right thing. This way Dex won't have to decide
anything or do anything. It will all be handled for us.

We walk up to the reservoir, circling it as we admire all the views of
the city. We pass a boy wearing head-to-toe army fatigues, walking an
aged beagle, and then an overweight woman panting along in a slow jog,
her elbows jutting out awkwardly. Otherwise, we have the usually popu-
lated path to ourselves. I listen to the gravel crunching beneath our
sneakers as we walk in perfect rhythm. I am content. The reservoir, the
views, the city, and the world belong to Dex and me.

Dark clouds are rolling in when we finally leave the park. We decide
not to change for dinner, heading straight for Atlantic Grill, a restaurant

near my apartment. Both of us are in the mood for fish and white wine and vanilla ice cream. After dinner, we dash back to my apartment in a downpour, laughing as we cross the streets midblock, splashing our way through the puddles formed on the sidewalks. Back inside, we strip off our wet clothes and towel each other off, still laughing. Dex puts on a pair of boxers. I wear one of his T-shirts. Then we play a Billie Holiday CD and open another bottle of wine, red this time. We stretch out on my sofa where we talk for hours, only getting up to brush our teeth and transfer to my bed for another satisfying sleep together.

Then suddenly, as it always happens, time accelerates. And just as being with Dex on our first night felt like the start of the summer, fearing the end of our time together reminds me of late August, when those daunting back-to-school commercials for Trapper Keepers would replace the ones featuring gleeful towheaded kids sipping Capri-Sun poolside. I remember the feeling well—a mixture of sadness and panic. This is how I feel now as we sit on my sofa on Saturday while afternoon bleeds into evening. I keep telling myself not to ruin the last night by being sad. I tell myself that the best is yet to come. He loves me.

As if reading my mind, Dex looks at me and says, "I meant what I said."

It is the first reference to our sacred exchange.

"I did too." I am filled with a deep longing, and am sure that our talk is coming. Our Post–Independence Day Talk. We are going to discuss ways to make this crazy thing work. How we can't bear to hurt Darcy, but that we must. I wait for his lead. It is his conversation to begin.

That's when he says, "No matter what happens, I meant that."

His words are like the sound of a needle dragging across a record. A sinking, sickening feeling washes over me. This is why you should never, ever get your hopes up. This is why you should see the glass as half empty. So when the whole thing spills, you aren't as devastated. I want to cry, but I keep my face placid, give myself a psychological shot of Botox. I can't cry, for several reasons, not the least of which is that if he asks why I'm crying, I won't be able to articulate an answer.

I fight to salvage the night, bring the golden cast back. *He loves me, he loves me, he loves me,* I tell myself. But it is not helping. He looks at me worriedly. "What's wrong?"

I shake my head, and he asks again, his voice gentle.

"Hey, hey, hey . . ." He lifts my chin, looks into my eyes. "What is it?"

"I'm just sad." My voice trembles tellingly. "It's our last night."

"It's not our last night."

I take a deep breath. "It's not?"

"No."

But that doesn't really explain much. What does "no" mean? That we will continue in this fashion for a few more weeks? Until the night before their rehearsal dinner? Or does he mean that this is only our beginning? Why can't he be more specific? I can't bring myself to ask. I am afraid of his answer.

"Rachel, I love you."

His lips stay curled up at the end of the last word, until I lean over to kiss him. A kiss is my response. I won't say it back until we have our talk. *Way to take a stand!*

We are kissing on my couch, followed by the unzipping and unbuttoning and attempting to gracefully slide out of denim, which is impossible. We move various sections of the *Times* out of our way and onto the floor. The sure fix, I think—the panacea. We are making love, but I am not in the moment. I am thinking, thinking, thinking. I can feel the dials of my brain whirring and rotating like the inside of a Swiss watch. *What is he going to do? What is going to happen?*

The next morning, when I wake up beside Dex, I hear him saying "no matter what happens." But during sleep my mind reprocessed the meaning of his words, landing on a perfectly logical explanation: Dexter just meant that whatever shit hits the fan, no matter what Darcy says or does, if we need some time apart in the aftermath of blood and guts, he will be waiting to love me and it will all be fixed in the end. That is what he must have meant. But still. I want him to tell me this. Surely he will say something more before he returns to the Upper West Side.

We get up, shower together, and go to Starbucks. Already we have a routine. It is eleven. Darcy and the others will be home soon. We are down to minutes and still no conversation, no conclusions. We finish our coffee and then stop at a toy store. Dex needs to buy a baby present for one of his work friends. Just a small token, he says. I can't decide whether I enjoy the feeling of being such an established couple that we run errands together, or whether I resent wasting our dwindling moments on this random task. It's more the latter. I just want to get back so that we have a few moments together. Time for him to share his plan.

But Dex lingers over various toys and books, asking me my opinion, laboring over a decision that doesn't matter one bit in the scheme of things. He finally decides on a stuffed, green triceratops with a cartoonish expression. It's not what I would choose for a newborn, but I admire his conviction. I hope he will have similar conviction about us.

"It's cute. Don't you think?" he asks, cocking its small head.

"Adorable."

Then, as he's about to pay for the dinosaur, he spots a plastic bin full of wooden dice. He picks out two red ones with gold-painted dots and holds them up in an open palm. "How much for a pair of dice?"

"Forty-nine cents per die," the man at the register says.

"A bargain. I'll take 'em."

We leave the store and walk toward my apartment. People are returning to the city in droves; traffic has resumed its normal pace. We are almost at my block. Dex is holding the bag with the dinosaur in his right hand and the dice in his left. He has been shaking them along the way. I wonder if his stomach hurts as much as mine does.

"What are you thinking?" I ask him. I want a long answer, articulating everything I am thinking. I want reassurance, some small nugget of hope.

He shrugs, licks his lips. "Nothing much."

ARE YOU MARRYING DARCY? The words roar in my head. But I say nothing, worrying that pressuring him is not strategically wise. As if what I say or don't say in the final minutes of our togetherness might make a difference. Maybe it is that tenuous—the fate of three people hanging in the balance like the cradle in the nursery rhyme.

"You like to gamble?" Dex asks, examining his dice while still walking.

"No," I say. Surprise, surprise. Rachel playing it safe. "Do you?"

"Yeah," he says. "I like craps. My lucky number is six—a four and a two. You have a lucky roll?"

"No . . . Well, I like double sixes," I answer, trying to mask my feelings of desperation. Desperate women are not attractive. Desperate women lose.

"Why double sixes?"

"I don't know," I say. I don't feel like explaining that it stems from playing backgammon with my father when I was little. I'd chant for double sixes and whenever I rolled them he'd call me Boxcar Willy. I still don't know who Boxcar Willy is, but I loved it when he called me that.

"Want me to roll you some double sixes?"

"Yeah," I say, pointing down at the filthy sidewalk, humoring him. "Go ahead."

We stop on the corner of Seventieth and Third. A bus lurches past us, and a woman with a baby nearly runs her stroller into Dex. He seems to ignore everyone and everything around him, shaking the dice with both hands, an expression of intense concentration on his face. If I saw him exactly like this, but in Atlantic City wearing polyester and a gold chain, I would wonder if he had his house and life savings on the line.

"What are we betting?" I ask.

"Betting? We're on the same team, baby," he says in a Queens accent, and then blows hard on his dice, his smooth cheeks puffing out like a little boy blowing the candles out on his birthday cake.

"Roll me double sixes right now."

"And if I do?"

I think to myself, *You roll double sixes, we end up together. No wedding with Darcy.* But instead I say, "It will mean good luck for us."

"All righty then. Double sixes coming right up for ya." He licks his lips and shakes his dice more vigorously.

The sun shines in my eyes as he tosses the dice in the air, catches them easily, and then dramatically lowers his arm toward the ground as if he's about to roll a bowling ball. He opens his hand, fingers splayed, as the cubes clatter to the concrete right at the busy Manhattan intersection.

One red die lands on six immediately. My heart skips with the thought,

What if? We are crouched over the landed die and its spinning twin, rotating on its axis for what seems like forever. If you tried to make a die go that long, you couldn't do it. But there it is, turning on its corner, a blur of gold dots and red background. And then it slows, slows, slows, and lands neatly beside the first one. Two rows of three dots on the second die.

Double sixes.

Boxcar Willy.

Holy shit, I think . . . *No wedding with Darcy!* . . . He wanted to talk about "no matter what happens" as if someone were steering from up above; well, here you go. Here you have it. Double sixes. Our fate.

I look up from the dice at Dex, debating whether to tell him what the roll had really been for. He looks at me with his mouth slightly open. Our eyes return to the dice as if maybe we got it wrong.

What are the chances?

Um, that would be precisely one in thirty-six. Just under three percent. So we aren't talking one-in-a-million odds. But those statistics are misleading when removed from our context. We have reached the end of a pivotal, meaningful weekend together. Right as we are minutes from parting ways (for the day? forever?), Dexter buys the dice on a whim, plays with them instead of putting them in the bag with his stuffed dinosaur, and adopts his boyish gambling persona. I play along, even though I'm in no mood for games. Then I decide, albeit silently, the terms of the roll. And he rolls double sixes! As if to say, we are foolproof, baby.

I look at his ninety-eight-cent (plus tax) dice with the reverence you would have for a crystal ball in a richly upholstered room with the world's greatest fortune-teller, wrinkled by the Persian sun, who has just told you how it was, how it is, and how it is going to be. Even Dex, who doesn't know what he just sealed for us, is impressed, telling me that he needs to take me to Atlantic City, Vegas, that we'd make a hell of a team.

Exactly.

He smiles at me and says, "There's your good luck, baby."

I say nothing, just pick up the dice and wedge them into the front pocket of my shorts.

"You stealing my dice?"

Our dice.

"I need them," I say.

We return to my apartment, where he collects his things and says good-bye.

"Thanks for an awesome weekend," he says, his face now mirroring mine. He is sad too.

"Yeah. It was great. Thank you." I strike the pose of a confident girl.

He bites his lower lip. "I better head back. As much as I don't want to."

"Yeah. You better go."

"I'll call you soon. Whenever I can. As soon as I can."

"Okay." I nod.

"Okay. Bye."

After one final kiss, he is gone.

I sit on my sofa, clutching my dice. They are a comfort—the roll is almost as good as a talk. Maybe better. We didn't have a talk because it is all so obvious. We are in love and meant to be together, and the dice confirmed everything. I place them reverently in his empty cinnamon Altoids container, nestled in the white paper liner with the sixes still facing up. I touch the rows of dots, like reverse Braille. They tell me that we will be together. It is our destiny. All of me believes it. I close the lid of the tin and push it against the base of my vase filled with lilies that are still clinging on. The dice, the tin, the lilies—I have created a shrine to our love.

I glance around my prim, orderly studio, perfectly neat except for my unmade bed. The sheets have molded against the mattress, revealing a vague outline of our bodies. I want to be there again, to feel closer to him. I slip off my sandals and walk over to the bed, sliding under the covers, which are chilled from the air conditioner. I get up, close my blinds, and hit the remote control on my stereo. Billie Holiday croons. I get back in bed, wriggle down toward the bottom of it, hooking my feet over the end of the mattress. I let my senses fill with Dex. See his face, feel him next to me.

I wonder if he is home yet or still stuck in crosstown traffic. Will he kiss Darcy hello? Will her lips feel strange and unfamiliar after kissing mine all weekend? Will she sense that something is wrong, unable to put her finger on exactly what has changed, never considering for a second that her maid of honor and a pair of dice might have something to do with the faraway look in her fiancé's eyes?

fifteen

Hillary arrives at work the next day, shortly before eleven, wearing wrinkled pants and scuffed black sandals. Her toenail polish is badly chipped, making her big toe resemble a squat candy cane. I laugh and shake my head as she hunkers down in her usual chair in my office.

"What's so funny?"

"Your wardrobe. They're going to fire you."

Our firm recently changed its dress code, from suits to business casual so long as there is no client interaction. But I'm pretty sure that Hillary's ensemble is not what the managing partner had in mind when his memo referenced "appropriate business casual."

She shrugs. "I wish they would fire me . . . Okay. So tell me about the weekend. Spare no details."

I smile.

"That good?"

I tell her we had an awesome time. I tell her about going to Balthazar and Atlantic Grill and our walk in the park and how nice it was to have so much time with Dex. I am hoping that if I talk enough, I will be able to avoid the obvious question.

"So is he going to call it off?"

That's the one.

"Well, I'm not sure."

"You're not sure? So he said he's thinking about it?"

"Well, no."

"He's *not* thinking about it?"

"Well . . . It didn't come up per se." I try not to sound too defensive.

She wrinkles her nose. Then she stares at me blankly. I wonder if her disapproval has more to do with my passivity or her growing suspicion that Dex is playing me for a fool. The former might be true, but the latter is not. "I thought you guys were going to discuss specifics," she says, frowning.

"I did too, but . . ."

"But what?"

"But he told me he loves me," I say. I hadn't planned on sharing this private detail, but I feel as if I must.

Hillary's expression changes somewhat. "He did?"

"Yes."

"Was he drunk?"

"No! He wasn't drunk," I say, glancing at my computer screen, hoping to get an e-mail from Dex. We have not yet spoken since his departure yesterday.

She isn't sold. "So did you say it back?"

"Yeah. I said it back. Because I do."

She gives me a respectful few seconds of silence. "All right. So you both love each other. What now? When does the little breakup happen?"

I take issue with the flippant characterization of his hurdle ahead. "Calling off a wedding and ending a long relationship is hardly a little breakup."

"Well, whatever. When is he going to do it?"

My stomach hurts as I say again that I don't know. I am tempted to tell Hillary about the dice, but I keep that to myself. That is between Dex and me. Besides, the story wouldn't translate well, and likely she would only be disgusted at me for relying on a dice roll instead of being direct.

I clear my throat. "So did Darcy mention him at all?"

"Not really . . . But I must admit, I kind of fell down on my lookout job. I have a good excuse." She grins.

"What's your excuse?"

"I met someone!"

"No way! Who? Do I know him?"

"No. He lives in Montauk. His name is Julian. Rachel—I didn't believe in the whole soul-mate thing until I met him."

"Start from the beginning," I tell her. There is no better audience for someone in love than someone in love.

She tells me that he's thirty-seven, a writer, never been married. She met him on the beach. She was going for a walk, he was going for a walk. Both of them were alone, moving in the same direction. He kept stopping to examine shells, and she finally caught up to him and introduced herself. They ended up going back to his house, where he made her tomato, mozzarella, and basil salad. Tomatoes and basil from his garden, fresh mozzarella. She says they couldn't stop talking—that he is brilliant, handsome, sensitive.

"So did you see him after that day?"

"Oh, yeah. We hung out the whole weekend . . . Rach, it's like we skipped all the bullshit. It's hard to explain . . . We are just together already. He is the best."

"When can I meet him?"

"He's coming this weekend. You can meet him then."

"I can't wait."

I am happy for her, but a little envious. I assume Julian isn't engaged. Les calls, interrupting our moment. I don't answer, feeling incapable of dealing with him. Hillary also seems unable to move out of her chair and go to her office to check her own messages. Our firm and all the drones in it can wait. We are talking about love.

After Hillary leaves my office, I go back to obsessing over Dex, waiting for an e-mail or call. When the phone finally rings, I jump.

But it's only Darcy, asking if I'm free for lunch.

I tell her yes. I hate the idea of seeing her, but I need to know what is going on. Maybe Dex has told her something.

We meet at Naples, a restaurant in the lobby of the MetLife Building. There is a line, so I suggest we go across the street to a deli. She says no, that she has been dying for pizza. I say fine, we'll wait for a table. I study her face for possible breakup signs. Nothing new, although her hair looks more sun-streaked. She is wearing it in a low, neat ponytail. Aquamarine earrings dangle just below her lobes.

"Do I have something on my face?" Darcy asks, swiping at her cheeks.

"I was just looking at your earrings. They're pretty. Are they new?"

"No. Dex gave them to me a long time ago."

"When? For your birthday?"

"No . . . I can't remember exactly. Just a random gift."

I feel a surge of jealousy, but tell myself that much has changed since then.

Darcy asks me how my weekend was.

"Fine," I say. My heart flutters just thinking about it. "You know. Lots of work . . . How was yours?"

"Awesome. You should have been there. Great parties. Great bands at the Talkhouse. Omigod, it was *so* much fun. You and Dex picked the wrong weekend to work."

You and Dex. You and Dex. You and Dex.

"Did Dex have to work the whole time?" I ask, for good measure.

She rolls her eyes. "Yeah, what else is new? I'm marrying a workaholic."

"He can't help his hours."

Or how he feels.

"Yeah, yeah, yeah," she says. "But I bet you anything he volunteers for half the stuff he gets stuck working on. I swear he enjoys it. It makes him feel important." Her voice is slightly snide. Perhaps this is the prelude to her story about their huge fight.

"You think?"

"I *know*," she says, as we are led to a table outside. "And I guess you know Hillary met a guy, right?"

"Yeah, she told me. Did you meet him?"

"Briefly."

"What did you think?"

"He's not bad-looking. Not my type—too artsy-fartsy. But still pretty cute. Wonders never cease."

"What's that supposed to mean?" I ask, knowing full well that she means Hillary meeting a cute guy is an unlikely event.

"Look at her. She doesn't care about her appearance at all. Half the time she doesn't even act like a girl."

"I think she's pretty."

Darcy gives me a "Get real" look.

I think of Hillary's wrinkled pants and chipped toenail. "Just because she's not a girly-girl doesn't mean she's not attractive."

"She's over thirty. She needs to start wearing makeup. The au naturel crap went out in the seventies."

"Well, apparently Julian doesn't agree."

"Yeah, well, we'll see how long that lasts," she says, dipping her bread into a plate of oil.

Yeah, we'll see how much longer you and Dex last. I think of the red dice, tucked safely into the Altoids tin, and am instantly overcome with remorse. I don't want her to be hurt. I wish there was a way for Dex and me to be together and for Darcy not to be hurt. Why are happy endings so hard to come by? I refocus on Hillary and Julian. "I think she's really into him," I say.

"Uh-huh," she says, rolling her eyes. "You *do* know her ex is with a new girl, right?"

"Yeah. Of course I know that. She couldn't care less about Corey anymore. And she dumped him, remember?"

"Well. Yeah. But then he started dating a twenty-three-year-old hottie and prancing around the Talkhouse right in front of her . . . and that's when she is suddenly so convinced that Julian is her guy. Coincidence? I don't think so."

I tell her that I think she's being mean. "Stop raining on her parade."

"Okay. Fine. Whatever. Next topic," Darcy says, dabbing her napkin at the corners of her mouth. "When did you last talk to Marcus?"

"Last week sometime."

She leans forward and tells me that he brought me up several times over the weekend.

"That's nice," I say, my eyes still on the menu. Marcus feels like ancient history.

She makes a face. "Why are you so lukewarm about him? Don't you think he's cute?"

"Yeah. He's cute," I say.

Our waiter arrives at the table to take our orders. Darcy asks for an individual pizza. I tell him that I'd like a Caesar salad.

Darcy objects. "Don't you want more than a salad?"

I can tell she's irritated that I'm getting a salad and she's ordering a pizza. She likes to be the dainty eater. So I appease her and say, "Caesar salads are substantial, and actually very fattening."

"Well, you'll have to eat some of my pizza. I can't eat the whole thing by myself." She is talking to me, but it is for the waiter's benefit. He smiles at her. She makes her expression friendly and open. I catch her moving her left hand under the table so he can't see her ring.

As he turns to leave, she says, "Oh, and can you make sure they don't burn the bottom of my pizza? Sometimes they burn the bottom. And I like my pizzas—how shall I say it—rare?" She moves her ponytail in front of one shoulder.

He laughs and winks. "No problem."

"He's too young for you," I say, not caring that he's still within earshot.

"What?" she says innocently. "Oh, puh-*lease*. I wasn't flirting."

Before she can launch into another topic, I must determine if there is any domestic trouble yet brewing. I use a wedding angle. "So what did you decide on the CDs?"

"The CDs?" She looks confused. "Oh, right, those things. I haven't given them another thought. I took the weekend off from wedding planning. Besides, I think those CDs might be too much trouble. Maybe I'll just do nuts or mints after all. They make these cute heart-shaped Altoids tins. Maybe we'll get those. You know how much Dexter loves his Altoids."

"Mmm . . . I didn't know that."

"Yeah," she says. "The cinnamon kind."

Dexter doesn't phone until late that night, and I miss the call because I am reviewing documents in a conference room. His message is brief: "Hi, Rach. Sorry I haven't called today . . . The whole day's been a fire drill getting ready for this pitch on Thursday. I really should have done some of this work over the weekend . . . Not that I'd do it differently. It was worth it to be with you. I miss you. I'll talk to you soon."

His message leaves me feeling hollow. *That's it?* A review of his work schedule? And using an annoying banker expression like "fire drill," no less. The next thing I know he's going to be telling me he's "in the weeds"— another one of those "I'm so busy" banker phrases. And more important, he doesn't say anything about Darcy, about when I will see him next, about anything. Just that he misses me. It feels as though he is slipping away, my shot at happiness dissipating. I start to get panicky, but then tell myself to be patient. Dex will do the right thing. He will be with me in the end.

I finally see Dex on Thursday night. He arrives at my place late, exhausted from work. We talk for a few minutes before he falls asleep with his head on my lap as I watch a *Sopranos* rerun. Tony is cheating on Carmella again. My empathy for her is huge and all-encompassing, ironic because she is the wife, and not the other woman. I think of Darcy, compare our feelings for Dex. She doesn't love him as I do. She can't possibly. This will be my final rationalization in the home stretch.

I nudge him a little after midnight, tell him he should probably get home. He reluctantly agrees and tells me again how sorry he is about his crazy work schedule. I tell him I understand, I know what it's like. He kisses me and gives me a long hug. And then he is off to be with Darcy again. As he's walking out the door, I ask him what he's doing over the weekend. I try to appear nonchalant, but in my heart I am grasping at straws, hoping that he will dole out a few hours for me.

"My dad and his wife are visiting. I didn't tell you that?"

"No. No. You didn't. That's nice though. What are you going to do?"

"You know—the usual. Dinners. Maybe a show."

I picture the four of them out on the town. It hurts that I can't meet his father, driving home the point all the more: I am not with Dex. I am the other woman. I think of all the other women who get the random Thursday nights, but never the holidays or the special family occasions or the important work dinners. Excluded when it really matters. Then I think to myself that Dex hasn't even given me any of the assurances, false or otherwise, that the other woman always gets in the movies. Nothing but a couple of "I love yous" and some red dice.

On Saturday night Hillary convinces me to join her and Julian. I feel guilty for crashing their dinner, but agree, not wanting to be alone with my thoughts about Dex. I have been obsessing about the cozy family weekend, Dex smiling amid all the inevitable wedding chatter, pretending that he is right on schedule with his nuptials. Maybe he *is* right on schedule. I have no idea what is going on, and the waiting and wondering is so much harder to take after our weekend together.

So I trek down to Gramercy and meet Hillary and Julian at I Trulli, an Italian restaurant. We sit at a small round table in the beautiful back garden, surrounded by brownstone walls, a patch of navy-blue sky above us. The patio is lit by candles, and tiny white lights are intertwined in the tree branches. The setting could not be more romantic. Except for the fact that I am the third wheel.

After fifteen minutes, I know I like Julian. He is not at all affected, but speaks slowly, choosing his words carefully—he uses "favor" instead of "like better," "pleasant" instead of "nice," and "outset" instead of "start." They are simple alternatives, not flamboyant thesaurus entries, so I know he is not showing off. (I once went on a date with a guy who used the words "salubrious," "sartorial," and "loquacious" in one evening. I declined his invitation for date number two, for fear that he would show up wearing an ascot.) And although Julian is not traditionally handsome, I like the way he looks. His curly, longish hair, tanned skin, and dark-brown eyes make me think of a Portuguese fisherman.

I watch Julian laughing at something Hillary just said, leaning toward her. Nobody would ever guess that they only met a week ago. Their interaction is fluid and natural, and she is doing none of the things that women do in the new stages of a relationship. She asks him twice if she has spinach in her teeth and she eats every last bit of her pasta, then insists that we order dessert.

Over our slices of cheesecake, Hillary and I tell Julian how much we hate our jobs. He asks why we don't just quit. We say it's not that easy, golden handcuffs, paying off our loans, blah blah blah. And besides, what else would we do? He looks at me and says yes, what else would you do? I glance at Hillary, wanting her to answer first.

"Hill would open an antiques shop," he says, touching her wrist. "Right?"

Hillary smiles at him. They have covered her dreams already. My bet is that she opens her shop in downtown Montauk.

"So what about you, Rachel?" Julian asks again, his dark eyes probing.

It is a common question during law-firm interviews, right up there with "Why did you decide to go to law school?" at which point you give the pat answer about the pursuit of justice, when what you are really thinking is *Because I'm a type-A high achiever with no idea of what else to do; I would have gone to med school, but blood makes me squeamish.*

I tell him that I don't know, embarrassed by the truth of it.

"Maybe if you quit your job, you'd figure it out more quickly," Julian says in his calm voice. "Poverty, hunger—these things help you think more clearly."

My cell phone rings. It is a jarring note. I apologize, say I thought I had turned it off before dinner. Maybe it is Dex. Maybe he sneaked off to the bathroom to call me.

"Who is it?" Hillary asks. I can tell that she, too, is wondering if it's Dex.

"I'm not sure."

"Well, check it out," she says. "We don't mind, do we?"

Julian shrugs. "Not at all."

I can't resist. I remove my phone from my purse and listen to the message. It's only Marcus. He says he knows it's late but wondered what I was up to.

"Marcus," I say, unable to hide my disappointment.

Hillary reminds Julian of who Marcus is—the guy from our house. He nods, says of course he remembers him.

"Why don't you call him? Ask him to come over," she says. "We'll order another bottle of wine."

She is sweet to offer, but I can tell that she is ready for the shared part of the evening to be over. And I don't want more charity. I say no, I'm tired, it has been a wonderful dinner but I should really get home. Julian makes eye contact with our waitress and asks for our check with a scribbling flourish in the air.

When we leave the restaurant, Hillary asks me if I'm going to take a cab. I tell her no, I think I'll walk.

"Forty-some blocks?"

"It's a nice evening."

We say good-bye on Twenty-seventh and Lex. Julian kisses my cheek. He is about my height, a full two inches shorter than Hillary. I'm surprised Darcy failed to mention this. I tell Julian it was a pleasure to meet him. He says likewise, and looks forward to seeing me in Montauk. I hug Hillary and give her an excited smile to let her know that I wholeheartedly approve of her new beau. As I turn for home, I realize that although I am truly happy for Hillary, her fledgling relationship makes me feel even emptier, more alone.

The cozy foursome is likely leaving the theater now, headed to a nice dinner out, strolling the avenues, laughing and singing the catchiest tunes from the show. Resentment fills me up. If I had the dice with me now, I would throw them in a gutter.

I continue on toward Third, checking my watch. It is just after ten and suddenly I don't want to go home. I consider calling Marcus back, worrying that it would be unfair, and I'd only be using him to get over Dex. But I am so miserable and angry that I dial Marcus's number anyway.

He answers on the first ring.

"What are you doing?" I ask.

"Hey! You got my message?"

"Yeah, I did. I was at dinner. I'm in your neighborhood. You want to meet me for a drink?"

"I'd love to. Where are you?"

I tell him Twenty-seventh and Third.

"Right there at Rodeo Bar?"

I look up. He has the correct coordinates. "Yeah, it's across the street."

"Well, go in and get me a Pete's Summer Brew, would ya? I'll be right over."

His voice is animated and cheerful and it makes me smile. I tell him I'll be at the bar waiting for him with his Pete's.

Rodeo Bar is as hillbilly as it gets in Manhattan. Old license plates frame the bar and a huge stuffed bison hangs from the ceiling. Peanut shells cover the floor.

"Hey, good-lookin'," I hear Marcus say behind me. "This seat taken?"

I laugh and tell him no, he is welcome to it. "Here's your beer."

"And it's still cold," he says, taking a long drink. "Thanks."

"You're very welcome."

"So where were you?"

"I Trulli."

He nods to say he knows the place. "Nice. Were you on a date?" he asks, with feigned jealousy. He lifts his fist as if he's about to become violent toward the guy who infringed on his territory.

I laugh. "No. I was with Hillary and Julian, her new boyfriend. You met him last weekend, right?"

"Oh yeah. That dude Hillary picked up on the beach."

I laugh again. "Something like that."

"She did. For real. It was a strong move."

"Hillary is more like a guy than a girl in a lot of ways," I say, thinking that I could never approach a stranger on the beach like that.

"Yeah," he says. "It's great, really. I'm still waiting for you to be aggressive with me."

I smile. "Oh, really?"

"Yes, really." He smiles, looking right at me.

"So," I say.

"So." He moves his arm against mine.

"I'm pasty," I say, comparing our skin tones.

"I like pale," he says. "It's feminine."

"So let me get this straight," I say, "you like aggressive women who look feminine?"

He snaps his fingers in the air and points at me. "You got it. Can you deliver?"

I laugh and sip my beer, wonder if Marcus will kiss me tonight. If he does, I might kiss him back. I might even enjoy it. *"If you can't be with the one you love . . ."*

We finish our beers. I say I am tired of country music and ask Marcus if he is ready to go. He says sure, do I want to go to another bar? Have I been to Aubette? It's only a few blocks away.

"Yeah. It's on the same block as I Trulli, right?"

"Yeah. I've only been there on weeknights so I don't know if it will be any good. But they have these killer apple martinis that would be right up your alley. You want to go?"

I laugh. How does he know what is up my alley? Dex is up my alley. "Sure. Let's go."

We walk quickly to Aubette, past the muscle-bound doorman clad in black at the entrance. We move inside. The crowd is hard to pinpoint—there is a bridge-and-tunnel element with a dash of Euro wannabes. I follow Marcus toward the cigar bar in the back and sit next to him on a buttoned leather couch with high arms. It is cozy, but would be cozier with Dex. I force him from my mind.

"What do you want?"

"An apple martini." I can feel the red wine and beers moving toward my head. A martini probably isn't a good idea, but I don't care.

"You won't be sorry. Be right back."

He returns with my apple martini and a glass of scotch for himself.

"How is it?" he asks, after I take a sip.

"It's good."

"Tastes just like a Jolly Rancher, doesn't it?"

I take another sip. "Yeah. It does. Want a taste?"

He sips from my glass and then licks his lips and looks at me. It is an invitation. For a second, in my semidrunk state, I am confused, unsure what to do next. I think of Dex. He hasn't broken off the engagement yet. He might never. I can kiss Marcus in the meantime. I must protect my heart. And something tells me that Marcus wouldn't mind being used in this manner. I lean toward him, initiate a kiss.

"Wow." He grins. "Didn't see that coming."

I kiss him again.

"Or that," he says.

I wonder if he will tell Dex. Part of me hopes he will. I kiss him a third time and add a little tongue for good measure. We talk some more. I am buzzed and vaguely attracted to him. He has nice forearms, with just the right amount of hair. We kiss several more times and it feels good, but nothing stirs inside me. And every time our lips touch, I miss Dexter a little bit more.

We finally leave Aubette and stand awkwardly in the street. A cab sails down Twenty-seventh toward Lex. Marcus doesn't stop me from hailing it, doesn't ask me to go back to his place. I am relieved, because I think I might have said yes. And that would be a mistake. It would only be the apple martini talking—that and a growing resentment in my chest that here I am, six days postroll, playing third wheel at a romantic dinner and kissing the wrong guy in a windowless lounge filled with cigar smoke.

sixteen

Kissing Marcus is what I need to give Dex more time. The logic is convoluted, but I feel that the small act of betrayal puts Dex and me on equal footing, at least in the short run. He is engaged; I kissed his friend.

Hillary doesn't buy the rationale. She is beside herself, telling me to cut it off. No more. Enough.

"Just a little more time," I say. "It's still only July. We're only in July."

She looks at me skeptically.

"Come on, Hill," I say. "Patience is a virtue . . . Good things come to those who wait . . . Time cures all things."

"Uh-huh," she says. "How about 'No time like the present'? Ever heard that one?"

"I'll say something soon. I will."

"Okay. Because you really can't put this off any longer. You need to nail him down," she says. "Move on with your life one way or the other.

This waiting-around stuff just isn't good for you, Rach. I'm seriously worried about you . . ."

"I know. I'll say something," I tell her. "You have to remember that I've only seen him one time since our weekend together. And that was late one night after work. He fell asleep on my couch."

"Well," she says knowingly.

"Well, *what?*"

"Well, isn't that somewhat telling?"

I know what she is implying. That if Dex loved me enough, he'd make more time for me. That I have lost momentum since July Fourth.

"No, actually, it's *not* telling," I say defensively. "Work has been crazy for both of us. Les is on a rampage. You know that. We've literally had no time to see each other."

"All right," she says. "But I'm giving him one more week. Then no more excuses."

"Two more weeks," I negotiate, and then explain that only a very shallow person would find it so incredibly easy to cancel an engagement. That the situation is vastly more complicated than she is acknowledging. That Dex would not string me along for the hell of it. That he values our friendship at the very least. That he also values my friendship with Darcy. That he has integrity. That he told me he loves me. And meant it. I pull out all the stops, trying to convince myself along the way.

"All right then," she says. "Two weeks. Absolute max."

I smile and nod, thinking that two weeks should just about do it. One way or the other.

In the meantime, I must face another hurdle: Darcy's shower/bachelorette party. It has been on the calendar forever—the third Saturday in July—but for obvious reasons I have yet to plan the evening. Claire calls that afternoon to press me on details. "Should we go to the Hamptons or stay in the city?"

"I don't know. What do you think?" I am distracted, noticing that my secretary put two *c*'s in "recommend" on a fax cover sheet that I failed to proofread. If Les sees it, he will go postal.

"It depends on what Darcy wants," Claire says.

Naturally. It always does.

"Right," I say.

"*So?* What does she want to do?" Claire asks in a tone that says, you should know this, you are the maid of honor.

I admit that I'm not sure.

"Let's conference her in and find out," Claire suggests in her sorority-social chair voice. She puts me on hold and returns with Darcy on the line.

We present Darcy with her options: Manhattan or the Hamptons. Claire outlines the pros and cons of each and assures her that either way it is going to be the best bachelorette party ever.

Darcy says she doesn't care. Both options sound great. She is subdued. Something is wrong. Maybe there is trouble brewing at home, a visible crack emerging in their relationship. Maybe Dex said something to her. I feel a surge of hope, which is followed by a larger dose of guilt. How can I so easily root for my friend's unhappiness?

"You don't care?" Claire asks. "That's a first."

"You guys decide. I'm fine either way."

"What's Dex doing?" Claire asks. Of course, I am wondering the same thing.

"I'm not sure," Darcy says. "He mentioned going to the Hamptons to golf."

"Well, if he does that, we should stay in the city. You don't want him around for your big night, do you?" Claire asks.

"No," Darcy says. "I guess not."

Something is definitely wrong. She does not sound the slightest bit excited about a night in her honor. My instinct to soothe her kicks in. "Claire and I will put it together and let you know where to show up," I say. "Does that sound good to you?"

"Yeah. That's fine." Her voice is flat.

"Is everything all right?" Claire asks.

"Yeah. I'm just a little tired."

"Okay. We'll work on this, Darce. It's going to be a great party," I say.

We all say good-bye and hang up. Claire calls me right back. "What is wrong with her? She sounds upset."

"I don't know."

"You think she's mad at us because we don't have this planned yet? It is pretty slack of us," Claire says, sounding worried. It is a scary thing to have Darcy mad at you.

"No. That can't be it. She knows we've told everyone about the date weeks ago . . . Everyone will be there. It's just a matter of nailing down final plans. I'll talk to her," I say.

I hang up with Claire and call Darcy back. She answers, her voice lifeless.

"You sure you're okay?" I ask, utterly conflicted as I wait for her answer.

"I'm fine. Just tired . . . Maybe a little down."

"Why? How was your weekend?" I ask tentatively.

"It was okay."

"Did you have fun with Dex's father?"

"Yeah. He's nice," she says.

"Do you like his stepmother?"

"She's okay. She can be a pain in the ass though."

Takes one to know one.

"What did she do?"

"Well, for example, she kept complaining about how cold she was at the theater. You should have heard her carrying on and on during the whole intermission, even after Mr. Thaler gave her his jacket. Dex and I were like, well, that's what you get for wearing a skimpy dress."

Dex and I were like . . . My stomach drops. I hope I'm not in for a lifetime of those words.

"But overall the weekend was okay?" I probe, pressing the phone against my ear.

"Yeah. It was okay."

"Then why are you down?"

"Oh, I don't know. I think it's just PMS. I'll be fine."

Ordinarily I would try and wheedle Darcy out of her mood, find a way to perk her up, but instead I just say, "Well, I better go. Got some party planning to do."

She giggles. "Yeah. You sure do. Make it a good one."

"Okay," I say, knowing that I will let Claire do the bulk of the organizing. She will be happy to undertake the project. I know she believes that she is more important to Darcy than I am, that she would have been named maid of honor but for the fact that I've known Darcy longer. She is probably right. The major thing Darcy and I have in common is the past. The past and Dex.

The rest of the week passes quickly. I don't see Dex, but only because he is in Dallas on a business trip. I try to convince Hillary that his deadline should be extended by three days because he can't really do anything about his situation while in Texas (although Dex and I do manage to log over four hours of phone time). She tells me that if anything, the time away should give him the chance to really sort through his feelings and come up with a plan of action. I tell her I'm sure that's what he's doing.

On Friday morning, only hours after Dex arrives back in New York, he calls and suggests that we meet for lunch before he heads out to the Hamptons. We arrange to meet at the Pick A Bagel near my apartment, to avoid the Midtown lunch crowds. I feel nervous as I take the uptown subway. I have not seen him in over a week—not since I kissed Marcus. I know that kissing Marcus was not a significant event (apparently it wasn't significant to him either, as we have barely talked since), yet I feel somewhat strange when I kiss Dex hello. Not quite guilty, just reticent.

"I've missed you *so* much," Dex says, shaking his head. "I kept hoping you'd fly down to Dallas and surprise me."

I laugh because the thought had actually occurred to me. "I missed you too," I say, feeling myself relax.

We stand there on the corner, grinning like crazy at each other, before moving inside the bagel shop. The place is jammed full of people, which gives us an excuse to touch. His fingers brush mine, the sides of our legs graze, his hand rests on my back as he guides me forward in line. I am basking in being near Dex, too distracted to order. We let three people go in front of us before we both decide on egg-salad sandwiches to go. We pay for the bagels and two Snapple lemon iced teas and then walk briskly toward my apartment. I tell myself not to get too swept up in emotion when we are finally alone. I really need to bring up Darcy before her bachelorette festivities get under way. I must do this over our egg salad. Unless of course he does it first.

Just as we are approaching my building, I spot Claire descending upon us half a block away. I hear Dex curse under his breath, just as I see a look of confusion on Claire's face. There is no time to consult Dex and formulate a story. Five steps later, she is upon us. We are cold busted.

"Hi, Claire!" Dex says robustly.

"What are you two doing here?" She switches her mustard-colored Prada bag from one shoulder to the other and smiles a bewildered smile.

I laugh nervously. "What are *you* doing here?" I ask. It is a feeble attempt to buy a few seconds. I am terrible under pressure, an absolute disaster. I should not be a litigator, at least not the kind who might ever see the light of a courtroom. I am better suited to my big boxes of documents in over-air-conditioned conference rooms.

"I left work early today to get ready for the party tomorrow. I was just at Kate's Paperie buying wrapping paper and a card for Darcy." She glances at our brown paper bags. I am carrying our Snapples; Dex has the sandwiches. "Are you having lunch?"

"No," Dex says. He is perfectly composed. "Well yes, we just bought lunch. But I'm headed to my car—about to leave for the Hamptons."

"Oh," she says, but is still not satisfied. Luckily she keeps her eyes on Dex. I have more faith in him than in myself.

"I had to give Rachel something to give to Darcy," Dex says.

She cocks her head to the side. "What's that?"

I don't think she's suspicious; she simply does not consider that what we are doing may not be her business. In her eyes, she is in the inner Darcy circle, privy to any information that concerns her friend. And Dex and I most certainly concern Darcy.

"A note," Dex says. "A little something I want Darcy to have before her wild and crazy night on the town."

"Oh." Claire smiles, clearly not wondering why Dex couldn't just leave the note in their apartment, why he would need to designate me as his messenger. "Well, it *is* going to be wild and crazy. Count on that."

"I can only imagine . . ." Dex says.

"So, Rachel, are you taking the afternoon off then?"

I stammer and stutter and say no, yes, I'm not sure, maybe.

"Oh, screw work. Just come with me and run my last-minute errands for the party. I'm on my way to Lingerie on Lex to get a few extra things," she says. We have designated tomorrow evening a hybrid lingerie shower–bachelorette party. "Please come?"

"All right. Sure. I just need to run up and change my clothes and make one phone call. I'll meet you in fifteen?"

"Great!" Claire says.

I wait for her to leave first, hoping that I can have a moment alone with Dex, but she is firmly rooted to the sidewalk. After a few seconds, Dex gives up and tells us good-bye. I am careful not to look at him as he leaves.

"All right then," I say to Claire. "See you in a few."

I walk home in a panic, telling myself we are fine, that surely Claire doesn't suspect such a monumental betrayal. Dex calls just as I close my apartment door. I answer the phone, my hands shaking.

"Hey," Dex says. "Can you believe that?"

"Omigod," I say. "I feel like I'm going to faint. Where are you?"

"Around the corner. In the car . . . Think we're okay?"

"I hope so," I say, feeling my pulse slowly return to normal. "You were good . . . How'd you come up with that excuse so quickly?"

"I don't know. She bought it, didn't she?"

"Seemed to . . . but what are we going to do about the note?"

"I'm writing one now . . . Shit, I have no idea what to write. This is ridiculous . . . I'm going to come up, okay?"

I tell him that it's not a good idea, that I have to go meet Claire.

He sighs. "I wanted to spend some time with you. Can't you get out of it?"

I feel myself weakening. "Don't you think it might look suspicious if I blow her off?"

"C'mon. Just for a few minutes?"

"Okay," I say. "Come up. But only to give me the note. Then I really have to go meet her."

He arrives at my door minutes later, handing me my sandwich and the folded note. I put them both on my coffee table next to our Snapples. We sit on my couch.

"How does stuff like that always happen in this city?" I ask.

"I know," he says, taking my hands. He tries to kiss me, but I am still too shaken to really reciprocate. I cannot relax. It is as if Claire is still with us.

"I really should go," I say, angry that she ruined our chance to have the big conversation, but also somehow relieved.

He keeps kissing me as he removes my suit jacket and rubs my shoulder.

"Dex!"

"What?"

"I *have* to go."

"In a minute."

"No. *Now.*"

But as he runs his fingers over my collarbone, I stop thinking about Claire. Moments later we are making love.

My cell phone rings immediately afterward. I jump. "Oh shit. That's gotta be Claire. I *really* have to go," I say, sitting up.

"But I wanted to talk about this weekend," he says.

"What about it?" I ask, avoiding his gaze as I button my shirt.

"Well, it's just that . . . I'm really sorry about this bachelorette party and everything—"

I interrupt him. "I know, Dex."

"Something has to be done soon. I just haven't had a free moment. I haven't had a chance . . . But I want you to know that I think about it—and you—all the time. I mean, *all* the time . . ." His expression is sincere, tortured. He waits for me to speak.

This is my opening. Words form in my head; they are right on my tongue, but I say none of them, reasoning that this is not the moment to delve. We don't have enough time for a real conversation. I reassure myself that I'm not a coward, I'm just being patient. I want to wait for the right moment to discuss the destruction of my best friend. So I give him and myself an out. "I know, Dex," I say again. "Let's talk next week, okay?"

He nods somberly and hugs me hard.

After he leaves, I call Claire and tell her that I got stuck on a work call but will be right over. I finish dressing, down my Snapple, and put my egg-salad sandwich in the refrigerator. I walk to the door as I eye the folded note. I can't help myself. I go back, unfold it, read it:

DARCY,

JUST WANTED YOU TO HAVE A LITTLE SOMETHING FROM ME BEFORE YOUR BIG NIGHT OUT. I HOPE YOU HAVE A GREAT TIME WITH YOUR FRIENDS.

LOVE, DEXTER

Why did he have to insert the word "love"? I comfort myself by thinking that he didn't just make love to her, and we will talk next week, still within Hillary's deadline. Then I scurry off to meet Claire, to help her prepare for Darcy's big weekend.

The whole situation is completely out of control, the stuff that happens to other people. Not to people like me.

The shower/bachelorette party is agony from start to finish, for obvious reasons, and also because I have nothing in common with Darcy's PR friends, all of whom are materialistic, shallow, bitchy egomaniacs. Claire is the best of the lot, which is scary. I tell myself to smile and suck it up. It is only one evening.

We meet at Claire's first to give Darcy her lingerie, an arsenal of black lace and red silk that I simply cannot compete against. If Darcy decides to wear any of this stuff before the wedding—particularly a La

Perla garter with fishnet stockings—I am dead. Unless she only debuts my gift, a long ivory nightgown with a high neckline, something that Caroline Ingalls might have worn on *Little House on the Prairie*. It screams sweet and wholesome, in contrast to the other sultry, skimpy gifts that scream, "Bend me over a chair and bust out the whipped cream." Darcy pretends to like my gift, as I catch a knowing glance between Claire and Jocelyn, an Uma Thurman look-alike. For one paranoid second, I believe that Claire suspects the truth after our chance meeting yesterday and has shared her suspicions with Jocelyn. But then I just chalk it up to this sentiment: *Darcy's dowdy friend Rachel strikes again. How can she be the maid of honor when she doesn't even know how to give a proper piece of lingerie?*

After the shower segment of the evening, we cab it to Churrascaria Plataforma, an all-you-can-eat Brazilian rotisserie in the Theater District, where waiters bring you endless servings of skewered meat. It is an amusing choice for a bunch of paper-thin women, half of whom are vegetarians and subsist on celery and cigarettes. Our group parades proudly into the restaurant, fetching plenty of stares from a predominantly male patronage. After a painful round of overpriced cocktails (put on my credit card) we are seated at a long table in the center of the restaurant where the PR girls continue to work the room, pretending to be oblivious to the attention they are garnering from all angles.

I watch a nearby table of women in conservative, Ann Taylor attire eye our group with a strange mix of envy and condescension. I make a bet with myself that before the evening is over, the Ann Taylor women will complain to their waiter that our table is being too loud. Our waiter will give us a saccharine suggestion that we bring the volume down just a tad. Then our table will get all huffy and declare the Ann Taylor women a bunch of fat losers. *I am seated at the wrong table*, I think, as Claire and I flank Darcy upon her command. She is still wearing a little veil constructed out of the ribbons and bows from her gifts, happy to be conspicuous, the hottest girl at a table full of gorgeous women. Except for me, that is. I pretend to care about the flimsy conversation swirling about me as I sip my sangria and smile, smile.

After dinner, we make our way to Float, a Midtown dance club complete with velvet ropes and self-important bouncers. Of course we are on a VIP list—compliments of Claire—and are able to power our way past the long line of nobodies (Darcy's description). The evening follows the stale, silly script for the typical twenty-something bachelorette party. Which would be okay, I guess, except for the fact that most of us are no longer twenty-somethings. We are too old for the shrieking and the shots and the wild dancing with any guy self-confident (or self-destructive) enough to penetrate our group of nine women. And Darcy is too old for the scavenger list that Claire has prepared: find red-haired boy to buy her a sex-on-the-beach, dance with a man over fifty (imagine this species who still frequents dance clubs), kiss a guy with a tattoo or body piercing.

The whole event is overplayed and unsophisticated, but Darcy shines. She is on the dance floor, glistening, her hair curling slightly from perspiration. Her tanned, flat stomach shows between her low-slung pants and halter top. Her cheeks are rosy, dewy. Everyone wants to talk to the bride-to-be. Single girls ask wistfully what her dress looks like and more than one guy tells her she should reconsider the marriage, or at the very least, have one final fling. I dance on the outskirts of the group, biding my time.

When the night is finally over, I am exhausted, sober, and five hundred bucks poorer. We file out of the club as Darcy turns to me and says that she wants to sleep over at my place, just the two of us, like old times. She is so thrilled with the idea that I cannot refuse. I smile. She whispers in my ear that she wants to shake Claire, that it won't be the same if she comes along. It reminds me of high school and how Darcy would decide who she wanted to include and exclude. Annalise and I seldom had a say and often could not figure out why someone failed to make the cut.

We hail a cab as Darcy thanks Claire, tells her the evening was a blast, and says to me loudly, with a nudge, "Why don't we share a cab back uptown? I'll drop you off first."

I say sure, and we head up to my apartment.

José is on duty. He is happy to see Darcy, who always flirts with him. "Where you been, girl?" he asks. "You don't visit me no more."

"Planning my wedding," she says in her beguiling way. She points to her now-crumpled veil that she is clutching like a precious souvenir.

"Aww. Say it ain't so! You gettin' maah-ried?"

I clench my teeth and hit the up button on the elevator.

"Yeah," she says, cocking her head to the side. "Why, do you think I shouldn't?"

José laughs, showing all his teeth. "Hell, no. Don't do it!" Even my doorman wants her. "Blow that guy off," he says.

Clearly he hasn't put the pieces of this puzzle together.

Darcy takes his hand in hers and twirls herself around. She finishes the move with a hip-to-hip bump.

"C'mon, Darce," I say, already in the elevator, holding the door-open button with my thumb. "I'm tired."

She twirls one last time and then joins me in the elevator.

On the ride up, she waves and blows kisses into the security camera, just in case José is watching.

When we get into my apartment, I immediately turn down the volume on my answering machine and switch off my cell phone in case Dex calls. Then I change into shorts and a T-shirt and give Darcy clothes to wear.

"Can I have your Naperville High shirt instead? So it will feel like old times."

I tell her that it is in the wash, and she will have to make do with my "1989 Indy 500" T-shirt. She says it is good enough, as it reminds her of home too.

I brush my teeth, floss, and wash my face as she sits on the edge of my tub and talks to me about the party, how much fun it was. We trade places. Darcy washes her face and then asks if she can use my toothbrush. I say yes even though I think it's disgusting to share with anyone. Even Dex. Okay, maybe not Dex, but anyone else. Through a mouthful of toothpaste, she remarks that she is not drunk, or even very buzzed, which is surprising considering the amount of alcohol we consumed. I tell her it must be all the meat we ate.

She spits into the sink. "Ugh. Don't remind me. I probably gained five pounds tonight."

"No way. Think of how much you burned off dancing and sweating."

"Good point!" She rinses her mouth, splashing water everywhere, before she leaves the bathroom.

"Are you all ready for bed?" I ask, wiping up her mess with a towel.

She turns and watches me, unapologetic. "No. I want to stay up and talk."

"Can we at least get in bed and talk?"

"If we keep the light on. Otherwise you'll fall asleep."

"All right," I say.

We get in bed. Darcy is closer to the window, on Dexter's side of the bed. Thank goodness I changed my sheets this morning.

We are facing each other, our bent knees touching.

"What should we discuss first?" she asks.

"You choose."

I brace myself for wedding talk, but instead she starts a long gossip session about the girls at the party, what everyone wore, Tracy's new short haircut, Jocelyn's struggle with bulimia, Claire's incessant name-dropping.

We talk about Hillary not showing up for her party. Of course, Darcy is red-hot mad about that. "Even if she is in love, she should have blown off Julian for one night."

Of course, I can't tell her that the real reason for Hillary's boycott has nothing to do with a new boyfriend.

Then we are on to Ethan. She wants to know if he's gay. She is always speculating about this, proffering flimsy bits of evidence: he played four square with the girls in grade school, he took home ec in high school instead of industrial arts, he has a lot of women friends, he dresses well, and he hasn't dated anyone since Brandi. I tell her no, that I am almost completely certain that he's not gay.

"How do you know?"

"I just don't think he is."

"There's nothing wrong with it if he is," Darcy says.

"I know that, Darce. I just don't think he is gay."

"Bisexual?"

"No."

"So you really don't think he's ever made out with another guy?"

"No!" I say.

"I have trouble picturing Ethan touching some guy's penis too."

"Enough," I say.

"Okay. Fine. What is your latest analysis on Marcus?"

"He's growing on me," I say, for added insurance—just in case she has the slightest intuition about my feelings for Dex.

"He is? Since when?"

"I kissed him on Saturday night," I say, and instantly regret it. She will tell Dex.

"You did? I thought you went out with Hillary and Julian on Saturday night."

"I did. But I met up with Marcus afterward . . . for a few drinks. It was no big deal, really."

"Did you go back to his place?"

"No. Nothing like that."

"So where did you kiss him?"

"At Aubette."

"And that was it? You only kissed?"

"Yeah. What do you think, we had sex at Aubette? Jeez."

"Well, this is noteworthy . . . I thought things had sort of tapered off with you two. So can you see yourself marrying him?"

I laugh. This is classic Darcy—taking a little bit of information and running like crazy with it.

"Why are you laughing? Is he not marriage material?"

"I don't know. Maybe . . . Now can we please turn out the light? My eyes hurt."

She says okay, but gives me a look of warning to say it's not yet time for sleep.

I turn off my bedside lamp, and as soon as we are in the dark, she brings up Dex and his note. She had been fairly dismissive of it when I gave it to her at the start of her party, but now she calls him thoughtful.

"Hmm-mmm," I say.

A long silence follows. Then she says, "Things have been sort of weird with us lately."

My pulse quickens. "Really?"

"We haven't had sex in a long time."

"How long?" I ask, crossing my fingers under the sheets.

She tells me the answer I want. Since before the Fourth.

"Really?" My palms are sweaty.

"Yeah. Is that a bad sign?"

"I don't know . . . How often did you have sex before?" I ask, grateful for the dark.

"Before what?"

Before he told me that he loves me. "Before the Fourth."

"It comes and goes. But when things are going well we have sex every day. Sometimes twice a day."

I force the sickening images out of my head, struggling to find something to say. "Maybe it's the pressure of the wedding?"

"Yeah . . ." she says.

And maybe it's because he's having an affair with me. I have a pang of guilt, which increases tenfold when she switches topics again and asks out of the blue, "Can you believe how long we've been friends?"

"I know it's been a long time."

"Think of all the sleepovers we've had. How many sleepovers would you say we've had? I'm not good at estimating things. Would you say a thousand?"

"That's probably close," I say.

"It's been a while since we've had one," she says.

My eyes have adjusted to the dark, so I can vaguely see her now. With her face freshly scrubbed and her hair pulled back into a ponytail, she looks like a teenager. We could be in her bed back in high school, giggling and whispering, with Annalise snoring softly beside the bed in her Garfield sleeping bag. Darcy always let Annalise fall asleep. I think she almost hoped she would. I know I sometimes did.

"You wanna play twenty questions?" I ask. It was one of our favorite games growing up.

"Yeah. Yeah. You go first."

"Okay. I got one."

"Same rules?"

"Same rules."

Our rules were simple: you must choose a person (instated after Annalise tried to do neighborhood pets), someone we knew personally (no celebrities, dead or living), and you must ask yes-no questions.

"From high school?" she asks.

"Yes."

"Male?"

"No."

"Our graduating class?"

"No."

"Class above us or below us?"

"That's two questions."

"No, it's a compound," she says. "If the answer's yes, I still have to break it down and use another question. Remember?"

"Okay, you're right," I say, remembering that nuance. "The answer is no."

"Student?"

"No. That's five questions. Fifteen to go."

Darcy says she knows she's on five, she's counting. "Teacher we both had?"

"No," I say, six fingers hiding under the covers. Darcy has been known to "miscount" during this game.

"Teacher you had?"

"No."

"Teacher I had?"

"No."

"Guidance counselor?"

"No."

"A dean?"

"That's ten. No."

"Other staff?"

"Yes."

"Janitor?"

"No."

"The nark?"

"No." I smile, thinking about the time the nark busted Darcy leaving school to go to Subway with Blaine at lunch. Darcy told him to get a real job as he escorted them to the dean's office. "What are you, thirty? Isn't it time you left high school?" The comment earned her an extra pair of demerits.

"Ohh! I think I got it!" She starts giggling uncontrollably. "Is she a lunch lady?"

I laugh. "Uh-huh."

"It's June!"

"Yep! You got it."

June was a high school icon. She was about eighty years old, four feet tall, and massively wrinkled from years of heavy smoking. And her main claim to fame was that she once lost a fake nail in Tommy Baxter's lasagna. Tommy ceremoniously marched back to the lunch line and returned the nail to June. "I believe this belongs to you, June?" June grinned, wiped the sauce and cheese off the nail, and stuck it back on her finger. Everybody cheered and clapped and chanted, "Go, June! Go, June!" Other than reapplying her nail, I'm not sure what she did to earn the respect of our student body. I think it was more that somebody in the popular crowd just decided along the way that it was cool to like June. Maybe it had even been Darcy. She had that sort of power.

Darcy laughs. "Good ole June! I wonder if she's dead yet."

"Nah. I'm sure she's still there, asking kids in her raspy voice if they want marinara or meat sauce on their rigatoni."

When she finally stops laughing, she says, "Aww. This feels just like a sleepover from way back."

"Yeah. It does," I say, as a wave of fondness for Darcy washes over me.

"We had fun as kids, didn't we?"

"Yeah. We did."

Darcy starts laughing again.

"What?" I ask.

"Do you remember the time we spent the night at Annalise's house and hanged her sister's Barbie dolls?"

I crack up, picturing the Barbies, tied with yarn around their necks, dangling from the doorways. Annalise's little sister cried hysterically to her parents, who promptly met with the two other sets of parents to come up with a suitable punishment. We could not play together for a week, which is a long time in the summer. "That was sort of sick now that I think about it," I say.

"I know! And remember how Annalise kept saying it wasn't her idea?"

"Yeah. Nothing ever was her idea," I say.

"We always thought of the cool stuff. She was a big-time coattailer."

"Yeah," I say.

I am quiet, thinking about our childhood. I remember the day we were dropped off at the mall with our paltry sixth-grade savings, racing to the Piercing Pagoda to purchase our "best friend" necklaces, a heart inscribed with the two words, split down the middle, each side of the charm hanging from a gold-plated chain. Darcy took the "Be Fri" half, I got the "st end" half. Of course, we were so worried about Annalise's feelings that we only wore the necklaces in secret, under our turtlenecks, or in bed at night. But I remember the thrill of tucking my half of the heart inside my shirt, against my skin. I had a best friend. There was such security in that, such a sense of identity and belonging.

I still have my necklace buried in my jewelry box, the gold plate turned green with grit and time, but now also tarnished with something impossible to remove. I am suddenly overcome with profound sadness for those two little girls. For what is now gone between them. For what might never be regained, no matter what happens with Dex.

"Talk more," Darcy says sweetly. There is no trace of the brash, self-centered bride-to-be whom I have come to resent, even dislike. "Please don't sleep yet. We never get to hang out like this anymore. I miss it."

"Me too," I say, meaning it.

I ask her if she remembers the day we bought our "best friend" necklaces.

"Yes. But remind me about the details," she says in her charming way.

Darcy loves to hear my accounts of our childhood, always praising my more complete memory. I tell her the story of the necklaces, give her the longest version possible. After I am finished, I whisper, "Are you asleep?"

No answer.

As I listen to Darcy breathing in the dark beside me, I wonder how we got to this. How we could be in love with the same person. How I could be sabotaging my best friend's engagement. In the final seconds before sleep, I wish I could go back and undo everything, give those little girls another chance.

seventeen

The next morning, I am awakened by the sound of Darcy rummaging through my medicine cabinet. I listen to her bang around as I try to piece together my dreams from the night before, a series of incoherent vignettes featuring a wide cast of the usual characters—my parents, Darcy, Dex, Marcus, even Les. The plot is unclear, but I recall a fair amount of running and hiding. I almost kissed Dex a dozen times, but never did. I can't even be satisfied in my dreams. Darcy emerges from the bathroom with a happy face.

"I'm not hungover at all," she announces. "Although I took some Advil just in case. You're out. Hope you didn't need any."

"I'm fine," I say.

"Not bad for the day after a bachelorette party! What do you want to do today? Can we spend the day together? Just doing nothing. Like old times."

"Okay," I say, somewhat reluctantly.

"Awesome!" She walks toward my kitchen, starts rooting around. "Do you have any cereal?"

"No, I'm out. You want to go to EJ's?"

She says no, that she wants to eat sugar cereal right here in my apartment, that she wants it to feel just like old times, no New York brunch scene. She opens my refrigerator and surveys the contents. "Man, you're out of everything. I'll just run out and get some coffee and some essentials."

"Should we really drink coffee?" I ask her.

"Why wouldn't we?"

"Because I thought we were going to be authentic. We didn't drink coffee when we were in high school."

She thinks for a second, missing my sarcasm. "We'll make an exception for coffee."

"Do you want me to come with you?" I offer.

"No. That's okay. I'll be right back."

As soon as she leaves, I check my voice mail. Dex has left me two messages—one from last night, one from this morning. In the first, he says how much he misses me. In the second, he asks if he can come over tonight. I call him back, surprised at how grateful I feel when I get voice mail. I leave him a message, telling him that Darcy is over and plans to stay for a while, so tonight won't really work out. Then I sit on my couch thinking about last night, my friendship with Darcy. Will I be able to live with myself if I get what I want at her expense? What would life be like without her? I am still thinking about it all when Darcy returns. Bulging plastic bags hang from her forearms. I take the coffees from her hands as she dramatically drops the bags to the floor and shows me the red indentations the bags made on her arms. I make a sympathetic noise until she smiles again.

"I got great stuff! Froot Loops! Root beer! Cranapple juice! And Ben and Jerry's Chocolate Chip Cookie Dough ice cream!"

"Ice cream for breakfast?"

"No. For later."

"Aren't you worried about your wedding weight?"

She waves her hand at me. "Whatever. No."

"Why not?" I ask, knowing that she will eat now and ask me later why I let her do it.

"'Cause I'm just not! Don't rain on my parade! . . . Now. Let's eat Froot Loops!"

She busies herself in the kitchen finding bowls, spoons, napkins. She brings them out to the coffee table. She is in her giddy, high-energy mode.

"Would you rather eat over there?" I say, pointing to my little round table.

"No. I want it to be just like my house after a sleepover. We always ate in front of the TV. Remember?" She aims the remote control at the television and flips through the channels until she finds MTV. Then she pours cereal into bowls, carefully making sure we have the same amount. I am not in the mood for Froot Loops, but it is clear that I do not have a choice in the matter. Although I find it somewhat touching that she wants to re-create our childhood, I am also annoyed by her bossiness. *Running roughshod*, Ethan said. Maybe it is a precise description after all. And here I am, a willing participant, letting her steamroll me.

"Tell me when," she says, pouring whole milk onto my cereal. I hate whole milk.

"When," I say, almost instantly.

She stops pouring and looks at me. "Really? They are barely moist."

"I know," I say, appeasing her, "but this is how I liked it in high school too."

"Good point," she says, pouring milk in her own bowl. She fills it to the brim.

I take a few bites as she stirs her cereal with her spoon, waiting for the milk to turn pink.

Dido's "Thank You" video is on. Of course, it makes me think of Dex.

"This song," Darcy says, still stirring. "You know the part when she says she's home at last and soaking and then 'you handed me a towel'?"

"Yeah."

"That line totally reminds me of you."

"Of me?" I look at her. "I think it's supposed to be a romantic song."

She rolls her eyes. "Duh! I know that. Don't worry." She takes a bite and continues to talk with her mouth full. "I'm not dyking out or anything. I'm just saying you really are always here for me. You know, when the chips are down."

"That's sweet." I smile, push away the guilt, sip my coffee.

We listen to the rest of the song as Darcy noisily eats her cereal. As she finishes her last few bites, she raises the bowl to her lips, gulping the pastel milk.

"Am I being too loud?" she asks, glancing up at me.

I shake my head. "You're fine."

"Dex calls me the Slurper whenever I eat cereal."

I get a pang as I always do when I glimpse a private part of their relationship—which I like to pretend does not exist. Then I realize with an even sharper pang that Dex doesn't have a nickname for me. Perhaps I am too bland to deserve one. Darcy doesn't have a bland bone in her body. No wonder it is hard to leave her. She is the type of woman who draws you in, holds your attention. Even when she is annoying, she is compelling, captivating.

Jennifer Lopez appears on the screen in all her voluptuousness. We watch wistfully as she gyrates over a rural landscape. "Is her butt that great?" Darcy asks.

"I'm afraid so," I say, although I actually enjoy telling Darcy this. She even views celebrities as competition, whereas no part of me begrudges Jennifer Lopez her fantastic ass.

Darcy makes a clicking sound. "Don't you think it's kind of fat?" she asks.

"No. It's great," I say, knowing that both of Darcy's cheeks equal one of Jennifer's.

"Well, I think it's kind of fat . . ."

I shrug.

"Dex loves her. He thinks she's totally hot."

New Dexter information. *Ding! Ding! Ding!* What might this mean in the equation? I am fuller-figured than Darcy, but she is darker. I decide to discard the tidbit as not particularly helpful. I mean, most guys appreciate J-Lo no matter what their type. It's like Brad Pitt for us. You might not like blond men with pretty features, but c'mon, it's Brad. You're not going to kick him out of bed for eating crackers.

"Don't worry, though, I'm sure she's not that pretty in real life," Darcy says, assuming all women are like her and need to be consoled whenever they run across someone prettier.

"Uh-huh," I say.

"I mean, makeup artists can work absolute wonders," she says knowingly, as if she has been in the industry for years. She pulls the blanket down from the back of my sofa and wraps herself in it. "I like it here."

So does Dex.

"You cold?" I ask.

"No. I just want to be all comfy-cozy."

We watch videos until I almost forget about Dex. As much as you can forget someone you're in love with. Then, out of the blue, during a Janet Jackson video, Darcy asks me a question I never anticipated:

"Should I marry Dexter?"

I freeze. "Why are you asking that?"

"I don't know."

"There must be some reason," I say, trying to appear calm.

"Do you think I should be with someone more laid-back? Like I am?"

"Dex is laid-back."

"No he's not! He's totally type A."

"You think?" I ask. Maybe he is. I guess I just don't see him that way. "Totally."

I mute the television and look at her as if to say, go on, I am ready to be a really good listener. I think of putting on your "listening cap" in elementary school, fastening the imaginary strap under your chin as the boys always did. I swallow, pause, and then say, "It concerns me that you're asking this question. What's on your mind?"

I can feel my heart thumping as I await her answer.

"I don't know . . . Sometimes the relationship just seems a bit tired. Boring. Is that a bad sign?" She looks at me plaintively.

This is my chance. I have an opening. I consider what I could say, how easily I could manipulate her. But somehow I can't do it. I am already doing the unspeakable, but at least I will be fair about it. I am conflicted out, as they say at my firm. I can't take her case.

"I really don't know, Darce. Only you and Dexter can know whether you are right for each other. But you should really examine your concerns carefully—marriage is a very serious step. Maybe you should postpone," I say.

"Postpone the wedding?"

"Maybe."

Darcy's bottom lip protrudes and her brow furrows. I am sure that tears are imminent when her eyes dart over to the television. She brightens. "Oh! I love this video! Turn it up! Turn it up!"

I unmute the television and turn up the volume. Darcy bobs up and down, doing a head and torso dance, singing a song I have never heard by some boy band. She knows every word. I watch her, marveling at her sudden transformation. I wait for her to bring up Dex again, but she does not.

I blew my chance to tell her to call the whole thing off, that Dex is all wrong for her. Why didn't I steer her in that direction, water the seed of discontent? I never play my hand right. Then again, I don't think Darcy really wants my advice. Other than to tell her that everything will be all right, that she should marry Dexter. And if I won't say what she wants to hear, she will find a video to cheer her up instead.

"That song's the bomb," Darcy says, tossing aside the blanket. She gets up and shuffles across my apartment. She surveys my bookshelf where I recently put the Altoids tin and dice.

"What are you doing?"

"Looking for your high school yearbook. Where is it?"

"Bottom shelf."

She squats and runs her fingers over the spines, stopping at the Husky Howler. "Oh yeah. Here it is." She stands back up and notices the tin, placed foolishly at eye level. "Can I have one?"

"It's empty," I say, but she has already deposited the yearbook onto the foot of my bed. Her long, sculpted arm darts toward the tin. She opens the lid. "Why do you have dice in here?"

"Um, I don't know," I stumble, remembering how Darcy used to tell me that I should never go on a timed quiz show. She used to lord it over me, saying that if she ever got picked to be on *The Family Feud* (never mind that we aren't in the same family) she'd have to think twice before selecting me to be on her team. And no way would I get to do the bonus round at the end.

"You don't know?" she asks.

"No reason, I guess."

She stares at me as one might look at a babbling schizophrenic on the subway. "You don't know why you put dice in an Altoids tin? Okay. Whatever, weirdo."

She removes the dice from the tin, shaking them as if she is about to roll them.

"Don't," I say loudly. "Put them back."

It is not a good idea to tell her what to do. She is a child. She will want to know why she can't roll them. She will want to roll them just because I told her not to.

Sure enough: "What are they for? I don't get it."

"Nothing. They are just my lucky dice."

"Lucky dice? Since when do you have lucky dice?"

"Since always."

"Well, why do you have them in an Altoids container? You don't like cinnamon Altoids."

"Yes I do."

She shrugs. "Oh."

I study her face. She is not suspicious, but she is still holding my dice. I will run across the apartment, tackle her, and wrestle them from her before I let her reroll them. But she just looks at them one more time and replaces them in the tin. I am not sure if they still have sixes facing up. I will check later. As long as they are not rolled again, I am okay.

She picks up my yearbook and carries it back over to the couch, flipping to the sports and intramural pages in the back. This will keep her busy for hours. She will find a thousand things to comment upon: remember this, remember that? She never tires of our high school yearbook, discussing the past and speculating about what has become of so-and-so who didn't show up at the reunion because either (a) he has now become a total loser or (b) the opposite phenomenon has occurred and he is so spectacularly successful that he doesn't have time to return to Indiana for a weekend (the category Darcy says I am in because, of course, I had to work that weekend and missed it). Or she plays one of her favorite games where she opens the book to a page, closes her eyes, scribbles her index finger over the page until I say stop, and whichever guy is closest to her finger will be the one I must have sex with. Those are classic Darcy games, and when our senior yearbook first came out twelve years ago, they were grand fun.

"Oh, my goodness. Look at her hair! Have you ever seen such poofy bangs?" Darcy gasps as she scrutinizes Laura Lindell's photo. "She looks so ridiculous. They must be a foot high!"

I nod in agreement and wait for her next prey: Richard Meek. Only she decides to give him more credit than she gave him in the twelfth grade. "Not bad. He's sort of cute, isn't he?"

"Sort of. He has a nice smile. But remember how he spit all over you when he talked?"

"Yeah. Good point."

Darcy flips the pages until she finally grows tired of it, casts it aside, and resumes control of the remote. She finds *When Harry Met Sally* and squeals. "It's just starting! Yes!"

We both recline on my couch, feet to head, and watch the movie we have seen together countless times. Darcy talks out loud constantly, quoting the parts she knows. I don't shush her once. Because even though she says talking during movies irritates Dex, I don't mind. Not even when she gets the line slightly wrong, so that I can't tell what Meg Ryan is really saying. It's just Darcy. This is what she does.

And like a favorite old movie, sometimes the sameness in a friend is what you like the most about her.

eighteen

The next evening Darcy calls me just as I am returning home from work. She is hysterical. A cold, calm feeling overcomes me. Could this be it? Has Dex told her that the wedding is off?

"What's wrong, Darcy?" I ask. My voice sounds tight and unnatural, my heart filled with conflict—love for Dex versus friendship with Darcy. I brace myself for the worst, although I'm not sure what the worst would be—losing my best friend or the love of my life. I can't fathom either.

Darcy says something that I can't understand, something about her ring.

"What is it, Darce? Slow down . . . What about your ring?"

"It's gone!" she sobs.

It doesn't seem possible that your heart can sink just as you feel tremendous relief, yet that is what happens as I register that this conversation is only about a missing piece of jewelry. "Where did you lose it? It's insured, right?"

I am asking the responsible-friend questions. I am being helpful. But I sound rote. If she were any less hysterical, she might be able to tell that I don't care a lick that her ring has been misplaced. I tell her that she is a slob, that she probably just put it somewhere and forgot. "Remember the time you thought it was gone and then found it in one of your slippers? You're always misplacing things, Darce."

"No, it's different this time! This time it's gone! It's gone! Dex is going to kill me!" Her voice is trembling.

Maybe not, I think. Maybe this will be the opening he has been waiting for. And then I hate myself for thinking such a thing. "Have you told him?"

"No. Not yet. He's still at work . . . What am I going to do?"

"Well, where did you lose it?"

She doesn't answer me, just keeps crying.

I repeat the question.

"I don't know."

"Where did you see it last?" I ask. "Did you have it at work today? Did you take it off to wash your hands?"

"No, I never take it off to wash my hands! What kind of dumbass would do that?"

I want to tell her not to snap at me, that she is the dumbass who lost her engagement ring. But I stay sympathetic, tell her that I'm sure it will turn up.

"No, it won't turn up." More loud sobs.

"How do you know?"

"'Cause I just know."

I have run out of suggestions.

"Can I come over? I really have to talk to you," she says.

"Yes, come right over," I say, wondering if there is more to this than a missing ring. "Have you eaten?"

"No," she says. "Can you order some wonton soup for me?"

"Sure."

"And an egg roll?"

"Yes. Come over now."

I call Tang Tang and order two wonton soups, two egg rolls, two Sprites, and one beef and broccoli. Darcy arrives at my door fifteen minutes later. She is disheveled, wearing a pair of Levi's that I recognize from high school—they still fit her perfectly—and a white tank top. She is wearing no makeup, her eyes are bloodshot, and her hair is thrown up in a sloppy ponytail, but she still manages to look pretty. I tell her to sit down and tell me everything.

"It's gone." She shakes her head, holding up her bare left hand.

"Where do you think you lost it?" I ask calmly, recalling that I have gone through this exercise a hundred times with Darcy. I am always helping her, cleaning up her messes, trailing loyally after her in her wake of turmoil and angst.

"I didn't lose it. Somebody stole it."

"Who stole it?"

"Someone."

"How do you know?"

"Because it's gone!"

We are getting nowhere. I sigh and tell Darcy again to give me all of the facts.

She looks at me, her eyes filling with tears and her lips quivering slightly. "Rachel . . ."

"Yes?"

"You're my best friend." She starts to cry again, tears streaming gracefully down her glistening cheeks and falling onto her lap. She has always been a pretty crier.

I nod. "Yes."

"My best friend in the world. And I have to tell you something."

"You can tell me anything," I say, feeling overcome with worry, suddenly sure that Dex has laid the preliminary breaking-up groundwork.

She looks at me and makes a whimpering sound. As confident as Darcy is, she can seem so pitiful and defenseless when she is down. And my instinct has always been—still is—to help her. "Tell me, Darce," I say gently.

"Rachel—I—I took off my ring in somebody's apartment."

"Okay."

"A guy's apartment."

I feel as though I'm looking through a camera, trying to focus. Is she saying what I think she's saying?

"Rachel," Darcy says again, this time in a whisper. "I cheated on Dexter."

I stare at her, unable to mask my shock.

Yes, Darcy is a flirt. Yes, she lives life on the edge. Yes, she is selfish. And yes, she loves male attention. The attributes add up and it makes sense. I should not be surprised that she would cheat. I mean, Dex is none of the above, and he is doing it. Still, I am floored. She is getting married in less than two months. She is a glowing bride-to-be with a stunning gown, the kind that you dream about when you're a little girl. And she is with Dexter. How in the world could anyone cheat on Dexter?

The five *w*'s and one *h* of journalism pop into my head. I am in high school reporter mode, interviewing for the *North Star*. "Who with?"

She sniffs. Her head is down. "This guy at work."

"When?"

"A couple of times. Today." She rubs her eyes with her fists and looks at me sideways.

I don't know what my face is giving away. And I'm not even sure exactly how I feel. Relieved? Outraged? Disgusted? Hopeful? I haven't had time to consider the implications for Dex and me.

"And that's how you lost your ring?"

She nods. "I went over there today after I left my apartment, on the way to work." She swallows and then lets out a small sob. "We hung out, you know, fooled around—"

"Did you sleep with him?"

Her ponytail jerks up and down.

"I took my ring off because . . . well, I felt too guilty wearing it while I had sex with someone else." She blows her nose into an already soggy tissue.

"You want a fresh one?"

She nods again. I jog the few steps to the bathroom to retrieve my Kleenex box.

"Here," I say, handing her the box.

She takes a tissue and blows her nose again loudly. "So anyway, I took off the ring and put it on his windowsill, next to his bed." She points to my bed in its alcove. "He has a studio sort of like yours."

A studio. So he's probably not an executive, which surprises me. I would have guessed that Darcy would go for the power type. An older man. I had been picturing Richard Gere in *Pretty Woman*. I change my mental image to Matt Damon in *Good Will Hunting*.

"So we hang out, you know." She waves her hand in the air. "Then we get dressed and walk to the subway. Go to work."

"Uh-huh . . ."

"So when I get to work, I realize that I forgot to put on my ring. So I call him and tell him I need to go back and get the ring. He says no problem, but that he has a meeting at three that is going to last a couple of hours. Can we meet there at seven? I tell him sure . . . So we meet back at his place at seven. And when we go in, the place is, like, totally clean. And when we left, it was a total dump. And he goes, 'Shit. The cleaning lady was here.' And we go over to the windowsill and the ring is gone!" She is crying harder now. "The bitch took it."

"Are you sure? I can't believe someone would do that . . ."

She gives me a "Don't be such a Pollyanna" look. "The ring is gone, Rachel. Gone. Gone. Gone!"

"Well, can't he just call his cleaning lady and tell her that he knows she took it?"

"We tried that. She doesn't speak English very well. She just kept saying that she 'didn't see no ring.'" Darcy imitates the maid's accent. "I even took the phone. I told her I would give her a big, big reward if she finds it. The bitch isn't stupid. She knows that two carats are worth about twenty million dirty toilets."

"Okay," I say. "But it's insured, right?"

"Yeah, it's insured. But what the hell am I going to tell Dexter?"

"I don't know. Tell him that it fell down the drain at work . . . Tell him that you took it off at the gym and somebody broke into your locker."

She gives me a half-smile. "I like the gym one. That's believable, right?"

"Totally."

"I just can't believe this happened."

That makes two of us. I can't believe that Darcy cheated on Dex with some random guy. I can't believe that I am helping Darcy cover up her affair. Does everyone cheat when they're engaged?

"Is this a full-fledged affair?" I ask.

"Not really. Just a couple of times."

"So it's not serious?"

"I don't know. Not really. I don't know." She shakes her head and then rests her forehead in her hands.

I wonder if Darcy's recent moodiness has anything to do with this guy. "Are you in love with him?"

"God, no," she says. "It's just fun. It's nothing."

"Are you sure you should be getting married?" I ask.

"I knew you would say something like that!" Darcy starts to cry again. "Can't you just help me without being all pious?"

Trust me, I'm not being pious.

"I'm sorry, Darce. I'm not trying to be pious . . . I was just offering you an out if you wanted one."

"I don't want an out. I want to get married. I just—I don't know—I just panic sometimes that this is *it*. That I will never be with anyone else ever again. And so I just had this little fling. It was nothing."

"Okay," I say. "All I meant was that if you are unsure of this whole marriage thing . . . I just want you to know that I fully support whatever decision—"

She interrupts me. "There's no decision to make! I'm getting married. I love Dex."

"Sorry," I say. And I *am* sorry. I'm sorry that I love Dex too.

"No. *I'm* sorry, Rachel," she says, touching my leg. "It's been a horrible day."

"I understand."

"I mean, *do* you understand? Can you imagine what it is like to be weeks away from a promise that is supposed to last forever?"

Oh, poor you. Does she have any idea how many girls would kill to make a promise like that to someone like Dexter? She is looking at one of them.

"'Forever is a mighty long time,'" I say, with a hint of sarcasm.

"Are you quoting a Prince song? You better not be quoting a Prince song in my time of need!"

I tell her no, although that was precisely what I had been doing.

"It *is* a long time," she says. "And sometimes I don't know if I can do it. I mean, I know I want to get married, but sometimes I don't know if I can go forty more years or however long it is and never feel that thrill of kissing someone new. I mean, look at Hillary. She is on cloud nine, isn't she?"

"Yeah."

"And it's not like that with Dexter anymore. Ever. It's all just the daily grind—him going to work all the time, leaving me with all the wedding plans. We're not even married and the fun part is already so far gone."

"Darce," I say. "Your relationship has evolved. It's not about the initial frenzy, the lust, the newness."

She looks at me as if she's really paying attention, taking mental notes. I can't believe what I'm saying. I'm convincing her that her relationship is this great, special thing. I don't know why I'm doing it. Probably just nerves. I keep going. "The thrill of the chase is always exciting. But that's not what a real, lasting, loving relationship is all about. And the initial infatuation, the 'I can't keep my hands off you' routine, it fades for everyone."

Except for Dex and me, I think. It would always be special with Dex and me.

"I know you're right," she says. "And I do love him."

I know she believes what she's saying, but I'm not sure she does love him. I'm not sure she's capable of truly loving anyone but herself.

José buzzes my intercom to tell me that my food has arrived.

"Thanks. You can send him up," I say into the speaker.

As I step into the hall to pay the delivery guy, my home phone rings. I panic. What if it is Dex? I thrust my bills at the guy and dash back inside, throw the bag on my coffee table, and lift up the phone right as the answering machine is about to click on. Sure enough, it's Dex.

"Hi," he says. "I'm so sorry I haven't called you today. It's been a nightmare of a day. Roger had me—"

"It's okay," I say, interrupting him.

"Can I come over? I wanna see you."

"Um, no," I say.

"I can't?"

"No . . ."

"Okay . . . Why? . . . Do you have company?" He lowers his voice.

"Yeah," I say, trying to monitor my tone of voice for both listening parties. "Actually I do."

I look at Darcy. She mouths, "Who is it?"

I ignore her.

"Okay . . . All right then . . . It's not Marcus, is it?" Dex asks.

"No . . . Darcy's here," I say.

"Ohhh. Shit. Good thing I called first," he whispers.

"So we'll talk tomorrow?"

"Yeah," he says. "Definitely."

"Sounds good."

"Who was that?" Darcy asks, as I hang up the phone.

"It was Ethan."

"C'mon, was it Marcus?" she asks. "You can tell me."

"No, it really *was* Ethan."

"Maybe he's calling to tell you that he's gay."

"Uh-huh," I say, opening our cartons of food.

As we eat our Chinese food, I ask about Dex, how he is doing.

"What do you mean?"

"I mean, does he suspect that anything is going on?"

She rolls her eyes. "No. He works too much."

I note that she does not change my word choice of "is going on" to "*was* going on."

"No?"

"No. He's just the same, normal old Dex."

"Really?"

"Yes, really. Why?" She opens her Sprite, sips from the can.

"I just wondered," I say. "I've read that when someone is cheating, the other person usually knows it on some deep, inner level."

She slurps wonton soup from her plastic spoon and looks at me blankly. "I don't believe that," she says.

"Yeah," I say. "I guess I don't either."

After we finish our dinner, I hold up two fortune cookies. "Which one do you want?"

She points to my left hand. "That one," she says. "And it better be good. I can't take more bad luck."

I feel like telling her that choosing to sleep with a coworker and carelessly leaving your ring behind in his apartment has nothing to do with luck. I pull the plastic wrapper off the stale cookie, crack it open, and silently read my sliver of paper. *You have much to be thankful for.*

"What's it say?" Darcy wants to know.

I tell her.

"That's a good one."

"Yeah, but it's not a fortune. It's a statement. I hate when they pass statements off as fortunes."

"Then pretend it says, 'You *will* have much to be thankful for,'" she says, opening her wrapper. "Mine better say, 'You will get your ring back from the Puerto Rican bitch.'"

She silently reads her fortune and then laughs.

"What?"

"It says, 'You have much to be thankful for.' . . . That's bullshit. Mass-produced fortunes!"

Yeah, and only one of us will have much to be thankful for.

Darcy tells me that she better get going, that she has to go face the music. She tears up again as she reaches for her purse. "Will you tell Dex for me?"

"Absolutely not. I'm not getting involved," I say, amusing myself with the absurdity of the statement.

"What do I say again?"

"That you lost it at the gym."

"Is there time to get a new one before the wedding?"

I tell her yes, realizing that she has not once expressed any sentimentality over *the* ring that Dexter picked for her.

"Rachel?"

"Hmm?"

"Do you think I'm a terrible person? Please don't think I'm a terrible person. I have never cheated on him before. I'm not going to do it again. I really do love Dex."

"Okay," I say, wondering if she will do it again.

"Do you think I'm awful?"

"No, Darcy," I say. "People make mistakes."

"I know, that's what it was. A *total* mistake. I really, really regret it."

"You did use a condom?" I ask her.

I picture the chart in health class explaining that for every sexual partner you have, there are essentially dozens of others that you don't even know about: everyone he slept with, and so on and so on . . .

"Of course!"

"Good." I nod. "Call me later if you need me."

"Thanks," she says. "Thank you so much for being here for me."

"No problem."

"Oh, and this goes without saying . . . don't tell anyone. I mean, anyone. Ethan, Hillary . . ."

But what about Dex? Can I tell Dex?

"Of course. I won't tell anyone."

She hugs me, patting my back. "Thanks, Rachel. I don't know what I'd do without you."

When Darcy leaves, I formulate my answer to the obvious dilemma—to tell or not to tell. I approach it as I would an exam question, keeping emotion to the side:

At first blush, the answer seems clear: tell Dexter. I have three major reasons motivating this decision. First, I want him to know. It is in my best interest for him to know. If he has not already decided to call off his wedding, having this piece of knowledge likely will sway him against marrying Darcy. Second, I love Dexter, which means that I should make decisions with his best interest at heart. Thus, I want him to have a full set of facts when making a pivotal life decision. Third, morality dictates that Dex be told; I have a moral obligation to tell Dexter the truth about Darcy's actions. (This should be distinguished from a retributive point of view, although certainly Darcy deserves a sound snitching.) As a corollary, I value and respect the institution of marriage, and Darcy's infidelity certainly doesn't bode well for a long and lasting union. This third point has nothing to do with my self-interest, as the same reasoning would apply even if I weren't in love with Dex.

The logic of point three, however, seems to indicate that Darcy should also know that Dex has been unfaithful, and that I should not be hiding my actions from Darcy (because she is my friend and trusts me, and because it is wrong to be deceitful). Thus, one might argue that thinking that Dex should know the truth about Darcy is fundamentally at odds with intentionally leaving Darcy in the dark about my own misdeeds. However, this reasoning ignores an essential distinction and one that my final analysis is dependent upon: there is a difference between thinking a person should know/be told and being that messenger. Yes, I think Dex should know what Darcy has done, and (perhaps? likely?) will continue to do. But is it my place to tell? I would argue that it is not.

Furthermore, although Dex should not marry Darcy, it is not because he cheated or because she cheated. And it is not because he loves me and I love him. These things are all true but are mere symptoms of the larger problem, i.e., their flawed relationship. Darcy and Dex are wrong for each other. The fact that both of them have cheated, although driven to do so by separate motivations (love versus a self-serving mixture of fear of commitment and lust) is just one indicator. But even if neither had cheated, the relationship would still be wrong. And if Darcy and Dex can't determine this essential truth based on their interactions, their feelings, and their years together, then it is their mistake to make and not my place to play informant.

And I might also drop a footnote, maybe under the morality discussion, where I would address the betrayal of Darcy:

Yes, telling Darcy's secret would be wrong, but in light of my far greater betrayal, telling a secret seems hardly worth discussing. On the other hand, however, one could argue that telling the secret is worse. Sleeping with Dex has nothing to do with Darcy per se, but telling Darcy's secret has everything to do with Darcy. Yet considering that the ultimate decision is not to tell, this point becomes moot.

So there's my answer. I think my reasoning might be a little shaky, particularly at the end, where I sort of fall apart and essentially say, "So there." I can just see the red marks in the margin of the blue book. "Unclear!" and "Why is it their mistake to make? Are you punishing them for their stupidity or for their infidelity? Explain!"

But regardless of my flawed rationale and the knowledge that Ethan and Hillary would accuse me of being my usual passive self, I'm not saying a word about this to Dex.

nineteen

The next day I return home from work, pick up my dry cleaning from José, and check my mailbox to find my Time Warner cable bill, the new issue of *In Style* magazine, and a large ivory envelope addressed in ornate calligraphy affixed with two heart stamps. I know what it is even before I flip it over and find a return address from Indianapolis.

I tell myself that a wedding can still be called off after invitations go out. This is just one more obstacle. Yes, it makes things stickier, but it is only a formality, a technicality. Still, I am dizzy and nauseated as I open the envelope and find another inner envelope. This one has my name and the two humiliating words "and Guest." I cast aside the RSVP card and its matching envelope and a sheet of silver tissue paper floats to the floor, sliding under my couch. I don't have the energy to retrieve it. Instead, I sit down and take a deep breath, mustering the courage to read the engraved script, as if the wording can somehow make things better or worse:

OUR JOY WILL BE MORE COMPLETE

IF YOU SHARE IN THE MARRIAGE OF OUR DAUGHTER

DARCY JANE

TO

MR. DEXTER THALER

I blink back tears and exhale slowly, skipping to the bottom of the invitation:

WE INVITE YOU TO WORSHIP WITH US,

WITNESS THEIR VOWS, AND JOIN US

FOR A RECEPTION AT THE CARLYLE FOLLOWING THE CEREMONY.

IF YOU ARE UNABLE TO ATTEND, WE ASK FOR YOUR

PRESENCE IN THOUGHT AND PRAYER.

DR. AND MRS. HUGO RHONE

RSVP

Yes, the wording can indeed make things worse. I put the invitation on my coffee table and stare at it. I picture Mrs. Rhone dropping the envelopes off at the post office on Jefferson Street, her long red nails patting the stack with motherly smugness. I hear her nasal voice saying, "Our joy will be more complete" and "We ask for your presence in thought and prayer."

I'll give her a prayer—a prayer that the marriage never happens. A prayer for a follow-up mailing to arrive at my apartment:

DR. AND MRS. HUGO RHONE

ANNOUNCE THAT THE MARRIAGE OF

THEIR DAUGHTER DARCY TO

MR. DEXTER THALER

WILL NOT TAKE PLACE

Now that is some wording that I can appreciate. Short, sweet, to the point. "Will not take place." The Rhones will be forced to abandon their usual flamboyant style. I mean, they can't very well say, "We regret to

inform you that the groom is in love with another" or "We are saddened
to announce that Dexter has broken our dear daughter's heart." No, this
mailing will be all business—cheap paper, boxy font, and typed computer
labels. Mrs. Rhone will not want to spend the money on Crane's stationery and calligraphy after already wasting so much. I see her at the
post office, triumphant no more, telling the mailman that no, she will not
be needing the heart stamps this time. Two hundred flag stamps will do
just fine.

I am in bed when Dex calls and asks if he can come over.

On the day I receive his wedding invitation, I still say yes, come right
on over. I am ashamed for being so weak, but then think of all the people
in the world who have done more pathetic things in the name of love.
And the bottom line is: I love Dex. Even though he is the last person on
earth I should feel this way about, I truly do love him. And I have not
given up on him quite yet.

As I wait for his arrival, I debate whether to put the invitation away or
leave it on my coffee table in plain view. I decide to tuck it between the
pages of my *In Style* magazine. A few minutes later, I answer the door in
my white cotton nightgown.

"Were you in bed?" Dex asks.

"Uh-huh."

"Well, let me take you back there."

We get in bed. He pulls the covers over us.

"You feel so good," he says, caressing my side and moving his hand
under my nightgown. I start to block him, but then acquiesce. Our eyes
meet before he kisses me slowly. No matter how disappointed I am in
him, I can't imagine stopping this tide. I am almost motionless as he
makes love to me. He talks the whole time, which he doesn't usually do.
I can't make out exactly what he is saying, but I hear the word "forever."
He wants to be with me forever, I think. He won't marry Darcy. He
can't. She cheated on him. They aren't in love. He loves me.

Dex spoons me as tears seep onto my pillow.

"You're so quiet tonight," Dex says.

"Yeah," I say, keeping my voice steady. I don't want him to know that I'm crying. The last thing I want is Dexter's pity. I am passive and weak, but I have some—albeit limited—pride.

"Talk to me," he says. "What's on your mind?"

I come close to asking him about the invitation, his plans, us, but instead I make my voice nonchalant. "Nothing really . . . I was just wondering if you're going to the Hamptons this weekend."

"I sort of promised Marcus that I would. He wants to golf again."

"Oh."

"I guess you wouldn't consider coming?"

"I don't think it's a good idea."

"Please?"

"I don't think so."

He kisses the back of my head. "Please. Please come."

Three little "please"s is all it takes.

"Okay," I whisper. "I'll go."

I fall asleep hating myself.

The next day Hillary bursts into my office. "Guess what I got in the mail." Her tone is accusatory, not at all sympathetic.

I completely overlooked the fact that Hillary would be receiving an invitation too. I have no response prepared for her. "I know," I say.

"So you have your answer."

"He could still cancel," I say.

"Rachel!"

"There's still time. You gave him two weeks, remember? He still has a few more days."

Hillary raises her eyebrows and coughs disdainfully. "Have you seen him recently?"

I start to lie, but don't have the energy. "Last night."

She gives me a wide-eyed look of disbelief. "Did you tell him you got the invitation?"

"No."

"Rachel!"

"I know," I say, feeling ashamed.

"Please tell me you aren't one of *those* women."

I know the type she is talking about. The woman who carries on a relationship with a married man for years, hoping, even believing, that he will one day come to his senses and leave his wife. The moment is just around the corner—if she only hangs in there, she won't be sorry in the end. But time passes, and the years only create fresh excuses. The kids are still in school, the wife is sick, a wedding is being planned, a grandchild is on the way. There is always something, a reason to keep the status quo. But then the excuses run out, and ultimately she accepts that there will be no leaving, that she will always be the second-place finisher. She decides that second place is better than nothing. She surrenders to her fate. I have new empathy for these women, although I do not believe that I have yet joined their ranks.

"That's not a fair characterization," I say.

She gives me an "Oh, really?" look.

"Dexter's not married."

"You're right. He's not married. But he *is* engaged. Which might be worse. He can change his situation like *that*." She snaps her fingers. "But he's not doing a damn thing."

"Look, Hillary, we are talking about a finite timetable . . . I can only be one of *those* women for a month more."

"A month? You're going to let this thing go down to the wire?"

I look away, out my window.

"Rachel, why are you waiting?"

"I want it to be his decision. I don't want to be responsible . . ."

"Why not?"

I shrug. If she knew about Darcy's infidelity, she'd be over the edge.

She sighs. "You want my advice?"

I do not, but nod anyway.

"You should dump him. Now. Do something while you still have a choice. The longer this goes on, the worse you are going to feel when you're standing in front of that church, watching them seal their vows with a kiss that Darcy will drag on for longer than is tasteful . . . Then watching them cut the cake and feed one another while she smears icing on his face. Then watching them dance the night away . . . and then—"

"I know. I know."

Hillary isn't finished. "And then darting into the night on their getaway to frickin' Hawaii!"

I wince and tell her that I get the picture.

"I just don't understand why you won't do something, force his hand. Something."

I tell her again that I don't want to be responsible for their breakup, that I want it to be Dexter's decision.

"It *will* be his decision. You won't be brainwashing him. You'll simply be going for what you want. Why aren't you being more assertive about something so significant and important?"

I have no explanation for her. At least none that she would find acceptable. My phone rings, interrupting our awkward silence.

I glance at the screen on my phone. "It's Les. I better take it," I say, feeling relief that the inquisition is over. It is a sad day when I am grateful to hear from Les.

Later that afternoon, I take a break from my research and roll my chair over to my window. I peer down on Park Avenue, watching people move about their daily lives. How many of them feel desperate, euphoric, or simply dead inside? I wonder if any of them are on the verge of losing something huge. If they already have. I close my eyes and picture the wedding scenes that Hillary painted for me. I then add my own honeymoon reel—Darcy clad in her new lingerie, posing seductively on their bed. I can see it all so perfectly.

And suddenly, all at once, it is clear to me why I won't force Dex's hand. Why I said nothing over July Fourth, nothing in the time since, nothing last night. It all comes down to expectations. In my heart, I don't actually believe that Dex is going to call off the wedding and be with me, no matter what I do or say. I believe that those Dex and Darcy wedding and honeymoon scenes will unfold while I am left on the sidelines, alone. I can already feel my grief, can envision my final time with Dex, if it hasn't happened already. Sure, I have occasionally scripted a different ending, one in which Dex and I are together, but those images are always short-lived, never escaping the realm of "what if." In short, I have no real faith in my own happiness. And then there is Darcy. She is a woman who believes that things should fall into her lap, and consequently, they do. They always have. She wins because she expects to win. I do not expect to get what I want, so I don't. And I don't even try.

It is Saturday afternoon, and we're in the Hamptons. I took the train out this morning, and now our whole group is reunited in the backyard. The togetherness is a recipe for disaster. Julian and Hillary are playing badminton. They ask if anyone wants to challenge them in a doubles match. Dex says sure, he will. Hillary glares at him. "Who do you want to be your partner, Dexter?"

Until this point, Dexter did *not* know that I told Hillary anything about us. I had two reasons for keeping him in the dark on this: I didn't want him to feel uncomfortable around her, and I didn't want him to have free license to tell a friend.

But Hillary makes her snide remark in a way that you simply cannot miss if you are aware of the situation. Which apparently Julian is, because he gives her a look of warning. It has become clear that he will be the steadying force in their duo.

She does not stop there. "Well, Dex, who is it going to be?" She rests her hand on her hip and points at him with her racquet.

Dex stares back at Hillary. His jaw clenches. He is pissed.

"What if two people both want to be your partner, then what?" Hillary's voice is dripping with innuendo.

Darcy seems oblivious to the tension. So do Marcus and Claire. Perhaps everyone is used to Hillary's occasional confrontational tone. Maybe they just chalk it up to the lawyer in her.

Dex turns around and looks at us. "Any of you guys wanna play?"

Marcus waves his hand dismissively. "Naw, man. No, thanks. That's a girly game."

Darcy giggles. "Yeah, Dex. You're a girly man."

Claire says no, she hates sports.

"Badminton is hardly a sport," Marcus says, opening a can of Budweiser. "It's like calling tic-tac-toe a sport."

"Looks like it's between Darcy and Rachel. Doesn't it?" Hillary says. "You want in, Rach?"

I am frozen at my post at the picnic table, flanked by Darcy and Claire.

"No, thanks," I say softly.

"You want me to be your partner, honey?" Darcy asks. She looks across the yard at Dex as she shades her eyes with her hand.

"Sure," he says. "C'mon then."

Hillary snorts as Darcy hops up from the table with a warning that she sucks at badminton.

Dex looks down at the grass, waiting for Darcy to take the fourth racquet and join him in the plot of grass outlined by various flip-flops and sneakers.

"We play to ten," Hillary says, tossing the bird up for her first serve.

"Why do you get to serve first?" Dex asks.

"Here," she says, tossing the bird over the net. "By all means."

Dex catches the bird and glares at her.

The game is cutthroat, at least every time Hillary and Dex have control. The bird is their ammunition and they smack it with full force, aiming at one another. Marcus does the color in a Howard Cosell voice. "And the mood is tense here in East Hampton as both sides strive for the championship." Claire is cheering for everyone. I say nothing.

The score is 9–8, Hillary and Julian lead. Julian serves underhand. Darcy squeals and swats with her eyes closed and through sheer luck happens to make contact with the bird. She sends it back across the net to Hillary. Hillary lines up her shot and hits a vicious forearm that conjures Venus Williams. The bird sails through the air, whizzing just over the net toward Darcy. Darcy cowers, preparing to swat at the bird, as

Dex yells, "It's out! It's out!" His face is red and covered with beads of sweat.

The bird lands squarely beside Claire's flip-flop.

"Out!" Dexter yells, wiping his forehead with the back of his arm.

"Bullshit. The line is good!" Hillary shouts back. "That's match!"

Marcus offers good-naturedly that he doesn't think a badminton game should be called a match. Claire is up off the bench, trotting over to the bird to examine its alignment with her shoe. Hillary and Julian join her from their side of the net. There are five pairs of eyes peering down at the bird. Julian says that it is a tough call. Hillary glares at him before she and Dex resume their shouting of "out" and "in," like a couple of playground enemies.

Claire announces a "do-over" in her best "let's make peace" voice. But clearly she was not an outdoor girl growing up because declaring a do-over is one of the biggest causes of dissension in the neighborhood. Hillary proves this to be the case. "Bullshit," she says. "No do-over. The line has been in all day."

"All day? We've been playing for twenty minutes," Dex says snidely.

"I don't think it's landed on the line yet," Darcy offers. But not as if she cares. As competitive as she is in real-life matters, sports and games do not concern her. She bought properties in Monopoly based on color; she thought the little houses were so much cuter than the "big, nasty Red Roof Inns."

"Fine. If you want to *cheat* your way through life," Hillary says to Dex, disguising her true intent with a friendly smile, as though simply engaging in playful banter. Her eyes are wide, innocent.

I think I might faint.

"Okay, you win," Dex says to Hillary, as if he could not care less. Let Hillary win her stupid game.

Hillary doesn't want it this way. She looks disoriented, unsure whether to reargue the point or savor her victory. I am afraid of what she will say next.

Dex tosses his racquet in the grass under a tree. "I'm gonna take a shower," he says, heading for the house.

"He's pissed," Darcy says, offering us a blinding glimpse of the obvious. Of course, she thinks it's about the game. "Dex hates to lose."

"Yeah, well he can be a big baby," Hillary says with disgust.

I note (with satisfaction? hope? superiority?) that Darcy does not defend Dex. If he were mine, I'd say something. Of course, if he were mine, Hillary would not have been so merciless in the first place.

I give her a measured glance, as if to say, enough.

She shrugs, plops down in the grass, and scratches a mosquito bite on her ankle until it bleeds. She swipes at the blood with a blade of grass, then looks up at me again.

"Well?" she says defiantly.

That night, Dex is so quiet at dinner that he borders on surly. But I cannot tell if he is mad at Hillary, or at me for telling her. He ignores both of us. Hillary ignores him right back, except for an occasional barb, while I make feeble attempts to talk to him.

"What are you ordering?" I ask him as he scans his menu.

He refuses to look up. "I'm not sure."

"Go figure," Hillary mumbles. "Why don't you order two meals?"

Julian squeezes her shoulder and shoots me an apologetic look.

Dex turns in his chair toward Marcus and manages to avoid all conversation and eye contact with me and Hillary for the rest of our dinner. I am seized by worry. *Are you mad? Are you mad? Are you mad?* I think as I struggle to eat my swordfish. *Please don't be mad.* I am desperate, frantic to talk to Dex and clear the air for our remaining time together. I don't want to end on such a sour note.

Later at the Talkhouse, Dex and I are finally alone. I am ready to apologize for Hillary when he turns on me, his green eyes flashing. "Why the hell did you tell her?" he hisses.

I am not well trained in conflict and feel startled by his hostility. I give him a blank look, pretending to be confused. Should I apologize? Offer an explanation? I know we had an unspoken vow of secrecy, but I had to tell someone.

"Hillary. You told her," he says, brushing a piece of hair off his forehead. I note that he is even hotter when he's angry—his jaw somehow more square.

I push this observation aside as something snaps inside me. How dare he be angry with me! I have done nothing to him! Why am I the one feeling frantic, desperate to be forgiven?

"I can tell anyone I want," I say, surprised by the hardness in my voice.

"Tell her to stay outta this," he says.

"Stay out of what, Dex? Our fucked-up relationship?"

He looks startled. And then hurt. Good.

"It's not fucked up," he says. "The situation is, but our relationship is not."

"You're *engaged,* Dexter." My indignation boils into fury. "You can't separate that from our relationship."

"I know. I'm still engaged . . . but you hooked up with Marcus."

"What?" I ask, incredulous.

"You kissed him at Aubette."

I can't believe what I'm hearing—he is engaged and is finding fault with a nothing little kiss! I fleetingly wonder how long he has known and why he hasn't said anything before now. I fight back the instinct to be contrite.

"Yeah, I kissed Marcus. Big deal."

"It's a big deal to me." His face is so close to mine that I can smell the alcohol on his breath. "I hate it. Don't do it again."

"Don't tell me what to do," I whisper fiercely back. Angry tears sting my eyes. "I don't tell you what to do . . . You know what? Maybe I should tell you what to do . . . How about this one: marry Darcy. I don't care."

I walk away from Dex, almost believing it. It is my first free moment of the summer. Perhaps the freest moment of my life. I am the one in control. I am the one deciding. I find a space on the back patio, alone in a massive crowd, my heart pounding. Minutes later, Dex finds me, grips my elbow.

"You don't mean what you said . . . about not caring." Now it is his turn to be anxious. It never ceases to amaze me how foolproof the rule is: the person who cares the least (or pretends to) holds the power. I have proven it true once more. I shake his hand off my arm and just look at him coldly. He moves closer to me, takes my arm again.

"I'm sorry, Rachel," he whispers, bending down toward my face.

I do not soften. I will not. "I'm tired of the warring emotions, Dex. The endless cycle of hope and guilt and resentment. I'm tired of wondering what will happen with us. I'm tired of waiting for you."

"I know. I'm sorry," he says. "I love you, Rachel."

I feel myself weakening. Despite my tough-girl façade I am buzzing from being this near him, from his words. I look into his eyes. All of my instincts and desires—everything tells me to make peace, to tell him that I love him too. But I fight against them like a drowning person in a rip-tide. I know what I have to say. I think of Hillary's advice, how she has been telling me to say something all along. But I am not doing this for her. This is for me. I formulate the sentences, words that have been ringing in my head all summer.

"I want to be with you, Dex," I say steadily. "Cancel the wedding. Be with me."

There it is. After two months of waiting, a lifetime of passivity, everything is on the line. I feel relieved and liberated and changed. I am a woman who expects happiness. I *deserve* happiness. Surely he will make me happy.

Dex inhales, on the verge of responding.

"Don't," I say, shaking my head. "Please don't talk to me again unless it's to tell me that the wedding is off. We have nothing more to discuss until then."

Our eyes lock. Neither of us blinks for a minute or more. And then, for the first time, I beat Dex in a staring contest.

twenty

It is two days after I delivered my ultimatum and one month before the wedding. I am still invigorated by my stand and filled with a soaring, positive feeling, stronger than hope. I have faith in Dex, faith in us. He will cancel. We will live happily ever after. Or something close to that.

Of course I worry about Darcy. I even worry that she might do something crazy when faced with her first dose of rejection. I have visions of her languishing in a hospital bed, hooked up to an IV, dark circles under her eyes, her hair stringy, her skin gray. In these scenes, I am there by her side, bringing her magazines and black licorice, telling her that everything is going to be okay, that everything happens for a reason.

But even if these scenes play out, I will never regret telling Dex the truth about what I want. I will never be sorry for going for it. For once, I did not put Darcy above myself.

As the days tick by, I go to work, come home, go back to work, waiting for the bomb to drop. I am sure that Dex will call at any moment with news. Good news. In the meantime, I steel myself, refusing to give in to my temptation to call him first. But after a full week passes, I start to worry and feel the shift back to my former self. I tell Hillary that I want to call him, knowing that she will talk me out of it. I remind myself of a woman on the wagon, dragging herself to an AA meeting in a last-ditch effort to resist her urges.

"No way," she says. "Don't do it. Don't contact him."

"What if he was drunk and doesn't remember our conversation?" I ask her, grasping at straws.

"His tough luck."

"Do you think he remembers?"

"He remembers."

"Well. I wish I hadn't said anything."

"Why? So you could have a few more nights with him?"

"No," I say defensively.

Even though that is exactly the reason.

After another few days of torture, of being unable to eat or work or sleep, I decide that I must get away. I have to be somewhere else, away from Dex. Leaving town is the only way that I will keep myself from calling him, retracting everything for one more night, one more minute with him. I consider going to Indiana, but that is not far enough. Besides, home will only remind me of Darcy and the wedding.

I call Ethan and ask if I can visit. He is thrilled, says come anytime. So I call United and book a flight to London. It is only five days away, so I must pay full fare—eight hundred and ninety dollars—but it's worth every penny.

After I type my vacation memo, I go to drop it off at Les's office. Mercifully, he is away from his desk.

"He's at an out-of-the-office meeting. Thank gawd," his secretary,

Cheryl, says to me. She is my ally, often warning me when Les is in a particularly foul mood.

"Just have a few things for him," I tell her, heading into his den of horrors.

I put a draft of our reply papers on his chair, the vacation memo under them. Then I change my mind and move the memo to the top of the pile. He will be so pissed. This makes me smile.

"What's that smirk for?" Cheryl asks as I leave his office.

"Vacation memo," I say. "Let me know how much he curses me."

She lifts her eyebrows and says, "Uh-oh," without losing her place on the document she is typing. "Someone's gonna be in *trou-ble.*"

Les calls me that evening when he returns to the office. "What's the big idea?"

"Excuse me?" I ask, knowing that my calm will nettle him further.

"You didn't tell me you were going on vacation!"

"Oh. I thought I did," I lie.

"When was that?"

"I don't know exactly . . . Weeks ago. I'm going to a wedding." Two lies.

"Christ." He breathes into the phone, waiting for me to offer to cancel my trip. In the old days, back when I was a first-year, the passive-aggressive trick might have worked. But now I say nothing. I outwait him.

"Is it a family wedding?" he finally asks. This is where he draws the line. Family funerals and family weddings. Likely only immediate family. So I tell him that it's my sister's wedding. Three lies.

"Sorry," I say flippantly. "Maid of honor, you know."

I let him rant for a few seconds and make an idle threat about getting another associate to take over the case. As if everyone is chomping at the bit to work with him. As if I would care if he replaced me. Then he announces with pleasure that this means no life outside the office for me until Friday. I think to myself that that won't be a problem.

Darcy calls minutes later. She is just as understanding. "How can you book a trip so close to my wedding?"

"I promised Ethan I'd visit him this summer. And the summer is almost over."

"What's wrong with the fall? I'm sure London is even more beautiful in the fall."

"I need a vacation. Now."

"Why now?"

"I just need to get out of here."

"Why? . . . Does it have anything to do with Marcus?"

"No."

"Have you seen him?"

"No."

"Why not?"

"Okay. Maybe it does have something to do with Marcus . . ." I say, just wanting her to shut up. "I don't think it's going to work out with him. And maybe I'm a little bummed. Okay?"

"Oh," she says. "I'm really sorry it didn't work out."

The last thing I want is Darcy's sympathy. I tell her that it really has more to do with work. "I need a break from Les."

"But I need you here," she whimpers. Apparently her ten seconds of sympathy have expired.

"Claire will be here."

"It's not the same. You're my maid of honor!"

"Darcy. I need a vacation. Okay?"

"I guess it'll have to be." I see her pouting face. "Right?" She adds this with a note of hope.

"Right."

She sighs loudly and tries another tactic. "Can't you go the week I'm in Hawaii on my honeymoon?"

"I could," I say, picturing Darcy in her new lingerie. "If my world revolved around you . . . but I'm sorry. It doesn't."

I never say things like this to Darcy. But times have changed.

"Okay. Fine. But meet me at the Bridal Party tomorrow at noon to pick up your bridesmaid dress . . . Unless you have plans to go to Venice or something."

"Very funny," I say, and hang up.

So now Dex will know that I am going to London. I wonder how he will feel when he hears this news. Maybe it will make him decide more quickly. Tell me something good before I fly far away.

I keep waiting, feeling increasingly tortured with every passing hour. No word from him. No call. No e-mail. I constantly check my messages, looking for the blinking red light. Nothing. I start to dial his phone number countless times, compose long e-mails that I never send. Somehow I stay strong.

Then, on the night before my flight, José buzzes me. "Dex is here to see you."

A flood of emotion rushes over me. *The wedding is off!* For once, my glass is not only half full, but it runneth over. My joy is temporarily clouded as my thoughts turn to Darcy—what will happen to our friendship? Does she know of my involvement? I push thoughts of her away, focus on my feelings for Dex. He is more important now.

But when I open the door, his face is all wrong.

"Can we talk?" he asks.

"Yes." My voice comes out in a whisper.

I sit stiffly as if I'm about to be told that someone very close to me has died. He might as well be a police officer, coming to my door with hat in hand.

He sits beside me and the words come. *This has been a really hard decision . . . I really do love you . . . I just can't . . . I've given it a lot of thought . . . feel guilty . . . didn't mean to lead you on . . . our friendship . . . incredibly difficult . . . I care too much about Darcy . . . can't do it to her . . . owe it to her family . . . seven years . . . summer has been intense . . . meant what I said . . . I'm sorry . . . I'm sorry . . . I'm truly sorry . . . always, always will love you . . .*

Dex covers his face with his hands, and I have a flashback to my birthday, how much I admired his hands while we were riding in the cab up First Avenue. Right before he kissed me. And now, here we are. At the very end. And I will never kiss him again.

"Say something," Dex says. His eyes are glassy, his lashes wet and jet black. "Please say something."

I hear myself say that I understand, that I will be fine. I do not cry. Instead I concentrate on breathing. In and out. In and out. More silence. There is nothing more to say.

"You should go now," I tell him.

As Dex stands up and walks to the door, I consider screaming, begging. *Don't go! Please! I love you! Change your mind! She cheated on you!* But instead I watch him leave, not hesitating or turning back for one final look at me.

I stare at the door for a long time, listening to the loud silence. I want to cry, so that something will fill the scary blank space, but I can't. The silence grows louder as I consider what to do next. Pack? Go to sleep? Call Ethan or Hillary? For one irrational second, I have those thoughts that most people don't admit to having—swallowing a dozen Tylenol PM, chasing them with vodka. I could really punish Dex, ruin their wedding, end my own misery.

Don't be crazy. It's just a little heartbreak. You will get over this. I think of all the hearts breaking at this moment, in Manhattan, all over the world. All of the overwhelming grief. It makes me feel less alone to think that other people are getting their insides torn to tiny bits. Husbands leaving wives after twenty years of marriage. Children crying out, "Don't leave me, Daddy! Please stay!" Surely what I feel doesn't compare to that kind of pain. It was only a summer romance, I think. Never meant to last beyond August.

I stand up, walk over to my bookcase, and find the Altoids tin. I have one final hope. If I get double sixes, maybe he will change his mind, come back to me. As if to cast a magic spell, I blow on the dice just as Dex did. Then I shake them once in my right hand and carefully, carefully roll them. Just as it happened with our first roll, one die lands before its mate. On a six! I hold my breath. For a brief second, I see a mess of dots, and think I have boxcars again. I kneel, staring at the second die.

It is only a five.

I have rolled an eleven. It is as if someone is mocking me, saying, *Close, but no dice.*

twenty-one

I am somewhere over the Atlantic Ocean when I decide that I will not tell Ethan all of the gory, pathetic details. I will not dwell and wallow once the plane lands on British soil. It will be the first step in getting over Dex, moving on. But I will give myself the duration of the flight to think about him and my situation. How I put myself on the line and lost. How it's not worth it to take risks. How it's better to be a glass-half-empty person. How I would have been so much better off if I had never gone down this road, setting myself up for rejection and disappointment and giving Darcy the chance to beat me again.

I rest my forehead against the window as a little girl behind me kicks my seat once, twice, three times. I hear her mother say in a sugary voice, "Now Ashley, don't kick the nice lady's seat." Ashley keeps kicking. "Ashley! That is against the rules. No kicking on the plane," the mother repeats with exaggerated calm as if to demonstrate to everyone around her what a competent parent she is. I close my eyes as we fly into the night, don't open them until the flight attendant comes by to offer us headphones.

"No, thanks," I say.

No movie for me. I will be too busy cramming all of the misery I can into the next few hours.

I told Ethan not to come to Heathrow—that I would take a taxi to his flat. But I am hoping that he comes anyway. Even though I live in Manhattan, I am intimidated by other big cities, particularly foreign ones. Except for the time I went to Rome with my parents for their twenty-fifth wedding anniversary, I have never left the country. Other than Niagara Falls on the Canadian side, which hardly counts. So I am relieved to see Ethan waiting for me just outside of customs, grinning and boyish and happy as ever. He is wearing new horn-rimmed glasses, like Buddy Holly's, only brown. He rushes toward me and hugs me hard around the neck. We both laugh.

"It's so good to see you! Here. Give me your bag," he says.

"You too." I grin back at him. "I like your glasses."

"Do they make me look smarter?" He pushes the frames on his nose and strikes a scholarly pose, stroking a nonexistent beard.

"Much." I giggle.

"I'm so glad you're here!"

"I'm so glad to be here."

A summer full of bad decisions, but at last I made a good one. Just seeing Ethan soothes me.

"It's about time you visited," he says, maneuvering my roller bag through the crowd. We make our way outside, into the cab line.

"I can't believe I'm in England. This is so exciting." I take my first breath of British air. The weather is exactly what I imagined—gray, drizzling, and slightly chilly. "You weren't kidding about the weather here. This feels like November, not August."

"I told you . . . We actually had a few hot days this month. But it's back to normal now. It's relentless. But you get used to it. You just have to dress for it."

Within minutes we are in the back of a black cab, my bags at our feet. The taxi is dignified and spacious compared to New York's yellow cabs.

Ethan asks me how I feel, and for a second I think he is asking about Dex, but then I realize it's the standard postflight questioning.

"Oh, fine," I say. "I'm really psyched to be here."

"Jet-lagged?"

"A little."

"A pint will fix that," he says. "No napping. We have a lot to do in a week."

I laugh. "Like what?"

"Sightseeing. Boozing. Reminiscing. Time-consuming, intense stuff . . . God, it's nice to see you."

We arrive at Ethan's basement flat in Kensington, and he gives me the brief tour of his bedroom, living room, and kitchen. His furniture is sleek and modern, and his walls are covered with abstract paintings and posters of jazz musicians. It is a bachelor pad, but without the I'm-trying-at-every-turn-to-get-laid feel.

"You probably want to shower?"

I tell him yes, that I feel pretty grimy. He hands me a towel in the hallway outside of his bathroom and tells me to be quick, that he wants to talk.

As soon as I am showered and changed, Ethan asks, "So how's the Dex situation? I take it they're still engaged?"

It's not as if I have stopped thinking about him for an instant. Everything vaguely reminds me of him. A sign for Newcastle. *Drinking Newcastles with him on my birthday.* Driving on the left side of the street. *Dex is left-handed.* The rain. *Alanis Morissette singing, "It's like rain on your wedding day."*

But Ethan's question about Dex still causes a sharp pain in my chest. My throat tightens as I struggle not to cry.

"Oh God. I knew it," Ethan says. He reaches up and grabs my hand, pulling me down on his black leather couch.

"Knew what?" I say, still fighting back tears.

"That your stiff-upper-lip, 'I don't care' thing was just a lot of bluster." He puts his arm around me. "What happened?"

I finally cry as I tell him everything, no editing. Even the dice. So much for my vow over the Atlantic. My pain feels raw, naked.

When I am finished, Ethan says, "I'm glad I RSVPed no. I don't think I could stomach it."

I blow my nose, wipe my face. "Those are the exact words Hillary used. She's not going either."

"You shouldn't go, Rachel. Boycott. It will be too hard. Spare yourself."

"I have to go."

"Why?"

"What would I tell her?"

"Tell her that you have to have surgery—you have to have an extraneous organ removed . . ."

"Like what kind of organ?"

"Like your spleen. People can get by without their spleen, right?"

"What's the reason for removing your spleen?"

"I dunno. A spleen stone? A problem . . . an accident, a disease. Who cares? Make something up. I'll do the research for you—we'll come up with something plausible. Just don't go."

"I have to be there," I say. I am back to rule-following.

We sit in silence for a minute, and then Ethan gets up, switches off two lamps, and grabs his wallet from a small table in the hall. "C'mon."

"Where are we going?"

"We're going to my local pub. Getting you good and loaded. Trust me, it will help."

"It's eleven in the morning!" I laugh at his exuberance.

"So? You got a better idea?" He crosses his arms across his narrow chest. "You want to sightsee? Think Big Ben's going to do you any good right now?"

"No," I say. Big Ben would only remind me of the minutes ticking down to what will be the most horrible day of my life.

"So c'mon then," he says.

I follow Ethan over to a pub called the Brittania. It is exactly how I expect an English pub to be—musty and full of old men smoking and reading the paper. The walls and carpet are dark red, and bad oil paintings of foxes and deer and Victorian women cover the walls. It could be 1955. One man wearing a little cap and smoking a pipe even resembles Winston Churchill.

"What's your pleasure?" Ethan asks me.

Dex, I think, but tell him a beer would be great. I am beginning to think that the boozing idea is a pretty good one.

"What kind? Guinness? Kronenbourg? Carling?"

"Whatever," I say. "Anything but Newcastle."

Ethan orders two beers, his several shades darker than mine. We sit down at a corner table. I trace the grain in the wood of the table and ask him how long it took for him to get over Brandi.

"Not long," he says. "Once I knew what she did, I realized that she wasn't what I thought. There was nothing to miss. That's what you have to think. He wasn't right for you. Let Darcy have him . . ."

"Why does she always win?" I sound like a five-year-old, but it helps to hear my misery simplified: *Darcy beat me. Again.*

Ethan laughs, flashing his dimple. "Win what?"

"Well, Dex for one." Self-pity envelops me as I picture him with Darcy. It is morning in New York. They are likely still in bed together.

"Okay. What else?"

"Everything." I gulp my beer as quickly as I can. I feel it hit my empty stomach.

"Like?"

How do I explain to a guy what I mean? It sounds so shallow: she's prettier, her clothes are better, she's thinner. But that is the least of it. She is happier too. She gets what she wants, whatever that happens to be. I try to articulate this with real examples. "Well, she has that great job making tons of money, when all she has to do is plan parties and look pretty."

"That schmoozing job of hers? Please."

"It's better than mine."

"Better than being a lawyer? I don't think so."

"More fun."

"You'd hate it."

"That's not the point. She loves her job." I know I am not doing a good job of showing how Darcy is always victorious.

"Then find one you love. Although that's another issue altogether. One that we will address later . . . But, okay, what else does she win?"

"Well . . . she got into Notre Dame," I say, knowing that I sound ridiculous.

"Oh, she did not!"

"Yes she did."

"No. She *said* she got into Notre Dame. Who picks IU over Notre Dame?"

"Plenty of people. Why do you always dump on IU?"

"Okay. Look. I hate Notre Dame more. I'm just saying if you apply to those two schools and get into both, presumably you want to go to both. So you'd pick Notre Dame. It's a better school, right?"

I nod. "I guess."

"But she didn't get in there. Nor did she get a, what did she say, thirteen hundred five and a half or something on her SATs? Remember that shit?"

"Yeah. She lied about her score."

"And she lied about Notre Dame too. *Trust* me . . . Did you ever see the acceptance letter?"

"No. But . . . well, maybe she didn't."

"God, you're so naïve," he says, mispronouncing it "nave" on purpose. "I assumed we were on the same page there."

"It was a sensitive topic. Remember?"

"Oh yeah. I remember. You were so sad," he says. "You should have been celebrating your escape from the Midwest. Of course, then you pick the second most obnoxious school in the country, and go to Duke . . . You know my theory about Duke and Notre Dame, right?"

I smile and tell Ethan that I have trouble keeping all of his theories straight. "What is it again?"

"Well, aside from you, and a few other exceptions, those two schools are filled to the brim with obnoxious people. Perhaps only obnoxious people apply there or perhaps the schools attract obnoxious people. Probably a combination, a mutually reinforcing issue. You're not offended, are you?"

"'Course not. Go on," I say. In part, I agree with him. A lot of people at Duke—including my own boyfriend—were hard to take.

"Okay. So why do they have a higher ratio of assholes per capita? What do those two schools have in common, you ask?"

"I give."

"Simple. Dominance in a Division-One, revenue-generating sport. Football at Notre Dame and basketball at Duke. Coupled with the stellar academic reputation. And the result is an intolerably smug student body. Can you name another school that has that combination of characteristics?"

"Michigan," I say, thinking of Luke Grimley from our high school who was insufferable in his chatter about Michigan football. And he still talks about Rumeal Robinson's clutch free throws in the NCAA finals.

"Aha! Michigan! Good one, nice try. But it's not an expensive private school. The public aspect saves Michigan, makes Michigan alums slightly less obnoxious."

"Wait a minute! What about your own school? Stanford. You had Tiger Woods. Great swimmers. Debbie Thomas, that skater, didn't she win a silver medal? Tennis players galore. Plus great academics—and it's private and expensive. So why aren't you Stanford grads as irritating?"

"Simple. We're not dominant in football or basketball. Yeah, we're good some years, but not like Duke in basketball or football at Notre Dame. You can't get as jazzed over nonrevenue sports. It saves us."

I smile and nod. His theory is interesting, but I am more intrigued with the realization that Darcy got rejected by Notre Dame.

"Mind if I smoke?" Ethan asks as he removes a carton from his back pocket. He shakes a cigarette free, rolling it between his fingers.

"I thought you quit."

"For a minute," he says.

"You should quit."

"I know."

"Okay. So back to Darcy."

"Right."

"So maybe she didn't get into Notre Dame. But she did get Dex."

He strikes a match and raises it to his lips. "Who cares? Let her keep him. He's spineless. Sincerely, you're better off."

"He's not spineless," I say, hoping that Ethan will convince me otherwise. I want to latch onto a fatal flaw, believe that Dex is not the person I thought he was. Which would be a lot less painful than believing that I am not the woman he wanted.

"Okay, maybe 'spineless' is too strong. But, Rach, I'm *positive* he'd rather be with you. He just doesn't know how to dump her."

"Thanks for the vote of confidence. But I actually think he just decided that he'd rather be with Darcy. He picked her over me. Everybody picks her." I gulp my beer more quickly.

"Everybody. Who besides spineless Dex?"

"Okay." I smile. "You picked her."

He gives me a puzzled look. "Did not."

I snort. "Ha."

"Is that what she told you?"

After all these years, I have never aired my feelings about their two-week elementary-school romance. "She didn't need to tell me. Everybody knew it."

"What are you talking about?"

"What are *you* talking about?"

"The reunion?" he asks.

"Our ten-year?" I ask, knowing of no other reunion. I remember the disappointment I felt when Les insisted that I had to work. Those were the days before I knew to lie. He had scoffed at me when I said I couldn't work, that I had to go to my ten-year reunion.

"Yeah. She didn't tell you what happened?" He takes a long drag, then turns his head, exhaling away from me.

"No. What happened?" I say, thinking that I am going to fall apart and die if Ethan slept with her. "Please tell me you didn't hook up with her."

"Hell, no," he says. "But she tried."

emily giffin

As I finish the rest of my pint and steal a few sips of Ethan's, I listen to him tell the story of our reunion. How Darcy came on to him at Horace Carlisle's backyard afterparty. Said she thought they should have one night together. What would it hurt?

"You're kidding me!"

"No," he says. "And I was like, Darce, *hell,* no. You have a boyfriend. What the fuck?"

"Was that why?"

"Why I didn't hook up with her?"

I nod.

"No, that's not why."

"Why then?" For a second, I wonder if he's going to come out of the closet. Maybe Darcy is right after all.

"Why do you think? It's Darcy. I don't see her that way."

"You don't think she's . . . beautiful?"

"Frankly, no. I don't."

"Why not?"

"I need reasons?"

"Yes."

"Okay." He exhales, looks up at the ceiling. " 'Cause she wears too much makeup. 'Cause she's too, I don't know, severe."

"Sharp featured?" I offer.

"Yeah. Sharp and . . . and overplucked."

I picture Darcy's skinny, high-arched brows. "Overplucked. That's funny."

"Yeah. And those hipbones jutting out at you. She's way too skinny. I don't like it. But that's not the point. The point is—is that it is Darcy." He shudders and then takes his beer back from me. "Hold on. Let me get another round." He crushes out his cigarette and strolls over to the bar, returning with two more beers. "There you are."

"Thanks," I say, and then set about chugging mine.

He laughs. "Man! I can't let you outdrink me."

I wipe the foam from my lips with the back of my hand and ask why he didn't tell me about Darcy and the reunion before now.

"Oh. I dunno. 'Cause it was no big deal. She was wasted." He shrugs. "Probably didn't even know what she was doing."

"Yeah, right. She always knows what she's doing."

"I guess so. Maybe. But it really wasn't significant."

That explains why she thought Ethan was gay. Turning her down—it must be the only explanation. "Guess her fifth-grade charms wore thin on you."

He laughs. "Yeah. We did go out once upon a time." He makes little quotes in the air as he says "go out."

"See. You picked her over me too."

He flashes his dimple. "What the hell are you talking about now?"

"On the note. The check-the-box note."

"What?"

I sigh. "The note that she sent you. The 'Do you want to go out with me or Rachel?' note."

"That's not what the note said. It didn't say anything about you. Why would it say anything about you?"

"Because I liked you!" Somehow I am embarrassed admitting it, even after all these years. "You knew that."

He shakes his head firmly. "Nope. Did not."

"You must have forgotten."

"I don't forget shit like that. I have a bomb-ass memory. Your name was *not* in the note. See. I'd know because I liked you back then." He peers at me from behind his glasses and then lights another cigarette.

"Bullshit." I feel myself blush. It's only Ethan, I tell myself. We are adults now.

"Okay." He shrugs and inverts the cover of his matchbook. Now he looks embarrassed too. "Don't believe me."

"You did?"

"Big time. I remember always helping you out in four square so that you'd get to be king. I'd always pound the king when you were in the queen position. Tell me you didn't notice that."

"I didn't notice that," I say.

"As it turns out, you're markedly less perceptive than I once thought . . .

Yeah, I liked you. I liked you all through junior high and high school. And then you dated Beamer. Broke my heart."

This is big news, but I still can't get past the fact that my name wasn't in that note. "I swear I thought Annalise saw it."

"Annalise is a sweet girl but such a lemming. Darcy probably told her to say that your name was in the note. Or somehow tricked her into thinking it. How is Annalise, anyway? Did she have her kid yet?"

"No. But any minute now."

"Is she going to the wedding?"

"If she's not in labor," I say. "Everybody is but you."

"And you. Terrible thing about your spleen."

"Yeah. Tragic." I smile. "So you're sure my name really wasn't in the note?"

I am focusing on evidence from twenty years ago. It is absurd, but I ascribe all kinds of meaning to it.

"Positive," he says. "Pos-i-tive."

"Damn," I say. "What a bitch."

He laughs. "I had no clue that I was the man. Thought it was all about Doug Jackson."

"You were not the man. It was all about Doug Jackson," I say. "That's the point—I was the only one who liked you. She copied me." Again, I notice how juvenile I sound whenever I describe my feelings about Darcy.

"Well, you didn't miss much. Going out with me consisted of sharing a few Hostess cupcakes. Wasn't very exciting. And I still hooked you up in four square."

"So maybe Dex will hook me up the next time we all play four square," I say. "That would be really . . ." I can't think of the right word. I can feel myself getting drunk.

"Nifty? Brilliant? Smashing?" Ethan offers.

I nod. "All of those. Yes."

"Feeling better?" he asks.

He is trying so hard. Between his efforts and the beer I feel somewhat healed, at least temporarily. I consider that I am thousands of miles away from Dex. Dexter—who *did* have my name as an option when he chose, instead, to check the box next to Darcy's name. "Yes. A little better. Yes."

"Well, let's recap. We determined that I never picked Darcy over you. And that she didn't get into Notre Dame."

"But she did get Dex."

"Forget him. He's not worth it," Ethan says, and then glances up at the menu scrawled on a blackboard behind us. "Now. Let's get you some fish and chips."

We eat lunch—fish, French fries, and mushy peas that remind me of baby food. Comfort food. And we have a couple more pints. Then I suggest that we go for a walk, see something England-y. So he takes me into Kensington Gardens and shows me Kensington Palace, where Princess Diana lived.

"See this gate? That's where they piled all the flowers and letters when she died. Remember those photos?"

"Oh yeah. That was here?"

I was with Dex and Darcy when I found out that Diana had died. We were at the Talkhouse and some guy walked up to us at the bar and said, "Did you hear that Diana died in a car crash?" And even though he could only have been talking about one Diana, Darcy and I both asked, Diana who? The guy said Princess Diana. Then he told us that she died in a high-speed crash while the paparazzi chased her through a tunnel in Paris. Darcy started bawling right on the spot. But for once it wasn't the give-me-attention tears. They were genuine. She was truly devastated. We both were. Several days later we watched her funeral together, waking at four A.M. to see all of the coverage, just as we had done with her wedding to Prince Charles sixteen years earlier.

Ethan and I meander through Kensington Gardens in a drizzle, without an umbrella. I don't mind getting wet. Don't care that my hair will frizz. We pass the palace and circle a small, round pond. "What's this pond called?"

"Round Pond," Ethan says. "Descriptive, huh?"

We walk past a bandstand and then over to the Albert Memorial, a huge bronze statue of Prince Albert perched on a throne. "You like?"

"It's pretty," I say.

"A grieving Queen Victoria had this thing built when Albert died from typhoid fever."

"When?"

"Eighteen sixty- or seventy-something . . . Nice, huh?"

"Yeah," I say.

"Apparently she and Al were pretty tight."

Queen Victoria must have been sadder than I am now, I suppose. I then have a fleeting thought that I'd prefer losing Dex to illness than to Darcy. So maybe it's not true love if I'd rather see him die . . . Okay, I wouldn't rather see him die.

The rain starts to come down harder. Other than a few Japanese tourists who are snapping pictures on the steps of the memorial, we are alone.

"You ready to head back?" Ethan points in the opposite direction. "We can explore Hyde Park and the Serpentine another day."

"Sure, we can go back now," I say.

"Your spleen acting up in this weather?"

"Ethan! I have to go to the wedding."

"Just blow it off."

"I'm the maid of honor."

"Oh, *right*! I keep forgetting that," he says, wiping his glasses on his sleeve.

As we walk back to his flat, Ethan chuckles to himself.

"What?"

"Darcy," he says, shaking his head.

"What about her?"

"I was just thinking about the time she wrote to Michael Jordan and asked him to our prom."

I laugh. "She actually thought he was going to come! Remember how she was worried about how she would break the news to Blaine?"

"And then Jordan wrote back to her. Or his people did, anyway. That's the part that I found unreal. I never thought she'd get a response." He laughs. No matter what he says, I know he has a soft spot for her, in spite of himself. Just as I do.

"Yeah. Well, she did. She still has the letter."

"You've seen it?"

"Yeah. Don't you remember how she taped it up in our locker?"

"And yet," he says, "you never saw the letter from Notre Dame."

"Okay. *Okay.* You might be right. But where were you twelve years ago with that insight?"

"As I said, I thought we were on the same page there. The whole thing was pretty transparent . . . You know, for a smart woman you can be pretty dim."

"Why, thank you."

He tips an imaginary hat. "Don't mention it."

We return to Ethan's flat, where I succumb to my jet lag. When I wake up, Ethan offers me a cup of Earl Grey tea and a crumpet. Lunch at a pub, a walk past Diana's old pad, an afternoon nap where I don't dream once about Dex, and tea and crumpets with my good friend. The trip is off to a good start. If anything can really be good with a broken heart.

twenty-two

That evening we meet up with Ethan's friends Martin and Phoebe, whom he met during his stint writing for *Time Out*. I have heard much about both of them: I know that Martin is very proper, went to Oxford, and comes from a ton of money, and that Phoebe hails from East London, once got fired for telling her boss to "piss off," and has slept with a lot of men.

They are exactly as I imagined. Martin is well dressed and attractive in an unsexy way. He sits with his legs crossed at the knee, nods and frowns a lot, and makes a "hmm" sound whenever anyone else speaks, showing rapt attention. Phoebe is Amazon-tall with untamed, tomato-red hair. I can't decide whether her orange lipstick clashes with her hair or complements it. I also can't decide whether she is very pretty or just plain weird-looking. Her body is definitely not ideal, but she doesn't try to hide it. One roll of her big white stomach shows between her shirt and jeans. Nobody in Manhattan would expose her stomach unless it was as hard as bedrock. Ethan told me once that British women are much less obsessed with appearances and being thin than American women. Phoebe is evidence of this, and it is refreshing. All night she talks about this bloke whom she wants to shag, and that bloke whom she has already shagged. She makes all the statements matter-of-factly, as you would tell someone that work has been very busy or that you are tired of all of the rain. I like her candor, but Martin rolls his eyes a lot and makes dry comments about her being uncouth.

After Phoebe has carried on for a while about this guy Roger, who "deserves to have kerosene poured on his balls," she turns to me and asks, "So, Rachel, how do you find the men in New York? Are they as bloody dreadful as English men?"

"Why, thank you, darling," Martin deadpans.

I smile at Martin and then turn back to Phoebe. "It depends . . . widely varies," I say. I have never thought in terms of "American men." They are all I know.

"Are you involved with anyone now?" she asks me, and then blows smoke up toward the ceiling.

"Um. Not exactly. No. I'm . . . unattached."

Ethan and I exchange a look. Phoebe is all over it. "What? There is a story here. I know there is."

Martin unfolds his arms, waves smoke out of his face, and waits. Phoebe makes a hand motion, as if to say, come on, out with it.

"It's nothing," I say. "Not worth discussing, really."

"Tell them," Ethan says.

So now I have no choice in the matter because Ethan has established that there is, indeed, something to tell.

I don't want to annoy everyone with a long session of "it's nothing," "tell," "really nothing," "*c'mon,* tell," and Phoebe does not seem the type to tolerate that evasive charade. She is Hillary-like in this regard—Hillary is fond of saying, "Well then, why'd you bring it up?" Only in this instance, Ethan brought it up. In any case I am stuck, so I say, "I've been seeing this guy all summer who is getting married in . . . less than two weeks. I thought he might call the wedding off. But he didn't. So here I am. Single once again." I tell my story without emotion, a fact that makes me proud. I am making progress.

Phoebe says, "Usually they wait until they're married to cheat. This bloke has a head start, eh? . . . What's his wife-to-be like? Do you know her?"

"Yeah. You could say that."

"A real bitch, is she?" Phoebe asks solicitously.

Martin clears his throat and waves away her smoke again. "Maybe Rachel doesn't wish to discuss it. Have we considered that?"

"No, *we haven't*," she says to him, and then to me, "Do you mind discussing it?"

"No. I don't mind," I say. Which I think is the truth.

"So? The girl he's marrying—how do you know her?"

"Well . . ." I say. "We've known each other a long time."

Ethan cuts to the chase. "In a nutshell, Rachel is the maid of honor." He pats me on the back and then rests his hand on my shoulder in a congratulatory way. He is clearly pleased to have offered his mates this nugget of transatlantic gossip.

Phoebe isn't fazed. I'm sure she's seen worse trouble. "Bloody mess," she says sympathetically.

"But it's over now," I say. "I made my feelings known. I told him to call the wedding off. And he picked her. So that's that." I try to mask the fact that I am a rejected mess; I think I am doing a good job of it.

"She's moving on marvelously," Ethan says.

"Yes. You don't look a bit ruffled," Phoebe says. "Never would have guessed."

"Should she be crying in her Carling?" Martin asks Phoebe.

"I would be. Remember Oscar?"

Ethan groans, and Martin winces. Clearly they remember Oscar.

Then Ethan tells them that he thinks I should blow off the wedding. Phoebe wants to know more about the bride, so Ethan gives the rundown on Darcy, including some color on our friendship. He even throws in the bit about Notre Dame. I answer questions when directly asked, but otherwise I just listen to the three of them discussing my plight as if I'm not present. It is amusing to hear Martin and Phoebe using Dex's name and Darcy's name and analyzing both in their British accents. People whom they have never met and likely will never meet. Somehow it helps put things in perspective. Almost.

"You don't want to be with him anyway," Phoebe says.

"That's what I tell her," Ethan says.

Martin offers that maybe he'll still call it off.

"No," I say. "He came over to my place the night before I left and told me in no uncertain terms. He's getting married."

"At least he told you outright," Martin says.

"At least," I say, thinking that that was a good thing. Otherwise I would be filled with hope on this visit. I have to give Dex limited credit for telling me face-to-face.

Suddenly Phoebe gets this fabulous idea. Her friend James is newly single, and he loves American women. Why not set that up and see what happens?

"She lives in New York," Martin says. "Remember?"

"So? That's just a minor logistical problem. She could move. He could move. And at the very least, they both will have a good time. Perhaps have a good shag."

"Not everyone sees a shag as therapy," Martin says.

Phoebe raises one eyebrow. I wish I could do that. There are times when it is such an appropriate gesture. "Oh, really? You might want to give it a go, Marty." She turns back to me, waiting to hear my position on this topic.

"A good shag can never hurt," I say, to win favor with Phoebe.

She runs her hands through her tousled hair and looks smug. "My point precisely."

"What're you doing?" Ethan asks, as Phoebe retrieves her cell phone from her purse.

"Calling James," she says.

"Fucking *hell*, Pheebs! Put your mobile down," Martin says. "Have some tact."

"No, it's okay," I say, fighting against my prudish instincts. "You can call him."

Phoebe beams. "Yeah. You boys stay out of this one."

So the next night, thanks to Phoebe, I am eating Thai food on a blind date with James Hathaway. James is a thirty-year-old freelance journalist. He is nice-looking, although Dexter's opposite. He is on the short side, with blue eyes, light hair, and even paler eyebrows. Something about him reminds me of Hugh Grant. At first I think it's just the accent, but then I realize that like Hugh, he has a certain flippant charm. And like Hugh, I bet he's slept with plenty of women. Maybe I should let him add me to his List.

I nod and laugh at something James just said, a wry comment about the couple next to us. He's funny. It suddenly occurs to me that maybe Dex is not very funny. Of course, I've always subscribed to the notion that if I want to laugh out loud, I'll watch a *Seinfeld* rerun, that I don't need to date a stand-up comic, but I contemplate revising my position. Maybe I *do* want a funny guy. Maybe Dex is lacking some crucial element. I try to run with this, picturing him as humorless, even boring. It doesn't really work. It's hard to trick yourself like that. Dex *is* funny enough. He is perfect for me. Other than the small, bothersome part about him marrying Darcy.

I realize that I have missed what James has been going on about, something about Madonna. "Do you like her?" he asks me.

"Not especially," I say. "She's okay."

"Usually Madonna elicits a stronger response. Usually people love her or hate her . . . Ever played that game? Love it or hate it?"

"No. What is it?"

James teaches me the rules of the game. He says that you throw out a topic or a person or anything at all, and both people have to decide whether they love it or hate it. Being neutral isn't allowed. What if you are neutral? I ask. I don't love *or* hate Madonna.

"You have to pick one or the other. So pick," he says. "Love her or hate her?"

I hesitate and then say, "Okay then. I hate her."

"Good. Me too."

"Do you really?" I ask.

"Well, actually, yes. She's talentless. Now you do one."

"Um . . . I can't think. You do another one."

"Fine. Water beds."

"So tacky. I hate them," I say. I'm not on the fence with that one.

"I do as well. Your turn."

"Okay . . . Bill Clinton."

"Love him," James says.

"Me too."

We keep playing the game as we finish our wine.

As it turns out, we both hate (or at least hate more than we love) people who keep goldfish as pets, Speedos, and Ross on *Friends*. We both love (or love more than we hate) Chicken McNuggets, breast implants (I lie here, just to be cool, but am surprised that he does not lie in the other direction—maybe he fears that I have them), and watching golf on television. We are split on rap music (I love; it gives him headaches), Tom Cruise (he loves; I still hate for dumping Nicole), the royal family (I love; he says he's a republican, whatever that means), and Las Vegas (he loves; I associate it with craps, dice-rolling, Dex).

I think to myself that I like (I mean, love) the game. Being extreme. Clear-cut. All or nothing. I do Dex in my mind, flip-flopping my decision twice—hate, love, hate, love. I remember that my mother once told me that the opposite of love isn't hate, it's indifference. She knew what she was talking about. My goal is to be indifferent to Dex.

James and I finish our dinner, decide to skip dessert, and go back to his place. He has a nice flat—larger than Ethan's—full of plants and cozy, upholstered furniture. I can tell that a woman recently moved out. To this point, half of the bookshelf is bare. The whole left side. Unless they kept their books segregated all along, which is doubtful, he has pushed all of his to one side. Maybe he wanted an exact percentage of how much more empty his life is without her.

"What was her name? Your ex?" I ask gingerly. Maybe I shouldn't be bringing her up, but I'm sure he assumes that Phoebe told me his situation. I'm sure she filled him in on mine as well.

"Katherine. Kate."

"How are you doing?"

"A bit sad. More relieved than anything. Sometimes downright euphoric. It's been over a long time."

I nod, as if I understand, although my situation could not be more different. Maybe Dex and I saved ourselves years of effort and pain if we were only going to end up like James and Kate anyway.

"And you?" he asks.

"Phoebe told you?"

I can tell that he is considering a fib, and then he says, "More or less . . . yes . . . How are you?"

"I'm fine," I say. "It was a short-lived situation. Nothing like your breakup."

But I don't believe my words. I have a flashback to July Fourth and feel a wave of pure, intense grief that catches me off guard with its intensity. I panic, thinking I'm going to cry. If James asks another thing about Dex, I will. Luckily, serious conversations seem not to be James's thing. He asks if he can get me something to drink. "Tea? Coffee? Wine? Beer?"

"A beer would be great," I say.

As he leaves for the kitchen, I breathe deeply and force Dex from my mind. I stand and survey the room. There is only one photograph in view. It is of James with an attractive, older woman who appears to be his mother. I wonder how many photographs of Kate and James were uprooted with the breakup. I wonder if he threw them away or saved them. That fact can tell you a lot about someone. I wish that I had a few photos of Dex. I have none of us together, only a few of him with Darcy. I'm sure I'll have a lot more after the wedding. Darcy will force me to order some, maybe even give me one in a frame, as a wedding keepsake. How will I ever get through it?

James returns with linen cocktail napkins, two beers poured into mugs, and a small glass bowl of mixed nuts. All nestled neatly on a square pewter tray. Well trained by Kate.

"Thanks," I say, sipping one of the beers.

We sit close to each other on the couch and talk about my job, his writing. It's not perfectly comfortable, but not horrible. Probably because we are in a dead-end situation. There will be no second date, so there is no pressure to perform. No expectations. We will never have to deal with that awkward period after all the getting-to-know-you topics are covered, the lulls in conversation that usually come on the second date, at which point both people must decide whether to fight their way through to the comfort zone or throw in the towel. Of course, Dex and I didn't have to deal with that. Another great thing about Dex. We were friends first. *Don't think about Dex. Think about now, being here with James!*

James leans in and kisses me. He uses a little too much tongue—working it in frantic circular motions—and his breath smells vaguely of cigarettes, which is odd because he didn't smoke this evening. Maybe he had one in the kitchen. I kiss him back anyway, faking enthusiasm. I even moan softly at one point. I don't know why.

How many times will I have to endure kissing someone for the first time? Although Darcy says she will miss this element of single life, I have no fondness for it. Except for my first real kiss with Dex, which was absolute magic. I wonder if James is thinking about Kate as much as I am thinking about Dex. After a reasonably long time, James's hand drifts up my shirt. I do not object. His touch is not altogether unpleasant, and I think, why not? Let him sample an American breast.

After a half hour of minor-to-significant groping, James asks me to spend the night, says that he doesn't want to sleep with me—well, he does, he says, but he won't try. And I almost agree, but then I learn that James has no saline solution. I can't sleep in my contact lenses, and I left my glasses at home. So that is that. It seems amusing that James's 20/20 vision prevents me from a potentially promiscuous move.

We kiss for a bit longer, listening to his Barenaked Ladies CD. The songs remind me of graduating from law school, dating Nate, being dumped by Nate. I hear the lyrics and remember the sadness.

Songs and smells will bring you back to a moment in time more than anything else. It's amazing how much can be conjured with a few notes of a song or a solitary whiff of a room. A song you didn't even pay attention to at the time, a place that you didn't even know had a particular smell. I wonder what will someday bring back Dex and our few months together. Maybe the sound of Dido's voice. Maybe the scent of the Aveda shampoo that I've been using all summer.

Someday being with Dex will be a distant memory. This fact makes me sad too. It's like when someone dies, the initial stages of grief seem to be the worst. But in some ways, it's sadder as time goes by and you consider how much they've missed in your life. In the world.

As James walks me back to Ethan's flat, he turns to me and says, "Do you want to go to Leeds Castle with me tomorrow? Ethan too?"

"What's Leeds Castle?" I ask, realizing that it's probably like asking what the Empire State Building is.

"It's a castle that was a Norman stronghold and a royal residence for six medieval queens. It's really quite lovely. There's an open-air theater nearby. It is a bit touristy, but you are a tourist after all, aren't you?"

I am beginning to notice that Brits put a little question tag at the end of every statement, looking for affirmation.

I give it to him. "I *am* a tourist, yes."

Then I tell him that Leeds Castle sounds perfect. Because it does sound nice. And because everything I do, every person I meet, puts a certain distance between Dex and me. Time heals all wounds, particularly if you pack a bunch of stuff into that time.

"Ask Ethan what he thinks about it. And call me." He writes his phone number on the back of a gum wrapper I find in my purse. "I'll be around."

I thank him for a nice night. He kisses me again, his hand on the back of my neck.

"Snogging someone new right after a big breakup. Love it or hate it?" he asks.

I laugh. "Love it."

James smirks. "I concur."

I unlock Ethan's door, wondering if James is lying too.

The next morning Ethan stumbles bleary-eyed into the kitchen, where I am pouring myself a glass of pulp-free orange juice.

"So? You in love with James?"

"Madly."

He scratches his head. "Seriously?"

"No. But it was fun."

I realize that I can't even recall exactly what James looks like. I keep picturing this guy from my Federal Income Tax class in law school instead. "He wants to meet up with us today. Go to some palace or castle together."

"Hmmm. A palace or castle in England. That narrows it down."

"Leeds or something?"

Ethan nods. "Yeah, Leeds Castle is nice. Is that what you want to do?"

"I don't know. Why not?" I say.

It seems like a waste of time and a lot of effort to make more conversation with James, but I call him anyway, and we all end up going to Leeds Castle for the day. Phoebe and Martin come too. Apparently all of Ethan's friends make their own work schedules because none of them seem to think twice about taking off on a random Wednesday. I think of how different my life is back in New York, with Les looming over me, even on the weekends.

It is a warm day, nearly hot by London standards. We explore the castle and grounds, have a picnic lunch in the grass. At one point, Phoebe asks me, loud enough for everyone to hear, if I've taken a shine to James. I look at James, who rolls his eyes at Phoebe. Then I smile and tell her, in the same volume, that he is quite nice, if only he lived in New York. I figure, what does it hurt to compliment him? If he genuinely likes me, he'll be happy to hear it. And if he doesn't, he will feel safe because of the distance.

"So why don't you move to London?" she asks. "Ethan says you positively despise your job. Why not move here and find something? It would be a nice change of scenery, wouldn't it?"

I laugh and tell her that I can't do that. But it occurs to me, as we sit by a peaceful lake and admire the fairy-tale castle in the English countryside, that I could, in fact, do exactly that. Maybe the thing to do after you roll the dice—and lose—is simply pick them up and roll them again. I imagine handing Les my letter of resignation. It would be incredibly satisfying. And I wouldn't have to deal with seeing Dex and Darcy on a regular basis. I wonder how a good therapist would characterize the move—as running away or creating a fresh, healthy start?

On my last night in London, Ethan and I are back at his favorite pub, which is starting to feel like my local. I ask Ethan what he thinks of the idea of my moving to London. Within fifteen minutes he has me all moved into his neighborhood. He knows of a flat, a job, and several guys, if James isn't ideal, all of whom have straight, white teeth (because I have commented on the Brits' poor dental work). He says do it. Just do it. He makes it sound so simple. It *is* simple. The seed is more than just planted. It is growing and sprouting a tiny bud.

Ethan continues. "You should get away from Darcy. That toxic friendship . . . It's unhealthy. And it's only going to be more destructive when you have to see them after the wedding."

"I know," I say, pushing a fry through mushy peas.

"And even if you stay in New York, I think it's *essential* that you pare back that friendship. It's not even a real friendship if she only wants to beat you."

"It's not as malicious as you make it sound," I say, wondering why I am defending her.

"You're right. It's not just for the sake of defeating you. I think she just respects you so much that she wants to beat you to win your respect . . . You'll note that she's not going out of her way to show up Annalise. It's just you. But sometimes I think you get sucked into it, and your whole dynamic becomes more about competing than true friend-ship." He gives me a knowing, parental look.

"You think that I like Dex for the same reason—to compete with Darcy. Don't you?"

He clears his throat and dabs his napkin to his lips, replaces it to his lap. "Well? Is it possible?" he asks.

I shake my head. "No way. You can't trick yourself into the feelings I have. Had," I say.

"Okay. It was just a theory."

"Absolutely not. It was the real deal."

But as I fall asleep that night in Ethan's bed (he insisted on taking the couch all week), I wonder about this theory of his. Is it possible that the thrill I felt when I kissed Dex had more to do with the titillation of being bad, breaking rules, having something that belonged to Darcy? Maybe my affair with Dex was about rebelling against my own safe choices, against Darcy and years of feeling deficient. I am disturbed by the idea, because you never like to think that you are a slave to these sorts of sub-liminal pulls. But at the same time, the idea consoles me. If I liked Dex for these reasons, then I don't love him after all. And it should be a whole lot easier for me to move on.

But the next day, as Ethan takes the tube with me to Paddington Station, I know, again, that I really do love Dex, and probably will for a very long time. I buy my ticket for the Heathrow Express. The board tells us that the next train will depart in three minutes, so we walk to the designated platform. "You know what you're doing, right?" he asks protectively.

For a second, I think he is asking me about my life, then I realize he is only inquiring about travel logistics. "Yes. This goes straight to Heathrow, right?"

"Yeah. Just get out at Terminal Three. It's easy."

I hug Ethan and thank him for everything. I tell him that I had a wonderful time. "I don't want to leave."

"Then move here . . . I really think you should do it. You have nothing to lose."

He is right; I do have nothing to lose. I'd be leaving nothing. A depressing thought. "I'll think about it," I say and promise myself I will keep thinking about it once I get home, rather than falling blindly into my old routine.

We hug one last time, and then I board my train and watch Ethan wave at me through the tinted train window. I wave back, thinking that there is nothing like old friends.

I arrive at Terminal Three and go through the motions of checking in, going through security, and waiting to board. The flight feels endless, and although I try, I can't sleep at all. Despite my week of distraction, I don't feel much better than I did on the flight over. Even the aerial views of New York City, which usually charge me with anticipation and excitement, don't do a thing for me. Dex is amid those buildings. I liked it better when the Atlantic Ocean separated us.

When the plane lands, I make my way through passport control, baggage, and customs to find a long cab line. It is meltingly hot outside, and as I get in my cab, I discover that the air-conditioning is barely blowing through the vent into the backseat.

"Could you make it cooler back here, please?" I ask my driver, who is smoking a cigarette, an offense which could fetch him a $150 ticket.

He ignores me and lurches us sickeningly sideways. He is switching lanes every ten seconds.

I ask him again if he will please turn the air up. Nothing. Maybe he doesn't hear me over his radio. Or maybe he doesn't speak English. I glance at my Passenger Bill of Rights. I am entitled to: a courteous, English-speaking driver who knows and obeys all traffic laws . . . air-conditioning on demand . . . a radio-free (silent) trip . . . smoke- and incense-free air . . . a clean trunk.

Maybe the trunk is clean.

See? It's all about low expectations.

The backseat keeps getting hotter, so I roll down the window and endure the dirty wind whipping my hair around my face. Finally I am home again. I pay my not-so-courteous cabbie the flat rate from JFK, plus toll and tip (even though the placard also states that I may refuse to tip if my rights weren't complied with). I heave my roller bag out of the backseat.

It is five-thirty. By this time on Saturday, Darcy and Dex will be married. I will have already helped Darcy into her gown and wrapped the stems of her calla lilies with my lace handkerchief, her something borrowed. I will have already assured her a thousand times that she has never looked so beautiful, that everything is just right. I will have already walked down the aisle toward Dexter without looking at him. Well, trying not to look at him, but maybe catching a fleeting look in his eyes, a mixture of guilt and pity. I will have endured that painful thirty seconds of watching Darcy, in all of her glory, walk toward the altar, as I hold Dexter's platinum band in my sweaty palm. In six days, the worst will be over.

"Hello there, Ms. Rachel!" José says as I close the cab door. Then he says to someone in the lobby, "She's back!"

I stiffen, expecting to see Darcy with her wedding folder, ready to bark demands my way. But it is not Darcy waiting for me in my lobby, in the lone leather wing chair.

twenty-three

It is Dex. He stands as I stare at him. He is wearing jeans and a gray "Hoyas" T-shirt. He is tanner than when I left. I resent his healthy glow and his placid expression.

"Hi," he says, taking a step toward me.

"Hi." I freeze, feeling my posture become perfect. "How did you know when I was getting home?"

"Ethan gave me your flight details. I found his number in Darcy's address book."

"Oh . . . What do you want? What are you doing here?" I ask. I don't mean to sound bitter, but I know that I do.

"Let me come up. I have to talk to you," he says quietly, but urgently. José is still beaming, perfectly clueless.

I shrug and push the arrow for the elevator. The ride up is endless, quiet. I look at him as he waits for me to exit first. I can tell by his expression that he is here to reapologize. He can't stand being the bad guy. Well, I will not give him the satisfaction. And I will not be patronized. If he goes down that road of telling me again how sorry he is, I will cut him off. Maybe even tell him about James. I will say that I am fine, that I will be at the wedding, but after that, I want minimal contact with him, and that I expect him to cooperate. *Make no mistake about it,* I will say, *our friendship is over.*

I turn the key in my lock and open the door. Entering my apartment is like opening a hot oven, even though I remembered to put my shades down. My plants have all wilted. I should have asked Hillary to water them. I turn on my air conditioner and notice that it won't operate on high. Whenever it gets above ninety-five, there is a deliberate citywide brownout. I miss London, where it's not even necessary to own an air conditioner.

"Brownout," Dex says.

"I can see that," I say.

I breeze by him and sit on my couch, cross my arms, try to raise one eyebrow as Phoebe did. Both rise together.

Dex sits beside me without asking first. He tries to take my hand, but I pull it away.

"Why are you here, Dex?"

"I just called it off."

"What?" I ask. Surely I heard him wrong.

"The wedding is off. I—I'm not getting married."

I am stunned, remembering the first time I heard that people pinch themselves when they think they're dreaming. I was four years old and took the concept literally, pinching my arm hard, as if maybe I was still two years old and had dreamed up the second half of my life. I remember feeling relieved that my skin hurt.

Dex continues, his voice steady and quiet. He stares at his balled fists in his lap as he talks, only glancing at me between sentences. "The whole time you were gone, I was going crazy. I missed you so much. I missed your face, your scent, even your apartment. I kept replaying everything in my head. All of our time together, all of our talks. Law school. Your birthday. July Fourth. Everything. And I just can't imagine never being with you again. It's that simple."

"What about Darcy?" I ask.

"I care about her. I want her to be happy. I saw marrying Darcy as the right thing to do. We've been together for seven years and most of the time we've been pretty happy. I didn't want to hurt her."

I don't want to hurt her either, I think.

He continues. "But that was before you. And I just can't marry her feeling this way about you. I can't do it. I love you. And this is only the beginning . . . If you still love me."

There is so much I want to say, but somehow I am speechless.

"Say something."

I force a question from my lips. "Did you tell her about us?"

"Not about us. But I told her that I wasn't in love with her and that it wasn't fair to marry her."

"What did she say?" I ask. I need to know every detail before I can believe this is real.

"She asked if there was someone else. I told her no . . . that it just didn't feel right between us."

"How is she?"

"She's upset. But mostly she's just upset about the damn wedding and what people are going to think. I swear that is what bothers her the most."

"Where is she now?" I ask. "She hasn't left me any messages."

"She went to Claire's, I think."

"I'm sure she thinks that you'll change your mind."

I am thinking this too. He will change his mind and when he does, it will be all the more cruel.

"No," he says. "She understands that I mean it. I called my parents and told them. And she and I are calling her parents together tonight. She says she wants me to tell them . . . and then we'll call everyone else." There is a catch in his voice, and for a second I wonder if he might cry.

I say that I'm sorry. I don't know what else to say. I can't digest this information quickly enough. I want to kiss him, to thank him, to smile. But I can't. It doesn't seem appropriate.

He nods, runs his hands through his hair, and then returns them to his lap. "It's hard, but I feel this tremendous load lifted. It's the right thing."

He looks at me, and I hold his gaze before I kiss him. As his arms encircle me, I think, *This is real.* Then I slowly relax into him, feeling happy and whole for the first time in what feels like forever. There was always a deep calm missing before, even during our July Fourth weekend together. We now have time. All kinds of time. Maybe even forever.

I wonder what it will be like without Darcy in the picture. Will making love be different? I am about to find out because Dex is unbuttoning my shirt. My heart is pounding as we move over to my bed, where we undress.

"I missed you, Rachel," he says. I can feel his heart beating against mine.

And then José interrupts, buzzing me, once, twice. I go to answer him, assuming that it is a package or dry cleaning, or something that he forgot to tell me about. I will tell him that I will get whatever it is later. But it is not a package. It is Darcy. And she has heard my voice over the intercom.

"Tell her I will be right down!" I say.

"Already on her way up!" José practically sings the news. Clearly he has no idea that Darcy's arrival means that my first guest and I are screwed. Then again, maybe he does know. Maybe doormen, even the ones who pretend to be your friend, secretly delight in any tenant drama.

"Oh shit!" I say, standing up and looking around. "She's coming up! Shit!"

Dex is calm, puts his boxers back on. He walks swiftly over to my linen closet and opens the door, carrying his jeans and T-shirt. The shelves line the closet the whole way to the bottom. No good.

"Get in the other one. The other closet!" I point, frantic and wild-eyed.

He walks around the corner and opens my other closet. There is room in this one. He crouches next to my hamper, holding his clothes. I shut the closet door just as I hear her knock.

"Coming!" I shout.

I throw my underwear back on and open the door. "Sorry. I was just changing."

"Omigod. Thank God you're back," she says.

I ask her what's wrong before I realize that she looks and sounds fine. No bloodshot eyes, no running mascara, no dejected gaze. Darcy moves into my apartment as I babble that I just arrived home and wanted to change into something more comfortable. I put on a pair of shorts and a T-shirt.

She still says nothing.

"So. Six days to go. You must be going crazy!" I laugh nervously. "Well, I'm here to help now. At your service. To help with any last-minute details for your wedding."

"There isn't going to be a wedding." She sniffs.

"What?" I gasp, widen my eyes, step toward her. Right as I am about to offer my full sympathy, I remember that I'm not supposed to know who called it off. So I ask.

"It was mutual."

"Mutual?" I ask, my voice louder.

I lead Darcy over to my bed and sit down. The closet is next to the bed. I want Dex to hear everything. *Mutual?* Dex said he did it. If it were mutual, or if she said it first, then perhaps it doesn't mean quite as much as I thought it did. Of course, I will still be happy. But I want this choice to be Dex's. Now I want to be the reason.

"Well. Technically Dexter was the one. He told me this morning that he couldn't go through with it. That he doesn't think he loves me." She rolls her eyes and smiles an ironic smile. I wish that Dex could see the look on her face. She no more believes that he doesn't love her than she believes that I could be capable of hiding a half-naked Dex in my closet.

"You're kidding me? This is crazy. How do you feel?"

Darcy looks down at her feet. *Now* she will start to cry. And I will comfort her and tell her that it will all be okay. Then I will suggest that we go for a little walk. Get some fresh air, even though it is disgustingly humid outside. Maybe I will suggest dinner. Her choice. A burger and fries now that there is no dress to fit into.

But still, Darcy does not cry. She takes a deep breath. "Rachel . . . I have something to tell you." Her voice is calm. She is not following the "I've just been dumped" script. Something is going on. For a second I think that she is going to tell me that she knows everything, that she understands, that true love must prevail, and that she sees clearly that Dex and I should be together.

"Yeah?" I ask, confused.

"This is very hard for me to tell you. Even harder than when I got into Notre Dame," she continues.

This is the first time she has brought up Notre Dame since college—which is crazy, considering my recent revelation. The conversation is definitely not making sense. Maybe she is going to confess that she, too, got rejected. That all her life she has been competing with me. And that she is finally acknowledging defeat.

"Do you remember when I told you about losing my ring?"

"Yeah?"

"How I lost it in my colleague's apartment?"

Now I am really confused. Dex must be even more confused. I am glad that I never told him how she really lost her ring. He canceled the wedding even without that information.

"How I hooked up with that guy and lost the ring?"

It's like a *Three's Company* episode where Jack and Chrissy are talking, and Janet is hiding somewhere listening to the conversation, full of misunderstandings and double meanings. I remember the close-ups of Janet's face, shocked and indignant. But there is no confusion here in my studio. There is only one meaning, and Dex is getting it right: she hooked up with someone else. *Why didn't you tell me?* he will ask me, perhaps accusatorily. *It would have made everything so much easier*, he will say. I will tell him that I didn't think it was right to sway him. Maybe it will make me look noble, and Darcy all the more wrong for him.

"Well, I didn't really hook up with a guy from work." She speaks slowly, enunciating every syllable.

"You didn't lose your ring?"

Is she about to confess to insurance fraud?

"The guy I was with wasn't a guy from work. It was someone else."

"Who was it?"

"It was Marcus," she says.

"Marcus?" I am floored.

"Your Marcus. Yes."

Of course. My Marcus. The Marcus I had to fly across the Atlantic to get over.

"Do you hate me?" she asks soulfully. "Please say something."

"You were with Marcus the day you lost your ring? You lost it in his apartment?" I am clarifying for myself and Dexter.

She nods. Then there is a fleeting second when she looks at me sideways—a brightening in her eyes, a slight upward movement in the corners of her mouth. She is enjoying this. This is her moment to shock. Shock and shine. Win again.

I give her what she wants. Pretend to be defeated. The gracious loser again.

"So you slept with him?" I keep my voice just south of accusatory, on the hurt side.

"Yes."

"More than once?"

"Yes," she whispers so softly that I know Dex can't hear her answer.

So I ask loudly and clearly, "You did?"

"Yes," she says.

I pretend to digest it all. Actually I am digesting it all. But on a level unknown to Darcy. "So," I say. "So."

I don't ask for further explanation, but she gives it to me anyway. "It all started over the July Fourth weekend. We came back from the Talkhouse, loaded. And one thing led to the other."

"July Fourth?" I ask.

This keeps getting better.

"Yes, but he felt terrible. And we swore that it would never happen again. Only we were totally into each other. It was intense . . . We just couldn't keep apart. We started to meet for lunch and sometimes after work. We felt awful every time because of Dex, and because of you. But then it would happen again and again . . . Do you hate me?"

I am at a crossroads. I am not sure how to play it. What would Ethan advise? Pretend to fly into a rage? *Yes, I hate you. Get out. Get out!* That would be one way to go. Or a soft, dejected, *How can I hate you? You are my best friend.* Or perhaps, *I don't know what to think. I need time.*

While I contemplate my response, she says she has something else to tell me. Something big.

"There's more?"

"Yes. There's more." Her voice sounds fragile, but her expression gives her away. She is definitely enjoying this.

I stare at my feet. "Go on."

"I am a few days late for my period. And you know that I'm always on a perfect twenty-eight-day schedule." She is touching her stomach fondly. It is still completely flat.

My own stomach lurches. "You're pregnant?"

"I think so. Yeah."

I am afraid to ask who the father is. If it is Dex, all of this might be taken back from me.

"I took a test . . . it was positive."

"Positive means you're pregnant?"

"Yes. Two pink lines. Yes, I'm pregnant."

I hold my breath, pray, make a deal with God. Never will I ask for anything else, if only . . . "Who is the father?" The question fills the room, circles over us, under the closet door.

"Marcus."

I exhale, feeling light-headed with relief. "Are you sure?"

"Yes. Positive. Dex and I haven't had sex since before my last period. Ages ago."

"Does he know?"

"Who? Marcus?"

"Yeah. Does Marcus know?"

"Yes. But Dex doesn't. Not yet."

He does now.

"I wanted to talk to you first."

I nod, still taking it all in. "So what are you going to do?"

"What do you mean?"

"Are you keeping it?"

"Yes. I want to have it." She rubs her stomach in small circular motions. "I want to marry Marcus and have his baby. I know it sounds crazy, but it just feels so right."

"Are you sure Marcus wants to get married?"

"Positive."

"Do you think Dex suspects anything?" I ask quietly. For some reason, I don't want him to hear this question.

"No. But to be honest, I think he sensed how distant I've been. That's probably why he called it off. You know, he said he didn't love me . . . because he felt that I had turned away from him first."

"I see."

"I'm shocked at how calm you are. Thank you for not hating me."

"Yeah . . . I don't hate you."

"I hope Dex takes it as well. At least as far as Marcus goes. He's going to hate him for a while. But Dex is rational. Nobody did this on purpose to hurt him. It just happened."

And right when I think that this story is winding up as neatly and tightly as a *Three's Company* episode, with its get-out-of-jail-free ending, I see Darcy stare at something behind me. By the look on her face, I think that Dex has emerged from his hiding place. I turn around, fully expecting to see him. But no, the door is still closed. I face Darcy again. She is still staring behind me, her expression stony and trancelike.

And then she asks, "Why is Dexter's watch on your nightstand?"

I follow her eyes again. Sure enough, his watch is most definitely on my nightstand. Dexter's watch. My nightstand. There is no way out. At least not one that I can think of.

I shrug and stammer that I don't know. If there were any doubt before this moment as to my ability to think on my feet, that is cleared up now. I mumble, "Oh, it's not his watch. I have one like it . . . I bought it in England." My voice is shaking. I am a complete mess, a dying calf in a hailstorm.

Darcy leaps from my bed and grabs the watch from my nightstand, flipping it over and reading the inscription. " 'All my love. Darcy,' " she says. Then she looks at me with pure hatred, demonstrating how I should have reacted to her Marcus news.

"What the fuck?" she asks. It is a cold, hard question. Her eyes narrow. "What the fuck!" she screams again, but this time it is a statement. Which means that I don't have to answer.

I stand as she pushes roughly past me into the bathroom. I follow her as she whips the shower curtain violently to the side. Only two tan Aveda bottles, a pink plastic razor, and a dwindling bar of soap.

I begin formulating a story: Dex came over to tell me about the break-up. He took his watch off, to woefully read the engraving. He was beside himself with grief. I comforted him briefly, at which point he left to wander in the park, alone.

But it is too late for explanations. The thirty-second window for explaining is over. Darcy's long, skinny fingers are gripping my closet doorknob.

"Darcy, don't," I say, clearly indicating that her ex-fiancé is behind door number two. I stand in the way, my back against the door.

"Move!" she bellows. "I know he's in there!"

I move, because what else am I supposed to do? She is right. We all know that he is in there. But as she opens the door, part of me actually thinks that Dex will have found a way to fold himself more neatly and tightly into a back corner of my closet. Or maybe he got out, somehow fled during the four seconds that Darcy and I stood gridlocked in my bathroom. Or maybe he miraculously found a secret opening in the back as in *The Lion, the Witch, and the Wardrobe*.

But no, he is there, crouched right where I last saw him, holding his jeans and his shirt, wearing striped navy boxers, staring up at us. He unfolds himself and stands upright.

"You liar!" Darcy screams, thrusting her finger into his chest.

He ignores her and dresses calmly, putting one foot into his jeans and then the other. The sound of his zipper is loud in the room.

"You lied to me!"

"You have got to be kidding me," Dex says, finding the armholes in his T-shirt. His voice is low and restrained. "Fuck you, Darcy."

Darcy's face grows red and she is spitting as she yells, "You said there was nobody else in the picture! And you're *fucking* my best friend!"

I whimper her name like a broken record. "Darcy. Darcy. Darcy."

She ignores me, staring at Dex. I wait for him to defend us, cast a spin on the facts, tell her that there has been no fucking. Nothing at all until today, when he came over to seek comfort. But Dex says calmly, "Isn't that a bit of the pot calling the kettle black, Darce? You and Marcus, huh? Having a baby? I guess congratulations are in order."

I expect her to make a statement about loyalty and love and friendship. I expect her to accuse us of doing it first. But she only looks at me and then Dex and then says that she knew it all along, and that she hates us both very much. And that she always will. She walks over to the door.

"Oh, Darcy?" Dex says.

"What?" She shouts the word, but the look in her eyes is needy, expectant.

"May I have my watch back, please?"

She hurls the evidence overhand at him. Clearly it is meant to strike and hurt him. But her aim is bad and it ricochets off my wall, skating across the parquet back to her feet, inscription up. She looks at it and then at me.

"And you! I never want to see you again! You are dead to me!"

She slams the door and is gone.

twenty-four

Darcy wastes no time in getting her version of the story out. Starting with José, apparently. On our way out of the building, minutes after Darcy's departure, we pass my doorman. For once, he is not grinning. Failing in the gatekeeping function is the stuff that can get a doorman fired. He looks worried.

"Hi, José," Dex and I say in unison.

"Aw, man, I'm really sorry I let her up," he says. "I, uh, didn't know . . . you know . . ."

"No. Not at all," I say. "Don't worry, José."

"Did she give you an earful?" Dex asks cheerfully, as if the whole thing were just a crazy little mix-up instead of a life-defining moment for at least four people.

José has tacit permission to smile again. "Uhh . . . you could say I got an earful. Heh, heh. But don't worry." He laughs. "I don't believe what she said about you . . . not most of it, anyway."

He slaps hands with Dex as though they are old pals, which I guess they are becoming. I walk Dex to the corner. He is going home to salvage as many belongings as he can fit into his luggage—we both believe that Darcy is a slash-and-burn kind of girl, fully up to the task of taking scissors to his wardrobe.

"I'll be back as soon as I can," he says.

I nod.

"And you're sure it's okay if I stay with you for a few days?"

He has asked me the question three times now.

"Of course. Stay as long as you want," I say, thinking that now he not only wants me, but he *needs* me too. It is a good feeling to be needed by Dex.

We stand facing each other in the street for a moment before Dex flags a cab and leans down to kiss me. Without thinking, I turn my head to give him a cheek. Then I remember that we no longer need to hide. I turn my face again, and our lips meet in daylight.

I return to my apartment in a state of semishock. I feel as if I should do something ceremonious. Write in my journal, which has been untouched for months (I could never bring myself to write about Dex, just in case something happened to me). Dance around my apartment. Cry. Instead I focus on the mundane, what I am good at. I shower, unpack, water my plants, open my mail, drag two fans out of my closet and plug them in near my bed, and eat a couple of stale Fig Newtons.

Dex returns an hour later with his full array of tan Hartmann luggage and two black Nike gym bags, all stuffed haphazardly with clothes, shoes, papers, toiletries, even some framed photographs. "Rescue mission accomplished," he says. "She wasn't home."

I survey the bags. "How did you haul all that stuff over here so fast?"

"It wasn't easy," he says, wiping sweat from his brow. His gray T-shirt is wet around the pits and across his chest.

"You can hang your suits in the front closet," I say, still focusing on the practical, unable to absorb everything, although the presence of Dex's belongings is helping with that.

"Thanks." He shakes out a few dark suits and white shirts and looks at me. "Don't be alarmed. I'm not moving in."

"I'm not alarmed," I say, as I watch him hang his clothes. Although in truth, I am filled with sudden trepidation. *What next? What now?* I never planned on this—the temporary living arrangement, the end of my friendship with Darcy, the strange and sudden change in the status quo. "I just can't believe it."

He puts his arms around me. "What can't you believe?"

"Everything. Any of it. Us."

I close my eyes just as my phone rings. I jump. "Shit. You think it's her?" I am almost afraid of Darcy, of what she will do.

"I doubt it. She's off with Marcus, I'm sure."

I answer it.

"Is this true?" my mother asks, in a panic. "What I hear from Mrs. Rhone? Say it's not so, Rachel. *Please tell me!*"

"That depends on what you heard." I choose my words carefully, and then mouth to Dex that it is my mother.

He makes a face and grabs the arm of my sofa as though he is bracing for a meteor to fall into my apartment. I'd prefer a meteor to this conversation.

"She tells me that Dex canceled the wedding?"

"That is correct."

"And that you are somehow *involved* with Dex? . . . I told her there must be some mistake, but she was sure. She's very upset. Your father and I were speechless."

"Mom, it is complicated," I say, an admission by any measure.

"Ra-*chel*. How *could* you?" She has never sounded more disappointed in me. All of my hard work, accomplishments, years of being a good daughter—it is all down the drain. "Darcy is your oldest friend in the world! How could you?"

I tell my mother that perhaps she would like to hear my side of the story before she casts judgment. I didn't think you needed law school to have the "innocent before proven guilty" concept down.

She says fine, please go on. I can see her shaking her head, pacing in the kitchen, waiting for an explanation, although none could ever suffice.

I am too mad to tell her anything. How can she take Darcy's side over mine before she even hears a thing from my mouth? "I'm not in the mood to discuss it with you," I say. Then I add, "Or Dad." Because I know she will use him as the ultimate weapon, just as she did when I was a child. "Wait until your father gets home," an oft-heard threat to many children, wasn't employed with the same meaning in our house. It was a threat to tarnish my reputation as Daddy's perfect little girl. One stern look from my father was worse than any punishment, and my mom knew it.

"Your father is in the garage, absolutely beside himself," she says, wavering between shrill and calm. "I don't think he could talk even if you wanted to speak to him. Did Darcy or Dr. and Mrs. Rhone cross your mind once?"

When I fell in love? No, they didn't! Neither did your bridge club, nor my third-grade teacher!

"Mom, it's not your life. Or Dad's . . . Look, I have to go."

I say good-bye and hang up before she can speak again. Let her be sorry when she learns that Darcy is having someone else's child. Let her do the math, subtract the months back to August. Maybe then she will phone me and apologize and toss out another one of her favorites—*People in glass houses . . .*

I hang up and contemplate phoning Annalise, getting to her before the spin doctor does. But I don't want to burden an expectant mother with this tale.

"So I gather that the news made its way west?" Dex asks me.

"Yup. Mrs. Rhone called my mom."

"That's bullshit," he says. "Darcy is *pregnant* with another man's baby! Did she share that part with the old neighborhood?"

"Clearly not."

"Think I should call Mrs. Rhone?"

"No . . . Let's just keep a low profile before everything shakes out. Screw them all."

"You're right," he says, and slams his fist into his palm. "Darcy! She's *fucking* unbelievable."

"I know," I say.

We are both quiet. I feel uneasy. For a fleeting second, I worry that maybe Ethan's theory could be right—that I only wanted Dex to beat Darcy, and now that I have him, I'm not sure what to do. But no, there is an unmistakable feeling of love surging beneath the layers of anxiety. It will just take some time for us to be normal again. Which is ironic, because we've never really *been* normal.

"Should we order dinner?" Dex asks, breaking the silence.

"I'm not really hungry. I think I might just go to bed," I say, even though it's only eight o'clock. "I'm feeling pretty jet-lagged. Besides, it's too hot to eat."

I think he knows the real reason I can't eat. "I'm not hungry either," he says.

I watch Dex as he listlessly tidies his belongings and finds his shaving kit. Then he showers while I brush my teeth, lock up the apartment, and climb into bed. My mind is working overtime, struggling to send a clear message to my heart. I hate feeling so much and yet being unable to categorize my dominant emotion. Am I mostly happy? Sad? Scared? I don't know. I think of Ethan. How surprised he will be. Spineless Dex isn't so spineless after all. Then I think of James. Was I kissing him when Dex was formulating a way to be with me? Should I feel guilty? Should I tell Dex?

Then I think about the four of us: Marcus was disloyal to Dex. I was disloyal to Darcy. Dex was disloyal to Darcy. Only Darcy did something to two people, to me and to Dex. She is the only one who was doubly disloyal. I think of my girl in the jury box. She is triumphant, pointing out this fact, telling Chanel Suit, "I told you so."

I watch Dex towel off, put on white boxer briefs, and walk toward me. He is beside the bed. I move over, taking his side. Maybe we will switch sides, our way of commemorating the change in our relationship, acknowledging its new legitimacy.

He switches off my lamp, and finds me under the sheets. His arm moves around me. Then he kisses my ear twice. But neither of us initiates anything more. Perhaps he, too, is contemplating the hugeness of what has happened.

"Good night, Dex," I say.

"Good night, Rachel."

For a long time, I listen to Dex breathe. When I am pretty sure he is asleep, I say his name softly.

"Yeah?" he answers, still wide awake.

"Are you okay?" I ask.

"Yes . . . Are you?"

"Yeah," I say.

Then I hear him make a noise. It sounds like crying at first. Then I realize with relief that he is laughing.

"What?"

"You." He imitates me. "'I bought the watch in London.'" He laughs harder.

I allow one small smile. "I couldn't think!"

"That was apparent."

"You're the one who left it on the nightstand."

"I know . . . Shit. I remembered it as soon as you let her in the apartment. Then I thought she might not see it. Then I heard the question . . . and was waiting for you to come up with something good. 'I bought it in London' wasn't what I had in mind. I was in there shaking my head in the dark, like, the jig is up, baby."

"Maybe it's for the best . . . Everything is out in the open now. She would have found out eventually."

I don't really mean this, though. Eventually would have been better than today. And maybe she never would have known that anything was going on this summer, while she was still with Dex.

"Yeah. An engagement and two friendships *finito*," he says.

I wonder which part Dex is sadder about. I hope that it is Marcus. "You really think you won't ever be friends with Marcus again?"

He sighs and adjusts his pillow. "I seriously doubt that we'll be grabbing a few beers anytime soon."

"Are you sad about that?"

"What's the point of being sad?" he says. "We're here now."

I want to tell Dex that I love him, but decide that it can wait until tomorrow. Or maybe even the next day.

Twelve hours later I am on my way to Hillary's office when Les ambushes me in the hall. "Good. You're back. I need to see you."

Yes, I had a lovely vacation. Thanks for asking.

"Now?" I ask.

"Yeah, now. Come to my office. Pronto."

I want to tell him that normal people do not use the word "pronto," unless they're kidding or playing Scrabble.

"I need to get a pad," I say. So much for easing into my old routine.

Seconds later I am sitting in his office, which smells of onions, furiously scribbling instructions for three new assignments. All time-consuming, mind-numbing, bullshit first-year research projects, riddled with false deadlines. It is my punishment for taking a vacation. He talks at me in aggressive run-on sentences, his tone condescending whenever I dare to interrupt to ask a pertinent question. As I study his bulbous nose, I am thinking that I don't need this. I remember how free I felt in London, being away from this place. I fantasize about quitting, getting another job in New York, or maybe moving to London with Dex. I will resign in mid-assignment. Leave Les high and dry. Tell him what I think of him on my way out the door. Tell him that he really should do something about those hairs in his nose.

After an hour of being held prisoner (he even takes three lengthy phone calls during my sentence), I am released. I head straight for Hillary's office. It is a war zone, worse than usual. Documents clutter up every square inch of floor space. Both of her guest chairs are covered with papers, and her desk is piled high with folders, treatises, and old newspapers.

She spins around in her chair. "Hey, you! Have a seat. Tell me about your trip!"

"Where do I sit?"

"Oh. Just dump that stuff anywhere . . . So how was England? How are you?"

"Well. Let's see," I say, as I clear off one of her chairs. "England was great. I made some progress in getting over Dex . . . But then I came home last night and learned that Dex called off the wedding after all."

She gives me a quizzical look. "He called it off? For sure?"

I tell her the whole story. She hangs on every word, and in the end she looks like one of those people who answers the door to find Ed McMahon with a big check and a television crew. She covers her eyes with her palms, laughs, shakes her head, and then comes around her desk and gives me a hug. I am not surprised by her reaction. I didn't expect her to get any of the subtleties—the fact that Darcy and I are no longer friends, the fact that my parents are upset, and that word of my treason is traveling at the speed of light all over Indiana.

"Well, that is awesome, awesome news. I owe Dex an apology. Shit. I really had him written off as another womanizing pretty boy."

"He's not like that."

"I can see that . . . I'm so happy for you."

I smile. "So what has been going on here?"

"Oh, not too much. Same old shit . . . Julian and I had our first big fight."

"What? Why?"

She shrugs. "We got into an argument that escalated."

"About what?"

"It's a long story . . . but basically we have this full-disclosure rule. No secrets whatsoever."

"Secrets about your past?"

"Yeah. And just anything. So anyway, he was talking to this girl at a party, and he introduced me to her. And the three of us had a big conversation about all sorts of things. And later that night, I asked him how he knew her . . . He told me he met her two summers ago . . . and that was it. Then kidding around, I said, 'Did you sleep with her?' And he just looked at me . . . He had!"

I don't try to hide my smirk. "You got mad because of an ex-girlfriend?"

"No. I got mad that I had to ask him if he slept with her. He should have brought it up first! That wasn't in the spirit of our agreement. So of course, I start to worry that he isn't as honest as he seems."

I shake my head. "You're a trip. So stubborn."

"He is too . . . We haven't talked in almost twenty-four hours."

"Hill! C'mon, you have to call him!"

"Not a chance. His finger isn't broken."

Her words and posturing are bold and defiant, but for the first time I see her as vulnerable. Something in her eyes gives her away.

"I think you should call him," I say. "This is silly."

"Maybe it is. I don't know—and then again, maybe we're not as perfect for each other as I first thought."

"Because of one fight?"

She shrugs.

"Hillary, I think you're overreacting. Pick up the phone and call him."

"No way," she says, but I can tell from the way that she glances at her phone that she is weakening.

I think to myself that when you're in love, sometimes you have to swallow your pride, and sometimes you have to fight to keep your pride. It's a balance. But when the relationship is right, you find that balance. I am sure that Hillary and Julian will.

When I return to my office, I dial up my only other unconditional ally. I know that Ethan won't miss the complexity of the situation, perhaps because he knows Darcy better than Hillary does. In some ways, he understands her better than I do.

He does not interrupt once as I tell him the story. "So did you suspect that? When Dex called asking about my flight?" I ask him after I finish.

"I hoped . . . That's why I gave him your information. But I didn't ask any questions. I just crossed my fingers."

"You hoped? Really? I thought you didn't like him."

"Aw, I just didn't like him for jerking you around all summer. I like him now. I mean, I actually *admire* him now. He didn't take the easy way out. I really respect him for that. So many people just let the engagement tide roll over them and get washed up into the hurrah of a wedding. Dex did the stand-up thing. I give him credit. I really do."

"I'm just glad he was the one to call it off, instead of Darcy making the decision for him after the pregnancy discovery. Then I'd always wonder, you know, if I was just the runner-up."

"So how do you feel?" His question is gentle, and I know he is asking about Darcy.

I tell him that I am happy, of course, but that I am devastated to lose Darcy, to realize that she will no longer be a part of my life. Although in truth, I don't think it has fully sunk in yet. "It's just not a fairy-tale ending," I say.

"No. It never is."

"And it all happened so fast. One minute I thought I was going to a wedding on Saturday. Next minute, no wedding, I get to be with Dex, Darcy is with Marcus, and she's having his baby. It is nuts."

"I can't believe she's pregnant . . . Shit! That girl!" he says, with some amusement.

"I know."

"Never a dull moment."

"I know . . . I think I might miss that about her."

"Yeah. Well. Maybe she'll come around."

"Maybe."

He clears his throat. "Although I doubt it."

"Me too."

"So Marcus and Darcy." He whistles. "That's certainly a twist."

"Yeah. You're telling me! But I can actually see it now . . . It makes sense. She was always railing at Dex for working too hard. And Marcus takes the opposite approach."

"And you're more like Dex."

"Yeah. So much for the 'opposites attract' theory."

"Sounds like everything may have worked out for the best. Except for James, that is. He'll be wrecked."

"Yeah, right," I say.

"And of course, I'm a little disappointed."

"Why?"

"I thought you were going to move here."

"Who knows? Maybe I still will."

"And leave Dex?"

"He can come with me."

"Think he'd do that?"

"Maybe."

Maybe he loves me enough to follow me anywhere.

I hang up and start my assignments, signing on to Lexis, skimming and highlighting case after case. I keep checking my e-mail and waiting for the phone to ring. At first I think it's Dex I am waiting for, but then I pick up the phone and call him, and still have an empty, aching feeling. That's when I realize that it's Darcy I am waiting to hear from. I expect her to call at any minute. Yell at me, say mean things to me, but talk to me. Communicate in some way. But my phone does not ring as I work through lunch. Around four o'clock, I finally get a call.

"Rachel?" Claire bellows into the phone.

I roll my eyes. "Hello, Claire."

"What in the world is going on?" she asks, pretending to be foggy on the exact details. I know that Darcy has put her up to this call. Maybe she is even listening to me now. It is pure, classic Darcy. I think of all the times in high school when she cajoled Annalise and me to undertake such assignments.

I do not take the bait. I briskly tell Claire that I have to be in court in thirty minutes, and don't have time to discuss the situation with her.

"Okay . . ." Her disappointment at the lack of juice is palpable. "Call me back when you can . . ."

Don't hold your breath.

"I just feel terrible for both of you. You've been friends for too long . . ." Her voice is dripping with false empathy. She is relishing her new position as Darcy's best friend. I picture them wearing the "best friend" necklaces. If anyone could bring them back into fashion, it is Darcy and Claire.

"Uh-huh." I give nothing away. Claire will be the one worthwhile casualty of my split with Darcy. I don't have to pretend to like her anymore.

It is Wednesday night. Three days after the confrontation. Dex and I are curled up in bed when the phone rings. This will be Darcy, I think. I both crave and fear her call, a call that might never come.

I answer nervously. "Hello?"

"Hi, Rachel."

It is Annalise. She sounds tired, and for a second I think it's because Darcy has dragged her into our saga. I prepare myself for a tentative, mousy, Annalise-style lecture. Instead I hear a baby unleash a wail in the background.

"It's a girl," Annalise says. "We had a girl!"

Darcy was right, is my first thought, before I become weepy. I am overcome by the news. My friend is a mother. "Congratulations! When?"

"Two hours ago. Eight-forty-two. She's six pounds, four ounces."

"What's her name?"

"Hannah Jane . . . Jane after you and Darcy."

Our friendship with Annalise and the middle name Jane are two of the only things that Darcy and I still share.

"Annalise, I am *so* touched," I say. "You never told me you were considering Jane."

"It was a surprise."

"Hannah Jane. It's a beautiful name."

"She *is* beautiful."

"Does she look like you?"

"I don't know. My mom says so. But I think she has Greg's nose and feet."

"I can't wait to see her."

"When are you coming home?"

"Soon. I promise."

For a moment I think that Darcy actually refrained from dragging Annalise into our scandal. But then she says, "Rachel, you and Darcy have to make up. She called me last night. I was going to call you but my water broke right afterward."

Leave it to Darcy to induce labor.

"Whatever happened—it can be fixed, right?" she asks.

I want to ask her what she knows, what Darcy reported. But obviously I am not going to pull a Darcy. This is not the time to delve into our soap opera. "Right," I say. "Don't worry about that . . . This is much more important. You have a baby!"

"I have a baby!"

"You're somebody's mother!"

"I know. It feels so nice."

"Did you tell Darcy yet?"

"Not yet. I'm calling her now . . ."

I think to myself that if Darcy discovers that Annalise called me first, she'd be even more enraged. "Yeah, I know you have a lot of calls to make. Tell Greg I said congratulations. And your parents . . . I'm so happy for you."

"Thank you, Rachel."

"I love you, Annalise." I feel the tears welling up.

"I love you too."

I hang up, overcome with emotion that I don't fully understand. I knew the baby would be here sooner or later. Yet I am still blown away by the reality of what has just happened. Annalise is a mother. She has a daughter. It is a moment that she, Darcy, and I talked about as little girls. Now Darcy is having a baby too, and I won't even get a phone call from her when it happens. I will hear about it secondhand. It wasn't supposed to be like this. Annalise's baby makes the rift all the more tragic. Never has good news seemed so bittersweet.

"Annalise had her baby?" Dex asks, as I get back into bed.

"Yes. A girl . . . Hannah Jane," I say, and then proceed to burst into tears. It is my first hard cry in front of Dex. The kind where your face gets all puffy and ugly and wet, and you can't breathe through your nose, and you feel the pressure building in your head. I know that I am going to have a migraine in the morning if I don't stop. But I can't. I turn away from Dex and sob. Dex keeps his arms tightly wrapped around me and makes consoling sounds, but he doesn't ask me why, exactly, I am crying. Maybe because he understands. Maybe because he knows that it's not the time for questions. Whatever his reason, I have never loved him more. I let him kiss me. I kiss him back. We make love for the first time post-Darcy.

twenty-five

The following day Darcy finally contacts Dex. He calls me straightaway with the update.

My heart jumps. I haven't let go of the fear that Darcy will somehow get Dex back, undo her pregnancy, change her mind, rewrite history. "Tell me everything," I say.

Dex summarizes their conversation, or rather, Darcy's demands: he is to get the remainder of his stuff out in seven days—during business hours—or it will be put out with the trash. He must leave the keys. The furniture will stay, except for the table that he "bullied" her into buying, the dresser he "brought into the joke of a union," and the "ugly lamps" from Dexter's mother. He must pay her parents back for her gown and the nonrefundable wedding deposits, which include just about everything, in excess of fifty thousand dollars. She will handle return of the wedding gifts. She is keeping the diamond ring he replaced only days before their breakup.

I wait for him to finish, and then say, "Pretty skewed terms, don't you think?"

"You could say that."

"You guys should split the wedding costs," I say. "She's pregnant with someone else's child!"

"Tell me about it."

"And technically, the ring is yours," I say. "Under New York law. You weren't married. She only gets the ring if you're married."

"I don't care," he says. "It's not worth fighting about."

"And what about the apartment? It was your apartment first."

"I know . . . but I don't even want it now. Or the furniture," he says.

I am glad that he feels this way. I can't imagine ever visiting him in Darcy's old apartment.

"Where do you think you'll move?"

"I'm just going to live with you."

"Really?"

"It was a joke, Rach . . . We'll hold off on that for a little while."

I laugh. "Oh . . . yeah. Right."

I am a little disappointed, but mostly relieved. I feel as if I could live with Dex immediately, but I want it to work, to be right, and I see no reason to rush things.

"I called a few places this morning . . . I found a one-bedroom on East End. I might just hit the bid."

Hit the bid. Just as you did with me.

"How is Darcy going to pay the rent alone?" I ask, more curious than concerned, although there is a part of me that is worried about her well-being, how she will manage, what will happen to her and her baby. I can't turn off the caring-about-Darcy switch after a lifetime of looking out for her.

"Maybe Marcus is moving in with her," Dex says.

"Do you think?"

"They *are* having a baby together."

"I guess so. But do you really think they're going to get married?" I ask.

"I have no idea. I don't care," he says.

"You haven't heard from Marcus, have you?"

"Nope . . . Have you?"

"No."

"I don't think we will."

"Are you going to call him?"

"Maybe someday. Not now."

"Hmm," I say, thinking that maybe I will someday call Darcy too. Although I can't imagine it happening for a very long time. "So was that it? Did she mention me?"

"No. I was shocked. Tremendous restraint for her. She must be getting some big-time coaching."

"No kidding. Restraint is not Darcy's style."

"But enough about her," Dex says. "Let's forget about her for a while."

"I will if you will," I say.

"So what do you want to do tonight?" Dex asks. "I think I'll be able to get out of here at a decent hour. What's your schedule?"

It is five now, and I have at least four hours of work remaining, but I tell him that I can leave whenever.

"Should we meet at eight?"

"Sure. Where?"

"Let's make dinner together at your place. We've never done that."

"Okay, but . . . I can't cook," I confess.

"Yeah you can."

"No, I really can't. Truly."

"Cooking is easy," he says. "You just sort of figure it out as you go along."

I smile. "I can do that."

After all, that is pretty much what I have been doing lately.

An hour later, I leave my office for home, not caring if I run into Les. I take the elevator down to the lobby, then two escalators down to Grand Central Station. I pause to admire the gorgeous main terminal, so familiar and so associated with work that I somehow miss its beauty on a daily

basis. I study the marble staircases at either end of the concourse, the
arched windows, the dramatic white columns, and the soaring turquoise
ceiling painted with constellations. I watch the people, mostly in business
attire, moving in every direction toward trains bound for the suburbs,
subways reaching every corner of New York, and a multitude of exits to
the busy city streets. I glance at the clock in the center of the terminal,
take in its intricate face. Six o'clock exactly. Early.

I walk slowly toward Grand Central Market, a food hall comprised of
individual stalls selling gourmet treats, located on the east end of the concourse. I have often passed through this corridor with Hillary, buying the
occasional chocolate truffle to go with our Starbucks coffee. But this evening, I am on a greater mission. I move from stall to stall, filling my arms
with delicacies: hard and soft cheeses, freshly baked breads, Sicilian green
olives, Italian parsley, fresh oregano, a perfect Vidalia onion, garlic, oils and
spices, pasta, red, green, and yellow produce, an expensive chardonnay, and
two exquisite, restaurant-perfect pastries. I exit the corridor on Lexington,
passing by a makeshift cab line and throngs of harried Midtown com-
muters. I decide to walk home. My bags are heavy, but I don't mind. I'm
not carrying a briefcase full of law books and cases; I'm carrying dinner for
Dex and me.

When I get back to my apartment, I tell José to let Dex up when he
arrives. "No need to buzz for him anymore."

He winks and hits the elevator door for me. "Aww. So it's serious!
That's good stuff."

"Good stuff," I echo, smiling.

A moment later, I am arranging groceries on my counter—more food
than my apartment has ever seen at one time. I put the chardonnay in the
refrigerator, play some classical music, and search for the recipe book that
my mother gave me at least four Christmases ago, a book I have never
before used. I flip through the glossy, pristine pages, finding a salad and
pasta recipe that contains my approximate ingredients. Then I find an
apron—another virginal gift—and set about peeling, chopping, and
sautéing. I glance at the book for guidance, but I do not follow every
instruction precisely. I substitute parsley for basil, skip the drained capers.

Dinner will not be perfect, but I am learning that perfection isn't what matters. In fact, it's the very thing that can destroy you if you let it.

I change my clothes, selecting a white sundress with pink embroidered flowers. Then I set the table, begin to boil water for our pasta, light candles, and open the bottle of chardonnay, filling two glasses, sipping mine. I glance at my watch. Ten minutes to spare. Ten minutes to sit and reflect on my new life, on how it feels to be Dex's legitimate, only love. I settle into my couch, close my eyes, inhale deeply. Good smells and beautiful, clear notes fill my apartment. Peace and calm rush over me as I process the lack of any bad feelings: I'm not jealous, I'm not worried, I'm not scared, I'm not lonely.

Only then do I acknowledge that what I am feeling might actually be true happiness. Even joy. Over the past several days, when I have felt the beginning of this emotion tugging at my heart, it has crossed my mind that the key to happiness should not be found in a man. That an independent, strong woman should feel fulfilled and whole on her own. Those things might be true. And without Dex in my life, I like to think I could have somehow found contentment. But the truth is, I feel freer with Dex than I ever did when I was single. I feel more myself with him than without. Maybe true love does that.

And I do love Dex. I have loved him from the very beginning, back in law school, when I pretended to myself that he wasn't my type. I love him for his intelligence, his sensitivity, his courage. I love him wholly and unconditionally and without reservation. I love him enough to take risks. I love him enough to sacrifice a friendship. I love him enough to accept my own happiness and use it, in turn, to make him happy back.

There is a knock at my door. I stand to open it. I am ready.

twenty-six

It is Saturday, what would have been Darcy and Dexter's wedding night. I am with Dex at 7B, the bar where it all began, back on the eve of my thirtieth birthday. We are sitting in our same booth. It was my idea to come back here. I suggested it in a playful way, but in truth I felt a strong need to return and revisit the way I felt before it all began. I want to ask Dex if he feels at all wistful on this night, but instead I tell him a Les story—how he blasted me in the hall for not using jump cites in a draft brief.

"That guy sounds like a miserable human being . . . Can't you work with someone else?"

"No. I'm his personal slave. He monopolizes my time, and now other partners won't ask me to work on their matters because Les inevitably pulls rank and leaves them high and dry. I'm trapped."

"Do you ever think about changing firms?"

"Sometimes. I just started revising my résumé today, in fact. Maybe I'll leave the law altogether, although I have no idea what I would do."

"You'd be good at so many things," Dex says, with a loyal nod.

I add "supportive" to the growing list of things I love about him.

I consider telling him about my idea of temporarily moving to London, wondering if he'd come with me. But tonight isn't the time for that conversation. We have enough going on right below the surface. He has to be thinking about her, thinking, *What if?* How could he not be?

"I'm going to play some songs on the jukebox," I say.

"Want me to come with you?"

"No. I'll be right back."

"Pick some good ones, all right?"

I give him a "have some faith in me" look. I walk over to the jukebox, past a couple smoking in silence. I slip a nappy five into the slot. The machine spits the bill back out at me three times, but I am patient, smoothing out the edges on my thigh before it finally takes. I flip through the songs, considering each one carefully. I choose songs that Dex likes, and songs that remind me of our first summer together. And of course I play "Thunder Road." I glance over at Dex, who appears to be deep in thought. He suddenly looks over at me and waves, a silly smile on his face. I go sit back down, sliding in beside him. As he drapes his arm around me, a wave of emotion leaves me breathless.

"Hi there," he says, in a way that tells me he knows exactly how I'm feeling.

"Hi," I say back, in the same tone.

We are one of those couples I used to watch, thinking to myself that I'd never be on the inside of something so special. I remember reassuring myself that it probably looked nicer than it actually was. I am happy to be wrong about that.

I smile up at Dex, my gaze resting on a tiny patch in his left eyebrow, a blank space where perhaps three or four hairs should be.

"What happened there?" I ask, reaching to touch his brow. My fingertips rest lightly on the spot.

"Oh, that. It's a scar. I fell playing hockey when I was a kid. Hair never grew back there."

I wonder why I never noticed it before and realize that I never knew he played hockey. There is so much that I still don't know about Dex. But now we have time. Endless time stretches before us. I study his face for other discoveries until he laughs self-consciously. I laugh too, and then our smiles fade away in unison. We drink our Newcastles in easy silence.

"Dex?" I say, after a long while.

"Yeah?"

"Do you miss her?"

"No," he says firmly. His breath is warm in my ear. "I'm with you. No."

I can tell that it is the truth.

"You aren't at all sad tonight?"

"Not one bit." He kisses the side of my head. "I'm a lot of things right now. But sad isn't one of them."

"Good," I say. "I'm glad."

"How do *you* feel? Do *you* miss her?" he asks.

I consider his questions. I am mostly happy, but with a soupçon of nostalgia, thinking of all that I have shared with Darcy. Until now, our lives have been so intertwined—she has been my frame of reference for so many events. Beating drums in the bicentennial parade. Tying yellow ribbons around the tree in my backyard during the hostage crisis. Watching the *Challenger* fall from the sky, the wall come down in Germany, the Soviet Union dissolve. Learning of Princess Diana's death, of John F. Kennedy Jr.'s fate. Grieving after September 11. All of it was with Darcy by my side. And then there is our personal history. Memories only we share. Things not another soul would ever understand.

Dex watches me intently, waiting for my answer.

"Yes," I finally say, somewhat apologetically. "I miss her. I can't help it."

He nods as though he understands. I wonder why I miss her and Dex does not. Perhaps it is because I've known her so much longer. Or maybe it's the very nature of a friendship versus an intimate relationship. When you are in a relationship, you are aware that it might end. You might grow apart, find someone else, simply fall out of love. But a friendship isn't a zero-sum game, and as such, you assume that it will last forever, especially an old friendship. You take its permanence for granted, which might be the very thing so dear about it. Even as Dex rolled those double sixes, I never imagined the end of Darcy and me.

I picture her now, wondering what she is feeling at this very moment. Is she as melancholy as I am? Or just angry? Is she with Marcus or Claire? Or is she alone, flipping sorrowfully through our high school yearbook and old pictures of Dex? Does she miss me too? Will we ever be friends again, tentatively agreeing to meet for lunch or coffee, rebuilding one small step at a time? Maybe she and I will laugh about that crazy summer when one of us was still twenty-something. But I doubt it. This one can't be bridged, particularly if Dex and I stay together. Our friendship is likely over forever, and maybe that is for the best. Maybe Ethan was right, and the time has come to stop using Darcy as a measuring stick for my own life.

I run my hands along my glass, marveling at how much has changed in such a short time. How much I have changed. I was a parent-pleaser, a dutiful friend. I made safe, careful choices and hoped that things would fall into place for me. Then I fell in love with Dex and still viewed it as something happening to me. I hoped that he would make things right, or that fate would intervene. But I have learned that you make your own happiness, that part of going for what you want means losing something else. And when the stakes are high, the losses can be that much greater.

Dex and I talk for a long time, covering virtually every moment of our summer, chronicling it all—the good and the gory. Mostly we laugh, and only once do I get teary, when we get to the part where he told me he was going to marry Darcy. I tell him how I rolled our dice after he left my apartment. He says he is sorry. I say that he has no reason to be sorry, that he didn't at the time, and certainly doesn't now.

And then, just before midnight, comes that sweet sound of the harmonica, playing slowly at first and then building momentum before Bruce sings, *The screen door slams, Mary's dress waves.*

A smile spreads across Dex's face, his eyes are bright and especially green. He pulls me against his chest and says into my ear, "I'm glad we're not eating cake right now."

"Me too," I whisper.

Dex holds me as we listen to Bruce, the words rich with our meaning:

Hey what else can we do now
Except roll down the windows and let the wind blow back your hair
Well the night's busting open
These two lanes will take us anywhere

It occurs to me that tonight is an ending and a beginning. But for once, I embrace both. The last line of "Thunder Road" fills the bar: *And I'm pulling out of here to win.*

"You want to go now?" I ask Dex.

He nods. "I do."

We stand and walk through the smoky bar, leaving 7B before the next song begins to play. It is a beautiful, clear night with a faint chill in the air. Fall is coming. I take Dexter's hand as we stroll up Avenue B, looking for a yellow cab headed in the right direction.

1. What do you think was the real impetus behind Rachel's decision to sleep with Dex after her birthday party? Was it about her desire to break out of her good-girl persona? Was it about a long-standing resentment toward Darcy? Or was it both?

2. How do you view Dex? How would you describe Dex and Rachel's relationship? What drew them together? Did you root for them to be together? Do you think they have true love?

3. Is anything about Rachel and Darcy's friendship genuine? Do you believe it has changed over time? Why does Rachel defend Darcy against attacks from Ethan and Hillary? Compare and contrast Rachel's friendship with Hillary and Ethan to her friendship with Darcy.

4. Do you think Dex and Darcy would have married if it weren't for Dex's affair with Rachel? Why did he stay with Darcy for so long?

5. How did Rachel's flawed self-image contribute to the dilemma that she faces? What do you see as her greatest weakness?

6. Was Rachel's moral dilemma made easier because of Darcy's personality? Would she have acted on her attraction to Dex if Darcy were a different kind of person and friend? If Rachel had fallen in love with Julian, would she have pursued the same course of action? How does Rachel rationalize her affair with Dex?

7. What risks does Rachel take when she pursues her relationship with Dex? What is the biggest moment of risk for her? How does Rachel grow and change in the novel?

St. Martin's Griffin

8. Disloyalty is a major theme in this novel. How differently do men and women view cheating on a friend? Why is Darcy so indignant when she catches Dex and Rachel together when she has been having an affair of her own?

9. Under what circumstances is it justified to choose love over friendship? How important is it for women to stick together? Have you ever been in a friendship like Darcy and Rachel's?

10. This novel is told from Rachel's perspective. How do you think Darcy would tell the same story? How do you think she would describe Rachel? How do you think she views their friendship?

something blue

For Buddy, always.

And for Edward and George.

acknowledgments

I would like to thank my family and friends for their love and support, especially my parents, who were a great source of strength to me over the past year. Thanks to my agent, Stephany Evans; my editor, Jennifer Enderlin; and my publicist, Stephen Lee, for being so professional, enthusiastic, and kind. Deep gratitude to my loyal triumvirate, Mary Ann Elgin, Sarah Giffin, and Nancy LeCroy Mohler, who read every draft of this book and offered so much valuable insight; thanks for always being there, in big ways and small. Thanks also to Doug Elgin and Brian Spainhour for joining the party late and offering their quality male perspective. To Allyson Wenig Jacoutot for being the best of confidantes. To Jennifer New for her enduring friendship. And to all the readers of *Something Borrowed*, who came to my signings, invited me to their book clubs, or took the time to share their very generous comments. Finally, my biggest and most heartfelt thanks go to my husband, Buddy Blaha, and our twin sons, Edward and George. I love being on your team.

prologue

I was born beautiful. A C-section baby, I started life out right by avoiding the misshapen head and battle scars that come with being forced through a birth canal. Instead, I emerged with a dainty nose, bow-shaped lips, and distinctive eyebrows. I had just the right amount of fuzz covering my crown in exactly the right places, promising a fine crop of hair and an exceptional hairline.

Sure enough, my hair grew in thick and silky, the color of coffee beans. Every morning I would sit cooperatively while my mother wrapped my hair around fat, hot rollers or twisted it into intricate braids. When I went to nursery school, the other little girls—many with unsightly bowl cuts—clamored to put their mat near mine during naptime, their fingers darting over to touch my ponytail. They happily shared their Play-Doh or surrendered their turn on the slide.

Anything to be my friend. It was then I discovered that there is a pecking order in life, and appearances play a role in that hierarchy. In other words, I understood at the tender age of three that with beauty come perks and power.

This lesson was only reinforced as I grew older and continued my reign as the prettiest girl in increasingly larger pools of competition. The cream of the crop in junior high and then high school. But unlike the characters in my favorite John Hughes films, my popularity and beauty never made me mean. I ruled as a benevolent dictator, playing watchdog over other popular girls who tried to abuse their power. I defied cliques, remaining true to my brainy best friend, Rachel. I was popular enough to make my own rules.

Of course, I had my moments of uncertainty. I remember one such occasion in the sixth grade when Rachel and I were playing "psychiatrist," one of our favorite games. I'd usually play the role of patient, saying things like, "I am so scared of spiders, Doctor, that I can't leave my house all summer long."

"Well," Rachel would respond, pushing her glasses up on the bridge of her nose and scribbling notes on a tablet. "I recommend that you watch *Charlotte's Web*. . . . Or move to Siberia, where there are no spiders. And take these." She'd hand me two Flintstones vitamins and nod encouragingly.

That was the way it usually went. But on this particular afternoon, Rachel suggested that instead of being a pretend patient, I should be myself, come up with a problem of my own. So I thought of how my little brother, Jeremy, hogged the dinner conversation every night, spouting off original knock-knock jokes and obscure animal kingdom facts. I confided that my parents seemed to favor Jeremy—or at least they listened to him more than they listened to me.

Rachel cleared her throat, thought for a second, and then shared some theory about how little boys are encouraged to be smart and funny while little girls are praised for being cute. She called this a "dangerous trap" for girls and said it can lead to "empty women."

"Where'd you hear *that*?" I asked her, wondering exactly what she meant by *empty*.

"Nowhere. It's just what I think," Rachel said, proving that she was in no danger of falling into the pretty-little-girl trap. In fact, her theory applied perfectly to us. I was the beautiful one with average grades, Rachel was the smart one with average looks. I suddenly felt a surge of envy, wishing that I, too, were full of big ideas and important words.

But I quickly assessed the haphazard waves in Rachel's mousy brown hair and reassured myself that I had been dealt a good hand. I couldn't find countries like Pakistan or Peru on a map or convert fractions into percentages, but my beauty was going to catapult me into a world of Jaguars and big houses and dinners with three forks to the left of my bone-china plate. All I had to do was marry well, as my mother had. She was no genius and hadn't finished more than three semesters at a community college, but her pretty face, petite frame, and impeccable taste had won over my smart father, a dentist, and now she lived the good life. I thought her life was an excellent blueprint for my own.

So I cruised through my teenage years and entered Indiana University with a "just get by" mentality. I pledged the best sorority, dated the hottest guys, and was featured in the Hoosier Dream Girls calendar four years straight. After graduating with a 2.9, I followed Rachel, who was still my best friend, to New York City, where she was attending law school. While she slogged it out in the library and then went to work for a big firm, I continued my pursuit of glamour and good times, quickly learning that the finer things were even finer in Manhattan. I discovered the city's hippest clubs, best restaurants, and most eligible men. And I still had the best hair in town.

Throughout our twenties, as Rachel and I continued along our different paths, she would often pose the judgmental question, "Aren't you worried about karma?" (Incidentally, she first mentioned karma in junior high after I had cheated on a math test. I remember trying to decipher the word's meaning using the song "Karma Chameleon," which, of course, didn't work.) Later, I understood her point: that hard work, honesty, and integrity always paid off in the end, while skating by on your looks was somehow an offense. And like that day playing psychiatrist, I occasionally worried that she was right.

But I told myself that I didn't have to be a nose-to-the-grindstone soup-kitchen volunteer to have good karma. I might not have followed a traditional route to success, but I had *earned* my glamorous PR job, my fabulous crowd of friends, and my amazing fiancé, Dex Thaler. I *deserved* my apartment with a terrace on Central Park West and the substantial, colorless diamond on my left hand.

That was back in the days when I thought I had it *all* figured out. I just didn't understand why people, particularly Rachel, insisted on making things so much more difficult than they had to be. She may have followed all the rules, but there she was, single and thirty, pulling all-nighters at a law firm she despised. Meanwhile, I was the happy one, just as I had been throughout our whole childhood. I remember trying to coach her, telling her to inject a little fun into her glum, disciplined life. I would say things like, "For starters, you should give your bland shoes to Goodwill and buy a few pairs of Blahniks. You'll feel better, for sure."

I know now how shallow that sounds. I realize that I made everything about appearances. But at the time, I honestly didn't think I was hurting anyone, not even myself. I didn't think much at all, in fact. Yes, I was gorgeous and lucky in love, but I truly believed that I was also a decent person who deserved her good fortune. And I saw no reason why the rest of my life should be any less charmed than my first three decades.

Then, something happened that made me question everything I thought I knew about the world: Rachel, my plain, do-gooding maid of honor with frizzy hair the color of wheat germ, swooped in and stole my fiancé.

one

Sucker punch.

It was one of my little brother Jeremy's pet expressions when we were kids. He used it when regaling the scuffles that would break out at the bus stop or in the halls of our junior high, his voice high and excited, his lips shiny with spittle: *WHAM! POW! Total sucker punch, man!* He'd then eagerly sock one fist into his other cupped palm, exceedingly pleased with himself. But that was years ago. Jeremy was a dentist now, in practice with my father, and I'm sure he hadn't witnessed, received, or rehashed a sucker punch in over a decade.

I hadn't thought of those words in just as long—until that memorable cab ride. I had just left Rachel's place and was telling my driver about my horrifying discovery.

"Wow," he said in a heavy Queens accent. "Your girlfriend really *sucker punched* you good, huh?"

7

"Yes," I cried, all but licking my wounds. "She certainly did."

Loyal, reliable Rachel, my best friend of twenty-five years, who always had my interests ahead of, or at least tied with, her own, had—*WHAM! POW!*—sucker punched me. Blindsided me. The surprise element of her betrayal was what burned me the most. The fact that I never saw it coming. It was as unexpected as a seeing-eye dog willfully leading his blind, trusting owner into the path of a Mack truck.

Truth be told, things weren't quite as simple as I made them out to be to my cab driver. But I didn't want him to lose sight of the main issue—the issue of what Rachel had done to me. I had made some mistakes, but I hadn't betrayed our friendship.

It was the week before what would have been my wedding day, and I had gone over to Rachel's to tell her that my wedding was called off. My fiancé, Dex, had been the first to say the difficult words—that perhaps we shouldn't get married—but I had quickly agreed because I'd been having an affair with Marcus, one of Dexter's friends. One thing had led to another, and after one particular steamy night, I had become pregnant. It was all hugely difficult to absorb, and I knew the hardest part would be confessing everything to Rachel, who, at the start of the summer, had been mildly interested in Marcus. The two had gone on a few dates, but the romance had petered out when, unbeknownst to her, my relationship with Marcus began. I felt terrible the entire time—for cheating on Dex, but even *more* for lying to Rachel. Still, I was ready to come clean to my best friend. I was sure that she would understand. She always did.

So I stoically arrived at Rachel's apartment on the Upper East Side.

"What's the matter?" she asked as she answered the door.

I felt a wave of comfort as I thought to myself how soothing and familiar those words were. Rachel was a maternal best friend, more maternal than my own mother. I thought of all the times my friend had asked me this question over the years: such as the time I left my father's sunroof down during a thunderstorm, or the day I got my period all over my white Guess jeans. She was always there with her "What's the matter?" followed by her "It's going to be all right," delivered in a competent tone that made me feel sure that she was right. Rachel could fix anything. Make me feel better when nobody else could. Even at that moment, when she might have felt disappointed that Marcus had chosen me over her, I was sure she'd rise to the occasion and reassure me that I had chosen the right path, that things happened for a reason, that I wasn't a villain, that I was right to follow my heart, that she completely understood, and that eventually Dex would too.

I took a deep breath and glided into her orderly studio apartment as she rattled on about the wedding, how she was at my service, ready to help with any last-minute details.

"There isn't going to be a wedding," I blurted out.

"What?" she asked. Her lips blended right in with the rest of her pale face. I watched her turn and sit on her bed. Then she asked me who called it off.

I had a flashback to high school. After a breakup, which was always a very public happening in high school, guys and girls alike would ask, "Who did it?" Everyone wanted to know who was the dumper and who the dumpee so that they could properly assign blame and dole out pity.

I said what I could never say in high school because, to be frank, I was never the dumpee. "It was mutual. . . . Well, technically Dexter was the one. He told me this morning that he couldn't go through with it. He doesn't think that he loves me." I rolled my eyes. At that point, I didn't believe that such a thing was possible. I thought the only reason Dex wanted out was because he could sense my growing indifference. The drifting that comes when you fall for someone else.

"You're kidding me. This is crazy. How do you feel?"

I studied my pink-striped jeweled Prada sandals and matching pink toenail polish and took a deep breath. Then I confessed that I had been having an affair with Marcus, dismissing a pang of guilt. Sure, Rachel had had a small summer crush on Marcus, but she had never slept with him, and it had been weeks since she had even kissed him. She just couldn't be *that* upset by the news.

"So you slept with him?" Rachel asked in a loud, strange voice. Her cheeks flushed pink—a sure sign that she was angry—but I plowed on, divulging full details, telling her how our affair had begun, how we tried to stop but couldn't overcome the crazy pull toward each other. Then I took a deep breath and told her that I was pregnant with Marcus's baby and that we planned on getting married. I braced myself for a few tears, but Rachel remained composed. She asked a few questions, which I answered honestly. Then I thanked her for not hating me, feeling incredibly relieved that despite the upheaval in my life, I still had my anchor, my best friend.

"Yeah . . . I don't hate you," Rachel said, sweeping a strand of hair behind her ear.

"I hope Dex takes it as well. At least as far as Marcus goes. He's going to hate him for a while. But Dex is rational. Nobody did this on purpose to hurt him. It just happened."

And then, just as I was about to ask her if she would still be my maid of honor when I married Marcus, my whole world collapsed around me. I knew that nothing would ever be the same again, nor had things ever been as I thought they were. That was the moment I saw Dexter's watch on my best friend's nightstand. An unmistakable vintage Rolex.

"Why is Dexter's watch on your nightstand?" I asked, silently praying that she would offer a logical and benign explanation.

But instead, she shrugged and stammered that she didn't know. Then she said that it was actually *her* watch, that she had one just like his. Which was not plausible because I had searched for months to find that watch and then bought a new crocodile band for it, making it a true original. Besides, even had it been a predictable, spanking-new Rolex Oyster Perpetual, her voice was shaking, her face even paler than usual. Rachel can do many things well, but lying isn't one of them. So I knew. I knew that my best friend in the world had committed an unspeakable act of betrayal.

The rest unfolded in slow motion. I could practically hear the sound effects that accompanied *The Bionic Woman*, one of my favorite shows. One of *our* favorite shows—I had watched every episode with Rachel. I stood up, grabbed the watch from her nightstand, flipped it over, and read the inscription aloud. "All my love, Darcy." My words felt thick and heavy in my throat as I remembered the day I had his watch engraved. I had called Rachel on my cell and asked her about the wording. "All my love" had been her suggestion.

I stared at her, waiting, but she still said nothing. Just stared at me with those big, brown eyes, her always ungroomed brows furrowed above them.

"What the fuck?" I said evenly. Then I screamed the question again as I realized that Dex was likely lurking in the apartment, hiding somewhere. I shoved past her into the bathroom, whipping open the shower curtain. Nothing. I darted forward to check the closet.

"Darcy, don't," she said, blocking the door with her back.

"Move!" I screamed. "I know he's in there!"

So she moved and I opened the door. And sure enough, there he was, crouched in the corner in his striped navy boxers. Another gift from me.

"You liar!" I shouted at him, feeling myself begin to hyperventilate. I was accustomed to drama. I *thrived* on drama. But not this kind. Not the kind of drama that I didn't control from the outset.

Dex stood and dressed calmly, putting one foot and then the other into his jeans, zipping defiantly. There wasn't a trace of guilt on his face. It was as if I had only accused him of stealing the covers or eating my Ben & Jerry's Cherry Garcia ice cream.

"You lied to me!" I shouted again, louder this time.

"You have got to be kidding me," he said, his voice low. "Fuck you, Darcy."

In all my years with Dex, he had never said this to me. Those were my words of last resort. Not his.

I tried again. "You said there was nobody else in the picture! And you're *fucking* my best friend!" I shouted, unsure of whom to confront first. Overwhelmed by the double betrayal.

I wanted him to say, yes, this looks bad, but there had been no fornicating. Yet no denial came my way. Instead he said, "Isn't that a bit of the pot calling the kettle black, Darce? You and Marcus, huh? Having a baby? I guess congratulations are in order."

I had nothing to say to that, so I just turned the tables right back on him and said, "I knew it all along."

This was a total lie. I never in a million years could have foreseen this moment. The shock was too much to bear. But that's the thing about the sucker .punch; the sucker element hurts worse than the punch. They had socked it to me, but I wasn't going to be their fool too.

"I hate you both. I always will," I said, realizing that my words sounded weak and juvenile, like the time when I was five years old and told my father that I loved the devil more than I loved him. I wanted to shock and horrify, but he had only chuckled at my creative putdown. Dex, too, seemed merely amused by my proclamation, which enraged me to the brink of tears. I told myself that I had to escape Rachel's apartment before I started bawling. On my way to the door, I heard Dex say, "Oh, Darcy?"

I turned to face him again. *"What?"* I spat out, praying that he was going to say it was all a joke, a big mix-up. Maybe they were going to laugh and ask how I could think such a thing. Maybe we'd even share a group hug.

But all he said was, "May I have my watch back, please?"

I swallowed hard and then hurled the watch at him, aiming for his face. Instead it hit a wall, skittered across her hardwood floor, and stopped just short of Dexter's bare feet. My eyes lifted from the watch to Rachel's face. "And you," I said to her. "I never want to see you again. You are dead to me."

two

Somehow I managed to make it downstairs (where I gave Rachel's doorman the gruesome highlights), into a cab (where I again shared the tale), and over to Marcus's place. I burst into his sloppy studio, where he sat cross-legged on the floor, playing a melody on his guitar that sounded vaguely like the refrain in "Fire and Rain."

He looked up at me, his expression a blend of annoyance and bemusement. "What's wrong *now*?" he said.

I resented his use of the word *now,* implying that I am always having a crisis. I couldn't help what had just happened to me. I told him the whole story, sparing no detail. I wanted outrage from my new beau. Or at least shock. But no matter how much I tried to whip him into my same frenzied state, he'd fire back with these two points: *How can you be mad when we did the same thing to them?* And, *Don't we want our friends to be as happy as we are?*

I told him that our guilt was beside the point and, *HELL NO, WE DON'T WANT THEM TO BE HAPPY!*

Marcus kept strumming his guitar and smirking.

"What's so funny?" I asked, exasperated. "Nothing is funny about this situation!"

"Well maybe not *ha-ha* funny, but ironic funny."

"There is nothing even *remotely* funny about this, Marcus! And stop playing that thing!"

Marcus ran his thumb across the strings one final time before putting his guitar in its case. Then he sat cross-legged, gripping the toes of his dirty sneakers, as he said again, "I just don't see how you can be so outraged when we did the same thing—"

"It's not the same thing at all!" I said, dropping to the cool floor. "See, I may have cheated on *Dex* with you. But I didn't do anything to Rachel."

"Well," he said. "She and I did date for a minute. We had potential before you came along."

"You went on a few lousy dates whereas I was *engaged* to Dex. What kind of person hooks up with her friend's fiancé?"

He crossed his arms and gave me a knowing look. "Darcy."

"What?"

"You're looking at one. Remember? I was one of Dexter's groomsmen? Ring a bell?"

I sniffed. True, Marcus and Dex had been college buddies, friends for years. But it just wasn't a comparable situation. "It's not the same. Female friendships are more sacred; my relationship with Rachel has been lifelong. She was my very best friend in the world, and you were, like, the very last one stuck in the groomsman lineup. Dex probably wouldn't even have picked you except that he needed a fifth person to go with my five girls."

"Gee. I'm touched."

I ignored his sarcasm, and said, "Besides, you never painted yourself as a saint like she did."

"You're right about that. I'm no saint."

"You just don't go there with your best girlfriend's fiancé. Or ex-fiancé. Period. Ever. Even if a gazillion years elapsed, you still can't go there. And you certainly don't hop in bed with him one day after the breakup." Then I hurled more questions his way: *Did he think it was a one-time thing? Were they beginning a relationship? Could they actually fall in love? Would they ever last?*

To which Marcus shrugged and answered with some variation of: *I don't know and I don't care.*

To which I yelled: *Guess! Care! Soothe me!*

Finally, he caved, patting my arm and responding satisfyingly to my leading questions. He agreed that it was likely a one-time thing with Rachel and Dex. That Dex went over to Rachel's because he was upset. That being with Rachel was the closest thing to me. And as for Rachel, she just wanted to throw a bone to a broken man.

"Okay. So what do you think I should do now?" I asked.

"Nothing you can do," Marcus said, reaching over to open a pizza box resting near his guitar case. "It's cold, but help yourself."

"As if I could eat now!" I exhaled dramatically and did a spread eagle on the floor. "The way I see it is, I have two options: murder and/or suicide. . . . It would be pretty easy to kill them, you know?"

I wanted him to gasp at my suggestion, but much to my constant disappointment, he was never too shocked by my words. He simply pulled a slice of pizza from the box, folded it in half, and crammed it in his mouth. He chewed for a moment, and with his mouth still full, he pointed out that I would be the prime and only suspect. "You'd wind up at a female corrections facility in upstate New York. With a mullet. I can see you now slopping out gruel with your mullet flapping in the prison yard breeze."

I thought about this and decided that I'd vastly prefer my own death to a mullet. Which brought me to the suicide option. "Fine. So murder is out. I'll just kill myself instead. They'd be really sorry if I killed myself, wouldn't they?" I asked, more for shock value than because I was really considering my own death.

I wanted Marcus to tell me that he couldn't live without me. But he didn't take the bait in the suicide game as Rachel had when we were in junior high, and she'd promise that she'd override my mother's classical music selections and see to it that Pink Floyd's "On the Turning Away" was cranked up at my funeral.

"They'd be so sorry if I killed myself," I said to Marcus. "Think they'd come to my funeral? Would they apologize to my parents?"

"Yeah. Probably so. But people move on fast. In fact, sometimes they even forget about you *at* the funeral, depending on how good the food is."

"But what about their guilt?" I asked. "How could they live with themselves?"

He assured me that the initial guilt could be assuaged by any good therapist. So after a few weeknights on a leather couch, the person, once racked with *what ifs*, would come to understand that only a very troubled soul would take her own life, and that one, albeit significant, act of betrayal doesn't cause a healthy person to jump in front of the number 6 train.

I knew that Marcus was right, remembering that when Rachel and I were sophomores in high school, one of our classmates, Ben Murray, shot himself in the head with his father's revolver in his bedroom while his parents watched television downstairs. The stories varied— but, bottom line, we all knew that it had something to do with a fight he'd had with his girlfriend, Amber Lucetti, who had dumped him for a college guy she met while visiting her sister at Illinois State. None of us could forget the moment when a guidance counselor ushered Amber out of speech class to give her the horrific news. Nor could we forget the sound of Amber's wails echoing in the halls. We all imagined that she'd lose it altogether and end up in a mental ward somewhere.

Yet within a few days, Amber was back in class, giving a speech on the recent stock market crash. I had just given my speech on why grocery-store makeup was the way to go—over more expensive makeup—as it all comes from the same big vats of oils and powder. I marveled at Amber's ability to give such a substantive speech, barely glancing at her index cards, when her ex-boyfriend was in a coffin under the frozen ground. And her competent speech was nothing compared to the spectacle she created when making out with Alan Hysack at the Spring Dance, fewer than three months after Ben's funeral.

So if I were striving to destroy Rachel and Dex's world, suicide might not be the answer, either. Which left me with one option: stay on course with my charmed, perfect life. Don't they say that happiness is the best revenge? I'd marry Marcus, have his baby, and ride off into the sunset, never looking back.

*"Hey. Give me a slice after all," I said to Marcus. "I'm eating for two now."

That night I called my parents and broke the news. My father answered and I told him to put Mom on the other extension. "Mom, Dad, the wedding is off. I'm so sorry," I said stoically, perhaps too stoically because they instantly assumed that I was solely to blame for the breakup. Dear ol' Dex would never cancel a wedding the week before it was to take place. My mother turned on her sob switch, wailing about how much she loved Dexter, while my father shouted over her in his "Now, Darcy. Don't be rash" tone. At which point, I dropped the closet-story bomb on them. A rare hush fell over the phone. They were so silent that I thought for a second that we had been disconnected. My father finally said there must be some mistake because Rachel would never do such a thing. I told them I never would have believed it either. But I saw it with my own two eyes—Dex in his boxers in Rachel's closet. Needless to say, I said nothing about Marcus or the baby to my parents. I wanted to have their full emotional and financial support. I wanted them to cast the blame on Rachel, the neighborhood girl who had duped them just as she had duped me. Perfect, trustworthy, good-hearted, loyal, reliable, predictable Rachel.

"What are we going to do, Hugh?" my mother asked my father in her little-girl tone.

"I'll take care of it," he said. "Everything will be fine. Darcy, don't you worry about a thing. We have the guest list. We'll call the family. We'll contact The Carlyle, the photographer. Everyone. You sit tight. Do you want us to come out on our same flight on Thursday or do you want a ticket to come home? You say the word, honey."

My father was in full-on crisis mode, the way he got during a tornado watch or a snowstorm or anytime our declawed, half-blind indoor cat would escape out the back door and dart out into the street, while my mother and I freaked out, secretly delighting in the drama.

"I don't know, Daddy. I just can't even think straight right now."

My dad sighed and then said, "Do you want me to call Dex? Talk some sense into him?"

"No, Daddy. It won't do any good. It's over. Please don't. I have some pride."

"That *bastard*," my mother chimed in. "And Rachel! I just can't believe that little tramp."

"Dee, that's not helping," my father said.

"Well, I know," my mother said. "But I just can't believe that Rachel would do such a thing. And how in the world could Dex *want* to be with *her*?"

"I know!" I said. "There's no way that they're *actually* together, right? He couldn't *really* like her?"

"No. No way," my mother said.

"I'm sure Rachel is sorry," my dad said. "It was a very inappropriate thing to do."

"*Inappropriate* isn't the word for it," my mother said.

My father tried again. "Treacherous? Opportunistic?"

My mother agreed with this assessment. "She probably wanted him the whole time you were with him."

"I know," I said, feeling a fleeting sense of regret that I had let Dex go. Everyone viewed him as such a prize. I looked at Marcus to reassure myself I had done the right thing, but he was eyeing his PlayStation.

"Has Rachel called to explain or apologize?" my dad continued.

"Not yet," I said.

"She will," my mom said. "And in the meantime, you stay strong, honey. Everything will be fine. You're a beautiful girl. You will find someone else. Someone better. Tell her, Hugh."

"You're the most beautiful girl in the world," he said. "Everything's going to be just fine. I promise you."

three

Ironically, it was Rachel who had introduced Dex and me. They were both first-year law students at NYU, and because Rachel insisted that she wasn't in school to date, but rather to learn, she passed her friend Dex, the most eligible man on campus, along to me.

I remember the moment well. Rachel and I were at a bar in the Village, waiting for Dex to arrive. When he walked in, I instantly knew that he was special. He belonged in a Ralph Lauren ad—the man in the glossy ads squinting into the sunlight on a sailboat or bending thoughtfully over a chessboard with a fire roaring in the background. I was sure that he didn't get sloppy, fall-down drunk, that he would never swear in front of his mother, that he used expensive aftershave products—and perhaps a straight-edge razor on special occasions. I just knew that he could enjoy the opera, that he could solve any

Times crossword, and that he ordered fine port after dinner. I swear I saw all of this in one glance. Saw that he was my ideal—the sophisticated East Coaster I needed in order to create a Manhattan version of my mother's life.

Dex and I had a nice conversation that evening, but it took him a few weeks to call and ask me out—which only made me want him more. As soon as he called, I dumped the guy I was seeing at the time, because I was *that* sure that something great was about to be launched. I was right. Dex and I fast became a couple, and things were perfect. *He* was perfect. So perfect that I felt a tiny bit unworthy of him. I knew I was gorgeous, but I sometimes worried that I wasn't quite smart enough or interesting enough for someone like Dex, and that once he discovered the truth about me, he might not want me anymore.

Rachel didn't help matters, because as usual, she seemed to have a way of highlighting my shortcomings, underscoring my apathy, my indifference to topics that she and Dex cared so much about: what was happening in third world countries, the economy, who stood for what in Congress. I mean, the two of them listened to NPR, for God's sake. Enough said. Even the sound of the voices on that station makes my eyes glaze over big time. Never mind the content. So after a few months of exhaustively feigning interest in stuff I cared little about, I decided to come clean with the real me. So one night, as Dex was engrossed in a documentary on some political happening in Chile, I grabbed the remote and switched the channel to a *Gidget* rerun on Nickelodeon.

"Hey! I was watching that!" Dex said.

"I'm so tired of poor people," I said, tucking the remote between my legs.

Dex chuckled fondly. "I know, Darce. They can be so annoying, can't they?"

I suddenly realized that for as much substance as Dex had, he didn't seem to mind my somewhat shallow outlook on the world. Nor did he mind my unapologetic zeal for pursuing quality goods and a good time. Instead, I think he admired my candor, my honesty about where I stood. I might not have been the deepest of gals, but I was no phony.

Bottom line, Dex and I had our differences, but I made him happy. And for the most part, I was a good and loyal girlfriend. Only twice, before Marcus, did my appreciation for the opposite sex spill over into something slightly more—which I think is a pretty admirable record for seven years.

The first minor slip happened a few years ago with Jack, a fresh-faced twenty-two-year-old I met at Lemon Bar one night while having a few drinks with Rachel and Claire, who was my best friend from work, former roommate, and the most well-connected girl on the East Coast. Rachel and Claire were as different as Laura Ingalls and Paris Hilton, but they were both my friends and both single, so we often went out together. Anyway, the three of us were standing at the bar chatting when Jack and his friends clumsily hit on us. Jack was the most outgoing of the group, full of boyish exuberance and charm, talking about his water polo tales from his very recent Princeton days. I had just turned twenty-seven and was feeling a bit tired and old, so I was flattered by young Jack's obvious interest in me. I humored him as the other guys (less cute versions of Jack) worked on Claire and Rachel.

We sipped cocktails and flirted, and as the evening wore on, Jack and his crew wanted to find a livelier venue (proving my theory that the number of times you change bars is inversely proportional to your age). So we all piled into cabs to find some party in SoHo. But, also in youthful fashion, Jack and his boys turned out to have the wrong ad-dress and then the wrong cell phone number of the friend of the friend having the party. They did the whole inept routine where they blame each other: *Dude! I can't believe you lost the shit,* etc. We ended up standing on Prince Street, in the cold, ready to call it a night. Rachel and Claire left first, sharing a cab to the Upper East Side. Jack's friends took off next, determined to find their party. So there Jack and I were alone on the street. I was buzzed, and Jack looked so smitten that I threw him a few harmless kisses. It was no big deal. It really wasn't. At least it wasn't to me.

Of course, eager little Jack called me repeatedly the next day, leaving a multitude of messages on my cell. Eventually, I phoned him back and confessed that I had a serious boyfriend, and that he couldn't call me again. I told him I was sorry.

"I understand," he said, sounding crushed. "Your boyfriend is a lucky guy. . . . If you ever break up with him, give me a call."

He gave me his work, home, and cell number, and I absentmindedly scribbled them on the back of a Chinese take-out menu that I ended up tossing later that night.

"Okay. Great. Thanks, Jack. And sorry again."

As I hung up, I felt a twinge of guilt and wondered why I had kissed Jack in the first place. There hadn't been much of a point. Even in my buzzed state, I had no delusions of real interest. The only thing that went into the calculation was, "Do I want to, at this moment, kiss this boy or not?" and because the answer was yes, I did it. I don't know. Maybe I was bored. Maybe I just missed the early days when Dex seemed to be crazy about me. I fleetingly worried that the thing with Jack was evidence of a problem in our relationship, but then I figured that a kiss was just a kiss. No big deal. I didn't even bother telling Rachel about Jack. It was over—there was no point in watching her mount her high horse as she had done when I cheated on my high school and college boyfriends.

After Jack, I was the portrait of the ideal girlfriend for a long stretch, close to a year. But then I met Lair at a launch party thrown by our PR firm for a new line of hip sportswear called Emmeline. Lair was a gorgeous model from South Africa with caramel-colored skin and eyes so blue they nearly matched the aqua sweatsuit he was wearing.

After he smiled at me twice, I approached him. "So, I have to know," I shouted over the music, "are those fake?"

"What?"

"Your eyes. Are you wearing blue lenses?"

He laughed a melodic South African laugh. "Jeepers, no. They're mine."

"Did you just say *jeepers?*"

He nodded and smiled.

"How quaint." I studied the edges of his corneas just to be sure he was telling the truth. Sure enough, no telltale contact lens lines. He laughed, exposing gorgeous white teeth. Then he extended his hand. "I'm Lair."

"Leah?" I said, sliding my hand into his strong, warm one.

"Lair," he said again, still sounding like *Leah*. "You know, *liar* with the *a* and *i* inverted, right?"

"Oh, Lair. What a cozy name," I said, picturing us both curled up in a little hideaway together. "I'm Darcy."

"Pleasure, Darcy," he said, and then glanced around the party that I had been planning for months. "This is quite an event."

"Thanks," I said proudly. Then I threw out some PR jargon. Something about what a challenge it is to make a client a real standout in today's competitive marketplace.

He nodded then bobbed his head to the bass.

"But . . ." I laughed, giving my long, dark hair a seductive toss. "It's a lot of fun too. I get to meet great people like you."

We kept talking, interrupted at regular intervals by my colleagues and other guests. Fellow model Kimmy, who was wearing pink fleece sweatpants with a navy *69* across her butt and a matching *69* jog bra, sought out Lair repeatedly and snapped pictures of him with her digital camera.

"Smile, honey," she'd say, as I did my best to squeeze into her photos. But despite Kimmy's overtures, Lair never diverted his attention, and our flirting evolved into more serious conversation. We talked about his home in South Africa. I admitted that I knew nothing about his country except that it used to have apartheid before Nelson Mandela was released from prison. As Lair explained more about South African politics, the problem with crime in his hometown of Johannesburg, and the amazing beauty of Kruger National Park, I realized that he was more than just a pretty face. He told me that he was only modeling to pay for school, even tossing out the word *sartorial.*

After the party, Lair and I hopped in a cab together. My intentions were basically pure—I wanted only a kiss on the street, Jack-style. But then Lair whispered in my ear, "Darcy, would you possibly consider joining me back at my hotel?" And I just couldn't help myself. So I went to The Palace with him, convinced that we would only engage in some heavy-duty making out.

And that is pretty much all we did. Then around three in the morning, I stood, dressed, and told him that I really needed to get home. Technically, I could have stayed, as Dex was out of town on a business trip, but somehow falling asleep with a guy made it seem like real cheating. And to that point, I felt that I wasn't a full-fledged cheater. Although in truth I think the threshold test of whether you have cheated is rather clear: if your partner could see a video of the event, would he or she think you had cheated? An alternative test is: if you could see a video of your partner in the identical situation, would you think he or she had cheated? On both counts, I clearly failed. But I had not crossed that bright sex line, and this fact made me proud.

I left a pining Lair that night, and after a few weeks of hot and heavy e-mailing, we gradually stopped talking and then lost touch altogether. The evening started to fade in my mind—and I nearly forgot those incredible eyes until I spotted him, in white boxer shorts, smiling down at me from a billboard in the middle of Times Square. I conjured the details of our tryst, wondering what would have happened if I had broken up with Dex for Lair. I pictured us living in Johannesburg amid elephants and carjackers, and decided, once again, that our relationship was best left at The Palace.

Dex and I got engaged a few months later, and I vowed to myself that I would be true to him forever. So we didn't have a ton in common, and he didn't thrill me every minute. He was still an amazing catch and a good guy to boot. I was going to marry him and live happily ever after on the Upper West Side. Okay, maybe we'd eventually move to Fifth Avenue, but other than such minor tweaking, my life was scripted.

I just hadn't planned on Marcus.

four

For years, I knew Marcus only as Dexter's slacker freshman roommate from Georgetown. While Marcus finished next to last in the class and got stoned all the time, Dex graduated summa and had never tried an illegal drug. But the freshman-roommate experience can be a powerful one, so the two stayed close throughout college and afterward, even though they lived on opposite coasts.

Of course, I never gave his college pal much thought until Dex and I got engaged and his name was thrown out as a groomsman candidate. Dex only had four clear-cut picks, but I had five bridesmaids (including Rachel as maid of honor), and symmetry in the wedding party lineup wasn't a negotiable point. So Dex phoned Marcus and bestowed the honor upon him. After the two yucked it up for a while, Marcus asked to speak to me, which I thought was good form, especially given the fact that we had never met face-to-face. He gave me the standard congratulations with some other remark about promising not to get the groom loaded the night before the wedding. I laughed and told him that I was holding him to that, never imagining that what he should have been promising was not to sleep with me before our wedding.

In fact, I didn't expect to see him at all before the wedding, but a few weeks later he took a new job in Manhattan. To celebrate, I made reservations at Aureole, despite Dexter's insistence that Marcus wasn't a fancy guy.

Dex and I arrived at the restaurant first and waited at the bar for Marcus. He finally walked in sporting baggy jeans, a wrinkled shirt, and at least two days' growth of beard. In short, he wasn't the kind of guy I usually look at twice.

"Dex-*ter*!" Marcus shouted as he approached us and then gave Dex a hearty, man-style hug, clapping him on the back. "Good to see you, man," Marcus said.

"You too," Dex said, gesturing at me with a gentlemanly sweep of his hand. "This is Darcy."

I stood slowly and leaned in to kiss the fifth groomsman on his whiskered cheek.

Marcus grinned. "The infamous Darcy."

I liked being called "infamous"—despite its negative connotations—so I laughed, put my hand to my chest, and said, "None of it's true."

"Too bad," Marcus said under his breath, and then pointed to the statuesque redhead hovering beside him. "Oh. This is my friend Stacy. We used to work together."

I had seen the woman come in at the same time as Marcus, but hadn't thought they were together. Nothing about them matched. Stacy was a total fashion plate, wearing a cropped teal leather jacket and a sweet pair of lizard pumps. As we were led to our table, I shot Dex a dirty look, irritated at him for suggesting that I might want to "tone it down" when I had busted out with my Louis Vuitton white cape and red tartan taffeta bustier. So now I was stuck in an understated black-and-white tweed jacket next to splashy Stacy. I assessed her again, wondering if she was prettier than I was. I quickly decided that I was more beautiful, but she was taller, which annoyed me. I liked being both. Incidentally, I had always believed that every woman wanted to be the most attractive in any group, but once when I admitted my feelings to Rachel, she gave me this blank stare followed by a diplomatic nod. At which point I backtracked somewhat and said, "Well, unless I'm friends with her and then I don't compare."

Fortunately, Stacy's personality wasn't nearly as scintillating as her wardrobe, and I succeeded handily in outshining her. Marcus was extremely entertaining, too, and kept our table in stitches. He wasn't an outright jokester, but was full of wry observations about the restaurant, the fancy food, and the people around us. I noticed that whenever Stacy laughed at him, she'd touch his arm in a familiar way, which made me fairly certain that if they weren't dating, they had at least hooked up. By the end of the night, I reevaluated Marcus's looks, upgrading him several notches. It was a combination of Stacy's obvious interest in him, his sense of humor, and something else. Something was just sexy about him: a gleam in his brown eyes and the cleft in his chin, which made me think of Danny Zuko in *Grease* (that first beach scene in the movie was my idea of romance for years).

After dinner, as Dex and I were cabbing back to the Upper West, I said, "I like Marcus. He's really funny and has surprising sex appeal."

Dex had grown accustomed to my candid commentary on other men, so it no longer fazed him. He just said, "Yeah. He's a character, all right."

I waited for him to say that he could tell Marcus approved of me as well, and when he didn't, I prompted, "What did Marcus say to you at the end of the night when you were getting our coats? Did he say something about me?"

Stacy and I had been chatting a few feet away and I had figured that Marcus was saying something like "You got yourself a hell of a woman" or "She's way hotter than your college girlfriend" or even a nice, straightforward "I really like Darcy—she's great."

But after I pressed Dex at length, he told me that what Marcus had shared was that he and Stacy had been dating, and despite the fact that she gave "bombass blow jobs," he was ending things because she was too demanding. Needless to say, the fact that Marcus garnered blow jobs from a girl like Stacy made him rise even more notches in my book of judgments.

And the more Dex and I hung out with Marcus, the more I liked him. But I still didn't think of him as anything other than Dexter's friend and a groomsman in our wedding until a few months later, the night of Rachel's thirtieth birthday, when I threw a surprise party for her at Prohibition, our favorite bar on the Upper West Side. I remember sometime that evening sidling up to Marcus and telling him that he may have been the party boy back in college, but that I could drink him under the table now.

He smirked and slapped the bar and said, "Oh, yeah? Bring it, big talker."

We proceeded to do Jägermeister shots. It was quite a bonding experience, not only because we were drinking together but because we hid the shots from Dex, who hates it when I get wasted. *It's unbecoming. It's immature. It's unhealthy. It's dangerous,* he would lecture. Not that it ever stopped me, especially not on that night. At one point, before our final round of shots, Dex found us at the bar and looked at me suspiciously. "Are you doing shots?" he asked, glancing at the empty shot glasses on the bar in front of us.

"That wasn't mine," I said. "Those were Marcus's. He did two."

"Yeah, man. Those were mine," Marcus said, twinkly eyed.

As Dex walked away, with raised eyebrows, Marcus winked at me. I laughed. "He can be so uptight. Thanks for the cover."

"No problem," Marcus said.

As of that moment, we had a secret, and having a secret—even a little one—creates a bond between two people. I remember thinking to myself how much more fun he was than Dex, who never lost control. On top of the fun factor, Marcus was looking hot that evening. He was wearing a navy polo shirt—nothing special—but for once it wasn't totally baggy so I could tell he had a pretty nice body. As I sipped a martini, I asked him if he worked out, which is a flirtatious question at best, downright cheesy at worst, but I didn't care. I wanted to go there.

"Once or twice," he said.

"C'mon. You have a great body. Do you lift? Run?"

He said only if he's being chased. He then proceeded to tell me that he had gone running with a girl the other day, despite his better judgment. "I never should have gone," he said, rubbing his thighs. "I'm still paying for it. And the date went nowhere."

"Was this with Stacy?"

"Who?"

"Stacy. You know, the redhead that you brought to Aureole?"

"Oh! *That* Stacy. Ancient history."

"Good," I said. "I wasn't a big fan. She was a bore."

Marcus laughed. "She wasn't your brightest bulb."

"So then, who was your jogger girl?" I asked.

"Just this chick."

"Does this chick have a name?"

"Let's call her Wanda."

"Okay. Wanda. . . . So did Wanda give you blow jobs as good as Stacy's?" I asked, proud of my outrageousness.

He smirked, poised for a comeback, but at this point, Dex and

Rachel both joined us and I never got my answer, only a sexy little wink. I remember thinking that I wished I could show him my talents in that arena. Not that I really wanted to go down on a groomsman in my wedding party—it was just one of those fleeting thoughts of alcohol-induced attraction.

Sometime after that, my memories of the night end, except for a vague recollection of Dex ushering me out of the bar and an even vaguer memory of puking in a paper bag beside our bed.

I didn't think of Marcus for a couple of days after that, until he called to talk to Dex. I told him Dex was still at work, feeling happy for the opportunity to talk to Marcus.

"He works too much," Marcus said.

"Tell me about it. . . . So how's it going? What's new? Think you stayed out late enough the other night?" I asked. After taking me home, Dex had gone back out with Marcus and they had ended up staying out that night until nearly seven in the morning.

"Oh. Yeah. Sorry about that," he said.

"Did you stay out of trouble?"

"Yeah."

"So you didn't talk to any girls?" I asked.

He laughed. "You know I always talk to the ladies."

I recalled that moment at the bar, my unmistakable attraction to him. "Oh. I *know*," I said flirtatiously. "So how is Wanda anyway?"

"Wanda?"

"You know. Wanda. The jogger."

"Oh, *that* Wanda! Right. It didn't work out with Wanda. . . . But I was wondering . . ."

"Wondering what?" I asked coyly, sensing that he was poised to flirt back with me.

But instead he asked, "What is the deal with Rachel?"

I was stunned to hear him say her name. "What do you mean?"

"Is she dating anyone?"

"No. Why?" I asked, feeling irrationally territorial and a little bit jealous that Marcus was interested in my friend. Perhaps, on some level, I even wished that he were pining after me. It was selfish, given the fact that Rachel was single and I was engaged. But you can't help your feelings.

Marcus continued, "She's pretty hot in that studious way of hers."

"Yeah, she's a cute girl," I said, thinking it was weird to hear her described as hot, although I had recently noticed that she seemed to be improving from our school days and early twenties. I think it was her skin. She didn't have as many lines around her eyes as other girls our age. And on a good day, when she put a little effort into her appearance, you might even call her pretty. But hot was going too far. "Well, if you want to go out with my friend, you have to go through me," I said jokingly, but actually meaning it. I was going to play gatekeeper on this one for sure.

"Fine. . . . Tell her I'm gonna ask her out. And tell her she'd better say yes. Or else."

"Or else what?"

"Or else it will be the biggest mistake of her life."

"You're *that* good?"

"Yeah," he said. "Actually, I am *that* good."

And then I got that wistful pang again. That feeling that it was just too bad that I couldn't sample Marcus before marrying Dex. Even beyond any minor feelings I felt for Marcus, I thought about what a shame it was that I would never experience another first kiss. That I'd never fall in love again. I think most guys experience such feelings in a relationship, typically right before they break down and buy the engagement ring. But from what I can tell, most women aren't like this—at least they don't admit to having such feelings. They find a good man, and that's it. They seem relieved that the search is over.

They are content, committed, totally in it for the long haul. I guess I was more like a guy in this regard.

Still, despite my occasionally chilly feet, I knew that nothing could happen with Marcus. So I set about doing the noble thing: I encouraged Rachel to go out with Marcus and took an active interest in their potential relationship. And when they actually did go out, I was happy for them.

But then both he and Rachel flatly refused to include me in any postdate gossip, and that irritated me as I was better friends with each of them than they could have become with each other on one stupid date. Rachel gave me nothing, wouldn't even tell me if they had kissed—which left me wondering if they had done much more than that. The more I pried, the more private they became, and the more intrigued with Marcus I became. It was a vicious cycle. Consequently, over the next few weeks, whenever Marcus called to talk to Dex, I made it my goal to keep him on the phone for as long as possible. Occasionally, I'd even call him to talk at work, under the pretext of asking about our Hamptons share or something related to the wedding. I'd hang up and follow up with a clever e-mail. He'd shoot one back at the speed of light, and we'd have a playful repartee that would last throughout the day. Harmless stuff.

Then over the July Fourth weekend, Dex and Rachel both stayed in the city to work rather than joining the rest of us in the Hamptons. Mostly I was annoyed and disappointed that my best friend and my fiancé were staying behind, but part of me was excited at the idea of spending unchaperoned time with Marcus. Not that I wanted anything to happen. I just wanted a little intrigue.

Sure enough, the intrigue bubbled up at The Talkhouse over part two of our little shot game, only this time it was without the Dexter safety net. I had a few too many, but managed not to get sick, black out, or become completely stupid. Still, I was unquestionably drunk. So was Marcus. We danced until two in the morning, when he,

Claire, and I returned home. Claire put on her Lily Pulitzer pajamas and went straight to bed, but Marcus and I kept partying, first in the den and then in the backyard.

It was all good fun—the teasing and the laughing. But then the boisterous put-downs gave way to playful slapping, which led to some wrestling around in the damp, cool grass. I remember yelling at Marcus to stop after he had tackled me under a tree. I told him that I was going to get stains all over my Chaiken white halter sundress. But I really didn't want him to stop, and I think he knew this because he didn't. Instead he pinned my arm behind my back, which I have to say is a huge turn-on. At least it was with Marcus. I could tell that he was turned on, too, because I felt him there on top of me. Which of course only turned me on more.

At some point, it started to rain, but neither of us made a move for the house. Instead we stayed glued on top of each other, almost frozen in place. Then the laughing stopped. We weren't even smiling, just staring at each other, our faces so close that our noses touched. After a long time like that, in sexual limbo, I tilted my head to the side and brushed my lips against his. Back and forth one time, lightly, innocently. I wanted him to kiss me first, but I had waited long enough. The brief seconds of contact were tellingly delicious. I could tell he thought so, too, but he pulled away and asked, "What's going on here?"

I found his lips again. This time it was a real kiss. I remember feeling completely alert, all my senses buzzing. "I'm kissing you," I said.

"Should you be doing that?" he asked, still on top of me, pressing slightly harder.

"Probably not," I said. "But here we are anyway."

I kissed him again, and this time he kissed me back. We made out for a long time with warm rain falling on us and thunder rumbling in the distance. I knew we were both thinking that we couldn't, shouldn't, do more than kiss, but we were both stalling to be sure.

Calling the other's bluff. He said stuff like *We gotta stop*, and *This is nuts*, and *We can't do this*, and *What if Claire busts us out here?* but neither of us changed course or even braked.

Instead, I took firm hold of his hand and moved it up under my sundress. And he sure knew what to do after that. If there had been any doubt in my mind before as to Marcus's expertise, I had no doubt anymore. He was just one of those guys. Dex might be handsome, I remember thinking, but he can't do this. Not like this. And even if he did, it wouldn't feel like this. And the thought that I'd never have with Dex what Marcus was offering me, made me whisper into his ear, "I wanna be with you."

"We can't go there," Marcus said, his hand still working between my legs.

"Why not?"

"You know why."

"But I *want* to."

"No, you don't."

"I do. I'm sure I do," I said.

"Hell, no. We can't."

But by then I was wriggling out of my thong and unfastening his jeans, reaching down into the warmth of his boxers, determined to make him breathe as hard as I was. We went through the whole high school charade of inching forward step by step, only delaying the inevitable. But the inevitable finally came. Right there under that tree in the pouring July rain.

I'd like to say that I was thinking big, important thoughts—about what I was doing, what it meant in the scheme of my life, the impact it would have on my engagement, my relationship. But no, it was more like, *Am I better than his other girls? Will Dex ever find out? Will Marcus ever go out with Rachel again? Why does this feel so damn good?*

We lasted a long time together, perhaps because of all that we had had to drink, but I decided that it had more to do with perfect chemistry and with Marcus's sexual prowess. Afterward, we rolled onto our backs, catching our breath, our eyes mostly closed. The rain came to a sudden stop, but we were both soaking wet.

"Wow," he said, moving a stick from under his back and flinging it several feet away from us. "Fuck."

I could tell I had made an impression, so I smiled to myself.

"We shouldn't have done that," he said.

"Too late," I said, intertwining my fingers with his.

He squeezed my hand. "Way too late. . . . *Ffffuck.*"

"You're not gonna tell Dex, are you?" I asked.

"Are you fuckin' nuts? No way. Nobody. You're not either," he said, looking slightly panicked.

"Of course not. Nobody," I said. Rachel flashed through my mind—her expression changing from shock to hurt to piousness. Especially not Rachel.

Marcus ran his hand over my wet thigh. "We should go in. Shower."

"Together?"

"No." He let out a nervous laugh. "Not together. I think we've done enough damage tonight."

I wanted to ask him what would happen from here. I wanted to know what it had meant to him, how he was feeling, whether it was a one-time thing or whether we'd have a repeat performance. But I was starting to feel groggy, confused, and a little bit worried. We went inside, kissed good night, and took separate showers. I couldn't quite believe what had happened—and although I didn't regret it, I still cried a little under the hot water when I looked at my beautiful diamond engagement ring and thought about Dexter asleep in our bed on the Upper West Side.

After my shower, I tried to rub the grass stains out of my dress with some Woolite that I found under the sink, but it was hopeless, and I knew bleach would only ruin the delicate fabric. So I wrung out the dress, crept down to the kitchen, and stuffed it into the bottom of the plastic trash bag under a banana peel and an empty box of Trix. I wasn't about to crash and burn over a dress like some kind of Monica Lewinsky.

five

The next day I awoke with a dry tequila mouth and a searing headache. I checked my watch; it was nearly noon. The night before seemed like a blurry dream. A blurry, *good* dream. I couldn't wait to see Marcus again. I got up, brushed my teeth, swept my hair up in a ponytail, added a hint of pink blush to my cheeks, put on a Juicy Couture lime-green skirt and a white tank, and sauntered out to find him.

He was in the den alone, watching television.

"Hiya," I said, taking a seat next to him on the couch.

He glanced over at me, squinted, and let out a hoarse, "Morning. Or afternoon, I guess." Then his eyes returned to the TV.

"Where is everyone?" I asked.

He told me that Claire went to brunch and that Hillary, our other housemate, hadn't returned home the night before.

"Maybe she got some action too," I said to break the ice.

"Yeah," he said. "Maybe."

I tried again. "So how do you feel?"

"Like ass," he said, changing the channel and still avoiding eye con-tact. "Those shots weren't such a hot idea."

"Ahh. I get it," I said. "We're blaming what happened on the alco-hol, are we?"

He shook his head and struggled not to smile. "Always knew you were trouble, Darcy Rhone."

I liked that that was his impression, but at the same time I didn't want him to think that I was a slut, or that I often cheated on Dexter, so I set the record straight, told him that nothing like that had ever happened before. It was, in a technical sense, the truth.

"Yeah. Well. It won't happen again. Back to reality," Marcus said.

It hurt my feelings and bruised my ego that he was treating me with no particular gentleness. We had, after all, shared a night of pas-sion. Passion that I hadn't experienced in years. Maybe not ever. I like to think of myself as a woman of the world, and I certainly had had sex in my share of interesting spots—including, but not limited to, a church parking lot, a cornfield, and the waiting room of my father's dentist office. But the thunderstorm hookup was a first, and I was an-noyed that Marcus wasn't giving our liaison its proper due.

"So you're sorry it happened?" I asked.

"Of *course* I am."

I sighed and tried another angle. "So you . . . didn't enjoy it?"

He finally cracked, looked up at me, and grinned. "Totally beside the point, Rhone."

"Don't call me Rhone," I said. "You weren't calling me Rhone last night."

"Last night," he said, shaking his head, "was fucked up. I think it's best we drop the whole thing."

"No," I said.

He looked at me. "No?"

"No. I can't drop it," I said. "It happened. We can't take it back."

"I know we can't take it back, but we gotta forget it," he said. "It was a shitty thing to do. You're engaged . . . and Dex is my boy . . . It's done."

"Right," I said, giving him a suggestive once-over.

He looked away, then crossed his legs, man-style. "It was fucked up."

It made me mad that he was worrying about Dex, instead of me. "Marcus," I said.

"What?"

"I think we should talk about what happened. I think we should talk about *why* it happened." I wanted to test the waters, determine how much he liked me and whether I could have him again if I wanted him. Which I sort of did. Maybe once or twice more. I mean, once you cheat, is it *that* much worse to cheat two or three times?

"It happened because we drank too much."

"That's not *why* it happened. There was more to it than that. You weren't out there with Claire."

He cleared his throat, but said nothing.

"What if I'm not *supposed* to be with Dex?"

"Then you better call off the wedding."

"You want me to do that?" I asked.

"No. I didn't say that. You should marry Dex." His voice was just cold enough to make me want to break him.

"What if I'm supposed to be with you?" I asked, staring purposefully into his eyes.

He looked away. "Ain't gonna happen."

"Why not?"

"Can't happen."

"Why?"

"Because." He got up and shuffled into the kitchen, returning with a bottle of orange Gatorade. "It was a mistake. One of those things."

"You have no feelings for me whatsoever?" I asked. It was a trap. He couldn't deny any feelings or he would be an asshole for sleeping with me. But if he admitted that he had feelings for me, then the door wouldn't be completely closed.

He thought for a second and skillfully replied, "Sure I like you, Darcy. We're friends."

"So you always do that with your friends?" I snapped back.

He turned the volume down one notch, crossed his arms, and looked at me. "Darce. I thoroughly . . . *enjoyed* last night. . . . But it was a dick move. And I regret it. . . . It was a mistake."

"A *mistake*?" I said, looking highly offended.

"Yeah," he said calmly. "A mistake. An alcohol-related *incident*."

"But it did mean *something* to you?"

"Yeah." He yawned, stretched, and smiled slightly. "Like I said, I enjoyed it. But it's done. Over."

"Okay. Fine," I said. "But you're not going to go out with Rachel again, are you?"

"I dunno. Maybe. Probably. Why?"

"You *are*?" I asked indignantly.

He just looked at me, took a swig of Gatorade. "Why not?"

"Don't you think that's sort of weird now?" I asked. "Like a conflict of interest or something?"

He shrugged, showing me that he saw no problem with it whatsoever.

"You aren't going to sleep with her, are you?" I asked, assuming, based on Rachel's track record, that he hadn't already.

He laughed and said, "Can't rule it out."

"Are you serious?" I asked, horrified. "That's just too weird. We're best friends."

He shrugged.

"Okay. Look. I gotta ask you this. One question . . . If I were single, who would you choose? Rachel or me?" I asked. I was pretty sure I knew the answer but wanted to hear him say it.

He laughed. "You're too much."

"C'mon. Answer me."

"Okay. Here's the truth," he said somberly. I anticipated his first soft words since our encounter. "I'd try to hook up with both of you at once."

I punched his arm and said, "Be serious."

He laughed. "You guys have never done that before?"

"No, we've never done that before! You're gross," I said. "I'm game for a lot, but I like my love one on one. . . . So c'mon, you have to pick. Rachel or me?"

He shrugged. "Close call."

"Close because of Dex, right? But you're more attracted to me?" I asked, looking for affirmation. It wasn't so much that I wanted to beat Rachel. It was more that she had her turf—the intelligent-lawyer thing—while being hot and desired by men was my domain, my main source of self-esteem. And I wanted—and needed—the lines to stay clear.

But Marcus wouldn't grant me any satisfaction. "You're pretty in different ways," he said as he turned the volume back up on the television to show me that our conversation was over. "Now. Let's watch some Wimbledon, what do you say? How about that Agassi?"

For the rest of the weekend, as Marcus did his best to avoid being alone with me, I found myself obsessing over him. And when we all returned to the city, my preoccupation only grew stronger. I didn't necessarily want to have an affair with him, but I wanted him to want me.

But that clearly wasn't happening. Despite a barrage of e-mails and phone calls, Marcus pretty much ignored me. So about a week later, I took drastic measures and showed up at his apartment with a six-pack of beer and *Pulp Fiction,* a movie all men love. Marcus buzzed me up to his apartment and was standing in his open door with his arms crossed. He was wearing gray sweats with a hole in the knee and a faded, stained T-shirt. Still, he looked hot, as one can only look after you've just had forbidden sex with them in the pouring rain.

"Well? Can I come in? I brought treats," I said, holding up the beer and the video.

"Nope," he said, still smiling.

"Please?" I said sweetly.

He shook his head and laughed, but didn't budge.

"C'mon? Can we please just hang out tonight?" I asked. "I just want to spend time with you. As friends. Strictly friends. Is that so wrong?"

He made an exasperated sound and moved over just enough to let me squeeze by him. "You're a trip."

"I just want to see you again. As friends. I promise," I said, surveying his stereotypically messy bachelor pad. Clothes and newspapers were strewn everywhere. A Stouffer's frozen lasagna sat thawing on his coffee table. His bed was unmade, the bottom sheet straining to cover a ratty blue mattress. And a large fish tank, badly needing a good scrub, sat next to a plasma screen television and dozens of video games. He saw me take it all in.

"Wasn't expecting company."

"I know. I know. But you wouldn't return my calls. I needed to take drastic measures."

"I know about you and your drastic measures," he said, pointing at a futon opposite his leather sectional. "Have a seat."

"Come on, Marcus. I think we can handle sitting on the couch together. I swear, nothing's going to happen."

It was a lie, and we both knew it.

So halfway through the movie, after a few smooth moves by me, Marcus and I were making our second big "mistake." And, I have to say, I liked him even better on a dry, soft couch.

six

After that night on the couch, Marcus stopped resisting and stopped referring to us as a mistake. Although he seldom initiated contact, he was always available when I asked to see him—whether during lunch in the middle of the day or at night whenever Dex worked late. All my free time involved Marcus. And when I wasn't with Marcus, I was thinking about him, fantasizing about him. The sex was ridiculous, over-the-top stuff I thought only existed in movies like *9½ Weeks*. I couldn't get enough of Marcus, and he clearly was just as obsessed with me. He tried to play it cool, but every now and then, I'd get a clue about his feelings by the sound of his voice when I'd call or the way he'd look at me after sex when I'd lounge naked in his apartment.

But despite our escalating romance, Marcus never so much as hinted that I should call off the wedding. Not once. Not even when I pressed him on it, asking him point-blank if I should go through with it. He'd just say, "That's up to you, Darce." Or, even more frustrating, he'd say that I should marry Dex. I know it was just his guilt talking, but I hated it anyway. Although I had no intention of canceling my wedding and should have been enjoying the freedom that came with a demand-free love affair, I still wanted Marcus to tell me that he *had* to be with me, that if I didn't tell Dex the truth about us, he would. Such measures would have matched the passionate idea of us—that unstoppable, unnameable force drawing us together. But that wasn't Marcus's style. Although he overcame the guy's guy hurdle by sleeping with a friend's fiancée, he wasn't willing to go the whole way and actually sabotage the wedding.

And so my engagement to Dex stayed on course, the partition between fiancé and lover firm. I'd leave Marcus's apartment and return to my own, completely switching gears, picking up my wedding files and ordering three hundred wedding favors without batting an eye. As into Marcus as I was, I still thought of myself as part of the golden couple and believed that nobody was better for me in the long run than Dex. At least on paper. Dex had it all over Marcus on paper. For one, he was better looking. If you polled a hundred women, Dex would get every vote. Marcus wasn't as tall, his hair wasn't as thick, and his features weren't as chiseled. And in other categories, too, Marcus came up short: he wasn't as neat, he had a terrible work ethic, he didn't make as much money, he didn't come from as good a family, his taste wasn't as refined, he had cheated on past girlfriends, and was capable of lying to a friend.

Marcus only prevailed in that fuzzy, intangible way that either matters a lot or not much at all, depending on whom you ask. We were all about all the stuff you can't really articulate. The lust, passion, the physical connection. He was irresistible, imperfections and all, and I couldn't stop going back for more. Not that I really tried. I breezed along, making wedding plans, returning home to Dex after having sweaty, intense sex with his groomsman. I reassured myself that I'd get my fix before the wedding, and that from that day forward, I'd be a loyal wife. I was just having a final fling. Just getting things out of my system. Plenty of guys did it. Why couldn't I?

Of course, I didn't tell a soul about my affair. Not my mother, with whom I usually shared all. Not Claire, who wouldn't even begin to understand why I would cheat on someone with Dexter's pedigree and jeopardize my future. And certainly not Rachel. Because she's so judgmental and because I knew she had a small crush on Marcus.

Only once did I come close to divulging the full truth. It was after I misplaced my ring in Marcus's apartment and accused his maid of stealing it. I was in a panic, worried about getting a replacement before the wedding, worried about telling Dex that the ring was missing, and suddenly worried about whether I should marry Dex at all. So in desperation, I turned to Rachel for guidance. She had always been my decision maker on even the most trivial matters, like whether to buy the chocolate or tan raw leather Gucci boots (although at the time, that didn't feel very trivial), so I knew she'd rise to the occasion in my hour of need. I confessed my affair, but downplayed its importance, telling her that it had only happened once. I also told her that I had slept with a guy from work—rather than Marcus. I just wanted to spare her feelings because at that point I didn't think the full truth would ever emerge.

As always, Rachel gave sound advice. Over Chinese delivery, she convinced me that the affair was simply a manifestation of cold feet, the cold feet that only a man—or a woman with endless options—can understand. She made me see that although the initial passion of an intense affair is hard to pass up, what I had with Dex was better, more enduring. I believed her, and decided that I was going to marry Dex.

Then, one night in August, about three weeks before my wedding, something happened that made me question my decision. I had a client dinner that was canceled at the last minute, so I showed up at

Marcus's apartment to surprise him. He wasn't yet home, but I convinced his doorman to give me his spare key so I could wait inside for him. Then I went upstairs, got undressed except for a pair of leopard-print heels, and sprawled out on his couch, anxious for him to come find me.

About an hour passed, and just as I was dozing, I heard unmistakable female giggling in the hallway and Marcus's low voice, obviously cracking up his companion. I scrambled to get dressed, but couldn't do so before Marcus and a blonde—who vaguely reminded me of Stacy from Aureole—walked inside. She had a pretty face but was pear-shaped, and worse, wearing Nine West footwear from about three seasons ago. The three of us stood there, mere feet apart. I was still completely naked but for my Blahniks.

"Darcy—you scared the shit out of me," Marcus said, looking not nearly scared enough as far as I was concerned. "My doorman didn't tell me you were up here."

I managed to throw on one of Marcus's dirty T-shirts that was draped over the back of his couch, but not before I caught the girl giving me an envious once-over. "I guess he forgot," I hissed.

"I'll leave," the blonde said, backing up like a trapped doe.

"You do that," I said, pointing at the door.

Marcus said, "Bye, Angie, I'll—"

"He'll call you tomorrow, Angie," I spit out caustically. "Toodle-oo."

As soon as the door closed, I tried to hit him, while screaming at him: *You bastard, you liar, you tainted my engagement, you ruined my life.*

I knew deep down that I had no right to be so enraged, that I was only a few weeks away from marrying somebody else. And yet, at the same time, I felt that I had every right. So I kept delivering inept blows while he effortlessly blocked each one with his hands or forearms just as my personal trainer does during a kickboxing session.

This battery went on for some time, until finally Marcus got angry.

He grabbed my wrists, shook me a little, and shouted, "What did you think was going to happen, Darcy?"

"With Angie?" I said, hoping that he was about to tell me that he and Angie were strictly friends, that *nothing* was going to happen.

"No," he said with disgust. "What did you think was going to happen after you got married? Have you even stopped to think about that?"

Of course I had, I told him, suddenly on the defensive. I hadn't expected this line of questioning.

"And?"

"I don't even know if I am getting married," I said. Of course, I had every intention of getting married but thought I had a greater right to be indignant if my nuptials were up in the air.

"Well, assuming you do," Marcus said. "Did you think we'd keep seeing each other?"

"No," I snapped back self-righteously.

"I mean, Jesus Christ, Darcy," he shouted. "It's bad enough that I've been seeing my friend's fiancée for almost two fucking months. But, you know, I draw the line there. I'm not gonna sleep with his wife in case that's what you had in mind."

"I did *not* have that in mind," I said. If he was going to take the high ground, then so would I—although the high ground was eroding quickly.

"So what then? Did you think I was going to be celibate after you got married? Pine away after you for the rest of my life? Hang out with you and Dex all the while thinking, 'Gee whiz, what a lucky guy he is. How I wish I could be him.'?"

"No," I said, although I did like the whole star-crossed lovers theme. Who doesn't? I mean, there is a reason why *Romeo and Juliet* is such a beloved tale.

"Then Christ, Darcy, what do you want from me?" he shouted louder, now pacing back and forth across his apartment.

I considered this for a moment and then said, in a pitiful, small voice with my dying-calf-in-a-hailstorm expression, "I want you to love me."

He made a *puh* sound and looked at me, disgusted. Everything was backfiring. Why was I suddenly the bad guy?

I sat down, pulling his T-shirt over my knees. Tears streamed down my cheeks. Crying always worked with Dex. But Marcus didn't fold. "Oh, *stop* crying!" he said. "Stop it *now!*"

"Well, *do you* love me?" I pressed, hopeful.

He shook his head. "I'm not playing your manipulative little games, Darce."

"I'm not manipulating you. . . . Why won't you answer the question?" I was suddenly on a singular quest.

"Why don't you answer *my* question? Okay? You tell me what the hell difference it would make if I did love you? Tell me that. Huh?" His face was turning red and his hands were moving all over the place. Unless it involved a sporting event or gambling, I had never seen him agitated, let alone angry or upset.

For a second, I was enchanted by the intensity of his reaction, as well as the word *love* coming from him. It was the closest he had ever come to telling me that he had real feelings for me. But then I pictured Angie and I was straight back to being furious. "Well, if you do love me, then what about *Angie?*" I pointed at the door, where my weak competition had exited. "Why was she here? Who is she, anyway?"

"She's nobody," he said.

"If she's such a nobody," I asked, "then why were you going to have sex with her?"

I expected a denial, but instead he looked at me defiantly.

"*Were* you going to have sex with her?" I asked.

He waited several beats, and then said, "Yup. Matter of fact, that was the plan."

I delivered a solid punch to his shoulder. My hand hurt, but he didn't flinch.

"You're such an asshole," I said. "I hate you *so much!*"

He gave me a blank stare and said, "Just go, Darcy. Leave now. This is over. We're done. I'll see you at your wedding."

I could tell he meant it. I was stunned, simply couldn't believe it would all end like this. "Is that what you really want?"

He spit out a disdainful laugh. "Has this ever been about anything other than what *you* want?"

"Oh, puh-*lease,*" I said. "As if you haven't been enjoying every second of it."

"Sure. It's been fun," he said flippantly.

"That's it? *Fun?*"

"Yeah. Fun. A blast. A real joyride. The time of my life," Marcus said. "What do you want me to say? What do you want from me?"

I considered the question and answered it honestly. "I want you to want me. For more than just fun. For more than just great sex. I want you to want me for real."

He sighed, laughed, and shook his head. "Okay, Darce, I want you. I *want* you. I want you all to myself. Are you happy now?"

Before I could answer, he turned the corner into the bathroom, slamming the door behind him. I waited a minute before I followed him, finding the door unlocked. He was leaning against his sink in the dark. From the light in the hall, I could see his face in the mirror. He looked sad, and that both surprised and softened me.

"Yes," I said quietly.

"Yes what?"

"Yes to your question. I am happy that you want me," I said. "And I love you too."

He gave me a disarmed look. I had my answer. Marcus loved me. I felt a rush of joy—a feeling of triumph and passion. "I'm calling off the wedding," I finally said.

More silence.

"Did you hear what I said?"

"I heard you."

"What do you think of that?"

"Are you sure you wanna do that?"

"Yes. I'm sure."

In truth, I wasn't at all sure, but it was the first moment I could actually picture doing it—cutting the long, safe cord with Dex and starting a new life. Maybe it took seeing Marcus with someone else and realizing that we were over in a matter of days if I didn't make a choice. Maybe it was watching him lean against his bathroom sink with those sad brown eyes. Maybe it was hearing him use the word *love*. And maybe it was the fact that the emotional ante had been so raised, I had nowhere else to go but there. It would have been anticlimactic to say anything else.

Moments later, Marcus and I were having intense, condomless sex.

"I'm going to come," Marcus finally breathed, after I had twice.

"Two more seconds," I said, crouching over him.

"Move now. I mean it."

So I moved harder, right down on him, not caring that I was in the middle of my cycle, probably at the most perilous millisecond of the month.

"What are you doing?" he shouted, his eyes wide and scared. "You wanna get pregnant?"

At that instant, it seemed like a great idea—the perfect romantic solution. "Why not?"

He gave me a half-smile and told me I was crazy.

"Crazy for you," I said.

"Don't *ever* do that again," he said. "I mean it."

"Okay, Daddy," I said, although I really didn't think we had hit the jackpot with our effort. There had been plenty of times in my life—especially in college—when I forgot to take my pill or hadn't been careful enough. But I had never gotten pregnant. In fact, part of me believed that I couldn't get pregnant. Which suited me just fine. When the time came, I would just hop on a plane and pick up a baby in China or Cambodia. Like Nicole Kidman or Angelina Jolie. And *presto,* I'd become a glam mom with my perfect body intact.

"That's not funny," Marcus said, smiling. "Go do something. Wash up or pee or something, would you?"

"No way," I said, tucking my legs underneath me, the technique my high school friend Annalise described using while she and her husband were trying to have a baby. "Swim, you little spermies, swim!"

Marcus laughed and kissed my nose. "You freak."

"Yes, but you love me," I said. "Say it again."

"Again? I never said it the first time."

"Pretty much you did. Say it again."

He exhaled and looked at me fondly. "I kinda love you, you freak."

I smiled, thinking that I had finally succeeded. Marcus was broken. He was mine if I wanted him. In the days that followed, I floundered, looking for a sign, any sign. Should I choose Dex or Marcus? Marriage or sex? Security or fun?

Then, one day in early September, a week before my wedding, I finally got my final answer in the form of two parallel pink lines on a plastic, urine-soaked stick.

seven

"What's it say?" Marcus asked, as I emerged from the bathroom with the plastic stick in hand. He was waiting for me on his couch while flipping through a *Sports Illustrated*.

"It says . . . 'Congratulations, Daddy.'"

"No way."

"Yes way."

"You're shitting me."

"Nope. I'm pregnant."

Marcus leaned back on his couch and closed his magazine. I sat next to him, took his hands, and waited for more. Perhaps an embrace, a gentle touch, a few tears.

"And . . . you're sure . . . that it's mine?"

"Yes," I said. "That question is insulting and hurtful. I haven't had sex with Dex since—well, since forever. And you know it."

"You're sure about that? Not even one time this month? It isn't the time to exaggerate, Darce."

"Yes, I'm sure," I said firmly. It was the truth, thank goodness.

I thought of my high school friend Ethan, who is fair and blue-eyed and how he had married his pregnant girlfriend, Brandi, also a blonde. Months later she gave birth to a dark-skinned baby with eyes the color of Oreos. Rachel and I felt so sorry for Ethan—for the heartache and humiliation he had to endure during his divorce. But I actually felt almost as bad for Brandi. For some reason, I identified with her in a kindred, fellow-rule-breaker way. I knew she must have suffered incredibly for nine months, hoping and praying that the baby would come out looking like her husband and not the Native Alaskan she was melting igloos with on the side. The waiting must have been agonizing. Just thinking about it made my stomach turn. So it was a very lucky thing that I hadn't had sex with Dex in at least a month. I was sure the baby was Marcus's.

I put the stick on his coffee table and stared at the two pink lines. "Wow," I said, feeling giddy. "A positive test. I've never seen one of those . . . and I've taken plenty."

"Should we do another test? Just to double-check?" Marcus asked, pulling another box of tests from the Duane Reade bag. "I got two brands."

"I don't think you get many false positives with pregnancy tests," I said. "It only works the other way."

"Humor me," Marcus said as he tore the plastic wrapper off another test.

I sighed loudly as I retrieved the mug full of my pee from his bathroom.

Marcus's face fell. "You peed in my Broncos mug?"

"Yeah. So?"

"That's my favorite mug," he said, cringing.

"Oh, for heaven's sake, just wash it," I said. "And anyway, haven't you ever heard that urine is completely sterile?"

Marcus made a face.

"Since when are you a stickler for germs?" I asked, looking around his sty of an apartment.

"I'll never be able to drink out of that mug again," he grumbled.

I rolled my eyes and stuck a fresh stick into his precious mug. Then I slowly counted to five aloud, before withdrawing it and placing it on the coffee table next to the first test.

Marcus studied the second hand on his watch until I said, "A cross! That means positive!"

"Lemme see," he said, looking stunned and wide-eyed as he examined the stick, comparing it to the diagram on the back of the box. "It looks kind of faint compared to the picture."

"A faint cross still counts," I said. "It's the whole 'you can't be a little bit pregnant' concept. Here. Read the directions."

Marcus scanned the page of fine print, obviously hoping to find a disclaimer—a section on false positives. A flash of fear crossed his face as he put the directions down. "So what now?"

"Well, for starters, we're having a baby in about nine months," I said jubilantly.

"You can't be serious." His voice had a hard edge.

I gave him a look that told him I was totally serious. Then I took his hands in mine.

Marcus stiffened. "Are you sure that's what you want? 'Cause we have other options."

The implication was clear. I raised my chin and said, "I don't believe in abortion."

I'm not sure why I said it, because I am actually as pro-choice as they come. Furthermore, I didn't particularly want to be a mother at this stage of my life. I had none of the biological cravings that so many of my friends had been experiencing lately as we reached our thirtieth year. And I certainly didn't want to gain a bunch of pounds. Or have all of that responsibility, and those restrictions on my freedom and night life.

But at that moment, I was inexplicably happy with my positive pregnancy tests. Perhaps because I was so wrapped up in Marcus that the idea of having his baby seemed thrilling. The ultimate romantic endeavor. Or maybe I liked the feeling of reeling him in just a little bit more. Not that I questioned his commitment to me. I could tell he was crazy about me in his own peculiar way. But he was one of those guys you could never quite control, and being pregnant with his child tightened my grip. Not that I consciously got myself pregnant. Not really. I thought back to our make-up sex. Clearly, it was just meant to be.

And even clearer to me at that moment was this: a positive pregnancy test meant that my wedding was off. The fact that my relief was so palpable meant that I had my true answer: I didn't want to marry Dex. In one instant, I felt over Dex and our fairy-tale wedding, only thrilled to be a part of an even greater drama.

"I'll tell Dex today," I said with an aplomb that surprised even me.

"That you're pregnant?" Marcus asked, aghast.

"No. Just that the wedding is off."

"Are you sure you wanna do that? Are you sure you wanna have a baby?" he asked, looking panicked.

"Positive." I looked over at the sticks. "*Positive.* Get it?"

Marcus just sat there, looking shell-shocked and a little bit pissed.

"Aren't you at *all* happy?" I asked him.

"Yeah," he said glumly. "But—but I think we need to slow down and discuss our . . . options."

I let him stumble on. "I could have sworn you said you were pro-choice?"

"Okay. So I *am* pro-choice," I said with an exaggerated nod. "And I *choose* to have this baby. *Our* baby."

"Well, take your time thinking it all over . . ."

"You're hurting my feelings," I said.

"Why?"

"Because I *want* to have this baby," I said, getting upset. "And I wish you felt the same. . . . I can't believe you haven't even hugged me yet."

Marcus sighed and put his arms loosely around me.

"Tell me you're happy. A little bit happy," I whispered in his ear.

Marcus looked at me again and said unconvincingly, "I'm happy. I'm just saying that maybe we want to slow down and think things through. Maybe you should talk to someone."

I gave him a scornful gaze. "You mean a shrink?"

"Something like that."

"That's ridiculous. People go to therapists when they are filled with despair. But I'm *thrilled*," I said.

"Still, you might have some issues around this thing," Marcus said. He always talked in generalities about our relationship—*some issues, this thing, our deal, the situation*—and sometimes with just a quick flourish of his hand. It always irritated me that he thought a hand motion could capture our essence. We were so much more than that. Especially now. We were going to be parents.

"I have no issues. I'm in love with you. I want to keep our baby. And that is that." Even as I said it, I knew that *that* was never just *that* in my world. *That* was *maybe that* or *some of that* or *that along with a dose of this*. But I kept going, resolute. "Now, if you'll excuse me, I have a wedding to cancel."

And that's exactly what I did. I marched right back over to the Upper West Side to break the news to my fiancé. I found Dex putting away his dry cleaning, stripping off the plastic coverings and separating his blue shirts from the white. For one moment, I couldn't do it, couldn't imagine telling Dex that after years of being together, we were finished. But then I thought about Marcus and drew confidence from him.

"We need to talk," I said, all business.

"All right," Dex said slowly. And I could tell he knew exactly what was coming. He had appeared clueless for weeks, but his expression at that moment told me that even men have intuition.

Mere sentences later our wedding was officially canceled. A seven-year relationship over. It was bizarre how fast and easy it was. Technically, Dex was the one to pull the cord, saying that it would be a mistake to get married. Hearing him use the word *mistake* in relation to me made me backtrack for a second, but then I convinced myself that he was simply acknowledging a reality I had created. He was reacting to my emotional and physical withdrawal from him. I watched him, with all that balled, dry-cleaning plastic at his feet, and felt sorry for him.

I kissed his clean-shaven cheek and said what people always say when they dump someone under amicable circumstances. I told him that I wished the best for him and hoped that he would find happiness. And I meant it on one level. After all, I certainly didn't want Dex to die alone. But if I'm completely honest, I'd say that I *did* want him to grieve for a good long while before seeking out his next girlfriend, a girlfriend I hoped would never quite measure up to me. Little did I know that he would be looking for that runner-up in my best friend's apartment.

eight

The morning after the great closet fiasco I awoke in Marcus's bed, momentarily disoriented. I had only spent the night with him once before, when Dex had gone on a business trip to Dallas, but I had left very early the next morning while it was still dark. So that really didn't count as a full-fledged sleepover.

This morning felt different. Everything felt different. I looked around, noticing how bright the morning sun was in his apartment. It was almost as if I were seeing it for the first time, seeing Marcus for the first time. I studied his profile and his receding (but still sexy) hairline as it hit me that the end of our saga had finally come. Marcus and I were a done deal with a baby on the way. There was no more Dex to creep back to. I felt a rush of adrenaline as I anticipated breaking the news to my friends, coworkers, and acquaintances. I wondered what explanation Dex would offer to his friends and family. I thought of all the celebrity breakups, wishing that I had a spokesperson to contact his spokesperson, to agree on one unified statement. Still, after seven years you know a person pretty well, and I was almost positive that Dex would keep the indelicate details to himself. So I could spin things pretty much my way. I considered my options. I could tell the whole truth, confess my relationship with Marcus. Or I could say nothing about Marcus and shift the blame to Dex and Rachel. Or I could maintain an aura of mystery.

It was tempting to divulge the closet tale and turn people against Rachel and Dex, but I certainly didn't want to look like some kind of tossed-aside loser. I had to safeguard my reputation in the city as a diva. After all, divas don't get played. So I decided that I would tell everyone that I broke up with Dex, simply announce that I was very sad to end our relationship, but it was for the best because we just weren't meant to be together. I would go for a somber, "I will survive" tone. It would elicit a certain degree of sympathy, but also inspire awe that I was the strong sort of woman who could voluntarily break free of a tall, dark, and handsome man. I'd omit the Marcus part of the equation for the time being. And of course I'd leave out my pregnancy. I was all for appearing to be a woman in charge, but not a full-on hussy. My public would know the truth at some point, but that was a worry for later.

In the meantime, I'd just cross my fingers and hope that nobody would find out about Dex and Rachel. I mean, *surely* they wouldn't keep seeing each other. It was an absolute impossibility. She wasn't his type. He was only using her in his moment of extreme sadness. He was a lost soul, she a familiar, comforting friend. As for Rachel, she had just succumbed to the most attractive man ever to cross her radar. A girl like Rachel only has such an opportunity once in her life. But she would come to her senses and return to the average Joes. She would never date such a significant ex of mine. It's a cardinal rule—and Rachel was all about rules. I was sure she was already racked with guilt for her fleeting weakness. Any day now she was going to come crawling back to me, eloquently detailing exactly how sorry she was. And if she begged long enough, talked of our friendship with enough passion, I might eventually let her back into the fold. But it would take a long, long time for her to win back the accolade of best friend.

I turned to look at Marcus again, now sleeping with one hand tucked behind his head, the other hanging off the bed. His brow was furrowed as if he were doing long division in his sleep. Then his lips curled into a sexy pout, accentuating the cleft in his chin. Suddenly his face morphed into Dexter's, like the faces at the end of Michael Jackson's "Black or White" video.

"Marcus, wake up," I said, shaking his arm. "I'm starting to freak out."

He kept snoring. I leaned over and kissed him. He made a low, throaty noise, opened one eye, and mumbled, "Mornin', Darce."

"Do you think they're together right now?" I asked.

"I told you already," he said. I guess he was referring to the *no* that he'd given a dozen times the night before.

"Tell me again."

"Nah . . . I highly doubt it. I'm sure you ruined the mood, and he probably left."

I decided to believe him. "Okay . . . But even so, I don't think I can go to work today. I'm too distracted. You wanna call in sick with me?"

In the seven years I had dated Dex he had never once called in sick unless he truly was extremely ill. Things were going to be different with Marcus. Our life was going to be so much more spontaneous and fun.

Sure enough, Marcus said, "All right, you twisted my arm. I'll sleep in."

I felt a fleeting sense of victory, but then realized that in some twisted way, I was actually looking forward to the wave I was about to create at work, so I said with a martyr's sigh, "I guess I *should* go in and get it over with."

"Get what over with?"

"You know . . . telling everyone that the wedding is off."

"Hmm-mmm."

"What exactly should I say?"

No response.

"Marcus!"

"You don't have to tell anyone anything," Marcus said, rolling over toward me. "It's nobody's business."

"Of course I have to tell them. They think I'm getting married on Saturday. Some of them are invited."

I admired Marcus's laid-back approach to life, but this was a perfect example of him underestimating the requisite effort something would take. It might even prove to be problematic later, if he underestimated my desire to have nice things on my birthday, Christmas, Valentine's, and randomly throughout the year. Dex knew the drill: flowers arrived like clockwork every other month, which meant a standing order rather than a rush of emotion, but that was fine with me. Attention was attention. Nice things were nice things.

But Marcus could be trained, I was sure of it. Every man can be trained. I welcomed the challenge of molding my new boyfriend into a responsible—but still sexy and spontaneous—husband and father. For now, I had to make him understand that breaking the news to my colleagues was going to be a huge, emotional ordeal and that I would need his support—i.e., phone calls and e-mails during my trying day. Maybe even a luxury good waiting for me upon my return to his apartment. I imagined him coming through the door with an orange Hermès box and a doting smile.

"I know you have to tell the people you invited," Marcus said. "I just think it's unnecessary to explain the whole thing in detail. Just send a mass e-mail and be done with it."

"But they're going to ask what happened," I said, thinking that I'd be disappointed if they didn't. "People want details."

"I know you would, you little information hound, but not everyone is like you."

"Everyone is like me in the world of public relations. Trust me. It's our business to gather, hoard, and disperse juicy details. And this is big-time juicy."

"Well, I'm just sayin' that it's your prerogative to tell people to mind their own fuckin' business," Marcus said.

I told him that wasn't my style. Then I got up quickly, resisting the urge to have sex. After all, I had a lot to accomplish in a day. I showered, put on my makeup, and then checked Marcus's closet, which was full of my clothes that I had brought over the night before. I opted for an Escada pencil skirt, a green Versace V-neck, and a pair of Ferragamo slingbacks. Then, I leaned into the bathroom to say goodbye to Marcus, who was singing "Purple Rain" at the top of his lungs, and, impressively, in tune.

"See you tonight, hon!" I called into the bathroom.

He stopped singing and poked his head around the shower curtain. "Sounds good. . . . C'mere and give me a quick kiss."

"Can't. The steam will ruin my hair," I said, blowing him a kiss from the doorway. Then I maneuvered through the busy city streets to the subway as I considered my strategy for how to break the news. I could tell Claire, coworker and new best friend effective immediately, that she was free to spread the word. Then I remembered that she had an out-of-office meeting with a potential new client this morning, and I couldn't stand the thought of waiting for her return. So I would send a mass e-mail as Marcus suggested, adopting just the right tone.

When I got to my office, I settled into my chair in front of my computer and quickly typed out my breaking news:

Good morning, everyone. I just wanted to let you all know that my wedding will not be taking place this Saturday. It was a difficult decision, but I think I'm doing the right thing. I know it's a bit odd to send out a group e-mail regarding such a personal matter, but I thought this was the easiest way.

Perfect. It was strong but emotional. And most important, it clearly signaled that I had done the dumping. I reread it, thinking that something was missing. I added an ellipsis at the end. Yes. Perfect touch. Those three little dots would conjure the sound of my voice trailing away mysteriously. Now for a subject line. Should it say "Wedding" or "Canceled" or "News"? None seemed right, so I kept the subject line blank. Then, as I selected my personal e-mail group and prepared to send the shocking nugget via cyberspace, my phone rang.

"Darcy," my boss, Cal, said in his breathy, effeminate voice. "How are ya?"

"Not so good, Cal," I said in my "I can't deal with taking instructions" voice. One that he knew well. It was the beauty of working for Cal. He was a complete pushover.

"Well, may I please see you in Conference Room C?"

"For what?"

"We need to talk about the Celebrity Golf Challenge."

"Right *now*?"

"Yes, if you could. Please?"

I sighed as loudly as possible. "Okay," I said. "I'll be there when I can."

Damn. Had I arrived a few minutes earlier, he'd be opening my e-mail and contacting someone else about the golf tournament. I was sure that once I told him the news, he'd pass the project elsewhere, especially if I could work up a few tears. In fact, I could probably squeeze a few leisurely weeks out of my purported hardship. Maybe Marcus and I could even take a vacation together. I minimized my e-mail, deciding that I'd give it a final tweaking and a spell-check before sending, and then made my way downstairs to the conference room. I pushed open the heavy door with a hangdog expression.

And there before me was the entire staff of Carolyn Morgan and Associates, all packed into the room, yelling *"Surprise!"* and hurling their heartiest congratulations at me from all directions. A gigantic blue box from Tiffany perched on one end of the lacquered table. An ivory-frosted cake with pink gel writing sat temptingly at the other. My heart raced. Talk about your audiences! Talk about your drama!

"We knew you'd expect your party later in the week!" Claire squealed. "Gotcha! And you believed I had that meeting!"

She was right. They had, indeed, gotten me. But I was about to get them right back. Top their surprise. I smiled hesitantly, and said, "You shouldn't have."

"Of course we should have," Claire said.

"No. You *really* shouldn't have," I said.

Cal stepped toward me and put his arm around me. "Speech," he said.

"I'm speechless," I said. "I'm literally without speech."

"Impossible," Cal said. "I've known you for years and never seen it happen yet."

Laughter rippled through the room, affirming that, indeed, I had the biggest mouth in the place. I cleared my throat again and took a step forward, smiling demurely. "Well. Thank you all so very much . . . but . . . there isn't going to *be* a wedding. I'm not getting married."

Cal and some others laughed again. "Yeah. Yeah. You're going down like the rest of us poor, married fools," he said.

I smiled bravely and said, "No. Actually, I called the wedding off this weekend."

Like a Red Cross volunteer during a fire at an orphanage, Claire sprang into action. *"Omigod! No! Way!"* She pressed one hand to her temple and whisked me out of the conference room back up to my office, her arm around my waist as if I might, at any moment, faint. "What in the *world* is going on?" she asked when we were alone.

"It's over." I sniffed.

"Why? You and Dex are perfect together! What happened?"

"It's a long story," I said, my eyes filling with tears as I thought about Dex in Rachel's closet. Despite all my plans to the contrary, I just couldn't resist telling her. I needed her sympathy and full support. I needed her to tell me that Dex could not possibly be interested in boring old Rachel. So I dropped the bomb on her. "We broke up this weekend, and then, yesterday afternoon, I caught Dex and Rachel together."

"What?" Claire's mouth fell open.

I nodded. "You're telling me."

"What do you mean 'together'? Are you sure?"

"Yes. I went over to talk to Rachel about this whole situation and Dex was there, in his boxers, all crouched down, hiding in her closet."

"No!"

"Yes," I said.

"Oh. My. God." Claire covered her mouth with both hands and shook her head. "I—I don't even know what to say. I just can't . . . what in the world was he thinking? What was *she* thinking? How *could they?"*

"Please don't tell anyone," I said. "It's all so humiliating. I mean, my maid of honor!"

"Of course not. Cross my heart," Claire said, making a big X over her bubble-gum-pink twin set. She gave me a few seconds of respectful silence before launching into Q&A mode. "Was it a one-time thing?" she asked.

"It *had* to be a one-time thing, don't you think?"

"Oh. I'm sure. Dex would *never* like her," she said.

"I know. I just can't see it. There's no way, right?"

"No way. He just couldn't go from you to her. She's just so plain, and . . . I don't know. . . . I know she's your best friend so I don't want to say anything bad—"

"What? She is *so* not my best friend anymore. I despise her."

"I don't blame you," Claire said solemnly, ready to step up and fill Rachel's bland shoes.

I threw her the bone she so craved. "You're my best friend now."

Claire clasped her hands together and looked at me as though she might cry. Ever since our roomie days together, Claire had jockeyed for position as my most favored friend. At times, she was downright obsequious. But it was what I needed at that moment, and she delivered. "Oh, Darce. I'm *totally* here for you."

"Thanks," I said. "I appreciate that."

"We're going to have the *best* time hanging out as single girls again," she said. "What are you doing tonight? Henry Fabuss is throwing a big bash at Lotus this evening—for his thirtieth. We should totally go. He's such a hoot—and he's so totally dialed in, you know? Everyone's going to be there. It would really get your mind off this."

"Not tonight," I said. "I think I just need some alone time. In fact, I think I'm going home now. I can't stand being here—and I don't want anyone to see me crying."

"Want me to come with you? I'm sure Cal would let me leave with you," she said. "We could go shopping. Retail therapy."

"No, thanks. I think I want to be alone," I said, even though I was actually planning to be with Marcus.

"Okay," she said, obviously disappointed. "I understand."

"I just need to get this e-mail out before I leave. Can you read it and see what you think?"

Proofing my e-mails used to be Rachel's role. She had been so good at it. I vowed to banish her from my thoughts. She was persona non grata until her apology came forth in skywriting. Meanwhile, Claire took her job seriously, leaning in close to my monitor, and reading the e-mail twice. She finally looked up, gave me a brisk nod, and said it was fine, just fine. So I hit send and sashayed down the hall, relishing the stares and whispers from my colleagues along the way.

nine

Marcus agreed to leave work early and meet me back at his apartment, where we had fantastic sex. Afterward, I rested my head on his chest and told him my conference room tale.

"I'm surprised you didn't jet with the Tiffany box," he said after I had finished the story.

"I wanted to," I said. "I bet it was something good. . . . Oh, well. We'll get a replacement when you and I get married."

No response.

"Do you want to talk about that?" I probed, stroking his arm.

"Talk about what?"

"Us getting married."

"Um—okay. What exactly do you want to talk about?"

"Well, don't you want to do it before the baby's born?" I asked, thinking that I couldn't even focus on my pregnancy until the details of our relationship were squared away. Besides, I was already in full-on wedding mode. There was no reason to let my preparations lapse. I even planned on keeping my dress, knowing that I couldn't find a better gown. "I think we should talk about it. Don't you?"

"I guess so," he said reluctantly.

I chose to ignore his tone and pressed on. "Okay—so when do you think we should do it?"

"I don't know. In six months?"

"When I'm totally showing? No, thanks."

"Five months?"

"Marcus!"

"Four?"

"No. Too long. I think we should do it right away. Or as soon as we can get some plans together."

"I thought you said that we were going to just get a justice of the peace?"

I had, in fact, said something like that somewhere along the line. But that was back when I actually worried about Dexter's feelings. Back when I wasn't even sure that Marcus and I were going to end up together. Now I wanted to have a big wedding just to spite Dex and Rachel and invite all of our mutual friends. I'd invite Rachel's parents too, and then they could report back to her how beautiful I looked, how thrilled I was in my new relationship, how moving Claire's toast was.

"Well, I was actually thinking that we could have a little ceremony. Just something small. Like fifty people or so." My count was more like one hundred, one twenty-five, but I would ease him into the idea.

"Fifty, huh? So pretty much immediate family?" he asked as he scratched the back of his neck.

"Yeah, pretty much. And our closest friends."

He smirked. "Like Dex and Rachel?"

I gave him a look.

"No?" he asked, grinning. "Not Dex and Rachel?"

"Be serious! What do you think about having a real wedding?"

He shrugged and then said, "I'm not sure about all that. That's not really my thing. I'm still kind of thinking that the justice of the peace is the way to go. Or we could elope. I don't know. Do we have to talk about this right now?"

"Okay, fine." I sighed, resigning myself to the fact that he probably wasn't going to be satisfying about a wedding. But what guy really is? Other than those repulsive, girly types on TLC's *A Wedding Story* who blubber their way through the ceremony. And who wants a guy like that?

Later that evening, after Marcus and I came back from dinner, I checked my messages. I had twenty-two at work, fourteen at home. Thirty-six messages in eight hours. And only two were work related. Which meant thirty-four personal messages. Likely an all-time personal record. I sat at Marcus's table, listening to the words of support as I took notes on a pad. When I got to the very last message, the third one from Claire, I looked up at Marcus. "They didn't call," I said, shocked. "Neither one of them."

"Did you think they would?" Marcus asked.

"Yes. They *owe* me a call. Especially Rachel."

"But didn't you say that you never wanted to speak to her again?"

I shot him a look of annoyance. "She should still *try* to call and apologize . . ."

Marcus shrugged.

"And as for Dex, I *have* to talk to him. About logistics. The wedding stuff," I said. "I just can't believe neither one of them called."

Marcus shrugged again. "I don't know what to tell you."

"Okay. For the record, I *abhor* that statement."

"What statement?"

" 'I don't know what to tell you.' "

"Well, I *don't* know what to tell you."

" 'I don't know what to tell you,' " I mimicked again. "It's what re-pairmen say when they can't fix what's broken. 'But I just bought this car/computer/dryer last month!' you say, at their mercy, and they shoot back with an 'I don't know what to tell you.' Translation: 'It's not my problem and I *really* don't give a shit.' "

Marcus smiled. "Sorry. I won't say it again."

"Thank you," I said, still clutching the phone. "So do you think I should call Dex?"

"Do you want to call him?" Marcus asked as he inspected the bottom of his foot and picked at a callus.

"It's not a question of *want*. It's a question of *need*. We have logistics to work out," I said, slapping his hand away from his foot. "Like canceling the photographer and caterer and band. And reaching everyone on our invite list. Like the honeymoon tickets. Like his moving out."

"So call him."

"But he should call me."

"So wait for him to call you."

"Look, mister. You better start taking a more active interest in these details. In case you forgot, you're an integral part of this whole saga, and you better start having an opinion on all related matters."

Marcus made a face as if to say, *I don't know what to tell you.*

The next few days, leading up to what would have been my wedding day, were jam-packed with nonstop drama. More phone calls, e-mails, and long drawn out conversations with Claire about why in the world

Dex would want to hook up with Rachel, even longer sessions with my mother, who still cried often and could not seem to accept that Dex and I were not going to reunite.

But there was still no word from Dex or Rachel. It infuriated me that they weren't calling. As much as I didn't want to be the one to phone first, I finally broke down and dialed Dexter's work number. We only discussed logistics—the money he owed me, the number of days he had to come remove his belongings from my apartment, that sort of thing. After I had given him my orders, I paused, waiting for him to tell me that the thing with Rachel was a fluke, and that he was only using her to get back at me. When he didn't, I reasoned that he was still so pissed about Marcus that he actually wanted me to think the worst. So I certainly wasn't going to give him the satisfaction of asking about her. Nor would I ask him where he was staying. Never one to impose on a friend, he had likely checked into a hotel. I pictured him ordering a club sandwich from room service and stirring whiskey from the minibar into a glass of Coke as he clicked his way through the Pay-Per-View selections.

"Well. Good-bye, Dex," I said as emphatically as possible. This was it. He had one more chance to tell me something, issue a final statement, plead his case. Maybe even tell me that he was sorry or that he missed me.

"All right, then. Bye, Darce," he said without the slightest trace of emotion. I told myself that it just hadn't hit him yet, the finality of it all. When it did, there was going to be some serious depression going on, some serious minibar bingeing happening somewhere in this city.

On what would have been my wedding night, Marcus and I hunkered down in his apartment, ordered Chinese, and had sex twice. Throughout the evening I kept announcing how happy I was not to be making "the biggest mistake of my life." In truth, I felt a bit wistful. Not because I wanted to be marrying Dex. Not because I missed Rachel. I had way too much indignation brewing to be nostalgic about either of them. It was more about the wedding, the party-that-almost-was. It would have been the event of the year, I told Marcus.

"I hear ya," Marcus said. "I could be hanging with my college buddies right now, drinking for free."

I punched him in the arm and told him to take it back. He obliged as he tilted back his third Miller Lite. "Besides, I wasn't in the mood to get dressed up. I hate wearing a tux."

I would have been miffed at the emotionless spin he was putting on our momentous evening together, but I could tell that deep down, he was really happy to have won the grand Darcy prize. I was in the heart of a "boy steals girl away from other boy" love-triangle thriller. Marcus was the victor, and Dex was so crushed that he was driven to hook up—or nearly hook up—with Rachel, a consolation prize if there ever was one. At least that's the way I saw things in those sweet early days.

ten

I don't think my pregnancy truly sank in until the following week, when I had my first prenatal doctor's appointment. Marcus came with me, but only after I guilt-tripped him into it. As we sat together in the waiting room, I filled out insurance forms while he flipped through a *Time* magazine, looking like he'd rather be anywhere else in the world. When the receptionist called my name, I stood up. Marcus stayed put. "Well, come *on*," I said impatiently.

"Can't I wait here?"

I caught a very pregnant woman, sitting with her husband, glance disdainfully at Marcus.

"Get up *now*," I hissed at him.

He did so, but with a loud sigh. More like a groan.

We followed a nurse to the corridor behind the waiting room, where she asked me to step on the scale.

"With all my clothes on?" I asked. I make it a firm policy only to weigh myself naked and first thing in the morning. Or after a long sweat at the gym.

"Yes," the nurse said impatiently.

I slipped off my Tod's, handed my heavy silver cuff bracelet to Marcus, and instructed him to turn around. He did, but not before he rolled his eyes.

The nurse skillfully adjusted the scale with several quick sweeps of her fingertips until it finally steadied at 126½.

"127," she said out loud.

I glared at her. Why did she think I'd wanted Marcus to turn around? "Looked like 126½ to me," I said.

She ignored me, recording 127 on my chart.

Still, this was good news. I was 127, which meant 124 or 125 without clothes. No weight gain yet.

"How tall are you?" the nurse asked.

"Five nine and a half."

She recorded this on my chart and led us to a small, chilly examining room. "The doctor will be with you shortly."

I got up on the table, while Marcus glanced at another magazine rack. Upon discovering that his only offerings were *Parents* and *American Baby,* he chose to read nothing. Minutes later a young, petite blond woman who looked no older than twenty-five bounced into the room. She wore her thick blond hair in a short, pixie cut that showcased huge, brilliant-cut diamond studs. Black leather knee-high boots met the edge of her crisp white doctor's coat.

"Hi. I'm Jan Stein. Sorry I'm running a little behind today." She beamed, reminding me of Tammy Baxter, our head cheerleader in high school—who always got to top the pyramid while I was stuck steadying her heel.

"Darcy Rhone," I said, sitting up straighter, noticing that she had an unusually large chest for such a small frame. Surely a doctor wouldn't get a boob job, though. So they had to be natural. As a relatively flat-chested woman, that is the one combination that has always irked me. Fine, give a gal her big chest if it comes with a cellulite-covered ass. But Jan's assets just weren't fair. Maybe Marcus wouldn't notice, I thought, as I introduced him as "the father."

"It's nice to meet you both." She beamed at Marcus as I noted with satisfaction that she had a slight smear of crimson lipstick on her right front tooth.

Marcus smiled broadly back. I wanted to kick myself for requesting a female doctor.

"Should I take my clothes off?" I asked impatiently, before Jan could engage Marcus further.

"No, I think we'll just chat for a bit first. I want to go through your medical history and answer your questions. I'm sure you have plenty."

"Sounds good," I said, although I actually had none except whether it was okay to have an occasional cup of coffee or glass of wine.

Jan took a seat across from us, rolled her chair closer, and pressed my chart into an old-school wooden clipboard and said, "So. First off. Can you tell me the first date of your last menstrual period?"

"Yes. I can," I said, proud that I'd thought to check the date on my calendar that morning. "August eighth."

She made a note on her chart as I studied the enormous emerald-cut rock on her finger. She had to have been wearing at least a hundred thousand dollars' worth of diamonds. I bet she was engaged to an older, gray-haired surgeon. I had a sudden pang for my engagement ring, which I planned to sell, but reassured myself that it was hip to be at a prenatal appointment with your partner, rather than your husband. I was like a celebrity. Plenty of them skipped the marriage and went right to having babies.

"So when is the baby due?" I asked. I knew she was due around early May, but I was eager to hear an exact date.

Jan pulled out a paper wheel, spun it, and squinted as she checked the dates. "Okay. Your estimated date of delivery, or EDD as you may hear me refer to it, is May second."

The second of May would be Dexter's thirty-fifth birthday. I looked at Marcus, who was clueless as to the implications of the due date. It's amazing to me how few guys know their friends' birthdays. So I announced to Jan and Marcus, "I hope I'm late—or early— because that's my ex-fiancé's birthday."

Marcus rolled his eyes and shook his head while Dr. Stein laughed and then reassured me that only about 10 percent of babies are born on their actual due date.

"Why's that?" I asked.

Jan looked stumped for a second—not a good sign if such an easy question threw her—and then said, "The due date is only a useful guide."

"Oh," I said, thinking that an older doctor would be able to come up with a better answer than that one. Or even a younger doctor who was less attractive. Ugly girls had more time to study in medical school. I bet Jan finished at the bottom of her class. I bet she wouldn't even be sitting here today but for her surgeon boyfriend. "I see."

"So," Jan said briskly. "I'd like to run through your medical history, ask you some questions."

"Sure," I said, catching Marcus examining Jan's toned left thigh.

I glared at him as Jan launched into her Q&A. She asked me my age (I was glad to say twenty-nine and not thirty), all about my medical history, what medications I was taking, and a bunch of questions about my lifestyle: how often I drank, exercised, whether I smoked, all about my diet, etc. After she had my life story fully recorded, she looked up, a smile plastered on her heavily made-up face.

"So, how have you been feeling?" Jan asked. "Any symptoms? Nausea?"

"My breasts are a little sore," I said.

Marcus looked embarrassed, so I added a gratuitous, "When he touches them."

Jan nodded earnestly. Marcus cringed.

I kept going. "And they're a little bigger, fuller . . . And the areolae are darker. . . . But other than that, I feel exactly the same. And my weight is the same," I said proudly.

"Well, you're only about five and a half weeks pregnant, so it would be a little early for weight gain," Jan said. "Although you might notice an increase in your appetite if you haven't already."

"Nope," I said proudly. "And I don't plan on being one of those chowhound pregnant women. I'm sure you see plenty of those."

Jan nodded again, making a note on my chart. Then she announced that we were ready for the physical examination.

"Should I go?" Marcus asked.

"You're fine to stay," Jan said.

"Told ya," I said to him. And then to Jan, "He feels all awkward."

"Well, he shouldn't. It's great that he's so involved."

"Yeah—we're not married yet," I said. "But he's still very into it."

Jan smiled and told me to change into the gown on the table, she'd be right back. As soon as she left, I asked Marcus if he thought our doctor was pretty.

"She's all right," he said. "Cute, I guess."

"How old would you say she is?"

"Twenty-eight?" he asked.

"Am I prettier?"

"Yes, Darce. You're prettier."

"Will I still be prettier when I'm twenty pounds heavier?"

"Yes," he said, but without much conviction.

Jan returned right as I was getting settled on the table. She took my blood pressure and then examined my heart, breasts, and lungs. "Now I'm going to examine your cervix."

"Does that confirm the pregnancy?"

"Well, we're going to give you a blood and urine test for that, but yes, this will give us further information about the approximate age of the pregnancy, as well as help us assess the size and shape of your pelvis."

I nodded.

"Now, just relax," Jan said.

I let my knees fall apart. "No problem," I said, looking past her at Marcus, who was clearly pretending that he was somewhere else.

After the physical examination was complete, I dressed, went to the bathroom, and peed into a cup, got my blood drawn in a small lab, and returned to the exam room, where Jan told me she'd be in touch with the results of my blood work.

"In the meantime, Darcy, I'm going to give you a prescription for prenatal vitamins. They contain folic acid. It is extremely important for your baby's spinal cord development. You're going to want to take them on a full stomach." She wrote out the prescription in un-characteristically neat handwriting for a doctor (another bad sign— real doctors should be messy) and handed it to me. "So congratulations to both of you. We'll see you in another four weeks for your first ultrasound."

Marcus and I shook Jan's hand and then headed off to Duane Reade to fill my prescription. For some reason, I remember that five-block walk well. It was a brilliant fall day—brisk but sunny, the sky bright blue and filled with cotton-candy clouds. I remember cinching my blue suede trench coat around my still tiny waist and skipping a few steps, feeling little-girl happy. As we waited at a crosswalk, Marcus took my hand without being prompted and smiled at me. That smile of his is frozen in my mind. It was warm and generous and sincere. It was the kind of smile a man gives you when he's happy to be with you, happy to be marrying you, happy that you are pregnant with his child.

eleven

My apartment's contents hadn't been too depleted when Dex moved out, but he had taken our kitchen table, two lamps, and a dresser. I was thrilled to see them all go, especially the rustic pine table that looked as if it belonged in an Amish home. I planned on going for a sleeker, more contemporary look that would complement the slick high-rise apartment with a view that Marcus and I would purchase together. Good riddance to Dexter's traditional taste, his insistence on prewar buildings long on charm and short on closet space.

So about two weeks after what would have been my wedding day, I dragged Marcus on a furniture-shopping expedition. We took the subway uptown to Fifty-ninth and Lex and walked over to Crate and Barrel on Madison Avenue. As we pushed open the glass doors, I felt a surprising wave of sadness, remembering my last visit to the store, when

Dex and I had registered for wedding gifts. I shared the memory with Marcus, who had developed a pat response to such recollections.

"Ahh. The good ol' days," he said, as he followed me to the second floor. At the top of the stairs, I admired an oblong cherry table with tapered legs. It was exactly what I had in mind for our table, but never imagined I would find it so easily. I swept my hand across the smooth surface. "This is perfect. Do you like it? What do you think? Picture it with upholstered chairs. Something in lime green, perhaps?"

Marcus shrugged. "Sure. Sounds good." He was staring at something behind me. "Um, Darcy . . . Rachel and Dex are here," he said in a tone that made me know it was not a joke.

"What?" I froze, and my heart stopped for several seconds. Then it began to race, beating faster than it does after a spinning class. "Where?" I whispered.

"At your nine o'clock. Over by that brown couch."

I turned around slowly, cautiously. Sure enough, there to my left, less than thirty feet away, was the enemy, scrutinizing a chenille couch the color of baby poo. They both had the whole casual Saturday look going—jeans and tennis shoes. Dex had his standard Saturday gray Georgetown sweatshirt, and Rachel was wearing a navy blue BCBG sweater that I helped her pick out at Bloomingdale's last year. The weekend before Dex had proposed, to be exact. A lifetime ago.

"Oh *shit*! How do I look?" I fumbled for the compact tucked into the side pocket of my Prada bag, and remembered that at the last minute I had removed it to add more blush and left it on Marcus's coffee table. I had no mirror. Instead I had to rely on Marcus. "How's my face?"

"You look fine," Marcus said. His eyes darted back to Rachel and Dex.

"What do we do? Should we get out of here?" I said. My knees felt weak as I leaned on my prospective table. "I think I'm gonna be sick."

"Maybe we should go have a chat," Marcus deadpanned. "It'd be the well-adjusted, mature thing to do."

"Are you crazy? I don't want to have a *chat*!"

Marcus shrugged. Dex had called Marcus a couple of days earlier to say "no hard feelings and congratulations on the baby." They had both glossed over the details, neither of them uttering my name or Rachel's. Marcus said the conversation was awkward, but had lasted fewer than three minutes. He said there was a tacit understanding that the friendship was over; even for guys, our situation was too much to get past.

"Okay, Darce. Let's get outta here," Marcus said. "I'm not in the mood for a reunion either." He pointed behind me at the staircase leading to the ground floor. We had an easy escape route. Clearly, we hadn't been spotted yet. Dex and Rachel were cheerfully chatting away, completely oblivious to the furniture-shopping coincidence of the century.

I wanted to turn and walk down the stairs, but I couldn't make myself go. It was like watching a gruesome scene in a scary movie. You don't want to see the girl get decapitated, but somehow, you always part your fingers to sneak a peek. I hid behind a bookcase and pulled Marcus down next to me. We watched Rachel and Dex stand and wander over to another couch, slightly closer to us. This one was boxier than the first, and as far as I was concerned, the better choice. Dex studied it and then made a face. It was too modern for him. I translated what had just transpired for Marcus. "See, he doesn't like clean lines. See?"

"Darcy, I don't give a shit about the couch they buy."

"*They buy?* You mean you think it's a *joint purchase?*"

"They buy. He buys. She buys," Marcus said, as if conjugating a verb in French class.

"Does she look good? Do they look happy?"

"Come on, Darce. Let's just go," he said.

I kept staring at them, my insides churning.

"Tell me," I demanded. "Does she look prettier than usual? Thinner maybe?" We watched Rachel and Dex return to their boring, brown couch. She sat and reclined smugly. Then she looked up at Dex and said something. His back was to us, but I could see him nod, run his fingers along the back of the couch. Then he stooped to flip through a book of color swatches on a coffee table next to the couch.

"Do you think they're moving in together?" I asked.

"How the hell should I know?"

"Did he say anything about that when you talked?"

He sighed. "I told you ten times every word of that conversation."

"He's just replacing our couch then, right? She's just helping him, right?"

He sighed harder this time. "I don't know, Darcy. Probably. Who cares?"

"Look. Don't lose your patience with me, mister," I said. "This is *major*." I thrust a finger toward them and then studied Dex and Rachel more, taking in every little detail. Three weeks ago, they were the people that I knew the best. My best friend and my fiancé. Now they seemed like strangers or estranged loved ones whom I hadn't heard from in years. As Rachel turned her head, I noticed that her hair was layered a bit at the bottom, a radical departure from her usual blunt ends.

"Do you like her hair like that?" I asked Marcus.

"Sure. It's great," he said dismissively.

I gave him a look that said, *Wrong answer.*

"Okay. It sucks. It's hideous."

"Come on. Look at it! Tell me your honest opinion!" I was feeling frantic, wishing that Claire were with me. She'd find *something* to criticize. Sneakers. Hair. Something.

Marcus thrust his hands in his pockets and glanced over at Rachel. "She looks the same to me."

I shook my head. "No. They both look better than usual," I said. "What is it? Is it just that some time has passed?"

Then, just as Dex sat down beside Rachel, it hit me. Dex was tanned. Even Rachel didn't have her usual white glow. The realization slashed through my heart. They had gone to Hawaii together! I gasped. "Omigod. They're tan. She went on *my* trip to Hawaii! She went on my honeymoon! Omigod. Omigod. I'm going to confront them!" You hear people say that rage can be blinding, and I learned at that moment that it was true. My vision became blurry as I took one step toward them.

Marcus grabbed my arm. "Darce—do *not* go over there. Let's just leave. *Now.*"

"He told me he was going to eat those tickets! How *dare* she go on my honeymoon!" I was crying. A couple standing near our bookcase bunker looked at me, then over at Dex and Rachel.

"You told me he offered them to you," Marcus said.

"That is totally beside the point! I wouldn't have taken you to Hawaii!"

Marcus raised his eyebrows as if to consider this. "Yeah—that is kind of fucked up," he conceded. "You have a point."

"She went on my honeymoon! What kind of a psycho bitch goes on her friend's honeymoon?" My voice was louder now.

"I'm leaving. Now." He took the stairs, two at a time, and as I turned to follow him, I got one more sickening visual: Dex leaning down to kiss Rachel. On her lips. Tan, happy, smitten, kissing couch consumers.

My eyes filled with tears as I rushed down the stairs, past Marcus, past the barware, out the door to Madison Avenue.

"I know, honey," Marcus said, when he caught up to me. For the first time, he seemed to have genuine empathy for my ordeal. "This has gotta be hard for you."

His kindness made me sob harder. "I can't *believe* she'd go to Hawaii," I said, hyperventilating. "What kind of person does that? I hate her! I want her to die!"

"You don't mean that," Marcus said.

"Fine. Maybe not death. But I want her to get a bad case of cystic acne that Accutane won't cure," I said, thinking that incurable acne would actually be worse than death.

Marcus put his arm around me as we jaywalked across Sixtieth Street, narrowly escaping a delivery guy on a bike. "Just forget about them, Darce. What does it matter what they do?"

"It *matters!*" I sobbed, thinking that there was no way around it: Dex and Rachel were a couple. I couldn't pretend otherwise. A wave of buyer's remorse washed over me. For the first time, I started to wonder if I should have stayed with Dex—if only to keep this from happening with Rachel. When my affair with Marcus began, the grass seemed so much greener with him. But after watching my former fiancé furniture-shop, Dexter's pastures seemed blissfully bucolic.

Marcus hailed a cab, and then helped me inside. I cried the whole way down Park Avenue, picturing Rachel and Dex in all of the scenes that I had studied from our honeymoon brochures: the two of them in a Jacuzzi sipping champagne . . . at a luau grinning over a roasted pig amid native dancers twirling flames . . . frolicking in turquoise water . . . having sex under a coconut tree.

I remembered saying to Dex that we were a better-looking couple than any of the featured honeymooners in those brochures. Dex had laughed and asked me how I got to be so modest.

"Can we go to Hawaii on our honeymoon?" I asked Marcus when we arrived back at his apartment.

"Whatever you want," he said, sprawling on his bed. He motioned for me to join him.

"We should go somewhere even more exotic," I said. "Dex picked Hawaii, and if you ask me, Hawaii is a trite choice."

"Yeah," he said, wearing his "I want sex" expression. "Everyone goes to Hawaii. Now c'mere."

"Where will we go, then?" I asked Marcus as I reluctantly lay down next to him.

"Turkey. Greece. Bali. Fiji. Wherever you want."

"You promise?"

"Yeah," he said, pulling me on top of him.

"And can we get a new, big apartment?" I asked, looking around at his stark white walls, his overflowing closet, and his hulking stereo equipment belching wires all over the scratched parquet floors.

"Sure."

I smiled a sad but hopeful smile.

"But in the meantime," he said, "I know how to make you feel better."

"Just one sec," I said, as I picked up the cordless phone next to his bed.

Marcus sighed and gave me an exasperated look. "Who are you calling? Don't you call them!"

"I'm *not* calling them. I'm over them," I lied. "I'm calling Crate and Barrel. I want that table."

Rachel may have stolen Dex and my trip to Hawaii, but I was sure as hell going to have a nicer table.

But even the table (which was in stock) and sex with Marcus (which was incredible) did nothing to repair my mood. I just couldn't believe that Rachel and Dex were actually together—that their relationship was real. Real enough to go shopping for couches together. Real enough to go to Hawaii.

And from that day forward, I was totally obsessed with Rachel and Dex. They were two people cut entirely from my life, yet from my perspective, the three of us had never been so inextricably and permanently bound together.

twelve

Things only got worse when I turned thirty. I woke up on the morning of my birthday to my first dose of morning sickness. I was in bed with Marcus, on the side farthest from the bathroom, and barely made it over him to the toilet before I puked up the fajitas I had eaten for dinner the night before at Rosa Mexicano. I flushed, rinsed my mouth with Listerine, and brushed my teeth. Another wave overcame me and more red and yellow bits of pepper descended. I flushed, rinsed, brushed again. Then I collapsed onto the floor and moaned loudly, hoping that Marcus would wake up and come to my rescue. He didn't.

I thought to myself that Dex would have heard me puking. He was a very light sleeper, but at the moment, I chalked it up to him having greater compassion. Maybe Marcus wasn't nurturing enough for me. I moaned again, louder this time. When Marcus still didn't stir, I picked myself up from the cold tile and returned to bed, whim-pering, "Hold me."

Marcus snored in response.

I nestled into the crevice between his arm and body and made some more needy sounds as I surveyed his clock. Seven thirty-three. The alarm was set for seven forty-five. I had twelve minutes before he offi-cially wished me a happy birthday. I closed my eyes and wondered what Rachel and Dex were doing at that moment—and more impor-tant, what they were going to do about my birthday. This was their *last chance,* I had ranted to my mother and Marcus the night before. I wasn't quite sure what I expected or wanted them to do—but a phone call or e-mail seemed a step in the right direction.

Surely Rachel and Dex had discussed the issue in recent days. My guess was that Dex voted to leave me alone, Rachel to call. "I've been celebrating her birthday for over twenty-five years," she would say to Dex. "I just can't blow this day off. I have to call her." I could hear Dex saying back, "It's for the best. I know it's hard, but no good can come of it." How long had they debated the point? Perhaps it had es-calated into an argument, maybe even a permanent rift. Unfortu-nately, neither Dex nor Rachel was particularly stubborn or argumentative. Since they were both pleasers by nature, I was sure that they had a calm, reasoned conversation and came to a unanimous con-clusion about how to approach the anniversary of my birth.

One thing I did know for sure was this: if Dex and Rachel did not wish me a happy birthday in some form, there would be no redemp-tion. Ever. My hatred for them was growing faster than the fruit flies had multiplied in our peanut butter jars in biology class sophomore year. I tried to remember what that experiment sought to prove, vaguely recalling something about eye color. Red eyes versus green eyes. I forgot the details. With Rachel as a lab partner, I hadn't needed to pay too much attention. She had done all the work. I suddenly wondered what color eyes my baby would have. I hoped for blue, or at least green like mine. Everyone knows blue eyes are prettier, at least on a girl, which is why there were so many songs about brown-eyed girls, to make them feel better. I listened to Marcus snore as I played with a tuft of hair on his chest. He had just the right amount.

"Hmm," he said, pulling me on top of him.

Having just puked fajitas, I wasn't in the mood for sex, but I caved. It seemed as good a way as any to begin my thirtieth birthday. So after a quick, perfunctory round, I waited for him to open his eyes and wish me a happy birthday. Tell me that he loved me. Reassure me that thirty wasn't old and that I had at least six good years left before I would need to think about plastic surgery. Ten, fifteen, twenty seconds passed with still no words from my boyfriend.

"Did you fall back asleep?" I demanded.

"No. I'm awake . . ." he mumbled, his eyelids fluttering.

The alarm clock sounded in a series of increasingly louder, high-pitched beeps. Marcus reached over and silenced his clock with a slap. I waited, feeling like Molly Ringwald in *Sixteen Candles* when her whole family forgot her birthday. Sure, it had only been a few minutes, whereas Molly's character had to endure a whole day of neglect, but after all I'd been through in recent weeks, all of the trauma and pain, those minutes felt like hours. It was bad enough that I had to turn thirty on a Monday and that I had to puke twice. But now the father of my child couldn't even muster a tiny, heartfelt "happy birthday" on the heels of gratuitous sex.

"I'm sick," I said, trying another angle for attention. "Morning sickness. I threw up twice."

He rolled over, his back toward me. "You feel better now?" he asked, his voice muffled under his comforter.

"No," I said. "Worse."

"Mmmmmm. I'm sorry, sweetheart," he said.

I sighed loudly and said in my most sardonic tone, "Happy birthday to me."

I expected his eyes to snap open, an immediate apology to spring from his lips. But he only mumbled again, still facedown in his pillow, "Happy birthday, Darce. I was getting to that."

"The hell you were. You *totally* forgot!"

"I didn't forget . . . I just gave you your present," he said. I couldn't see his face but knew he was smirking.

I told him I wasn't amused and then announced that I was going to take a shower. "By all means," I said, "you just stay in bed and relax."

Marcus tried to redeem himself after I had showered, but he didn't have much ammunition. It was clear he had not yet bought me a card or a present. Nor had he purchased my Pillsbury sticky cinnamon buns and pink candles even though I had told him that this was my family tradition, a tradition that Dex had continued over the past seven years. Instead, Marcus only offered me a few *sweeties* and *babies,* along with a pack of saltines from his delivery from the diner the night before. "Here," he said. "In case you start to feel morning sickness again. I heard once that these do the trick."

I wondered where he had heard that before. Had he ever gotten another girl pregnant? I decided to broach the topic later and snatched the crackers from his outstretched hand, saying, "You're way too good to me. Really, Marcus, you have to tone this down. I can't handle all the over-the-top gestures."

"Oh, relax. I got you covered, Darce. You'll get your present tonight," Marcus said as he sauntered naked toward the bathroom. "Now go play nice with the other kids."

"Buh-*bye,*" I said, as I slipped on my favorite Marc Jacobs pumps and walked toward the door. "Have fun shopping for my gift!"

"What makes you think I don't have it already?" he said.

"Because I know you, Mr. Last Minute . . . and I mean it, Marcus. I want something good. Think Fifty-seventh Street!"

When I got to work, Claire was waiting in my office with yellow roses and what appeared to be a professionally wrapped gift. "Happy birthday, hon!" she trilled.

"You remembered!" I said. "What gorgeous roses!"

"Of course I remembered, silly," she said, placing the fishbowl vase of flowers on my desk. "So how do you feel today?"

I looked at her, worried that she could tell I had morning sickness. "Fine. Why?"

"Just wondering if it feels any different being thirty?" she whispered. Claire was still twenty-eight for another few weeks, in the safety zone, buffered by twenty-nine.

"A little," I said. "Not too bad, though."

"Well, when you look as good as you do, what's a little thing called age?" Claire said. She had been full of compliments since my breakup with Dex. I enjoyed them, of course, but sometimes I had the sense that they verged on pity remarks. She continued, "You could easily still pass for twenty-seven."

"Thanks," I said, wanting to believe her.

Claire smiled sweetly as she handed me my gift. "Here! Open! Open!"

"I thought you were going to make me wait until lunch!" I said, eagerly eyeing the present. Claire had excellent taste and never skimped in the gifting department. I ripped open the paper and saw a satisfying, red Baccarat box. I lifted the hinged lid and peered down at the chunky green crystal heart threaded with a black silk cord.

"Claire! I love it! I love it!"

"You do? Really? I have a gift receipt if you want to get a different color. The purple one was really pretty, too, but I thought this one would look nice with your eyes . . ."

"No way! This is perfect!" I said, thinking that Rachel probably would have picked some boring limited edition book. "You're the best." I hugged her, silently taking back every mean thing I had ever thought about her, every petty criticism. Like how annoying and clingy she got after too many drinks, always needing to accompany me to the bathroom at bars. How she bragged about her hometown of Greenwich and her debutante days. And how she stayed so hopelessly lumpy despite daily visits to the gym. What was she doing, I used to ask Rachel, eating Ho Hos in the locker room?

"The green matches your eyes," Claire said again, beaming.

"I *love* it," I said, as I admired the necklace from my compact mirror. The heart fell at just the right spot, accentuating my thin collarbone.

Claire took me to lunch later that day. I kept my cell phone on, just in case Dex or Rachel decided that lunchtime was the appropriate time to phone, apologize profusely, beg for my forgiveness, and wish me a happy birthday. It rang five different times, and every time I'd say to Claire, "Do you mind?" and she'd wave her hand and say, "Of course not. Go on."

All of the calls (except Bliss Spa reminding me of my five o'clock facial) were from birthday well-wishers. But no Rachel or Dex.

I know it was on Claire's mind, too, as she mouthed, "Who?" each time I answered.

After the fifth call, she asked, "Have you heard from Rachel today?"

"No," I said.

"Dex?"

"Nope."

"How rude not to call on your birthday and try to make up."

"I know!"

"Any sightings since Crate and Barrel?" she asked.

"No. Have you seen them?"

"No. *Nobody* has seen them," Claire said—which was saying something as her network was expansive. The next best thing to hiring a private investigator (and believe me, I had considered it) was having Claire as my new best friend.

"Maybe they broke up," I said.

"Probably so," she said. "Out of guilt if nothing else."

"Or maybe they just went on another exotic trip together," I said.

She patted my arm sympathetically and ordered me a second glass of chardonnay. I knew I shouldn't be drinking—but Dr. Jan had specifically said that I could drink on special occasions. Besides, plenty of French babies were born undamaged, and I was sure their mothers kept up with their daily intake of wine.

"I do have a little nugget for you, though," I said, inhaling deeply, excited to drop the Marcus news on her. Minus the pregnancy, of course.

"Oh, really?" Her bangle bracelets clinked together as she crossed her arms and leaned toward me.

"I'm seeing someone," I said proudly.

"Who?" she asked, wide-eyed. I detected a hint of jealousy. Claire, bless her heart, was a fast and furious matchmaker, but she never seemed to make much progress in her own right.

I smiled mysteriously, took a sip of water, and wiped the lipstick off my glass with my thumb. "Marcus," I said proudly.

"Marcus?" she asked with bewilderment. "You mean, *Marcus* Marcus?"

I nodded.

"Really?" she asked.

"Uh-huh. Isn't that crazy?"

Something flashed across her face that I wasn't sure how to read. Was it jealousy that I had someone new so fast on the heels of a broken engagement? Did she, too, find him sexy in an unorthodox way? Or was it disapproval? My heart fluttered over the possibility of the latter. I desperately needed affirmation that Marcus was acceptable to a member of the Manhattan elite. I needed to be with someone whom everyone else wanted.

"When did this come about?" she asked.

"Oh, recently . . ." I said vaguely.

"I'm . . . I guess I'm a little bit surprised."

"I know," I said, thinking that she would have been less surprised if she hadn't been such a sound sleeper that night over our July Fourth weekend. "Who would have thunk it? . . . But I *really* like him."

"Really?" This time I definitely pegged her expression as disapproving.

"Why are you so surprised?"

"It's just . . . I don't know. I just didn't think Marcus was your type."

"You mean his looks?" I asked. "You mean the fact that I'm better looking than he is?"

"Well, that," Claire said, struggling for tactful wording. "And, I don't know, just everything. He's a nice, fun guy—don't get me wrong . . ." She trailed off.

"You don't think he's sexy?" I said. "I think he's *so* sexy."

Claire looked at me blankly. Her answer was clear. She did not find Marcus sexy. Not in the least.

"Well, I think he is," I said again, feeling highly offended.

"That's all that matters, then," Claire said, patting my hand condescendingly.

"Right," I said, knowing that that was *not* all that mattered. "I can't believe you don't think he's cute."

"I guess," she said. "In a . . . I don't know . . . 'guy's guy' kind of way."

"Well, he's great in bed," I said, trying to convince Claire—and myself—that this single fact could make up for all of his shortcomings.

By five o'clock, I had received a dozen or more birthday e-mails and phone calls, and a stream of chipper office visits from colleagues. Still nothing from Rachel or Dex. There was one last possibility: maybe they had sent a card, note, or gift to my apartment, which I hadn't returned to in several days. So after my facial, I cabbed it across the park to my apartment, anticipating the apologies that were surely awaiting me.

Minutes later I grabbed my mail from the lobby, unlocked my door, and surveyed my stash. I had cards from the usual lineup: my parents; my brother, Jeremy; my still-smitten high school boyfriend, Blaine; my grandmother; and my second-oldest friend from home, Annalise. The final one had no return address. It had to be from Rachel or Dex! I ripped open the envelope to find a picture of wriggling golden retriever puppies piled into a white wicker basket. A "Happy Birthday" banner stretched over the basket, each letter written in a different shade of pink. My heart sank, as I realized that the card was likely from my aunt Clarice, who still treated me as if I were ten. Unless Rachel was playing on the whole "friends since childhood" theme. I slowly opened the card, feeling hopeful until I saw the telltale ten-dollar bill taped inside and Aunt Clarice's wobbly signature below the greeting "Hope your day is a basket of fun!"

And that was that. There was no getting around it—Rachel and Dex had blown off my thirtieth birthday, a day we had talked about for at least the past five years. I started to cry, undermining the treatment for puffy eyes that I had added to my regular facial. I called Marcus's cell to garner some sympathy.

"Where are you?" I asked.

"That's for me to know—and you to find out," he said, the noise of heavy traffic in the background. I pictured him tripping down Fifth Avenue, his arms filled with packages.

"They didn't call. Neither of them. No calls, e-mails, cards. Nothing."

He knew who I meant. "The *nerve* of some ex-boyfriends," Marcus joked.

"It's not funny!" I said. "Can you believe them?"

"Darcy, didn't you tell them that you never wanted to speak to them again? That they were—what were your words?—'dead to you'?"

I gave him credit for recalling my precise wording. "Yes—but they could at least try to *redeem* themselves. They didn't even try. It's my thirtieth birthday!"

"I know, babe. And we're gonna celebrate. So bring your skinny ass down here."

He was right, my ass *was* still skinny. This observation cheered me up a drop. "Am I going to be a basketball girl?"

"What's a basketball girl?"

"One of those girls who looks as if she has only a basketball under her shirt. You know, with thin limbs and a still-pretty face? And then the ball falls out and she is, *voilà,* perfect again?"

"Sure you will. Now get down here!"

He hung up before I could ask him where we were going for dinner, how dressed up I needed to be. Well, there's no such thing as being overdressed, I told myself, as I selected my slinkiest black dress, highest Jimmy Choo stilettos, and gauziest wrap out of my closet, lining the ensemble up on my bed. Then I showered, blew my hair out straight, applied makeup to my glowing skin, opting for neutral lips and dramatic, smoky eyes.

"Thirty and ab-so-lute-ly stunning," I said aloud to the mirror, trying not to look at the tiny crow's feet around my eyes. Or worry about the fact that I was no longer in my twenties, and therefore on the road to losing my two most valuable assets: beauty and youth. I was filled with an unfamiliar sense of self-doubt that I pushed aside as I grabbed Aunt Clarice's ten for cab fare and headed out the door.

Fifteen minutes later I sauntered into Marcus's apartment, catwalk-style.

He whistled. "You look great."

"Thanks." I smiled as I noticed that he was wearing old brown cords, a pilled gray sweater, and scuffed shoes. I pictured Claire's disapproving frown when I told her about Marcus. Maybe this was part of the reason why. He was sloppy. But not *couture* sloppy—you know, the whole low-hanging Dolce & Gabbana jeans with a cool Hanes wifebeater. Just *bad* sloppy.

"No offense, but you do not look so great," I said, remembering that Rachel once told me that anytime I had to preface a statement with "no offense" I was probably saying something I shouldn't be saying.

"No offense taken," Marcus said.

"Please change and kick it up a notch. And FYI, brown and gray don't generally go together . . . although somehow Matt Lauer manages to pull it off."

"I'm not changing," he said stubbornly.

"C'mon, Marcus. Couldn't you at least put on some khakis and a sweater purchased within the last six years?"

"I'm wearing this," Marcus said.

We argued for a few seconds, and I finally gave in. Nobody was going to be looking at Marcus anyway. Not with me on his arm. On our way out the door, I heard a clap of thunder. I asked Marcus for an umbrella.

"I don't have one," he said, sounding curiously proud of himself. "Haven't for years."

I told him that I truly didn't get how one can not own an umbrella. Fine, people lose umbrellas all the time, leave them in shops or cabs when the rain has cleared, not realizing it until the next rainy day. But how could you simply not own one?

"What am I supposed to use to keep dry?" I asked.

He handed me a plastic Duane Reade bag. "Take this."

"Really classy," I said, snatching it from him.

The evening wasn't off to a roaring start.

It only got worse as we stood on the corner struggling to find a cab, which is close to impossible when it's raining. Nothing frustrates me more about living in Manhattan than being stranded on the sidewalk in inclement weather and very high heels. When I expressed this to Marcus, he suggested we make a run for the subway.

I scowled and told him that I couldn't run in heels. And besides, Jimmy Choos shouldn't tread the underworld. Then, when a cab finally arrived, my left shoe got stuck in a gutter, wedged in so tightly that I had to remove my foot from the shoe, bend down, and yank. As I examined the scratched heel, the Duane Reade bag flew up and rain splattered across my forehead.

Marcus chuckled and said, "The shoes would have been better off in the underworld, eh?"

I glared at him as he slid in the cab ahead of me and told the driver the address. I couldn't determine the restaurant from the address but thought to myself that it had better be a good choice, appropriate for a thirtieth birthday. An all-caps Zagat entry I had forgotten about.

But minutes later, I discovered that Marcus's idea of an appropriate thirtieth-birthday dinner was my idea of an appropriate twenty-sixth birthday dinner if the guy is near broke and/or not that into the girl. He had picked an Italian restaurant I had never heard of on a street in the Village I had never bothered to walk down. Needless to say, I was the only one wearing Jimmy Choos in the joint. Then, the food was awful. I'm talking stale, recycled bread plopped onto the table in a red plastic basket with a waxed-paper liner, followed by overcooked pasta. The only reason I braved it and ordered dessert was to see if Marcus had at least thought to request a candle in my cake, do something ceremonious or special. Of course, my tiramisu arrived sans accoutrement. No drizzle of raspberry, no presentation whatsoever. As I picked at it with my fork, Marcus asked if I wanted my gift. "Sure," I said, shrugging.

He handed me a Tiffany box, and for a moment, I was excited. But like his choice of venue, he had bombed in the gift department. Elsa Peretti bean earrings in silver. Not even platinum or white gold. Sure, they came from Tiffany, but those bean earrings were mass-produced, suburban Tiffany. Again, appropriate for a twenty-sixth birthday, but not a thirtieth. Claire had done better. At least her gift was shaped in a heart rather than a gas-causing vegetable.

As Marcus signed the check, I resisted making a snide remark on the off chance that the bean-earring stunt was designed to throw me off the scent of the diamond ring, hidden in the pocket of his leather jacket. Instead, I graciously thanked him for the earrings, replacing them in the box.

"Aren't you going to wear them?" Marcus asked.

"Not tonight," I said. I wasn't about to switch out of my diamond studs, which, ironically, were given to me by Dex on my twenty-sixth birthday.

After dinner Marcus and I had a drink at the Plaza (my idea) and then returned to his apartment and had sex (his idea). For the very first time with Marcus, I didn't have an orgasm. Not even a tiny hiccup of one. What was worse, he didn't seem to notice, not even when I furrowed my brow and sighed, the portrait of a frustrated woman. Instead, his breathing grew deep and steady. He was falling asleep. My day was beginning and ending in the same frustrating way.

"Well, I guess this means no engagement ring," I said loudly.

He didn't respond, so I shot him another pointed barb, something about winning some and losing some.

Marcus sat up, sighed, and said, "What's your beef now, Darcy?"

And that was that. We were on our way to a full-on fight. I called him insensitive; he called me demanding. I called him mean; he called me spoiled. I told him that the bean earrings were not acceptable. He said he'd gladly return them. And then I think I said that I wished I were still with Dex. And that maybe we shouldn't get married. He said nothing back. Just gave me a cold stare. It wasn't the reaction I was after. I thought about what Rachel always said: *The opposite of love isn't hate; it's indifference.* Marcus's expression was the embodiment of utter indifference.

"You want to be off the hook!" I shouted. I turned away from him and sobbed quietly into my pillow.

After a long while, Marcus broke and put his arm around me. "Let's not fight anymore, Darce. I'm sorry." His tone was unconvincing, but at least he was apologizing.

I told him that I was sorry for the mean things I had said, especially the part about Dex. I told him I loved him. He told me, for only the second time, that he loved me too. But as Marcus fell asleep again, his arm still around me, I knew that our relationship wasn't quite right. Moreover, I think I knew that it had never really been right in the first place. Sure, we had shared some passion under a tree in East Hampton. And we had had a few good times after that, but what else did we have together? I reminded myself that Marcus was the father of my baby, and I vowed to make things work between us. I tried to come up with names for our daughter. Annabel Francesca, Lydia Brooke, Sabrina Rose, Paloma Grace. I envisioned our life together, pictured the pages of the scrapbook: rosy snapshots on creamy, linen pages.

But in the final seconds before I drifted off to sleep, in that time of semiconsciousness when what you think dictates what you dream, I thought of Claire's disapproving stare and my own feelings of dissatisfaction. Then my mind was elsewhere, rooted in the past. Fixed on Dex and Rachel and what would never be again.

thirteen

In the following weeks, my relationship with Marcus disintegrated further. Even the sex—the cornerstone of our relationship—was starting to feel routine. I tried to tell myself that it was only the stress caused by the life changes hurtling our way: the apartment we had yet to look for, the wedding we had yet to plan, and our baby on the way.

When I asked Marcus why he thought we were fighting so much, he blamed it all on my "fixation" with Rachel and Dex. He said he had grown weary of my endless Q&A, that he didn't think it was healthy to spend so much time speculating over what they were doing, and that I should focus on my own life instead. I vowed to talk less about them, believing that in a matter of weeks, I would no longer care what they were doing. But a worry tugged at my heart that it wasn't that simple, that despite my efforts to make things work with Marcus, we were on the brink of a breakup.

What nagged at me even more than any relationship woes was the accompanying regret about the baby. I talked a big game, but deep down, I wasn't so sure I wanted a baby. Since I had been a teenager, my identity was about being thin and beautiful and fun and carefree. A baby threatened all of that. I didn't know who I was going to become. And I certainly didn't feel like anyone's mother.

My own mother called me every other hour in those transitional weeks, just to check on me, her voice filled with pity and worry. Being without a man was a fate worse than death to her, so I finally put her out of her misery and told her that I had a new boyfriend.

I was at Marcus's apartment, talking on his phone while he ate a slice of pizza. I was skipping dinner, as I had far surpassed my carb and fat allocation for the day.

When I told her the good news, she said, "That was fast," with not a hint of disapproval. Only pride that I was back on my horse. "What's his name?"

"Marcus," I said, hoping that she wouldn't remember that there had been a groomsman named Marcus. I wanted to ease her into that part of the story. Of course, I had no intention of breaking the baby news anytime soon.

"Is he black? Marcus sounds like a black name."

"No. He's white," I said.

"Does he go by Mark?"

"No. Just Marcus," I said, looking up at him and smiling.

"Marcus what?"

"Marcus Peter Lawson," I said proudly.

"I *like* the full name. *A lot.* I was never too keen on the name Dexter. Were you?"

"Not really," I said, even though I actually loved the name Dex. It had panache. But the name Marcus did too.

"What does he look like? Tell me all about him. How did you meet?"

"Well, Mother, how about you just meet him yourself? We're coming home this weekend. I got flights today."

Marcus's head jerked up to look at me. This was news to him. I hadn't quite gotten around to telling him about our travel plans.

"Fantastic news!" she shouted.

I heard my father ask in the background if I was getting back with Dex. My mother covered the phone, but I could still hear her say, "No, Hugh. Darcy has a *new* boyfriend."

Marcus frantically whispered something. I held up my hand and shushed him. He took an imaginary golf swing and mumbled that he had plans.

I shook my head and mouthed, "Cancel."

"Well, just give me a short prelude," my mom said. "What does he look like?"

"He's handsome," I said. "You'll love him. And as a matter of fact, he's here right now. So I better run."

"Oh! Let me say hello to him," she said.

"No, Mom. You'll meet him soon enough!"

"I can't wait," she said.

"You'll like him way more than Dex," I said, winking at Marcus. "I know you will."

"Dex?" My mother giggled. "Dex who?"

I smiled as I hung up the phone.

"What's the big idea?" Marcus demanded.

"I forgot to tell you," I said breezily. "I booked us flights to Indy."

He threw his slice of pizza back into the greasy box and said, "I'm not goin' to Indy this weekend."

"I asked you if you had plans. Remember? You said you didn't."

"You asked about Friday or Saturday nights. I'm golfing Saturday afternoon."

"With whom? Dex?"

Marcus rolled his eyes. "I have other friends in this town, ya know."

Very few, I thought. Another problem in our relationship. When I was with Dex, we traveled in a pack, a big group of friends. But Marcus and I spent all of our time alone, most of it holed up in his apartment. I knew I needed to stage our coming-out party, but I wasn't quite ready for my discerning crowd to sit in judgment of my new boyfriend. And in any event, I needed to buy him some new clothes first.

Marcus continued, "Darcy, you just can't book a trip like that without telling me. That's not cool."

"C'mon, Marcus. This is *really important.* Just play ball on this one," I said, using one of his many sports expressions.

He shook his head.

I smiled and said in my sweetest voice, "You need to meet your in-laws. We need to get this show on the road."

He sighed wearily and said, "In the future, don't go signing me up for shit without asking me. But this time, I'll do it."

As if you ever had a choice, I thought.

For the first time in my long dating history, I could tell my parents actually wanted to like the boy I was bringing home. Their instinct in the past was always to judge and disapprove. My father would follow the script of the living room interrogator, the staunch enforcer of curfews, the guardian of my virtue. Although I'm sure he really did have some protective instincts, I always had the feeling that it was mostly for show. I could tell my mother loved the routine by the way she would re-hash it all later. "Did you see the way your father put Blaine back on his heels?" she would ask me the morning after a date. I think it reminded her of her own teenage years, when she was the big prize in her sleepy Midwestern town and my grandfather had to chase away her suitors.

While my father was a tough customer on the outside, my mother was harsh in private, after being all sugar and spice to the boy's face. She had high standards for me. Specifically, any man of mine had to be as handsome as I was pretty. He had to be mainstream handsome at that. No quirky good looks would do. He also had to be smart, although she would let this one slide if he had money. And he had to have a certain well-mannered slickness. I called this "show quality"—the "impress the neighbors" factor. Dex had this one in spades. He passed with flying colors in every category.

Marcus, on the other hand, was far from perfect, but he had one significant thing going for him: my parents had a strong *need* to like him. What was their alternative? Have their daughter thirty and alone? I knew the thought made both of them shudder. Well, it made my mother shudder, and therefore it became my father's problem too. My mother loved that I had a glamorous job and made good money, but she made it perfectly clear that she thought I should get married, have babies, and live a life of leisure. She wasn't going to hear an argument from me over that game plan. My job could be fun, but not as much fun as a massage at Bliss, shopping at Bendel's, and lunch at Bolo.

So that Friday, Marcus and I flew to Indianapolis for the big introduction. We found my father waiting at baggage claim, all smiles. My father is what you would call polished. Full head of dark hair always in place, polo shirts and sweaters with pressed khakis, loafers with tassels. Glow-in-the-dark teeth befitting the best dentist in town.

"Daddy!" I squealed as we approached him.

"Hi, baby," he said, opening his arms wide to embrace me. I inhaled his aftershave and could tell that he had just showered before his drive over.

"It's so good to see you," I said in my "daddy's little girl," borderline baby-talk voice.

"You too, sweetie pie."

My father and I didn't know any other way to interact. When we were alone for any length of time, we'd fall silent and awkward. But on the surface, in front of an audience, we fulfilled our conspicuously traditional roles—roles that made us both feel comfortable. I don't think I would have even noticed this dynamic but for watching Rachel with her own father. They talked like real friends, equals.

My dad and I separated as I turned to Marcus, who was shifting from foot to foot and looking most uncomfortable. "Daddy, this is Marcus."

My dad squared his shoulders, stepped forward, and gave Marcus's hand a hearty pump. "Hello, Marcus. Hugh Rhone. Welcome to Indianapolis. It's a pleasure to meet you," he boomed in his chipper dentist's-office voice.

Marcus nodded and mumbled that it was nice to meet him too. I gave him a look, widening my eyes as if to say "Is that the best you can do?" Had he ignored my lecture during the flight, my tireless explaining that my parents were all about image? "First impressions are last impressions" was one of my father's favorite expressions. I had told Marcus this.

I waited for Marcus to say something more, but instead he averted his eyes to the luggage belt. "Is that your bag?" he asked me.

"Yes," I said, spotting my Louis Vuitton suitcase. "Grab it for me, please."

Marcus leaned down and heaved it from the belt. *"Sheesh,"* he said under his breath, the fourth comment he had made about my overpacking since we had left the city.

"Oh, Marcus, let me," my dad said, reaching for my bag.

Marcus shrugged and gave it to him. "If you insist."

I cringed, wishing he had protested at least once.

"So that's it, Daddy. Marcus just has his carry-on bag," I said, glancing at his nasty pea-green satchel with a frayed strap and some defunct Internet logo emblazoned on the side. I saw my father take it in too.

"Okeydokey. We're off," my dad bellowed, rubbing his hands together vigorously. Then, as we found his BMW in the parking garage, he told us of his speeding ticket on the way over. "Was only going seven over."

"Daddy, was it really just seven?" I asked.

"Cross my heart. Seven over. Marcus, the cops in this town are relentless."

"That's what I told you in high school!" I said, hitting his arm. "A lot of good *that* excuse ever did me."

"Drinking vodka in the Burger King parking lot at sixteen? That is hardly what I'd characterize as overzealous police work." My dad chuckled. "Marcus, I have a lot of stories to tell you about our girl here."

Our girl. It was a big concession. That combined with his chipper mood on the heels of a ticket was only further proof of his determination to like my new boyfriend.

"I can only imagine," Marcus said from the back seat, his voice detached, bored. Was he missing my dad's cues, or was he simply unwilling to go along with the jovial routine?

I glanced back at him, but his face was in shadow and I couldn't read his expression. For the rest of the ride home, Marcus said virtually nothing despite plenty of effort from my father.

As we pulled into our cul-de-sac, I pointed out Rachel's house to Marcus. He made an acknowledging sound.

"Are the Whites away?" I asked my father, noticing that all of their lights were out.

He reached over and squeezed my knee with one hand and then clicked our garage door opener with the other. "No. They're around, I think."

"Maybe they knew I was coming home and couldn't bear to face me," I said.

"Just remember, it's not their fault," my dad said. "It's Rachel's."

"I know," I said. "But they *did* raise a traitor."

My dad made a face as if to say, "Fair point."

"Think Mom will mind if we go in through the back way?" he asked me. My mother believes that visitors should always be brought through the front door—not that Marcus would ever notice the difference.

Sure enough, my mom peered into the garage and whispered, as if Marcus and I couldn't hear her, "Hugh, the *front* door."

"The kids have bags," he said.

My mother forced a smile and said in her turbocharged, company voice, "Well then, come in! Come in!" As always, she was in full makeup—she put her "face" on even to go to the grocery store. Her hair was swept up in a jeweled clip I had bought for her at Barneys, and she was dressed in ivory from head to toe. She looked beautiful, and I was proud for Marcus to see her. If he subscribed to the whole "a daughter will end up looking like her mother" notion, he had to be exceedingly pleased.

Marcus and my father fumbled with our bags, maneuvering them between our car and the lawnmower as my mom lectured my father about pulling the car in too far to the left.

"Dee, I'm perfectly centered," he said, agitation creeping into his voice. My parents bickered constantly, more with every passing year, but I knew that they would stay together for the long haul. Maybe not for love, but because they both liked the image of the proper home—the good, intact family. "I'm perfectly centered," he said again.

My mom resisted a retort, and opened the door wide for us. As she kissed me, my nose filled with her heavier-than-usual application of Chanel No. 5. She then turned to Marcus, putting one hand on each of his cheeks and planting a big kiss just to the right of his mouth. "Marcus! Welcome! It's so nice to meet you."

"Nice to meet you too," Marcus mumbled back.

My mother hates mumblers. I silently hoped that the shame of greeting a guest between our dark garage and laundry room would distract her from noticing my boyfriend's poor enunciation. She quickly ushered us into the kitchen. A spread of cheese, olives, and her famous shrimp puffs was laid out on the counter.

My brother, Jeremy, and his girlfriend, Lauren, suddenly bounded around the corner like two overeager house pets. Neither of them was ever in a bad mood. My father once said that the pair had two modes: chipper or asleep. True to form, Lauren wasted no time postintroduction and launched into an inane tale about one of our neighbors. I have known Lauren since she was a baby—she lived down the street from us and Rachel occasionally babysat her—so I knew that she was the kind of girl who could dominate a conversation by saying absolutely nothing in the sort of way you expect from an old lady in church, not a twenty-five-year-old. The weather, the big sale at JoAnn Fabrics, or the latest winner of bingo at Good Haven, the nursing home where she worked.

As Lauren concluded her story, my father offered Marcus a drink.

"A beer would be great," he said.

"Get him a chilled glass, Hugh," my mother said, as my dad flicked off the top of a Budweiser.

"Oh, I don't need a glass. Thanks, though," Marcus said, taking the bottle from my father.

I gave him a look to indicate that he should have taken the glass as we all followed my mother to the living room. Lauren sat close to my brother on the couch, clutching his arm in a death grip. My brother is a bit of a dork, too, but as I studied his girlfriend's sweatshirt with the Good Haven logo, acid-washed, cropped jeans, Keds with no socks (a look I couldn't even stomach during its brief acceptable stint in high school), I determined for the hundredth time that he could do better. Marcus and I took a seat on the opposite couch, and my parents took the two armchairs.

"So," my mother said, crossing her ankles. I assumed she was ready to interrogate Marcus. I felt nervous, but also excited, hopeful that he would rise to the occasion and make me proud. But instead of focusing on Marcus, my mother said, "Lauren and Jeremy have some news!"

Lauren giggled and threw out her left hand, revealing what appeared from my seat on the opposite couch to be a princess-cut diamond ring set in white gold or platinum. "Surprise!"

I looked at my brother. I was surprised, all right. Surprised that it wasn't a marquis cut set in yellow gold.

"We're getting married," Jeremy confirmed.

Marcus spoke before I could. "Congrats." He raised his beer.

Jeremy returned the gesture with his glass of Coke. "Thanks, man."

Jeremy shouldn't say *man*. He just can't pull it off. He hasn't a cool bone in his body.

"Congratulations," I said, but my voice sounded stilted, unnatural. I stood to survey the goods, quickly determining that although the diamond was a decent size, it was slightly yellowish. I pegged it as a J in color.

"Very nice," I said, returning Lauren's hand to my brother's knee.

My mother started to gush about a May wedding in Indy and a reception at our country club.

I told them how happy I was for them, my mouth stretched into a fake smile as I tried to suppress a stab of envy. I wondered how I could possibly be jealous of my dorky little brother and this girl with bad bangs and thick thighs shoved into acid-washed jeans. Yet incredibly, I was. I was bothered by my mother's enthusiasm. Bothered that Lauren was replacing me as the bride-to-be, my mother's focal point. And what annoyed me the very most was that their spring wedding was going to shift the focus from my baby and me.

"Should I ask her now?" Lauren looked eagerly at Jeremy.

"Go ahead." Jeremy beamed.

"Ask me what?"

"We want you to be a bridesmaid," Lauren chirped. "Because you've always been like a big sister to me." She looked at Marcus and explained further, "Darcy used to babysit for me."

"I never babysat for you. Rachel did," I said.

"Well, true," Lauren said, her smile fading slightly. Mention of Rachel sombered up the room. I liked the effect—liked reminding everyone of my suffering. But the result was short-lived. Lauren's grin quickly returned in full force. "But you were always there helping her. You were *so* fun."

"Thanks," I said. "I try."

"So will you?"

"Will I what?" I asked, pretending to be puzzled.

"Be a bridesmaid?"

"Oh. Yeah. Sure thing."

Lauren clapped and squealed. "Goody! And I want your help. I *need* your help."

She could say that again, I thought. And sure enough, she did. "I need you to help because you're so good at this stuff."

"Why? Because I'm the wedding expert now that I just spent almost a year planning one?" Another reminder of my pain.

Lauren flinched, but then recovered. "No. Not that. Just because you have the most excellent taste." She turned to Marcus again. "Incredible taste. Nobody has taste like Darcy."

This much was true.

Marcus nodded and then took another swallow of beer.

"So I need your help," she continued excitedly.

Okay. Let's start with those jeans. And the Keds. And your bangs.

I looked at my mother, hoping she was thinking the same thing. She was usually right on board with the Lauren criticism, recently ranting about her application of blush: two round circles of pink missing her cheekbones altogether. Not that Lauren had much in the way of cheekbones. She wasn't bringing the best genes to the table. But clearly my mother was not in her usual critical mode; she was hypnotized by the rosy glow of a new wedding to plan. She looked at Jeremy and Lauren adoringly. "Lauren has been dying to call you. But Jeremy and I convinced her to wait to tell you in person."

"I'm so glad you did," I said flatly.

"You were right, Mom," Lauren said.

Mom? Had I heard that right? I looked at Lauren. "So you're calling her 'Mom' now?" Pretty soon she was going to lay claim to my mother's jewelry and china.

Lauren giggled, pressed Jeremy's hand to her cheek in a nauseating display of affection. It looked like a bad Kodak commercial, the kind that's supposed to make you cry. "Yeah. I've felt that way about her for a long time, but now it feels right to call her that."

"I see," I said, with what I hoped was maximum disapproval. Then I glanced over at Marcus, who was finishing his beer.

"You want another?" I asked, standing for the kitchen.

"Sure," he said.

I gave him a look. "Come with me."

Marcus followed me into the kitchen, where I went off on my family. "How could they go on and on about this wedding after what I just went through? Can you believe how insensitive they're all being? I wanted to tell them about *us* getting married. Now it just doesn't feel right. Probably because I don't even have a ring," I said. I shouldn't have shifted the blame to Marcus like that, but I couldn't help it. Casting the blame net wide is just my natural instinct when I'm upset.

Marcus just looked at me, and then said, "Can I get another beer?"

I opened the refrigerator with such force that a bottle of Heinz ketchup flew from the side shelf onto the floor.

"Everything all right in there?" my mother asked from the living room.

"Just dandy!" I said, as Marcus replaced the ketchup and grabbed another beer.

I took a deep breath, and we returned to the living room, where my mother and Lauren were talking about the guest list.

"Two hundred seems just about right," Lauren said.

"I think you're going to realize that two hundred is the bare minimum. It adds up fast. If your parents invite twenty couples, and we invite twenty couples, that's eighty guests right there," my mother said.

"True," Lauren said. "And I'm going to want to invite a lot of people from Good Haven."

"Well, that should cut down on the liquor bill," Marcus joked.

Lauren shook her head and tittered. "You'd be surprised how much they can put away. Every year at the Christmas party, they get lousy drunk."

"Sounds like a wild and crazy time," I said.

"Do they ever . . . you know . . . hook up?" Marcus asked. His first substantive contribution to the conversation was about geriatric sex. Lovely.

Lauren giggled and then launched into a story about Walter and Myrtle and their recent escapades in Myrtle's room. After she exhausted the nursing-home romance tales, my mother finally turned to my boyfriend and said, "So, Marcus. Tell us a little about yourself."

"What would you like to know?" he asked. Dex would have posed the same question, but with a completely different tone.

"Anything. Everything. We want to get to know you."

"Well. I'm from Montana. I went to Georgetown. Now I work at a pointless marketing job. That's about it."

My mom raised her eyebrows and recrossed her ankles. "Marketing? How interesting."

"Not really," Marcus said. "But it pays the bills. Barely."

"I've never been to Montana," Jeremy remarked.

"Neither have I," Lauren said.

"Have you ever been out of the state?" I muttered under my breath. Then, before she could tell us about her childhood trip to the Grand Canyon, I said, "So what's for dinner?"

"Lasagna. Mom and I made it together," Lauren said.

"You and Mom, huh?"

Lauren was unfazed. "Yeah! And you'll be my sister! Like the sister I never had! It's just too, too wonderful."

"Uh-huh," I said.

"So Marcus, do you have brothers and sisters?" my mother asked.

"Yeah," he said. "One brother."

"Older or younger?"

"Four years older."

"How nice."

Marcus gave her a stiff smile, took another sip of beer. I suddenly remembered how much I wanted to kiss him the night of Rachel's birthday as I watched him drinking a beer at the bar. Where had those feelings gone?

The cocktail hour mercifully ended, and the six of us made our way into my mom's Ethan Allen dining room. Her china cabinet was polished to a high gloss and filled with her Lenox china and crystal.

"Take your seats, everyone. Marcus, you may sit there." She pointed at Dexter's old chair. I saw a pained look flash in my mother's eyes. She missed Dex. Then another look crossed her face—one of determination.

But despite her efforts, dinner was painful. There were stilted questions from my parents and terse answers coupled with more beer-guzzling from Marcus. Then he made the comment that will go down in history.

It started with Jeremy talking about one of his patients, an older man who had just left his wife for a much younger woman. Thirty-one years his junior.

"What a shame," Lauren clucked.

"Shocking," my mother added.

Even my father, whom I sometimes suspected of committing his own indiscretions, shook his head with apparent disgust.

But for some reason, Marcus couldn't just get on board and disapprove along with the rest of the group. Or simply say nothing at all, which he had mastered up until that point. Instead he chose to open his mouth and say, "Thirty-one years, huh? Guess that means that my second wife hasn't even been born yet."

My father and Jeremy exchanged glances, wearing identical raised-brow expressions. My mother deflated as she stroked the stem of her wine glass. Lauren laughed nervously and said, "That's really funny, Marcus. Good one!"

Marcus smiled halfheartedly, realizing that his joke had not gone over.

Suddenly, I was in no mood to salvage the night or my new boyfriend's image. I stood and carried my dishes into the kitchen, my posture ramrod erect. I heard my mother excuse herself and click after me in her heels.

"Sweetheart, he was only trying to be funny," my mother said under her breath when we were alone in the kitchen. "Or perhaps he's just nervous, meeting your parents for the first time. Your father can be intimidating."

But I could tell that she didn't believe her words. She thought Marcus was crass, subpar, nowhere close to Dexter's caliber.

"He's not usually like this," I said. "He's just as charming as Dex when he wants to be."

But as I tried to convince my mother, I realized that I knew that

Marcus was absolutely nothing like Dex. Nothing. The last remaining drops of coffee dripped into the pot in time with my one and only thought: *I. Picked. Wrong.*

We returned to the dining room, where everyone pretended to enjoy a strawberry cream pie from Crawford's Bakery. My mother apologized twice for not baking one herself.

"I love pies from Crawford's! They taste homemade," Lauren said.

My father whistled the theme from *The Andy Griffith Show* between bites until my mother glared at him to stop. After another few painful moments I said, "I'm not in the mood for pie. I'm going to bed. Good night."

Marcus stood, drummed his fingers on the edge of the table, and said he was "bushed" too. He thanked my mother for dinner and followed me silently, leaving his plate at the table.

I walked up the stairs ahead of him, then down the hall, stopping abruptly at our guest room. "Here's your room. Good night." I was too exhausted to gear myself up for a big fight.

Marcus massaged my shoulder. "C'mon, Darce."

"Are you proud of yourself?"

He smirked—which only further riled me.

"How could you embarrass me like that?"

"It was a joke."

"It *wasn't* funny."

"I'm sorry."

"No you're not."

"I *am* sorry."

"How am I supposed to tell them that we're getting married and that I'm pregnant with your baby?" I whispered. "The man who plans to leave me in thirty years for another woman?" I felt a stab of vulnerability, something I had never felt before I got pregnant. It was an awful feeling.

"You know it was a joke."

"Good night, Marcus."

I went to my room, hoping he would follow me. He didn't. So I sat and stared at my lavender walls covered with photos from happier days. Photos that were yellowing and curling at the edges, reminding me of how much time had passed, how far removed I was from high school. I studied one picture of Rachel, Annalise, and me after a foot-ball game. I was in my cheerleading uniform, and they were both wearing Naperville High sweatshirts. Our cheeks were painted with little orange paw prints. I remembered that Blaine had just caught a long touchdown pass to win the game and advance our team to the state quarterfinals. I remember how he took off his helmet, his hair and face drenched with sweat like the sexy star of a Gatorade commer-cial. Then, as the crowd roared, he beamed up at me from the sidelines and pointed, as if to say, "That one was for you, sweetie!" It seemed as though everyone in that stadium followed his finger right to me.

Life was good then, I thought, as I started to cry. Not so much be-cause I missed the good times, although I did. It was more that I knew I was turning into one of those girls who, upon looking at high school photos, feels wistful.

fourteen

The next morning I heard a light rapping at the door and my mother's voice. "Darcy, are you awake?" Her soothing tone—an unnatural one for her—made me feel even worse.

"Come in," I said, as I felt a wave of morning sickness.

She opened the door, crossed my room, and sat on the foot of my bed. "Sweetheart. Don't be so upset," she said, patting my legs through the covers.

"I can't help it. I know you hate him."

"I like Marcus," she said unconvincingly.

"No you don't. You couldn't possibly after last night. He barely said anything—except to announce that he plans to leave me someday."

She gave me a puzzled look. "Leave you?"

"The 'second wife' comment," I said, rearranging my head on my pillow.

"Well, you don't have plans to marry *this boy* anyway, do you?" she whispered.

The way she said "this boy" told the full story.

"Maybe," I whimpered.

My mother looked anxious and continued to whisper. "Marcus is probably just your *rebound* boyfriend."

I sniffed, stared back at her, wondering if I should tell her the big news. *You are months away from being a grandmother.* Instead I said, "He's just going through a difficult stage."

"Well, if he doesn't straighten up, just dump him and start over," she said, snapping her fingers. "You can get anybody you want."

If only it were that easy. If only I could go back to the drawing board and fix my mistake. The realization that I couldn't, that I was stuck with Marcus, made me feel even more nauseated. I told my mother I wasn't feeling so well, and that I thought I should get a few more hours of sleep.

"Sure, dear. You get your rest . . . I'll just get your laundry."

Our housekeeper always did the laundry, so my mother's offer was further confirmation of how much she pitied my current state of affairs.

"My dirty stuff is all in that turquoise mesh bag," I instructed as I closed my eyes. "And please don't put my La Perla bras in the dryer. They're very delicate."

"Okay, honey," she said.

I heard her unzip my suitcase and pull my clothes from it. Then I heard her gasp. My mother's gasp is one of her trademarks. A dramatic inhalation with more noise than you'd ever imagine possible. For a moment I thought she was making a point about my volume of dirty clothes. And then I remembered what I had popped last minute into my luggage: *What to Expect When You're Expecting.*

"What in the world is *this*?"

I had no choice but to fess up. I opened my eyes, sat up, and said, "Mom. I'm pregnant."

She gasped again, pressing her hands to her temples. "No." She shook her head. "No, you're *not*."

"Yes I am," I said.

"Dex?" she asked hopefully. She wanted desperately for me to tell her that Dex was the father. She wanted to believe that I could reconcile with the ideal man. Get my charmed life back.

I shook my head. "No. Marcus."

My mother collapsed onto the bed, dug her fists into my mattress, and wept. It wasn't exactly the "Mom, I'm pregnant" moment I had imagined.

"Mother, puh-*lease*! You're supposed to be happy for me!"

Her expression changed from mournful to angry. "How could you ruin your life like this? That boy is *awful*."

"He is *not* awful. He can be charming and *really* funny," I said, realizing that he hadn't been charming or even a little bit funny in a very long time. "And I'm marrying him, Mother. End of story."

"No. No. *No!* You can't do that, Darcy!"

"Yes, I can."

"You're throwing your life away. He's not good enough for you. Not even close," she said, her eyes filling with fresh tears.

"Because of *one* comment?"

"Because of a lot of things. Because you are not right for each other. Because of his behavior last night. Dex would never behave in such a deplorable—"

"Stop bringing up Dex! I'm with Marcus now!" I shouted at her, not caring who overheard me.

"You're ruining your life!" she yelled back at me. "And your father and I are not going to stand by and watch you do it!"

"I'm not ruining my life, Mother. I love Marcus and we're going to get married and have this baby. And you better just get used to it. Or else you're going to be one of those women on *Oprah* talking about how she's never met her grandchildren," I said, roughly pushing aside the covers and marching over to the guest room, into the arms of my husband-to-be.

After all, there is nothing like a mother telling you that you're making a bad decision to convince you that what you are doing is the absolute best course of action.

Minutes later, Marcus and I had packed our bags and were standing on the corner of the cul-de-sac waiting for the cab I had called. Nobody—not even my chipper little brother—tried to stop us from leaving. The cab dropped us off at the Holiday Inn next to the airport, where Marcus at least pretended to be contrite. I accepted his apology, and we spent the remainder of the weekend having sex and watching television in a darkened room that smelled of bleach and cigarette smoke. The whole scene was undeniably depressing, but strangely romantic and unifying. Marcus and I rehashed my fight with my mother, both of us agreeing that she was a heartless, shallow bitch.

And when we returned home, things continued to be good between us—or at least not altogether bad. But the peace was short-lived, and within a few weeks, we were at it again. Fighting about everything and anything. My chief complaints were his far-too-frequent poker nights with his newly acquired friends from the underbelly of Manhattan, his shabby wardrobe, and his unwillingness ever to make the trip up to my apartment. His chief complaints were my sudden lack of interest in giving him blow jobs, my keeping the thermostat too low in his apartment, and my obsession with Dex and Rachel.

Then one Saturday morning, after a doozy about baby names (he deigned to suggest the name Julie, when I knew that he had lost his virginity to a girl named Julie), Marcus kicked me out of his apartment, saying that he needed some time alone. So I left his place and went to

Barneys, chalking it up to yet another lover's quarrel. Later that night, I expected him to call and apologize. But that didn't happen. In fact, he didn't call at all. Instead, I called him. Over and over. I left him angry messages. Then I left him threatening messages. And then I resorted to hysterical, pathetic, begging messages. When Marcus finally called me back, my venom and tears were gone. I only felt a cold uncertainty.

"Where have you been all weekend?" I asked, feeling pitiful.

"Thinking," he said.

"About us?"

"Yup."

"What exactly were you thinking?" I asked. "Whether you want to be with me?"

"More or less . . ."

At that moment, I knew that Marcus had all of the power. Every drop of it. I thought of all the times I had dumped guys, particularly remembering my breakup speech with my high school boyfriend Blaine. I remember how he had asked, "I want to stay together and you want to break up? How come you get your way?"

"Because, Blaine," I had said. "That's just how it works. The person who wants out of the relationship always gets her way. It's definitional."

The sad truth of the statement hit me in the gut now. If Marcus wanted out, there was absolutely nothing I could do to stop him.

I tried anyway, my voice shaking. "Marcus, please! Don't do this!"

"Look. We should talk face-to-face. I'll be over soon," he said.

"Are you going to break up with me? Just tell me now. Please!" I had waited for him all weekend, but the thought of waiting another twenty minutes was too much to bear.

"I'll be there soon," he said. His voice was flat, emotionless.

He arrived an hour later, wearing a Hooters T-shirt.

"You're dumping me, aren't you?" I asked, before he could even sit down.

He twisted the cap off a plastic bottle of Sprite, took a swig, and nodded twice.

"Omigod. I just can't believe this is happening. How can you dump me? I am pregnant with your baby! How can you do this?"

"I'm sorry, Darcy . . . but I just don't want to be with you."

It was the most surprising sentence I had ever heard. It was even more shocking than when Dex came out of the closet, so to speak. Perhaps because it was so utterly one-sided. I wanted Marcus. He did not want me. End of story.

"Why?" I asked. "Because of one fight?"

He shook his head. "You know it's not about any one fight."

"Then why?"

"Because I just can't ever see marrying you."

"Fine. We don't have to get married. We'll be like Goldie Hawn and what's his name?"

He shook his head again. "No."

"But I'm pregnant with your baby!"

"I know. And that's a problem." He raised his eyebrows and looked at me. "A problem with several different solutions."

"I've told you a million times, I'm *not* getting an abortion!"

"That's your decision, Darcy. Just like getting pregnant was *your* unilateral decision. Remember that?" he said angrily. "And now, here we are . . . and I just want you to have all the facts about the future—"

I interrupted him. "What does *that* mean?"

"It means I don't want to be with you, and I certainly don't want a kid. I'll help support it financially if you insist on having it, but I don't want to be . . . involved," he said, looking relieved. "At all."

"I don't believe what I'm hearing!"

"I'm sorry," he said, looking anything but sorry.

I begged. I cried. I pleaded. I promised that I would try harder.

Then he gave me the ultimate insult—"I'm just not that into you anymore"—before leaving my apartment.

It was Dex all over again. Only this time, I had no backup. No suitor waiting in the wings. I was, for the very first time in my life, completely on my own.

fifteen

The next day I caved and did the unthinkable. I phoned Dex. It was a pathetic and desperate move, but there was no denying it, I had become pathetic and desperate.

"Hi, Dex," I said when he answered his work line at Goldman Sachs.

He made a sound that was either a laugh or a cough, followed by silence.

"It's Darcy," I said.

"I know who it is."

"How are you?" I asked, keeping my voice steady.

"I'm fine. You?" he said.

"I'm . . . okay," I said. "I was just wondering . . . can you talk? Is this an okay time?"

"Um . . . Well, I actually have to run—"

"Well, how about later? Can you meet me after work?"

"I don't think so," he answered quickly.

"Please. I really need to talk to you about something," I said.

As I said the words, I realized that Dex likely no longer cared about my needs. Sure enough, he said again, "I don't think so."

"Why not?"

"I just don't think it's a good idea."

"Because of Rachel?"

"Darcy," he said, annoyed. "What do you want?"

"I just need to see you. Can't you just see me? Please? I just want to talk to you. I'm sure she'd understand," I said, wanting him to tell me that he wasn't seeing Rachel anymore. That they had broken up. I was hungry to hear the words.

But instead he said, "Rachel would be fine with me seeing you."

The statement wasn't clarifying. It could mean she was secure in their relationship. It could mean there was no relationship. I decided not to press. For now. "Well, then, why won't you see me?" I asked.

"Darcy, you need to move on."

"I *have* moved on," I said. "I just need to talk to you about something."

He sighed and then folded. "Fine. Whatever."

I brightened. My plan was going to work. He gave in because he secretly wanted to see me too. "So let's meet back at our place at eight," I said.

"*Our* place?"

"You know what I mean," I said.

"No. I'm not going there. Pick somewhere else."

"Like where?" I asked, wondering if he had a nice restaurant in mind. "You choose."

"How about Session 73?"

The fact that the bar was mere blocks away from Rachel's apartment was not lost on me. "Why there?" I asked snidely. "Is that your new Upper East hangout?"

"Darcy. You're on thin ice," he said. It was something he always used to say to me in jest. I felt a wave of nostalgia and wondered if he felt it too.

"Why can't we meet at the apartment?"

"Don't press your luck."

"But I have some stuff to give you."

"What stuff? I got it all."

"Just a box of stuff you left. Stuff from the filing cabinet."

"Like what?"

"Maps, instruction booklets, a few letters . . ."

"You can toss that stuff."

"Can't you just meet me back at the apartment? We can talk for ten minutes. I'll give you your stuff and you can go."

"No. Bring it to Session 73."

"It's too heavy," I said. "I can't lift it, let alone carry it all that way—"

"Oh. Right. You're pregnant," he said bitterly. It was a good sign; he wouldn't be bitter if he didn't still care.

"So I'll swing by your place at eight," he said. "Please have the stuff ready."

"Okay," I said. "See you tonight, Dex."

Later that afternoon, I left work and zipped over to Bendel's, where I picked up a fabulous sea-foam-green cashmere sweater that plunged in the back. Dexter was a huge fan of my back. He always told me that I had the best back and that he loved how strong it was and the way I had no fat around my bra strap. Rachel definitely had her share of back fat, I thought, as I raced across Fifth Avenue to my hair appointment at Louis Licari. After a fabulous blowout, I changed into my new sweater in the salon bathroom. In case Dex made it back to my place before I did, I wanted to be ready.

Sure enough, when I returned home, there he was, sitting on our front stoop, leafing through a document. He looked gorgeous. My heart raced just as it had when I first saw him walk into that bar in the Village so many years before. His tan had faded somewhat, but his skin still glowed. He had olive skin that would make any woman jealous. A perfect, even color, never a blemish. His sideburns were longer than usual—which gave him a sexy edge. I liked the subtle change. But with or without the sideburns, Dex was gorgeous. I had to get him back.

"Hello, Dex," I said, smiling a slow smile. "You're early."

Dex grimaced and tossed his document into his briefcase. Then he snapped it closed, stood up, and looked me straight in the eye. "Hi, Darcy."

"Come on up," I said, walking as enticingly as possible up the stairs to our third-floor apartment. Dex used to hate when I took the elevator three floors up, so I would show him that people could change. He followed me silently and then stood waiting with a grim expression as I unlocked the door. I walked inside, but he waited just outside the doorway.

"Well? Aren't you going to come in?" I asked, making my way over to the couch.

"Where's my stuff?" he asked, refusing to take another step.

I rolled my eyes. "Can't you please just come in and sit down? I want to talk to you for one second."

"I have plans at nine," he said.

"Well, it's only eight."

He glanced around nervously. Then he sighed, walked toward me, and perched on the very edge of the couch, placing his briefcase between his feet. I thought of all the times he had plopped down on that exact spot, kicked off his shoes, and reclined. We had eaten countless dinners on that couch, watched hundreds of movies and television shows there, even made love a few times in the early days. Now he looked out of place and stiff. It was weird.

I smiled at him, trying to alter the mood.

"Let's get this show on the road, Darcy. I gotta get going."

"Where are you going?"

"That is none of your business."

"Are you going out with Rachel? How are things going with her?" I asked, hoping to hear that their ill-advised romance—one based on hurt feelings and confusion—had fizzled, destroying their friendship along the way.

Dex said, "Let's not go through the charade of inquiring about each other's lives as if we're friends."

"What's that supposed to mean?" I asked.

"What part didn't you get?" he said.

"The part about us not being friends?"

"We're *not* friends," he said.

"We date for seven years and now we're not even *friends*? Just like that?" I asked.

He didn't flinch. "That's right. Just like that."

"Well. Regardless of whether we're friends, why can't you tell me if you're still with Rachel? What's the big deal?" I paused, praying that he would say, *Don't be ridiculous. Rachel and I don't have a relationship. That afternoon was just something that happened* . . . or even better . . . *almost happened.* Maybe I had even imagined their tans in Crate and Barrel.

"It's not a big deal," he said. "I just think it's best if we don't discuss our personal lives." He gripped the handle on his briefcase, pushing it from side to side.

"Why? I can handle it. You can't?"

He exhaled hard, shook his head, and said, "Fine. If you insist. Things with Rachel are very good. Great, in fact."

"So you're *actually* dating?"

"See? That's exactly why I don't want to discuss my life with you," Dex said, rubbing his hand along his jaw.

"Fine." I sniffed. "Let's just get your things. They're in the bedroom. You remember where that is, don't you?"

"You get them. I'll wait here."

"Dex, please," I said. "Just come with me."

"No," he said. "I'm not going back there."

I sighed, striding toward our bedroom, where I had planned on seducing him after a glass or two of wine. That clearly wasn't going to happen. So I grabbed a shoebox, dumped a pair of Jimmy Choos on my bed, and rummaged through my desk until I found a few instruction booklets. One for a fancy calculator he had bought for his home office. Another for our stereo. And a few maps of the D.C. area where his father lived. I put the papers in the shoebox. Then, just to add some heft, I threw in our studio engagement picture, expensive sterling silver frame and all. I knew it was one of Dexter's favorites of me, so it had surprised me when he took other pictures of us and left that one behind. I waltzed back into the living room, thrust the box toward him, and said, "Here."

"That's the heavy box you couldn't carry?" he asked, disgusted. He stood, poised to leave.

That's when it all sank in and I started to cry. Dex was serious with Rachel. He was leaving me to go meet her. Through tears, I begged. "Don't go. Please don't go," I said, wondering how many times I'd say those words.

"*Darcy,*" he said, as he sat back down. "Why are you doing this?"

"I can't help it," I said as I blew my nose. "I'm so sad."

He sighed loudly. "You act as if I did this thing to you."

"You *did* do this thing to me."

"You did it too. Remember?" He pointed at my stomach.

"Okay. Fine. I did it too. But . . ." I struggled to think of some way to keep him with me a bit longer. "But I need some answers before I can move on. I need closure. Please, Dex."

He stared at me blankly. His eyes said: "You don't have a choice about moving on. I'm outta here."

I asked my question anyway. "When exactly did you start dating? On the very day we broke up?"

"Darcy, that is entirely immaterial at this point."

"Tell me. Were you looking to be consoled? Is that why you went to Rachel's?"

"Darcy, just stop it. I want you to be happy. I want you and Marcus to be happy. Can't you want the same for me?"

"Marcus and I broke up," I blurted. All pride was out the window now.

Dex raised his eyebrows, his mouth forming the beginning of a question—*when* or maybe *why*. But he changed his response to, "Oh. I'm sorry to hear that."

"I miss you, Dex," I said. "I want us to be together again. Isn't there any way?"

He shook his head. "No."

"But I still love you." I linked my arm around his. "And I think that we still have something—"

"Darcy." He pulled roughly away, his features rearranging in a preachy expression. I knew this face well. It was his "my patience has expired" face. The face he got after I posed the same question a dozen times. "I'm with Rachel now. I'm sorry. There's no chance of us ever getting back together. Zero."

"Why are you being so *cruel*?"

"I'm not trying to be cruel. You just need to know that."

I put my face in my hands and sobbed harder. Then, suddenly, I had an idea. It was an awful, low thing to do, but I decided that I had no choice. I stopped crying, cast him a sideways glance, and said, "The baby is yours."

Dex was unfazed. "Darcy. Don't even start with that Montel Williams DNA-testing crap. That baby is *not* mine, and we both know it. I heard what you told Rachel. I know when we last had sex."

"The pregnancy is further along than I thought. It's yours. Why do you think Marcus and I broke up?"

"Darcy," Dex said, raising his voice. "Do *not* do this."

"Dex. The baby is yours. My doctor did an ultrasound to confirm the fetus's age. It happened earlier than I thought. It's yours," I said, shocking even myself with the disgraceful tactic. I told myself that I would come clean later. I just needed to buy some time with Dex. I could get him back if I just had time to work my magic. He wouldn't be able to resist me as Marcus had. After all, Marcus was impossible, weird about commitment. But Dex had been mine forever. There had to be some lingering feelings.

"If you're lying about this, it is unforgivable." His voice was almost shaking, and his eyes were wide. "I want the truth. Now."

I sucked in my breath, exhaled slowly, and maintained eye contact while I lied again. "It's yours," I said, feeling ashamed.

"You know I'm going to want proof."

I licked my lips, stayed calm. "Yes. Absolutely. I want you to take a blood test. You'll see that it's yours."

"Darcy."

"What?"

Dex put his head in his hands and then ran them through his thick, dark hair. "Darcy . . . Even if it *is* mine, I want you to understand that this baby won't change a thing between us. Not a thing. You got that?"

"What does that mean exactly?" I asked, even though it was pretty clear what he was driving at. After all, Marcus had just made the same point to me the night before. I had the concept down.

"We're over. Finished. It's never going to happen again with you and me. Baby or no baby. I'm with Rachel now."

I stared at him, feeling outrage well up inside of me. It was all so unbelievable! So utterly inconceivable! How could he be with Rachel? I stood and paced over to the window, trying to catch my breath.

"So tell me the truth right now. Is it mine?" he asked.

I turned and looked at him. He wasn't going to fold. You come to know a person well in seven years—and I knew that once Dex made up his mind, there was absolutely nothing that I could say to change it. His jaw was clenched. There was no opening for me. Besides, as brazen as I could be, I knew I could never actually go through with a ploy like this one, even as a temporary measure. It was just too awful, and I only felt worse for having tried it.

"Fine," I said, throwing up my hands. "It's Marcus's baby. Are you happy?"

"Actually yes, Darcy. I am happy. No, *ecstatic* is more the word." He stood and pointed angrily at me. "And the fact that you could lie about such a thing confirms to me—"

"I'm sorry," I said before he could finish his sentence. I was crying again. "I know it was *really* low . . . I just don't know what to do. Everything is falling apart for me. And—and—you're with Rachel. You took her on our honeymoon! How could you take her on our honeymoon? How could you do that?"

Dex said nothing.

"You did, didn't you? You went to Hawaii with her?"

"The tickets were nonrefundable, Darcy. Even the hotel was already paid for," he said, looking guilty.

"How could you do that? How? And then I see you two in Crate and Barrel, shopping for couches. That's how I knew about Hawaii. You were all tan. Shopping for couches . . . All tan and happy and buying couches." I was babbling now, a total mess. "Are you moving in together?"

"Not yet . . ."

"Not *yet*?" I said. "So you are eventually? Are you *serious*?"

"Darcy, please. Stop this. Rachel and I didn't do this to hurt you.

Just like you didn't get pregnant to hurt me. Right?" he asked in his "please be reasonable" tone.

I looked out the window again at a pile of trash on the curb. Then I returned my gaze to Dex. "Please be with me again," I said softly. "Please. Give me another chance. We had seven good years together. Things were good. We'll forgive each other and move on." I walked back over to him and tried to hug him. He stiffened and recoiled like a puppy resisting the grasp of an overzealous child.

"Dex? Please?"

"No, Darcy. We don't belong together. We aren't right for each other."

"Do you love her?" I asked under my breath, truly expecting him to say no or that he didn't know or that he wouldn't answer the question.

But instead he said, "Yes. I love her." I could see in his eyes that he wasn't saying it to be mean; he was saying it out of a sense of loyalty to her. It was that committed, resolute look of his. It was Dex being a good person, being true to his new girlfriend. I marveled at how fast old loyalties, ones that took years to build, could be ripped apart and replaced. I knew I had lost him, but I felt desperate to recruit a small piece of his heart back to me. Make him feel even a sliver of what he used to feel for me. "More than you ever loved me?" I asked, looking for one small scrap.

"Don't do this, Darcy."

"I need to know, Dex. I really need to know the answer to that," I said, thinking that he couldn't possibly love her more in a few weeks than he had loved me when he had proposed after years together. It just wasn't possible.

"Why do you need to know, Darce?"

"I just do. Tell me."

He stared down at the coffee table for a long minute in that dazed way of his where he doesn't blink. Then he looked around the apartment, his eyes resting on an oil painting of a dilapidated, pillared

house surrounded by terraced fields and a solitary oak. We had purchased the painting together in New Orleans right at the beginning of
our relationship. We had spent nearly eight hundred dollars on it,
which seemed like a huge sum of money at the time, as Dex was in law
school and I had just begun to work. It was our first big purchase as a
couple—an implicit acknowledgment of our commitment to each
other. Sort of like buying a dog together. I remember standing in that
gallery, admiring our painting, as Dex told me that he loved the way
the early evening shadows fell across the front porch. I remember him
saying that dusk was his favorite time of day. I remember we grinned
at each other as the clerk bubble-wrapped our painting. Then we returned to the hotel, where we made love and ordered a banana split
from the room service menu. Had he forgotten all of that?

I guess I had forgotten such moments when my affair began with
Marcus. But I remembered every such occasion now. Regret surged
through me. What I would have given to have a big ol' redo, take back
everything with Marcus. I looked at Dex and asked the question
again. "Do you love her more than you ever loved me?"

I waited.

Then he nodded and said so softly that it was nearly a whisper,
"Yes. I do. I'm really sorry, Darcy."

I stared at him incredulously, trying to process what he was saying,
how it could be possible that he could love Rachel so much. She
wasn't that pretty. She wasn't that fun. What did she have that I
didn't have besides a few measly IQ points?

Dex spoke again. "I can tell you're in a bad place right now, Darcy.
Part of me would like to help you, but it just won't work. I can't be
that person for you. You have friends and family you need to turn
to. . . . I really have to go now." His voice was distant, his gaze detached. In a few seconds, he would walk out, hail a cab, and cross the
park to see Rachel. She would greet him at her door, her brown eyes
sympathetic, probing for details about our meeting. I could hear her

asking, "How did it go?" and stroking Dexter's hair as he told her everything. How I had lied about the baby, then begged, then cried. She would feel both pity and disdain for me.

"Fine. Get out. I don't want to talk to you or her ever again," I said, realizing that I had said pretty much the same thing in Rachel's apartment. This time, my words had a watered-down, weak effect.

Dex bit his lower lip. "Please be well," he said, gathering up his briefcase and the shoebox of junk he didn't want any more than he wanted me. Then he stood and walked out of his old apartment, leaving me for good.

sixteen

It was incomprehensible. In my entire lifetime—throughout high school, college, and my twenties—I had never been dissed by a guy. Not dumped. Not stood up. Not even slighted. And there I was—a two-time loser all in a week's time. I was completely alone, didn't even have a prospect in sight.

I also didn't have Rachel, my steadfast source of comfort when other things, unrelated to romance, had unraveled in my life. Nor did I have my own mother—whom I refused to call back and hear some variation of "I told you so." That left Claire, who came to my apartment after I had called in sick to work for three straight days. I was surprised that it took her so long to rush to my aid, but I guess she had no way of suspecting my depth of despair. Up to that point in my life, my definition of down-and-out was a bad case of PMS.

"What has gotten into you?" Claire asked, glancing around my messier-than-usual apartment. "I've been so worried about you. Why haven't you returned any of my calls?"

"Marcus dumped me," I said mournfully. I had sunk too low to try to put a triumphant spin on the facts.

She raised the blinds in my living room. "*Marcus* broke up with *you*?" she asked, appropriately shocked.

I sniffed and nodded.

"That's ridiculous! Has he taken a look in the mirror? What was he thinking?"

"I don't know," I said. "He just doesn't want to be with me."

"Well, the whole world's gone mad. First Dex and Rachel and now *this*! I mean—come on! This is *nuts*. I just don't get it. It's like an episode of *The Twilight Zone*."

I felt a tear roll down my cheek.

Claire rushed over to give me a hug and a "buck up, little camper" smile. Then she said briskly, "Well, it's a blessing in disguise. Marcus was so *bush league*. You're better off without him. And Rachel and Dex are dullsville." She headed for my kitchen, holding up a plastic bag filled with all the fixings for margaritas. "And believe me, this whole situation is nothing that a few drinks won't cure . . . Besides, I have a much finer man all cued up for you."

I blew my nose and looked at her hopefully. "Who?"

"You remember Josh Levine?"

I shook my head.

"Well, I have two words for you. Hot and loaded," she said, rubbing her thumb against her fingers. "His nose is rather large, but not offensively so. Your daughter might need a minor nose job, but that's the only issue," she said brightly. She rolled up her sleeves and set about rinsing my dishes covered with day-old Kraft macaroni and cheese residue. "You briefly met him at that house in the Hamptons with the eighteen-person hot tub? Remember? He's friends with Eric Kiefer and that whole crowd?"

"Oh, yeah," I said, conjuring a well-dressed, thirty-something banker with wavy brown hair and big, square teeth. "Doesn't he have a girlfriend who is a model or actress or something?"

"He *did* have a girlfriend. Amanda something or other. And yes, she's a model . . . but the low-rent catalog kind. I think she wore some pleated cords in Chadwick's of Boston or something. But Josh dumped her two days ago." Claire looked up smugly. "How's that for hot off the presses?"

Claire loved being the first to get a scoop.

"Why'd they break up?" I asked. "Did Josh catch his best friend hiding in Amanda's closet?"

Claire chuckled. "No. Word is she was just too dumb for him. She is as vapid as they come. Get a load of *this one* . . . I heard that she actually thought *paparazzi* was the last name of one particular Italian photographer. Apparently she said something like, 'Who is this Paparazzi guy and why didn't they arrest him years ago after he killed Princess Diana?' "

I laughed for the first time in weeks.

"So anyway, Josh is *a-vail-a-ble*," Claire sang and spun around ballerina-style.

I became momentarily suspicious. "Why don't you want him?"

"You know my uptight Episcopalian parents would never let me go down the Jewish-guy road or I would have claimed him for myself. . . . But you better act fast because the girls in this city are ready to *pounce*."

"Yeah. Don't let Jocelyn catch wind of this," I said.

Jocelyn Silver worked with Claire and me, and although I liked her in small doses, she was a total alpha female, way too competitive for me ever to trust. She also bore a strong resemblance to Uma Thurman, and if I had to watch her pretend to be annoyed when one more stranger approached her to ask if she was Uma, I was going to puke. Which, incidentally, was what Jocelyn did after every meal.

"No kidding . . . I haven't mentioned anything about the breakup to her. Even if I did, Josh would *totally* go for you over her."

I smiled with false modesty.

She continued, "So how about this? I'll make sure Josh comes to our club opening next week—the one Jocelyn's going to miss for her cousin's wedding . . ." She winked at me. "So stop this sniveling over Marcus. I mean, Christ, what was the deal there anyway? He could be fun, but he's certainly not worthy of macaroni-and-cheese-level grief."

"You're right," I said. I could feel myself cheering up as I thought of how Jewish men were supposed make great husbands. "Josh sounds divine. I'm sure I could convince him to have a Christmas tree, don't you think?"

"You can convince anyone to do anything," Claire said.

I beamed. That theory had been proven wrong a few times in recent days, but surely I was going to get back on track with my charmed life.

"And I had another thought on my way over . . ." Claire smiled mysteriously, poised to reveal another terrific surprise.

"What's that?"

"Well," she said as she uncorked the bottle of Patrón, our favorite brand of tequila. "What do you say we move in together again? My lease is up, and you have a spare bedroom. We could save a ton on rent and have a blast together. What do you say?"

"That's a fantastic idea," I said, remembering fondly our roomie days before I had moved in with Dex. Claire and I had shared the same shoe size, the same taste in music, and the same love of fruity mixed drinks that we consumed in quantity as we primped for our big nights out. Besides, it would be great to have her around when the baby arrived. I was sure she wouldn't mind getting up occasionally for nighttime feedings. I watched as she sliced a lime and hung perfect twists on our glasses. She had a nice touch when it came to entertaining, another perk of living with her. "Let's do it!"

"Excellent!" she squealed. "My lease expires next month."

"There's just one thing I should tell you," I said as she crossed the living room over to my couch, drinks in hand.

"What's that?"

I swallowed, reassuring myself that although Claire could be snobbish and judgmental, she had only demonstrated a sense of absolute loyalty to me over the years. I had to believe that she would be there for me in my hour of need. So as she handed me a temptingly perfect margarita on the rocks, salt lined evenly along the rim of the glass (an engagement present from Dexter's Aunt Suzy), I blurted out my big secret. "I'm pregnant with Marcus's baby." Then I took one tiny sip of my drink, inhaling the sweet smell of tequila, licking the salt from my lips.

"Get outta here," she said, her crystal drop earrings swinging as she plopped down next to me and curled her legs up under her ample bottom. "Oh—we didn't do a toast. Here's to being roomies again!"

She clearly thought I was joking. I clinked my glass against hers, took another tiny sip, and said, "No. It's true. I *am* pregnant. So I probably shouldn't drink this. Although a few more sips couldn't hurt. It's not that strong, is it?"

She looked at me sideways and said, "You're kidding, right?"

I shook my head.

"Darcy!" She froze, a fearful smile plastered on her face.

"I'm not joking."

"Swear."

"I swear."

It went on like that for some time before I could convince her that I wasn't putting her on, that I was, indeed, pregnant with the child of a man whom she had deemed woefully inadequate. As she listened to me ramble about my morning sickness, my due date, the problems with my mother, she gulped her margarita—which was highly unusual for Claire. She had finishing-school manners even when wasted. She never forgot to cross her legs on a bar stool or keep her elbows off a table, and she never gulped. But at that moment, she was rattled.

"So what do you think?" I asked her.

She took another swallow, then coughed and sputtered, "Whoa! Excuse me! I think it went down the wrong pipe."

I waited for her to say something more, but she only stared back at me with a plastered smile, as if she were no longer quite sure who it was she was having a drink with. I guess I expected her to be surprised, but I wanted the *giddy* brand of surprised, not the *freaked-out* version. I reassured myself that I had just caught her off guard. She needed a minute to digest the news. In the meantime, I gave a short, noble speech about how I never once considered having an abortion or giving the baby up for adoption. In truth, I had given some consideration to both options in the past forty-eight hours, but something made me stay on track. I'd like to say it was strength of character and good morals, but it also had a lot to do with stubborn pride.

"Congratulations. That's fantastic news," Claire finally said, in the tinny, insincere voice of a game show host informing the losing contestant that they weren't going to walk away completely empty-handed, but rather with a gift certificate for Omaha Steaks. "I know you'll do a great job with this . . . And I will be here for you to help in any way I can."

I could tell she added the last sentence as an afterthought, its generality smacking of obligation rather than any earnest desire to be involved in my baby's life. Or even mine, for that matter.

"Thank you," I said, my mind spinning to analyze the moment. Was I being too critical of her? Too paranoid? What exactly did I want her to say? Ideally, she could ask to be the baby's godmother or offer to throw me a big shower. At the very least, I wanted her to mention moving in with me again, or say something about Josh, how we needed to act fast while my body was still spectacular. Claire only laughed nervously and said, "This is all so . . . *so* exciting."

"Yes," I said defensively. "It really *is*. And I see no reason why I can't still date."

"Of course you will date," she said, pumping one fist in the air. But no further mention of my Jewish Prince Charming.

"Do you think Josh will mind?" I asked.

More nervous laughter. "Mind that you're pregnant?"

"Yeah. Mind that I'm pregnant?"

"Well, I . . . I'm not sure . . . I don't know him *that* well."

It was perfectly clear that she was quite sure that Josh would mind very much indeed. About as much as she would mind living with me and a newborn. She downed the rest of her margarita, chattering about how excited the girls in our office would be. Could she tell them? Was it public knowledge yet?

I said no, not yet, I wasn't quite ready for the world to know.

"I understand. Mum's the word," Claire said, pinching her lips between thumb and index finger. She giggled. "No pun intended."

I insisted that I wasn't ashamed of my pregnancy. It wasn't that at all. I babbled about how I would maintain my sense of self, referencing Rachel on *Friends* and Miranda on *Sex and the City*. Both women had managed to keep their lives and looks intact while embracing single motherhood. I saw no reason why I couldn't do the same.

"Oh, I know," Claire said in a condescending tone. "There's no reason you can't do it all, have it all. Be a modern woman!"

As I studied her big, fake smile, the exact contours of our shallow friendship came into focus. Sure, Claire liked me, but she liked me because I was fun to go out with and because I was a guy magnet, even when I had worn my engagement ring from Dex. She liked me because I was an invaluable asset. With her pedigree and my looks and personality, we had been unstoppable. The glamorous PR duo everyone either knew or wanted to know.

But in the time it took to down a margarita, my stock had plummeted in her eyes. I had been transformed into nothing but a struggling single mother. I might as well have had curlers in my hair and a welfare check in my callused hand. I was of no use to her anymore.

As she finished her drink, she eyed mine. "Well? May I?" she asked.

"Go ahead," I said.

She took a few sips from my glass and then glanced at her watch. "Oh, shoot. Look at the time!"

"Did you have to be somewhere?" I asked. Usually it was impossible to shake Claire.

"Yes," she said. "I told Jocelyn I'd give her a call. She wants to go out tonight. Didn't I mention that?"

"No," I said. "You didn't mention that."

Claire smiled tightly and said, "Yeah. Dinner and a few drinks. Of course, you can come if you want. Even though you can't drink. We'd love your company."

Claire was offering me, Darcy Rhone, a charity invite. I was tempted to go, to prove that I could still be fun. But I was too indignant to accept the invitation so easily. So I told her no, that I had some phone calls to return. I waited for a little coaxing, but she just stood, carried her glass over to the sink, swung her Prada bag over her shoulder, and said with all the cheeriness in the world, "All righty then, hon. . . . Congratulations again. Have a great night. You take good care of yourself, okay?"

Needless to say the next week passed and Claire never mentioned moving in with me again. Instead, I heard from another girl in our office that Claire and Jocelyn were apartment-hunting in the Village. I also heard from Jocelyn herself, in the office restroom after her postlunchtime purge, that she had met a great guy—Josh Levine—did I know him? It was the final straw, the salt in my open, bleeding, infected wound. Even dependent and doting Claire had joined the ranks and betrayed me. I hurried back to my office, stunned and teary, my mind racing about what to do next. Without even fully thinking it through, I found myself propelled down the hall to Cal's office, where I informed my boss that I needed to take a leave of absence, effective immediately. I told him I was having some personal issues. He asked if there were anything he could do. I said no, I just needed some time away. He told me they were overstaffed these days, anyway, and the economy was socking the PR business right in the gut, so I could take as much time as I needed and could come back whenever I was ready. Then he gave my midsection an unmistakable once-over. He knew my secret.

Claire, the biggest gossip hound in Manhattan, had added me to her inside scoop. So I added her to my ever-growing list of enemies—of people who would be sorry to have crossed me.

seventeen

For the next few days I cranked up "I Will Survive," Ace of Base's "I Saw the Sign," and other inspiring songs as I racked my brain, trying to come up with a plan, a way to escape the shame of so much rejection. I needed a fresh start, a change of venue, a new cast of characters. I scoured my list of contacts in the city, but everyone was somehow linked to Dex or to Claire or to my firm. I seemed to be without options. And then, just as true despair set in, a call from Indianapolis showed up on my caller ID. It was Annalise, my last girlfriend standing.

"Hi, Annalise!" I answered, feeling guilty for all the times in the past that I had dismissed her as boring, neglected to call her back, even scoffed at her suburban, kindergarten-teaching existence. I felt especially bad for not meeting her new baby, Hannah, when I was back in Indy.

"I'm so glad you called!" I told her. "How are you? How is Hannah?"

I listened patiently as Annalise gushed about her baby and complained about the lack of sleep. Then she asked how I was doing, her tone implying that she already knew my tale of woe. Just in case she was missing some details, I filled her in on everything. "My life is falling apart, and I don't know what to do," I cried into the phone.

"Oh, wow, Darce," Annalise said in her heavy Midwestern accent. "I don't know what to say. I'm just . . . really worried about you."

"Well, you *should* be worried," I said. "I'm at the absolute end of my rope. And this is all Rachel's fault, you know."

I was yearning for one derogatory comment about Rachel, her other best friend. Just a tiny dig would have felt like a cooling salve. But Annalise was not one to be mean, so she only made a concerned clucking noise into the phone and then said, "Can't you and Rach just try to work things out? This is just too sad."

"Hell, no!"

Annalise made another remark about forgiveness, one of those annoying religious comments that had become her trademark after marrying Greg, a Bible beater from Kentucky.

"Never," I said. "I'll never forgive her."

Annalise sighed as Hannah Jane fussed in the background, making an annoying, and escalating, *ehh, ehhh, ehhhhhh* sound that wasn't exactly igniting my mothering instinct.

"So, anyway, I just think I need a change of scenery, you know? I thought about the Peace Corps or some outdoorsy type of adventure, but that's not really my scene. I like my creature comforts. Especially now that I'm pregnant . . ."

That's when Annalise suggested that I return home for a few months, live with my parents, and have the baby in Indianapolis. "It'd be so fun to have you here," she said. "I'm in this amazing playgroup at church. You'd love it. It might be really grounding for you."

"I don't need to be grounded. I need the opposite. I need an *escape*.

Besides, I can't go back to Indy. It just feels like such a downgrade. You know, like I'm selling out, settling, cashing in my chips, admitting defeat."

"Okay!" Annalise giggled good-naturedly. "I get the picture. We know we're small potatoes, don't we, Hannah?"

Hannah howled in response.

"You know what I mean. You like it there, and that's great for you. But I'm just not a small-town kind of girl . . ."

"You're far from small-town," Annalise said.

"And besides, I'm not speaking to my mother," I said, explaining what a bitch she had been upon hearing my news.

"Why don't you go to London and stay with Ethan?" she said, referring to Ethan Ainsley, our high school friend who was in London, writing some book.

The second she said it, I knew it was the answer. It was so obvious, I marveled that I hadn't thought of it first. I would sublease my apartment and head off to jolly ol' England.

"Annalise, that's a marvelous idea," I said, imagining everyone catching wind of my transatlantic move. Claire, who fancied herself such a world traveler, would eat her heart out. Marcus, who had yet to call and check on me, would be filled with guilt and second-guessing when he discovered that his baby was going to be born thousands of miles away. Rachel, who had always been closer to Ethan than I, would be jealous of my intense bonding with her dear childhood pal. Dex would wonder how he could have ever let such an independent, adventurous, gutsy woman go.

It was an idea whose time had come. I only had to convince Ethan to let me stay with him.

I had known Ethan since the fourth grade, when he moved to our town in the middle of the school year. There was always a flurry of intrigue when a new kid arrived, with everyone excited at the thought of fresh blood. I remembered Ethan's first day well. I could still see our teacher, Mrs. Billone, resting her hand on his scrawny shoulder and announcing, "This is Ethan Ainsley. He comes to us from Long Island. Please join me in welcoming him."

As we all muttered, "Welcome, Ethan," I found myself wondering where this island of his was located—in the Atlantic or Pacific?—and how a boy from the tropics could have such fair skin and light hair. I pictured Ethan running around half-naked, shimmying up trees to collect coconuts for all of his meals. Had he been rescued by a search team? Sent to foster parents in Indiana? Perhaps this was his first day in proper clothes. I suspected that it was torture for him to feel so restricted.

At recess that day, Ethan sat alone on the curb near the monkey bars, writing in the dirt with a twig as we all cast curious glances his way. Everyone else was too shy to talk to him, but I summoned Rachel and Annalise and the three of us approached him. "Hi, Ethan. I'm Darcy. This is Rachel, and this is Annalise," I said boldly, pointing to my timid sidekicks.

"Hi," Ethan said, squinting up at us over his oversized, round glasses.

"So how far away is your homeland?" I asked him, cutting right to the chase. I wanted the full scoop on his exotic childhood.

"New York is about eight hundred miles from here." He enunciated every word, making him sound very smart. It wasn't the voice I expected from a native islander.

"New York?" I was confused. "But Mrs. Billone said you're from an island?"

He and Rachel exchanged an amused glance—their first of many superior moments.

"What's so funny?" I asked indignantly. "She did so say you're from an island. Didn't she, Annalise?"

Annalise nodded somberly.

"*Long* Island," Ethan and Rachel said in unison, with matching smirks.

So it was a *long* island as opposed to a short one? That didn't clear anything up.

"Long Island is part of New York," Rachel said in her know-it-all voice.

"Oh. Yeah. Right. I knew that. I just didn't hear her say *long*," I lied. "Did you, Annalise?"

"No," Annalise said, "I didn't hear that part either."

Annalise never made you feel dumb. It was one of her best qualities. That and the fact that she was always willing to share anything. In fact, I was wearing her pale pink Jellies on that very day.

"Long Island is the eastern part of New York State," Ethan continued. His condescending tutorial made it clear that he didn't believe me about not hearing the word *long*. That really got my fur up, and I instantly regretted any attempt to be nice to the new kid.

"So why'd you move here?" I asked abruptly, thinking that he should have stayed back on his faux island.

He reported that his parents had just divorced, and that his mother, originally from Indiana, moved back to be closer to her parents, his grandparents. It was hardly a glamorous tale. Annalise, whose own parents were divorced, asked him if his father still lived in New York.

"Yes. He does," Ethan said, his eyes returning to his dirt doodling. "I'll see him on alternating holidays and during the summers."

I would have felt sorry for him—divorce seemed just about the worst thing that could happen to a kid—right up there with having to wear a wig after leukemia radiation treatments. But it's hard to feel sorry for someone who makes you feel stupid for not knowing some insignificant geographical fact.

Rachel changed the subject from divorce and asked Ethan questions about New York, as if it were her idea to talk to him in the first place. The two rattled on about the Empire State Building and the Metropolitan Museum of Art and the World Trade Center, all places Ethan had visited and Rachel had read about.

"We have big buildings and museums in Indianapolis too," I said defensively, pegging Ethan as one of those annoying people who always say, "Back where I come from." Then I steered Annalise away from their big-shot conversation over to a game of four square.

After that day, I didn't give Ethan much thought until he and Rachel were placed in the academically gifted program called "T.G." for "talented and gifted" at the start of the following school year. I hated the T.G. program, hated the feeling of being excluded, of not making the cut. I couldn't stand the smugness of the T.G.ers, and resented them with a burning in my chest every time they trotted merrily down the hall to their mystery room and then returned, buzzing about their dumb experiments—like constructing clay boats in an attempt to hold the maximum number of tacks. Incidentally, Ethan won that contest, engineering a vessel that held nineteen tacks before sinking. "Big deal," I remember telling Rachel. "I stopped playing with Play-Doh and clay when I was four." I always sought to burst her bubble, insisted that T.G. really stood for "totally geeky." And just in case it looked like sour grapes, I reminded Rachel often that I had only missed the T.G. test score cutoff by one point and that was only because I had strep throat the day of the test and couldn't concentrate on anything other than my inability to swallow. (The part about strep throat was the truth; the part about one point was probably not—although I never knew for sure how far I had missed the mark, because my mother had told me that it wasn't important what my score was, that I didn't need the T.G. program to be special.)

So in light of my irritation over Ethan's superiority, it was surprising when he turned out to be my first real boyfriend. It was also surprising because Rachel had had a crush on him since the day he arrived, while I was firmly in the Doug Jackson camp. Doug was the most popular boy in our class, and I was sure that he and I were going to become a hot-and-heavy item, until he taped a picture of Heather Locklear to his Trapper Keeper, announcing that he preferred blondes to brunettes. The sentiment put me in a huff and I decided to look for another candidate, perhaps even a sixth-grader. Skinny, pale Ethan was the farthest thing from my mind.

But one day, as I watched him search the card catalogue for Peru, I suddenly saw in Ethan what Rachel was always carrying on about. He was pretty cute. So I waltzed over and bumped into him on purpose under the pretense of trying to find a card on Paraguay, one drawer over. He gave me a funny look, smiled, and flashed his dimples. I decided right then and there that I would like Ethan.

When I delivered the news to Rachel later that week, I assumed she'd be pleased, happy that I was finally agreeing with her and that we'd have one more thing in common. After all, best friends should agree on all topics, certainly ones as major as who to have a crush on. But Rachel was not happy at all. In fact, she was furious, becoming strangely territorial, like she *owned* Ethan. Annalise pointed out that she and I had shared our crush on Doug for months, but Rachel wasn't persuaded. She just kept saying that Doug was somehow a different case, and she stayed huffy and self-righteous, muttering about how she had liked Ethan first.

That was true enough; she did like Ethan first. But the way I saw it was this—if she liked him so darn much, she should have done something about it. Taken some real action. And by action, I didn't mean writing his initials in the condensation on her mother's car window. But Rachel was never one for action. That was my department.

So a few days later, I wrote Ethan a note, asking if he wanted to go out with me, with instructions to check a box next to *yes, no,* or *maybe.* To be fair, I included Rachel's name as a fourth option. But at the last minute, I tore off that part of the note, reasoning that she shouldn't be the benefactor of my get-up-and-go. Besides, I didn't want to lose to Rachel when she was already beating me in so many other arenas. She was in T.G. after all. So I passed the note, and Ethan said yes, and just like that we were a couple. We talked on the phone and flirted during recess and it was all a tingly thrill for a few weeks.

But then Doug changed his mind, announcing that he liked brunettes better than blondes after all. So I dumped Ethan and put myself back on the fifth-grade market. Luckily, our breakup coincided with Ethan's Loch Ness Monster obsession; it was all he talked about for weeks, even planning a summer trip to Scotland or Switzerland or wherever the thing supposedly lived. So he had another focus and got over me relatively quickly. A short time later, Rachel got over Ethan too. She said she was no longer interested in boys, a convenient decision because she wasn't exactly being pursued by any.

So we all forged our way into junior high and high school. Annalise, Ethan, Rachel, and I formed a little clique (although I ran in more popular circles too) and none of us ever mentioned the fifth-grade love-triangle saga again. After high school graduation, I continued to keep in touch with Ethan, but mostly I did so through Rachel. Those two stayed very close, particularly during his divorce. Ethan came to New York often during his crisis, so much so that I wondered if he and Rachel might get together. But Rachel insisted that there was nothing romantic between them.

"Do you think he could be gay?" I'd ask her, referencing his close female friendships, his sensitivity, and his love of classical music. She'd say that she was sure he was straight, simply explaining that they were strictly friends.

So as I dialed up Ethan in London, I worried that he'd turn me down out of loyalty to Rachel, a sense that he had to take her side. Annalise loved us both equally, but Ethan clearly favored Rachel. Sure enough, when he finally called me back more than a week later, after I had left him two phone messages and sent him a well-crafted, slightly desperate e-mail, his hello was tight and tentative.

I worked up a stirring preemptive strike. "Ethan, I can't take it if you're going to shoot me down. I just can't take it. You gotta help me out. I know you're better friends with Rachel—I know you're on her side . . ." I hesitated, waiting for him to say he wasn't on anyone's side. When he didn't, I kept going. "But I'm begging you, Ethan. I have to get away from here. I'm pregnant. My boyfriend dumped me. I took a leave of absence from work. I can't go home, Ethan. It would be way too humiliating. Way." I said it all, knowing the risk—that he would call Rachel and tell her what a loser I was. But it was a chance I had to take. I said one final *please* and then waited.

"Darce, it has nothing to do with Rachel. It's just that I like living alone. I don't want a roommate."

"Ethan, please. Just for a few weeks. Just for a visit. I have nowhere else to go."

"What about Indy? You could stay with your folks."

"You know I can't do that. Could you have crawled back to Indy after you divorced Brandi?"

He sighed, but I could tell that I had hit an empathetic chord. "A few weeks? Like how many?"

"Three? Four? Six tops?" I said and held my breath, waiting.

"All right, Darce," he finally said. "You can stay here. But only temporarily. My place is really small . . . and as I said, I really relish solitude."

"Oh, thank you. Thank you. Thank you!" I said, feeling like my old victorious self. I just knew that my problems were solved and that his saying yes was the equivalent of bestowing me with a chance to fix my life, infuse it with European glamour. "You won't be sorry, Ethan. I'll be the perfect guest," I said.

"Just remember—a *short* visit."

"A short visit," I echoed. "I got it."

I hung up and envisioned my new life . . .

Strolling around cobblestone streets in Notting Hill, through the mist and fog, my basketball of a stomach peeking out between a cropped, cowl-neck sweater and chic, low-slung pants. A plaid Burberry cap is perched on my head, cocked slightly to the side. Beautifully tousled hair with chestnut highlights, compliments of the finest London salon, spills down around my shoulders. I stop by a charming patisserie, where I carefully select a pumpkin mousse tart. As I pay at the counter, I spot my future beau. As he glances up at me from his paper, his face lights up in a sexy smile. He is outlandishly handsome, with Dexter's strong features and Lair's light eyes and cute body. (His father is from Northern Italy—hence the blue eyes; his mother, British—hence the impeccable grooming, fine manners, and Oxford education.) His name is Alistair, and he is wickedly smart and sophisticated and ultra-wealthy. He might even be a duke or earl. He will top Dex in all categories. And he'll be sexier than Marcus. Of course, he'll fall madly in love with me at first sight. My pregnancy won't deter him in the slightest. In fact, it will turn him on—as I have heard is the case with some highly evolved men. Within weeks of our first meeting, Alistair will ask for my hand in marriage. I will move out of Ethan's charming flat into Alistair's enormous and perfectly appointed home, complete with a maid, cook, butler, the works.

And then, one night in late April, when spring has come to London, as we sleep naked in his canopied, carved-wood bed handed down through four generations, on his eleven-hundred-thread-count sheets, I will feel the first gentle stirrings of labor. "I think it's time," I will whisper, gently jostling Alistair. He will bolt out of bed, help me dress in my cashmere pajamas, run a silver brush through my hair, and summon his driver before we whisk off into the London night. Then he will hover by my hospital bed, stroking my brow and planting tiny kisses along my hairline, while murmuring, "Push, dahling. Push, my treasure."

It will be love at first sight all over again when he sees my daughter, who will look exactly like me. The daughter he will want to adopt. "Our daughter," he will tell people. By the time her first tooth appears, we will have both forgotten that a boorish American is the biological father. And by that time, I surely will have forgotten all about Rachel and Dex. I will be too caught up in my happily-ever-after to give them even a cursory thought.

eighteen

For the next two weeks, I was all about preparation and action, single-minded in my quest to shut down my New York affairs and get myself to London. I placed a classified ad and found a young couple to sublet my apartment. Then I sold my tainted engagement ring in the diamond district and my wedding gown on eBay. When I combined the proceeds with the balance in my checking account, I calculated that I had enough money to get through my pregnancy in London without a day's work.

Finally, I was all ready, my bags packed full of my finest belongings, on the way to JFK for my red-eye flight to London. As I boarded the plane, I felt a sense of absolute satisfaction, knowing that I was leaving the city without a word to the people who had betrayed me. I hunkered down in my business class seat, slipped on a pair of cashmere slippers, and fell into a deep and peaceful sleep.

Seven hours later, I awoke as the plane hovered over green meadows and a winding ribbon of blue that had to be the Thames. My heart galloped with the realization that my new life had begun. I only grew more excited as I made my way through passport control (fibbing about the length of my stay just as I had to Ethan), withdrew British money from an ATM machine, and took a black cab from Heathrow to Ethan's apartment.

I was invigorated on our drive into London, feeling more worldly already. I sat up straighter, speaking properly to my cabbie, and injecting plenty of niceties into our chitchat, instead of barking my usual yellow-cab orders. This was a civilized land, and in it I was going to find the good life. A more cultured existence. People like Madonna and Gwyneth Paltrow, who could live anywhere in the world, chose to live in London, instead of tired old New York City and Los Angeles. I had some significant things in common with these women. Style. Beauty. A certain je ne sais quoi. Maybe I'd even befriend Madge and Gwynnie. Along with Kate Moss, Hugh Grant, and Ralph Fiennes.

Forty minutes of polite conversation later, I arrived on Ethan's street. My cabbie got out of the car, came around to the passenger side, and helped me with my bags, lining my Louis Vuitton luggage up on the curb. I handed him two purple twenties and a pretty green five—all oversized, colorful bills adorned with a young Queen Elizabeth. Even the money was more interesting and lovely in England. "Here you go, sir. Please keep the change. Thank you kindly for your help," I said, curtsying ever so slightly. It seemed a very British thing to do.

My cabbie smiled and winked at me.

I was off to a good start. I took a deep breath and exhaled, watching my breath fog up in the chilly November morning. Then I marched up the six weathered marble steps to Ethan's building, located his flat number, and pushed the bronze button next to it. I heard an anemic buzzer followed by a "Yes?" over the intercom.

"Ethan! I'm here! Hurry! I'm freezing!"

Seconds later Ethan grinned at me through the beveled pane in the front door. He swung the door open and gave me a big hug. "Darcy! How are you?"

"Wonderful!" I said, doling out a double Euro-kiss, planting one on each of his pink cheeks. I ran my hand through his honey-colored hair. It was longer than usual, his curls loopy like a lion's mane. "Love the 'do, Ethan."

He thanked me, said he hadn't had time for a cut. Then he smiled and said in what seemed to be a sincere tone, "It's good to see you, Darce."

"It's *great* to see you, Ethan."

"How do you feel?" His hand moved in a comforting circle on my back.

I told him I'd be fine as soon as I got in out of the cold and cleaned my pores. "You know how flights wreak havoc on your skin. All of that nasty, recirculated air," I said. "But at least I wasn't stuck back in the cattle car. It's disgusting back there with the common folk."

"You're far from a common folk," he said, his smile fading as he looked beyond me and spotted my bags on the curb. "You gotta be kidding me. All of that for a few weeks?"

I had yet to tell him that my plan far exceeded a few weeks, and that I was thinking more along the lines of a few months, perhaps a permanent change. I'd ease him into that, though. By the time I told him the truth, our friendship would have supplanted his bond with Rachel. Besides, I'd be finding my Alistair in no time.

Ethan rolled his eyes. Then he heaved my two largest suitcases up his front steps. "Damn, Darce. You have a body in this bag?"

"Yes. Rachel is in this one," I said proudly, pointing to one bag. "And Dex is in that one."

He shook his head and gave me a look of warning, as if to tell me that he wasn't going to bash his precious Rachel. "Seriously. What is all of this crap?"

"Just clothes, shoes. A lot of toiletries, perfumes, that sort of thing," I said, scooping up my lighter bags, explaining that pregnant women shouldn't lift anything heavier than twenty pounds.

"Gotcha," Ethan said, struggling his way through the front door. Four trips later, he had all of my bags inside the building. I followed him into the dark, mothball-smelling lobby complete with seventies-green carpeting. I must have made a face, because Ethan asked me if something was wrong.

"Mothballs," I said, wrinkling my nose.

"Better than moths," Ethan said. "Wouldn't want them to ruin your expensive jumpers."

"Jumpers?"

"Sweaters."

"My jumpers. Right," I said, feeling excited to adopt British slang for everything. Maybe even pick up an English accent.

Ethan led me to the back of the dark, cold hall and then, to my disappointment, down a flight of stairs. I couldn't stand basement apartments. They made me claustrophobic. They also translated to inadequate light and no terrace or view. Maybe the inside would compensate, I thought, as Ethan pushed open his door. "So this is it. Home sweet home," he said.

I looked around, trying to mask my disappointment.

"I told you it was small," he said, giving me a nonchalant tour. Everything was clean and neat and well decorated, but nothing struck me as particularly European except for some decent crown molding around fairly high ceilings. The kitchen was nondescript and the bathroom downright grim—with wall-to-wall carpeting (bizarre in a bathroom, but not uncommon according to Ethan) and an absolutely miniature toilet.

"Cute flat," I said with false cheer. "Where's my room?"

"Patience, my dear. I was getting to that," Ethan said, leading me to a room off the kitchen. It was smaller than a maid's room in a New

York apartment, and its sole window was too narrow to squeeze through, yet it was still covered with a row of corroded iron bars. There was one white dresser in the corner that somehow clashed with the white walls, each making the other look sickly gray. Against the adjacent wall was a small bookshelf, also painted white, but peeling, exposing a mint-green underbelly. Its shelves were empty save for a few paperbacks and a huge pink conch shell. There is something about seashells displaced from the beach that has always depressed me. I hate the hollow, lonely sound they make when you press them to your ear, although I am always compelled to listen. Sure enough, when I picked up the shell and heard the dull echo, I felt a wave of sadness. I put it back on the shelf, then walked over to the window, peering up to the street level. Nothing about my view indicated that I was in London. I could just as easily have been in Cleveland.

Ethan must have read my reaction because he said, "Look, Darce. If you don't like your room, there are plenty of hotels . . ."

"What?" I asked innocently. "I didn't say a word!"

"I know you."

"Well, then you should know that I'm endlessly grateful and thrilled beyond belief to be here. I love my cozy little cell." I laughed. "I mean, room."

Ethan raised his eyebrows and shot me a look over the top of his tortoiseshell glasses.

"It was a joke! It's not a cell," I said, thinking that John Hinckley Jr. probably had better accommodations.

He shook his head, turned, and dragged my bags into the room. By the time he was finished, there was barely room left to stand, let alone sleep.

"Where will I sleep?" I asked him, horrified.

Ethan opened a closet door and pointed to an air mattress. "I bought this for you yesterday. Luxury blowup. For a luxury girl."

I smiled. At least my reputation was intact.

"Get organized. Shower if you want."

"Of course I want. I'm *soo* gross."

"Okay. Shower up and then we'll get a bite to eat."

"Perfect!" I said, thinking that perhaps his flat wasn't what I hoped it would be, but everything else would surpass my expectations. The London scene would more than make up for the mothball odor and my cramped quarters.

I took a shower, disapproving of the water pressure and the way a draft in the bathroom blew the plastic curtain against my legs. At least Ethan had a nice array of unisex bath products. Plenty of Kiehl's goodies, including a pineapple facial scrub that I have always enjoyed. I used it, careful to replace it on the tub exactly as it was so as not to give myself away. Nobody likes a houseguest who saps their best toiletries.

"Is there something wrong with your water?" I asked Ethan as I emerged from the bathroom in my finest pink silk robe, finger-combing my wet hair. "My hair feels gross. Stripped."

"The water here is very hard. You'll get used to it. . . . Only annoying thing is that it leaves stains on your clothes."

"Are you serious?" I asked, thinking that I'd have to dry-clean everything if that was the case. "Can't you get a water softener?"

"Never looked into it. But you're welcome to undertake the project."

I sighed. "And I assume you don't have a hair dryer?"

"Good assumption," he said.

"Well. Guess I'll have to go with the natural look. We're not hanging out with other people today, are we? I want to look my best when you introduce me to your crowd."

Ethan busied himself with a stack of bills on his dining room table, his back to me. "I don't really have a crowd. Just a few friends. And I haven't planned anything."

"*Phew*. I want to make a good first impression. You know what they say—first impressions are last impressions!"

"Uh-huh."

"So I'll pick up a hair dryer at Harrods today," I said.

"I wouldn't go to Harrods for a hair dryer. There's a drugstore up on the corner. Boots."

"Boots! How sweet!"

"Just your standard drugstore."

"Well, I better go dress then."

"Okay," Ethan said without looking up.

After I had changed into my warmest sweater and my hair had dried somewhat, Ethan took me to lunch at a pub near his house. It was charming on the outside: a small, ancient-looking brick building covered with ivy. Copper pots filled with tiny red flowers framed the doorway. But like Ethan's flat, the inside was a different story. The place was dingy and reeked of smoke, and it was filled with undesirable workman types with grungy boots and even grungier fingernails. This observation was especially noteworthy because I had read a sign on the front door that said: CLEAN WORKING CLOTHES REQUIRED. I also noticed a small placard near the bar that read: PLEASE REPORT ANY SUSPICIOUS BAGS OR PACKAGES TO THE PROPRIETOR.

"What's up with that?" I asked Ethan, pointing to the sign.

"The IRA," Ethan said.

"The who?"

"Irish Republican Army?" Ethan said. "Ring a bell?"

"Oh, that," I said, vaguely recalling some incidents of terrorism in years past. "Sure."

As we sat down, Ethan suggested that I order fish and chips.

"I'm feeling sort of queasy. Either from being pregnant or from the trip. I think I need something more bland. A grilled cheese, perhaps?"

"You're in luck," he said. "They have great croque monsieurs."

"Croque misters?" I said. "What's that?"

"Fancy French name for ham and cheese."

"Sounds like a delight," I said, thinking that I should brush up on my high school French. It would come in handy when Alistair and I took our weekend jaunts to Paris.

Ethan ordered our food at the bar, which he said was standard practice at English pubs, while I perused a newspaper someone had left on our table. Victoria and David Beckham, or, as the Brits called them, "Posh and Becks," were plastered across the front page. I knew David Beckham was a big deal in England, but I just didn't get it. He wasn't that cute. Sunken cheeks, stringy hair. And I hated the earrings in both ears. I made my observations to Ethan, who pinched his lips, as if David were a personal friend of his.

"Have you ever seen him play soccer?" Ethan asked me.

"No. Who watches soccer?"

"The whole world watches soccer. It happens to be the biggest sport in every country but America."

"Well, as far as I'm concerned this David guy," I said, tapping his picture, "is no George Clooney. That's all I'm sayin'."

Ethan rolled his eyes just as an ill-kempt waitress brought our food to the table and handed us each a set of cutlery wrapped in a paper napkin. She briefly chatted with Ethan about his writing. Obviously he ate here often. I noticed that she had dreadful, crooked, yellow teeth. As she walked away, I couldn't refrain from commenting. "So it's true what they say about the dental work over here?"

Ethan salted his fish and chips and a pile of green mashed potatoes. "Kiley is really nice," he said.

"Didn't say she wasn't. Just said that her teeth are bad. *Sheesh*," I said, wondering if he was going to be so touchy about everything. "And what's with the green mashed potatoes?"

"They're peas. Mushy peas, they're called."

"Gross."

Ethan didn't respond. I took a tiny bite of my croque monsieur. As I chewed, I found myself bursting to say Rachel's name, get the full scoop from Ethan, find out everything he knew about her relationship with Dex. But I knew I had to tread carefully. If I launched into a tirade, Ethan would shut down. So after a few minutes of silent strategizing, I brought her up under the pretense of a shared high school memory, one that involved the three of us going to a Cubs game the summer after we graduated from high school. Then I cocked my head and said, very nonchalantly, "How is Rachel anyway?"

Ethan didn't take the bait. He looked up from his mushy peas and said, "She's fine."

"Just fine?"

"Darcy," he said, not fooled at all by my look of wide-eyed innocence. It was hard to pull one over on Ethan.

"What?" I asked.

"I'm not going to do this with you," he said.

"Do what?"

"Discuss Rachel."

"Why not? I don't get it," I said, dropping my sandwich onto the plate.

"Rachel is my friend."

"You're friends with me, too, you know."

He poured some vinegar on his fish and said, "I know that."

"Annalise is friends with both of us, and she'll talk to me about . . . what happened," I said, choosing my words carefully. "Why won't you tell me what you think? I won't be offended. I mean, clearly you're on her side." Reverse psychology was always worth a try, even with someone as smart as Ethan.

"Look, Darcy, I just don't feel comfortable with this whole topic. Don't you have anything else to talk about besides Rachel?"

"Trust me. Plenty," I said, as if my world were as chock full of glamorous intrigue as it had always been before tough times had befallen me.

"Well, then . . . stop trying to get me to bash her."

"I'm doing no such thing. I just wanted to talk to you, my child-hood friend, about our other childhood friend and . . . the current state of affairs. Is that so wrong?"

He gave me a long look, and then finished his lunch in silence. When he was finished, he lit a cigarette, took a long drag, and exhaled in my general direction.

"Hey! Watch it! I'm with child!" I squawked.

"Sorry," he said, turning his chair and exhaling in the other direc-tion. "You're going to have a rough time in this country, though. Everybody smokes."

"I can see that," I said, looking around. "It stinks in here."

He shrugged.

"So. Can I just ask a few questions?"

"Not if they're about Rachel."

"C'mon, Ethan, they are perfectly harmless questions. Please?"

He didn't respond so I asked my first question. "Have you talked to her recently?"

"Fairly recently."

"Does she know I'm here?"

He nodded.

"And she's okay with that?" I asked, hoping that she was decidedly *not* okay with it. I wanted her to be jealous that I was here in London with her precious Ethan. I wanted her to feel territorial stabs. I couldn't wait for Ethan to send her postcards from our trips together—jaunts to Vienna, Amsterdam, Barcelona. Perhaps I'd scratch out a haphazard PS on the occasional card. "Wish you were here," I'd write. To show her that I was *so* over the whole Dex thing. That I had moved on big time.

"She's fine with it. Yes."

I made a snorting sound to indicate that I highly doubted that that was the case.

Ethan shrugged.

"So what's new with her?"

"Not much."

"Is she still with Dex?"

"Darcy. No more. I mean it."

"What? Just tell me! I don't care if they're together. I'm just curious, is all . . ."

"I *really* mean it," he said. "No Dex questions."

"Fine. Fine. I think it's bullshit that we—two friends—can't talk frankly. But whatever. Your issues."

"Right. My issues," Ethan said, looking drained.

After lunch I unpacked while Ethan retreated to his bedroom to write. I made several trips to his room to request more hangers, and every time I'd pop in, he would glance up from his laptop with an annoyed expression, as if one little hanger request somehow threw him off his whole train of thought.

By midafternoon, my room was as organized as it could be considering the lack of space. I had stuffed my closet full of clothes, lined my favorite shoes in two rows along the bottom, and had set up all of my makeup, toiletries, and lingerie on the bookcase. It wasn't pretty, but it was functional enough. Just as I was in the mood to call it quits for the day and round up Ethan for some fun, I caught him in the living room stuffing papers and a pack of cigarettes into a messenger bag.

"Are you going somewhere?" I asked him.

"Yeah."

"Where?"

"Out. To write."

"What exactly are you writing again?"

"A chapter in a book on London architecture. And I recently

started writing a novel. And I have a ton of freelance articles due. You know, stuff to pay the rent."

"What's your novel about?" I asked, thinking that my life would make for an excellent read. I was sure I could provide him with some good material.

"It's about a guy who loses his whole family in a carbon monoxide accident and goes to live in the woods alone to heal."

"Sounds cheery."

"It's ultimately uplifting."

"If you say so. . . . But do you have to work on my first day?"

"Yes. I do," he said unapologetically.

I frowned, asked him why he couldn't stay at home and write. I told him I'd be extra quiet. "Like a church mouse," I whispered.

He smiled. "You? A church mouse?"

"C'mon, Ethan. Please," I said. "I'll be lonely here."

He shook his head. "I can't think here."

No wonder. It's a cramped little shit hole, I thought to myself. Instead I just threw up my hands and said, "Fine. Fine. But just so you know . . . glasses and caps don't go together. Pick one or the other. It's like . . . overaccessorizing or something. Edit your look."

He shook his head as I followed him to the door.

"Where do I find you if I need you?" I asked.

"You don't," he said.

"Seriously, Ethan! Where will you be?"

"I don't know. I just wander around until I find a café with a good vibe. Nothing too quiet. Nothing too clamorous. Just a nice dull din. I left my mobile number on that pad," he said, pointing to a tablet on the hall table. "Call only if absolutely necessary."

"Can't I come with you?"

"No."

I sighed. "What am I supposed to do for the rest of the day without you? I didn't think I'd be all alone on my first day here."

He shifted his bag to the opposite shoulder and looked at me, poised to lecture.

"Okay. Okay. Sorry . . . I'll make do."

He handed me a set of keys and a spiral book with a map on the front. "The small key works the front door. The brass one goes in the top lock. Skull key for the bottom. All turn to the left. And take this *A to Zed*. Your bible to the London streets."

"I hate maps," I said, flipping through the book. "And this one looks impossible. There are too many pages."

"*You're* impossible," Ethan said.

"Just tell me where I should go to shop," I said.

"There's an index in the back of the *A to Zed*. Look up Knightsbridge. You have plenty of shopping in that general area. Harrods. And Harvey Nichols, which is more your bag."

"How so?" I asked, anticipating a compliment.

"More fashionably elite."

I smiled. I was nothing if not fashionably elite. "How far away is Knightsbridge?"

"A long walk. Or short cab ride. I'll explain the tube another day. No time now."

"Thanks, Ethan," I said, kissing his cheek. "I'll see you tonight. And in the meantime, I'm going to find some cute clothes!"

"Sounds like a swell plan," he said with a supportive smile. It was as if Ethan understood that if I were going to start a new life, I needed a whole new wardrobe too.

nineteen

As it turned out, Ethan was right. Harvey Nichols was *exactly* my bag. I started out at Harrods, but it was too large and packed with touristy riffraff in much the same way Macy's is at home. Harvey Nics, as I overheard one British girl call it right outside the Sloane Street entrance, was more upscale and boutiquey, reminding me of Henri Bendel or Barneys in New York. I was in heaven, going from rack to rack, gathering various gems by Stella McCartney, Dolce & Gabbana, Alexander McQueen, Jean Paul Gaultier, and Marc Jacobs. Then I threw some new names into the mix, finding splendid, wintery garments from designers I had never heard of.

My only bad moment of the afternoon came when I discovered that I could no longer squeeze into a size six. I was seventeen weeks pregnant, and my initial few pounds of pregnancy weight had already propelled me up from my usual size four, but when even the sixes didn't fit, I panicked. I examined my ass and thighs in the dressing room mirror, and then simulated the old pencil test, where you stand with your feet together, place a pencil between your legs, and see if it stays put between your thighs or drops to the ground. I was relieved to see that there was still adequate space—a pencil would definitely fall to the ground. So how could it be that my size had changed so significantly, seemingly overnight? I poked my head out of the dressing room and summoned a striking salesgirl wearing a funky leather skirt and orange vinyl boots.

"Excuse me, but are the sizes a bit off in Dries Van Noten?" I asked her.

She gave me a melodious laugh. "American?"

I nodded.

"The sizes run different here, love. Are you a four at home?"

"Yes," I said proudly. "I am normally. But lately I take a six at home."

"That's a ten here typically."

"Oh, what a relief!" I said.

"Would you like me to get you some new sizes?"

I nodded gratefully, handed her my stash, and asked her if she would add a skirt like hers to my pile. Then I waited, half naked, in the dressing room, studying the small bump protruding from my stomach. It had popped out seemingly overnight, but my body was otherwise still trim and well toned. I had fallen off my rigorous, prewedding workout schedule, but I reasoned that as long as I was careful with my diet, I could maintain my figure for at least a few more months.

When the salesgirl finally returned, she squealed, "Oh, my, you're pregnant! How far along are you?"

"Four months and change," I said, running my hand down along my bump.

"You look *smashing* for four months," she purred in her chic accent.

I thanked her as I moved aside to let her hang my size tens in the dressing room. An hour later, I was buying five amazing outfits that would have made Claire drool. As I forked over my Visa, I remembered that my spree added up to many more dollars than pounds, but I told myself not to bother with the conversion. I would just pretend to be spending dollars. And anyway, what was a few thousand dollars in the scheme of things? Nothing. Not when I thought of it as a kick start to my new life. It was an investment.

And as long as I was investing in myself, I figured that I might as well throw in a couple pairs of Jimmy Choos, which after all had great practicality as I could wear them throughout my pregnancy, maybe even tapping home in them from the hospital with Alistair by my side.

I left Harvey Nics and found my way back out to glorious Sloane Street, visiting my old friends—Christian Dior, Valentino, Hermès, Prada, and Gucci—discovering with delight that each store had slightly different inventory than what the New York stores carried. So I treated myself to a gorgeous Gucci tan leather hobo bag with the most satisfying brass hardware.

After my final purchase, I hailed a cab and returned to Ethan's flat, exhausted but thrilled with my purchases, anxious to show him what I had discovered, conquered, and made my own. Ethan wasn't yet back at the flat so I helped myself to a cup of raspberry sherbet and turned on the television. I discovered that Ethan only had five channels, and I ended up watching a string of remarkably unfunny British sitcoms and a reality television show based in a hair salon. Ethan finally walked in the door just after ten o'clock.

"Where have you been?" I asked, hands on my hips.

He glanced at me as he tossed his bag on the floor. "Writing," he said.

"This whole time?"

"Yes."

"Are you sure? You smell like a bar," I said, burrowing my nose in his jacket. "Don't discount my ability to party just because I'm pregnant."

He jerked his arm away, his blue eyes narrowing. "I wasn't partying, Darce. I work in cafés. Smoky cafés. I told you that."

"If you say so . . . but I'll have you know I've been bored stiff here. And I'm famished. I only had some sherbet all night. I really shouldn't be skipping meals like this when I'm pregnant."

"You could have eaten without me," he said. "I have stuff here—and there are plenty of places to eat up on the High Street. For future reference, there's a good Lebanese joint called Al Dar. . . . They don't deliver but you can call ahead for takeout."

I was a little annoyed that he wasn't being more nurturing, but I decided not to pout. Instead, I embarked on a mini fashion show, showing Ethan all my purchases, twirling and posing while he watched the news. I got a lot of cursory compliments, but mostly he seemed disinterested in my goods. During one clip on a suicide bomber in Jerusalem, he even shushed me, holding up the palm of his hand inches from my face. At that point, I let the dream of a bonding session die and retired to my room to blow up my air mattress. Sometime later, Ethan appeared in the doorway with a sheet, blanket, and small, flat pillow. "So you figured that thing out?" he asked, pointing down at my mattress.

"Yeah," I said, sitting on the edge and bouncing slightly. "It had a little pump. Much easier than blowing."

"Told you it was luxury."

I smiled, yawned, and politely requested a good-night kiss. Ethan leaned down and planted one on my forehead. " 'Night, Darcy."

"Good night, Ethan."

After he closed the door, I turned off the light and struggled to get comfortable on my mattress, arranging and rearranging my pillow and blanket. But I couldn't fall asleep despite how tired and jet-lagged I was. After an hour of tossing, I took my blanket and pillow and shuffled into the living room, hoping that Ethan's couch would be more comfortable. It wasn't. It was too short by several inches, which gave me that desperate feeling of needing to straighten my knees. I tried to drape my feet over the edge of the couch, but the arms were slightly too high and after several minutes with elevated legs, I felt as if all my blood were rushing to my head. I sat up, whimpered, and stared into the still, dark room.

Only one option remained. Still swaddled in my blanket, I tiptoed down the hall toward Ethan's room, pressing my ear against his door. I could hear his radio and realized that the quiet in my room might be part of the problem. I was used to the lulling sound of New York City traffic. I knocked softly, hoping he was still awake and willing to talk for a few minutes. Nothing. I knocked again, more loudly. Still nothing. So I tried the doorknob. It was unlocked. I pushed the door open and whispered Ethan's name. No response. I walked over to the bed and peered down at him. His mouth was slightly open, his hands tucked under one cherubic cheek.

I hesitated and then said in a normal tone, "Ethan?"

When he still didn't stir, I walked around to the other side of the bed. There was plenty of room for me so I got in bed next to him, on top of the covers, still wrapped in my own blanket. Although I would have preferred a long conversation, I instantly felt less lonely just being close to a familiar friend from home. Just as I was drifting off, I sensed movement. When I opened my eyes, Ethan was squinting over at me.

"What are you doing in my bed?"

"Please let me stay," I said. "It's too lonely sleeping in that room with bars on the windows. And I think the air mattress is bad for my back. Take pity on a pregnant girl. Please?"

He made an exasperated sound but didn't protest. So of course I pressed my luck. *Quit while you're ahead* is advice I've never been able to follow. "Can I get under the covers with you, please? I need a human touch. I'm dying inside."

"Don't be so dramatic." Ethan grunted wearily, but then shifted slightly, lifting the covers for me.

I shed my blanket and crawled in beside him, nestling against his slender, wiry frame.

"No funny business," he mumbled.

"No funny business," I said cheerfully, thinking how nice it was to have a good male friend. I felt grateful that we had never hooked up— so it didn't feel at all weird to be in the same bed together. In fact, unless you count elementary school, we had only had one close call over the years. We were at a party following our ten-year reunion. I was a little tipsy and something came over me—perhaps it was the realization that Ethan, although slightly nerdy in high school, had become the most popular guy in our class. Everyone was clamoring to talk to him. The adulation made me appreciate him on a whole new level. So I guess I got a little carried away for a few seconds and thought it might be fun to make out with him. The details are blurry, but I remember running my hands through his curly hair and suggesting that he give me a lift home. Luckily, Ethan showed superhuman restraint in the name of our friendship. Or maybe he really *was* gay. Either way, the lines of our friendship were clear now—which was a good thing.

"I'm glad I'm here," I whispered happily.

"Yeah. Me too," he said unconvincingly. "Now go to sleep."

I was quiet for a few minutes but then realized that I had to pee. I tried to ignore it, but then kept myself up debating whether to get up. So I finally got up, and tripped over a pile of books next to Ethan's bed.

"Darcy!"

"I'm sorry. I can't help it that I *have* to pee. I'm pregnant. Remember?"

"You might be pregnant, but I have insomnia," he said. "And I better be able to fall back asleep after all your shenanigans. I have a *lot* to do tomorrow."

"I'm sorry. I promise I'll be quiet when I get back," I said. Then I scurried down the hall to the bathroom, peed, and returned to his bed. Ethan lifted the covers again for me, his eyes still shut. "Now be quiet. Or it's back to your cell. I mean it."

"Okay. I'll be quiet," I said, cuddling next to him again. "Thanks, Ethan. I needed this. I really needed this."

For the next couple of weeks, my routine stayed the same. I shopped all day, discovering a wide array of fashion boutiques: Amanda Wakeley and Betty Jackson on Fulham Road, Browns on South Molton Street, Caroline Charles on Beauchamp Place, Joseph on Old Bond Street, and Nicole Farhi on New Bond Street. I bought fabulous designer pieces: playful scarves, beautiful jumpers, chic skirts, unusual handbags, and sexy shoes. Then I sought out the bargain spots on Oxford Street—Next, River Island, Top Shop, Selfridges, and Marks & Spencer—because I've always maintained that it is totally effective to work such low-end pieces into an otherwise couture wardrobe. Even overt knockoffs, if paired with high-end pieces and worn with confidence, can look positively fabulous.

Every night I would return home with my purchases, and wait for Ethan to finish his day of work. Then we would eat takeaway together, or he would whip us up a meal, followed by a little bit of television and conversation. When it was time for bed, I always retired to my room first, pretending to give my air mattress a good-faith try before transferring to his bed. Ethan would act exasperated, but I could tell he secretly enjoyed my company.

On my third Wednesday in town, after much nagging on my part, Ethan finally promised to take the following day off and hang out with me.

"Awesome! What's the special occasion?" I asked.

"Um. Thanksgiving? Remember that holiday? Or have you been in England too long?"

"Omigod. I totally forgot about Thanksgiving," I said, realizing that it had been days since I had consulted a calendar or talked to anyone from home. I had yet to call my parents or brother and notify them that I had left New York, and I felt satisfied knowing that I would be a topic of conversation at the dinner table the following day.

"What would you like to do?" Ethan asked me.

"Well, the stores will all be open, right?" I asked. "Since it's not a holiday here?"

He made a face. "You want to shop more?"

"We could shop for you," I said, trying to entice him. "I love men's clothing." I thought of all the times I had shopped for Dex—how gorgeous he had looked in the outfits I had assembled. Now with only Rachel to help him, I was sure he was sporting Banana Republic clothing. His wardrobe was definitely going to take a hit without me.

"I was thinking more along the lines of a nice, long walk along the Thames. Or a stroll around Regent's Park. Have you been there yet?"

"No," I said. "But it's freezing out there. You really want to spend the day outside?"

"Okay. Then how about a museum? Have you been to the National Gallery?"

"Yes," I fibbed, in part because I didn't want to be dragged there. Museums make me weary, and the dim lighting depresses me. But I also lied because I didn't want any attitude about the number of days I had spent in stores in lieu of museums. If he called me out on it, I had a rationale ready—the museums and cathedrals weren't going any-where, whereas fashion was changing by the second.

"Oh, really? You didn't mention you'd been there," he said, with a hint of suspicion. "What did you think of the Sainsbury Wing?"

"Oh. I *loved* it. Why? What do you think of it?" Deflection is al-ways a good technique when you're in mid-fib.

"I love it . . . I wrote an article about it."

I struck a thoughtful pose. "What was the article about?"

"Oh, I wrote about how the modernists criticize it because they prefer a streamlined simplicity in architecture. You know, 'less is more' . . . whereas the postmodernists, including Robert Venturi, the American who designed it, believe that a structure should be in sync with its surroundings . . . so the rooms in that wing reflect the cultural context of the Renaissance works housed within it." Ethan spoke ex-citedly despite the dull topic.

He continued, "Thus you have this grand interior with all sorts of things going on, like this perspective illusion where these aligned arches get smaller in the distance, just as they do in the Scala Regia, at the Vatican Palace . . . because in Venturi's words, 'Less is a bore.'"

"Hmmm," I said, nodding. "Less *is* a bore. I'd have to agree with Venturi on that point."

Ethan adjusted his glasses and said, "So would Prince Charles. Upon seeing the initial design plans for a much more simple design by modernists, he made the comment that the wing would be 'a mon-strous carbuncle on the face of a much-loved friend.'"

I laughed. "I don't know what a carbuncle is, but it doesn't sound pleasant. I wish one upon Rachel's nose."

Ethan ignored the remark and asked me what were my favorite paintings in the National Gallery.

"Oh, I couldn't begin to choose just one."

"Did you see *The Supper at Emmaus?*"

"Yes. Brilliant."

"And how about Jan van Eyck's Arnolfini Portrait?"

"Oh, I loved that one too," I said.

"Did you notice the inscription on the back wall in the painting?" he asked.

"Refresh my memory?"

"The inscription over the mirror . . . Its English translation is 'Jan van Eyck was present' and sure enough you can see his reflection in the mirror, along with the couple getting married and another guest. I've always wondered why Jan van Eyck wanted to include his own image in that painting. What do you suppose he was trying to say?"

I had the sudden feeling that I was back in college, being put on the spot by an art history professor. "Hmm. I dunno."

"I don't either . . . but it does make you think . . . And don't you just love how huge that painting is? Just dominating the room?"

"Uh-huh," I said. "It's huge, all right."

Ethan shook his head and laughed. "You're full of shit, Darce. That painting is tiny. You've never been to the National Gallery, have you?"

I tossed my hair off my face and smiled sheepishly. "Okay. No. You got me. You know I don't like museums, Ethan! I'd rather live life than walk around some dark rooms with a bunch of dorky American tourists." It sounded like a good excuse. Sort of like people who say they don't read the newspaper because the news is too depressing. I had subscribed to that one in the past too.

"I'd agree that when you go to a new city, you shouldn't spend every moment in a museum, but you'll miss a lot if you blow off *all* museums. . . . In any event, I'd like to show you something of London. Something other than Harrods and Harvey Nichols. What do you say?"

I thought to myself that what I really wanted was to return to Joseph for a leather jacket I had resisted the day before. It was over four hundred pounds but classic enough to last forever, the kind of purchase you never regret. I was sure it would be gone if I didn't get back there tomorrow. But I relished the idea of having daytime companionship, so if Ethan wanted London culture, I'd oblige.

The next day Ethan woke me up at eight, chirping excitedly about the full day he had planned for us. We showered and dressed quickly, and by nine, we were making our way up to Kensington High Street. It was a frigid, gray day, and as I slid on my aubergine leather gloves trimmed with rabbit fur, I asked Ethan why London always felt so much colder than the actual temperature.

"It's the dampness in the air," he said. "Permeates every layer of clothing."

"Yeah," I said, shivering. "It's downright bone-chilling. Glad I wore my boots."

Ethan made an acknowledging sound as we walked at a faster clip to keep warm. Moments later we were at the entrance of Holland Park, both of us slightly out of breath.

"Of all the parks in London, this is my favorite," Ethan said, beaming. "It has such an intimate, romantic aura."

"Are you trying to tell me something, Ethan?" I joked, as I linked my arm around his.

He smiled, rolled his eyes, and shook me off. "Yeah. I'm about to propose. How'd you know?"

"I hope you have an emerald-cut diamond in your pocket. I'm so over brilliant cuts," I told him as we walked along a wooded path that curved around a big, open field.

"Brilliant cuts are the round ones?" he asked.

"Yeah."

"Damn. I bought you a fat, round diamond. Guess we'll have to stay friends then."

I giggled. "Guess so."

"So anyway, this," he said pointing to the field, "is called the Cricket Lawn."

"People play cricket here?"

"Historically, yes. And I've seen the occasional cricket game here, but more often it's football—soccer. And in the summer, it's a giant lounging ground. People spread out everywhere on blankets. It only takes about sixty degrees before the Brits will be out here sunning. . . . My spot is right there," he said, pointing to a shady area on the outskirts of the field. "I've had many delicious naps under that tree."

I pictured Ethan with his various notebooks, trying to write, but succumbing to sleep. I thought how nice it would be to come here with him in the summer with my baby and a picnic lunch. As we circled the top of the field next to an outdoor theater, I thought about how contented I was to be hanging with Ethan. Then I thought of Rachel, and wished that she could see a snapshot of us together, strolling around a London park on Thanksgiving morning. I wondered what she and Dex were doing, whether they had gone back to Indianapolis for the holiday. Perhaps they were in Rachel's kitchen now, sitting by her bay window with a cup of coffee and a view of my house.

I told myself not to corrupt my good mood and turned my attention back to Ethan, who was spouting off all kinds of facts, as he often does. He told me that the park comprised the former grounds of Holland House, which used to be a social and political hot spot in the city. He explained that it was bombed and damaged during World War II. He said that it currently provided shelter for several peacocks that we were bound to see.

"Oh, I *love* peacocks."

He looked at me sideways and snickered. "You sort of remind me of one."

I told him that I'd take that as a compliment.

"I figured you would," he said, and then pointed out a restaurant called the Belvedere. He told me they had the most elegant brunch, and that if I were good, he might take me there.

Beyond the restaurant was a beautiful, formal garden, which Ethan told me was planted in 1790 by Lady Holland with the first English dahlias. I asked him how he could remember so many names and dates and facts, and if his mind didn't ever feel cluttered with useless information.

He told me that history wasn't clutter. "Clutter is knowing all of the things that you absorb through your fashion magazines. Clutter is knowing which celebrities broke up with whom and why."

I started to explain that today's celebrities would be tomorrow's historical figures, but Ethan interrupted me. "Check it out. A peacock!"

Sure enough, a gorgeous bird in brilliant blues and greens was strutting around a fenced-in grassy area, his feathers splayed just like the NBC mascot. "Wow. So pretty," I said. "I wouldn't mind having a coat in those colors."

"I'll keep that in mind when I'm Christmas-shopping for you," Ethan said. Although I knew he was joking, it made me happy to hear him reference Christmas. I hoped that I could extend my stay at least that long. If I could make it until then, I was home free until my baby arrived. He surely wouldn't banish me as I approached my third trimester. "Okay. This is my favorite part of the park coming up. The Kyoto Garden, built during the Japan festival."

We climbed a few steps and passed a placard on our way to the garden.

"Isn't it lovely?" Ethan asked, pausing at the entrance of the garden.

I nodded. It was. The tiny garden was a tranquil enclave with a pond, bonsai-like trees, wooden walkways, and waterfalls. I told Ethan that the whole scene reminded me of Mr. Miyagi's garden in *Karate Kid*. Ethan laughed as he led me across one footbridge. He stopped on the other side and sat on a wooden bench. Then he closed his eyes, propped his hands behind his head, and said, "This is the most peaceful spot in London. Nobody ever comes here. Even in warm weather, I always seem to have it all to myself."

I sat down next to Ethan and looked at him as he inhaled deeply, his eyes still closed. His cheeks were pink and his hair was curled up around the edges of his navy wool hat, and suddenly, out of nowhere, I felt a flicker of attraction to him. It wasn't the sort of physical attraction I had felt toward Marcus, nor was it the objective admiration I had felt for Dexter. It was more a welling of fondness for one of my only remaining friends in the world. Ethan was both a tie to my past and a bridge to my new life, and if gratitude can make you want to kiss a person, at that moment I had an unmistakable urge to plant one on him. Of course I resisted, telling myself to stop being crazy. Ethan wasn't my type, and besides, the last thing I wanted to do was disrupt our living (and sleeping) arrangement.

A moment later, Ethan stood abruptly. "You hungry?"

I told him that I was, so we walked back to Kensington High Street, past his flat, and over to a tea shop on Wright's Lane called the Muffin Man. The inside was shabby but cozy, filled with little tables and chairs and waitresses wearing floral aprons. We took a table by the window and ordered toasted sandwiches, tea, and scones. As we waited for our treats, we talked about my pregnancy. Ethan asked me about my last trip to the doctor. I told him it was right before I came to live with him and that I was due for another one soon.

Ethan caught my slip and raised his eyebrows. "To *live* with me?"

"I mean to visit," I said, and then quickly changed the subject before he could inquire about my departure and discover that I had bought a one-way ticket. "So at my next appointment, I'll find out the gender of the baby. . . . But I just *know* that it's a girl."

"Why's that?" Ethan asked, as the waitress arrived with our treats.

"It's just a very strong feeling. God, I hope it's a girl. I'm not a big fan of men these days. Except for you, of course. And gay men."

He laughed.

"You're not gay, are you?" I asked. It seemed like as good a time as any to broach the subject.

"No." He smiled and shook his head. "Did you think I was?"

"Well, you don't have a girlfriend," I said. *And you've never hit on me,* I thought.

He laughed. "I don't have a boyfriend either."

"Good point . . . I don't know. You have good taste, you know so much about artsy things. I guess I thought maybe Brandi would have turned you off women."

"She didn't turn me off *all* women."

I studied his face, but couldn't read his expression. "Did I offend you?"

"Not at all," Ethan said, as he buttered a scone.

"Oh, thank goodness," I said. "I'd hate to offend my best friend in the world."

I wanted him to be flattered, maybe even reciprocate by saying "Why, you're my best friend too." But he just smiled and took a bite of his scone. After our tea break, Ethan led us back to Kensington High Street over to the tube stop.

"We're taking the tube?" I asked. "Why not a cab?" I wasn't a big fan of the subway in New York, always favoring cabs, and I had not changed the practice in London.

"Suck it up, Darce," Ethan told me, as he handed me a pink ticket. "And don't lose your ticket. You'll need it to exit on the other side."

I told him that I didn't think that was a particularly good system.

"Seems to me an awful lot of people would misplace their ticket during their journey and be stuck floundering on the other end."

Ethan stuck his ticket in a slot, went through a turnstile and down some stairs. I followed him and found myself on the very cold, outdoor platform. "It's freezing," I said, rubbing my gloves together. "Why don't they have enclosed platforms?"

"No more complaining, Darce."

"I'm not complaining. I'm simply commenting that it's a very chilly day."

Ethan zipped his fleece jacket up around his chin and looked down the tracks. "Circle Line train coming now," he said.

Moments later we were seated on the train, a woman's voice announcing the next stop in a very civilized British accent.

"When are they going to say 'mind the gap'?" I asked. "Or do they not really say that?"

Ethan smiled and explained that they only give that caution at certain stops where there is a substantial gap between the train and the platform.

I looked up at the tube map over us and asked him where exactly we were going.

"Charing Cross Station," he said. "We're off to cover some basics, including the National Gallery. I know you aren't a big fan of museums, but tough. It's a must. You're going to see some Turners, Seurats, and Botticellis whether you like it or not."

"I like it," I said, meaning it. "Please enlighten me."

So that afternoon, we hit some more London highlights. We lingered by Nelson's Column, in the middle of Trafalgar Square amid all the people and pigeons, as I got a lesson about Lord Horatio Nelson's naval victory over the French. (Ethan was astonished when I admitted that I had no idea that the French and British were ever at odds.) We visited Ethan's favorite church, St. Martin-in-the-Fields, which he said was famous for its social activism. Then we had another tea break in the Café-in-the-Crypt, located in the basement of the church. Afterward, we made our way over to the National Gallery. Ethan showed me a smattering of his favorite works, and I have to admit, I enjoyed myself. His commentary made the paintings almost interesting. It was as if I were seeing things through his eyes, noticing details of color and shape that otherwise would have been lost on me.

We returned home just after dark, and prepared our untraditional Thanksgiving dinner of salmon, asparagus, and couscous. After we ate, I crawled in bed next to Ethan and thanked him for my tour of London.

He rolled over to face me and gave me a strange, serious look. "You're welcome, Darcy."

"It was my best Thanksgiving ever," I said, surprised to feel my heart beating faster. Our eyes remained locked, and my thoughts returned to that moment on the park bench. I wondered if Ethan occasionally felt a vague attraction to me too. If he did right now.

But as he turned away abruptly, leaning up to switch off his lamp, and repositioning himself farther away from me, I told myself that I was being crazy. It was likely just my pregnancy hormones making me imagine things.

After several minutes, Ethan said quietly, his voice muffled against his pillow, "I had a nice time, too, Darce."

I smiled to myself. It may not have been Ethan's best Thanksgiving ever, but I was pretty sure that the day would buy me some more weeks in London. He wasn't going to send me packing just yet.

twenty

One morning the following week I told Ethan I was desperate for a night out on the town and a little social interaction. I insisted that he take me somewhere other than his pub and introduce me to his friends.

"After all," I said, "a pregnant girl shouldn't be forced to go to a bar alone, should she?"

"I suppose not," he said, and then reluctantly promised that he'd invite a few people out to dinner on Saturday night.

"Let's go somewhere *fabulous*!"

"I don't generally do fabulous. Would you settle for a slightly upscale gastropub?" he asked, as he gathered up his cigarettes and lighter and headed outside for a smoke.

I wasn't a big fan of pubs, gastro or otherwise, but I'd take what I could get, so I lightheartedly called after him, "Whatever you want. Just invite your coolest friends. Preferably male!"

So on Saturday night, I got all decked out in my favorite Seven jeans (which I could still button right under my belly), an ivory silk brocade coat, a new pair of Moschino leather pumps, and the perfect tourmaline drop earrings.

"How do I look?" I asked.

He gave me a cursory glance and said, "Nice."

"Can you tell I'm pregnant?" I asked, following him into the hall outside his flat. "Or does this jacket sort of hide my stomach?"

He looked at me again. "I don't know. I know you're pregnant, so I see it, I guess. Why? Are you trying to hide it?"

"Well, naturally," I said. "I don't want to scare off all the eligible men before they get to know me."

I caught Ethan rolling his eyes before he ran to the corner to hail a passing cab. I took my time catching up to him, deciding to let his eye-roll slide. Instead I told him that he looked very nice too. "I really like your Levi's," I said.

"Thanks. They're so old."

I nodded and then said, "Guys fall into two camps, you know."

"How's that?" he asked with a bemused expression.

"Those who wear good jeans and those who don't. . . . And it's not about the brand *per se*. It's more about the fit, the wash, the length. All those subtleties. And you, my friend, have the art of the blue jean mastered." I kissed my thumb and index finger and made an okay sign in the air.

Ethan laughed and ran the back of his hand along his forehead. "I was worried."

I smiled, squeezed his thigh, and said, "This is fun . . . Where are we going again?"

"The Admiral Codrington. In Chelsea."

I was worried when I heard the stodgy name of the restaurant, but there was an excellent vibe when we walked inside. It was nothing like Ethan's nasty local pub. The bar area was packed with a smartly dressed, professional crowd, and I instantly spotted two prospects, one leaning on the bar, smoking, the other telling a story. I smiled at the guy talking. He winked at me, still talking to his smoking friend. The smoking friend then turned to see who was winkworthy, spotted me, and raised his eyebrows as if to second his friend's judgment. I gave him a smile too. Equal opportunity for all Brits.

"Either one of those guys your friend Martin?" I asked, pointing at the cute pair.

"No," Ethan said, giving them a quick look. "My friends are out of their teens."

"Those guys are not teenagers!" I said, but upon second glance, I saw that they were probably in their early twenties. That is one of the problems with getting older. There is a distinct lag time between how you see others and how you view yourself. I still thought of myself as looking about twenty-four. "So," I asked Ethan, "where are Martin and Phoebe?"

"Probably seated already," Ethan said, glancing at his watch. "We're late."

Ethan hated being late, and I could tell he was annoyed that I had taken a bit too long getting ready for our outing. As we made our way to the back of the restaurant, I remembered one night in the tenth grade, just after Ethan got his driver's license, when he took Rachel, Annalise, and me for his inaugural spin to the movie theater. Like tonight, I guess I had taken a bit too long primping, so the whole way to the theater, Ethan kept ranting, saying things like, "By God, Darcy, we better not be stuck seeing some inane chick flick because everything else is sold out!" Finally, I had had enough of his verbal abuse and told him to stop the car immediately and let me out, never mind that we were cruising down Ogden Avenue, a busy street with very little shoulder. Rachel and Annalise tried to smooth things over from the back seat, but Ethan and I were both too fired up. Then, in our escalating battle, Ethan ran a red light, nearly smashing into a minivan. The driver looked like a prim, well-coiffed soccer mom, but that didn't stop her from leaning on her horn with one hand and flipping Ethan the bird with the other just as a cop pulled Ethan over to issue him his first ticket. Despite the incident, we *still* made it to the theater in time to see Ethan's first choice of movies, but he brought the night up often anyway, saying that it was "emblematic of my inconsiderate nature."

I remembered the night with a mixture of nostalgia and sheepishness as Ethan spotted his friends. "That's Martin and Phoebe," he said, pointing to his two closest friends in London. My heart sank as I studied them because, to be frank, I judge books by their covers, and neither of them was impressive. Martin was a thin, balding guy, with a prominent Adam's apple. He was wearing a lackluster corduroy jacket with dark patches at the elbow, and cuffed jeans (which, incidentally, placed him in the bad-jean camp). Phoebe was a large, ruddy woman with man hands and hair like Julia Roberts in *Pretty Woman* (before she becomes refined).

My face must have registered disappointment because Ethan made a disgusted sound, shook his head, and walked past me toward his unpolished pals. I followed him, smiling brightly, deciding to make the most of the evening. Maybe one of them had a hot, single brother.

"Martin, Phoebe, this is Darcy," Ethan said when we reached the table.

"Darcy. Pleasure," Martin said, standing slightly to shake my hand. I tried not to look at his Adam's apple as I gave him a demure smile and said, "Likewise" in the Jackie O, finishing-school voice I had mastered from Claire.

Meanwhile, Phoebe's face was frozen into a knowing little smirk that made me instantly, and intensely, dislike her.

"Darcy. We've heard *so* much about you," she said, her voice loaded with sarcasm and innuendo.

My mind raced. What had Ethan told them that would cause Phoebe to smirk? I considered the possibilities: *Pregnant and alone?* No. That didn't warrant a smirk, especially from a hulking woman with orange hair whose best hope of offspring sat in a Petri dish at a sperm bank. *Mooching roommate?* No. I hadn't been in the country long enough to achieve that status. Besides, I was still (barely) self-sufficient. *Shallow New Yorker?* Perhaps that was it, but I wasn't about to feel ashamed for being well-groomed and wearing fine clothes.

Then it hit me. Phoebe was smirking about Rachel and Dex. Ethan must have told them the whole story. Sure enough, as I talked about how much I was enjoying my visit to London, Phoebe's smile evolved into a full-on jackal grin, and I became convinced that she was amused by my plight, amused that my former best friend was shagging my former fiancé.

"What's so funny here? Am I missing something?" I finally asked, glancing around the table.

Martin muttered that nothing was funny. Ethan shrugged, looking flustered and guilty. Phoebe hid her smile with her pint of frothy Guinness, a fitting drink for a beast of a woman. *At least I don't have fat sausage limbs. At least I'm pretty and not wearing a nappy puce turtleneck.* How could she not see that I had it all over her? As I watched Phoebe guffaw at her own bad jokes and order pint after pint to wash down her pork chops covered with thick, oniony sauce, I marveled at her abundance of misplaced confidence. To make my displeasure known to Ethan, I remained mostly silent.

Then, as we waited for our bill, Phoebe confirmed my hunch as she turned to me and slurred, "I met your friend Rachel a few months back. She was lovely."

I inhaled sharply and held her gaze, struggling to remain calm. "Oh, you met Rachel? That *is* lovely. . . . Ethan didn't mention that." I glared at Ethan as he flinched, recrossed his arms, and averted his eyes to a nearby raucous table.

"Yeah," he said. "Martin and Phoebe met Rachel when she visited me . . ."

My heart pounded with indignation, and I could feel my face tighten and contort in an attempt not to cry. How dare Ethan bring me out with these people after introducing Rachel to them—and not give me any warning? And worse, from the way Phoebe was acting, I just knew that Rachel had had feelings for Dex during her visit to London, and that she had shared her thoughts with Ethan and his friends. Before tonight, I was sure that Rachel had not confessed much to Ethan. At least not anything too incriminating. I had assumed this because when we were kids Rachel once told me that she didn't divulge anything embarrassing or controversial even in her own diary because she feared an early demise from a fluke accident—something undignified like dropping her hair dryer in the bathtub or choking on a hot dog. And upon her death, she couldn't bear the thought of her parents reading an entry that might make them think less of her. "But you'd be dead," I remember saying to her. "Even worse," she'd say. "Because if I were dead, I wouldn't be able to change my parents' opinion of me. That would be their final impression."

So, because of Rachel's heretofore unflagging morality, coupled with her anxiety over what people might think of her character, I had assumed that if she had had feelings for Dex prior to our breakup, she surely hadn't shared them with anyone. I think I also wanted to believe that Ethan, although closer to Rachel, was my friend, too, and that he therefore wasn't holding out on me in any significant way. It was sickening to realize that not only did he likely know much more than he had let on—but that total strangers in London knew everything too. I felt like a fool—and feeling foolish is one of the all-time worst emotions. Suddenly I was burning up, fanning at my face with my small Chanel purse, panicking that perhaps Rachel and Dex had hooked up even before the day I caught them together.

In an attempt to ferret out the truth, I looked Phoebe straight in the eye and asked in a volume way louder than necessary, even in a noisy restaurant filled with a bunch of drunken Brits, "When you met my friend Rachel, did she happen to mention that she wanted to fuck my fiancé? Or had she already fucked him at that point?"

Martin looked pained as he intently studied our bill. Ethan shook his head. Phoebe let out a gleeful chortle.

"I'm glad that somebody here is amused," I said, standing angrily from the table. My heel caught on the edge of my chair, causing it to crash to the ground. Everyone—including the two cute twenty-something guys who were now joined by two cute twenty-something girls—turned to stare, looking embarrassed for me. I fumbled in my purse for money, realizing that I had left my wallet on the floor next to my air mattress. This was unfortunate, because it would have been a way stronger statement to throw down a wad of bills before exiting. Instead I had to mumble to Ethan that I'd pay him back later. Then I stomped off, wondering if I could find my way home, and how much my feet were going to ache walking all that way in my new shoes. As I spilled onto the dark street, I realized that I had no idea where I was. I walked in one direction, then turned in the other, and was hugely re-lieved when Ethan appeared from the door of the restaurant.

"Darcy, just wait here. I have to pay our part of the bill," he said, as if he were the one who had the right to be annoyed.

"You owe me an apology!" I shouted.

"Just wait here. I'll be right back. Okay?"

I crossed my arms, glared at him, and said fine, I'd wait. As if I had much of a choice. A minute later Ethan was back on the street, his lips set in an angry line. He hailed us a cab and opened the door roughly. How dare he be mad at me! I was the wronged party here. My instinct was to unleash, but I bit my lip, literally, waiting for him to talk first. He said nothing for several minutes and then spoke in a wry tone. "So you and Phoebe got along brilliantly."

"She's such a miserable cow, Ethan!"

"Calm down."

"Don't tell me to calm down!" I shouted. "How dare you bring me out with them when they know everything about me! You should have told me they had already met Rachel! I can't believe you all had a good laugh at my expense! I thought you were my friend!"

"I *am* your friend," he said.

"Then tell me what you told them, Ethan! And while you're at it, tell me *everything* you know about Dex and Rachel!"

His neck muscles twitched. "We'll talk about it at home, okay?"

"No. We'll talk about it *now*!" I shouted, but Ethan looked resolute, and I was afraid of pressing my luck. I wanted the truth too much to jeopardize pissing him off. It took all of my resolve, but I managed to keep my mouth shut the rest of the way home.

When Ethan and I arrived back at his flat, he disappeared to his bedroom, possibly to call Rachel and seek permission to divulge her dirty little secrets. I paced in the living room, wondering what he was going to tell me. How bad the truth was. After a few minutes, he returned to the living room and began rummaging through his CDs. I took off my jacket and heels and sat cross-legged on the floor, keeping my face placid, as I waited for the truth. The *whole* truth. Ethan calmly selected a Coldplay CD, turned the volume higher than I thought appropriate, and sank into his couch. He gave me a steely gaze. "Okay. Look," he said over the music. "I'm really tired of this shit, Darcy. I am *really, really* sick of it."

"So am I," I said, reaching over to turn down his stereo.

He held up his hand as if to warn me that interrupting was not an option.

"So we're going to discuss this tonight and then never again, okay?"

"Fine," I said. "That's all I wanted in the first place."

"Okay. When Rachel came here to visit me, she told me that she . . . that she had feelings for Dex."

"I knew it!" I said, pointing at him.

"Are you going to listen or not?"

I swallowed hard and nodded.

"And she had been having those feelings for some time, but not that long a time."

"How long?"

"A few weeks . . . maybe a few months."

"A few *months*?" I shouted.

He gave me a look of warning, as if he were poised to exit the conversation.

"Sorry. Go on."

"I don't have much else to say."

"When did they first hook up?" I asked, petrified of the answer, but needing to know just how big a fool I had been.

He paused and then said that he didn't know.

"I can tell you're lying," I said. "I know you know!"

"What I do know is this," Ethan said, dodging the question. "Rachel didn't want to feel the way she did. She was in agony over the whole thing. She had every intention of going back to New York after her visit here and being your maid of honor. She was prepared to move on, force herself to get over Dex, and be your friend. Which is more than most people would do in her shoes."

My heart pounded in my ears. I was fixated on one thing. One fact. "Give me a date, Ethan. When did they first hook up?"

He crossed his arms and exhaled loudly.

"Was it before or after Rachel's birthday?" I asked. I honestly don't know what made me pick that date. Perhaps because Rachel's birthday is in late May, always coinciding with the start of summer. I could have just as easily said Memorial Day. But I didn't. I said, "Rachel's birthday," and by the look on Ethan's face, I knew I had hit the jackpot. My mind raced back to the night, how I had thrown a surprise party for her. Suddenly, I remembered with horror how Dex hadn't come home until nearly seven in the morning. How he had said he was with Marcus. And how Marcus had backed him up. They had *all* lied to me! My fiancé had spent the night with my best friend! Months before I had ever cheated on him!

Suddenly everything came into sharp focus: Dexter's later-than-usual nights working, how Rachel had dragged her feet during my wedding plans, and the July Fourth weekend! My God, Rachel and Dex had both stayed home from the Hamptons! They had been together that entire weekend! It was too horrible to be true, but I was certain that it was true.

I laid it all out for Ethan who didn't deny a thing. He just looked at me, without a trace of compassion or remorse.

"How could you, Ethan? How could you?" I sobbed.

"How could I what?"

"How could you be friends with her? How could you take me out with those people who knew the whole story? You made me look like a fool! All of you were probably laughing behind my back!"

"Nobody was laughing behind your back."

"Yeah, right. That mad cow laughed up a storm."

"Phoebe was a bit rude. I'll admit that."

"And admit the rest! Admit that Rachel told all of you what she was doing to me."

He hesitated and then said, "Her relationship with Dex *did* come up. But obviously I didn't think you'd ever meet Martin and Phoebe. And besides, we weren't discussing the situation in a 'ha ha what a fool Darcy is' kind of way. It was more of a 'gosh, how bad it sucks to have feelings for your best friend's fiancé' sort of way."

"*Right.* She *really* suffered."

"Well, didn't you suffer when you started seeing Marcus? While you were still with Dex?"

"It's not the same thing, Ethan."

How was it that everyone had such difficulty grasping the obvious difference between cheating on one's fiancé and screwing over your very best girlfriend?

"This isn't about me and Dex. It's about me and Rachel. And I would never have done that to her," I continued, feeling shocked that my mousy friend had it in her.

He looked at me, folded his arms, and cocked his head with a knowing smile. *"Really?"*

"Never," I said, taking mental inventory of Rachel's utterly unappealing ex-boyfriends. Her law school boyfriend and most significant ex, Nate, had a unibrow, sloping shoulders, and an effeminate voice.

"If you say so," Ethan said skeptically.

"What is that supposed to mean? I have never, *ever* tried to steal one of Rachel's boyfriends."

He smiled an oblique, private smile. I knew what he was driving at: I had hooked up with Marcus even though Rachel was interested in him.

"Oh, give me a freaking break, Ethan. Marcus was *not* Rachel's boyfriend! They had kissed, like, one time. It was never going to go anywhere."

"I wasn't thinking of Marcus."

"So then what *were* you thinking of?"

"Well . . . I just think that you would do the same thing to Rachel if the circumstances presented themselves. If you had fallen in love with one of her boyfriends, nothing would have stopped you from going after him. Not Rachel's feelings, not the stigma of taking your best friend's man. Nothing."

"No," I said firmly. "That's not true."

Ethan continued. He was on a roll now, leaning forward on the couch, thrusting his index finger at me as he talked. "I think you have a long, *long* history of going after exactly what you want, Darcy. Whatever that is. Come hell or high water. Until now, Rachel has always played second fiddle to you. And you shamelessly let her do the whole lady-in-waiting routine. All through high school she was at your beck and call, letting you show off. You liked it that way. And now that it is all over, you can't handle it."

"That's just . . . not true!" I sputtered, feeling my face burn. "You're being so unfair!"

Ethan ignored me and kept going, now pacing in front of his faux fireplace. "You were the star of the show in high school. The star of the show in college. The star of the show in Manhattan. And Rachel let you shine. Now you can't step back and be happy for her."

"Be happy for her for *stealing* my fiancé? You've got to be kidding me!"

"Darce—*you* did the same thing. It might be a different story if you were deeply in love with Dex, if you hadn't cheated on him also."

"But they did it first!"

"That is beside the point," he said.

"How can you say that?"

"Because. Because, Darcy, you never examine your own behavior. You just look to blame everyone else."

He then proceeded to bring up this ancient history from high school. Like why I had applied to Notre Dame when I knew that it was Rachel's dream to go there, and how crushed she was when I got in and she didn't.

"I didn't know she owned Notre Dame!"

"It was her dream. Not yours."

"So let me get this straight, she can go after my fiancé, but I don't have the right to apply to a stupid college?"

He ignored my question and said, "While we're on this topic,

Darcy, why don't you tell me one thing . . . Did you *really* get in there?"

"Did I get in where?" I asked.

"Were you or were you not accepted at Notre Dame University?"

"Yes. I was," I said, almost believing the lie I had told all of my friends so many years ago. Notre Dame had been Rachel's first choice, but I had applied, too, thinking how great it would be if we could be roommates. I remember getting that rejection letter, feeling like a failure. So I told a harmless fib to my friends, and then covered by saying that I was going to Indiana anyway.

He shook his head. "I don't believe you," he said. "You did *not* get into Notre Dame."

I started to sweat. How did he know? Had he seen my letter? Had he hacked into the Notre Dame admissions office's computer system?

"Why is my choice of colleges relevant here?"

"I'll tell you why it's relevant, Darcy. I'll tell you exactly why. You have always competed with Rachel. From way back in the day until now. Everything has always been a contest with you. And part of what's eating you up inside is that Dex picked Rachel. He picked her over you."

I tried to speak but he kept going, his words cruel, stark, and loud. "Dex wanted to be with her and not you. Never mind that you didn't want to be with him either. Never mind that you cheated on him too. Never mind that clearly you and he weren't at all right for each other and you both saved yourselves a divorce by calling it quits. You can only focus on one thing: the fact that Rachel somehow beat you. And it kills you, Darce. I'm telling you, as your friend, that you need to let it go and move on," he finished in his debate-team tone.

I shook my head. I told him that he was wrong. I told him that nobody, nobody in my position, could be happy for Rachel. I felt myself getting shrill, desperate to make him see things my way, just as I had tried to do with Marcus.

"It's like this, Ethan . . . even if they hadn't done a thing behind my back, even if this relationship had begun *after* we broke up, it would still be . . . just *wrong*. You just don't go there with a friend's ex. Period. How is it that men have trouble seeing that? It's a basic life principle."

"She *loves* him, Darce. *That* is a basic life principle."

"Would you stop rubbing it in! I don't want to hear the word *love* again. Whether they *love* each other is totally beside the point. . . . You don't understand *anything* about friendship."

"Darcy. No offense—and I'm not saying this to be mean, because I care about you, which is why you're here right now for this pur-ported *visit*," he said, making quotation marks in the air as he said the word *visit*. "But—"

"But *what*?" I asked pitifully, afraid of what he would say next.

"But I think *you're* the one who doesn't understand friendship," he said, speaking fast and furiously. "Not at all. Which is why you're sit-ting here essentially friendless. At war with Rachel. At war with Claire. At war with the father of your child. At war with your *own mother*, who, as far as you know, has no clue where you are! And now you're mad at me too."

"It's not my fault that you all betrayed me."

"You need to take a long, hard look in the mirror, Darce. You need to realize that there are consequences to your basically shallow existence."

"I'm *not* shallow," I said, only half-believing it.

"You *are* shallow. You're utterly selfish and misguided, with totally screwed-up values."

He had gone too far. I might be a bit on the shallow side, but the rest of his accusations were ridiculous. "What the hell is that supposed to mean? Misguided?"

"It means that you're, what, five months pregnant now? And as far as I can tell, you're doing nothing to prepare for this child. Nothing.

You come to London for this so-called visit, but I see no signs of you returning to New York—and meanwhile, you have made no effort to seek any prenatal care here in London. On top of that, you don't eat particularly well, probably in an effort to stay thin at the expense of your baby's growth. You had two glasses of wine tonight. And instead of saving for the child you have to raise alone, you are throwing money to the wind on positively frivolous purchases. It's simply staggering to watch how utterly irresponsible and totally self-absorbed you're being."

I sat there, completely speechless. I mean, what do you say when someone tells you, essentially, that you're a shit friend, a horrible, irresponsible mother-to-be, and an empty, self-absorbed woman? Unless I counted some of the accusations I'd received from scorned lovers (which don't have much credibility), this was an unprecedented attack. He had said so many mean things, come at me from so many angles, that I was unsure how to defend myself. "I *am* taking prenatal vitamins," I said meekly.

Ethan looked at me as if to say, *If that's the best you can do here, I rest my case.* Then he announced that he was going to bed. His expression told me not to follow him, that he did not want me in his room.

But just to be sure, after I sat in the living room for a long while, licking my wounds and replaying his speech, I decided to go down the hall and check his door. Not that I would have opened it on a bet—I had some pride—I just had to know whether he had boxed me out for real. Did he regret his harsh words? Had he softened his opinion of me as his beer-buzz dissipated? I put my hand around the glass doorknob and turned. It didn't budge. Ethan had shut me out. There was something about that door, cold and unyielding, that made me feel angry and sad and determined all at once.

twenty-one

The next morning I awoke on my air mattress and felt my baby kick for the first time. There had been other times when I thought I felt her—only to realize that it was likely just indigestion, hunger pangs, or nerves. But there was no confusing that odd, unmistakable sensation of tiny feet moving inside me, churning up against my organs and bones. I put my hand on the spot, right under my rib cage, waiting to feel her again. Sure enough, there was another small but distinct nudge and twitch. I know it sounds crazy, especially considering that my stomach was quickly becoming the size of a basketball, but I think it took that flutter of baby feet for my pregnancy to move beyond the theoretical and feel real. I had a baby inside me, a little person who was going to be born in a few short months. I was going to be a mother. In a way, I already was.

I curled up in a fetal position and squeezed my eyes shut as I was bombarded by a riot of emotions. First I felt a burst of pure joy. It was an indescribable happiness, a kind that I'd never experienced before, a kind that can't be found by purchasing a Gucci bag or a pair of Manolo Blahniks. A smile spread across my face, and I almost laughed out loud.

But my happiness quickly commingled with an unsettling melancholy as I realized that I had no one to share my huge milestone with. I couldn't call my baby's father or her grandmother. I wasn't in the mood to talk to Ethan after all the mean things he had said to me. And most important, I couldn't call Rachel. For the first time since I found Dex in her closet, I really missed her. I still had Annalise, but she just wasn't the same. I thought of all the times in the past when I'd had good news, bad news, in-between news. How I could barely digest it before I was running next door or speed-dialing Rachel's number. When we were kids in Indiana, Annalise was always the runner-up, always the afterthought, always the second to know. With Rachel out of the picture, you'd think that Annalise would just replace her. But I was beginning to see that it didn't work like that. Rachel wasn't replaceable. Claire hadn't replaced her. Annalise couldn't either. I wondered why that was. After all, I knew Annalise would say all the right things, be as nice as she could be. But she would never be able to quench that deep-seated need to share.

As I turned over on my mattress to face the window, I heard Ethan's words: the part about me being a bad friend, the part about me being selfish and self-centered and shallow. A warm shame spread over me as I acknowledged that there was a ring of truth to his accusations. I looked at the facts: I had no doctor, no income, no close girlfriends, no contact with my family. I was on the verge of depleting all my savings, and all I had to show for myself was a closet full of gorgeous clothing, most of which no longer fit. I had moved to London to find change, but I hadn't really changed at all. My life was stagnating. I needed to do more. For myself and for my baby.

I stared out my barred window into the dreary London morning, and vowed to make the day I first felt my baby kick a turning point in my life. I would prove to Ethan that I was not the person he had described the evening before. I got to my feet (which was becoming more difficult to do, particularly from a horizontal position on a soft air mattress) and found a pad of paper in the bottom of one of my suitcases. I ripped out a page and wrote: "Steps to Becoming a Better Darcy." I thought for a second, replaying Ethan's speech. Then I wrote:

1. Go to an ob-gyn in London and prepare for motherhood!
2. Be more healthy, i.e., eat better, no caffeine or alcohol
3. Find some new girlfriends (no competing with them!)
4. Let my family know that I'm in London and that I'm okay
5. Get a job (preferably a "do-gooding" job)
6. Stop buying clothes (and shoes, etc.) and start saving money!

Then, because something still seemed to be missing, I threw in a catchall:

7. Refine my character (i.e., be more thoughtful, less selfish, etc.)

As I reread my list, I found myself wondering what Ethan would say if he saw it. Would he praise my effort or would he scoff, "Don't be so naïve, Darcy. You can't just make a list and fix yourself overnight! It doesn't work like that."

Why did I care so much about what Ethan thought anyway? Part of me wanted to hate him. Hate him for siding with Rachel. Hate him for lying to me. Hate him for the awful things he had said about me.

But I couldn't hate him. And in a bizarre, surprising way, all I wanted to do was see him, or at the very least set about changing his opinion of me.

I rocked once to gain momentum before standing again. Then I made my way down the hall to Ethan's room. Upon discovering that he had already left for the day, I went to the kitchen and whipped up a healthy egg-white omelet. Then I consulted my list and decided to clean his flat. I dusted and vacuumed, scrubbed the toilet, took out the trash, did two loads of laundry in his ridiculously small washer/dryer unit (the Brits have miserable, third-world appliances), carefully stacked his magazines and newspapers, and soaped down the kitchen floors.

After the place was spotless, I wrote my mother a quick note, telling her that I was staying with Ethan in London. "I know we're not happy with each other right now," I wrote, "but I still don't want you and Daddy to worry about me. I'm doing fine." Then I wrote Ethan's phone number in a PS just in case she wanted to call me. I sealed and stamped my letter, showered, and headed out in the London drizzle, wandering up Kensington Church Street to Notting Hill. I resisted the urge to stop in a single store, gaining strength from my list, which was folded in neat thirds and tucked into my coat pocket. I even stopped in a charity thrift shop to ask for a job. No positions were available, but I felt proud of myself for trying.

On my way home, I ducked inside a coffee shop for a short rest, ordered a decaffeinated latte, and hunkered down in a big overstuffed armchair. On the couch next to me sat two women—a blonde and a brunette—who looked about my age. The blonde was balancing a baby on one knee as she struggled to eat a brownie with her free hand. Both girls wore tiny diamonds on their left ring fingers, and I recalled that Ethan had mentioned that the Brits are less ostentatious about engagement rings than Americans. Maybe that sort of thing was emblematic of what Ethan liked about London. The Brits' understated quality was the opposite of what he said I was—more or less a shameless show-off.

From the corner of my eye, I continued to study the women. The blonde had a weak chin but good highlights; the brunette wore gripping velour sweats but was holding an enviable Prada bag. I felt a pang of worry that I was being shallow, but reassured myself that it was okay to be observant; I just shouldn't draw conclusions about the women as people. I thought of how many times I had judged people by their footwear, and vowed that I would never do so again. After all, wearing a square-toed shoe in a pointy-toed season was not a crime. To prove the point to myself, I resisted looking down at their feet. I could feel myself turning into a more solid person already, and my spirits soared.

As I sipped my coffee and flipped through *Hello* magazine, I listened to the women talk, noting that their conversation sounded much more interesting in their British accents. The theme of their chat was marital woes—both had issues with their husbands. The blonde said that having a baby makes everything worse. The brunette complained that since she and her husband started trying to conceive, sex had become a chore. Every few seconds, I turned the pages of my magazine, which was filled with Hollywood stars, as well as people I had never seen before, presumably British television actors. And more photos of Posh and Becks.

The blonde sighed as she repositioned her squirming baby. "At least you're having sex," she said to her friend, as she reached down and pulled a pacifier out of a side pocket in her stroller and popped it into the baby's mouth. The baby sucked vigorously for several seconds before letting the pacifier drop to the ground. An apparent subscriber to the three-second rule, the blonde picked it up, swiped it across her sleeve, and reinserted it in her child's mouth.

"How long has it been?" the brunette asked, in a candid way that told me these two were not new or casual acquaintances. It made me ache for Rachel, for the way things used to be.

"I couldn't even say," the blonde answered. "Ages."

The brunette made a sympathetic clucking noise as she wrapped her tea bag around a plastic stirrer and squeezed with her thumb and index finger.

I closed my magazine and made eye contact with the blonde. She smiled at me, giving me an opening.

"She's really cute," I said, gazing at her baby and then realizing with panic that the baby could be a boy. It was impossible to tell. Yellow outfit, bald head, no gender-based accoutrement.

"Thank you," the blonde said.

Good. I guessed right. "What's her name?"

"Natalie."

"Hi, Natalie," I said in a high, singsongy voice. Natalie ignored me, kept straining to grasp her mother's brownie. "How old is she?"

"Twenty-two weeks." The blonde smiled as she jiggled her up and down on one knee.

"So . . . that's what? Five months?"

She laughed. "Yeah, right. Sorry. I remember before I had Natalie I wondered why mums gave their child's age in weeks. I guess it's an extension of the pregnancy."

I nodded as I noticed the brunette giving me a curious once-over as if to say, "What is your deal, American girl, sitting here alone on a weekday?"

"Yeah, I know what you mean. I'm eighteen weeks along myself—"

"Pregnant?" both women squealed at once as if I had just told them that I was dating Prince William. It felt great to finally have a little enthusiasm over my news.

"Yes," I said, moving aside my coat and rubbing my stomach with my ringless left hand. "In fact, I just felt a kick for the first time this morning."

It struck me as a bit sad that I was first sharing such monumental news with strangers, but I told myself that they were potential new friends. Perhaps they would even become lifelong, to-the-grave mates.

"Congrats!" the blonde squealed.

"You look amazing for eighteen weeks!" the brunette said.

I smiled with what felt like sincere modesty. "Thank you."

"Boy or girl?" the brunette asked.

"I don't know yet for sure, but I'm fairly certain that it's a girl."

"I was too," the blonde said, rubbing Natalie's fuzzy head. "I just knew she was a girl."

"Did you find out ahead of time?"

"No, I wanted to be surprised," she said. "My husband knew, though."

I raised my eyebrows. "He knew and you didn't?"

She nodded. "Our doctor showed him the relevant anatomy on the sonogram while I closed my eyes. My husband swore that he wouldn't tell another soul. Not even our mums, who were positively dying to know."

"I can't believe he kept it a secret! That's amazing," I said.

"Her husband is great that way," the brunette said.

"Hmm." The blonde nodded. I had begun to notice that the Brits make that *hmm* sound often, in lieu of saying *yes* or *uh-huh* or *yeah*. She continued, "Never one slip with the pronouns. He was always very careful to say 'he or she' or just 'the baby.'"

"What about baby names? Wasn't it obvious when you'd discuss names?"

"Not at all. He covered both equally. . . . In fact, he pushed Gavin so hard that if anything, I thought we were having a boy."

"Wow. Your husband sounds like a great guy," I said.

She turned to look at her friend and they both burst into laughter. "We were just tearing him to shreds. He's being a bit of a prat these days."

I wasn't sure what a *prat* was, but I nodded empathetically and said, "I know how that is!"

A few seconds of silence passed and I could tell that the girls were again wondering about my situation.

"I'm Darcy, by the way," I said, with what I hoped was a disarming, "I won't compete with you" smile.

"I'm Charlotte," the blonde said.

"And I'm Meg," the brunette said.

"It's so great to meet you both. I've been dying to have some female interaction since moving here," I said. It was the truth, although I don't think I consciously realized it until that moment.

"When did you move to London?" Meg asked.

"About a month ago."

"Did you move here alone?" she asked. It was as close as she could come to inquiring about the father of my child.

"Yes, I'm going it alone," I said.

Meg and Charlotte both stared at me, with what I detected as admiration. I gave them a warm, open smile, tacit permission to inquire further, which they did, tentatively. I answered each of their questions, only embellishing occasionally. For example, I told them that I caught Rachel in bed with Dex—and I left out Marcus altogether, thereby implying that Dex was the father. It just seemed easier that way, and frankly, what was the difference at this point? Both men were out of the picture. My audience of two was riveted. Charlotte even ignored Natalie, who was gumming the corner of an *Evening Standard*. I continued my tale, telling them I had quit my job, and come to London to live with my childhood friend Ethan. "He's straight, but we're just friends," I told them. A gay friend might be more interesting, and certainly more entertaining, but there was something compelling about an aboveboard, straight male–female friendship. Besides, it gave me more credibility as a nice girl. I could hear them saying later, "She's beautiful, but she doesn't go around stalking every available man."

Charlotte asked if I had any interest in Ethan. I shook my head vigorously. "Absolutely not . . . We're strictly friends. Although we did go out in the fifth grade!"

They laughed.

"So I'm entirely single . . . if you know anyone?" I said, fleetingly worrying that finding a man shouldn't be important to me. I dismissed the concern; a boyfriend needn't detract from my other, loftier goals.

Meg and Charlotte exchanged a thoughtful glance as if doing a mental inventory of all their male acquaintances.

"Simon?" Charlotte posited to Meg.

Meg made a face.

"You don't like Simon?" Charlotte asked her.

"I like Si well enough . . ." Meg said with a shrug.

I resisted the temptation to inquire about Simon's looks, but Meg seemed to read my mind because she giggled and said, "I doubt that Darcy is attracted to gingers!"

"Meg!" Charlotte said, reminding me of Rachel. Rachel must have said "Darcy!" in that same tone close to a million times. "Besides, I'd say Si is more of a strawberry blonde."

"He's a ginger and you know it!" Meg said, sipping her tea.

"What's a ginger?" I asked.

"You know, orange hair? I think you call it a 'redhead'?" Meg said.

I laughed. "Oh. Right."

"So? Do you like gingers?" Charlotte asked.

"Probably not my favorite," I said diplomatically, rationalizing that chemistry is beyond one's control. And for a relationship to work, the chemistry has to be there.

"I suppose gingers aren't sought after on either side of the pond," Meg opined.

Charlotte looked disappointed, so I said, "But there are exceptions. Look at cute little Prince Harry. I like his devilish little smile. It depends entirely on personality."

I couldn't help thinking of Marcus. It had been a misguided (to use Ethan's word) decision to start a relationship with him, a decision based largely on intrigue, lust, and competition with Rachel. But at least I wasn't driven by appearances. Marcus was far from perfect looking. So I knew I had it in me to look beyond the mere physical.

Charlotte smiled at me. "Precisely," she said, nodding. Then she turned to Meg. "Why don't you invite Darcy to your party? Isn't Si coming?"

"What a fab idea! You must come, Darcy. I'm having a few friends over this Saturday night. Won't you join us?" Meg asked.

"I'd love to," I said, thinking how satisfying it would be to tell Ethan I had been invited to a party *by women*. I took a mental inventory of my list. In just one short day, I had ticked off several items already. I had helped Ethan (by cleaning his apartment), I was being healthy (by not ordering a caffeinated beverage), and I had made a couple of new friends. I still needed to find a job and a doctor, so after a few more minutes of polite conversation, I asked Meg and Charlotte for a recommendation on both fronts.

"Oh, I have the perfect chap for you. Mr. Moore is his name," Charlotte said, consulting her address book and jotting down his number on the back of one of her own calling cards. "Here you go. Give him a ring. He's really lovely."

"How come he goes by 'mister' and not 'doctor'?" I asked, feeling a bit skeptical about the British health care system.

Meg explained that in England only nonoperating physicians are called doctors—something that goes back to medieval times, when all surgeons were butchers and therefore mere misters.

"As for the job," Charlotte said, "what is it that you did in New York?"

"I worked in public relations. . . . But I'm looking for something different here. Something that would help the poor, old, or sick," I said earnestly.

"That is *so* nice," Charlotte and Meg said in unison.

I smiled.

Meg told me that there was a nursing home right around the corner. She jotted down some directions on a napkin, and then wrote her own address and phone number on the other side. "Do stop by on Saturday," she said. "We'd love to see you. And so would Si." She winked.

I smiled, took my last sip of coffee, and said good-bye to my new friends.

That evening, when Ethan returned home, I was waiting for him with a homemade Greek salad, a glass of red wine, and softly playing classical music.

"Welcome home!" I said, smiling nervously as I handed him his glass.

He took it from me tentatively, sipped, and then looked around his apartment. "It looks great in here. Smells good too. Did you clean?"

I nodded. "Uh-huh. I scoured the place. I even cleaned your room," I said, and then couldn't resist adding, "Still think I'm a lousy friend?"

He took another sip and sat on his couch. "I didn't say that exactly."

I sat next to him. "Yes you did."

He gave me a half-smile. "You can be a good friend when you try, Darce. You tried today. Thank you."

The old me would have held out for an over-the-top apology coupled with a complete retraction and a small gift. But somehow Ethan's simple "thank you" was enough for me. I just wanted to make up and move on.

"So guess what happened this morning?" I said, bursting to share my news with him. Before he could guess, I blurted out, "I felt my baby kick!"

"Wow," Ethan said. "That was the first time you felt it?"

"Yeah. But I haven't felt her since. Should I be worried?"

Ethan shook his head. "No. I remember when Brandi was pregnant . . . she would feel a kick one day and then nothing for several days. The doctor told her that when you're active, the baby is less likely to move around, because you're essentially lulling it to sleep," he said with a somewhat pained expression, as if it still hurt to think of Brandi's betrayal.

"Does it make you sad to think about her?" I asked.

He kicked off his wet Pumas, peeled off his socks, and propped his feet up on the coffee table. "I'm not sad about Brandi, but sometimes I am sad when I think about Milo."

"Milo? Was that the guy Brandi cheated on you with?"

"No. Milo's the baby."

"Oh," I said sheepishly, knowing that I should have remembered that detail. I looked at Ethan, wondering what empathetic words Rachel would offer. She always had a way of saying the right thing, making someone feel better. I couldn't think of anything good so I just waited for Ethan to continue.

"For nine months, I thought I was going to be a father. I went to every doctor's appointment and fell in love with those ultrasound pictures . . . I even picked the name Milo." He shook his head. "Then we had the baby, and I realized he wasn't mine."

"When did you know for sure that he wasn't yours?"

"As soon as he was born. I mean, he was dark-skinned with black eyes and all this crazy black hair sticking up everywhere. I kept thinking of my own baby pictures. Bald and pink. Brandi's a blue-eyed blonde too. It didn't take a genius to figure out what was going on."

"So what did you do?"

"For the first few days, I think I was in shock. I pretended that it wasn't true, that it was just a fluke genetic thing. . . . All the while, in the back of my mind, I remembered that 'big b, little b' chart from high-school biology. . . . Two blue-eyed parents just couldn't make a Milo."

I touched his arm lightly. "That must have been so hard."

"It was awful. I mean, I loved that little boy. Enough so that I almost stayed with her. In the end . . . well . . . you know the rest." His voice cracked. "I left. It felt as though someone had died."

I remembered Rachel telling me about Ethan's divorce and the baby that wasn't his. At the time, I think I had been preoccupied with some crisis of my own and hadn't been particularly empathetic to his pain.

"You did the right thing," I said now, taking his hand in mine.

He didn't pull away. "Yeah. I guess I did."

"Do you think I did the right thing? Keeping my baby?"

"Absolutely."

"Even though you think I'm being a bad mother so far?" I asked, resisting the urge to tell him about my list. I wanted to make more progress before confiding in him.

"You'll get it together," Ethan said, squeezing my hand. "I have faith in you."

I looked at him, and felt the same way I did on Thanksgiving, sitting on our bench in Holland Park. I wanted to kiss him. But of course I didn't. I wondered why I resisted, when in the past I had always followed my impulses with not much thought of the consequences. Maybe because it didn't feel like a game with Ethan, the way it had with Marcus and so many guys before him. Maybe because I had more to lose. Blurring the line between friendship and attraction was a surefire way to lose a friend. And losing one good friend was enough this year.

Later that night, after Ethan and I watched the news, he turned to me and said, "C'mon, Darce. Let's hit the hay."

"The hay in your room?" I asked hopefully.

Ethan laughed. "Yeah. In my room."

"So you missed me last night?" I asked.

He laughed again. "I wouldn't go *that* far."

But I could tell by his expression that he *had* missed me. I could also tell that he was a little bit sorry for our fight, even though much of what he had said about me was true. Ethan liked me in spite of my flaws, and as I fell asleep next to him, I thought of how much more he was going to like the new and improved Darcy.

twenty-two

The next morning, prodded by another series of kicks from my baby, I decided that I would go apply for a job at the nursing home Meg and Charlotte had told me about. Ethan had already left for the day, so I used his computer to type up my résumé and a quick cover letter, which articulately explained that my success in the world of public relations had everything to do with my outgoing personality, and that certainly this quality would translate well in the group bingo setting. After I spell-checked the letter, opting for the British spelling of the words *colourful* and *organised,* I showered, dressed, and headed out into the London chill.

When I arrived at the nursing home, I was blasted with the distinct and depressing odor of old people and institutional food, and felt my first wave of morning sickness since my first trimester had ended. I found a mint in my purse and drew a deep breath through my mouth as I studied two little old ladies in matching floral smocks parked in wheelchairs in the lobby. Watching them laugh and chat together made me think of Rachel and how we used to say that when we were old and widowed we wanted to be put in a nursing home together. I remembered her saying that I would still be a guy magnet well into my nineties and could help her get dates with the cutest old men in the home. I guess she decided to play that one out sixty years early, I thought, as a gnomelike man, whom I'd assumed was a resident, came to the door and introduced himself as the manager.

"I'm Darcy Rhone," I said, shaking his hand.

"Bernard Dobbs," he said. "How may I help you?"

"The question is, Mr. Dobbs, how can *I* help *you*? You see, I have come today to find a position at this fine institution," I said, redecorating the shabby, poorly lit lobby in my mind.

"What sort of experience do you have?" he asked.

"I have a background in public relations," I said, handing him my résumé. "Which is a very interactive, people-driven business." Then I paraphrased my cover letter, concluding with, "Most importantly, I just want to help spread cheer to the elderly folk in your fine country."

Mr. Dobbs looked at me skeptically and asked if I had a work permit.

"Um . . . no," I said. "But I'm sure 'wink, wink, nudge, nudge' we could deal with that problem, couldn't we?"

He gave me a blank stare and then asked if I had ever worked in a nursing home. I considered lying. After all, I seriously doubted that he would place an international call to check my references. But I made a split-second determination that lying was not in keeping with the new Darcy, and that deceit wasn't necessary to get a job. So I told him no, I hadn't, and then added, "But believe me, Mr. Dobbs, I can handle anything here. My job in *Manhattan* was quite challenging. I worked long hours and was very successful."

"Hmm. Well. I'm so sorry, Dicey," he said, without sounding the slightest bit apologetic.

"It's Darcy," I said.

"Yes. Well. I'm sorry, Darcy. We can't have just *anyone* working with our residents. You must be qualified." He handed me back my résumé.

Just anyone? Was he for real? I pictured my future sister-in-law wiping up old-person drool as she hummed "Oh, Susanna." Her job hardly required much skill.

"I understand where you're coming from, Mr. Dobbs . . . but what experience do you really need to relate well to others? I mean, you either have that or you don't. And I have that in spades," I gushed, noticing a woman with a horrifying case of osteoporosis, inching her way down the hallway toward us. She craned her neck sideways and looked at me. I smiled at her and uttered a high, cheery "Good morning" just to prove my point.

As I waited for her to smile back at me, I imagined that her name was Gert and that she and I would forge a beautiful friendship, like the one in *Tuesdays with Morrie,* one of Dexter's favorite books, one of many that I had never found time to read. Gert would confide in me, tell me all about her childhood, her wartime remembrances, her husband, whom she had sadly outlived by several decades. Then, one night, she would pass quietly in the night, while I held her hand. Later, I would learn that she had bequeathed to me all of her worldly possessions, including her favorite emerald brooch worth tens of thousands of pounds. At her funeral, I would wear the pin over my heart and eulogize her to a small but intimate gathering. *Gertrude was a special woman. I first met her one wintery day . . .*

I smiled at Gert once more as she approached us. She muttered something back, her ill-fitting dentures wobbling slightly.

"Come again?" I asked her, to show Mr. Dobbs that not only was I kind and friendly, but that I also had a never-ending supply of patience.

"Go away and don't come back," she grumbled more clearly.

I smiled brightly, pretending not to understand her. Then I returned my gaze to Mr. Dobbs. "Well, then. As I was saying, I think you'll see upon careful review that I'm really quite qualified for any position you might have for me."

"I'm afraid I'm not interested," Mr. Dobbs said.

As Gert passed us, her eyes danced triumphantly. I was tempted to tell her and Mr. Dobbs off. Something along the lines of "Get a life," which I thought was particularly apropos for Gert, who appeared not to have many days left in her. Instead I politely thanked Mr. Dobbs for his time and turned to go.

Back outside, I embraced the cold day, clearing my nose of the sour nursing home stench. "Well. Back to the drawing board," I said aloud to myself as I headed for the High Street to buy a newspaper. I would check the classifieds and regroup over breakfast at the Muffin Man. I wouldn't let Mr. Dobbs or Gert get me down.

When I arrived at the tea house, I pushed open the door and said hello to the Polish waitress who had served Ethan and me on Thanksgiving. She gave me a perfunctory smile and told me I could sit anywhere. I chose a small table by the window, sitting on one chair and setting my purse, newspaper, and leather binder on the other. Then I consulted the sticky laminated menu and ordered herbal tea, scrambled eggs, and a scone.

As I waited for my food, I glanced around the flowery room decorated with Monet prints, my eyes resting on a petite girl sipping coffee at a table near mine. She had incredibly wide-set eyes, an auburn bob, and porcelain skin. She wore a wide-brimmed canary-yellow hat. She reminded me of Madeline, the character in the children's books, which I used to read with Rachel twenty-five years ago. When the girl's mobile phone rang, she answered it, speaking in a husky voice with a French accent. The French part fit the Madeline image, the husky part did not, as she seemed too diminutive to have such a deep voice. I strained to hear what she was saying—something about how she shouldn't complain about the London weather because it is even colder and rainier in Paris. After a few more minutes of chatter about Paris, she said, "I'll see you soon, *mon petit chou.*" Then she laughed affectionately, snapped her phone shut, and stared dreamily out the window in a way that made me think that she had just conversed with a new lover. I tried to remember what *chou* meant in French. Was it a puppy? No, I was pretty sure that dog was *chien.*

I glanced around the Muffin Man again, hoping to find my Alistair, my own *chou.* But there were no solo male diners, handsome or otherwise. Only Madeline and an American couple consulting a Fodor's guidebook on Great Britain. The two were sporting matching, bulging purple fanny packs and bright white Reeboks. I couldn't help wondering why so many Americans (other than New Yorkers) have such a distinct lack of fashion sense, but the new Darcy didn't hold it against them.

After my waitress brought my breakfast, I studied the tea strainer and peered into the silver pot at the floating tea particles, trying to remember how Ethan had prepared it for us. To a coffee drinker, it all seemed pretty complicated. Then, right as I was wishing he were here with me to pour my cup of tea and listen to my Mr. Dobbs tale, in he strolled, looking adorable in a red cap and a brightly colored striped sweater. His cheeks were pink, as they always were in the cold—which made his eyes look even bluer.

"Ethan!" I spoke in a normal voice, but it registered loud in the small, quiet room. "Hey, there!"

I caught Madeline giving me a look, perhaps disapproving of my outburst. I fleetingly regretted being the loud American in the room.

"Hey, Darce," Ethan said, as he approached my table. "How did it go at the nursing home?" He must have returned to the flat, because I had left him a note about my job-hunting mission.

"Not so well. But I bought a paper to check the classifieds. Have a seat," I said, moving my purse and binder to clear a chair for him. "I'm so glad you're here. I was just thinking about you. How do you work this little contraption again?" I asked, motioning toward the tea strainer. Without sitting down, he leaned over my table, efficiently placed the strainer over my cup with one hand, and poured from the silver pot with the other.

"Have a seat," I said again.

He cleared his throat, looking uncomfortable. "Um . . . actually, I'm meeting a friend here."

"Oh . . . who?" I asked, worried that Phoebe was on her way.

"She's right over there." Ethan gestured toward Madeline and then, as she looked up at him, he winked at her—not in the smooth, sleazy way that some guys wink—more the cute, friendly sort of wink. Like Santa Claus if he were thin and young.

Madeline gave Ethan a pinky wave as she sipped her cappuccino from a glass mug. She then flashed him a small, private smile. I combined her smile with her *mon petit chou*, digesting the implications. . . . *Ethan has a girlfriend. And she's not only attractive, but she's French to boot!*

Ethan smiled back at Madeline and then looked down at me. "You're welcome to join us, Darce."

But I could tell he didn't mean it. "That's okay. You go ahead," I said quickly, feeling embarrassed for assuming he was ever-available for me.

"Are you sure?" He gave me a furtive, borderline sympathetic look.

"Yeah. Yeah. I have to run in a sec anyway. Check out the leads in my paper. You go on . . . really," I said.

"All right, then. I'll see you a little later, okay?"

"Yup. Sounds good," I said breezily.

As I watched Ethan amble toward Madeline's table, I felt strangely territorial. Almost jealous. The emotion caught me off guard. I mean, why should I care if Ethan had a girlfriend? I certainly wasn't interested in him. Sure, I had thought about kissing him, but that didn't mean I was in love with him or anything crazy like that. Perhaps seeing him with someone just made me long for a companion of my own. Perhaps I was worried about my standing in his flat. My rights to his comfortable bed.

From the corner of my eye, I saw Madeline stand and kiss her *chou* on one cheek and then the other. I know it is a European practice, but it still looked pretentious, and I vowed never to dole out the double kiss again. Ethan pulled off his cap, exposing his tousled curls. Then he sat and angled his chair toward her. Their knees touched.

I looked away and ate quickly, feeling queasy and hurt that Ethan hadn't told me about his relationship. I wondered what exactly was going on between them. Was he always off meeting her under the guise of finishing his book? Were they making mad love back at her place as I waited for him to come home every night? Why had he not told me about her? As I stood to pay my bill, I debated whether to say good-bye on my way out. On the one hand, I was curious to meet this girl and glean some insight into their fledgling (or was it established?) relationship. At the same time, I felt awkward, like I'd rather just sidle out the door unnoticed. It wasn't like me to be anything other than gregarious, and I wondered again why Ethan's having a girlfriend could affect me in this way.

As I stood by the cash register, a few yards from the lovebirds' table, I could hear Madeline's throaty French accent followed by Ethan's happy chortle. I presented my bill to the waitress along with a ten-pound note. She gave me my change, which I dropped into a little dish for tips. Then, just as I was heading out the door, I heard Ethan call out, "Hey, Darce. C'mere for a sec."

I turned around, pretending to be momentarily disoriented, as if I had forgotten altogether that he was there with a woman. Then I smiled warmly and took the few steps over to their table.

"Hey, there," I said casually.

"This is Sondrine," Ethan said. "Sondrine, this is Darcy."

Sondrine? What kind of name was that? I examined her closely. Her skin was poreless, and she had perfectly arched eyebrows. I hadn't had my own brows done since I had left New York.

"Nice to meet you, Sondrine," I said, catching myself in the pregnant-girl stance: knees locked, hands resting on my stomach. I dropped my arms to my sides, assuming a more attractive pose.

"And you," Sondrine purred in a phone-sex voice.

We exchanged a few more pleasantries, and then, just in case Ethan had downplayed my importance in his life—or failed to mention me altogether—I told him that I'd see him back home. I checked Sondrine's face for a flash of surprise or insecurity, but saw neither. Just pleasant indifference. As I departed the Muffin Man and rounded the corner back to Ethan's flat, I felt inexplicably wistful, almost sad. I felt my baby kick again, and I confided in her, whispering, "Ethan has a girlfriend. And I don't know why that upsets me."

I didn't see Ethan until much later that night when he finally returned to the flat, sans Sondrine. I was sprawled on his couch, half-asleep, waiting for him with a pit in my stomach as I listened to a Norah Jones CD.

"What time is it?" I asked.

"Tenish," he said, standing over me. "Have you eaten?"

"Yes," I said. "You?"

He nodded.

"Where've you been?" I asked, feeling like a suspicious wife who just found a smear of pink lipstick on her husband's starched white shirt.

"Writing."

"*Sure* you were," I said, trying to sound nonchalant and playful.

"What's that supposed to mean?" he asked, motioning for me to move over and clear a space for him.

I lifted my legs long enough for him to sit and then rested my feet on his thighs. "It means, were you *really* writing or were you hanging out with Sondrine?" I asked the question in the singsongy way that kids say, *"Ethan and Sondrine sitting in a tree, K-I-S-S-I-N-G!"*

"I really was writing," he said innocently. Then he tried to change the subject by asking what I did with my day.

"I looked for a job. Called some places. Surfed the Net."

"And?"

"All to no avail," I said. "Very frustrating . . . So what's the deal with Son-*drine*?" I pronounced her name as un-Frenchy as possible, making the word sound clunky and unattractive.

"She's cool. Fun to hang out with."

"Don't play dumb with me, Ethan."

He gave me a quizzical look.

"Is she your girlfriend or what?"

He yawned and stretched. "No, she's not my girlfriend."

"But you're her *petit chou*." I grinned.

"What?"

"I heard her on the phone talking to you right before you showed up at the Muffin Man. She called you her *petit chou*."

"You're too much," Ethan said, smiling.

"By the way, are you aware that a *chou* is a cabbage?" I asked, rolling my eyes. I had looked the word up on the Internet as soon as I had returned to the flat, and could not believe that she was using such a dumb pet name.

Ethan shrugged. "I had no idea. I took Spanish. Remember?"

"Too bad for you."

"Why?"

"Because your girlfriend's French, that's why."

"She's not my girlfriend, Darce," Ethan said unconvincingly. "We've just gone out a couple of times."

"When was that?"

"Once last week . . . and then today."

"Was last week a dinner date?" I asked, trying to remember which nights Ethan had stayed out late.

"No. We met for lunch."

"Where?"

"At a bistro in Notting Hill."

"Did you go dutch?"

"No. I paid. . . . Is your inquisition almost over?"

"I guess so. I just don't get why you didn't tell me about her."

He shrugged. "I don't know why I didn't mention her. It's really not a big deal," he said, as he kneaded my left heel and then my right. I couldn't remember the last time someone had given me a foot massage. It felt better than an orgasm. I told Ethan this. He gave me a proud smile that I translated as: "You've never had an orgasm with me." An image of Ethan and Sondrine, naked and sweaty, popped into my head. I pictured them postcoitus, sharing a cigarette. She had to be a smoker with that raspy voice.

"So tell me about her," I probed.

"There's not much to tell . . . I met her at the Tate Gallery. We were both there to see this exhibit," he said as he made a fist and rolled it along my arches.

"So what, did you meet in front of a painting?" I asked, thinking of my own trip to the National Gallery with Ethan and wondering why he hadn't invited me to the Tate.

"No. We met in the café at the museum. She was behind me in line. I got the last free table. She asked if she could join me," he said. I could hear the story being retold later, whenever anyone asked how they had met. I could see Sondrine linking her arm through his, concluding the tale with a coy, "He got the last Caesar salad *and* the last table!"

"What a sweet story," I said.

He ignored my sarcasm. "And then we walked around the museum together afterward."

The whole thing was a little too close to my Alistair fantasy for comfort. I swallowed, trying to identify the knotted feeling in my chest. It felt like envy and worry and loneliness all blended together.

I formulated a dozen more questions but decided against asking any of them. I had heard enough. Instead we just listened to Norah Jones. Ethan's eyes were closed, his hands still on my feet when he finally spoke. "You looked really pregnant in the Muffin Man today," he said.

"You mean fat?" I asked, thinking of Sondrine's delicate bird wrists. I was downright sturdy next to her.

"Not *fat*. *Pregnant*."

"Pregnant and fat," I said.

He shook his head, opened his eyes, and gave me a funny look. "No. Pregnant and *radiant*."

I felt all tingly and knew that I was beaming. I thanked him, feeling shy.

Ethan kept looking at me with concentration, the way you study someone when you're trying to place them, remember their name. He finally said, "You really do have that glow."

"Thank you," I said again. Our eyes locked for a second, and then we both looked away at the same time.

There was no more conversation for a long time after that. Then Ethan suddenly turned to me and said, "Darce, I was wondering . . . why did you go to the nursing home today?"

"I told you—to get a job," I said.

"I know. But why a nursing home when you have a public relations background?"

"Because I want to help people. Be more compassionate and stuff."

Ethan chuckled and shook his head. "You're such a little extremist, aren't you?"

"What do you mean? *You're* the one who said I needed to change. Be a less shallow person and all that," I said, realizing how very much I wanted him to recognize the effort I was making.

"You don't have to change *everything* about yourself, Darce. And you certainly don't need to go working in a nursing home to be a good person."

"Well, it's a good thing. Because I didn't get hired." I smiled. "And to be perfectly honest, I don't particularly want to work with old people."

"Yeah. You don't have to be a martyr. Just find an enjoyable job and make a little loot. If you can add some value to the world in the process, all the better. But you have to be yourself."

"Be myself, huh?" I said with a smirk.

"Yeah," he said, grinning as he stood and walked toward his bedroom. "It ain't *all* bad."

I stood to follow him and then hesitated. I knew nothing had changed overnight, but there was something about seeing Ethan with a girl that made sleeping in bed with him feel strange, somehow wrong. I reassured myself that despite an occasional, fleeting attraction on my part, we were strictly friends. And friends could share beds. I used to have sleepovers with Rachel all the time.

Still, just to be sure, I waited for Ethan to turn around and say, "Are you coming?" before bounding (as much as a pregnant girl can bound) down the hall after him.

I didn't know how much longer I had before Sondrine would make her presence known in the flat, but I was going to savor every minute of it.

twenty-three

The next morning I called Mr. Moore, the doctor Meg and Charlotte had recommended. As it turned out, he had a cancellation in his morning schedule, so I took the Circle Line to Great Portland Street and followed my *A to Zed* to his office on Harley Street, a block of beautiful, old town houses, most of which appeared to have been converted to medical offices.

I opened the heavy red door to Mr. Moore's practice and walked into a marble foyer, where a receptionist handed me a form to fill out and pointed to a waiting room with a fireplace. Moments later, a plump, grandmotherly woman who introduced herself as Beatrix, Mr. Moore's midwife, collected me in the waiting room and led me up a winding, grand staircase to another room that looked as if it should have been roped off in a museum.

Beatrix introduced me to my doctor as he rose behind his mahogany desk, stepped around it, and gracefully extended his hand. I shook it and studied his face. With high cheekbones, wide-set brown eyes, and an interesting Roman nose, he was quite handsome. And he was elegantly dressed in a sharp navy suit and a green tie. He nodded toward a wing chair in front of his desk, inviting me to have a seat.

We both sat down, and for some reason I blurted out, "I expected a white coat."

He gave me a hint of a smile and said, "White is not my color." His refined accent seemed to transform the friendly quip into a line right out of a Shakespeare play.

Beatrix murmured that she'd be back shortly, and Mr. Moore asked me polite, getting-to-know-you questions: stuff about where I was from, when I had arrived in England, and when I was due. I answered his questions, telling him matter-of-factly that I had become pregnant unexpectedly, broken up with my boyfriend, and moved to London to start over. I also told him that I was due on May second, and that I had not been to the doctor in several weeks.

"Have you had an ultrasound?" he asked.

I was embarrassed to report no, remembering that I had blown off my ten-week ultrasound appointment in New York.

"Well, we'll do an ultrasound today and check on everything," Mr. Moore said, making a note on my chart.

"Will you be able to tell the gender?"

"I will . . . assuming your baby is cooperative."

"Really? Today?"

"Hmmm," he said, nodding.

My heart pounded with excitement and a dash of fear. I was about to see my daughter for the first time. I suddenly wished that Ethan were with me.

"Let's get started then," Mr. Moore said. "Shall we?"

I nodded.

"Just go right behind that screen, get undressed from the waist down, and pop onto the table. I'll return with Beatrix in a moment."

I nodded again and went to undress. As I slid off my skirt, I regretted not getting a bikini wax before my appointment. I was going to make a poor first impression on the impeccably groomed Mr. Moore. But as I got up on the table and tucked the paper cover neatly around me, I reassured myself that surely he had seen much worse. Minutes later, Mr. Moore returned with Beatrix, knocking on the partition that separated the examination room from his parlor.

"All set?" he asked.

"All set," I said.

Mr. Moore smiled as he perched on a small stool beside me while Beatrix hovered primly in the background.

"All right then, Darcy," Mr. Moore said. "Please slide down for me and place your feet in the stirrups. I am going to have a peek at your cervix. You'll feel a little pressure."

He put on latex gloves and checked my cervix with two fingers. I winced as he murmured, "Your cervix is closed and long. Wonderful." Then he removed his gloves, deposited them into a small waste can, slid my paper covering down, and squeezed a blob of gel onto my stomach. "I apologize if this feels a bit cold."

"No problem," I said, grateful for his sensitivity.

He slid the ultrasound probe over my stomach as a murky black-and-white image appeared on the screen. At first it looked like nothing but an ink blot, the kind that a psychiatrist uses, but then I made out a head and a hand.

"Omigod!" I shouted. "She's sucking her little thumb, isn't she?"

"Hmmm," Mr. Moore said, as Beatrix smiled.

I got all choked up as I told them that I had never seen anything so miraculous. "She's perfect," I said. "Isn't she absolutely perfect?"

Mr. Moore agreed. "Beautiful. Beautiful," he murmured. He then squinted at the screen and carefully inched the probe along my stomach. The image disappeared for a second, then reappeared.

"What?" I asked. "What do you see? She *is* a girl, right?"

"Just give me a moment . . . I need to have a closer look. Then I'll take some measurements."

"What do you need to measure?" I asked.

"The head, abdomen, and femur. Then we'll look at the various structures. The brain, chambers of the heart, and so forth."

It suddenly occurred to me that something *could* be wrong with my daughter. Why had I not considered this before? I regretted all of the wine I had sipped, the coffees that I wasn't able to resist in the morning. What if I had done something to harm her? I anxiously watched the screen and Mr. Moore's face for clues. He calmly examined different parts of my baby, reading out numbers as Beatrix took notes on my chart. "Is that normal?" I asked at every turn.

"Yes. Yes. It's all terribly, beautifully normal."

At that moment, *normal* was the most wonderful word in the English language. My daughter didn't have to be a beauty like me. She didn't have to be extraordinary in any way. I just wanted her to be healthy.

"So. Are you ready to hear the big news?" Mr. Moore asked me.

"Oh, I know it's a girl," I said. "I've never had a moment's doubt, but I'm dying for confirmation so I can start buying pink things."

Mr. Moore made a clucking sound, and said, "Ahhh. Well, now. I should warn you that pink might not be the best choice."

"What?" I asked, straining to make out the image on the screen. "It's *not* a girl?"

"No. You are *not* having a girl," he said, turning to me with the proud smile of a man who assumes that a boy is always the preferred gender.

"It's a *boy*? Are you sure?"

"Yes. I'm sure. You're having a boy . . ." he said, pointing to the screen with his right index finger, the other hand still holding the probe against my stomach. "And *another* boy."

He turned away from the screen and beamed down at me, waiting for a reaction.

My mind churned wildly, landing on a once common word now infused with a crazy, new meaning: *twin*. I managed to spit out a question. "Two babies?"

"Yes, Darcy. You're pregnant with twin boys." Mr. Moore's smile grew wider. "Congratulations!"

"There must be some mistake. Look again," I said. He had to be wrong. Twins didn't run in my family. I hadn't taken any fertility drugs. I didn't *want* twins. And certainly not twin *boys*!

Mr. Moore and Beatrix exchanged a knowing glance and then chuckled their restrained English chuckles. That's when I thought maybe they were just pulling my chain. Playing some cruel little trick on me. Tell the unmarried Yank she's having twins. Good one. Ethan had told me that the sense of humor is different in England.

"You're kidding, right?" I asked, completely stunned.

"No," Mr. Moore said. "I'm quite serious. You are having two boys. Congratulations, Darcy."

I sat upright, my paper cover slipping off me and floating to the floor. "But I wanted a girl. *One* girl. Not *two boys*," I said, not caring that I was completely exposed from the waist down.

"Well. These things can't be ordered up like a mince pie," Mr. Moore said wryly, as he stooped to retrieve my covering and handed it to me.

I glared at him. In no way did I appreciate his analogy or his apparent amusement.

"Are you ever wrong about these things?" I asked desperately. "I've heard of that happening. I mean, have you ever made a mistake?"

Mr. Moore said he was quite sure I was having twins. Then he explained that occasionally girls are mistaken for boys, but rarely does it happen the other way.

"So you're *positive*?"

With the patience of Annie Sullivan teaching Helen Keller the alphabet, he pointed to the floating images on the screen. Two heartbeats. Two heads. And two penises.

I started to cry, as my visions of sugar and spice and all things pink and nice evaporated, replaced by horrid remembrances of my little brother, Jeremy. His lips vibrating together as he made endless, monotonous bulldozer sounds. I was about to have that times two. It was inconceivable.

Sensing my mounting despair, Mr. Moore switched into sympathetic mode, explaining that the news of twins is often met with something less than enthusiasm.

I fought back tears. "That is a gross understatement."

"It will just take some getting used to," he said.

"*Two boys?*" I asked again.

"Two boys," he said. "Identical twins."

"How in the world did this happen?"

Mr. Moore took the question literally because he gave me a quick biology lesson, pointing to the screen and explaining that my babies appeared to be sharing one placenta, but two sacs. "Or diamnionic monochorionic twins," he said. "Which means your fertilized egg divided between four and seven days postconception."

"*Shhhit*," I whispered.

He pushed a button, explaining that he was taking an ultrasound picture for me. He then moved the probe, snapped again. He handed me the two photographs, one labeled Baby A and the other Baby B. I reluctantly took them from him. Mr. Moore asked if I would like to get dressed and share a soothing cup of mint tea with Beatrix, who inched her way toward the table and smiled down at me.

"No. No, thank you. I have to go," I said, standing and dressing as quickly as I could.

Mr. Moore tried to coax me back on the table for further discussion, but I had to get out of there, irrationally believing that his office and its imposing Victorian formality had transformed my girl baby into a boy baby and then multiplied her by two. If I escaped, maybe it would all fix itself. I would go seek a second opinion. Surely there was a good American physician in London. One who had the title *doctor,* for heaven's sake.

"I'm sorry, Mr. Moore," I stammered. "But I have to go."

Mr. Moore and Beatrix watched as I finished dressing, collected my purse, and said, as I headed out the door, that he should bill me for the visit, and thank you very much. Then I made my way back to Harley Street, where I felt numbed by Mr. Moore's news and the biting London drizzle.

I walked all over town in a daze, the word *twins* drumming in my skull. I walked down to Bond Street, then over to Marble Arch, then across to Knightsbridge. I walked until my lower back ached and my hands and toes grew numb. I did not stop in a single store, no matter how tempting the window display. I didn't stop at all except for a few minutes at a Starbucks during the worst of the rain. I thought the familiar burnt-orange-and-purple décor would offer me some sort of solace. It didn't. Nor did the hot chocolate and bagel I hungrily swallowed. The thought of having one baby was intimidating. Now I was full-on scared. How would I be able to take care of twins—or even tell them apart? It felt surreal.

Around three o'clock, just as it was getting dark, I arrived home, frozen and exhausted.

"Darcy? Is that you?" I heard Ethan call from his bedroom.

"Yeah," I yelled back as I took off my jacket and kicked off my boots.

"Come on back!"

I walked down the hall and opened Ethan's door. He was stretched out on his bed with an open book resting on his chest. The lamp next to his bed cast a warm, soft glow on his blond hair, creating a halo effect.

"Can I sit down? I'm kind of wet," I said.

"Of course you can."

I sat cross-legged at the foot of his bed, rubbed the soles of my feet, and shivered.

"Did you get caught in the rain?" he asked.

"Yeah. Sort of. I've been walking in it all day," I said pitifully. "I left my umbrella at home."

"Not a good thing to leave behind in London."

"So. You'll never believe what happened to me today . . ."

"Were you mugged?" he asked, drumming his fingers on the spine of his book.

"No. Worse."

Ethan snickered. "Worse than someone stealing your Gucci bag?"

"This isn't funny, Ethan." My voice trembled.

His smile disappeared as he closed his book and tossed it on the bed next to him. "What happened?"

"I went to the doctor this morning . . ."

He sat up, a concerned look on his face. "Is everything okay with the baby?"

I uncrossed my legs and brought them up to my chest, resting my chin on my knees. "Everything is fine . . . with the ba-*bies.*"

Ethan's eyes widened. "Babies?"

I nodded.

"Twins?"

"Yes. Twins. Identical twin *boys.*"

Ethan stared at me for a few seconds. "Are you kidding?"

"Do I look amused?"

The corners of his mouth twitched, as if he were trying not to laugh.

"It's not funny, Ethan. . . . And please don't tell me that I deserve this either. Because, believe me, I've already considered that I'm being punished. Maybe I was engaging in some frivolous behavior in Manhattan. Maybe shopping too much," I said. "Or railing on someone's appearance. Or having sex with Marcus behind Dexter's back. . . . And God frowned down upon me and *whazzam* split my embryo . . . giving me identical twin boys." I started to cry. It was really sinking in. Twins. Twins. *Twins.*

"Darcy. Chill, hon. I wasn't going to say anything like that."

"Then why are you smiling?"

"I'm smiling because . . . I'm happy."

"Happy that I'm getting screwed?"

"No, Darce. I'm happy *for* you. If one baby is a blessing, then you have twice the good fortune. Two babies! It's a small miracle. Not a punishment." His words were convincing, his tone and expression even more so.

"Do you think?"

"I *know*. . . . It's wonderful."

"But how will I do it?"

"You just *will*."

"I don't know if I can."

"Of course you can . . . Now. Why don't you go take a hot shower, put on warm pajamas, and I'll make you some dinner."

"Thanks, Ethan," I said, feeling soothed even before I got out of my damp clothes. Ethan's nurturing quality was one of the things I liked most about him. He had this in common with Rachel. I thought of how Rachel used to bring pistachios over to my house whenever I needed some good cheering up. She knew pistachios were my favorite treat, but the best part was how she always assumed the role of the nut cracker, handing me filet after filet. I remember thinking they were that much tastier without the interruption and aggravation of peeling.

Ethan's offer to make me dinner reminded me of those pistachio days.

"Just get in the shower and start thinking of boy names. Wayne and Dwayne might be just the ticket. What do you say?"

I giggled. "Wayne and Dwayne Rhone . . . I like it."

Later that night, after Ethan and I had eaten his homemade beef stew for dinner and spent much time admiring my boys' sweet, matching profiles in their ultrasound photos, we went to bed.

"How come you never spend the night with Sondrine?" I asked as I slid under the covers.

Ethan switched off the light, got in bed next to me, and said, "It's not that serious yet."

The *yet* gave me a small pang, but I just said, "Oh," and dropped the subject.

After a long silence, Ethan whispered, "Congratulations again, Darce. Twin boys. Awesome."

"Thank you, Ethan," I said, as I felt a kick from one of my little guys.

"Are you feeling a bit better about it?"

"A tiny bit maybe," I said. I wasn't yet thrilled with the news, but at least I no longer viewed it as a curse or a punishment. "Thank you for acting happy about it."

"I *am* happy about it."

I smiled to myself and slid my leg across the cool sheets, finding Ethan's chilly foot. "Love you, Ethan." I held my breath, worried that despite dropping the *I* in *I love you* (which always makes the sentiment seem safe and platonic), I had still said too much. I didn't want to give him the impression that I wanted more than his friendship.

"Love you too, Darce," Ethan said, wiggling his toes against mine.

I smiled in the dark, letting go of my worries, and falling into a very deep and peaceful sleep.

twenty-four

The next morning I awoke in a fresh panic. How in the world was I ever going to manage twins? Would Ethan let us live with him? Would two cribs even fit in my tiny room? What if I couldn't find a job? I had less than two thousand dollars left in my account—barely enough to cover my hospital bills, let alone baby supplies, food, rent. I told myself to calm down, stay focused on my list, and take things one day at a time.

So for the rest of the week, I was all about the job hunt. I kept an open mind, diligently seeking any kind of work: high-minded jobs, jobs in PR, even menial jobs. I checked the papers, made phone calls, hit the pavement. Nothing turned up—except some disappointing findings regarding the difficulty of securing a work permit. Even worse, I learned that all female employees in England are entitled to twenty-six weeks' maternity leave. Not exactly promising news. Who would hire me so far along in my pregnancy, knowing they'd have to let me go for six months? I began to worry that I was going to have to return to New York. To my old job and my old life. It was the last thing I wanted to do.

By Saturday evening, I was totally drained and disheartened and ready to let my hair down at Meg's party, stop worrying for one night. I took my time getting ready, trying on several maternity outfits that I had purchased at H&M (which didn't count as frivolous shopping as my regular wardrobe no longer fit) before settling on a simple black dress. I stood in front of the mirror, admiring the way it hugged my stomach and hips, showcasing my bump. I added a touch of mascara and gloss, deciding not to hide my glow of pregnancy behind a veil of heavy makeup. Then I slid on a pair of simple black heels and my diamond studs from Dex. The result, if I do say so myself, was understated elegance.

Ethan returned home just as I was heading out the door.

He whistled as he rested his open palm on my stomach and then patted. "You look great. Where are you off to?"

I reminded him that I had been invited to a dinner party. "Remember? The girls I met at the coffee shop last week?"

"Oh, yeah. The English girls," he said. "I'm impressed that you got the invite. Most Americans don't get invited into a Brit's home until their going-away party." It wasn't his first comment on the closed nature of British society, one of the few things he did not like about the country.

"I am very excited about it," I said. "I hope it feels like a night out with Bridget Jones."

"You mean a bunch of neurotic women chain-smoking, talking about losing weight and shagging their bosses?"

"Something like that," I said, laughing. "So what are you up to tonight?"

"Didn't I tell you? . . . I'm going to dinner with Sondrine." I felt a stab of envy as he gave me a sheepish look. He knew full well that he hadn't mentioned his date with her. In fact, he hadn't mentioned her at all since the day I met her at the Muffin Man.

"No. You didn't tell me." I nodded toward the plastic bag he was holding from Oddbins, a wine shop near us. "And apparently you have plans for after dinner too?"

He said maybe, he'd see how dinner went.

"Well, have fun. I'm off," I said, telling myself not to dwell on his relationship.

As I headed out the door, Ethan asked if I planned on taking a cab.

"No. The tube," I said, holding up my tube pass. "I'm very frugal these days—in case you hadn't noticed."

"It's too late for you to take the tube alone."

"I thought you said the tube was safe at night?" I asked.

"It is. But . . . I don't know. You're pregnant. Here you go." He opened his wallet, pulled out a few bills, and tried to hand them to me.

"Ethan, I don't need your money. I'm operating perfectly well within the confines of my budget," I said, even though one of my credit cards had been declined at Marks & Spencer that morning when I tried to buy a new bra to support my burgeoning, pregnant-girl D cups.

He slipped the money back in his wallet and said, "Okay . . . but please take a cab."

"I will," I said, feeling touched that he was being so protective. "You be careful too." I winked.

He gave me a puzzled look.

"Wear a condom."

He rolled his eyes and gave me a dismissive wave, which I translated to mean: "Don't be crazy. I'm not sleeping with her anytime soon." Then he kissed me good-bye on the cheek and I caught a whiff of his cologne. The scent was nice, and it made me feel strangely melancholy. I reminded myself that Simon the Ginger was waiting for me at an English dinner party in Mayfair.

But as I sat in the back of the cab on my way to Meg's flat, psyching myself up for the evening ahead, I couldn't get rid of the pit in my stomach. It wasn't just my seeming jealousy over Sondrine and Ethan's date, or my overarching worry about mothering twins. I was also just plain nervous for the party. Anxiety was not an emotion I could ever remember feeling when I went out in New York, and I wondered why tonight felt so different. Maybe it was because I no longer had a boyfriend or fiancé. I suddenly recognized that there was a safety in having someone, as well as a lack of pressure to shine. Ironically, this had cultivated a certain free-spiritedness that had, in turn, allowed me to be the life of the party and hoard the affection of *additional* men.

But I was no longer attached to someone and no longer in my comfort zone of Manhattan and the Hamptons, where I knew exactly what to expect at any bar, club, party, or gathering. Where I knew that no matter what the venue, I could have a few drinks and I would not only be the most beautiful woman in the room (except for the one time that I happened to be at Lotus when Gisele Bundchen walked in), but usually the most scintillating too.

But that had all changed. I didn't have a boyfriend, a perfect figure, or alcohol-induced outrageousness to fall back on. So I was more than a little apprehensive as we pulled up to Meg's town house. I got out of the cab and paid the driver through the front window (a practice I preferred to the New York way of passing bills over the seat). Then I took a deep breath, walked up to the door, and rang the buzzer.

"Hello, darling! So nice to see you again," Meg said as she answered the door. She gave me a kiss on the cheek as I noticed with minor relief that she was also wearing a black dress. At the very least, I had dressed appropriately.

"Great to see you too! Thanks so much for having me," I said, feeling myself relax.

Meg smiled and introduced me to her husband, Yossi, a rail-thin, dark-skinned guy with an unusual accent (I later learned he was Israeli but went to school in Paris). He took my coat and offered me a drink. "A glass of champagne perhaps?"

I rested my hand on my stomach and politely declined.

"How about a Perrier?" he asked.

"That would be lovely," I said, as Meg led me into her living room which looked like a spread in a magazine. The ceilings were higher than any I had seen in a private residence—they must have been at least sixteen feet high. The walls were painted a dark, romantic red. A fire was flickering in the fireplace, casting a soft light on the jewel-toned Oriental rug and dark, antique furniture. Faded hardcover books filled the shelves that lined one entire floor-to-ceiling wall of the room. There was something about all of those books that intimidated me, as if I might be quizzed on literature later.

The guests, too, were somehow intimidating. They did not resemble my homogenous New York crowd. Instead, the dozen or so people in the room seemed so culturally and racially diverse that they looked like a Benetton ad. As Yossi returned with my sparkling water in a crystal goblet, Meg asked if I had had any luck in finding a job.

"No luck so far," I said. "But I did make it to the doctor."

"Did you find out the gender?" she asked eagerly.

"Yes," I said, realizing that I had forgotten to prepare for the question.

"A girl?"

"No. A boy," I said, making the split-second decision not to tell her about the twins just yet. Being single and expecting one baby seemed acceptable, maybe even au courant, but there was something about being single and having twins that seemed sort of embarrassing, almost low-rent, and certainly not the kind of news you want to broadcast at an elegant dinner party.

"Oh! A *boy!* How delightful!" Meg said. "Congratulations!"

I smiled, feeling vaguely guilty for not telling Meg the full story. But by then, she was leading me around the room, introducing me to the other guests. There was Henrik, a Swede, and Cecilia, his French wife, both cellists. Tumi, a jewelry designer from Cameroon. Beata, a handsome woman who was born in Prague, raised in Scotland, and now spent much of her time working in Africa with AIDS patients. Uli, a strapping German who worked with Yossi in banking. An older Arab man whose name was so full of odd consonants that I didn't catch it even after he repeated it twice. A handful of Brits, including Charlotte and her husband, John. And Simon the Ginger, who had a zillion freckles to go with the shockingly red hair. To my relief, he ignored me in favor of Beata, who, incidentally, was also a redhead (which always raises the interesting question of whether redheads pursue other redheads in a narcissistic way, or simply because they have no other choice, as nonredheads aren't interested).

In any event, I was the odd woman out. The only person at the mini UN convention who had nothing to contribute to the geopolitical conversation. I had no clue whether Asia was a market bubble or still a buy. No opinion on how the threat of terrorism and various elections were going to cause stock prices to tumble. Or whether the slump in luxury travel was nearly over. I knew nothing about the conflict in the Sudan that had caused a hundred thousand refugees to cross the border into Chad. Or the conversion of the pound to the euro. Or France's chances at the next World Cup. Ditto for rugby (something about the Five Nations?) and *Breakfast with Frost* (whatever that is). Nor did I realize that Tony Blair's "shameless love affair with America" was so offensive to the rest of the world.

I kept waiting for someone to bring up the royal family, the one topic that I knew a thing or two about. But when the royals were finally raised, it wasn't to comment on Fergie's yo-yo dieting, the conspiracy theory surrounding Di's death, William's latest love interest, or Charles and Camilla. Instead, they chatted about whether England should continue to have a monarchy at all. Which I didn't even know was up for debate.

After at least two hours of cocktails for everyone but me, we were all seated to a Moroccan feast, where people continued to drink heavily. In fact, the sheer amount of alcohol consumed was the only real similarity between my old world and this one. But unlike New York, where the more you drank, the more stupid you became, these people just got smarter. Not even Dex and Rachel talked about this heavy stuff when they were drunk. I found my mind drifting, wondering what Ethan was doing with Sondrine.

Then, toward the end of dinner, a very late guest arrived. I was sitting with my back to the dining room entryway when Meg looked up and said, "Why, hello there, Geoffrey, darling. Fashionably late again, are we?" At which point I heard Geoffrey apologize, explaining that he had been paged for an emergency C-section. That's when I turned around and found my one and only Mr. Moore looking incredibly handsome in a tweed sport coat, a cashmere turtleneck, and gray twill pants.

I watched as my doctor greeted his friends, shaking hands with the men and bending down to kiss the women. Then, his eyes rested on me. He gave me a funny look, and after a few beats, he smiled with recognition. "Darcy, right?"

Charlotte and Meg exchanged a look, as if remembering the connection.

"Oh, right! I forgot you two would have met," Meg said. "Darcy told us the fantastic, exciting news!" She was, of course, referring to my *one* boy.

Mr. Moore looked at me, as I realized with horror what was about to transpire. I tried to preempt it by saying, "Yes, he told me I was having *a* boy," but before I could, Mr. Moore blurted out, "Yes. Twins! Marvelous, isn't it?"

For the first time all evening, a hush fell over the room. Everyone looked at me. For someone who had spent three decades basking in attention, I should have been savoring the moment, but instead I was mortified as I confessed, "Um . . . I'm actually pregnant with twins."

"*Twins!*" came the collective roar at the table.

"Oh, my," Geoffrey said, looking horrified as he took the empty seat next to me. "Meg said 'fantastic news.' I just assumed . . . I'm truly sorry."

"No problem," I said quietly, but wanted to melt away as Meg stood and made a toast: "To our new American friend and her *two* babies! Congratulations, Darcy!"

So I was not only the dumb American, but an unwed, lying mother of two. I gave the group a large, fake smile and then mumbled with all the grace and dignity that I could muster, "Mr. Moore—Geoffrey—did give me a bit of a jolt last week when he told me I'm having two boys . . . I suppose I haven't fully digested it yet . . ."

Then I waited for the group to turn to other matters—which took a surprisingly long time considering their interest in much loftier topics. But when they finally did, my discomfort did not subside. I said very little. Just focused on eating my foreign, too flavorful food. Geoffrey, too, seemed just as uncomfortable and spent most of the evening avoiding me. When he did address me, it was in a formal and awkward manner, to ask things such as, "Are you enjoying your lamb shank tagine and apricot couscous?"

So I was very surprised when, at the end of the evening, as everyone was thanking Meg and Yossi and putting on their coats to leave, Geoffrey offered to drive me home. I accepted, assuming that he was trying to make amends. Clearly this was his way of apologizing for outing me. But the way he rested his hand gently on my back on our walk to his car suggested the possibility of something more. And despite the awkward fact that he had had his fingers in my vagina, I couldn't help feeling a flutter of excitement as he opened the door to his hunter-green Jaguar. After all, he *was* the most eligible man I had met in London. I told myself that I could always find a new doctor.

I lowered myself into the tan leather seat, catching Geoffrey glancing down at my ankles before he turned to walk around the car and slide in beside me. He started the engine and negotiated his way out of the tight parking spot as he said, "I feel just awful about tonight, Darcy. I am so sorry. That was incredibly unprofessional of me. I just assumed that you had told everyone. A terrible assumption indeed."

"No worries, Mr. Moore," I said, testing the waters. If he let the *Mr. Moore* stand, then he still saw me only as a patient he had wronged. And I would know that my ride was strictly a pity lift.

But instead he said, "Geoffrey. Please call me Geoffrey." He looked at me with his almond-shaped brown eyes rimmed with thick, dark lashes.

"Geoffrey," I said in a slightly flirtatious tone. "You are forgiven."

He looked over at me, nodded, and grinned. Then, after he had driven the equivalent of three New York City blocks, he asked, "So how are you feeling about . . . everything?"

"I'm getting used to the idea. Maybe I'm even a tiny bit excited."

"Well, I think little boys are positively marvelous," he said earnestly. "I have one. He's called Max."

"Oh, really? How old is he?" I asked, wondering if Geoffrey also had a wife.

"He just turned four. They grow so quickly," Geoffrey said. "One second you're changing nappies. And the very next, you're watching them go off to school, too proud to even hold your hand." He laughed and then worked in somewhat awkwardly that he was "no longer with Max's mum."

I looked out my window, smiling to myself, knowing now that Geoffrey was *definitely* interested. And I couldn't help feeling smug. I still had it—pregnant with twins and all.

When we arrived at Ethan's flat, I asked Geoffrey if he'd like to come inside for a drink and talk some more.

He hesitated and said, "I would like that very much."

So a few minutes later, after discovering that Ethan was not yet home, I struck a provocative pose on the couch and engaged Geoffrey in pleasant conversation. We talked about New York and London. My job search. His profession. Identical twins. Parenthood. Then we segued into more personal matters. We discussed Max's mother and their amicable split. We covered Marcus. Even an abridged version of Rachel and Dex. Geoffrey was a bit stiff, but still easy to talk to. And very easy on the eyes.

Then, right around midnight, he asked if I wouldn't mind enlisting his partner, Mr. Smith, as my new doctor. I smiled and said I had been thinking the very same thing.

"Well, then . . . now that we have cleared up that little conflict, might I kiss you?" he asked, leaning in closer to me.

I said that he could. So he did. And it was nice. His lips were soft. His breath sweet. His hands gentle. All the boxes were checked. His name might as well have been Alistair.

Yet right in the heat of the first real kiss I'd had in months, with Geoffrey, a British doctor, dallying about my newly acquired cleavage, my mind was elsewhere, fixed on Ethan and Sondrine. Was his face buried in her neck or some such spot? Was he falling for her? Was she equally overcome by his spicy, yet subtle, cologne?

twenty-five

Geoffrey called me before noon on the following day, proving that he was man enough not to subscribe to any silly waiting games. Or perhaps only American men make you wait. In any event, he told me that he enjoyed my company and would love to see me again. I found his candor immensely attractive, which in turn made me feel that I had matured.

I shared this observation with Ethan later that night as he stood at the stove making us fried eggs and bacon for dinner. We both loved breakfast foods any time of day. In fact, one of the few things that Ethan and I agreed on in high school was that going to IHOP after football games was a better choice than the infinitely more popular Taco Bell.

"Yeah," he said. "Sounds like you might be ready for a real, healthy relationship."

"As opposed to pursuing someone like Marcus?" I asked.

He nodded. "Marcus was all about rebellion." He flipped one egg with a spatula and then probed gently at the yolk of the other. "You subconsciously knew that Dex was wrong for you, so you cheated on him to escape your engagement."

I considered this statement, and told him I thought he was right. Then I said, "So what about you and Sondrine?"

Ethan had not returned home the night before, and I had spent a long, restless night checking the clock and wondering what was happening between them.

Ethan blushed while he kept his eyes on our eggs.

"So? How was last night?" I asked.

He turned down the gas flame with a flick of his wrist and said, "We had a nice time."

I decided to cut to the chase. "Did you sleep with her?"

His cheeks turned a shade pinker. Clearly he had. "None of your business," he said. "Now make the toast, please."

I stood from the table and put two slices of wheat bread in his toaster. "It is *sort of* my business."

He shook his head and asked, "How do you figure?"

"I'm your roommate . . . and your bedmate . . . I need to know if my status is in any way threatened," I asked, treading carefully.

"Your status?"

"My spot in your bed?" I said, in my "no duh" tone.

"You can stay in my bed," he said.

"I can? Why's that?" I asked, perhaps a tad hopeful that Ethan had determined that Sondrine wasn't the woman for him in the long term.

"Because I'm not going to throw a pregnant woman to the wolves. . . . I'll just stay at her place," he said quickly, as if he had already given much thought to the issue.

Maybe he had even decided that it was no longer appropriate for us to sleep next to each other. At least I still had my bed for the short term, but what if Ethan and Sondrine became more serious and moved in together? What then? I felt anxious at the thought of it—and maybe even a little sad. I liked how close Ethan and I were, and didn't want that to change.

I decided that I had to prepare for the worst. If Ethan and Sondrine did become serious, I sure as hell wanted to be in a relationship too. From an emotional standpoint (I mean, who wants to be alone?), and as much as I hated to admit it, from a financial standpoint. I so wanted to add "be self-sufficient and independent" to my list, but in practical terms, how could I stay in London, jobless, with two children on the way?

So I threw myself into dating Geoffrey, catching myself fantasizing about a big wedding and the blissful life after with our three boys and a couple of Cavalier King Charles spaniels. I could hear myself saying, years later, every time I would tell the convoluted story of how we met: "See? Things happen for a reason. My life was hell and then it all fell neatly, magically into place."

I told Charlotte and Meg of my hopes for the future as we strolled through Hyde Park with Natalie one afternoon. They both seemed thrilled with the idea of Geoffrey and me being together. They sang his praises, calling him a "wonderful father," a "brilliant doctor," and the "rare, highly evolved man who is not scared off by a pregnant woman."

"And," said Charlotte, as she maneuvered Natalie's pram around a cluster of Japanese tourists snapping photos of the Peter Pan statue, "he's gorgeous and rich to boot!"

I laughed. "Yeah. And you wanted to set me up with a damn ginger!"

Meg laughed. "I don't know why we didn't think of Geoffrey in the first place. I guess because we were thinking of him as your doctor."

Charlotte agreed. "I know! But it's so *obvious* now. Clearly you're perfect together."

Meg nodded. "He adores you . . . and you even *look* amazing together."

I had a second of uneasiness. "You look amazing together" was the kind of thing people always said to Dex and me, and look how we turned out. But I pushed the comparison out of my head and said with a chuckle, "Yeah. Well. Now I just have to find out whether he's good in bed. If so, this whole thing is a done deal!"

So a few nights later, I set about finding out. Our evening began at the Ivy, one of the most popular restaurants in London. The head chef was a friend of Geoffrey's, so we had a tasting menu prepared especially for us, followed by a magnificent slice of flourless chocolate cake for dessert, and some very expensive port for Geoffrey.

While we waited for the bill, Elle MacPherson and her husband sauntered in for a late reservation. They sat one table over from us. I caught Geoffrey inspecting her, and then glancing back at me as if comparing us feature by feature. When I asked him what he was thinking, he said, "You truly are prettier than she. I much prefer your eyes."

I smiled, and told him that he was more handsome than Elle's husband too. *Handsome* was the right word for Geoffrey's looks. He reached across the table and put his hand on mine. "What do you say we go back to my place?"

I leaned seductively across the table and said, "I thought you'd never ask."

We left the Ivy and returned to Geoffrey's flat, my first visit to his place. I pictured him living in a traditional town house, like Meg's, but instead it was a sleek, minimalist loft decorated with interesting sculptures, monochromatic paintings, and contemporary furniture. I thought of Marcus's sloppy apartment, relishing the absence of video games, fish tanks, dirty sneakers, and beer cans.

"I love your flat. It's *exactly* my taste," I said.

He looked pleased with the compliment, but confessed that he had used a decorator. "She's quite good. I don't have the patience for it."

I glanced around again, noticing a little red table and chairs covered with crayons, scraps of paper, and a half-assembled puzzle of a cartoon character I didn't recognize. "Max's play area?" I asked.

He nodded. "Although his stuff usually spreads from his bedroom to every corner of the flat."

I smiled.

"Could I see a picture of him?"

He pointed to his mantel. On it was a photo of Max walking along a pebbled beach, squinting up in the sunlight. "He's two and a half in that photo. It was taken at my cottage at St. Mawe's."

"What a beautiful little boy. He looks a bit like you," I said, glancing from the photo back to Geoffrey.

"He actually looks more like his mum," Geoffrey said. "But he got my nose. Poor chap."

I laughed and told him that I loved his nose. "It has character," I said, reminding myself of Rachel. She always talked of the character in someone's face, saying that small, pretty noses on men turned her off. I sort of knew what she meant. I liked the strong statement that Geoffrey's nose made.

He put his arms around me and kissed my nose. "And I love yours."

The exchange was one of those very early precursors to *I love you.* You know—when a couple goes around saying that they love certain things about each other. *I love your eyes. I love spending time with you. I love the way you make me feel.* And then out of the blue—a straight-up *I love you.*

Geoffrey offered me a drink. "Juice? Water? Tea?"

"Nothing, thank you," I said, shifting a Tic Tac from one side of my mouth to the other.

I watched him stride over to his wet bar and pour himself a glass of bourbon. Then he turned on his stereo. African music that reminded me of the background singers in Paul Simon's *Graceland* filled his flat. We sat on his modern leather couch, he draped his arm around my shoulder, and we talked. As I listened to his charming accent, punctuated by the atmospheric clinking of ice in his rock-cut tumbler, I tried to figure out who he reminded me of. I finally decided that he was a mature Hugh Grant, a straight Rupert Everett, and an English Dex Thaler. He was exactly what I would have ordered off a menu: an absolute gentleman—no part guy or boy.

And as always, he waited just long enough before he kissed me, not delving in too quickly. We were half-reclined, but every few minutes, Geoffrey would stop the tide, straighten up, sip his bourbon, and sort of silently gather himself. Then he'd kiss me again. The last such session concluded with him standing and issuing a formal invitation to his bedroom. I obliged, thinking how much I wanted to have sex. I missed it a lot. It had been my longest drought in at least a decade, maybe ever. More important, I wanted to take things to another level with Geoffrey. I wanted to infuse intensity and intimacy into our somewhat formal relationship.

Moments later I got my wish. Geoffrey and I were standing by his bed, undressing each other slowly. We faced each other, alternating pieces of clothing like a game of strip poker where you can't decide if you want to be the one naked and vulnerable or the one in control. I wanted everything, all at once. But I was patient, letting the suspense build. Finally we were both naked. For the first time, I was with a guy and feeling self-conscious about my body, but Geoffrey quickly dispelled any lingering worry I had that my pregnancy would turn him off. He knelt in front of me and kissed my navel. The sensual gesture made me feel lush and beautiful.

Then he took my hand and led me over to his bed. The transition was smooth, like a scene in a movie where everything flows just right.

After some quality foreplay, the somewhat awkward production of a condom, and Geoffrey's reassurance that sex was perfectly safe during this stage of my pregnancy, he entered me from behind, which was practical given my stomach issues, but nonetheless quite nice. Geoffrey lasted a very long time. A very, *very* long time. In addition to his impressive staying power, he was definitely less reserved between the sheets. At some point I stopped observing and just let myself go.

Then, in the sweaty aftermath, while listening to an a cappella tribal chorus of *tu lu lus,* he curled his body around mine, kissed the nape of my neck, and said, "You're amazing."

I thanked him and returned the compliment. He *was* amazing.

We both fell asleep and repeated everything in the middle of the night and then again in the very early morning. After our third time together, I looked into his eyes and saw something. Saw a look I recognized. It took a moment to place it, but when I did, I was certain of what it was. It was addiction. Geoffrey was addicted to me. And this fact alone felt like a very significant triumph in a season of heavy losses.

A short time later, I met Geoffrey's son, Max. Geoffrey went to pick him up at his mother's house in Wimbledon while I waited in his flat, resisting the strong temptation to snoop through his drawers. In the past, I wouldn't have been able to stop myself, but in the past, I think I *wanted* to find some fodder for a fight. A photo of another woman, an old love letter, a condom that predated me. Something to rile me up, fuel my jealous instincts, get my competitive juices flowing. I wasn't sure whether my pregnancy had matured me, mellowed me, or simply sapped my strength. But in any event, I was enjoying the ease of my new, tranquil relationship. I wasn't interested in barriers, only smooth sailing and a happy ending.

When Geoffrey and Max returned, I stood to greet them, my face stretched out in a huge smile. Max was adorable—cute enough to be in a Gap ad in his little navy overalls and fire-engine-red turtleneck. I felt my first wave of excitement over having sons instead of daughters.

"Hi, Max," I said. "How are you?"

"Fine," he said, avoiding eye contact as he got down on his knees and rolled his toy truck along the hardwood floor. I noticed that he had blue eyes, but lashes as dark as Geoffrey's.

I tried again to engage Max, lowering myself to the floor, where I sat back on my heels. "It's so nice to meet you."

Geoffrey mouthed, "He's shy," before gently prompting Max, "Can you tell Darcy it's nice to meet her too?"

"Nice to meet you, Darcy," Max mumbled, giving me a suspicious glance.

I suddenly wished that I had more experience talking to children. I struggled for a second and then said, "That's a great truck—lorry—you have there." I lowered myself further, sitting cross-legged.

Max glanced at me again, slightly longer this time. He gripped the cab of his truck and pushed it a few inches toward me. "It has big tires. See?" he said, almost as if he were testing me.

"It sure does. Some really, *really* big tires."

Max didn't seem too impressed with my answer. I tried to dig up any scrap of information I had stored in my memory on trucks. "My brother, Jeremy, had a red lorry just like this one," I finally said. "Only the steering wheel was on the other side!"

"On this side?" he asked, pointing to the passenger side.

"Exactly!" I said, resting my hands gently over his and trying to remember the throaty sounds that Jeremy used to annoy me with when he played with his trucks. I cleared my throat, hoping that I could get them right.

"*Vroom,*" I started, realizing that such a noise belonged more to a sports car. I tried again. "*Grrrrrrr. Grrrrrrrrrrr,*" I growled, easing the front wheels over my right knee. I felt slightly foolish, like a man must feel when prompted by his daughter to play with a Ken doll.

Fortunately, Max seemed to approve of my sound effects. I saw the corners of his mouth twitch into the smallest of smiles. This gave me confidence. So I made more motor noises, followed by the sound of an engine idling. *"Buh. Buh. Buh. Buh."* That had been one of Jeremy's favorites.

"Do it again," Max squealed.

I did, forgetting that Geoffrey was watching, perhaps even critiquing me.

"Grrrrrrrrrrrrrr," I said more robustly, as the rear wheels completed the bouncy climb over my leg. Then, I slipped off my socks, balled them up, and stuffed them into the cab of the truck. "Here. Some . . . cargo for you to drive . . . to the factory in . . . Liverpool," I said. It all sounded feasible, and I felt relieved that boy games might be easier and more fun than I had once thought.

"The factory in Liverpool," Max repeated happily.

And from that moment on, Max and I were fast friends. He didn't stop saying my name in his adorable English accent, leading me around by the hand, showing me his toys, even insisting that I take a tour of his bedroom. I basked in his acceptance, feeling thrilled that Geoffrey and I had cleared the final hurdle.

Later that night, after Geoffrey put Max to bed, he rejoined me in the bedroom, all smiles. "Well. You did it! He loves you."

"He does?" I asked, wondering if his father loved me too.

"Yes," Geoffrey said, grinning.

"Does that make you happy?" I asked, snuggling up to him.

"Over the moon," Geoffrey said as he smoothed my hair away from my face. "A million miles over the moon."

twenty-six

Geoffrey invited me to go to the Maldives with him and Max for Christmas, even offering to buy me a plane ticket.

I hesitated before asking, "Where are the Maldives exactly?"

He gave me the sort of affectionate gaze Dex had given me in the beginning whenever I confessed ignorance. "In the Indian Ocean, darling," he said, stroking my hair. "Think white-sand beaches, crystal-clear water, palm trees swaying in the breeze."

As tempting as a vacation in the sun was and as eager as I was to push things even further along with our relationship, I politely declined the invite, telling him that I thought he should spend quality father-son time with Max. The truth was, I didn't want to leave Ethan all by himself in London. He didn't have the extra cash to fly home for the holidays, and Sondrine was going to Paris for the week, so

I think he was counting on spending time with me. Part of me was even excited that it would just be the two of us. I figured it might be our last hurrah—and our last flurry of sleepovers—before things really took off for each of us on the romance front.

I think Ethan felt the same way because on Christmas Eve morning, he went to Sondrine's to say good-bye and returned home in high spirits, suggesting that we go buy a tree together. "Better late than never!" he chirped. So we put on our warmest clothes and strolled over to the nursery near his house. Of course, the best trees were long gone, so we had to settle for a small fir with mangled branches and several bald patches around the base. As we dragged the tree home, it lost even more needles.

But between Ethan's ornament collection and a few pairs of my most sparkly chandelier earrings, our little tree became more than respectable. Ethan said the transformation reminded him of the tree in *A Charlie Brown Christmas*. I agreed and told him that it was the prettiest one I had ever owned, even though I had always made Dex buy grand eight-footers for our New York apartment.

We dimmed the lights in the living room and then switched on the white tree lights, spending the longest time just gazing at the tree, listening to Harry Connick Jr. croon Christmas carols, and drinking hot apple cider. After a long, cozy stretch of silence, Ethan turned to me and asked me if I had come up with any baby names.

I told him that I had a short list, but nothing concrete. I rattled some of them off. "Trevor. Flynn. Jonas. What do you think?"

"Honestly?"

I nodded.

"Hmm . . . Well, let's see . . . a guy named Trevor got caught stealing clothes from the dryers in my dorm at Stanford. Flynn sounds like *phlegm*, and Jonas conjures whales . . ."

I laughed, and said that I'd have to go back to the drawing board.

"Don't change on account of me."

I shook my head. "Nope. I want you to love my names."

He smiled and then suggested that we exchange our presents.

"Okay," I said, clapping excitedly.

He got up from the couch, sat cross-legged on the floor next to the tree, and handed me a large box wrapped with silver paper. "You first," he said.

I sat down beside him and carefully sliced open the paper the way my grandmother always did, as if to save it for future use. Then I opened the white box and the turquoise tissue paper inside to find a beautiful gray cashmere sweater coat from Brora, a store I had passed many times on the King's Road.

"It's not technically a maternity sweater, but it's quite roomy, and the lady at the store said that lots of pregnant women buy them," he explained.

I stood up and tried it on over my sweats. It fit perfectly, with room to grow, and the cashmere was positively luxurious. "I love it, Ethan!"

"See? It's belted," Ethan said earnestly. "So you can just loosen the belt as you get bigger . . . I thought you could wear it when you bring the boys home from the hospital. It will look really nice in photos."

"I will definitely do that," I said, loving that Ethan cared about photos. He was one of the few guys I knew who bothered to put them in albums. I looked at him and asked if he'd be there to take those photos.

"I wouldn't want to step on Geoffrey's toes . . . but I'd like to be there. It's your call."

"Geoffrey understands our friendship," I said, not knowing whether that was exactly true, but hoping that it was the case. It was the only way our relationship would work.

Ethan smiled and said, "There's another gift under there." He pointed to a white envelope. On it, he had written, "To Darcy, Baby A and Baby B." Inside was a small square of blue paper. I studied it, puzzled. "What is it?"

"It's a paint swatch," he said. "I want to paint your room that color. For the nursery. I was going to just surprise you and do it, but then I worried that blue was too obvious for you. Would you rather do something more . . . unexpected?"

"I *love* this shade of blue," I said, feeling all warm inside and thrilled that Ethan wanted me to stay with him even after the babies arrived. I had been wanting to broach the subject for weeks, and now I had my answer. I threw my arms around his neck and kissed his cheek.

Ethan went on to tell me that he had measured a crib at Peter Jones and had determined that two would fit along the long wall. And that we could put a pad on top of that bookshelf and use it as a changing table.

I grinned and told him it was an excellent plan. "Now open your gift!" I said, handing him his package.

He opened it with exuberance, tearing off the paper, tossing it aside, and holding up the leather messenger bag I had found to replace his tattered nylon one. My only splurge in weeks. I could tell he loved it, because he immediately went to his room and brought out his old bag, unloading his papers and folders and transferring them to his new one. He swung it over his shoulder, then adjusted the strap slightly. "It's awesome," he said. "I look like a real novelist now."

He had begun to make a lot of comments like this lately. I could tell he felt anxious about the progress—or lack of progress—he was making on his book.

"Still having writer's block?" I asked sympathetically.

"Yeah. I feel like Snoopy stuck on that one line: 'It was a dark and stormy night.'"

I laughed and reassured him that surely all great authors struggled with occasional writer's block, and that I knew he'd make some good headway in the new year.

"Thanks, Darce. I appreciate that," he said sincerely.

Then we curled up under a big blanket on the couch and watched a video of *It's a Wonderful Life*. Right around the part where the uncle accidentally gives the envelope of money to Mr. Potter, Ethan hit the pause button and asked if he could fast-forward to the end. "I can't stand this part. It's too frustrating."

I agreed. As we watched the grim scenes blur forward, I couldn't help thinking about my own life—specifically the rift with my mother. She had not contacted me once since I had sent her the note from London. I firmly believed that the ball was in her court, but by the end of the movie, as we watched the happy family scene where George Bailey's youngest daughter says, "Every time a bell rings an angel gets his wings," I decided to let go of my pride and call home.

Ethan was supportive of the idea, so I nervously dialed up my home in Indy. As the phone rang, I almost hung up, but grabbed Ethan's hand instead. My mom answered after five or six rings.

"Hi, Mom," I said, feeling scared and small.

She said my name icily and then silence floated over the wires. My mother was a champion grudge holder. I thought of my own grudge against Rachel, figuring that you didn't get these things from strangers.

"Did I interrupt dinner?" I asked.

"Not really. We were just finishing. Jeremy and Lauren are here."

"Oh," I said. "How are their wedding plans coming?"

"Just fine."

I waited for her to ask how I was, whether I was still in London. When she didn't, I offered it up awkwardly. "I'm still here in London. . . . You got my note, right?"

She said that she already knew I was in London, even before receiving the note, as she had run into Annalise's mother at the mall. She added that it had been embarrassing to hear of my whereabouts from someone else, which I thought was a petty point to raise given the fact that I had written her a note, and that I had been the one to phone her first. But I didn't let this deter me from telling her how sorry I was for disappointing her. I told her that it was understandable how shocked she had been upon my news. That no mother would want her daughter to get pregnant so fast on the heels of a broken engagement to another man. I also told her that she was right about Marcus. "He was a big jerk, Mom. I'm not with him at all anymore. I see now that you just wanted what was best for me."

Ethan squeezed my hand and nodded, as if to say, "Keep going. You're doing great."

I swallowed, took a deep breath, and said, "So anyway, I had an ultrasound here in London . . . and I found out what I'm having."

"A girl?"

"No. Not a girl. I thought it would be a girl too. But it's not a girl."

"So a boy then? That's great," she said emotionlessly.

"Well, yes. But . . . it's actually . . . *two* boys. I'm having twins. Identical twin boys! Isn't that just the *most craziest* thing ever?"

In my mind, I could hear Rachel instructing me that it's either "the craziest" or "the most crazy"—not "the most craziest." But this seemed an appropriate time to break the grammar rule. To me, having twin boys *was* the *most craziest*. "Can you believe that, Mom?"

I braced myself for the worst, but it didn't hurt any less when I got just that. She did not congratulate me. She did not ask about names. She did not ask how I was feeling. She did not say that she was happy for me. She only asked how in the world I was going to manage twins. Tears stung my eyes as I calmly reassured her that I intended to make things work in London. I told her that I was looking for a job and was sure something would turn up. I told her of our plans to fix up a nursery in Ethan's flat, smiling at him gratefully. I told her how much I loved London, rain and all. Then I wished her a merry Christmas and told her that I loved her. I told her to tell my dad and Jeremy, and even Lauren, that I loved them, and that I'd be sure to call again soon. She said she loved me, too, but she said so briskly, with no warmth at all.

When I hung up, I lowered my head into my hands and cried. Ethan stroked my hair and said softly, "You did good, Darce. You did the right thing by calling her. I'm proud of you."

"I shouldn't have called. She was *awful!*"

"Yes. You should have. . . . Don't let her get you down. You can only control your own actions. Not other people's reactions."

I blew my nose and said, "I can't help feeling this way. She's my *mother.*"

"Parents often let you down," he said. "You'll just have to do a better job being a mother to your boys. I know you will."

"How do you know that?"

"Because, Darce, you've shown your true colors lately."

I blew my nose again. "What do you mean by 'true colors'?"

"I mean . . . you are a good person." Ethan touched my arm gently. "A strong person. And you're going to make a wonderful mother."

Over the years, I had received endless compliments and ego-stroking words from countless men. *You're beautiful. You're sexy. You're incredible. I want you. Marry me.* But this sentiment from Ethan was the nicest thing I had ever heard from a man. I put my head on his shoulder, basking in it.

"I'm going to try, Ethan. I'm really going to try."

The next morning Ethan and I awoke and sleepily wished each other "Merry Christmas."

"What are we going to do today?" I asked him.

"We're gonna chef it up," Ethan answered joyously.

We had gone grocery-shopping two days earlier, and his small English refrigerator was packed to the gills with all of our ingredients.

"What else?"

"Cooking Christmas dinner will take most of the day," he said.

I asked if he wished we had waited to open our gifts. I knew that

Christmas wasn't about presents, but there is always a bit of a letdown when that part of the holidays has passed. Although, for once, I had enjoyed giving more than receiving.

Ethan said he preferred opening gifts on Christmas Eve, and then said, "I could give you something else though . . ."

I looked at him, and I think my face registered surprise. Was it my imagination or was his tone suggestive? Was Ethan coming on to me? Before I could answer, he continued innocently, "How about a poem?"

"Oh. Yeah. Sure," I said, feeling relieved that I hadn't responded inappropriately and embarrassed myself. "What's the title of this poem?"

He thought for a second and then said, " 'Hot Mama.' "

I smiled and told him to go on, remembering his funny impromptu rhymes in high school. He cleared his throat and started rapping, inserting little rhythmic sputters and head bobbing along the way:

> You're one hot mama in your sexy gown.
> The cutest little preggers girl in town.
> You envisioned buying girly toys.
> But instead you're having two bouncing boys.
> You took the news in stride and did not cry or pout.
> 'Cause you know what motherhood's really about.
> And no one will make a finer mutha.
> Your baby is lucky and so is his brutha!

We both cracked up. Then he threw one arm over me and hugged me just as one of my babies delivered a sharp kick.

Ethan's face lit up.

I laughed. "You felt that?"

"Yeah. Wow."

"He got you."

"He sure did," Ethan murmured. He rested his hand on my stomach and gently pushed.

One baby responded with an impressive jolt. Ethan chuckled. "That's wild. I still can't believe you have two babies in there!"

"Tell me about it," I said. "I feel like I'm running out of room. It's starting to get really tight."

"Does it hurt?"

"Sort of. It's just this weird pressure down there. And I'm starting to get this annoying back pain."

Ethan asked me if I wanted a massage.

"Are your back massages as good as your foot massages?"

"Better," he said.

"Hell yeah, then," I said, as I rolled onto my side.

Ethan rubbed his hands together. Then he slid my nightgown up, exposing my bare back and apple-green thong. I felt my heart race with the realization that Ethan was seeing me essentially naked for the first time. I held my breath as he pressed his warm palms against the middle of my back and slowly worked upward between my shoulder blades. Then he firmly massaged my shoulders. "Is this too hard?" he asked softly.

"Nooo. It's awesome," I moaned, feeling all the tightness and tension drain from my body. As he kept massaging, I couldn't stop imagining sex with Ethan. I tried to dismiss the thought, remind myself that it would ruin our friendship, to say nothing of what it would do to our respective relationships—relationships that were actually working. No matter what, I didn't want to be a cheater ever again. I wondered if any such thoughts were crossing Ethan's mind as his hands drifted down my back, his thumbs kneading my muscles along the way. He spent a lot of time in the small of my back and then went even lower to the top edge of my thong, just over my tailbone. His touch became gentler as his hands swept out over my hips. He lingered there and then stilled, signaling the end of the massage.

"There," he said, patting my hips twice.

I turned around to face him, feeling oddly breathless. "Thanks. That was awesome."

He didn't respond, just looked at me with those clear, blue eyes. He was feeling something too. I was almost sure of it. I think I even saw his chest rising and falling under his T-shirt, as if he, too, were short of breath.

Then, after a long, strange moment, just as I thought he was poised to utter something meaningful, maybe even kiss me, he took a deep breath, exhaled loudly, and said, "Well, what do you say we hit the kitchen?"

Ethan and I spent most of the day in our pajamas, preparing our Christmas dinner. I played the role of sous-chef, diligently taking his instructions. I chopped and peeled vegetables while Ethan focused on the turkey and fancier trimmings. Other than burning my finger in the goose fat when I removed the parsnips from the oven, everything went remarkably smoothly. Almost like a cooking show, Ethan bragged at one point.

Then, just as it was getting dark outside, I took a shower. Under the hot water, I allowed myself to revisit his massage that morning, marveling that Ethan could make me feel the way he had. I found myself speculating about what he had been thinking. When I got out of the shower, I even craned to check out my back in the mirror, feeling relieved to see that my ass was still rather small and—knock on wood—stretch-mark and cellulite-free. I felt a wave of guilt and confusion. Was I grateful to have a nice ass for Geoffrey's sake, Ethan's, or my own? As I changed into a fresh pair of sweats, I told myself that I was being crazy, likely even imagining the erotic component of the whole massage.

When I returned to the living room, I discovered that Ethan had moved the kitchen table in front of the tree, and set it with his best dishes and an ivory damask tablecloth.

"How pretty," I said, kissing his cheek and feeling relief that I felt nothing more than affection for a good friend.

He smiled, adjusted the volume on his classical music, and pulled out my chair for me. "Let's feast."

And what a feast it was. Restaurant-worthy, for sure. We had a smoked-salmon salad with mustard and dill dressing as a starter, followed by our main course: a roast turkey seasoned with pink peppercorns, sage, and lemon. Our side dishes were roasted potatoes, pan-fried brussels sprouts with chestnuts, orange-glazed carrots, spiced red cabbage with apples, and parsnips seasoned with sea salt. And for dessert we had a delightful strawberry macaroon tart that Ethan had picked up from Maison Blanc, a bakery on Kensington Church Street.

We ate and ate until we literally couldn't take another bite, applauding our efforts along the way. Afterward, we rolled our way over to the couch, where we cozied up under a blanket in our standard head-to-feet position and watched the candles burn down to their nubs. Just as we were nodding off to sleep, the phone rang and jarred us awake. I silently hoped that it wasn't Sondrine—or Geoffrey for that matter. They had both already called earlier in the day, and I saw no reason why further conversation was necessary.

"You wanna get that?" I asked Ethan.

"Not really," he mumbled, but he picked up the phone and said hello.

He shot me a furtive glance and then said, with a strained expression, "Hi, there, Rachel."

I sat numbly next to him as I listened to him wish her a merry Christmas. He gave me another concerned look. I smiled to indicate that I was just fine. Then I went back to his bedroom and curled up under the covers. I tried to put Rachel out of my mind, but clearly that was impossible. I wondered if she was calling from Indiana. Whether Dex had come home with her. Seconds later Ethan appeared in the doorway. His face was solemn.

"Is it Rachel?" I asked.

"Yeah."

"Are you off?"

"No, not yet . . . I just wanted to check on you . . ."

"I'm fine," I said, reburying my face in the covers.

"Okay . . . I also wanted to ask you . . . can I tell her about your twins? She's asking about you . . ."

"It's none of her business," I snapped. "I don't want her to know anything about my new life."

Ethan nodded. "I respect that. I won't tell her anything."

I thought for a beat and then peered up at him. "Oh, go ahead. It makes no difference to me."

"Are you sure?"

"Yeah. Whatever."

Ethan nodded, closed the door, and then returned to the living room. I suddenly felt overcome with grief and had to fight back tears. Why was I so upset? Hadn't I moved beyond Rachel's betrayal? I had a new boyfriend, new girlfriends, a new best friend in Ethan, and two babies on the way. And I was sure that I would find a job in the new year. I was doing fine. So why was I sad? I thought for a few minutes, dug down to a very deep place, and came up with an answer that I didn't like. I didn't want to admit it to myself, but I knew that it had something to do with missing Rachel.

Against my better judgment, I got out of bed, opened the door, and strained to hear Ethan's end of the conversation. He was talking in a low voice, but I heard some snippets. "Twins . . . Boys. Identical boys. Amazing . . . Believe it or not, yes . . . Really great . . . She's really changed . . . Like a different person . . . Yeah. Her doctor [laughter]. Yeah, she switched doctors, of course . . . Uh-huh, good for her, you know? . . . So what about you and Dex? . . . Sure, yeah. That makes sense . . ." Then came a long silence. And finally, a bone-chilling word: *Congratulations.*

I could only think of one thing he could be congratulating her on. *Holy shit! Dex and Rachel got engaged!* How could they have gotten engaged so quickly? I wanted to hear more, but I forced myself to close the door and crawl back under the covers. Then I repeated over and over: *I don't care about Rachel and Dex. I've moved on.* By the time Ethan returned to his bedroom, I half-believed my pep talk and, miraculously, was able to resist asking any questions about his conversation. I could tell Ethan was amazed by my restraint. He rewarded me with a kiss on my forehead and a gentle gaze. Then he told me to stay in bed. "I'll clean up. You stay here and rest."

I nodded, feeling drained and weary. "Thanks, Ethan."

"Thank *you,* Darcy."

"For what?" I asked.

He thought for a second and then said, "For a very memorable Christmas."

I gave him a brave smile and waited for him to leave before weeping silently into my pillow.

twenty-seven

Ethan, Sondrine, Geoffrey, and I
did the whole double-dating thing for the first time on New Year's
Eve. Geoffrey made reservations for us at Gordon Ramsey, the posh,
Michelin-starred restaurant at Sloane Square, which was the perfect
venue for a special occasion. Throughout the meal, we all praised the
New French cuisine. Geoffrey called it "sublime" and Sondrine re-
ferred to it as a "symphony of flavors." I thought they both sounded a
bit pretentious, although it was a fair description of my pot-roasted
belly of West Country pork with aubergine caviar, and of Ethan's
roast Scottish gray-legged partridge with braised red cabbage—which
I tasted more than once.

Unfortunately, the interpersonal dynamic did not live up to the
food. I think the measure of success of any double date is how well the
women get along, and Sondrine and I just did not jell. On the sur-

face, everything was pleasant enough. She was extremely nice to me and very easy to talk to, but she came across as condescending. It was almost as if she thought I needed reassurance on every front. She must have said four times, "You hardly look pregnant at all," which was no longer the case. I actually looked quite pregnant, and was comfortable with my new shape. And every time her career as a curator came up, she'd turn to me and purr, "I'm sure something will turn up for you very, very soon!"

I also had the distinct sense that Ethan had told her what a sybarite I had been in my old life, as she incessantly questioned me on my favorite clubs, designers, wines, and hotels. Of course, I still enjoyed those topics, but I would have appreciated at least a passing mention of my unborn sons.

Ethan and Geoffrey's interaction, too, seemed strained beneath a friendly exterior. If I had to bet on it, I would have said that Ethan thought Geoffrey was overly reserved and colorless, and I think Geoffrey was just generally annoyed by my relationship with Ethan, and specifically our unconventional sleeping arrangement. It had been the root of our first argument the night before. Somehow it had come up that I had slept in Ethan's bed over the holidays, and Geoffrey had grown quiet, almost sullen. After I coaxed it out of him, he told me that he thought it was "more than a bit odd" to sleep in a bed with a male friend. I reassured him that my relationship with Ethan was 100 percent platonic, feeling relieved that I could say so honestly. But I could tell he still felt somewhat threatened. This was evident at dinner whenever I tasted Ethan's food. After my third bite, Geoffrey aggressively offered me a taste of his entrée, and when I declined, he seemed a bit miffed. As if it were my fault that I didn't like the sound of filet of monkfish wrapped in Parma ham.

But the four of us made it through dinner, and then to Annabel's, an exclusive club on Berkeley Square, where we were joined by a dozen or so of Geoffrey's upper-crust pals. Sondrine was in her element amid the elegant crowd, and she made a point to talk to an array of strangers, mostly men. I knew what she was doing, because I had done it myself many times; she was showing Ethan that she was desired by other men. At one point, when she was engrossed in conversation with a tuxedoed gentleman who looked like a young Frank Sinatra, I asked Ethan if he was at all bothered. He gave me a confused look and then said, "Why? Because she's talking to that guy?"

I nodded.

He glanced at Sondrine, his face a mask of indifference. "Nah. Not at all," he said with a shrug.

I couldn't help feeling pleased with his answer. I wanted him to be happy, just not head over heels in love, and it seemed clear that that wasn't the case.

Geoffrey, on the other hand, *did* seem smitten. He introduced me proudly to all of his friends. He repeatedly pulled me aside to ask how I was feeling and if he could get me anything. And just before midnight, with the crowd counting down the seconds to the new year, he gave me a passionate kiss, whirled me around a full turn, and shouted above the din, "Happy New Year, *darling!*"

"Happy New Year, Geoffrey!" I said, feeling flushed and happy to be ushering in a monumental year with my dapper English beau. But I couldn't help feeling distracted, wondering what Ethan and Sondrine were up to. I glanced around the room and spotted them lounging on a sofa, holding hands, while he ordered more drinks from a waiter. As I watched them together, I silently willed him to look over at me. When he finally did, I discreetly blew him a friendly kiss. He grinned and blew one back, and I suddenly had an overwhelming urge to be next to him, to exchange our first words of the new year. I wanted to thank him for everything, for being such a good friend when I needed one the most.

At that very second, Geoffrey whispered in my ear, "I'm falling in love with you, Darcy."

I felt goose bumps rise all over my arms. Geoffrey's words were the answer to all of my wishes. But as I tried to say the words back—that I was falling in love too—I caught another glimpse of Ethan, and I couldn't get them out of my throat.

Much later that night, after we had said good-bye to Ethan and Sondrine, I was in Geoffrey's bed making love to him. I sensed that he wasn't entirely in the moment.

"Are you worried about the babies?" I finally asked. "Are you sure this is still safe?"

"Yes. Perfectly safe," he breathed. "I just worry anyway."

Proving that this was the case, he told me he would rather just cuddle anyway. "If that's okay with you?"

I told him it was fine with me, but I was a bit worried too. Then after a long, silent stretch, he said the words outright. "I love you, Darcy." His breath was warm in my ear, and I could feel the little hairs on my neck standing at attention. This time, I whispered that I loved him too. Then, I silently listed all of the reasons: I loved him for his gentleness. I loved him for being an amazing catch yet still vulnerable enough to be insecure. But most of all, I loved him for loving me.

As the winter in London dragged on and my due date neared, Geoffrey doted on me more and more. It was as if he had consulted every article ever written on how to treat a pregnant woman. He took me to the most fabulous restaurants: Mirabelle, Assagi, and Petrus. He bought me lavish gifts—Jo Malone bath oils, a Valentino clutch, lingerie from Agent Provocateur—which he'd leave for me on his bed, pretending to be just as surprised as I when I'd emerge from the bathroom to discover them. He reassured me that I was only becoming more beautiful with every passing day, insisting that he could not see the zits (or "spots" as he called them) that were frequenting my nose and chin. All the while, he would talk of our future. He promised to take me to see the exotic places he had traveled: Botswana, Budapest, Bora Bora. He promised me a wonderful life and made me feel like a lucky woman. A saved woman.

Yet as I lay next to him every night, I couldn't shake the feeling that something was very wrong. That no matter how perfect my life was becoming, something was missing. I suspected that it had something to do with my dire financial situation. I had never had such money worries in my life. Even in college, and my early days in New York, before I found my bartending job, all I'd had to do was phone my father and he'd help me out, wire me a few hundred dollars or send me a fresh credit card. Obviously, calling my dad was out of the question this time, so I finally swallowed my pride and confessed my situation to Geoffrey. My voice cracked with shame as I told him how I had blown my savings on a new wardrobe.

"Don't worry about money, darling," he said. "I can take care of you."

"I don't want you to have to do that," I said, unable to make eye contact.

"But I *want* to."

"That is so nice. Thank you," I said, my face growing hot. I knew I had to accept his help, but it wasn't easy. I told him I missed having a job, feeling completely independent.

He reassured me that I'd find a wonderful career after the babies were born. "You're bright, talented, beautiful. When the babies are six months old, you can begin your search again. I can put you in touch with so many people . . . And in the meantime, I'm here for you."

I smiled and thanked him again. I told myself that I wasn't using Geoffrey. I loved him, and if you love someone, you can't use them. Not really. Besides, I knew I would pay him back someday, somehow.

I went to sleep that night feeling tremendously relieved to have had the difficult conversation, relieved that I had a safety net when my last pound was spent. My peace of mind was short-lived, however, and the pit in my stomach returned full force just days later.

This time, I confessed my misgivings to Charlotte and Meg over tea at Charlotte's flat. We were sitting at her small kitchen table, watching Natalie ignore her vast array of toys in favor of pots and pans that she had scattered all over the kitchen. I kept picturing how much more chaos *two* Natalies could inflict. "I just don't know what's wrong with me. Something's just *plaguing* me."

Charlotte nodded. "You're just feeling general anxiety over childbirth and motherhood. The whole scary journey ahead. And it can't help watching this!" She pointed at Natalie, rolled her eyes, and laughed.

"That has to be it," Meg agreed. She had just recently announced the wonderful news that she, too, was pregnant. But she was still in her very early weeks, with her own set of worries about miscarrying. "There's always something to fret about," she said.

"Hmm," Charlotte agreed. "The responsibility that is barreling toward you is bound to make you feel a bit insecure."

"Maybe you guys are right," I said, telling them about my crazy nightmares about losing or misplacing one, sometimes both, of my babies. I also dreamed about SIDS, kidnappings, *Sophie's Choice*, deadly fires, cleft palates, and missing thumbs, but the losing-a-baby motif was the most common. In one dream, I actually shrugged and said to Ethan, "Oh, well. Still got one left. And this one looks just like the lost one anyway."

"It's totally normal to have those dreams," Charlotte said. "I know

I did. They'll go away . . . Just throw yourself into preparing for motherhood. You'll feel more confident that way."

I took her advice over the next few weeks, calling her and Annalise often to ask for advice. I also read articles and books on parenting philosophies, breast-feeding, and scheduling. And I signed up for a birthing class, where I learned everything from how to breathe during labor to how to bathe my babies.

But despite all of the assurances given to me and all of my preparation for motherhood, I *still* felt unsettled. I honestly had no idea what it was, but my mind kept drifting to Ethan. I barely saw him at all anymore. Every time I went to his flat to pick up clothing, he was gone, either out working or at Sondrine's. Or worse, I'd hear her husky laughter emanating from his bedroom. I wasn't jealous, because I was very happy in my own relationship. It was more just a pang of missing the way things used to be. I suppose that's the way you always feel when a close friend develops a romantic relationship that threatens to impact your friendship—or at least the everyday nature of it. I vaguely remembered feeling the same way when Rachel spent all of her time with her law school boyfriend, Nate. I reassured myself that although things would change in the upcoming year, Ethan and I would always remain close. Much closer than we'd ever been before my move to London. We just had to make the effort to see each other. So after a week of not connecting, I phoned his mobile and arranged a dinner alone.

"You seem down," Ethan said over our Thai takeaway back at his flat.

"Maybe a little," I said. "I think it's all the changes on the horizon. Meg and Charlotte said it's normal to feel apprehensive."

He nodded as he transferred our dinner from Styrofoam containers onto plates. "Yeah. Your life *is* about to change dramatically." Then he thought for a second and said, "Maybe it's also your unresolved conflict with your mother?"

"No," I said, blowing on my Pad Thai. "And I don't think it's Rachel, either, in case that's what you're thinking." I looked at him, expecting him to say something more about her. He still had not told me—nor had I asked—about their conversation on Christmas Day. Which was fine by me. I didn't want the confirmation of her engagement to upset the delicate balance in my life. I looked up at him and said, "I don't know. I can't put my finger on exactly what I'm feeling. Something just isn't quite right."

He suggested that perhaps I needed to nest. "You're prepared mentally . . . but now you have to get there physically." He took a sip of beer. "I think we need to get the nursery set up. I was thinking that I'd paint this weekend."

I smiled, thrilled that he still wanted us, but then hesitated and said, "What about Geoffrey?"

"What about him?"

"Well, I think he might want me to move in with him," I said. "He's been talking about finding a bigger flat," I said nervously, as if I were somehow betraying Ethan by moving out. We had come a long way since my frantic phone calls from New York when I had to practically beg to stay with him for a few weeks.

Ethan jabbed at a green pepper with one chopstick. "Is that what you want? To live with Geoffrey?" he asked in a judgmental tone.

"Why do you say it like that?"

"I'm not . . . I mean . . . I just didn't know you two were *that* serious," Ethan said. "It seems like it's really happening fast."

I felt myself getting defensive as I told him yes, we were getting quite serious and that Geoffrey was everything I was looking for.

"As long as you're happy," Ethan said. "That's all I want for you."

"I *am* happy."

Ethan looked pensive as he took a bite of brown rice. He chewed, swallowed, sipped his beer, and then said, "Well, I still think we should go ahead and paint your room . . . just in case."

"Just in case Geoffrey and I break up?"

"No. I didn't mean that. I just meant . . . well . . . just in case it takes longer than expected for you and Geoffrey to feel ready to live together. In any event, I want the boys to have a room here too."

"That is *so* sweet, Ethan. You're such a good friend," I said.

So that weekend, while Geoffrey was on call, Ethan painted the nursery walls blue, touched up the bookcase with a coat of fresh white paint, and assembled the spindle cribs I had charged a few weeks earlier. Meanwhile, Meg and Charlotte took me shopping for more supplies. I stuck to the essentials—nappies, wipes, bottles, bibs, onesies, a changing pad, and a double stroller—and charged the items on my last remaining credit card. But as I paid, Meg and Charlotte sneaked off and surprised me by purchasing some gorgeous and way too expensive blue toile crib bedding and a matching curtain for the small nursery window.

"We saw you admiring it," Meg said.

"Thank you, guys, *so* much," I said, accepting the gift. It was the kind of thing Rachel always did for me—generosity I had taken for granted in my selfish past.

"You're *so* welcome," they said, looking as happy as I felt.

I told them how lucky I felt to have such close friends in London.

Later that night, as Ethan and I put the finishing touches on the nursery, I thanked him again too.

He smiled and said, "You feel better now?"

"Yeah," I said. "I do."

He rested his arm on the edge of Baby A's crib. "See? It was nothing that a little shopping spree couldn't cure."

I laughed, and said that he was right. "Yeah. Nothing that a little blue toile couldn't fix."

But as I packed my bag for Geoffrey's, I had a strong suspicion that things weren't that simple.

twenty-eight

I had my epiphany on Valentine's Day.

It was my idea to go on another double date with Ethan and Sondrine. Although our first effort wasn't an overwhelming success, I wanted to give it another try. Geoffrey protested a bit, saying that he preferred to be alone with me. I told him that where I came from, Valentine's was a cheesy, amateur nonevent and therefore we had two options: blow it off altogether and order a pizza, or share the evening with another couple. I told him I wasn't going to be one of those silly couples sitting alone at a table, all dressed up and eagerly ordering off a jacked-up, prix-fixe menu, and that going to dinner with another couple would temper the whole cheese factor. He reluctantly saw my point and made reservations for four at Daphne's, an Italian restaurant in South Kensington.

On the evening of the fourteenth, Geoffrey and I drove to the restaurant, arriving right on time. Sondrine and Ethan showed up nearly thirty minutes late with that telltale "I just had sex" look about them: messy hair, flushed cheeks, flustered expressions and all. Of course, I couldn't resist rubbing it in to the always-punctual Ethan, asking, "What were you two up to that you couldn't get here on time?"

Sondrine smirked, looking exceedingly pleased with herself, and Ethan mumbled guiltily, "Bad traffic. I'm really sorry, guys."

I raised my eyebrows and said, "Uh-huh. *Sure* it was the traffic," while Geoffrey found the maître d' and told him our party was "finally present." On the way to our table we made small talk—which with two women always includes some obligatory compliments. I praised Sondrine's Chanel ballet flats, and she told me for the zillionth time how marvelous I looked. Then she touched my stomach without asking permission first (something I did *not* appreciate from anyone other than Ethan or Geoffrey) and said, in an exaggerated tone, "This is *so* exciting!" Her words did not sound sincere. Perhaps because I remembered issuing similar statements to Annalise during her pregnancy while thinking, *Better you than me, sister.*

"How much longer do you have?" Sondrine asked.

"Geoffrey says term for twins is about thirty-six or thirty-seven weeks, so I guess I have about six weeks to go."

Geoffrey looked up from the wine list and gazed adoringly at me. He found my hand under the table and laced his fingers with mine. "We can barely stand the suspense," he said.

I saw a tightening in Ethan's face—a look he gets when he's upset where his mouth sort of twitches. I wondered what he was thinking. Just in case he felt excluded by Geoffrey's *we,* I said to Sondrine, "Yeah. It's really starting to feel real now. Especially when Ethan and I set up the nursery last weekend. It's adorable. Have you seen it yet?"

"No," she said stiffly, glancing at Ethan. Now it was her turn to be annoyed. I guess I could empathize with her. If I were dating a guy, I wouldn't want his female friend and her twins aboard in the flat. So she did what I would have done—she elicited disapproval from Geoffrey, her ally apparent. "Have you seen the room yet?" she asked him.

The tactic worked, because Geoffrey's lips fell into a sharp line. Then he said, "No. I haven't seen it yet . . . I've been really busy at work . . . and looking at flats. I'm trying to find something with a bit more room for us."

Sondrine lit up. "You and Darcy are moving in together?"

Geoffrey moved our clasped hands to the top of the table and gave me a look, the English equivalent of "aw shucks," while I said, "Yeah. We're thinking about moving in together."

"More than thinking about it, darling. . . . We're actively pursuing it, aren't we?"

"Right," I said. "That's the plan."

An awkward silence befell the table where we all just sort of smiled at each other and then looked down at our menus with seeming concentration. A moment later the waiter appeared to take our orders. As it turned out, we all wanted the filet mignon, medium rare. Sondrine and Geoffrey seemed to think that ordering four identical steaks was some sort of breach of etiquette so they changed their orders at the last second, Sondrine opting for the sea bass and Geoffrey going for the rack of lamb.

Throughout dinner, we all made a great effort to keep the conversation lively, but as on New Year's Eve, there was an unmistakable tension, a lot of fake smiles. Bottom line, nobody was having a particularly good time, and I had the feeling that it would be our last double date.

Then, right before our desserts arrived, I excused myself, announcing that it was the longest I had held my pee in nearly two weeks. To my dismay, Sondrine said that she would join me. We weaved our way through the maze of overdressed couples to the bathroom, where she tried to make interstall small talk with me, saying something about what a cute couple Geoffrey and I made. I couldn't bring myself to reciprocate the comment, so I just thanked her instead. That's when I turned to flush and saw a bright red ribbon in the water below. For one brief second, I was confused. Then it registered. I was bleeding. I panicked and wiped. Another smear of blood appeared on the white tissue.

The next few minutes were hazy, but I remember gasping so loudly that Sondrine asked if I was okay. I remember saying no, I wasn't okay. And I remember feeling my heart thudding in my ears, as I crumbled onto the edge of the cold, enamel toilet seat.

"What's wrong, Darcy?" Sondrine asked over the sound of flushing, an automatic hand dryer, and happy female chatter.

I managed to say, "I'm bleeding." Then I remember just sitting there in my stall with my underwear down at my ankles, holding my legs together, as if the babies would fall out otherwise. All the while, I visualized the passages I had skimmed over in my pregnancy books. I could see the words on the page: phrases such as "placenta previa" and "premature rupture of the membranes" and even the horrifying acronym CLIMB, which stood for "Center for Loss in Multiple Birth." I couldn't catch my breath, let alone stand and leave the bathroom.

Some minutes later I heard more commotion as Sondrine announced that a man was entering the restroom. Then I heard Geoffrey's voice outside the stall and the sound of his knuckles rapping hard against the metal door. Somehow I managed to stand, pull up my pants, and swing open the door. I saw Sondrine hovering at Geoffrey's side, and a few other women standing near the sinks, mouths agape.

"Sweetheart, what is it?" he asked me.

"There's blood," I said, feeling faint at the sound of the word.

"How much blood?" he asked, his brow furrowed.

I turned and pointed downward. The strands of red were dissipating, turning the water a frightening pink hue.

Geoffrey glanced down and then spoke with measured calm. He told me that third-trimester bleeding, particularly with multiples, was not uncommon. He said that everything was going to be fine, but that I needed to go to the hospital.

"Right now?" I said.

"Yes. Ethan's getting my car now."

"So this is really bad, right?" I asked. "You're scared, aren't you?"

"No, I'm not scared, sweetheart," he said.

"Could I be losing my babies?"

"No."

"Are you sure?"

I knew he couldn't possibly be sure of such a thing, but felt grateful when he said yes anyway.

"If I delivered now, would they live?"

He told me that it wouldn't come to that, but that if I had to deliver the babies, I was far enough along that they would survive. "Everything's going to be just fine," he kept repeating as he put one arm around me, the other hand at my bent elbow, and guided me out of the bathroom, through the dining room, and past our four plates of beautiful desserts. At the front door, Geoffrey handed the maître d' his credit card and said, "We're having a small emergency. I'm very sorry. I'll send someone to collect my card later."

The drive to the hospital was a blur, but I remember catching glimpses of Ethan's pale, worried face in the rearview mirror. I also remember Geoffrey repeating that everything was going to be fine, just fine. And most of all, I remember thinking that if he turned out to be wrong, if things weren't fine in the end, I wouldn't be able to bear the grief.

When we arrived at the hospital, Geoffrey and I went immediately to a small room on the labor and delivery wing, where a nurse handed me a hospital gown and instructed me to change and wait for my doctor to arrive. Mr. Smith came in minutes later, consulting with Geoffrey for a moment before examining me. He felt inside me with a look of intense concentration. Geoffrey hovered by my side.

"What?" I asked. "What's happening?"

Mr. Smith told me that although I was slightly effaced, my cervix was still closed. Geoffrey looked relieved, but I asked Mr. Smith the question anyway, "Does that mean the babies are okay?"

"Yes. But we're going to hook you up to the fetal monitor just to be absolutely sure," he said, and then motioned toward the nurse. I shivered as she slid my hospital gown up and strapped three monitors around my stomach. She told me one monitor would measure contractions, and the other two would trace the babies' heartbeats. I held on to the cold bar next to my bed and kept asking her if she could hear them.

Geoffrey told me to be patient, that the babies were still small and that sometimes it takes a moment to locate them. I waited, still imagining the worst. Finally, a joyous galloping sound filled the room. Then another. Two heartbeats. Two *distinct* heartbeats.

"So they're both still living?" I asked, my voice trembling.

"Yes, darling." Geoffrey's face broke into a smile. "They're both fine."

In that moment of relief, something in my mind clicked, and I realized what had been troubling me in recent days. It was all so clear. Maybe a crisis will do that for you—make you see things that were there all along. Or maybe it was the connection I felt to my sons, hearing the *whooshing* sound of their movements and the thumping of their tiny hearts. Or maybe it was the sense of enormous gratitude I felt for the miracle of not only one but two lives inside of me. Whatever it was, I had my awakening at that moment, right there in my hospital room.

Just to be sure, I asked Geoffrey if he wouldn't mind getting Ethan for me.

"Certainly," he said. "I'll send him back while Mr. Smith and I have a chat." He leaned down and kissed my forehead before leaving the room with his partner.

A moment later, a still pale Ethan opened my door and walked hesitantly toward me. His eyes were watery, as if he had been crying or trying hard not to cry.

"Didn't Geoffrey tell you? Everything is fine."

"Yes. He told me." Ethan sat tentatively at the foot of my bed. He squeezed my foot through the sheets.

"Then why do you look so upset?"

"I don't know . . . You just had me so worried . . ." His voice trailed off.

I adjusted my bed to a more upright position and then lifted my arms to indicate that I wanted a hug. Ethan obliged, his cheek resting against mine as his arms encircled me. In that simple but soulful embrace, one simple truth was confirmed in my heart: I was in love with Ethan.

twenty-nine

Geoffrey barged back into the room in the middle of my transforming hug with Ethan. At least it seemed as if he were barging, given my mind-set, but more likely it was his usual dignified entry. In any event, I felt flustered and guilty. I told myself that for once, I had not cheated. I couldn't control my feelings, and Geoffrey couldn't read my mind. Neither could Ethan for that matter. By all appearances, I was only hugging a friend. Yet inside I was reeling.

I watched Ethan stand and walk over to the window, as if to give Geoffrey and me privacy. I wanted to yell out, "No. You stay here. *You* belong next to me." But instead I looked at Geoffrey, standing at the foot of the hospital bed with his erect posture, in his starched white shirt and perfect suit and tie. Despite our ordeal, he remained composed, unruffled, and steadfast. It was clear to me why I had been confused about loving him, why I had wanted so much to love him. On paper, he was perfect: handsome doctor, committed lover, seeming savior.

"What happens now?" I asked Geoffrey as I fiddled nervously with the unraveling hem of my hospital gown. Of course, I meant what would happen in the next few minutes and hours, but to myself, I was also wondering about the long-term future. I had been fooled into falling in love with what was on paper once before. Dex had been all about the checked boxes, the fine fiancé résumé—good guy, chiseled cheekbones, careful grooming, fat bank account. And look how disastrously that relationship had ended. I vowed to myself not to make another seven-year mistake. Or even a seven-day mistake. I needed to break up with Geoffrey within a week.

My soon-to-be-ex-boyfriend informed me in a brisk, professional tone that Mr. Smith had decided, and he agreed, that as a precautionary measure, I was to be on bedrest until the babies arrived. He said that they didn't want any unnecessary pressure on my cervix. I had read that bedrest was common in twin pregnancies, but I still felt shaken by the news.

"So I have to stay in bed all day?" I asked.

Geoffrey said yes, except to use the bathroom or shower. He said that I had to avoid all stress, as stress can cause contractions.

"Can I get up to fix meals?" I asked.

"No, darling. I will hire someone to come in and cook and look after you while I'm at work." He thought for a second and said, "I know a wonderful Portuguese woman who helped after Max was born. You will love her."

Ethan turned to face us, his eyes flashing. "That won't be necessary, Geoffrey." His tone was emphatic and take-charge. Sexy even. He continued, "I'll write at home and take care of her."

I smiled, feeling touched, and also tremendously relieved. I didn't want to stay in Geoffrey's flat. I wanted to be home with

Ethan. I wanted to be with him forever. I marveled at how such a monumental realization can unfold in an instant and change every single thing in your life. I loved Ethan. It was crazy, but there it was anyway. Even if he never loved me back, my feelings for him negated any possibility of a future with Geoffrey. I had never understood what people meant when they said they'd rather be alone if they couldn't be in the right relationship. Now I got it. I wanted Ethan or no one.

"You don't mind writing from home?" I asked him tentatively.

"Not at all."

"But I thought you said you couldn't think in your flat?" I asked him. "I don't want to infringe on your creative process."

Geoffrey, who seemed to sense what was happening, seized on this opening and said, "Yes. We don't want to impose on your writing."

I held my breath and felt my muscles tense as Ethan walked over to my bed and squeezed my shoulder. "Darcy and her babies are not an imposition."

"Darcy?" Geoffrey looked at me plaintively, his palms pressed together in front of his chest. "Is this arrangement okay with you?"

"Yeah," I said apologetically.

"It's settled then," Ethan said. "Let's go home."

It was after midnight when Ethan, Sondrine, and I spilled wearily onto the dark, narrow street outside the hospital and waited for Geoffrey to swing his Jaguar around from the short-term parking lot. He got out of the car, hurried around to the passenger side, and helped me into the front seat. Ethan and Sondrine sat in the back.

On the drive to Ethan's flat, Sondrine chirped about how she'd come over and cook for me, and Geoffrey thanked Ethan half a dozen times for his "generous spirit" and his "willingness to help in a pinch." I stared silently out my window, trying to process exactly what I was feeling. There was guilt over my impending breakup with Geoffrey. There was relief that my babies were okay. There was worry that I still had a long road ahead of me. Most of all, there was my love for Ethan, a love that reached down to my core and made me feel both queasy and exhilarated.

When we arrived home, Ethan awkwardly invited Geoffrey and Sondrine inside. Of course, they had no choice but to decline. I mean, what were we all going to do? Pile in Ethan's bed for a midnight snack of tea and biscuits? I heard Ethan whisper an apology to Sondrine. She murmured something back that I didn't quite catch— something about how she'd miss him—and then there was the sound of a quick kiss. Geoffrey followed suit, brushing his lips against mine and saying that he would call me in the morning. Then he said, "Drink as much water as you can because dehydration can trigger contractions. And stay in bed." By his expression, it was clear that he had not forgotten that there was only one proper bed in Ethan's flat.

Ethan and I got out of the car and stood on the curb as Sondrine took my spot in the front seat. Geoffrey promised Ethan through his half-open window that he'd get Sondrine home safely. Then she gave us a little wave and slammed her door. A second later, the disgruntled duo was gone. I turned to face Ethan, feeling strangely shy in front of the boy I had known since the fourth grade.

I waited a beat and then said, "Did they seem . . . a bit miffed?"

A smile tugged at the corners of Ethan's mouth. "A little. Yes . . ."

His expression made me erupt into nervous laughter. "They were totally pissed," I said.

"They sure were," he said, grinning.

As Ethan helped me up the front stairs to his flat, we both insisted that there was nothing funny about Geoffrey and Sondrine being upset. To reinforce the point, I apologized to Ethan for ruining his

Valentine's Day. He told me not to be silly, that I hadn't ruined anything.

"Sondrine might disagree with that."

He shrugged as he unlocked his door. "Sondrine will get over it . . . They'll both get over it."

I thought about how Sondrine and Geoffrey had become the *they*, and, if only for the time leading up to my delivery, Ethan and I would be the *we*. I liked being a *we* with Ethan, I thought, as he led me down the hall to his room. When he switched on his light, I saw his unmade bed, as well as the foil condom wrapper on his nightstand. The predinner romp was confirmed. Ethan looked embarrassed as he asked if I wouldn't mind hanging out on the couch while he changed the sheets. Something about his pained expression made me want to throw my arms around him, kiss him, and tell him how much I loved him.

Instead, I went and sat on the couch, feeling jittery and excited about sleeping next to Ethan. My heart refused to slow even after I reminded myself that the giddy brand of anxiety was still stress and that Geoffrey had said that stress causes contractions. A few minutes later, Ethan appeared in his T-shirt and boxers. I couldn't help gazing down at his legs. They were the same as they'd always been, thin calves covered with fine, light hair, but now they held incredible appeal.

"All set," Ethan said. "Did you want to change into some pajamas?"

I told him that none of mine fit anymore. I had been sleeping naked with Geoffrey for the past several weeks, but I didn't offer this part up.

"Do you want to borrow some of mine?" Ethan asked.

I told him yes, even though I doubted they would fit either. Ethan was only slightly larger than my normal size. He produced a plaid flannel pair and said, "Here. Try these."

I took them from him and said that I'd change in the bathroom. "Okay. Hurry. You should be in bed."

I nodded and said that I would be back in a jiffy. I went to the bathroom and took off my clothes and stood sideways in front of the mirror. My stomach was huge. So huge that I could no longer see my feet without bending forward. I prayed that I would get even bigger over the next few weeks. The bigger the better. I peed and held my breath as I inspected the toilet. Much to my relief, there was no more blood.

I quickly brushed my teeth, washed my face with cool water, and put on Ethan's soft, worn pajamas, pushing the elastic waistband below my stomach. They fit—barely. I inhaled a sleeve, hoping to smell Ethan's cologne, but only got a whiff of fabric softener.

When I returned to Ethan's room, he was turning down the sheets, hotel-style. "Climb in," he said as he plumped my pillow with his fist.

I slid under the covers and asked if he was coming to bed soon. He said yes, soon, after he brushed his teeth and did a few other things. I wondered if one of the things he had to do was phone Sondrine.

If he did call her, the conversation didn't last long, because a few minutes later, he was back in the room, flicking off his lamp and getting in bed next to me. I longed to touch him, debating whether to seek out his hand under the covers. Just as I decided that I'd better not, he leaned over and planted a quick kiss just to the left of my mouth. His breath smelled of Listerine and his mouth left a trace of wet on my skin. I touched the spot as he said, "I'm so glad your babies are okay, Darce. And I'm glad you're here."

"Me, too, Ethan. Thank you."

In the darkness of his room, I squeezed my eyes shut and made everything black. I pretended that Ethan and I were really together, a permanent *we,* on the verge of becoming a real family.

I awoke the next morning to the ringing phone. My first thought was, *I hope it's not Geoffrey.* My next thought was, *I still love Ethan.* So, my feelings weren't just an illusion rooted in near tragedy. I felt the mattress jostle as Ethan reached down to grab the phone. I could hear Sondrine's French accent on the other line. I think she must have asked where I was sleeping because Ethan answered, "Right here."

The controlling, jealous, break-of-dawn maneuver was something I would have pulled in my former life, and I silently vowed that no matter what the circumstances of my future relationships, I would never behave that way again. It was selfish and unattractive. Ethan reacted as I knew he would—with restrained annoyance. I pretended to be asleep as he got out of bed and whispered fiercely in the hall that she was being ridiculous.

"Were you not there witnessing the same ordeal last night?" he asked. "What do you think? Something is going on? . . . No. No! She's my *friend,* Sondrine. . . . She doesn't want to stay over there . . . I don't know—would you like to ask her?"

The conversation went on like that for some time, until he said he had to go. When he hung up, I opened one eye and saw him in the doorway, his hair messy, sticking up all over the place like a Native American headdress. I asked if everything was okay.

"Yeah," Ethan said, but he looked agitated as he crossed the room to his closet and pulled out a pair of jeans and a navy roll-neck sweater.

"Is Sondrine mad that I'm staying here?" I asked.

"No. She's cool with it," he lied. "How are you feeling?"

"Fine, but I have to go pee."

Ethan nodded, looking nervous. We both knew what I really had to do: check for blood. He sat on the edge of the bed and waited for me. A moment later I returned and gave him the good report.

"All clear," I said, giving him the thumbs-up signal.

He smiled and told me to get back in bed. I did.

"Now," Ethan said. "What can I get you for breakfast?"

I didn't want to be any more trouble than I already was, so I said instant oatmeal would be great, even though I was really craving eggs.

"Okay," he said. "I'll be right back."

After he left I flipped through my *When You're Expecting Twins* book, which I had conveniently left next to his bed several weeks earlier. I studied a graphic on weeks of gestation and head circumference, determining that my babies' heads were currently the size of lemons. If I reached my goal of thirty-six weeks, they would grow to the size of grapefruits. I told myself I could do it.

Moments later Ethan returned carrying a wooden tray. On it was a plate of scrambled eggs, sliced tomatoes, and wheat toast, all beautifully presented with a sprig of parsley. "I overrode your cereal order. You need protein." I sat up and straightened my knees as he placed the tray as close to me as my stomach would allow—which wasn't very close. He sat down next to me on the bed.

"Thank you," I said. "Where's your breakfast?"

"I'm not hungry," he said. "But I'll just keep you company."

I smiled and took a bite of my eggs.

"Do they need more salt or pepper?" he asked.

"No. They're perfect," I said. "Thank you."

As I took my first bite, I felt both babies move simultaneously. Baby A jabbing hard under my rib cage, Baby B swimming calmly below, creating his standard rippling sensation. Of course, it could have been one baby, waving an arm as he kicked. But I didn't think so. It felt like both of them in tandem. I was starting to believe I could actually distinguish their movements, and from this, I read things into their personalities. Baby A seemed more assertive. Fittingly, a Type A. He'd be my athlete, my go-getter. Baby B seemed mellow and easygoing. The tenderhearted artist. I imagined them together, spilling off the school bus, identical figures from a distance. One bouncing his basketball, the other swinging his trumpet case.

No matter what their interests, I just hoped that my sons would be good, happy boys who would always have the wisdom and courage to follow their hearts.

For the rest of the day, except for a five-minute shower interrupted by Ethan who kept knocking on the bathroom door and yelling at me to hurry up, I stayed horizontal. I napped, read my *Twins* book, and flipped through my accumulation of *Hello* magazines. Mostly, though, I just thought about Ethan, imagining what it would be like to share a slow, passionate kiss with him. To make love to him. To hear him introduce me as his girlfriend, and then his fiancée. I briefly questioned whether this wasn't just one of my challenges, if it wasn't about my needing to have every man love me.

But I knew, deep down, that it had nothing to do with any of that. For the first time in my life, I was truly in love. It wasn't about what Ethan could give me or how we would look together as we walked into a room. It was just about Ethan. Good, quirky, adorable, passionate, smart, witty Ethan. I was crazy about him, and so revved up with emotion that I had to resist calling him back to the bedroom as he had insisted I could do anytime. Instead, I patiently waited for him to take breaks from his writing and poke his sweet towhead into the room to check on me. Sometimes he'd just say a quick hello or get me a water refill. Other times he'd bring me plates of wholesome snacks: cheese and crackers, sliced pears, olives, homemade pasta salad, and peanut butter sandwiches cut in quarters. He'd always talk to me while I ate. And once, in the late afternoon, when it was raining really hard outside, he climbed under the covers and took a short nap with me. He fell asleep first, which gave me the chance to study his face. I loved everything about it. His curly, full lips, his long, sandy eyelashes that grew straight down, his regal nose. As I admired his features, his mouth twitched in his sleep, his lone dimple making a flash appearance. In that second, I knew what I really wanted for my boys. I wanted them to have Ethan as their father.

thirty

Over the next week, I relished my
cozy existence with Ethan while tolerating the seemingly incessant in-
terruptions from Geoffrey. He phoned every few hours and visited
daily on his way home from work. Sometimes he'd bring dinner, and
I'd be forced to spend the evening with him instead of Ethan (who
would promptly depart for Sondrine's). Other times I'd pretend to be
sleeping, and he'd simply leave me a note on his personal stationery,
which, incidentally, was adorned with an engraving of his family coat
of arms. It was the sort of touch that would have been right up my alley in the Alistair-fantasizing days. But now I preferred Ethan's no-
nonsense, ruled yellow notepads. Now I preferred everything about
Ethan.

One afternoon during my thirty-first week, Geoffrey paid me a
surprise visit during his lunch break. I had fallen asleep reading an

Us Weekly that Annalise had so thoughtfully sent me from home along with a tin of her famous oatmeal raisin cookies and a bottle of antistretch-mark body oil. When I awoke, there was Geoffrey perched oddly in a straight-backed dining chair pulled up next to the bed. I could tell by his expression that he felt the way I did whenever I watched Ethan sleep, and I knew that it was time to end things.

"Hello, darling," he said as I stretched and sat up. His voice was low and nurturing. "How are you feeling?"

"Fine. Just tired and generally uncomfortable," I said.

"Did Mr. Smith stop by this afternoon?"

"Yeah," I said, smiling. "Love the house calls doctors make in this country."

"And?" Geoffrey asked. "What did he say?"

"He said everything still looks good."

He nodded. "Good. Any cramping or spotting or contractions since then?"

I shook my head.

"Good girl." He reached out and smoothed my hair back from my forehead. Then he gave me a tiny, mysterious smile and said, "I've got something for you." He handed me three real estate flyers featuring wondrous, spacious flats in posh neighborhoods. The stuff of my dreams upon my move to London. My eyes lingered on the descriptions: five bedrooms, terrace, park view, working fireplace. I forced myself to hand them back to him. I couldn't wait another moment, couldn't risk letting those brochures reel the old Darcy back in.

"You're not in the mood to have a look?" Geoffrey asked.

"I don't think it would be a good idea," I said.

"Is something wrong?"

He knew there was. People always know. I searched for the right words, compassionate words. But it is very hard to sugarcoat a breakup when you're in another man's bed wearing his plaid pajamas.

So I just blurted it out, the verbal equivalent of ripping off a Band-Aid: "Geoffrey, I'm really sorry, but I think we need to break up."

He shuffled the flyers and glanced down at the one on top, showcasing a flat in Belgravia that looked exactly like the block where Gwyneth Paltrow and Chris Martin resided. I felt a pang thinking that if I stayed with Geoffrey, I could be one of Gwyneth's gal-pals. I pictured sharing her clothes, her linking arms with mine and saying, "What's mine is yours." We'd be photographed together in *Hello*. As a huge Coldplay fan, Ethan would benefit too. I saw my boys in a playgroup with young Apple. Maybe one of them would someday marry her. I'd plan the rehearsal dinner, Gwynnie would do the wedding. We'd phone each other daily, discussing flower arrangements, cake tastings, wine selections. I snapped back to reality. Not even the lure of Gwyneth was enough to change my mind about Geoffrey.

He finally spoke. "Is it Ethan?"

I felt caught off guard and nervous hearing Ethan's name. I wasn't sure how to answer, but I finally said, "I just don't have the right feelings for you. I thought I did . . . but . . . I'm not in love with you. I'm sorry."

The straightforward, dressed-down words sounded familiar, and I realized how close they were to Dexter's breakup speech with me. It suddenly occurred to me that no matter when his affair with Rachel had begun, she hadn't been the cause of our breakup. Dex and I had split because we weren't right for each other, and because of that fact, he had been able to fall in love with her. Had we been on solid ground, Dex wouldn't have cheated on me. The realization was somehow freeing, and it enabled me to let go of another sliver of resentment toward both of them. I'd think about it more later, but for now, I refocused on Geoffrey, waiting for him to respond.

"That's okay," he finally said with an elegant wave of his hand.

I must have looked confused by his nonchalance because he clarified. "You're just in a very difficult situation right now. Being in bed like this is bound to confuse you. We can sort it out later—after the babies arrive. And in the meantime, I really want to take care of you. Just let me do it, darling."

Coming from most men the words would have sounded either condescending or pathetic—a last, desperate attempt to hold a relationship together at its seams. But from Geoffrey it was just a dignified, pragmatic, and sincere declaration. For one beat, I was sold. After all, he was my ticket to staying in London for the long term. But even more important, Geoffrey was my emotional security blanket. It is impossible to overstate the unique brand of vulnerability that comes with pregnancy, particularly the circumstances of my pregnancy—and Geoffrey assuaged much of my anxiety. He was a good person who took excellent care of me, and implicit in his every touch was the promise that he always would.

But I wasn't in love with him. It was that simple. The concept of being with a man strictly for love used to seem naïve and high-minded, the kind of thing I used to scoff at Rachel for saying, but now I subscribed to the notion too. So I forced myself to stay on track.

"That is really very sweet," I said, reaching out to take his hand. "And I cannot tell you how much I appreciate your kindness, everything you have done for me. But we have to break up. It just isn't right to stay together when my feelings aren't there . . ."

Then to reinforce the point, I told him that I would miss him, although I knew I'd miss the fringe benefits that came along with him a bit more than I'd actually miss him. I let go of his hand.

Geoffrey squinted. His eyes were sad but dry. He said, without a trace of bitterness, that he was very sorry to lose me, but that he understood. He swung his briefcase onto his lap, snapped it open, and tossed the glossy brochures inside. Then he stood and headed for the door.

"Can we still be friends?" I called after him, feeling slightly frantic after his easy surrender. I worried that the question emanated from the old Darcy, the needing-to-be-worshipped-at-any-cost Darcy. Maybe I just wanted to retain control over Geoffrey. But as he turned to look at me over his shoulder, saying that he would like that very much, I knew that my intentions were pure. I wanted to remain friends with Geoffrey because I liked him as a person. Not because I wanted a single thing from him.

Later that night as Ethan lay next to me reading an article in *National Geographic* on global warming, I told him that Geoffrey and I had broken up that afternoon. I told him everything except Geoffrey's question about him.

Ethan listened, eyebrows raised. "Wow. I didn't even know you two were on shaky ground," he said, but his tone gave him away. Like Geoffrey, he wasn't all that surprised.

I nodded. "Yeah. I just wasn't feeling it."

"Was he okay?"

"I guess so," I said.

"And you?" he asked.

I shrugged. "I don't know. I feel guilty after all he's done for me. And I guess a tiny bit sad too . . . But mostly I think it's a good thing, even though it means I'll have to move back to New York sooner than I'd like."

Ethan blinked. "What?"

"I said I feel guilty—"

"No. The part about moving back?"

"I don't have a job, Ethan. I'll probably have to go back to my old one after the babies are born. I just don't have the money to stay here."

"You can stay here for as long as you want," Ethan said.

"I can't do that. I've been enough of a burden . . . And it's not like you're rolling in it." I smiled.

"I *love* having you here, Darcy. I can't wait for those babies to get here. I'm unbelievably pumped. Don't let money constraints force your hand. We'll work it out. I have money saved."

I looked at his earnest face and had to swallow back the urge to confide my feelings. It wasn't that I was afraid of rejection. It was more that for once, my feelings were selfless, and I didn't think it was fair to Ethan to unload everything on him. He was already in a relationship. He didn't need the pressure of worrying about me and how hurting my feelings might impact my pregnancy.

So I just smiled and said, "Thank you, Ethan. We'll see what happens."

In my mind, though, I knew that my time in London, as well as my time with Ethan, was running out.

thirty-one

The next day I hit the thirty-two-week benchmark, significant according to my *Twins* book in that my children would be "unlikely to suffer long-term health consequences as a result of their premature births." This felt like an enormous hurdle, which seemed ironic considering that I had achieved the goal by doing absolutely nothing but hanging out in bed, reading magazines and snacking.

To celebrate the milestone, Ethan surprised me with a homemade chocolate cake, bringing it back to the bedroom on his wooden tray. The cake was decorated with thirty-two blue candles, one for each week of my pregnancy, which he lit while singing, off-key, "Happy birthday, Baby A and B!"

I laughed, made a wish, and blew out the candles in two tries (which he said counted as I was having two babies). Then he cut the cake and served us each a big slice. I had seconds and then thirds, praising his baking efforts, especially the icing. When we finished eating, he cleared our plates and the tray and returned with a big box wrapped in mint-green and white polka-dotted paper.

"You shouldn't have," I said, hoping that he hadn't spent too much on the baby gift.

He ceremoniously rested the box on my lap. "I didn't . . . It's from Rachel."

I stared down at the package. Sure enough, the present-wrapping was unmistakably Rachel: perfect and pretty, but restrained enough not to look professionally wrapped. I observed her neat corners, the short strips of tape all parallel to the edges of the box, and her full, symmetrical bow. For some reason, that package unearthed all kinds of good memories, moments shared with Rachel over the years.

Ethan shot me a furtive glance. "Are you upset? Should I not have given it to you? I debated it for some time . . ."

"No. It's fine," I said, my hand running across the wrapping paper. Rachel's hand had touched this box, I thought, and I was overcome with the most absurd sensation that I was connecting with someone from the dead.

"Are you going to open it?" he asked.

I nodded.

"She sent it a few weeks ago, but she wanted me to wait until closer to your due date. I thought today was good . . . because I'm not worried anymore. Your babies are going to be fine."

My heart pounded as I carefully untied the white bow, peeled back the paper, and opened the box to find two white receiving blankets trimmed with light blue silk. They were the softest, most sumptuous things I had ever touched. I remembered that Rachel had given Annalise a similar blanket at her baby shower, but mine were even nicer. After a long moment, I removed the card from the envelope. It was letter-pressed with two baby carriages. I opened the card slowly and saw her familiar, neat cursive. I could hear her voice as I read silently:

Dear Darcy,

First, I want to tell you how sorry I am for everything that has happened between us. I miss our friendship, and I regret that I cannot share in this very special time in your life. But despite the distance between us, I want you to know that I think of you often. Many times a day. I am so pleased to learn from Ethan that you are happy and well. And twins! It is so you to turn an already wonderful event into something doubly exciting! And, finally, I just want to wish you heartfelt congratulations as you embark upon motherhood. I hope someday to meet your sons. I know they will be beautiful, amazing little boys, just like their mother.

Best wishes and much love always,
Rachel

Still clutching the card, I leaned my head back on my pillow. For months now, I had been waiting to hear something from Rachel, but I didn't realize how *much* I wanted to hear from her until I read her card. I looked up at Ethan. His face was placid, patient.

"Huh. Imagine that," I said, filling the silence.

"What'd she say?" Ethan asked.

I downplayed my emotion by rolling my eyes. Then I twisted my hair up in a knot, secured it with an elastic band, and said nonchalantly, "Let's just say, she is trying to make a comeback." My words were cavalier, but the catch in my voice gave me away. And against my best efforts, I could feel myself softening. I tried to mask my feelings by flinging the card his way, Frisbee-style. "Here you go. Read it for yourself," I said.

His lips moved as he read silently. When he got to the end, he looked up at me and said, "It's really nice."

"Yeah. These blankets are pretty nice too," I said, stroking the silk border with my thumb. "I guess I no longer want her to go hell." I laughed. "Just a dingy place in heaven."

Ethan smiled.

"Does this mean I have to call her?" I asked him.

Part of me wanted his response to be, "Yes, you must call her now," because I wanted an excuse to swallow my pride and give in. But Ethan just said, "You don't have to call. Just send her a thank-you note." He handed the card back to me.

I couldn't resist rereading it aloud, parsing every sentence for its meaning.

"She said she's 'sorry for what happened between us.' Not *what she did*."

"I think that's implied."

"So what does that mean exactly? That she'd take back what she did with Dex if she could?" I asked, redoing my bun.

"She probably just wishes she had handled things differently," Ethan said.

"Like how?" I asked.

"I don't know . . . like waiting until after you and Dex broke up to start seeing him?"

"Did she tell you that? Do you know that for a fact?"

"Not for a fact. No."

"Okay," I said, my eyes scanning the rest of the card. "Moving on here . . . 'Despite the distance between us,'" I read aloud. "Do you think she means emotional distance or geographic distance?"

"Probably both," Ethan said.

"She thinks of me *every* day? Do you think she's exaggerating?"

"No. I don't, actually," Ethan said. "Don't you think of her every day?"

The answer was yes, but I pretended not to hear the question as I rattled on. " 'Pleased to learn from Ethan?' " I said, remembering the bits of the conversation I had overheard on Christmas. "What exactly did you tell her?"

"Well, obviously I told her you were having twin boys. You said I could . . . and I just told her that you're doing well here. That you've made some friends. And I told her about Geoffrey too."

"Have you talked to her since Geoffrey and I broke up?"

"No."

I briefly considered asking him about Rachel's engagement, but I decided that I still wasn't ready to have it confirmed. I closed the card and tucked it back into the envelope.

"She can't honestly think that we could really be close friends again?" I asked, my voice trailing off.

"She knows you pretty well, Darce. I don't think she expects you to fold," he murmured. His tone was matter-of-fact, but his expression said, "I think you will fold." Or maybe, "I think you already have folded."

I put off writing Rachel's thank-you note for nearly two weeks because I couldn't decide on the content or tone. Should I forgive her outright? Tell her that I missed her, too, and that although I would never fully accept her relationship with Dex, I wanted to repair our friendship? Was that even the case?

One evening, on the Saturday night of my thirty-fourth week, something compelled me to get out of bed and retrieve a small leather album in the closet nursery, stuck down in a side pocket of one of my suitcases. I had put together the album several summers before and had packed it at the last moment. I brought it back to bed and flipped through it, skipping past the photos of Claire and Dex and various other friends, and finding one of Rachel and me taken in the Hamptons right after she and Dex had graduated from law school. I studied our carefree poses, our broad smiles, our arms draped casually around each other as we stood by the water's edge in our bikinis. I could practically smell the salty air, feel the ocean breeze and the sand shifting under my feet. I could even hear her laughter. I wondered why beach photos taken of lost loved ones always seemed so much more poignant than other photos.

As I looked at that picture of us, I thought about everything that had happened between Dex and Rachel and me, deciding again that the cracks in our relationships had been a breeding ground for deceit. Dex and I had cheated on each other because we weren't right together in the first place. Rachel betrayed me because our friendship was a flawed one. I lied to her about Marcus because of the same negative undercurrent—the unspoken competition that can corrupt even the best of friendships. That had ruined ours.

As much as I wanted to hold them responsible, I knew that I was not blameless. We were all accountable. We had all lied and cheated. But despite everything, I knew we were still good people. We all deserved a second chance, a chance to be happy. I considered the expression "Once a cheater, always a cheater," and I dismissed it as a fallacy. People generally didn't cheat in good relationships, and I couldn't imagine Dex and Rachel cheating on each other. I also knew that if I were ever with Ethan, I would never cheat on him. I would be true to him, no matter what, always.

And at that moment, there on the doorstep of forgiveness, I went into labor. It started out as an intense cramping in my lower abdomen, and when I got up to pee, fluid ran down my leg. My water had broken. I felt a strange sense of calm as I phoned Mr. Smith and reported my symptoms. He confirmed that I, indeed, was in labor, and he instructed me to come to the hospital as soon as possible. He said he would meet me there.

Ethan was at a sports bar in Piccadilly watching Stanford play in the NCAA basketball tournament. I hated to interrupt the game— he took March Madness very seriously—but he had made me promise to call for "the smallest of reasons," and I figured that my water breaking qualified. He answered on the first ring, shouting into the phone with bar noise in the background. "Darcy? Are you okay?"

"I'm fine . . . Is Stanford winning?"

"They haven't tipped off yet," he said. "I'm watching Wake Forest now. They're looking pretty solid—which is good because I have them going to the Final Four in my pool." I pictured him perched on a barstool gripping the yellow highlighter he used to mark up his brackets torn from *USA Today*.

"When does your game start?" I asked, debating whether I should wait until the game was over to have him meet me at the hospital.

"Soon. Why? Are you okay?"

I hesitated and then said, "I'm really sorry, Ethan. I know how much you look forward to this tournament and Stanford playing and everything . . . but my water broke. Do you think you could come home and take me to the hospital?"

"Oh, Christ! Don't move!" he shouted into the phone. "I'll be right there!"

Ten minutes later he burst through the door and streaked down the hall toward the bedroom, yelling, "Cab's waiting outside! Cab's waiting outside!"

"I'm right here," I called out to him from the living room. My small duffel, which I had packed weeks earlier, was resting at my feet.

He ran into the living room, kissed my cheek, and breathlessly asked how I was.

"I'm fine," I said, feeling relieved to see him. "Would you mind tying my shoes? I can't reach."

"Oh, God. I'm so sorry I wasn't here," he said as he stooped down to tie my Nikes. His hands were shaking.

"Where's your jacket?" I asked, noticing that he had come home wearing only his lucky Stanford T-shirt. "It has to be freezing outside."

"I left it at the bar."

"Oh, Ethan, I'm sorry," I said. "And I'm really sorry about interrupting your game too."

He told me not to be silly, he'd get the jacket later, and the game wasn't important. As he bent down to pick up my bag, I noticed a clear patch adhered to his arm, peeking out from under his T-shirt.

"You've quit smoking?" I asked, realizing that I hadn't seen him with a cigarette in ages or, for that matter, detected any telltale tobacco odor on his clothing.

"Yeah. Can't have smoke around you or the babies." He nervously rubbed his patch as if to give himself a needed boost of nicotine.

I thanked him, feeling moved by his effort.

"Don't mention it. I needed to quit anyway. Now let's go!" He pulled me to my feet and shouted, "Schnell! Schnell!" which I figured meant "hurry" in another language, maybe German. He helped me to the door, where he grabbed his only other jacket, a bright yellow raincoat. Then he inhaled sharply, rubbed his hands together, and said, "Well. This is it."

During our cab ride to the hospital, Ethan helped me with my breathing exercises, which was amusing because he seemed to need more help breathing than I did. We determined that my contractions were six minutes apart and lasting about thirty seconds each.

"How bad does it hurt?" Ethan asked every time I winced. "On a scale of one to ten?"

My pain threshold was normally quite low, and I'd been known to bawl even during the removal of a splinter, so the pain actually felt like an eleven. But I told him a four because I wanted him to be proud of my strength. I also told him I wasn't scared—which is really saying something coming from a former pessimistic drama queen. But it was the truth—I *wasn't* scared. I just knew everything was going to be all right with my babies. I had made it to thirty-four and a half weeks. And I had Ethan with me. What more could I ask for? I felt like the luckiest woman in the world. I was ready to meet my sons.

We checked in at the hospital, and Ethan pushed my wheelchair to our assigned birthing room. He then helped me undress and change into my hospital gown. He blushed as I stood naked in front of him, and for a second I was embarrassed too.

"You ain't seen nothing yet," I said to ease the awkwardness. I laughed. "There is no modesty from here on out . . . And I sure hope you're not squeamish."

He smiled, held my hand, and said he could handle it. Then he helped me recline in bed. I felt relieved to stretch out—and overcome with a profound sense of fatigue. All I wanted to do was sleep, but the pain was too intense for napping. About five minutes later, Mr. Smith and his midwife arrived. She started my IV while he checked my cervix and informed me that I was nearly five centimeters dilated.

Shortly after that, an anesthesiologist brought my epidural. I'd never been so excited to see a needle, anticipating a marvelous high, something akin to laughing gas at the dentist. Instead of a tingly, floating sensation, however, the epidural only caused the absence of pain. But on the heels of my vicious contractions, the absence of pain felt downright euphoric.

Everything happened very quickly after that. I remember Ethan holding one leg, under my knee, my midwife gripping the other, while Mr. Smith coached me to bear down and push. I did—as hard as I could. Again and again. I remember panting and sweating like mad, and making all kinds of ugly faces and guttural cries. After a very long time, my doctor announced that the first baby was crowning. I sat up, straining to see, catching a glimpse of dark, matted hair, then shoulders, torso, and two skinny legs.

"It's a boy," Mr. Smith confirmed.

Then I heard my son's first plaintive note in the world. His voice was hoarse, as if he had been crying in the womb for hours. My arms ached to hold him. "I want to see him," I said through sobs.

"Just one moment," my doctor said. "We have to cut the cord. . . . Ethan, do you want to do the honors?"

"May I?" Ethan asked me.

I nodded and cried harder. "Of course you can."

Ethan took the big metal scissors from my midwife and carefully snipped the cord. Then my doctor tied it and briefly examined my baby before bundling him in a blanket and resting him on my chest. I shifted his head over my heart, and he instantly quieted while I continued to sob. I gazed down at his angelic face, taking in every detail. The curve of his cheeks, his tiny but still full lips, the dimple in his left cheek. Strangely enough, he looked an awful lot like Ethan.

"He's perfect. Isn't he perfect?" I asked everyone and no one.

Ethan rested his hand gently on my shoulder and said, "Yes. He *is* perfect."

I consciously savored the moment, deciding that everything I had ever read, seen, and heard about childbirth paled in comparison to what I was actually feeling.

"What's his name?" Ethan asked.

I studied my son's face, searching for the answer. My earlier flamboyant choices—names like Romeo and Enzo—seemed ridiculous and utterly wrong. His name suddenly came to me. "John," I said. "His name is John." I was certain that he would live up to the straightforward but strong name. He was going to make a wonderful John.

That's when Mr. Smith reminded me that I had more work to do, and my midwife scooped up John and handed him to a nurse. I tried to keep my eyes on my firstborn, but a fresh wave of pain enveloped me. I closed my eyes and moaned. The epidural seemed to be wearing off. I begged for another dose. My doctor told me no, offering some explanation I couldn't begin to focus on. Ethan kept repeating that I could do it.

Several minutes of agony later, I heard another wail. John's brother was born seconds after midnight. Identical twins with their own, separate birthdays. Although I knew the babies were identical, I was no less eager to see my second born. Ethan cut the umbilical cord, and my midwife swaddled the baby and handed him to me. Through more tears, I instantly surmised that this baby shared his brother's features, but his were slightly more defined. He was also a bit smaller, with slightly more hair. He wore a determined expression that struck me as amusing on such a tiny, new baby. Again, his name just came to me.

"You are Thomas," I whispered down at him. He opened one eye and peeped at me with apparent approval.

"May I hold them both together?" I asked my doctor.

He nodded and brought John back to my chest.

Ethan asked me if I had settled on middle names. I thought of Ethan's middle name, Noel, and decided that each of my sons should have a part of the best man I knew.

"Yes," I said. "Their names are John Noel and Thomas Ethan."

Ethan took a breath, blinking back tears. "I'm so . . . *honored*," he said, looking both surprised and touched. Then he leaned down to embrace us. "I love you, Darcy," he whispered in my ear. "I love all three of you."

thirty-two

For the next twenty-four hours, I had no sense of day or night. It was just a blur of time with John and Thomas. Ethan never left my side, unless on a specific mission for peanut butter crackers from the vending machine, painkillers from the nurses, or booties from the gift shop in the lobby of the hospital. He slept on a cot next to my bed, helped me to the bathroom, and snapped roll after roll of black-and-white film.

Ethan also saw to it that I phoned my mother. When I balked, saying I was too exhausted and hormonal to deal with her, he dialed my home number on his mobile and said, "Here. You'll regret it if you don't do this."

I took his phone just as my mother answered.

"Hi, Mom. It's me," I said, feeling defeated before the conversation even began.

"Hello, Darcy." Her voice was as formal and stiff as it had been on Christmas Eve.

I refused to be hurt and instead swiftly delivered my news. "I had my babies, Mom." Before she could respond, I covered the basics, giving her their full names, as well as their weights, lengths, and times of birth.

Then I said, "Can you believe it, Mom? Twins born on separate days?" I looked down at John, sleeping on my chest, and then over at Thomas, whom Ethan was holding.

My mother asked me to repeat everything so she could write it down. I did, and then she said, "Congratulations, honey." A softness crept into her voice.

"Thanks, Mom," I said, as Ethan prompted me to share the smaller, but in many ways more important, details. "Tell her how John cries more than Thomas and has a birthmark in the shape of Italy on his knee. Tell her how Thomas peeps at you with one eye," he whispered.

I followed his lead, and although it could have gone either way, my mother chose to be satisfying, nearly joyful.

"I can't stand the thought of you being alone," my mother said in a nurturing and repentant tone.

"Thank you, Mom. That means so much to me. . . . But I'm not alone. I'm with Ethan," I said, not to be contrary, but because I wanted her to understand Ethan's importance in my life.

Ethan smiled as he repositioned Thomas in his arms and then kissed the top of his fuzzy head.

"Still. There is no substitute for a mother," she said firmly.

"I know, Mom," I said, feeling moved by the truth of her statement.

"So I'll come visit as soon as I can . . . In early June. As soon as we get through Jeremy and Lauren's wedding."

"Okay, Mom," I said. "That would be *really* great. Thank you."

"And Darcy?"

"Yeah?"

"I'm *so* proud of you."

I basked in her words. "Thanks, Mom."

"I love you, honey," she continued, her voice cracking.

"I love you too, Mom. And tell Dad and Jeremy and Lauren I love them. I'm really sorry I won't be able to come to their wedding."

"Jeremy understands," she said. "We all do."

As we said good-bye, I found myself pondering what Thomas and John's birth meant in the larger scheme of things, in the fabric of our family. I had created a new generation. The responsibility of it was awesome. My eyes filled with tears for what felt like the hundredth time since I had arrived at the hospital.

"This postpartum thing is no joke," I said to Ethan as I wiped my eyes with the sleeve of my nightgown.

Ethan brought Thomas over to me, and the four of us crowded into bed together. "Is she coming to visit us?" he asked.

The *us* was not lost on me. I smiled and said, "Yeah. After Jeremy's wedding."

"How do you feel about seeing her?" he asked.

"I can't wait, actually," I said, surprised by how much I wanted to share John and Thomas with her.

Ethan nodded and then glanced at me sideways. "Any other calls you want to make?"

I could tell that he was thinking of Rachel so I said her name as a question, the two syllables lingering in the room, sounding both comforting and menacing at once.

"Well?" he asked. "What do you think?"

"As a matter of fact, I think I *will* call her," I said resolutely. "And then Annalise. And then Meg and Charlotte."

It was the right order.

"Are you sure you want to talk to Rachel?" he asked.

I nodded. I couldn't put it into words, but in some inexplicable way, I felt compelled to forge an official truce with my ex–best friend. No matter what had happened in the past, or what the future held for us, I wanted Rachel to hear the news of Thomas and John's birth from me. So I dialed her number on Ethan's mobile before I could change my mind. As I listened to her phone ring, I couldn't decide whether I wanted her to answer or for her machine to pick up.

I got the one thing I hadn't banked on.

"*Hell*-o," Dex said cheerily.

I panicked, gave Ethan a wide-eyed look of horror, and frantically mouthed, "Dex!"

He grimaced empathetically and then made a motivating fist in the air and whispered, "Go on. Do it. Ask to speak to Rachel."

So I did, gathering strength by glancing down at John, who was making a soft, sucking noise in his sleep. Dex was ancient history. Literally two lifetimes ago.

I took a deep breath and said, "Hi, Dex. It's Darcy. Is Rachel there?"

"Hello, Darcy," Dex said formally. Then he paused as if he were some kind of gatekeeper, suspecting trouble from abroad. "Rachel's right here," he finally said.

There was another long pause, and a rustling on the line. I pictured him covering the phone and coaching her, saying something like, "Don't let her suck you into a conflict."

I thought back to the last time I had seen Dex, in our old apartment, and felt ashamed of the stunt I had tried to pull. I guess my reputation was deserved, and I couldn't blame him for being wary of me now.

"Hi, Darcy," Rachel said timidly, her voice crackling over the distance. It was a voice I had heard nearly every day for twenty-five years, and I felt amazed at how it could now sound both familiar and utterly foreign.

"Hi, Rachel . . . I had something—I wanted to tell you something," I babbled as my heart raced. "I had my babies last night. Two boys."

"Congratulations, Darcy," she said. Her voice was warm and sincere. "I'm *so* happy for you."

"Thank you," I said.

"What are their names?" she asked tentatively.

"John Noel and Thomas Ethan."

"I *love* those names," she said, and then hesitated. "After Ethan?"

"Yeah," I said, wondering if Ethan had told her how close we had become. If he hadn't, she was likely thinking that I was trying to infringe on her turf as Ethan's close female friend. It wasn't beyond the pale of my old tricks, and I felt another flicker of embarrassment over the person I used to be. Still, I resisted the urge to explain why the names were appropriate, and instead, rattled off the other birth statistics.

"How do you feel?" she asked softly.

I could feel myself relaxing as I said, "I'm fine. It wasn't a bad delivery . . . I'm just *really* tired now, but from what I hear, it only gets worse."

I laughed, but Rachel stayed serious. She asked if my mother was coming to help.

"Uh-huh. I just talked to her," I said. "You are only the second person I've called."

I wanted her to know the order. I wanted it to count as my between-the-lines apology. I didn't feel up to a full-blown examination of our friendship, but I wanted her to know that I was sorry about what had happened between us.

After a long pause, she said, "I'm *really* glad you called, Darcy. I've been thinking of you so much lately, wondering how you are."

"Yeah. I got your note. And the blankets," I said. "They're really special. I love them. Thank you."

"You're so welcome," she said.

"So how are you?" I asked, realizing that I wasn't ready to let her go just yet. I wanted more of her.

"Fine. I'm fine," she said somewhat hesitantly.

"What has been going on in your life?" I asked, referring to Dex, but also everything else.

"Well . . . I paid off my loans finally, and quit my job. I do legal work for an AIDS foundation in Brooklyn now."

"That's great," I said. "I know you must be much happier."

"Yeah. I like it a lot," she said. "It's so nice not to worry about billable hours. . . . And the commute's not too bad."

I could tell she was avoiding any mention of Dex, so after another few seconds of silence, I said, "So you and Dex are doing well?"

I wanted to show her I was fine with the status quo. And although it still felt funny to think of them together, I really *was* remarkably okay with things. How could I begrudge anyone happiness when I felt so fulfilled and contented?

She made an *umm* sound, hesitated, and then said, "Didn't Ethan tell you?"

"About your engagement?" I guessed.

"Um . . . well, actually . . . Dex and I are . . . married," Rachel said softly. "We got married yesterday."

"Wow," I said. "I didn't know."

I waited for a wave of jealousy or bitterness to hit me. Or at least a healthy dose of wistfulness. Instead, I felt the way I do when I read about a celebrity wedding in *People*. Interested in the details, but not wholly invested in it.

"Congratulations," I said, understanding why Dex sounded wary of my call. The timing was definitely suspect.

"Thank you, Darcy," she said. "I know . . . this is all so bizarre, isn't it?" Her tone was apologetic.

Was she sorry for marrying Dex? For not inviting me? For everything?

I let her off the hook, and said, "It's fine, Rachel. Truly. I'm happy for you."

"Thank you, Darcy."

My mind filled with questions. I considered censoring them, but then thought, why not ask?

"Where was your ceremony?" I asked first.

"Here in the city. At the Methodist church on Sixtieth and Park."

"And your reception?"

"We had it at The Inn at Irving Place," she said. "It was very small."

"Was Annalise there?"

"Yeah. Just a few friends and our families . . . I wanted you to be there, but . . ." Her voice trailed off. "I knew you wouldn't come. *Couldn't* come, I mean."

I laughed. "Yeah. That would have been sort of weird, huh?"

"Yeah. I guess so," she said wanly.

"So where are you guys living now?" I asked.

She told me they had bought an apartment in Gramercy—which had always been Rachel's favorite neighborhood in the city.

"That's awesome. . . . And are you going on a honeymoon?" I asked, thinking of their trip to Hawaii, but refusing to succumb to negative emotion.

"Yeah . . . We leave for Italy tonight," she said.

"Oh. That's great. I'm glad I caught you."

"Yeah. Me too," she said.

"So I hope you have a good time in Italy. Give Dex my best too. Okay?"

She said that she would do that. Then we congratulated each other again, and said good-bye. I hung up and looked at Ethan through fresh tears. The kind that come after you've survived an or-deal.

"I was going to tell you," Ethan said. "But with your preterm labor,

I didn't want to upset you, and yesterday wasn't the day for it. . . . Besides, I thought Rachel should tell you herself."

"It's fine," I said. "I'm surprisingly fine with it . . . I guess you were invited?"

He nodded. "Yeah. But I never planned on going."

"Why not?"

"You think I would have left you?"

"You could have."

He shook his head emphatically. "No way."

"You're closer to her," I said, perhaps to gauge his feelings for me, but also because I felt guilty that he had missed one of his best friend's weddings because of me.

"I'm closer to *you*," he said earnestly.

I smiled, feeling no sense of victory over Rachel, just an incredible closeness to Ethan. I wondered if he felt the way I did—or whether it was only love for a friend.

"And just look what I would have missed," Ethan said, gazing down at John and Thomas.

I thought about the two events—the birth of my babies and Rachel's wedding—transpiring virtually simultaneously, on opposite sides of the Atlantic.

"Can you believe it all happened on the very same day?" I asked him.

Ethan shook his head. "Frankly, no. I cannot."

"Guess I'm never going to forget their anniversary."

Ethan put his arm around me and let me cry some more.

On the day of our discharge from the hospital, Geoffrey stopped by to visit us during his rounds. He shook Ethan's hand, kissed me on the cheek, and admired my sons.

"What a nice guy," Ethan said after Geoffrey had left the room.

"Yeah, he could win the ex-boyfriend-of-the-year award," I said, thinking that as nice as Geoffrey was, I was still certain that I had done the right thing in breaking up with him. The fact that our relationship had weathered the transition to friendship so seamlessly was just further confirmation.

I put on the sweater that Ethan had given me for Christmas as he reswaddled John and Thomas in Rachel's blankets, handing me both bundles, one in each arm. Then Ethan finished packing our belongings, which had spread to every corner of the room.

"I don't want to go," I said.

"Why not?" he asked.

I tried to explain my feeling of wanting to stay in the hospital forever, with a fleet of nurses and doctors catering to me and my children. I felt envious of the women just going into labor, and told Ethan that I'd take the pain all over again for a few more nights at the inn.

Ethan reassured me that I had nothing to worry about. "We'll be fine," he said. "You'll see."

It was that *we* that held me together through those first crazy days and weeks at home. It got me through the fear that my babies would suddenly stop breathing, the frustration with breast-feeding, my insecurity during bath time, and all the other mundane but seemingly insurmountable tasks. Most of all, it got me through the agony of the sleepless nights. You hear parents of *one* newborn talk about how grueling the lack of sleep is, but experiencing the endless cycle of waking-feeding-changing with twins is simply not to be believed. Let's just say I understood why sleep deprivation is the number-one form of torture for political prisoners.

Our days weren't much easier. Laundry and dishes and bills accumulated at an alarming rate. Food disappeared even more quickly, and we often resorted to opening dusty canned goods rather than schlep-

ping our delirious selves the few blocks to the grocery store. There
were many days when we didn't even change out of our pajamas or
brush our teeth before late afternoon. And I certainly didn't have the
energy to put on makeup or blow-dry my hair or even look in the
mirror except in passing, catching horrific glimpses of my matted
hair, sunken eyes, and a lingering fifteen pounds, mostly around my
middle.

In short, it wasn't exactly a breeding ground for romance, but there
it was anyway, blooming between Ethan and me, evident in every
small act of kindness. It was love as a verb, as Rachel used to say. Love
that made me more patient, more loyal, and stronger. Love that made
me feel more complete than I had ever felt in my glamorous, Jimmy
Choo–filled past.

Yet on the surface, Ethan and I remained "just friends." They were
two words that haunted me, especially when Ethan went off, every
few days, to spend time with Sondrine. She was still his girlfriend. I
was just his friend. Sure, we were friends who exchanged soulful
glances, friends who slept in a bed filled with sexual tension, friends
who found any excuse to touch, but I worried that we'd never take
that perilous leap of faith toward becoming a real couple, a permanent
team. I had nightmares of a tragic ending: Ethan marrying Sondrine
while I returned to New York with Thomas and John. I would
awaken, sweating and teary, tasting the grief and heartbreak I'd face if
I had to spend the rest of my life wondering just how incredible we
could have been together, if only one of us had stepped up and taken
the chance.

Then, one afternoon in late April, as Ethan and I took the boys out for
our daily walk around Holland Park, he solemnly reported that the
night before, over oysters at Bibendum, he had ended things with

Sondrine. I felt a rush of excitement and opportunity. I also sensed uneasiness between us. Our last obstacle was gone, but now what?

I let out a nervous laugh and said in a teasing tone, "Kind of weird to dump someone over oysters, isn't it?"

"Well," Ethan said, his eyes focused on the path ahead of us. "I'm not always the slickest guy . . . as you well know."

His "as you well know" seemed loaded with meaning and made me even more anxious. So I stumbled on, rambling about how I thought you weren't supposed to eat oysters in months containing the letter *r*.

"We had rock oysters—fins de clair—which you can eat year-round. But thanks so much for your concern," he said, yawning with feigned nonchalance.

"Anytime," I said, as we strolled around the top of the Cricket Lawn. A long minute passed, the silence between us thickening.

"How do you feel?" I finally asked, choosing my words carefully. "About the breakup?"

Ethan glanced at me with raised brows. "It was a long time coming. I think I was just too sleep-deprived to get around to it sooner, you know?"

I nodded. I knew.

"I just didn't feel that close to her," he continued. "After this long, I should have felt closer to her. Or at least had the sense that I knew her . . . I mean, I knew her taste in music, art, food, travel, literature. But I still didn't know *her*. Or maybe I just didn't want to know her badly enough."

I nodded again, noticing that we were both walking at a faster clip and avoiding eye contact.

"There was other stuff too," he chattered nervously. He stopped pushing the pram long enough to reach down and adjust John's cap, which had slipped down over his eyes, and then said, "She was so relentlessly anti-American. I'm the first guy to step up and criticize our government. But it raised my hackles when she did it. I found myself constantly grinding my teeth to keep from saying, 'Your ass'd be speaking German if it weren't for us.' "

I smiled, pretending to be distracted by a nearby three-on-three football game.

"And then there's her scent . . . ," he said.

"What? She doesn't bathe enough?"

He shook his head. "No. She's perfectly clean. And she wears nice perfume and all of that. But there's something about her actual, *natural* scent. The way her skin smells. I just didn't like it. . . . So you know, it's hard to fix that one."

"Do I have a scent? When I'm not wearing perfume?" I asked, suddenly worried that Ethan didn't like mine either, and that I was only imagining our physical, chemical connection.

Ethan glanced at me, blushing scarlet. "Yeah. You do have a scent," he said slowly.

"And?" I asked, my heart pounding.

He stopped walking, turned to face me, and stared into my eyes. "You have an almost citrusy scent. Sweet, but not too sweet."

His expression removed my last trace of doubt. I was sure now— Ethan loved me as much as I loved him. I smiled, feeling light-headed and breathless as he wrapped his hand around mine, his other still gripping the handle of the pram. We had held hands many times before, but this time was different. It was a precursor to something more. Sure enough, Ethan pulled me against him. Then he closed his eyes, buried his face in my neck, and inhaled.

"Yeah. You smell like an orange," he whispered. "An orange in your stocking on Christmas morning."

An electrical charge passed through my body, and I learned what it means to be weak in the knees. I closed my eyes and put my arms around Ethan's shoulders, holding on tightly. Then, right in the middle of Holland Park, amid footballers and dogs and babies, Ethan and I shared our first real kiss. I'm not sure how long it lasted—ten seconds or five minutes or something in between—but I do know that everything in the world seemed to halt, except our hearts, thudding against each other. I remember his warm hand slipping up under my jacket and shirt, his long, slender fingers pressing into my back. I remember thinking how much I wanted to feel all of his skin against mine.

When we finally separated, Ethan said my name in a way nobody had ever said it, his voice filled with equal parts affection and desire. My eyes welled as I looked into his. He was still Ethan, the scrawny kid on the playground and my best friend. But he was also someone new.

"I think you know the real reason Sondrine and I broke up," he said. "Yeah. I think I do," I whispered.

I could feel myself beaming, bursting with anticipation of what was to come. That afternoon and every day to follow. I hooked my hand over his elbow, as we turned the pram around and headed toward home.

two years later

It is a brilliant summer day in London. I am waiting in Holland Park, wearing an ivory gown made of chiffon so soft I can't stop touching it. The dress comes to a V in the back, and the front is gathered over the bustline and accented with a shimmering of beads. The skirt is a loose A-line—romantic and simple—and it sways just right in the breeze. The woman at the Kensington bridal shop told me that the design was inspired by the Edwardian era—which sounded like something Ethan would love. It was the first dress I tried on, but when you know something is right, you just know.

As the string quartet begins to play, I peek around the corner of the Belvedere, into the gardens, and allow myself a glimpse of Ethan. We've only been apart twenty-four hours, but for us, it is a long stretch. Whether it is our separation, his Armani suit, or the emotion of the day, he has never looked more handsome. I feel a tightening in my chest, and take rapid, shallow breaths to keep from crying. I don't want to ruin my mascara so early in the day. For a moment, I wish I had my father to lean on or a bridesmaid to trail behind. But no, I made the right decision. I am walking solo on my wedding day, not out of spite or to make a statement, but rather as my own private symbol of how far I've come.

I take a deep breath and round the corner toward the gardens. Ethan is now in full view. I can see in his face that he thinks I look beautiful, and I can't wait to hear him put his feelings into words later. No one can express himself as he can. I keep my eyes locked with his. I am finally beside him.

"Hi," he whispers.

"Hi," I whisper back as the minister begins to speak.

The ceremony is short, despite the hours Ethan and I spent crafting our vows. We kept some parts traditional, discarded the rest, but every word is imbued with our own meaning. At the end, Ethan's eyes are damp and red-rimmed. He leans forward and brushes his lips against mine. I kiss my husband back, memorizing the moment, the feel of the sun on my skin, the scent of wildflowers in the arch around us, the sound of applause and snapping cameras and the jubilant notes of Beethoven's "Ode to Joy."

I feel buoyant as Ethan and I turn, hand in hand, and face our guests. I see my mother first, dabbing at her eyes with a lace handkerchief. My dad sits beside her, holding Thomas and John. My parents are thrilled that I found true love, and that I found it with a Stanford-educated novelist, whose book about finding love in unexpected places is an international bestseller. I doubt if my parents will ever change—they will always care a lot about money and material things and image, but I also know that part of our rift was caused by worry and concern for a child. I understand these emotions now.

As Ethan and I walk down the garden path, we smile at our other guests. I see my brother and Lauren, who is newly pregnant . . . Ethan's mother and father, who by all appearances were rekindling a romance at last night's rehearsal dinner . . . Annalise, Greg, and sweet, little Hannah, who is about to turn three . . . Martin and his new girlfriend, Lucy . . . Phoebe, whom I have grown to appreciate, and almost like after a few cocktails . . . Charlotte and John with Natalie . . . Meg, Yossi, and their son, Lucas . . . Geoffrey and Sondrine, who, much to Ethan's and my amusement, are recently engaged.

Then I spot them in the back row. Rachel and Dex with their baby daughter, Julia, a clone of her mother, but with Dexter's dark, wavy hair. She is wearing the pink smocked dress I sent for her first birthday. As I pass them, I point to the blue silk trim from Thomas and John's worn-out baby blankets, now a ribbon tied around my bouquet of white lilies. Rachel and I don't talk often, but I did tell her about my plan to use the ribbon as my "something blue." I could tell she was touched, pleased to play an indirect role in our day.

"You're gorgeous!" she mouths to me now.

Dex smiles at me, almost fondly, and I acknowledge him with a pleasant nod. It is hard to believe we were together for seven years. He now seems to be nothing more than an acquaintance with exceptionally good hair.

As we come to the end of the path, I turn back to face Ethan. Then we scoop up Thomas and John, who have broken free of my dad and chased after us.

"Are we married yet, Mummy?" they ask in the British accent they did not learn at home.

"Yes!" I laugh.

"Yes! We *are* married!" Ethan says.

At last.

I think back to that autumn day when Ethan proposed. We were on a weekend trip to Edinburgh, celebrating my new job as a fundraiser for the Adopt-A-Minefield organization. After checking into our hotel, we decided to climb Arthur's Seat, a small mountain over-looking the ancient city. As we rested on the hillside and admired the sweeping views below, Ethan presented me with a tiny slip of paper so worn it felt like velvet. Upon closer examination, I could see that it was the note I had given him in the fifth grade. The "Will you go out with me?" note, its *yes* box checked with a red-colored pencil.

"Where in the *world* did you find this?" I said, feeling giddy that he had preserved the oldest piece of our history together.

"I found it in a box of old papers," he said, smiling. "I thought I had given it back to you, but I guess I never did?"

"No. You just told me yes at recess. Remember?"

"I guess so." Ethan nodded and then said, "Turn it over."

I did, and on the other side, I could see that he had written a question of his own.

Will you marry me?

I looked up, startled. Then I cried and said yes, *yes*! Ethan's hands trembled slightly as he removed a small box from his jacket pocket, opened it, and slid a sparkling cushion-cut diamond ring onto my finger.

"It doesn't take vows or genetics to be a family. We are one already," Ethan said. "But I want to make it *official*. I want to make it *forever*."

Then, always one to capture a moment on film, he extended his arm and snapped our engagement photo. I knew my hair was messy from the wind and that both of our noses were red and running from the cold, but I didn't care. I had learned to let those surface issues go, to value content over form. I knew that every time I'd look at that picture of us on the mountain in Scotland, I would see no imperfections, and would only think of Ethan's words. *I want to make it official. I want to make it forever.*

So on this joyful June day, below skies so blue they look airbrushed, we are just that: an official family, embarking on our forever.

Later, after we all have moved into the Belvedere for a champagne brunch, the toasts to Ethan and me begin. Some people joke about our fifth-grade romance. Others reference our hectic life as the parents of twins, marveling at how we do it all. Everyone says how happy they are for us.

Then, when I think that the last toast is over, Rachel stands tentatively and clears her throat. She seems nervous, but perhaps I just know how much she hates giving speeches.

"Nothing could make me prouder or happier than being here to witness the marriage of two such close friends," she starts, looking up from an index card and glancing around the room. "I have known Darcy and Ethan for what feels like forever, and so I know what fine people they are. I also know that they are *that* much better together." She pauses, her eyes meeting Ethan's, then mine. "I guess that's the power of true love and true friendship. . . . I guess that's what it's really all about." She raises her glass, smiles, and says, "So here's to Ethan and Darcy, true love and true friendship."

As everyone applauds and sips champagne, I smile back at Rachel, thinking that she got it just right. Love and friendship. They are what make us who we are, and what can change us, if we let them.

1. Many readers of *Something Borrowed* expressed doubts at being able to read and enjoy a book written from Darcy's point of view. Were you reluctant to read her story? Did your feelings about her ever change? If so, at what point in the story?

2. What do you view as Darcy's greatest weakness? Could this also be considered her greatest strength? If so, how?

3. What do you think caused Darcy's breakup with Marcus? Do you think Marcus was more or less responsible for it than Darcy was?

4. In many ways this is a story about personal growth and transformation. Do you think people can fundamentally change? How difficult did it seem for Darcy to change? What role did Ethan play in those changes? What role did her pregnancy play?

5. What do you think would have become of Darcy if she had not become pregnant? If she hadn't gone to London? What would some of the key differences be living in London as opposed to New York? Do you think some of these differences helped Darcy evolve?

6. How do you think Darcy's relationship with her mother plays a role in the person she is?

7. In what ways are Dex, Marcus, and Ethan different? In what ways are they similar? Do you think their similarities are true of men in general?

8. Where do you see Darcy and Rachel in five years? Ten?

St. Martin's Griffin

9. If you were Darcy, would you have been able to forgive Rachel? Would you have invited her to your wedding? Do you feel there is a line that can be crossed in friendship where forgiveness isn't possible?

10. What are your views regarding the closing sentences of the book: "Love and friendship. They are what make us who we are, and what can change us, if we let them"?

read all of **emily giffin**'s novels

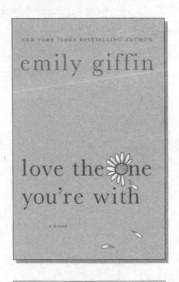
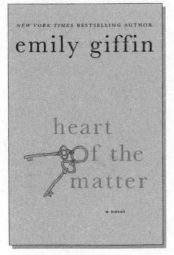
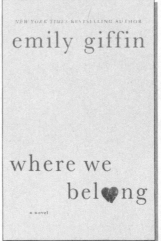